Catherine Alliott
After graduating from Warwick University she moved
to London where she worked as a copywriter in advertising. She lives with her husband, who is a barrister,
and their three children in Hertfordshire.

Catherine's first novel, THE OLD-GIRL NETWORK,
was chosen by W H Smith for their Fresh Talent Promo-
tion in 1994 and became an instant bestseller across the
country, as did her second novel, GOING TOO FAR.

'A tongue-in-cheek romance intelligently laced with
humour' *Radio Times*

'A compulsive page turner' *Today*

'A wickedly funny romance' *Liverpool Daily Post*

'Well-produced frothy fun in the "naughty-girl" mould
of Jilly Cooper' *Manchester Evening News*

'Fans of Jilly Cooper will warm to this wickedly funny
romance' *Bookcase*

'A fun, frothy romantic saga in the tradition of early Jilly
Cooper' *Books* magazine

'Great fluff' *Company*

The Old-Girl Network
Network
The Real Thing

Catherine Alliott

HEADLINE

First published in this omnibus edition in 2001 by
HEADLINE BOOK PUBLISHING

10 9 8 7 6 5 4 3 2 1

ISBN 0 7472 6787 1

Printed and bound in Great Britain by
Mackays of Chatham plc, Chatham, Kent

HEADLINE BOOK PUBLISHING
A division of Hodder Headline
338 Euston Road
London NW1 3BH

www.headline.co.uk
www.hodderheadline.com

The Old-Girl Network

For George

Chapter One

I sat down and ran a practised eye over the ten people sitting opposite me. I saw at once that it wasn't a good day. In fact, it was a particularly bad day. Six women and only four men, and as if that wasn't bad enough, all four of the men looked as if they'd narrowly survived major car crashes. A singularly unpromising selection and I had to go to bed with one of them. Damn.

I sat back in my seat narrowing my rather myopic eyes and studied the four contenders: Too Fat, Too Young, Too Chinese and Too Ginger. Typical. Where was Too Handsome when I needed him most? Still, it was no good belly-aching about lack of talent; rules were rules, and one of these lucky guys was about to get even luckier. I gritted my teeth and appraised them individually, searching for hidden depths. I was going to have to dig pretty deep.

Number one was a fat slob masquerading as a businessman. The buttons of his blue nylon shirt were doing sterling work as they strained under the pressure of his ample bosom, and the waistband of his trousers was nowhere to be seen as his gut spilled out over the top of it. Lovely. Not only that, but he was bald too. Long flowing locks had been grown from somewhere beneath his left ear and swept carefully over the top à la Bobby Charlton, but that didn't fool anyone. Sensing early depression I dismissed him out of hand and moved smartly on to number two.

1

I suppressed a shudder. This callow youth was still grappling with something I'd got to grips with long ago and I didn't fancy going through it again. Puberty. As I cast a cold eye over his acne-festooned, hormone-infested face, his upper lip suddenly curled into a leer, a lazy eye winked at me, and a lolling hand scratched at the fly of his jeans. Good grief, the very idea! I tossed my head in disgust. Bloody nerve.

I swiftly turned my attention to number three. Ah. Now this was a tricky one. You see, I've nothing against Chinese men per se, in fact the one in my local takeaway couldn't be nicer, it's just that − well, on balance I prefer my men to be, er, you know − English. I'm quite sure the Chinese make wonderful lovers but, as I said, my personal preference is for something a little closer to home, like − well, like Harry, of course.

For one blissful moment I allowed a fleeting glimpse of the divine Harry Lloyd-Roberts to seep into my consciousness. Ah yes, there he was, with his mop of blond hair, his tanned, smiling face, his bright blue eyes, his long lean legs, his broad shoulders, his − I gave myself a little shake. Concentrate, Polly, Harry is not on the menu this morning, but this Oriental gentleman is and you'll have to do a little better than simply admitting to a preference for Englishmen.

I grudgingly appraised him again and realised, with joy, that he had a mighty peculiar set of teeth. I seized gratefully on his unusual dental arrangement. Oh no, I'm sorry, I simply have to have straight teeth; they must be regular and they must be white, I make a point of insisting on it. No, I wasn't being racist at all, I was just − yes, I was just being a little toothist, that was it!

As I rejected him I realised with a sinking heart that I was now left with only one contender and − oh, horrors, I was about to be gingerist too. I studied the red-headed gentleman before me and sighed. But not deeply. Because,

2

hold on a minute, Polly McLaren, not so fast. On closer inspection this one wasn't so bad. Ginger, certainly, but not flaming carrots or nasty nasturtium red, more of a — well, more of an autumnal russet really. And was I seeing things, or weren't those features remarkably regular? And wasn't that face rather attractively tanned? And didn't we have here a particularly piercing pair of blue eyes? We did! Complete with crinkle-cut laughter lines at each corner! That very nearly did it, I'm a sucker for crinkle cuts, but I had the good sense to run an eye over the rest of the goods before I clinched the deal. Shoulders broad, legs long, no sign of a paunch, good.

He was wearing a pale blue Brooks Brothers shirt topped with an expensive navy jacket, a good quality leather belt and heavy cotton trousers — not too baggy, not too tight — and, more to the point (and how foolish of me not to have spotted it before), he was sporting a signet-ring on the little finger of his left hand. I leaned back in my seat, heady with relief. I had myself a winner.

There was no true competition, but I gave the opposition another cursory glance just to ensure fair play. Too Chinese and Too Young had never got off their starting blocks, Too Fat was definitely Too Bald and, let's face it, a girl has to have something to run her fingers through, even if it is red, so Ginger — I charitably omitted the 'Too' — it was. He'd run an easy race and won by an absence of baldness, hormones and buck teeth. What a lucky guy!

I stood up, flushed with success and pleased with my prize. So pleased, in fact, that I did something unforgivable. I smiled at the victor. It slipped out before I had a chance to retract it or even to turn it into something like a nasty little twitch. There it was, all turned up at the corners, wide and welcoming, teeth flashing away like beacons. Ginger looked up in surprise and returned the smile, blue eyes crinkling as predicted.

Horrified with myself, I wrapped my scarf around my

3

flushing neck and made for the sliding doors, just as – thank God – the tube pulled into South Kensington station. There was a nasty moment when the doors stuck for a second, but a minute later I was off and running – well, walking fast – in the direction of the escalator.

How ghastly! He must have thought I was sizing him up for real, propositioning him even! I glanced nervously over my shoulder as I joined the moronic trudge for the exit, but thankfully there was no sign of his russet locks hovering hopefully behind me.

But that was a lucky escape, Polly, I told myself sternly; don't do it again, for God's sake – who knows what sort of trouble it could get you into? It's bad enough that you stare at them every morning, without giving them the come-on too.

I grinned sheepishly as I thought of the way I amused myself on the way to work. Blind date without the blindfold, and without, of course, the actual date. Harmless fun, but these days increasingly depressing. Take yesterday, for example. I shuddered as I recalled. Yesterday, due to an unprecedented number of women commuters, I'd been forced to climb between the imaginary sheets with a slack-jawed octogenarian with bubbles on his lower lip. There'd been a moment back there when I could have become a lesbian, but no, I played the game. After all, it was my game, and I couldn't cheat on myself, could I?

As I jostled for position in the line up to the escalator, I spotted the leering Too Young ahead of me in the queue. Oh dear, he really didn't know the ropes did he? There he was, pushing his way through, and committing the unpardonable sin of standing firmly on the left which, as every urbane traveller knows, is for climbers only. I had the satisfaction of seeing him being bundled over to the right by a hoard of embattled commuters amidst a sea of shaking heads and tutting tongues. 'You stand on the right,' someone muttered by way of explanation — only muttered you understand, no one who did this on a regular basis would be so gauche as to talk. I joined in the 'glare past' on the way up to complete the ritual humiliation. To my surprise, he had the balls to leer back at me.

Oh well, I thought, as I trudged on up the moving staircase, its always nice to be ogled, even if it is by a spotty fourteen-year old: I must be looking quite good today.

We reached the top and I geared myself up to catch a glimpse of my reflection in the photo-booth mirror that everyone looks in and pretends not to. Christ, I thought as I caught my millisecond's worth, he must be desperate. Bad hair, bad make-up (too hurried) and a very bad jacket covered in dog hairs. Lottie's fault for buying a bloody Yorkshire Terrier. I brushed myself down, cursing my impulsive flatmate. At least it was all superficial. The hair could be washed, the jacket changed, and the make-up carefully reapplied in time for tonight's little excursion with the divine Harry. Please God, let there be an excursion! Please God, let him ring!

I allowed myself a moment's luxury as I considered the joys of going out with the utterly mouth-wateringly delicious Mr Harry Lloyd-Roberts. My heart pranced around in its usual foolish manner, but after an initial burst of skippy enthusiasm, sank a little too. I sighed. If only he wasn't so elusive. If only every date wasn't such a trumpet-blowing-red-carpeted-big-deal because they were so few and far between. If only — oh well. Don't bang on, Polly.

And that was another thing, I thought bitterly as I barged and elbowed my way towards the ticket barrier, it was all so time-consuming. I really didn't want to be the sort of girl who only thought about boys, but until I'd well and truly ensnared this one, I honestly didn't think I could get my mind around anything else. Of course it went without saying that once he was as besotted with me as I was with him I'd spend a lot more time thinking about – oh well, you know – Shakespeare, art, starving orphans, charity work, that kind of thing; but until that glorious, glorious day came, I'm afraid I just didn't have the time.

As I approached the barrier, I dug into my pocket for some change. The diminutive ticket collector already had his hand out, palm upward. It was a tacit agreement we had. He knew I was a lazy slut who couldn't be bothered to buy a ticket at the right station, and I knew he was a thieving bastard who pocketed my sixty pence. We smiled sweetly at one another, both happy with the arrangement, and London Transport was none the wiser.

As I walked up the few remaining steps to the main road, I felt as if I was walking into a Persil advert. South Kensington was awash with bright, primary colours bathed in sunshine. Tall white houses soared up into a bright blue sky, and the little patches of green grass at their feet played host to the very first signs of spring as snowdrops, crocuses and a few lonely daffodils bobbed around in the sunshine. It was a beautiful day, and my spirits rose.

They rose even higher as I turned the corner into Cresswell Gardens, for this was where I'd met Harry and it never failed to please. Number twenty-four, to be precise – yes, this was the one. I paused outside, allowing myself a moment of sentimental nostalgia.

If I say so myself, I'd looked pretty damn sexy that night; seductively clad in a black Alaia dress which clung to every curve – of which I have a few; some would say too many – and with a liberal sprinkling of Butler and Wilson's finest baubles at my ears and around my neck, my long, wavy blond hair freshly highlighted, and the remains of a tan still glowing . . . I hadn't looked bad.

The occasion had been a birthday drinks party, but to this day I can't remember being invited, although I do remember the hostess's look of surprise as I kissed her

6

warmly on both cheeks. I'd obviously crashed it, probably with Lottie, who knows everyone. It had been a small, select gathering, and the venue had been the drawing room of this majestic townhouse. It was chock-a-block with original oil paintings, tasteful antiques, and other expensive and eminently breakable family heirlooms, and in fact the atmosphere had been so rarefied that people were talking in whispers. They didn't stray from their own little groups of two or three, and it seemed to me that everyone was in danger of turning to stone and joining the rest of the precious treasures dotted around the room.

Thankfully, as the evening limped along, the hostess was suddenly alive to this possibility, and hastily poured a two-litre bottle of brandy into the insipid punch. A rather horsy girl standing next to me said she thought it was the stupidest thing she'd ever seen. I thought it was inspired. Within twenty minutes the party was revving up like nobody's business, and I delved deep to summon up all the Dutch courage I possessed to chat up the most attractive man in the room.

He was standing by the window wearing a pair of ageing beige cords, a blue shirt and a bright red skiing jumper. An unruly mop of floppy blond hair was constantly falling into the bluest eyes I'd ever seen. He was such a cliché it was untrue. He was calmly eating pistachio nuts and staring out of the window to the street below, pretending he didn't know how divine he looked and what a commotion he was causing.

No less than three knock-out looking girls were prowling and circling around him, tossing back metres of silky hair and adjusting their hemlines up or down, according to whether they had good or bad legs. I decided to skip these formalities and move in for the kill. Buoyed up by too much bevvy and my revealing little black dress, I took a deep breath and dived in.

Somehow, and to this day I know not how, I managed to

monopolise him totally for the rest of the evening, engaging him with my witty repartee whilst at the same time staving off the competition. The circling harpies evidently decided I'd scored and limped away to nurse their egos and, within the hour, I'd secured myself a seat opposite him in a restaurant of my choice somewhere on the Fulham Road. Before you could say your place or mine, it was back to his for Rémy and rumpy-pumpy – and the rest, as they say, is history. Unfortunately I was under the distinct impression that, unless I could recapture some of that original wit and vitality, I was in danger of becoming history too. I bit my lip miserably. Why was love such bloody hard work? Perhaps I should have a few sun-beds.

I turned the corner into Egerton Street where the houses are even taller, even whiter and even lovelier. My second pause on the walk to work was just coming up, right . . . here. I stopped in front of one of the tallest and whitest and gazed up at it, for this was where Harry and I were going to live when we were married. I'd picked it out ages ago as being the perfect house. I could almost hear my Manolo Blahnik heels tip-tapping around the highly polished wooden floors as I checked on my beautiful blond children asleep in their bedrooms and adjusted my Chanel suit in the enormous hall mirror before skipping off to join my husband for dinner or the theatre – or both.

Before I went I would dispense a few last-minute instructions to the Swedish nanny – did I say Swedish? Lord, no, I meant Rumanian or, um . . . yes, Mongolian. Or did Mongolians have those rather attractive high cheekbones? I was rattled. Well then, we wouldn't have one at all, why bother? Baby-sitters were just as good, and cheaper. But younger. I sighed. Even I could see the poverty of my situation, when even in my fantasies Harry was incapable of keeping his hands to himself.

With these weighty problems still preying on my mind, I

climbed the steps to my workplace, Penhalligan and Waters, number thirty-three. I pressed the buzzer urgently, as if I'd been waiting there for some time and wasn't late at all.

'S'me!' I yelled into the metal squawk box, and another buzzer obligingly let me in.

The only delay I was now likely to encounter was Bob. I looked nervously around the marble hallway. Bob was a large black labrador who belonged to Maurice, the aged and grumpy commissionaire who fielded visitors and clients up to the various offices in the building. They say a dog resembles his owner, but these two really couldn't have been more different.

Maurice was a Yorkshireman; dour, miserable, grizzled and past it. Bob, on the other hand, was well-bred, bouncy, friendly, in peak condition and well up to it. He greeted most people simply with enthusiasm and affection, which was fine as long as his paws were clean and you weren't wearing white, but I was a different matter. Bob adored me. Let's face it, Bob had the hots for me. The mere smell of me would make his nose twitch with delight, and the sight of me would have him yelping with joy. Within seconds, his front paws would be up on my shoulders, his tongue frantically licking every scrap of make-up off my face. If I pushed him away, he'd think it was all part of the foreplay. He'd goose me in the crutch, whimpering with delight, and it wasn't funny because Bob was a big dog. There I'd be, pinned to the Regency staircase or the Georgian hall-table, with Bob on top of me, pleading with him, or Maurice, or both, to give me a break.

'Wants to play, by the look of things,' Maurice would observe at length from the safety of his chair.

'Yes – yes, he does, doesn't he?' I'd pant as Bob's big black head would give me another excruciating buck in the groin. 'Ooof! Geddof, Bob! But the thing is, Maurice, I'm

9

just a teensy bit late, could you possibly — you know, call him off? Aarrhh!'

'Humph,' Maurice would grunt in an offended fashion. 'He's only being friendly like, better than being all aggressive like one of them Rottweilers, i'n't it?'

'Oh yes, yes, absolutely, much better,' I'd gasp, nodding furiously. 'It's just that — well, you know, I do have to get to work and I am rather late . . .'

'C'mon then, Bob,' Maurice would growl grudgingly, jerking his head. 'She don't want your attentions. Save them for them that do.'

Luckily Bob was remarkably obedient to Maurice's commands — probably terrified of him like the rest of us — and he'd respond immediately, slinking back to his basket. Muttering my thanks to Maurice, I'd then back gratefully up the stairs, flapping my skirt in a vain attempt to get the air to it and dry the nasty wet patch where he'd slobbered before I got upstairs.

This morning, thank goodness, there was no sign of the amorous Bob. Maurice appeared to be asleep behind his desk, so I tiptoed past, hoping Bob was also kipping deadly in his basket beside him or, even better, at home with a bad case of doggy flu.

I looked at my watch and leaped up the stairs two at a time — Christ! I hadn't realised I was that late. I flew down one of the many corridors in the grand old house, which at one time would have been full of oil paintings and family portraits. Now that the second floor housed an advertising agency, the walls were lined with stills from cat-food commercials and Tampax ads. I barged through reception shouting, 'Morning!' to Josie the receptionist, then, out of breath and panting heavily, shouldered open the nearest door and fell into the pit I share with Pippa.

Even by my standards it was a mess. It was a small office, dominated by two enormous desks which were almost totally obscured by magazines, newspapers, TV

10

scripts, show reels, voice-over tapes, commercials, and the odd word processor or two. The walls were plastered with polaroid photos which appeared to chart the progress of a particularly debauched office party – a veritable collage of tongues, silly hats, bare bottoms, gin bottles and suspender belts. The windowsill, the filing cabinet, and any other spare surface area, spewed over with rampant Busy Lizzie plants and their offspring; cuttings of cuttings of cuttings had taken over in triffid-like proportions. The floor was covered with yet more magazines; in piles, in bundles, in general disarray. In the midst of this chaos, a young girl in a blue coat was slumped in a heap at her desk.

Pippa had obviously died at her typewriter. She was sitting with her head cradled in her arms, her face pressed nose-down on to her blotter. She was one of those girls who had an amazing capacity to look ravishingly attractive one day and hideously atrocious the next. Today it was obviously the latter. Her insatiable appetite for night clubs, late nights, gin and tonics and men – not necessarily in that order – was also instrumental in determining how she looked in the morning. My best friend, soul-mate and partner in grime at Penhalligan and Waters raised a pale green face from the blotter and peered at me through severely bloodshot eyes. 'Don't talk to me,' she whispered.

'Chocolate milk and bacon sandwich?' I ventured sympathetically.

'Please, if you're going.'

It was all she could manage. Her head dropped back on to her desk like a stone. I dumped my bag and moved a few papers around on my own desk to make it look as if I'd been in for hours.

'If Nick gets back from his meeting, say I've been in for ages and I've just popped out to the bank,' I commanded.

Pippa moaned in agreement and I galloped downstairs,

11

this time escaping through the back entrance, thereby avoiding Maurice and Bob.

I exchanged the usual pleasantries with the friendly Italians in the sandwich bar, in pidgin Italian on my part and in pidgin English on theirs, and with '*Arrivederci, Bella*!' still ringing in my ears, sped back to the patient, hangover cure in hand.

As I deposited it on her desk, I decided she'd improved, but only marginally. She was still wrapped up in her navy blue winter coat, even though it was a warm spring day, but her head was off the desk and she was at least indulging in some sort of activity. She was smoking her one, two, three — fourth cigarette of the morning, judging by the ashtray. If Pippa were having a frontal lobotomy, she'd find time to light a fag.

'Was he worth it?' I asked smugly, from my frightfully healthy position at the opposite desk.

'Oh, very definitely,' whispered Pippa, fumbling to open the chocolate milk and quietly ramming home the fact that I might be the picture of health, but I'd earned it by spending a mind-bendingly boring evening in front of the television, working my way through two chocolate oranges and a box of Maltesers. I'd suffered the added indignity of dog-sitting for Lottie whilst she too pursued life in the fast lane. Between them, Pippa and Lottie went to more clubs and parties than I'd had hot dates. What was the point of having a boyfriend if I never went out with him? I didn't voice this last complaint to Pippa, as I already knew her jaundiced views on the subject of Harry.

'And you?' It was a supreme effort on Pippa's part, but she managed to form the two short syllables. After all, the morning ritual of, 'What did you do last night?' had to be gone through, come hell, high water or hangover.

'Oh, you know, just a quiet evening in. Quite nice for a change,' I lied. I hoped she wasn't going to ask, 'With Harry?' but she was opening her mouth ominously, so I cut in quickly, 'No, not with Harry. Something came up.'

Pippa sighed. 'Probably his dinner.'

'What do you mean?' I pounced quickly, realising she had classified information.

'He was in the same restaurant as me last night, absolutely plastered.' It was still an effort to speak, but our code of honour meant this horrendous piece of news had to be transmitted as soon as possible. I felt cold as I waited for the inevitable bombshell.

'No, don't worry, he wasn't with anybody, just a whole crowd of hoorays having a bun fight.'

I breathed a sigh of relief and my heart slipped out of my mouth, down my throat, and back to a more normal position. So it hadn't been a candlelit tête-à-tête but, even so, why hadn't I been there? I like restaurants, I don't mind hoorays, and I'm game-on for a bun fight. I quizzed Pippa mercilessly, ignoring her frail condition, but she either didn't know much or was being very kind. Her answers were suspiciously diplomatic.

' . . . About ten of them, mostly men.'

' . . . No, he didn't see me.'

' . . . Um, a blondish girl on one side and a man on the other.'

' . . . No, not very pretty, more mousy than blonde actually.'

' . . . Oh, a blue dress, very Top Shop.'

' . . . Um, about twelve-thirty, I think, in a taxi.'

' . . . No, not with Top Shop, on his own — Polly, please don't bully me any more, you know he's a dead loss, what more can I tell you?'

Her body slumped forward again and her head dropped back into position. The interview was over. I sighed and lit what was for me a very premature cigarette. She was right, of course, he was a dead loss. Always out, but never with me. I decided for the millionth time to end what passed as our relationship the next time I saw him. For sure. Yes,

13

definitely. The very next time. He simply wasn't worth it. Having made that little porky-pie of a resolution I felt better, and even had the appetite to tuck into my own daily fix of egg mayonnaise on brown and the *Daily Mail*.

Nick, my boss, and in fact *the* boss, was still in a client meeting, and when Nick was away the rest of the agency played. We lounged around on desks, sofas and — after a heavy lunch — floors. We draped ourselves decoratively around the reception area watching the television, exchanged dirty jokes, made calls to Australia, drank the 'strictly client meetings only' drinks cupboard dry, threw up in loos (new boys only), and generally behaved like any other normal advertising agency. When Nick was around we did exactly the same but made sure he didn't notice.

Which brings me to another sore point. Another bitter blow to add to my long and doleful list of disappointments. Nick Penhalligan.

When I switched from the overworked and underpaid world of publishing to the sexy and glamorous world of advertising six months ago, I had very definite ideas about what life at Penhalligan and Waters was going to be like. OK, it was a small agency, only fifteen people, but small agencies were by all accounts great fun. I was also going to be working for the chairman, which of course guaranteed me an enormous slice of the action.

I daydreamed about being an indispensable girl Friday to a wild and wacky ad-man full of crazy impulsive ideas like, 'Let's get out of the agency today and go and bounce a few ideas around in the wine bar.' I imagined a snappy sartorial dresser with a fine line in enormous red-framed spectacles and swivelling bow-ties who lived in a creative dreamworld and needed a sensible, reliable girl by his side to guide him through his hectic day.

I foresaw long boozy lunches in dimly lit Soho restaurants, where he'd confide in me and tell me all his marital problems, after which we'd pile into a taxi together

14

and charge off to a shoot. As we swept into the studio, the crew would mutter, 'That's Nick Penhalligan: he's brilliant, but of course he can't *move* without Polly, she's his right arm; in fact I don't know where he'd be without her.' To illustrate this point, Nick would then discover he'd lost the script for the commercial and would rummage frantically through his briefcase as everyone waited.

'It's not here!' he'd cry, 'but I'm sure I put it in!'

There'd be an awkward silence, then I'd smile indulgently and produce a wad of paper from my handbag. 'Don't worry, Nick,' I'd say soothingly, 'I've got a copy.'

Everyone would heave great sighs of relief and say things like, 'Gosh, thank goodness for Polly,' and I'd spend the rest of the afternoon being chatted up by the director, the producer and Nigel Havers who happened to be starring in the commercial, before being whisked away to the Zanzibar for several large gin and tonics by my grateful boss. As you can see, I have quite a stranglehold on reality.

The real Nick Penhalligan turned out to be about as wacky as a filing cabinet, and the nearest I got to a shoot was nearly being fired on my first day.

I had arrived on day one of my employment dressed in what I imagined people in the ad-racket probably wore. Short leather mini-skirt, white Katherine Hamnett T-shirt complete with anti-establishment slogan, black biker's jacket, Doc Marten-type shoes and an extraordinary pair of dangly white earrings which Pippa later told me she'd thought were tampons. Dead trendy, or so I believed.

Pippa's eyes were out on stalks when she collected me in reception in her navy blue Puffa, Liberty print skirt and velvet hairband. She eyed what passed for my skirt in disbelief and mumbled something incoherent like 'shit', before leading me into Nick's office.

Nick didn't recognise me. Hardly surprising really, since the girl he'd interviewed for the job had been buttoned up to the eyeballs in Laura Ashley and bore no resemblance whatsoever to the apparition sitting in front of him now. He gaped at me for a long time, opening and closing his mouth a lot, and then very slowly the penny started to drop.

'Ah, yes, you're um . . . you must be Polly, is that right?'

Ah yes, just as I'd thought: short memory; mind on higher, more creative things. Any minute now I'd be producing the forgotten script from my bag.

'That's right.' I smiled and helped him out as one would help a small child. I leaned forward and spoke very slowly. 'You interviewed me last week, remember?' I smiled encouragingly and nodded.

'Yes, yes, of course I did. It's just that last week you looked, um, different . . . more sort of businesslike.' Nick coughed and adjusted his extremely businesslike navy blue tie which I could tell was never going to swivel.

Now, I'm sensitive to atmosphere, and the one we had here was not good. In fact it dawned on me that I'd cocked up. I surreptitiously slid the bubble-gum from my mouth to my hand and pulled the leather skirt down from around my knicker-line, trying to make it look less like a belt.

Nick was shifting around in his chair looking uncomfortable. 'I suppose I'd better make it clear right now that we have quite a lot of important clients coming in and out of here, and whilst some of them I'm sure are very broad-minded, they're probably not used to seeing quite such, um, unusual clothing in an office. I don't want to appear dogmatic or old-fashioned, but I was wondering if in future you could, um, well – tone it down a little?'

'Oh, it's OK,' I said quickly, 'I can explain. I know exactly what you mean about the clothes, but you see I stayed at my sister's place last night and had to borrow some of her things. She's only sixteen and going through a rather rebellious stage, hence the – well, hence the rather avant-garde style! Not me at all!'

'Oh, I see.' He wasn't totally convinced.

'Yes,' I hurried on, 'she's such a worry to my parents: thinks life is just one big party, you know; sex, drugs, rock and roll.'

'Drugs?' he looked alarmed.

'Oh well, not strong ones, no,' I laughed nervously. 'Just, you know . . . recreational.' Was that the word? Nick's eyebrows shot into his hairline. Obviously not.

'No, no, not recreational, I don't mean that, just aspirin really, oh, and the odd paracetamol or two,' I nodded sagely, 'nothing to worry about really.'

'Ah.' Thankfully his eyebrows were coming down from orbit and it seemed his alarm had turned to mere surprise.

I was desperate to change the subject and get away from my fictitious junkie sister. I slapped my thigh in true jolly-hockey-stick style. 'But don't you worry, I'll be back in my own wardrobe tomorrow.'

'Ah good, so tomorrow we can expect to see something a little more, er, restrained?'

'Back to the tweeds and the brogues!' I grinned. And so, I seem to remember, did he, which must have been a first and only.

It wasn't that I didn't like Nick, it was just that he was so bloody difficult to get to know. He was always so incredibly busy, and when I did manage to speak to him, he was invariably abrupt, off-hand, and sometimes downright rude. He would nod his thank-yous and bark out his orders.

A normal opening gambit of a Monday morning would be, 'There's a meeting in half an hour, I'd like tea, coffee and an agenda,' not, 'Good morning, Polly, how was your weekend? If you've got a moment could you possibly find time to make some coffee and then maybe type a little agenda if it's not too much trouble,' to which I would have smiled sweetly and acquiesced. As it was, I barged around

17

in the kitchen slamming cups on to saucers and invariably breaking something.

He was still pretty young to be in his position – about thirty-three or thirty-four – and I had to admit quite good-looking, if you liked that sort of thing. Of course, I didn't. He was tall and slim but with broad shoulders, very dark hair and dark bushy eyebrows. His eyes were dark brown and deep-set and he had very striking angular features, including a rather hooked nose which somehow suited his face. Unfortunately he spoiled the effect by looking continually tired and harassed which he probably was since he was the only one in the agency who appeared to do any work.

As far as sharing conspiratorial lunches in groovy restaurants was concerned, the only thing I'd ever seen him eat was a hastily grabbed sandwich at his desk in between meetings. By all accounts he was screamingly intelligent, or so Pippa – whose brother had been up at Cambridge with him – told me, so he naturally despised the rest of us who survived on one brain cell between us.

As I inanely filled in the D of Dempster with Tipp-Ex and yawned with boredom, in he swept with a face like reinforced concrete. His old tweed coat streamed out behind him like Batman as he flew past at speed, his black eyebrows knitted together in fury.

'Good presentation?' I ventured, closing the paper and trying to look intelligent.

'Bloody client didn't pitch up!' he bawled as he charged into his office slamming the door behind him.

'Oh dear,' I said lamely.

'Happy days,' murmured Pippa, grimacing.

I was just about to grab my notebook and take his messages in, when the door opened again and he poked his head round. 'By the way, Polly, there's a chap downstairs waiting to see you.'

'A chap?' I said in surprise. 'Downstairs?'

It's a bit of a habit of mine to repeat what people say, especially when I'm nonplussed. It obviously irritated the hell out of Nick. He ground his teeth together and shut the door without replying.

Who on earth could it be? No one ever came to see me at work. Suddenly my heart leaped into my oesophagus. Of course! Harry! Harry had come to see me. He knew Pippa had spotted him last night and he'd come to explain himself, to ask my forgiveness and implore me to go out with him tonight, that was it! But why hadn't he telephoned? Why had he come all the way from his computer screen in the city just to see me? Love? Impulse? Even I was clued-up enough to realise he didn't know the meaning of either word. All the same, I jumped up from my chair with joy in my heart and a kiss ready and waiting on my lips. Just in case.

'How extraordinary, Pippa, a man downstairs to see me! Who on earth d'you think it could be?' I babbled excitedly as I brushed my hair and scrabbled around in my drawer for my lipstick.

'I don't know. But I'll tell you one thing, it's not who you think it is,' she said caustically, eyeing my preparations with suspicion.

'Oh God, you're such a killjoy, how do you know?'

'Take it from me. I just know.'

I sighed. Why couldn't any of my friends share my enthusiasm for the man I loved? Never mind. Wouldn't it just show her if it were Harry? I snapped my make-up mirror shut and bounced off down the corridor.

I leaned over the banisters and peered down to the marble hallway below. Whoever it was was sitting on the sofa, most of which was obscured from my view by the stairwell, so all I could make out was a pair of long slim male legs clad in beige trousers with a pair of Docksiders at the end of them. Not Harry's, definitely not Harry's; his Docksiders were brown, not blue; but funnily enough I thought I recognised them. I craned my neck, but couldn't see any more of the body without doing myself a serious injury.

I shrugged. Oh well, it wasn't Harry, but the legs didn't look too bad, so I bounced down the stairs in what I hoped was an attractive, skippy manner, with my blonde hair bobbing around behind me.

'Can I help you?' I inquired in my most imperious, up-market, I-just-bash-a-word-processor-for-a-lark, I-don't-need-the-money, voice.

At that moment the beige trousers uncrossed, the Docksiders hit the deck, and the legs straightened. As he stood up and turned to face me, I realised why the trousers had looked familiar. I'd seen them less than half an hour ago; sat opposite them, in fact. I gasped and my hand shot to my mouth. Good God, it was Ginger!

Chapter Two

I gasped in amazement and gripped the banister rail. Oh
Christ, he'd followed me. He'd seen me giving him the
glad-eye on the tube and got completely the wrong idea.
Now he was going to force himself on me right here on the
cold marble stairs and I was too frightened to scream. I
looked around desperately. Where was Maurice? Where
was Bob? Even a sex-crazed dog was preferable to this. I
wasn't even carrying the rape alarm that Mummy had
given me for Christmas. Ginger walked towards me. I
moaned softly and backed upstairs.

'Hi,' he said.

'What do you want?' I whispered in a very small, un-
imperious voice.

He took another menacing giant stride in my direction
and placed a large freckled hand on the banister rail. I
whimpered in terror and jumped back up another step. He
smiled in an extremely un-threatening way and the blue
eyes crinkled.

'Hey, I'm sorry, I'm not trying to frighten you or
anything, I just want to talk to you.'

Pure Ivy League. I'm very hot on accents, especially
American ones. I was somewhat relieved, but keen to be
totally relieved.

'But you followed me,' I squeaked. 'You followed me
from the station, I saw you on the tube.'

'You're right, I did follow you, but hey –' he laughed

— 'there's a perfectly innocent reason. I'm not a mad rapist or anything; I'm certainly not after your body, if that's what you're thinking!'

'Oh.'

He made the very idea sound so absurd I was rather miffed. I drew myself up to my full five feet three inches and adopted a second-position ballet stance, which I've been told gives one poise. Dignity and composure were slowly beginning to course through my veins again.

'So what exactly do you want, only I'm rather busy. I was in a meeting,' I said haughtily.

I had to admit he didn't look like the mad axe-man and, anyway, now I'd got my breath back, I was sure I could scream the place down if I felt like it.

'Actually, I need your help,' he said. 'Look, I'm sorry I followed you, but I couldn't help noticing your scarf.'

'My scarf?' I clutched my neck. I wasn't wearing a scarf. Sometimes I wear a silk scarf under my shirt, but today I definitely wasn't. He *was* mad. A madman with a scarf fetish. Perhaps he wanted to strangle me. 'I'm not wearing a scarf!'

'Your woollen scarf,' he said patiently. 'You were wearing it on the tube this morning.'

'Oh, that one!'

'Yes, that one.'

'What about it?' Was this guy for real? He liked my old school scarf? OK, it was about the only decent legacy I'd got from St Gertrude's, a rather dashing college-style affair with bright red and green stripes, but even so, come *on*. 'It's just my old school scarf, St Gertrude's.'

'Yes I know, I recognised it, that's why I followed you.' Suddenly he reached inside the front of his jacket and went for his gun. Christ! I ducked down on the stairs, hands on head, Miami Vice-style. He pulled a wallet out of his breast pocket.

'Hey, calm down, I just want to show you something.'

He produced a rather crumpled photograph and put it under my nose as I straightened myself out with the help of the banisters. Feeling more than a tad foolish, I took the photo. It was a girl of about my age, maybe younger, with wavy fair hair and quite a sweet face. Pretty-ish, but nothing special.

'Do you know her?' He looked at me intently.

'No . . . I don't think so.' I shook my head.

'Her name's Rachel Marsden, she was at school with you,' he said with some urgency.

'Really? At St Gertrude's?' I had another look. 'Can't say I do, I'm afraid. How old is she?'

'Twenty.'

'Ah well, that's a little bit younger than me, and if she wasn't in my house, which I don't think she was, I wouldn't know her from Eve.'

'I'm pretty sure her house was called something like Finch or Fich—'

'Finches. No, well in that case she definitely wasn't in my house. Well, there you go, sorry. Can't help you, I'm afraid.' I handed back the picture.

He looked crestfallen. 'Are you absolutely sure?'

'Absolutely.'

'Perhaps you'd remember some of her friends?'

'Who were they?'

'Well, that's the problem, she was a bit of a loner really. I'm finding it pretty hard to locate anybody.'

He put the photo back in his wallet and ran his hands through his hair. He really was rather good-looking. Especially when he did that. I was intrigued.

'So um, you're looking for her, is that it?'

He sighed. 'Yeh, that's it.'

'Why, has she done something wrong?' What was he, Special Branch, MI5?

He laughed hollowly. 'No, she hasn't done anything wrong, she's my . . .' He hesitated ' . . . My fiancée.'

'Your fiancée!' I was flabbergasted. Some mousy nobody probably a year or so below me at school who I didn't even remember had got herself engaged to this yummy American hunk, done a bunk, and left him moving heaven and earth to find her? And how in God's name do you loose a fiancé? I know if I had one I'd have him locked in a little cage in my bedroom with a heavy padlock on the door.

'Well, if she's a missing person, why don't you go to the police?'

He sat down on the bottom step and shook his head. He looked all in. He was also getting cuter by the minute. I quickly sat down next to him and looked sympathetic, sweeping my hair back from my forehead so he could see my profile, and opening my eyes wide.

'Well, she's not a missing person exactly,' he said. 'Her father knows where she is, but he won't let me see her.' He gave a wry smile and scuffed the toe of his Docksider on the marble. 'He doesn't exactly approve.'

'Oh! Why ever not, you don't look like too much of a reprobate to me.'

He laughed. 'I'm not, he just doesn't . . . Well, let's just say we don't see eye to eye.'

I looked at him warily. Perhaps he had done something terrible after all. Walked off with the family silver, seduced the parlourmaid, made a pass at the dog – it would have to have been something in that line for my own parents to disapprove. Mummy practically tripped men like this up in the street for me, so desperate was she to shorten my shelf-life and climb into her mother-of-the-bride outfit.

'Why on earth doesn't he like you?' I asked nosily.

He hesitated and I thought he was about to tell me, but he obviously thought better of it. 'Oh, it's a long story.'

I took the hint and got to my feet briskly. 'Well, I'm sorry I can't be more helpful, but I honestly don't

24

remember er, whatsername, Rachel thingamy.'

He stood up immediately and held out his hand. I shook it. What charming manners.

'That's OK,' he said, 'thanks a lot for trying, anyway. I really appreciate it.'

'Not at all.' I almost said, Do come again.

'Well goodbye, and thanks.' He turned to go and was walking towards the door when he suddenly swung around and stared at me intently. He looked desperate.

'Look, if you see anyone from school who remembers her or who might have seen her recently, would you please let me know? I'd be really grateful. You see, I've got nothing to go on at the moment, and to be honest I'm really at the end of my rope, I just don't know what the hell's happened to her. I mean, maybe if you rang a few people up? You know, old schoolfriends? I don't want to be a nuisance but I just . . . I just don't know what to do next. I'm staying at the Savoy till the end of the week, so you could get me there if you come up with anything. My name's Adam Buchanan, by the way. Shall I write that down?'

'No, it's OK.' Adam Buchanan. Somehow I thought I'd remember. Savoy, eh? I smiled. 'I promise I'll ring you if I hear anything.'

'Thanks. It would mean so much, really. Well, goodbye, it was good to meet you.'

'Um, you too. Bye,' I smiled.

This time he went, closing the door softly behind him. Well! I stood on the stairs for a moment, inwardly digesting. Then I walked slowly back upstairs. Poor chap, what a shame, and how horrid Rachel Thingamy's father must be not to like him. Fancy searching London for his girlfriend; he must be crazy about her. I couldn't see Harry looking under the bed if I went missing.

'Well?' asked Pippa eagerly as I wandered into the pit, chewing my thumbnail thoughtfully. 'Was it him?'

'Who?'

'Harry, you goon.'

'Oh, Harry, no, but it was quite interesting . . .' I explained at length, embellishing the story a bit here and there for her benefit. She was suitably horrified at the potential rape situation, clapping her hands over her mouth and rolling her eyes in terror, and then was almost moved to tears, as I knew she would be, by the futility of the lover's quest.

'Oh Polly, how awful! You mean he's an innocent abroad, combing the streets of London and grilling complete strangers in an effort to find her,' she said dramatically. 'God, he must have been desperate to follow you.'

'Thanks a bunch,' I said dryly, but I knew what she meant.

'Well, ring up some old schoolfriends and see if they remember her!' she said eagerly.

'Oh, come on, Pippa,' I said, eyeing the enormous pile of typing Nick had obviously just deposited on my desk, 'I have enough trouble sorting out my own life, let alone someone else's.'

'But you could really help him, Polly, someone might have seen her. Just ring a couple of people, please,' she impassioned.

'I will later, if I have time,' I lied. 'Just let me get through some of this first.'

I went on to auto-pilot and started bashing out the first contact report of the day. One of only two million, I was sure. Pippa always made me feel like such a heel. She'd help every lame dog she came across and positively went looking for them. There was an old tramp at South Ken station who should have been wearing designer labels saying, 'Clothes by Pippa Harvey', she threw so much money at him. I bashed away, taking my lack of humanity out on the typewriter. Suddenly my hands froze in mid-air.

How had he known my name? How on earth had he known who to ask for, for God's sake? Bloody hell, there was something fishy going on here! I pushed back my chair and charged into Nick's office without bothering to knock.

'Who did he ask for, Nick? Did he know my name?' I gasped.

Nick was behind his desk, and sitting opposite him was Mr Hutchinson, probably our most important client. He could have been the Queen for all I cared.

'Did he say Polly? Or Polly McLaren, or what?' I urged.

They both stared at me. Mr Hutchinson was on the edge of his seat: he liked a bit of drama because he led such a dull life. He was a little rat of a man with thin grey hair, a pale waxy face, and thick pebble glasses through which he blinked a great deal. On rare occasions he gave a tight little smile, but mostly his expression was similar to that of an undertaker's. His front teeth protruded slightly, just like a rat's, and he did a lot of slurping and sucking in an effort to cover them with his upper lip. He was a great one for giving Pippa and me the vicar's handshake, a two handed ever-so-sincere jobby, and we decided that was probably the closest he ever got to sex. A hell of a nasty thought. We always washed afterwards. He was blinking away at me now like a Belisha beacon, but the tight little smile had yet to surface.

Nick looked at me coldly, keeping his own eyelids well under control. They didn't bat once. 'If you mean the gentleman downstairs,' he said evenly, 'he simply asked for Miss McLaren. I've no idea how he knew your name.'

'But that's so spooky, isn't it, don't you see?' I was raving now. 'I mean, he must have been on to me for days, he probably knows where I *live*, for God's sake, and there I was falling for his story and even trying to *help* him when all the time—'

'*Polly*!' Nick cut in furiously and with volume. It did the trick. I'd never heard him raise his voice and I ground to a halt. He glared at me. 'I've no idea how he knew your name, nor, come to that, what the hell you are talking about. Now let's sort this out later, shall we?' It was said with about six inches of solid steel blade running through the middle of it.

My P45 fluttered briefly through my fuddled brain and I saw his point. I retreated, closing the door quietly.

Pippa looked at me with horror as I came out. 'Mr Hutchinson's in there!' she hissed.

'I know,' I whispered, 'but how did he know my name?'

'Who, Hutchinson?'

'No, idiot, scarf-spotter downstairs.'

'Oh! Did he?'

'Yes! He asked for Miss McLaren!'

'Oh!' Pippa looked almost as shaken as I did for a moment, then she suddenly swung round and grabbed my scarf from the hat stand.

'You said it yourself, he's a scarf spotter! It's got your name on it, see?' she said, waving it under my nose. 'Here, look!'

And of course there it was. P. E. McLaren, red letters on a little strip of white tape, sown on by my ever-loving mother, years before I embarked on my career as a job-wrecker.

'He'll sack me!' I wailed. 'I was like a loony in there!'

'No he won't,' said Pippa doubtfully. 'He'll just be furious.'

And so he was. Bloody furious. When Mr Hutchinson had gone he asked me, murderously, to come into his office. 'Now please!'

I slunk in meekly and sat down opposite him at his vast, leather-topped desk. I decided to get my story in quickly before he had a chance to ask, thereby deflecting the shit from the fan.

'Look, Nick, I'm terribly sorry about bursting in on you and Mr Hutchinson, but the guy downstairs followed me from the tube, can you believe it? I mean, OK, I was staring at him first, but only as a joke — you know it's this game I play every morning, which man would you fancy going to — er, well anyway — I thought he'd got the wrong idea, and that was why I was so alarmed, but in fact he's lost his fiancée and was following me because he recognised my old school scarf and the reason he knew my name is that—'

'Stop!' Nick had his hand up like a policeman stopping traffic. His eyes were tightly shut. 'Just stop!'

I stopped. He opened his eyes. Except they didn't look like eyes, more like bits of flint. I had a feeling the shit was making a detour my way. He leaned forward and folded his arms on his desk. His face was about a foot from mine. A muscle was going in his cheek and he looked deadly.

'Listen to me, Polly,' he said quietly. I listened. 'This is not a large agency: in fact it's extremely small. We have a few minor clients who provide us with a smattering of income, but we have one major client who happens to bill a great deal of money with us, namely Mr Hutchinson. He is, as you know, a total jerk but, be that as it may, he has us by the short and curlies. Because if he decides, for whatever reason, to take his revolting instant coffee away to another agency, we're sunk. Snookered. Finished. Washed up. Bankrupt. Am I making myself clear?'

'Yes,' I whispered, feeling about twelve.

'Our image is extremely important. Like it or loathe it, it sells us. It is therefore absolutely imperative that we create a good impression in front of clients. You come charging into my office, ranting and raving like a banshee, and we look like a Mickey Mouse agency. D'you get my drift?'

'Yes,' I whispered again, squirming in my seat. What did he think I was, a moron?

Nick leaned back in his seat and surveyed me, tapping the desk with a pencil. 'And another thing, Polly. If you ask me, your private life is intruding too much on your

29

work. You just haven't got your mind on the job, have you? If you're not sitting at your desk filing your nails, you're mooning around thinking about your boyfriend and waiting for the telephone to ring. Well, that's harmless enough as long as you've done all your typing, but now I find you're picking up men on trains, bringing them into the agency, and chatting them up downstairs. I'm afraid that's just not on. I don't give a damn if you behave like that in your spare time, although frankly I'm surprised, but for God's sake don't bring these guys into the agency.'

Steam was pouring from my ears now, and I opened my mouth to speak, but the policeman's hand flew up again.

'Let me finish! It's quite simple, Polly, and we don't need to discuss it any further. I simply ask that you don't bring your men friends into the office, and that you don't burst into important client meetings raving like a lunatic. Is that clear?' The telephone rang, he picked it up instantly. 'Yes, hello? Oh, Mr Rawlings, yes, I was going to get back to you . . .'

My mouth was wide with indignation, which I was bloody well going to voice in no uncertain terms, but Nick waved me out of the office. I ignored him and sat tight. He was not getting away with this. He carried on talking, saw me still sitting there, and frowned, waving me off again. Still I sat there, determined to have my two penny-worth.

Suddenly he put his hand over the mouthpiece. 'Polly, if you don't get out of my office this minute and let me talk to Mr Rawlings, I will really lose my temper!' he hissed.

I ran. But by golly was I livid. Exactly who did he think he was talking to? Mooning about my boyfriend! Picking up men! Filing my nails! I don't even have a nail-file — come to that, I don't even have any nails! He'd just thrown that in to make me sound like a Sharon, the bastard.

Pippa tried to placate me with numerous cups of strong, sweet tea, but the steam was gushing out of every orifice now, and I gnashed my teeth in fury, waiting for my chance to set Mr Penhalligan straight.

Unfortunately, Nick shut himself away for the rest of the day to work on a presentation, giving the strict instruction that under no circumstances was he to be disturbed. I don't have that much of a death wish, so I left him alone and finally went home on the dot of five-thirty, seething with rage and plotting my revenge.

Chapter Three

I marched up the steps to our front door in Tregunter Road, slammed it behind me, and stomped up the innumerable stairs to the garret flat I share with Lottie. I was still steaming. *No one*, I repeated to myself, *no one* has *ever* spoken to me like that. *No one*. I viciously shouldered open the flat door which always sticks, flung my bag on the floor and collapsed on the sofa in a deep depression. Fine Young Cannibals assaulted my eardrums at full volume. The flat was in the most disgusting mess: dirty glasses, wine bottles and overflowing ashtrays covered every conceivable surface area, a line of bras and knickers in varying shades of sock-grey were drying on the radiator, bits of chocolate digestive had been trodden into the rug, there were dog hairs everywhere, and penicillin was sprouting from the various coffee mugs that were littered around. Why doesn't anyone ever tidy *up*? I thought savagely.

'Harry rang!' shouted Lottie from the bathroom.

I sprang to my feet, eyes shining. Suddenly the flat seemed beautifully cosy and lived in and − oh, just charmingly Bohemian, and the music was joyous and uplifting. I ran to the bathroom where Lottie was brushing her teeth in her underwear. A bath was running, bad sign, I'd have to have her water.

'When! What did he say? Is he ringing back?'

Lottie paused, her mouth full of froth. 'Ten minutes

ago, he's coming over in an hour to take you out to supper and no, he's not ringing back.'

She gargled, making sure she didn't swallow any toothpaste — we'd read somewhere that it was full of calories — and then went back for some more vigorous brushing, her D-cupped boobs bouncing up and down under the strain and her long dark hair dripping in the basin.

'Oh joy! Oh joy! Oh thank you God!' I did an ecstatic little dance and wrapped the shower curtain around me in a dramatic Grecian sweep.

Lottie put her toothbrush down and looked at me accusingly. 'So you're going,' she said grimly.

'Well of course I'm going.' I dropped the curtain in disbelief. 'I've been waiting for this phone call for six days now!'

'Exactly.' Lottie rinsed her mouth. 'If you were really cool you'd ring back and say you were busy. Look at the way he just assumes you're free!'

'Oh I know.' I felt deflated. 'But don't make me do it, Lottie. I can't, I'm mad about him,' I wailed.

She sighed. 'I know. And the worst thing is he knows it too. Rung up for his weekly bonk, I suppose.'

She peered in the mirror, looking apprehensively at potential blackhead areas. I watched her reflection as I perched on the side of the bath. Her round sweet face was framed with long dark silky hair and she had beautiful huge dark eyes that looked at me critically now. Oh dear, I was in trouble.

Lottie was my only truly sensible friend. She ran her life in an orderly, no-nonsense fashion, and boy did she get results. I once analysed the secret of Lottie's success and realised it was mind-blowingly simple. During the day, she focused her mind on the job in hand, which in her case was that of being a solicitor in a large city practice. That was what she was there to do and that was what she did. She didn't loll all over her desk nursing a hangover, eating chocolate and dreaming about men. She didn't block the office phone-lines gossiping endlessly to girlfriends, neither did she go shopping in office hours searching for that elusive little black number. No, no. Lottie did something that was anathema to me. She worked. Consequently she was well respected, well liked and well paid. A simple formula, you might think, but one that had yet to filter down to my neck of the woods.

Then there was Lottie's love life to consider. OK, she was experiencing a temporary lull at the moment, but purely at her own instigation. A particularly sweet (but rather short) antique dealer was probably at this very moment throwing himself off Blackfriars Bridge because Lottie had gently but firmly eased him out of her life. Lottie finished with men. They did not finish with her. Lottie was pursued into cupboards, behind sofas, into expensive restaurants: you name it, she'd been there.

Now admittedly she's a good-looking girl. But if I say so myself, and she would say it too, I'm not bad looking either. Granted, I'm prone to pushing the scales over nine stone, but who isn't? And I have nice blue eyes, a good complexion, a pair of rather stylish cheekbones (a rare commodity these days, I've noticed), longish, blondish hair, a thankfully unremarkable nose and pretty remarkable legs, so how do I manage to get it so wrong?

Do I have an unattractive personality? Am I perhaps lacking in humour, or a sartorial sense of style? My friends tell me no. As far as humour's concerned I like nothing better than a good laugh and, as for style, if they handed out O-levels in how to accessorise, I'm sure I'd have a shed-full.

Ah, so perhaps it's something more sinister, I hear you whisper. Perhaps there's a personal hygiene problem lurking nastily under the armpits. Again, the answer, I assure you, is no. I happen to be a rigorous pit sniffer –

just my own — and I'm also an avid, and noisy, mouthwash gargler. So what exactly is my problem?

Simple, says Lottie, I aim too high. Way, way too high. Apparently I should be aiming lower — much, much lower; underground preferably, somewhere around pit level, amongst the slugs and the worms. Lottie is actually the greatest exponent of her theory, her maxim at a party being, 'Go ugly early.' Why waste valuable time, she says, lining up behind all the other prospective female candidates to chat up the best-looking man in the room, when you know you're going to end up with that short, balding insurance broker in the corner?

All this, of course, makes huge sense, but sense and I have never made very good bedfellows. The one and only time I took Lottie's advice, sense did indeed turn out to be huge, about six feet nine inches, in fact; more of a giraffe than a human being. And hard though I tried to keep his 'good personality' to the forefront of my mind, I couldn't help being distracted by his colossal nostrils (of which I had an excellent view from my low vantage point), and his enormous expanse of smooth white forehead which seemed to go back and back in an uninterrupted fashion almost to the nape of his neck. Needless to say he had to go and, as he went, my feet went dancing off to the sunny side of the street again, where the beautiful people live.

Of course, this side of the street is harder work. Back on the sensible side I'm way up in the pecking order, but over here with the stunners, I'm only fair to middling. I had to fight my corner, and fight I did, until one day I went home with the prize. Harry. Now this should have been my moment of glory. I should have been able to dangle his delectable personage in front of Lottie's sensible nose crying, 'You see! You see! I hooked one in the end!' But no. The more I dangled, the more Lottie was able to shake her head at me and sigh. Like now. Oh-oh.

Lottie set aside her toothbrush and sat on the linen

basket facing me. She folded her arms in an ominously businesslike manner. 'Polly, let me ask you something. Do you honestly enjoy your dates with Harry?'

'Enjoy them? Of course I do! What a question! Enjoy them? I positively live for them!'

'Yes, I know that, I know you spend every waking hour dreaming about them and listening for the phone, but when you actually go out, do you relax? Is he good company? Does he make you laugh? Does he – I don't know – look after you, see that you're having a good time?'

'Lottie, don't be absurd; we never stop laughing, he's marvellous company!'

'But do you feel relaxed? I mean really? Or d'you feel that you're constantly making an effort with him? It's just that whenever I see you with him it all seems such a strain, so sort of – artificial really. I mean you never just get a video out and curl up on the sofa with him, do you? You never just have a quiet evening in. It's always night clubs and parties and restaurants; and you always have to look marvellous, and it's not as if you've just met him, you've been going out with him for ages now, and I shouldn't think he's even seen you without lipstick, let alone no make-up at all.'

'Oh Lottie, what's make-up got to do with it? You know I wear a lot anyway.'

'Not around the flat, you don't, and not when you go to your parents.'

'Oh well, that's different—'

'But why? Why aren't you more natural with him? Let him see what you're really like instead of, I don't know, always being perfect. I'm not trying to spoil things, and I know you're excited because he's phoned, but honestly Polly, it's been about nine months now and I sometimes wonder if you really know this guy at all!'

I sighed and picked my nails, feeling hemmed in. 'I

37

know what you mean, Lotts, but honestly, everything's fine. Harry just likes me to be like that, you know, made up and dressed up and—'

'Exactly! That's exactly what I mean!'

'I know, I know, but, well, if Harry likes it, well then I like it too . . .' I trailed off lamely. I could see from Lottie's face how pathetic that sounded, but my argumentative powers were fading fast. I rallied myself.

'The thing is, I can't explain why, but I enjoy it all. The preparation and − and the excitement, the build up. I don't want us to be mundane and boring − living on takeaways and watching telly and taking each other for granted.'

'No but surely there's a happy medium. I mean—'

'Please, Lottie. I know what you're saying, but seriously, I reckon I've nearly cracked it with Harry. A couple more weeks and he'll be eating out of my hand! In fact, I'm pretty sure he's mad about me already,' I lied.

Lottie looked totally unconvinced. I took a shifty look at my watch. Christ, quarter-past six already.

'Look, I promise, everything's fine, I couldn't be happier! And honestly, I'd love to talk about it more with you, but the thing is he'll be here in about an hour and I desperately need a bath,' I said, eyeing her water enviously. 'I couldn't possibly . . . ?'

'Yes, yes, go on, have it,' she said, caving in dramatically, 'I'll have it after you. I'm only going to the cinema with Sophie, I'm sure she won't mind if I'm covered in scum and leg shavings.'

I hugged her, grateful for the water and for her submission. 'Thanks, you're an absolute star, and I promise I'll think about what you've said.'

'Promise?' she said, knowing I wouldn't.

'Promise,' I said, knowing she knew that I wouldn't.

When she'd gone, I quickly poured half a bottle of my most expensive bubble-bath into the water, hoping it would overpower her Radox, and leaped in. Only an hour! Even less, in fact! I didn't have much time and there was so much to do! I scrubbed and shaved and plucked and washed and rinsed and sloshed around a bit, then jumped out and ran dripping to the bedroom where I emptied the entire contents of my wardrobe on to the bed.

I looked at the mountain of clothes and groaned. 'Oh God, I've got nothing to wear!' I wailed. 'Lottie, can I borrow your suede trousers?'

'They're at the cleaners,' she yelled back.

'Oh no! What else have you got?'

I ran into Lottie's bedroom where she obligingly emptied her own wardrobe on to the bed. I wriggled in and out of things like a maniac, but eventually ran back to my own mountain and settled on a short black skirt and a silky red jumper with a slashed neckline which slipped seductively off one shoulder. I clinched it all in with a black suede belt. The shoulder looked a bit anaemic, so I rubbed on some fake tan with tiny pieces of make-up sponge which Wellington, Lottie's Yorkie, had thoughtfully chewed into little bits. I ran into the sitting room where Lottie was ironing a shirt.

'What d'you think?' I said, balancing on the sofa and peering into our only decent mirror above the fireplace. I'd coaxed my hair into mad gypsy curls of the blonde variety, and completed the look with some enormous gold hoop earrings which had eaten up most of last month's salary and were so heavy that they almost made me walk with my head bowed.

'Wow!' Lottie was genuinely impressed. 'That should knock him for six.'

'Really?' I was pleased, Lottie was a tough critic. 'Not too tarty?'

'Oh well, it's tarty all right, but you can't have it both ways.'

I hoiked the jumper up a bit to cover the shoulder. 'Better?'

'Well, it'll come off later anyway, so what does it matter? I take it you're playing away tonight?'

I ignored Lottie's disapproving tone, and jumped around on the sofa with excitement. 'I expect so! Don't double-lock, but don't expect me either – and stop looking at me like an old fishwife with a rolling pin. Haven't you ever been wild and irresponsible?'

Lottie sighed and said truthfully, 'Just give me half a chance. Seriously though, Polly, don't hang on to his every monosyllable, and don't race him back to his flat when he suggests coffee, and don't iron every single shirt he possesses, and don't—'

The doorbell rang in the middle of the lecture. I leaped off the sofa, then leaped back on again, yelping with panic.

'He's early! You go, Lottie.'

'Oh sure, then he'd really think it was his lucky night.' Lottie was still in her underwear. 'A flat full of push-overs.'

She went off to dress and I buzzed Harry in, my heart beating as loud as the thump-thump-thump of his feet coming up the stairs.

I knew I'd settle down eventually, but for the first half an hour with him you'd think I was on drugs. I'd leap around like a maniac, talking in a strange high-pitched voice, breathing heavily, offering him cigarettes when he didn't smoke, and pouring him large gins when he drank whisky. Anyone else, said Lottie, would get terribly insecure and think there was a chain-smoking, gin-swilling hunk knocking around the rest of the week, but not Harry.

He came bounding into the flat like a golden retriever puppy, all long-legged and blond and floppy-haired. He looked, as usual, divine. He was tanned from a long weekend skiing, and his hair was blonder and streakier than ever from the sun. I could feel my much touched-up roots sizzling with jealousy.

'Polyester!' he yelled as he came charging through the door, rugby tackling me on to the sofa. 'How the devil are you? Hang on, we're off!'

I shrieked with laughter as the sofa got under way and we slid across the room on the coasters. Lottie wandered in wearing her dressing gown and munching a jaffa cake. She sidestepped the cruising sofa with weary indifference. She'd seen it all before.

Harry looked up as we came to a standstill next to her. 'Hi, Lottie, how's your sex life?' he said, pulling her dressing gown cord undone.

'Not as complicated as yours, I suspect,' said Lottie dryly, tying the cord up again.

Harry laughed nervously. He wasn't sure about Lottie, she was a bit too smart for him. He swept his hair back in a practised gesture. 'I see it's nice and tidy in here as usual,' he said, taking in the debris-strewn flat. 'That ironing board seems to be a permanent fixture! Modern art, is it? Ha-ha!'

'No, we're looking back in anger,' Lottie quipped, but it was lost on Harry.

He turned his cornflower-blue gaze on to me. God he was attractive. I bit my hand to stop myself from giving him the first kiss. Wait for it, Polly, wait for it . . . Ah, here it come. He leaned down and kissed me briefly on the mouth. He always started with a little one, a teaser, then bent his head down again for the big clinch. I responded enthusiastically, considering Lottie was still in the room.

When I eventually let him go, his lazy, sexy grin spread over his face and his blue eyes roamed all over me as we lay on the sofa. He took my chin in his hand. I smiled, overwhelmed with love.

'So, young Polly,' he murmured, 'what have you been

41

up to all this time? I haven't seen you for absolutely ages. Been a good girl?'

He made it sound as if I'd been deliberately avoiding him instead of staring at the phone willing it to ring.

'Oh, I've been out and about,' I said as casually as I could. Harry liked independent girls. 'A couple of drinks parties, out to supper once or twice.'

'Terrific, that's what I like to hear. Got to keep your finger on the pulse.'

My own pulse was going like a bongo drum as he ran his fingers through my hair. He was making slow progress, and I leaped up as I realised he was wading through half a ton of mousse and gel. 'Must have a ciggy,' I said quickly.

He sat up and watched me as I lit a cigarette. I knew I was being appraised, so I lit it slowly, then stood with my back to the fireplace – chest out, tummy in – reclining against the marble shelf. Quite uncomfortable really, but it worked. He looked me up and down approvingly.

'You're looking extremely tasty tonight, Poll. Where shall we go to eat before I ravage you? Or shall we skip the meal and I'll ravage you here, much easier!'

'Easier on your wallet,' muttered Lottie.

Harry missed it, but I caught it and said bravely, more for sisterhood than for myself, 'Actually, I'm quite hungry.'

'Of course you are, my little pumpkin, I was only joking. Where d'you want to go?'

'Oh, I don't know. How about Giovanni's?'

'Right, Giovanni's it is. Let's go then.' He drained his glass and stood up, ready for a change of scene.

I was always staggered by his low boredom threshold. He was like a small child, constantly needing to be amused by new toys.

I jumped up too, hurriedly stubbed out my cigarette, and knocked back my drink, throwing most of it down my jumper and choking on the rest. Lottie shook her head in disbelief.

'Steady darling!' Harry patted me on the back, laughing. 'Don't choke on it! Right, we'll be off then. Packed a bag?'

'Er, no, not yet.'

I hadn't, because the last time I'd packed one he'd dropped me back at my flat at ten-thirty saying he was going on to a dance – hadn't he mentioned it? He hadn't, and I'd felt like a complete berk trudging up the stairs to the flat, overnight bag in hand.

'Won't be a minute!' I said, grabbing a pair of knickers from the radiator and stuffing them in my handbag. 'There.'

Harry raised his eyebrows. 'That's it?'

Yes, that was it, or did that look slutty?

'Er, well no, not quite, hang on a sec . . .' I ran into my bedroom.

'No rush, no rush!' he called after me, but I was too wound up to slow down now.

Nothing seemed to be clean, so I rummaged through my dirty linen basket and recycled a navy blue shirt that didn't show the dirt, and grabbed my cleanser, moisturiser and toothbrush, although I always liked to use his. I rummaged under the bed, found an old carrier bag, and shoved everything in.

When I got back to the sitting room he was standing by the door, jangling his keys and looking impatient.

'Sorry,' I panted, 'couldn't find a shirt.'

'No worries. All set now?'

'Yes – bye Lottie!'

I gave her a backward wave, not having the nerve to meet her judgemental eyes; and anyway, I had to run, because Harry seemed to be half-way down the stairs already. I pounded down the stairs after him. Funny how he's always one step ahead, I mused, as I jumped the last few and ran out on to the pavement. He was already revving up the car. I ran around to the passenger door and limbo-danced my way into his low-slung crumpet-catcher. With a good deal of throttle we set off for the restaurant.

And that's another thing, I thought as I settled back into the impossibly-difficult-to-get-out-of bucket seat, how come I never rip him off? How come I never have the nerve to say, 'Well actually, I thought we'd go to Le Gavroche tonight.'

On the other hand, I reflected, as he pulled up outside the extremely reasonable little Italian I'd picked, this was where he'd fallen for me on that first magical night, and I always hoped he'd remember and fall for me all over again.

As we ploughed our way through the only edible food on the menu – avocado, mozzarella and tomato followed by veal marsala – I had him rolling in the aisles as I recounted various anecdotes, apocryphal or otherwise, that I'd saved up and made up during the week. My efforts were rewarded handsomely.

He leaned back in his chair wiping his eyes at one of my more outrageous witticisms. 'Polly, that's hysterical. I don't know where you get these stories from!' he cried.

From my imagination, of course, was the answer to this, but why tell the boring truth when you can tell a good lie? Flushed with success, I helped myself to another glass of wine by way of celebration, although I couldn't help thinking that things were slightly arse about tit here. Wasn't he supposed to be laughing me into bed? And how come I was pouring the wine? Lottie's wise words came briefly to mind, but I banished them hastily. Utter rubbish, I was having a marvellous time.

Oh God, he was off and I hadn't been listening. I rearranged my face so that it took on an absorbed expression as we had our weekly bulletin of Stockbroking News.

I didn't understand stockbroking, but since Harry had explained it twice already, the second time in a painstaking, stockbroking-for-morons tone of voice, I didn't feel I could ask again. I just smiled knowingly and nodded a lot, and when there was a gap in the monologue, made what I thought were appropriate remarks like:

'Really, as much as that?'

'Forty-two per cent, my goodness.'

'No, of course not, that would be insider dealing.'

'Isn't that what they call a bear market?'

It was all pretty hit or miss stuff, but he never seemed to suss me. Once he'd got into his stride he was unstoppable, and he didn't really notice what I said anyway. It suited me because it gave me a chance to catch my breath and think of some more outrageous lies to amuse him with later.

'Polly?'

Harry was wiping his mouth with his napkin and looking none too pleased. Oh God, he'd come to the end of his story which I now remembered he'd prefixed with the words, 'I think you'll find this rather amusing', and I couldn't for the life of me remember what he'd been talking about. Too late for a belly laugh? Definitely. I shook my head and twisted my mouth into what I hoped was a wry little smile.

'How funny, but when you come to think about it, sad too, don't you think?'

Harry looked rather taken aback. 'Er . . . well, I suppose so, for his wife maybe. You can bet your bottom dollar the bra wasn't hers.'

It was my turn to look mystified, but before he'd had time to rearrange his brain cells, I charged off on a completely different tack and told him about my encounter with Adam Buchanan. Of course I hammed it up like mad, and had the distraught man practically crying on my shoulder, begging me to help him find his girlfriend. I naturally expected Harry to laugh like a drain and sneer at such love-struck, unmanly behaviour, but not for the first time in my checkered career with him, I was wrong. Harry was on the edge of his seat; in fact, Harry was leaning forward, keen to hear more. Now this was a first. Harry always leaned back. I was the one who leaned forward. I once tried leaning back in the hope that he'd come in, but we just ended up yelling at each other across the table in an effort to make ourselves heard. But here he was now, eager for details, gripped, engrossed and, wait for it, sympathetic.

'How extraordinary. You say they're engaged?'

'Apparently.'

'And now she's just vanished?'

'That's what he says.'

'And the father thinks he's a bad influence. You can bet your life Daddy's hiding her somewhere, the bastard. And presumably this American guy doesn't know where to start looking for her; he probably doesn't know anyone in London, does he?'

'No, he doesn't, that's why he followed me, you see, because of the school scarf.'

'So what are you going to do?'

'Do?'

'Yes, to help. Didn't you say you'd try and help?'

I fidgeted a bit. 'Well, no, I didn't really.'

'Why not?'

'Well, for a start I didn't even know the girl at school; and secondly, well secondly, what on earth can I do?'

'More than he can in a strange country, that's for sure. I don't know, use your imagination!'

This stung. I smiled sweetly. 'Yes, but it's none of my business really, is it?'

'Except that he's made it your business by following you to work and asking you to help. God, Polly, aren't you intrigued? I mean, how amazing to fall in love and find the person you feel you can spend the rest of your life with, but then have her vanish into thin air! Pretty irritating, don't you think?'

I snorted with derision. 'Hardly thin air, Harry. She's probably shacked up with some hunk in Bayswater. I mean, who knows if this guy's telling the truth? Who knows what's going on?'

'Not you, obviously,' said Harry, helping himself to more wine.

I took a sharp intake of breath and reached for my wine glass. My God, he was pissed off. Pissed off because I couldn't end the story, couldn't give him the punchline. Harry's new toy had been taken away from him just when he was enjoying it. Well gosh, I'm sorry.

But my indignation was misdirected and I knew it. What had really knocked me sideways was that all-revealing sentence of his: 'to find the person you feel you can spend the rest of your life with.' Had he really said that? Harry, the happy hunter, who couldn't even commit himself to a quick drink in the pub, let alone the rest of his life with a wife? Harry, who I'd naturally assumed was an emotional cripple because he'd never come up trumps in the love and slush department?

I'd convinced myself that it all stemmed from his childhood. In fact I'd spent many happy hours fantasising about a strict and puritanical upbringing at the hands of uncompromising and no doubt brutal parents – too many smacks as a child, not enough chocolate, not enough telly – comparing it to my own cuddly, chocolatey, telly-viewing childhood. I was sure that this had soured his outlook, but that with a little patience I could show him the way, lead him up the Mills and Boon path of true romance, teach him what love was all about. But he knew! He knew about it, and what's more – and this was where I nearly gagged on my courgettes – he thought it was 'wonderful'! Harry, like the rest of the human race, was on the prowl for that elusive love match, and all along I'd put his compulsive prowling down to an insatiable desire to stick his hand up girls' skirts.

I struggled womanfully with the courgettes, pushing them firmly down my throat and trying desperately to remember what had brought about this earth-shattering revelation. Oh yes, Rachel Whatsername.

'Anyway,' I said, swallowing hard, 'I don't suppose I could have helped. I mean, I didn't know the girl at school. I only know what she looks like from that photo he showed me.'

'That's it,' said Harry snidely, 'put your head in the sand as usual.'

I was furious. 'How dare you! What do you expect me to do, ring up all the old girls I can find in the phone book and quiz them rigid?'

'Wouldn't hurt,' he said. 'Give you something to do at work for a change.'

Harry was enjoying himself now. I'd worked myself up into a nice little state, and he was steadily winding me up.

Like a moron I took the bait. 'Well for your information,' I said furiously, 'I said I'd look into it for him!'

Harry threw back his head and roared with laughter. 'Oh, really? Inspector McLaren's looking into it, is she? Off to sniff the pavements, eh? Well I shall look forward to hearing how you solve the case!'

The waiter arrived to take our order for pudding. I fumed and tore my napkin into a million pieces. We sat in stony silence as Harry demolished a delicious-looking crême-brûlée which I'd petulantly refused. Just you wait, I thought. It'll take me exactly two minutes to find that girl. Just you wait. I downed the rest of my glass in one gulp, which seemed to have a calming effect. Get a grip, Polly old girl. This is ridiculous. This is no way to end the evening.

Harry was obviously thinking along the same lines. After all, it's not much fun going to bed with a grumpy girlie. He crowbarred his way back into my good books. 'So, how are your parents?' he asked with a glittering smile.

I smiled back reluctantly. I was potty about my family and, given half a chance, could bore for England about my wonderful parents and my gorgeous older brothers.

'They're really well, thanks.'

'Still living in the country?' he grinned maliciously.

He had to spoil it, didn't he? When I'd first met Harry, I'd told him I was going home to the country one weekend. He'd roared with laughter when he discovered we lived in Esher.

'Esher's not country, Polly! You might as well live in Surbiton!'

I'd blushed hotly; I'd always rather liked Esher. Harry's parents lived in Derbyshire, in 'proper country', where his father was a farmer, a gentleman farmer, of course, none of that ploughing the fields and scattering lark for him: he employed people to do that. No, Harry's father strolled around his thousands of acres doing important things like ordering fences to be put here and ditches to be dug there, shooting the odd recalcitrant pheasant; or peasant probably, if he felt like it.

My father wasn't nearly so grand, he was just a consultant at the local hospital. A humble doctor who did little more than save lives every day and bring people back from the dead, that sort of thing. His work was very mundane: a brain tumour one day, a heart attack the next; run-of-the-mill stuff. I'd always been terribly proud of Daddy, but Harry had shown me the error of my ways.

'Very middle-class, Polly, like all the professions.'

He'd once introduced me to some smart friends of his as 'the doctor's daughter from Esher', and laughed. Why? No matter, I was keen to learn. Luckily I'd learned enough already to know that one house just wasn't enough. It was with this in mind that I answered his question.

'Yes, they are in Esher at the moment,' I replied. 'Just back from our place in London, actually.'

'Oh really?' Harry looked surprised. 'I didn't know your parents had a house in London.'

Neither did I, but apparently I'd just invented one.

'Oh yes,' I lied, 'we've always kept a little place up here. So useful.'

'Ah,' he grinned, 'a little place. What is it, a flat?'

'No, it's not actually. I say "a little place" out of habit, but it's quite a big house.'

'Really?' He looked startled. 'How big?'

'Oh I don't know, about six or seven storeys, the usual sort of townhouse.'

'Six or seven storeys!' He was incredibly impressed. I'd obviously overdone it. 'Whereabouts?'

'Oh, um, Knightsbridge.'

'Really? Whereabouts in Knightsbridge?'

Whereabouts again? We'd just done that one, hadn't we? Wasn't he being just a touch nosy? I began to panic. Think of a street, any street, but make sure it's in Knightsbridge.

'Montpelier Street.'

'No! Montpelier Street? My aunt lives in Montpelier Street. What number?'

What number? Christ! Pick a number, any number, just don't let it be Auntie's. I hesitated, this was like Russian Roulette.

'Don't you know?' asked Harry.

'Yes, of course I know, it's number twenty-thre— four!'

'Twenty-four! But that's right next door. Aunt Rose lives at number twenty-six! How extraordinary!'

'Well, not really. I mean someone has to live next door, why not Aunt Rose?'

'But she must know your parents. I'm seeing her on Sunday, I'll ask her, she's bound to!'

'No! I mean, um, I wouldn't ask her, because she won't

50

necessarily know them. You see the thing is — the thing is, it's rented! It's rented on a sort of permanent basis to other people.'

'Rented? But I thought you said your parents had just come back from there?'

Ah yes, Polly, you did, you did.

'Oh! Oh yes, well, they were there for a few days last week, that's true, but that's because, um, that's because they know the people it's rented to. Old family friends, you see, known them for years, so they let my parents stay whenever they're in London.'

'What are they called?'

'My parents?'

'No, idiot, the friends, who are they? Aunt Rose will probably know them.'

Yes, Polly, who are they? These very old trusty family friends, practically your godparents, who exactly are they?

'Well, I er, I don't exactly know them myself, they're friends of my father's really. Daddy's the one who's known them for years, they're colleagues of his, you know, doctors.'

'Ah.' Harry looked more than a little confused, and who can blame him. 'So you never actually use the house yourself?'

'No, oh no, never.' It was such a relief to say something truthful that I said it with a vengeance, with gusto even. I shook my head vehemently. 'Never ever, in fact.'

'Oh. Seems a bit odd really.' God he *would* go on. Couldn't we talk about something else? His ego perhaps? Or his sex appeal? 'I mean, to have a house in London that you can't use . . .' He looked thoughtful, then he sneered. 'I suppose your parents need the money.'

I bristled furiously. 'Certainly not! Need the money? Good gracious, no. In fact these people don't even pay the rent, they just borrow it.'

51

'Oh!'

Oh indeed. So what do we have here now, Polly? A massively philanthropic gesture, is that it? On behalf of some poor impoverished doctors who have been close to your family for many years but whose names escape you? A nice, rent-free, six-, nay seven-storey house in the middle of Knightsbridge for which they pay not a sausage? What are your parents anyway, missionaries? Born-again Christians?

Happily, in the nick of time, the waiter arrived with a bottle of wine which, according to Harry, was corked. This took Harry's mind off things as he sent the waiter scurrying back and forth with new bottles. I blessed the hapless waiter from the bottom of my heart. But I also realised I'd done irreparable damage. It was quite obvious that Harry could never meet my parents now. I imagined him settling down to a quiet chat with Daddy after Sunday lunch in Esher. 'Polly tells me you have a house in Montpelier Street, Mr McLaren.' Oh no, that would never do. They must never meet. Oh dear, so I couldn't marry him! Or if I did my parents wouldn't be able to come to the wedding! It was too horrrific.

I'd talk to Mummy, she'd understand, if a little vaguely. I'd catch her while she was gardening; I could see her pausing for a moment as she pruned the roses. 'Yes, of course I'll pretend, darling, but I don't understand why you said we had a house in London in the first place. Whatever made you imagine we had? We haven't, have we?'

Daddy would be a different matter, glaring at me over his glasses in the study, stern and unamused. 'No, Polly, I'm sorry. If you're ashamed of our house here, that's too bad, but I will *not* become a millionaire overnight just to please your playboy friends.'

I sighed as Harry tasted the new bottle. Oh well, something would come up. Perhaps we could sell it. Yes, that was it, we'd sell it! Get rid of the sodding house once and for all. I brightened considerably. It would be sold tomorrow — but quietly. So Aunt bleeding-nosy-parker Rose didn't get to hear about it.

The new wine had obviously been deemed drinkable and was apparently on the house, so Harry was agreeable now and wanting me to be agreeable too.

'And how is that dreadful boss of yours? Still bullying you and Pippa and throwing his weight around?' he asked.

I smiled. This at least was a subject we both agreed on. As far as Harry was concerned, any man who spent his working days west of the City and certainly west of Fleet Street was either a shirt-lifter or an estate agent. Failing that, he had to be an ad-man, which was the lowest of the low. If he felt like it, Harry could put on a high moral tone and pontificate for hours about the immorality of off-loading unwanted products on to an unsuspecting, gullible public through the medium of advertising. Then he'd put the boot into spineless individuals like Nick who, failing to get a proper job, had gone into advertising to propagate this corruption and earn enormous salaries.

Of course, he'd concede, it was all right for girlies. Girlies had to work in the West End to be near the shops and to have lunch with each other and discuss their boyfriends in the City. But for a man, advertising was the pits.

I told Harry how Nick had shouted at me today when I had simply knocked on his door and very politely interrupted his meeting to ask a pertinent question.

Harry leaned across the table and took my hand. He stroked it sympathetically. 'But he's an ad-man, poppet, that's what you have to remember, he's not like the rest of us. He wouldn't have the first idea how to talk to a lady. He probably didn't even go to public school.'

Nick had gone to Harrow, but I let that pass. I liked the hand-stroking bit and I also liked the bit about the lady.

Harry ordered me a Cointreau without even asking, and I sipped it while he signed the Access slip, feeling decidedly perkier.

I even kept my cool when a drop-dead blonde in a spray-on black lycra dress walked passed us and Harry nearly knocked the table over, so desperate was he to spring to his feet and kiss her very enthusiastically on both cheeks.

'See you tomorrow at Ransome's,' he called after her swaying bottom as it undulated off to the loo like a metronome, mesmerising most of the men in the room.

I tried not to but I couldn't help it. 'What's happening at Ransome's?'

'Oh, it's just a little party. A guy I've known for donkey's years is having a birthday dinner there. He's paying for the whole bash so it's invitation only, of course. Sorry, my sweet, I'd love you to come, but there it is. Actually, it'll probably be rather boring, but I've got to go.' He drained his glass. 'Ready, darling?' He stood up and held my coat out for me.

Again, I was taken by surprise, but I obediently knocked back the Cointreau and stood up. 'Ready.'

And with that I slipped into my coat, slipped into the front seat of his car, slipped into his flat, slipped down a Rémy and slipped into bed.

Well, that's how it always was with Harry, I reflected as I lay there waiting for him to brush his teeth. I felt like a well trained poodle jumping through the hoops as he skilfully manoeuvred me round the course. From restaurant, to car, to flat, to bed. You know the rules, Polly. Not that I was complaining, of course. Perish the thought.

Harry appeared in the doorway looking like a toothpaste commercial — tall, blond, brown, and with a whiter-than-white smile. I giggled because I knew what was coming next. Harry had pinched a child's diving board from his parent's swimming pool and screwed it into the floorboards at the end of his bed. He would bounce up and down on it before launching himself, with a blood-curdling scream, on to his victim. It always reduced me to fits of giggles, but when I'd told Lottie about it she'd looked at me with horror, her eyes like saucers, as if I'd said he dressed up as the fairy queen and cried, 'Beat me, beat me!'

The dive from the board very much set the tone for the rest of the evening, because what always ensued can only be described as a romp. Our particular form of rumpy-pumpy was punctuated with great gales of laughter from him and screams and giggles from me. Pillow fights would occur on a regular basis and even, on one memorable occasion, a water fight with squeezy bottles. Anything, basically, to stop Harry from getting bored. It was certainly fun, and I reckon I lost pounds in the process – one had to be reasonably confident figure-wise, as there was never any question of the light going off – but it was never, by any stretch of the imagination, romantic.

It would have been quite out of place, for example, for me to murmur anything more romantic than, 'Oh no, not on the chest-of-drawers again!' or, 'Come and get me!' from the top of the wardrobe.

I did once, in an extremely drunken and foolhardy moment and after a particularly passionate bout of love-making half-way out of the window, venture, 'Oh Harry, I do love you,' but it was met with such a look of mock horror and surprise that I never tried it again.

This evening was no exception. The Squire and his wench, for wenchy was how I always felt, romped and rolled and screeched and chortled until oh, two-thirty in the morning.

And that was when Harry sat up in bed and gave me a strange and questioning look. 'What would you like to do now, Polly?' he asked.

What would I like to do? Well, sleep was pretty high on my list of priorities. After all, it was two-thirty a.m. and I had to go to work in a few hours. I also felt we'd pretty much run the gamut as far as re-enacting the raunchiest of *The Canterbury Tales* was concerned but, not wishing to be a party-pooper, I opened my eyes wide and let an inquiring little smile play around my lips.

'I don't know, Harry, what would you like to do?'

'Well, how about a little shave?' he asked, innocently enough.

A shave? I sat up and stared at him. What on earth did he mean? I thought I had shaved. I felt my legs . . . fine. One or two bristles, but that was only to be expected considering the time I'd been given to get ready. I frowned. Under-arms! I gasped in alarm, had I forgotten? Was I sitting in Harry's bed like an Italian shot-putter, unmanageable pits flowing on to his whiter-than-white Conran bed linen? My hands shot under my arms. No, false alarm, smooth as a baby's bottom. So what did he mean, a shave? I looked at him quizzically, keen to learn.

'Down there Polly.' He pointed downwards.

I followed his finger and almost gagged on my tonsils. Down there? A shave down there? What, off? All of them? Surely not! He couldn't be serious. I looked up at him again, wary of falling for a practical joke which would later be relayed to a group of friends in the pub. 'Polly thought I wanted to shave her! Can you believe it?' I studied his face. I'd better believe it. A huge grin was spreading slowly from one ear to the other. Harry had thought of a new game. It was called disfiguring Polly. I gulped.

'So what d'you think?' he asked.

Yes, what d'you think, Polly, eh? Baldy? Eh? What do you think? I stalled and played for time.

'Well, I'm not really sure. I mean won't it be a bit, um, prickly, you know, afterwards? For both of us really?' I didn't want to appear selfish.

'Well, a bit maybe, but it won't take long to grow.'

'Really?'

Stupid, very stupid. Harry instantly took this mad impulsive 'Really?' as a sign of accord; in fact he obviously regarded it as being tantamount to a 'Yes please!' He jumped out of bed with alacrity.

'Great!' he cried, joyfully making for the bathroom.

With trepidation I listened to him clattering around in there; taps were running, blades were being changed, probably sharpened too. Oh Lord. I peeped under the bedclothes and gave myself a last lingering look. In a trice he was back, stark naked, armed with a large bowl of steaming water, a fluffy white towel, a razor and a mad, Jack Nicholson grin. He arranged his equipment on the bed in an unnervingly practised fashion. I half expected him to pull a pair of rubber gloves out from under the bed.

'Now hold still, Polly, there's a good girl.'

'I've changed my mind!' I squeaked.

'Don't be silly, you won't feel a thing.'

Won't I, I thought, feeling a lot of hot soapy water sloshing around my nether regions? All of a sudden I knew I'd gone past that point. The one you can return from. Harry was humming a merry tune as he went about his business, 'Tum-ti tum-ti tum-ti tum.' I dared not move. I lay there as if I'd been turned to stone, not moving a muscle, not even lifting my head from the pillow to view the operation because *what if he slipped*! Yes, dear God, what if his hand slipped a millimetre? It just didn't bear thinking about.

'More soap!' cried Harry joyfully, and I looked up to see him trotting off to the bathroom for supplies, whistling away, happy in his work.

I took a sneaky look down. Great Scott! I was receding rapidly; in fact I was half bald. I looked about eight years old on one side and twenty-two on the other. Maybe, I thought desperately, maybe if he stopped now I'd still be in with a chance. Maybe I could sweep one side across to hide

57

the bald patch, yes, that's it! That would do the trick!

Too late. The demonic barber was back again, a razor shining in his hand and madness glinting in his eye. I thought long and hard of England as he deftly completed his task before giving me a wash and . . . no, no brush up this time.

'There you go!' he said, busily putting away his equipment. 'All finished!'

I sat up and gazed down at the alien territory below my tummy. Was that me? And if so where were my knickers – quick, it was obscene! Ah, there they were on the diving board. I grabbed them and whipped them on inside out.

'Polly, don't . . .' He pulled at them; I pulled back. I won.

I sat there in my knickers, forcing a smile.

'So what do you think?' he grinned. 'Something for the weekend, madam?'

'How about a toupee?' I said with forced jollity, rallying a brave smile.

'So you like it?'

'Oh yes, it's great, yes, thanks a lot!'

Should I tip him? I thought wildly. I mean, what does he expect? He deprives me of my womanhood with one quick flick of the wrist and wants to know what I think. I think I'm going to cry, that's what. Tears were welling. One even escaped down my cheek. Harry spotted it.

'Oh Polly, what's wrong? Don't you like it? You should have said!' He put his arm around me. 'You are an old silly!'

Yes, I am, aren't I? But then I'm in love, and love makes us do crazy things. I snuffled a bit and nuzzled into his shoulder.

'Look, don't worry. If you don't like it, it'll grow soon!' he said cheerfully.

Now where had I heard those words before? They sounded very familiar. Ah yes, that was it, about twice a year at my hairdresser's. Of course, it was all just a bad dream and in fact Harry was just Raymond in disguise, taking two inches off my split ends before I left, as usual, in tears.

'Yes, of course it will grow,' I smiled bravely. And it'll hurt like hell too, I thought grimly.

When I woke up the next morning I realised he'd made a pretty awful job of it too. I already had the makings of designer stubble. George Michael, I thought, would be proud of that. Harry wasn't.

'Oh sorry Polly, I've made a bit of a mess of that, haven't I? Tell you what, I'll have another go.'

I stood my ground very firmly this time and clutched my George Michael possessively. 'No bloody fear.'

I pulled the bedclothes around me. Harry looked slightly miffed. 'Polly, really . . .'

Don't upset him. 'I mean, no thanks. Thanks awfully, jolly kind of you to offer, but no more, thanks all the same.'

He accepted this, albeit sulkily and reluctantly, but he accepted it, and anyway he was late for work.

'Oh well, if you must go around looking like a diseased hedgehog,' he said as he jumped out of bed.

Yes, I must, I thought. It's all your fault, but I must, if I want to stand any chance of looking like a normal twenty-two-year-old again, that is. Thank God I wasn't in a rugby team or something. At least I wouldn't have to suffer the indignity of communal showers.

Harry bathed quickly, then raced around the bedroom throwing his clothes on while I dragged myself out of bed and into the bathroom. I peered blearily into the mirror and lanced a spot before it even had time to surface. Splat. Harry appeared just as I was cleaning it off the mirror.

'Must dash, darling — doing a spot of housework? Thanks so much, the washing-up needs doing if you've got a moment. See you in a day or two.' He kissed me noisily, goosing me at the same time. 'Bye Polyester!'

'Bye!' I called down the stairs after him, wishing for the millionth time I'd never told him that the 'E' in my initials stood for Esther. It had been a practical joke of my father's way back in the swinging sixties when I'd been born. A friend of his had given his daughter the singularly groovy name of Silk, so Daddy, for a laugh, had called me Polly Esther. What a wag. Stupidly I'd told Harry, who'd laughed like a drain and couldn't leave it alone. Ah well, my fault again, I suppose.

I dragged myself away from the mirror and looked at my watch. God, eight forty-five already, I didn't have much time. I had a quick shower, jumped into my clothes, and set about my weekly task of looking for 'signs'.

These 'signs' were unspecified in appearance, but could take the form of jewellery — perhaps a pair of earrings or a necklace; scent bottles; clothing — especially underwear, anything of that nature; all of which would have sent me completely ballistic. Thus far I'd never found anything, but one could never be too careful and I always had to look.

It wasn't a long job, because Harry had such a trendy minimalist flat with very few searchable places. A couple of cupboards, one or two drawers, no shelves. His walls were full of urgent white space with just one or two obscure pictures hanging in strange places, like near the skirting boards or above a window. The floor was polished and wooden and bits of twisted chrome or knotted leather were dotted about here and there making statements, about what I don't know. Occasionally you'd come across something made of both chrome and leather which could be a chair or a sofa, but was certainly uncomfortable. It wasn't my sort of flat at all but, because it was Harry's, I bullied myself into thinking it was beautiful.

Consequently, the search for 'signs' was really confined to the bedroom and the bathroom. I went through both with a fine tooth-comb, terrified of what I might find but totally unable to stop myself.

There was the usual dried-up lip gloss in the bathroom cabinet and the tarnished silver bracelet in the second drawer down in the bedside table, but they both pre-dated me, so that was OK. No letters, no earrings, no scent bottles; in fact no sign at all of any other female visitor. Good.

Feeling much perkier, I threw a cup of tea down my throat, made the bed roughly, almost washed up but just managed to stop myself, grabbed my handbag and charged off to work, putting my lipstick on as I ran downstairs.

Chapter Four

Pippa was rolling her eyes and gesticulating madly when I arrived panting like a dog at nine forty-five a.m.

'He's been waiting for you since nine-thirty!' she hissed, jabbing her finger in the direction of Nick's office.

'Oh Christ!' I wriggled out of my coat, leaving it where it fell on the floor, and dashed into his room, grabbing my shorthand book on the way.

'Sorry, Nick,' I gasped as I flopped down on his leather sofa. 'I had a bit of trouble with the tubes.'

'For someone who lives two tube stops away you seem to spend a hell of a lot of time commuting,' he said sardonically. 'Anyway, let's get on, I've got a lot to do today. Letter to Dick Appleby. Dear Mr Appleby, Further to our conversation yesterday . . .' and he was off.

He paced around the room, talking to the walls, the window, the carpet, his shoes, dictating like a steam train while I scribbled away like mad, trying to keep up.

'Slow down!' I screeched in desperation when I was at least a paragraph behind. I was fast, but I wasn't that fast.

He stopped pacing and turned, surprised. Then he grinned sheepishly. 'Sorry – getting a bit carried away.'

'Can't imagine that ever happening,' I said without thinking, and then blushed, instantly wishing I hadn't said it.

Nick raised his eyebrows. He looked at me inquiringly, a slight smile playing on his lips. 'Oh really? It's something you've thought about then, is it?'

'No, of course not.' My blush deepened and spread to my neck. I squirmed around uncomfortably on the sofa. Well really, this was most unlike Nick. Indulging in friendly banter and sexual innuendo first thing in the morning, or for that matter at any time of day. Whatever was the matter with him? I glared studiously at my notebook and let my hair fall over my flushing face.

He grinned. 'Right! Well I'll try to go a bit slower then.'

He set off again at a slightly more sedate pace, and then the telephone rang. It was our media buyer. I doodled on my pad as I waited, and drew a rather unflattering picture of him. It just showed, though, I thought, as I added a large and rather phallic nose to my portrait; when he loosened up a bit he could be almost human. I drew a pair of bushy eyebrows, Dennis Healey-style, and studied him as he sat in his big leather chair, sideways-on to the window. His profile jutted out against the skyline of tower blocks behind. It had to be said that his nose was definitely on the large side, but then again his jaw was very square, which seemed to balance it. The eyes were deep set and slightly slanted, and his hair was thick, straight and very dark. Somehow it all worked rather well if you liked a lot of angles on your man. Personally I was much more into soft, boyish good looks with melting baby-blue eyes and honey-gold hair. Funny that.

Nick was issuing instructions down the phone in a quiet, authoritative way, his voice deep and thoughtful. A lock of dark hair flopped into his eyes and he pushed it back impatiently. Suddenly he swivelled round in his chair to consult his diary and caught me staring at him. He smiled. He smiled! I mean, for God's sake, whatever next? And not just a little twitch, a dazzlingly broad grin. Good grief, perhaps he was flesh and blood after all, and not just a collection of old memo pads and documents held together with paper clips. That smile had definitely been directed at me, hadn't it? I had a quick look over my shoulder just to make sure — no, there was definitely no one else here.

Well well. Could it be that he was finally coming round to the discreet and subtle charms of one Polly McLaren? Had a beam of sunlight darted through the window and lingered becomingly on my blonde curls for a moment, making them shine like spun gold and reminding him of a cornfield in summer perhaps? Had he at last noticed my finely chiselled features, my sparkling eyes, and that attractive dusting of freckles over my pert little nose? Odd that he'd never noticed all this before, but no matter. He'd got there in the end. And if it was going to make him all smiley and agreeable, I would obviously have to draw more attention to my assets, thereby ensuring myself an easier, happier, and hopefully bollock-free working environment.

First a smile, heavens, whatever next? Intrigued, I carefully arranged myself in what I believed to be a seductive manner. I rested my elbow on the back of the sofa and balanced my chin on my hand. Then I curled my legs up beneath me in a kittenish style, failing to notice that I'd also curled some papers up with my feet. Once in position I sucked my cheeks in and stared moodily out of the window, pouting slightly as I sucked the end of my pencil. I made sure I could still see him out of the corner of my eye in order to clock his reaction and — good grief! He was doing something with his hand, flapping it around from side to side, could it be — yes, he was, he was *waving* at me. How odd! Gosh, he was really letting himself go now. Well there was nothing else for it, was there? Rude not to. I raised my hand and fluttered back, eyes wide, smiling encouragingly. Was that OK, I wondered? This waving lark was a new one on me. Winking yes, smouldering looks, fine, I could cope with all that, but waving? He barked a final order down the phone, making me jump slightly, and slammed the receiver down.

'For goodness sake, Polly, stop lolling around over those papers. I've got to sign them later.'

He flapped his hand again, gesturing for me to move. Oh Christ!

'And sit up properly, please, you're not at home now.'

Bastard! I flushed furiously and sat bolt upright. Who did he think he was, my father?

The telephone call had obviously put him in a filthy mood. His brows were knitted together now and a thundercloud settled in its usual position on his face.

'Right, let's go again. Dear Mr Hutchinson, Please find enclosed a pre-production schedule . . .'

Once again we raced off at breakneck speed, and this time I didn't have the nerve to slow him down. Luckily, I was saved by the bell again, and I scribbled away, making up lost ground as he answered the phone.

'Yes?' he shouted impatiently. God, he was charming. 'Oh it's you, sorry, darling.'

Darling? I felt like Dr Spock as my ears sprang into action. It was obviously the bird, Serena. I kept my head well down, pretending I was still writing.

'I know I said I would,' he was saying wearily, 'but honestly, I'm so snowed under here I'll probably be working till about midnight.'

I carefully studied the spiral binding in my notepad. A low profile was all-important if I was to go unnoticed.

'Well, can't you go on your own, or get Hugh to take you?' He was irritated now, and so was she, judging by the long silence at this end as he listened to the monologue. The Hugh suggestion had obviously gone down like a cup of cold sick.

'Look, I said I'd try, I can do no more. I'll ring you as soon as I know how long I'll be, but don't bank on it because I think it's highly unlikely. For one thing—' He broke off suddenly, remembering I was still in the room.

He put his hand over the mouthpiece.

'Polly, if you don't mind, we'll carry on with this later.'

I nodded, smiled sweetly, and went back to my desk, closing his door softly behind me.

'Serena saved my bacon,' I said to Pippa, who was buried in *Harpers and Queen*. 'He was going for the world shorthand speed record in there.'

'Mmmmm . . .' she murmured as she stared longingly at London's twenty most eligible men, salivating slightly as she digested the profusion of titles, bank balances and good looks assembled before her.

'I can't imagine him with a girlfriend,' I said, flicking through a pile of TV scripts that had been put on my desk for typing. 'I wonder what she's like.'

'A bit of a handful, by all accounts,' said Pippa, licking her lips greedily as she dissected one particularly affluent viscount. 'Keeps him on his toes.'

'Really? Well he certainly wasn't giving an inch on the phone. I wonder if she lives with him.'

Pippa didn't answer. She was miles away — in Dorset, in fact — walking slowly up the aisle of a private chapel on her father's arm. Resplendent in an ivory silk wedding dress, a flurry of little bridesmaids behind her in matching ivory with apricot sashes, she smiled shyly at her guests from beneath her veil. As she neared the altar, the organist reached his crescendo and her viscount turned to watch her, bursting with pride at her beauty. She smiled at him serenely . . .

'I wonder what she looks like,' I mused.

But Pippa was still walking, her head held high to Purcell's 'Trumpet Voluntary'.

'I shouldn't think she's much of a beauty,' I went on. 'Blue-stockinged I expect, with buck teeth and a smattering of acne.' I giggled.

Pippa stuck her finger firmly in the viscount's bank balance, determined to keep her place. 'You know what she looks like,' she said, tearing herself away from her future husband for a second.

'I don't. I've never met her.'

'No, but you know what she *looks* like.'

'What d'you mean?'

'Serena Montgomery, you've seen her in films, haven't you?'

'Serena Montgomery! Nick Penhalligan is going out with Serena Montgomery! I don't believe you!' I shrieked.

'Shh, he'll hear you. He's been going out with her for ages.'

'Good grief! How did he meet her? What does she see in him? Are you sure, Pippa?'

But Pippa was already in her receiving line, a countess now, standing next to her husband and graciously greeting all her friends – particularly those friends who thought themselves rather grand and who, at one stage or another, had snubbed her, left her off their drinks party lists, or failed to send a Christmas card, and who, at a later date, would no doubt be grovelling to be guests at her balls and shooting parties. She smiled at them benignly, tiara twinkling.

I left her to her dreams as I picked my jaw up from somewhere around bra level, digesting this bombshell. Serena Montgomery, no less! Miss Montgomery was a startlingly beautiful English actress who had up and come at the tender age of about twenty-five. She only appeared in frightfully tasteful arty films, usually English or continental, and had achieved her fame without getting her hands dirty with any gratuitous smut or violence. She was extremely successful and extremely sought-after, and Nick Penhalligan, my boss and cross to bear on a daily basis, was going out with her! My mind was boggling so much I thought it would boggle out of my earholes.

I simply had to drag Pippa away from her wedding

reception. 'But what on ea   does she see in him?' I repeated.

'Well, you know, he isn't bad 'ooking, Polly, and he's probably totally different out of t.e agency. I mean, you work for him, so you're bound to be jaundiced.' She looked thoughtful. 'I think he's rather cute, actually, and, you never know, he might be a demon lover.'

'Demon lover! That lump of rock-solid granite in there. He hasn't an ounce of sensibility! Are you mad?'

I shook my head in disbelief and began to bash away at my scripts. As I waded through coffee plantations in Kenya, where the highly optimistic creative team had set their commercials in the hope of wangling a trip abroad, my thoughts oscillated between Nick and Serena and, just for a change, Harry. I went over our little débâcle in the restaurant. I hadn't forgotten. I was determined to find Rachel Thingamy, just to show him. Just to show him what, I wasn't sure, but just to show him something.

Every so often I caught a glimpse of Nick through his glass door, scribbling away. I tried to imagine him in a clinch with Serena Montgomery. Hidden depths, all right. I was jolted out of my daydreams by the telephone. It was Lottie.

'Polly? It's me. Listen, I completely forgot, Caro's coming round for supper tonight and I haven't got any food. You couldn't be an angel and get something on the way home, could you? I'm up to my eyeballs here.'

'Sure, I'll go to Safeway's.'

'Great, get a lasagne and some salad stuff. How was last night?'

'Brilliant,' I lied. 'We went to—'

'Tell me later, I can't talk now.' Lottie couldn't rabbit on for hours like the rest of us.

'OK, oh Lottie – ' I suddenly remembered ' – very quickly, d'you remember someone at school called Rachel Marsden?'

69

'No, why?'

'Curly fair hair, bit mousy looking, a year or so below us. Have a quick think.'

'Can't say I do, but Caro might, ask her tonight. Polly, I must go. Bye.'

I put the phone down. Of course, Caro might know. She was Lottie's younger sister and would probably have been in the same year as Rachel. Caro made occasional visits to our flat, principally to view the latest collections in our wardrobes and walk off with most of them. I'd ask her.

I left the agency, as is my wont, at five-thirty on the dot — I don't believe in unpaid overtime — and made my way to Safeway's. Wednesday night is late-night shopping and, being in the middle of the King's Road, it takes on the atmosphere of a drinks party rather than a supermarket. I reapplied my lipstick at the door and grabbed a basket. True to form, the aisles were already throbbing with bright young things snapping up dinner party fodder.

A shriek of delight rang out as someone rounded a corner and bashed trollies over the dog food with a neighbour they hadn't seen for at least a day. There was lots of noisy kissing and, 'Darling! How lovely to see you!' as they compared trolley loads, exchanged gossip and threw in the Lapsang Souchong.

There were always plenty of single men sniffing around, advertising their availability with a solitary cod steak and a packet of frozen peas. Predictable chat-up lines would pop out over the freezers as lone males exclaimed, 'Oh, I see you've got Chicken Kiev. Is that good?' or some such other notable opening gambit, whereupon the lone female would reply, 'Oh, frightfully, haven't you tried it?' to which the response would come, 'Well, I'm not very good with ovens . . .' hoping that the offer of a practical demonstration would come his way.

I always reckoned you could tell a lot by what a man had in his basket — his wire basket, of course. Fillet steak and peas were fine, and a bottle of Sancerre wouldn't go amiss, but it was always a good idea to steer well clear of the Pot Noodles, Carlsberg Special and extra-strength deodorant brigade.

I threaded my way through the usual merry throng, throwing necessities into my basket along the way: avocado pears, gravadlax and quails' eggs, as well as one or two frivolous little luxuries like oven cleaner and washing powder.

Having located the lasagne and salad, I made a detour to a less fashionable part of the shop to chuck in some loo paper, which should have been a necessity but in our forgetful household was often a luxury. It always made a nice change from the *Evening Standard* or Lottie's dressmaking patterns. Maddeningly, they always put the loo paper high up on a shelf above a freezer, so that midgets like me had to stand on tiptoe and pretend to be a tree to reach it.

I was just stretching up and trying vainly to flick a couple of rolls off the shelf, when suddenly I teetered wildly, completely lost my balance and fell, with a mighty shriek, head first into the freezer. I lay there, pole-axed with shock, my nose pressed up against the Arctic Roll, my legs sticking straight up in the air behind me. The freezer was deep and relatively empty and I'd landed at a pretty acute angle; so acute, in fact, that I couldn't move. Jesus Christ, I couldn't move! And apart from anything else it was bloody cold and my jumper was sticking to the ice.

'Help! Could somebody help me?' I wailed feebly as I eyeballed the Arctic Roll. I waited a second, but didn't detect the sound of pounding feet running towards me, and no helpful hands appeared to be winging their way down, so I desperately tried to rock backwards and heave myself out. I spread my hands on the floor of the freezer and pushed hard. 'Huurmphhh!' Alas! Too much of my vast weight was freezer-bound and, strong and meaty though my thighs are, they didn't have the muscle to lever me out. It was no good, I would have to climb in, turn around, and then climb out again.

I set about this task with a vengeance, curling my legs round and down into the frozen wastes – my skirt at this stage was somewhere up around my earrings. I scrambled to my feet and from here began the tricky ascent up the south face of the freezer.

By now I was aware that, far from being alone as I'd assumed, a small army of shoppers had broken off from selecting their mid-week groceries and were collecting in a gawping, open mouthed semi-circle around me.

'What's happening?' someone at the back asked.

'There's a girl in the freezer,' came the muttered response from the front.

'Oh, thanks very much, don't help, will you!' I spat furiously at no one in particular, glimpsing out of the corner of my ice-packed, bloodshot eye, an extremely attractive girl who looked terribly familiar. She was laughing her head off.

Puce with shame I brushed my wet hair out of my eyes, swung a leg over the side, and began to clamber out. Unfortunately, in my haste, I was unlucky enough to catch the heel of my shoe in a wire basket full of oven chips.

'Bugger!' I shook my foot furiously, straddled, as I now was, over the side of the freezer, but I couldn't for the life of me shake the basket free. Finally, in desperation, I leaned down and wrenched it off, pulling the heel of my shoe off with it. No matter, at least I was liberated. I swung my leg over, knickers no doubt flashing wildly, and landed, pretty unsteadily, on the other side. With shaking hands I straightened out my skirt, pulled down my jumper – which had ridden up to bra level and was covered with little bobbles of ice – and, with my head held high, I turned on my broken heel and marched, or rather hobbled, through the gawping crowd, shopping basket in one hand, broken heel in the other.

By the time I'd arrived at the check-out desk my teeth were chattering like a monkey's, my hair was dripping wet and the ice bobbles on my jumper were beginning to melt.

I slammed my groceries down on the conveyer belt, muttering oaths and obscenities under my breath. The gum-chewing check-out girl raised her eyebrows in surprise as she took in my dishevelled, damp condition. Of all the snooty, stuck-up people — what did they think I was doing in there? Stealing fish fingers? Stuffing frozen peas up my jumper? Jesus, it was unbelievable. I could have died of frostbite and no one so much as raised a finger to help!

Safely back in the flat half an hour later, I wrapped myself in a blanket, poured myself a large gin and tonic, and lit a rather shaky cigarette. When I'd consumed about half of each, I recounted my miserable expedition to Lottie and Caro.

Lottie cried with laughter. 'At least you didn't knock yourself out: you could still be there now, lying unconscious in the raspberry ripple. Imagine someone reaching in for some ice-cream and grabbing hold of your nose or something.' She wiped her eyes with her shirt. 'Oh God, Polly, you are an idiot!'

Caro smiled politely, staring at me with naked incredulity. She was so self-possessed and perfect, she'd be incapable of tripping over a rucked-up piece of carpet, let alone falling into a freezer.

Caro and Lottie were obviously sisters, with their long dark hair, hazel eyes, pale skins and sooty lashes and eyebrows, but Caro was very definitely the beauty. Lottie's eyes were big and round, but Caro's were almond-shaped with long sweeping lashes. Her mouth was a perfect little rosebud and, whereas Lottie was prone to plumpness and had a round, sweet face, Caro was reed slim with a little heart-shaped face. She had the sort of dark silky hair that looks so good spread out on pillows, and she wouldn't know a split end if it ran her over.

Like her sister, she had an enormous bust, which I didn't envy her for; but, unlike her sister who tried to disguise it with baggy T-shirts and sloppy jumpers, young Caro positively flaunted hers. Most of her tops were snug-fitting clingy numbers, and she was very fond of stretching up and locking her arms behind her head, or lying with her back on the floor, propping herself up with her elbows, chest to the fore.

She didn't have a line on her face, principally because she betrayed very little emotion. When she smiled it was a controlled, tight little smile, like the one she was giving me now. She wouldn't dream of rocking around like Lottie, who was clutching her stomach and roaring with laughter. I am quite sure that Caro has never, ever farted.

Lottie doted on her little sister and spoilt her rotten. Their mother was dead and Lottie had always felt responsible for Caro. Caro took everything Lottie had to offer and, as far as I could see, gave very little in return. Let's just say she wasn't my favourite person.

This evening, as usual, Caro had her eyes firmly on our wardrobes. 'Can I see what you've bought recently, Lottie?' she said, making a bee-line for Lottie's bedroom. I stuck to her like glue. As usual, half my wardrobe was in Lottie's room and vice versa. I didn't want her to get her thieving hands on anything precious.

'Yes, but tell me what you're borrowing,' shouted Lottie, who was glued to an old 'Dallas' repeat.

Caro was already riffling through her sister's drawers. I sat on the bed and lit a cigarette.

'Ooh, this is nice, I'll have this,' she said, pulling out the only cashmere jumper I'm ever likely to possess.

I snatched it out of her hot little hands and smiled sweetly. 'Sorry, Caro, that's mine.'

Caro pouted sulkily. 'You obviously lent it to Lottie, it was in her drawer.'

'Yes, but then I know that Lottie won't come home doused in red wine and aftershave.'

'Oh, all right.' She threw it back in the drawer and added cattily, 'Black's a bit old for me anyway.'

I smiled, suddenly remembering that I needed her help. 'I have got a lovely red polo neck you could borrow, though.'

'Oh?' Caro was interested. She tried it on and looked infuriatingly stunning. I stood next to her as she admired herself in the mirror, and then stepped hastily away again to avoid the comparison. My tatty old candlewick dressing gown with make-up stains down the front and holes in the bottom where Wellington had chewed it didn't really stand up against her slimming black ski pants and the red jumper stretched tight across her ample bosom. Neither, I thought, looking at her clean silky hair, did my rather dirty blonde curls, streaked with grease rather than highlights.

'Yes, I'll take this,' she said, as if she were in a shop. I gritted my teeth, thinking that a please or a thank-you wouldn't be out of place, but since I needed to pick what passed as her brain, I wisely held my tongue.

'Listen, Caro, d'you remember someone at school called Rachel Marsden?'

'Mmmm, vaguely,' said Caro, picking up a skirt of mine and holding it up against herself in the mirror.

'What was she like?'

'Very quiet, brainy, musical, not my type at all.'

That figures, I thought.

'D'you know what she's doing now?'

'Haven't the foggiest,' said Caro, slipping off her skirt and stepping into mine. I prayed it wouldn't fit. 'Why?'

'Oh, someone I know was asking after her. Who were her friends at school, can you remember?'

'She didn't really have many, she was a bit of a loner, but I suppose Sally Lomax was her closest friend. She lives in Paris now.'

'Do you know where?'

'No, but her parents live in Godalming, you could ring them and find out, I suppose.'

Well, that at least was a start. Adam could get in touch with Sally if I got her number for him, but Paris seemed awfully remote.

'Anything else? What about her family?'

Caro took off my skirt which was miles too big for her — a mixed blessing — and sighed. She was getting a bit bored by this inquisition.

'Well, her father is ghastly, I know that. He's a judge, and a pretty Victorian one at that. He doesn't agree with girls having too much education — thought needlework and a few French lessons was good enough for Rachel, can you believe it? Anyway, he dragged her out of school before her A-level year saying she didn't need to pass exams. There was a terrible row, because of course she was so bright. I remember he came up to the school and they were all locked in Miss Harper's study for ages with Rachel crying her eyes out. Anyway, he got his way and Rachel left. Whose is this?' she said, holding up a yellow shirt.

'Mine,' I said wearily. 'Yes, I suppose so, Caro.' She folded it and put it on top of the little pile she was collecting.

Well, this was getting more interesting. And now I came to think about it I vaguely remembered someone's father storming up to school and dragging his daughter out before A-level year. There was quite a row about it. Old man Marsden sounded like a complete nightmare. Not only didn't he approve of very passable boyfriends, but education too. I had one last shot.

'What about the teachers, did she get on with any of them particularly well?'

'Well she was brilliant at music, played the piano and one of those fluty things, so you might try Mr Saunders. Oh, and she was good at maths too, so that would be Mrs

Compton . . . Polly, why are you so interested in Rachel Marsden? She was bloody boring, you know.'

Caro had obviously had enough, so I left it at that and started smearing on a mud face-pack.

'Oh, no reason really, thanks Caro; oh, and can I have my red jumper back in a couple of weeks, please?' I said without much hope of success.

'Sure.' She gathered all my clothes together and went into the sitting room to catch the end of 'Dallas'. Just then the doorbell rang.

'I'll get it,' yelled Lottie.

I padded into the kitchen in my cosy old slippers, trying to keep my face still as the mud-pack began to set like a rock. I was dying to wash it off, but the packet had said ten minutes. I mulled over the information Caro had given me. Quite good for starters; at least I could give Adam a few snippets, I thought, as I shoved the frozen lasagne in the oven.

I lit a cigarette with difficulty, then spotted a rather scrummy-looking chocolate cake sitting on the side. Caro had obviously brought it. I cut a large piece and couldn't decide whether to eat that first or finish my cigarette, so I did both, trying to keep mouth movement to a minimum on account of the concrete on my face. I paddled off down the corridor back to the telly. My slippers were flopping around like boats and I had to clutch my dressing gown like a bag lady because it had long since lost its cord. As I shuffled through the sitting-room door, cake in one hand, dressing gown in the other, cigarette therefore in my rather muddy mouth, I suddenly stopped dead in my tracks. For bounding through the front door, in his own inimitable, puppy-dog style, was Harry.

Chapter Five

Understandably, Harry didn't recognise me at first, but then slowly the penny started to drop. If I hadn't been the freak show, it would have been pretty to watch. His eyes glazed over, his forehead puckered thoughtfully, his jaw fell. Then it dawned. He bent double, clutched himself with his arms, his eyes bulged, his mouth got wider and wider, and he ultimately let rip with an enormous bellow of what I supposed was laughter. So enormous, in fact, was the animal-like bellow he'd summoned up, that poor Harry had to hold on to his stomach to stop it from falling apart at the seams. As he clutched his aching belly with one hand, he grabbed the door frame for support with the other, obviously in imminent danger of losing control of his legs. Was he going to have a hernia?

'Oh God, Polly, you look like – you look like you've just stepped out of a horror movie or something! What's that muck all over your face?' he gasped between convulsions.

I felt like running into my bedroom and sobbing uncontrollably into my pillow, but I kept as cool as I could with my face burning away beneath the mud. Any minute now the bloody thing would melt with the heat. I couldn't actually speak properly but, depositing cake and cigarette in a nearby ashtray, I flashed my brave old eyes, wiggled my hands about Al Jolson style and, old pro that I am, threw myself into a spirited rendition of the opening bars of 'Maa-amie — Maa-amie!' Then I gave him a quick flash of George Michael, just for good measure. When in doubt, play it for laughs. This had him rolling in the aisles.

'Oh God, you look such a sight!' he gasped. 'What is it?'

'It's a face-pack, you berk, haven't you ever seen one before?' I mumbled in my ventriloquist's voice.

'And there was I thinking it was all natural,' he spluttered. 'I didn't realise you had a face-lift every other night, and what an incredibly sexy negligée that is!'

Once again he dissolved into a helpless heap as he took my ten-year-old candlewick on board. I did a catwalk twirl in response and he roared even louder. He was easily pleased. I turned to my flatmate.

'Perhaps you'd get Harry a drink, Lottie?' I said with as much dignity as I could muster under the circumstances. 'Meanwhile, I shall get changed into something less hysterical.'

Lottie, who'd been horror-struck when she first saw me, was now beside herself with giggles. She ran around getting ice and whisky, glad of something to do.

Right on cue, Caro sauntered in with freshly applied make-up, looking as if she'd just walked out of *Vogue*. She was still wearing my red jumper — and good grief! Weren't they my new black leggings?

Harry had collapsed in a heap on the sofa where he was still convulsing but, as she sauntered in, the bellowing ceased, and he looked up in wonder. There was a rather too meaningful silence. His eyes lit up like a pinball machine as they took in one attraction after another. The face — those eyes — that mouth — that figure — those — those boobs! Bloody hellfire, those enormous, gigantic, socking great boobs! The poor fellow tried desperately to tear himself away from the upper torso to smile at the face. Who was this divine creature?

'Caro Hamilton, Harry Lloyd-Roberts,' I said by way of

explanation, flipping my hand from one to the other and trying to keep the misery from my voice.

Caro, realising she'd made something of an entrance, milked it for all it was worth. The saunter became a swagger, a slow, bottom wiggling, undulating stroll, which finally came to rest in *my* favourite position, propped up against the mantelpiece, back to the fire, chest out, tummy in, etc, etc. She got out a cigarette, lit it slowly and, raising her chin and pursing her rosebud lips, blew the smoke seductively into the air. It was more than I could bear. She did it so much better than I did. With a strangled little yelp which I turned into a cough, I ran for the safety of the bathroom.

I slammed the door and yelped for real, adding one or two muffled wails for good measure. Oh, why had he come? I couldn't have looked more repulsive if I'd tried! I scrubbed away at the face-pack, which wasn't going to relinquish its position easily. I looked around wildly, desperate for a hammer and chisel, and hit upon a nail-file which would do just as well. I chipped and scrubbed and chipped and scrubbed until finally something vaguely resembling a face was revealed, albeit a pretty blotchy one. Oh God, I looked diseased! I frantically slapped on a bit of Polyfilla foundation, added a shaky black line under each eye, and applied the only lipstick I could find – which was Lottie's and too red for me. I whimpered in dismay at my by now trollopy little reflection, and ran a comb through my hair.

Lottie poked her head round the door. 'You'd better get in there quick,' she hissed. 'They're getting on like a bloody mansion on fire!'

'But I look so disgusting!' I wailed.

'No you don't,' said Lottie doubtfully. 'A bit of make-up might help, though.'

'I'm covered in make-up!'

'Oh. Oh well, never mind, just hurry up! You've been in

here for ages, he'll know you're upset.'

She was right. I ran into my bedroom, shed the hateful dressing gown, and pulled on a pair of jeans and a jumper.

When I eventually returned, it was quite obvious that Harry wouldn't have noticed if I'd sprung another head, let alone been a little upset. He was reclining in the corner of the sofa with his arm resting along the back, his hand within about an inch of Caro's hair. For Caro had relinquished her position by the fireplace in favour of an altogether more cosy one. She'd curled herself up into a cute little ball, not at the other end of the sofa where most newly acquainted people would sit, but in the middle, right next to Harry. So close – without actually touching, and so snug – without actually snuggling, that she was in danger of disappearing up his armpit. I was in danger of throwing up.

I fought back the bile as it rose in my throat, and forced a bright little smile on to my unwilling face. I sat down on the sofa opposite the happy couple, next to Lottie who, appalled at her sister's antics, was looking decidedly grim. We faced them across the coffee table and watched, spellbound, as the show unfolded before us. A bag of popcorn might have come in handy, but I settled instead for a lungful of nicotine.

Meanwhile, on the Harry and Caro show, the protagonists were busy unearthing mounds of mutual friends as a front for their outrageous flirtation.

'Oh the Watson-*Smith's*!' Caro was saying with lots of Sloaney random emphasis. 'Yes of *course* I know them, they're *really* good friends of mine – I simply *adore* Hugo and Amanda. Gosh, so you're a *cousin*! I'm surprised I haven't met you *before*!'

'They must have been keeping you from me,' murmured Harry, devouring her with his baby blues.

'I quite often go there for the weekend, actually, they have the *most* beautiful house, don't they?' Caro gushed on. 'I must ask them all about you!'

'Don't believe a word they say,' he flashed her his most winning smile. 'It's all lies, every word of it!'

'Ah-ha! Got a bit of a reputation, have we?' She prodded his chest playfully. 'Bit of a playboy, eh?'

I ground my teeth, still smiling broadly.

'Oh well,' he feigned modesty. 'I wouldn't say that . . .'

'I think I'm going to puke,' muttered Lottie sotto voce on my right.

Caro giggled. 'Well, I've certainly heard a lot about you from Polly!'

'Oh, really?' Harry grinned. 'Such as?'

'Oh well, I know for instance that you're a stockbroker, and you live in Flood Street, and you've got a beautiful flat all sort of minimalist and trendy, and you drive a Porsche − oh, and a motorbike, and − oh gosh, all sorts of things!'

'Well, well,' drawled Harry, 'I had no idea I was such a topic of conversation!'

I flared my nostrils most becomingly and made a sort of strangled chicken noise. Thanks, Caro. No, really, thanks a lot. I made a mental note that the red jumper was leaving this flat over my dead body. I pushed the corners of my mouth up again and tested my voice for cracks with what I thought was a surreptitious little hum.

'Hrmmm . . . so what brings you so far from Chelsea, Harry?' I sounded like Kermit the frog. 'Slightly off the beaten track for you, isn't it? I trust you've brought your barley sugars for the journey home?'

Harry pulled a little yellow pill packet out of his trouser pocket and waved it in the air. He grinned. 'Well, talking of sweeties, darling, you forgot your smarties.'

I flushed unattractively. 'I've got plenty more where those came from, thank you!' I snatched them out of his hand.

'Well we don't want any, ha-ha, cock-ups, do we? I

83

thought it best to be on the safe side.'

Caro giggled.

Typical, I thought, seething: the only thing that gets Harry over to my flat in a flaming hurry is a paranoiac fear of becoming a father. I composed myself with difficulty.

'Well, I'm sure I can rely on you to face up to your responsibilities should the situation ever arise, God forbid; but in the meantime I dare say you'll be wanting to get off to the dinner party at Ransome's — it is tonight, isn't it?' I said sweetly.

Harry had returned his lust-glazed eyes to my jumper, the one I wasn't wearing, but he managed to tear them away for a second. He looked at me in surprise.

'Oh yes, that.' He'd forgotten. 'Yes, I suppose I'd better go at some stage — don't suppose they'll miss me for a bit, though.'

His eyes seemed to be on a piece of elastic which was inexorably twanging them back to the red cable-stitch. And who could blame the poor boy? For the red cable-stitch was being stretched to within an inch of its life. Caro was uncurling herself languidly from her little ball, yawning widely and str-e-tching her arms up, way, way up in the air, arching her back and sticking her ample bosom out further and further — gracious, there was so much of it, it was almost obscene! She reached the climax of her stretch, gave a little moan, then relaxed her elbows and rubbed the back of her neck, thereby still keeping her assets well to the fore. It was one helluva routine.

'Ooooh, I'm so stiff!' she groaned.

'Really? Perhaps you should have a massage,' murmured Harry.

'Mmmm . . . I suppose I should really, it's sitting at a typewriter all day that does it. Oooh . . . gosh, I've got quite a crick in my neck.'

She unfurled her legs, splayed them out in front of her, pointing her bare little toes, then brought them in again to

84

sit cross-legged on the sofa, back ramrod straight now, hands on her knees. Now what? She shut her eyes and dropped her head forward, then she rolled it around rhythmically on her swan-like neck. Round and around it went.

'Mmmm . . .' She sighed in what can only be described as an orgasmic fashion. 'That's better . . .'

By now we were all totally mesmerised. Even Lottie and I had our mouths open. Any minute now she'd slip into the lotus position, or even, I thought in wonder, that one with the ankles behind the ears. Saliva was positively dripping from Harry's mouth, and he was making no effort to hide it.

'Better?' he murmured salaciously, as his boggling eyes roamed around her gyrating figure, savouring the swaying bosom, the tiny waist, the firm thighs spread akimbo on the sofa . . .

'Mmmm . . . much . . . a little bit of yoga works wonders, you know. You should try it, it's so relaxing and really easy.'

'Really?' He leaned in, keen to receive his tuition right now if she had a moment. 'D'you, er, practise a lot?'

'Quite a lot. Keeps me supple.'

'I should say . . .' Harry drooled.

'Um, Harry, I thought you were supposed to be going out to dinner?' Lottie burst in desperately, eyeing her sister's contortions with horror.

Caro took a break from the head-rolling routine and opened her eyes wide. 'Oh, I always think dinner parties are so boring. All that talking and not enough action.'

'Well, I suppose some people might find them a little taxing if they're not used to exercising the brain!' I spat in what remained of my voice as I ground my teeth to powder.

'And there's nothing worse than turning up late, it's so incredibly rude, don't you think?' said dear Lottie, jumping up quickly. 'I'll get your jacket, Harry.'

She rushed off and returned in a flash, brandishing the jacket like a matador shaping up to a young bull. Harry drained his glass unwillingly and allowed himself to be helped into his jacket, eyes still glued to Caro. He pecked me perfunctorily on the cheek and patted my bottom.

'Bye Polyester,' he grinned. 'Keep taking the pills.' He kissed Lottie. 'Look after your little sister, Lottie, or someone else will!' He winked at Caro who squirmed and giggled; I tried to ignore the electric current that seemed to be zig-zagging between them. 'Goodbye, Miss Hamilton, it was a great pleasure to have made your acquaintance.'

Caro giggled and simpered, fluttering her hand in a dinky little wave. 'Bye, Harry!'

As soon as he was out of the front door, Lottie rounded on her sister furiously. 'Why didn't you take all your clothes off and wriggle around on the floor? You might just as well have done!'

But Caro was unmoved. 'Don't be silly, Lottie,' she said yawning widely, 'I was just doing a bit of yoga. He is rather cute, though, I'm not surprised you keep him to yourself, Polly. What's happened to your face, by the way? It looks a bit blotchy.'

I didn't trust myself to speak. I stared at her perfect face, the corners of the rosebud mouth turned up in a mocking little grin, and a wave of pure hatred swept over me. I wondered for a moment if I was perhaps about to commit murder. How interesting, I'd never killed anyone before. I looked around for a handy implement, but by the time I'd decided that the heavy china fruit bowl, hurled forcefully and accurately, was just the thing to bash her brains out with, the wave of hatred dissipated and was replaced by one of misery. Why take it out on Caro? I was the one who'd made a comprehensive laughing stock of myself. Why not just kill myself? Ah, so it was suicide, was it? Again, interesting, but not so much fun, I hazarded.

Just me, a large tub of paracetamol, and then a wafty little float through the stratosphere in a white nightie. Hang on a minute, a large tub of . . . Suddenly a think bubble appeared over my head — of course! I knew exactly what I was going to do. It was less messy, less drastic, and ultimately more satisfying than either murder or suicide could ever be.

I leaped up and strode purposefully into the kitchen, making straight for the fridge. There was something inside shouting to be let out. Lottie was after me in a trice, five years at school and two in the flat had left an impression. She raced ahead and flattened herself possessively against the fridge door, arms spread out defiantly, shielding it from the imminent onslaught. It was a spirited defence, but doomed to failure from the outset. My hand was already firmly on the handle.

'Out of my way, Lottie,' I said between clenched teeth. 'I don't want to have to hurt you.'

Lottie suppressed a giggle. 'Don't do it, Polly,' she implored, 'he's not worth it!'

'OUT OF MY WAY, LOTTIE!' She stood her ground for a moment, but only a moment. There was a dangerous glint in my eye and Lottie wasn't very brave. She hesitated, then stood aside. I flung the door open dramatically and made for the ice-box. Ahhh . . . there was my prize, nestling innocently between the frozen peas and the ice-cubes. A family sized tub of Häagen-Dazs chocolate ice-cream, ready and waiting for just such an emergency. I removed it carefully using both hands, slid a knife around the outside of the precious confection and up-ended it ceremoniously on to a large plate — plop! What a divinely decadent noise. I stood back, arms in the air as if I'd just produced a rabbit from a hat. It got a ripple of applause from Lottie and more giggles. I felt better already.

'There,' I said triumphantly, and then, in case anyone was in any doubt, 'and it's all mine!'

'Not the family-sized, Polly,' wailed Lottie, wringing her hands in mock despair. 'Look,' she delved into the ice-box and pulled out a meagre little choc bar, waving it around in front of my nose like a carrot. 'What about one of these nice big choc ices: that'll do the trick, won't it?'

I brushed it aside scornfully. 'Don't be ridiculous, I'm feeding a crisis, not a minor incident. Now for the topping, ooh look!'

A large slab of cooking chocolate had found its way like magic from the back of the fridge to the palm of my hand. I tore open the wrapper like a five-year-old on Christmas morning, and broke it savagely into little pieces, sprinkling them with greedy abandon over the ice-cream.

'Now, what next?' I murmured thoughtfully. 'Ah yes, the cream.'

I strode purposefully back to the fridge, enjoying myself hugely, and seized a carton. I was just about to pour it all over the top when – oh-oh, not so fast, Polly old girl, take a look at the label. My suspicions were confirmed, it was only single. I sniggered. Lucky I spotted that before it was too late, I thought, as I replaced it and returned with the double. Lottie was eyeing the proceedings with deep concern.

'He's not worth it, Poll!' she cried as I poured the cream from a dramatic height, making nice big swirly dollops over my feast.

'Now for the nuts!' I cried, ignoring her pleas. I tore open a large packet of roasted peanuts – I could almost see the monosodium glutamate crawling all over them as I threw them on top. I rubbed my hands with glee: that should do it! I went to sit down. But wait a minute now – I paused in mid-sit – had I got enough calories here? I eyed my plateful with suspicion. I had to have at least two thousand five hundred, it was no good going off half cocked.

I got up again and prowled slowly around the kitchen,

looking for inspiration, searching for hidden carbohydrates. There was definitely something missing, an elusive little *je ne sais quoi*. I scratched my head, what could it be? Of course! The maple syrup! I rounded on my hapless flatmate.

'Have we got any maple syrup, Lottie?'

'I, I, I'm not sure, no, I don't think—' So we *had*!

I ran to the cupboard she was so obviously shielding, threw it open, and spied a tin, glinting in the fluorescent strip-lighting. Only about a third of a tin, but no matter. I scooped away, scraping it to within an inch of its life. A little metal poisoning wouldn't go amiss either. I sat down with a spoon poised over the top of the mound. Did I need a tablespoon? I dithered.

Lottie saw my hesitation and misread it. She was beside me in an instant. 'You don't really want to do it, do you, Polly?'

I grinned demoniacally. Did I!

'A moment on the lips, a lifetime on the hips?' she ventured. I gave her a withering look. 'You'll have to do better than that.'

She tried harder. 'Remember Monica Stewart?'

I remembered, and wavered for an instant, but only an instant. Monica Stewart was far and away the largest girl we had ever known. She'd been in our year at school and we used to fight to sit next to her at lunch so as to marvel at what she put away. Half a steak-and-kidney pudding, mounds of mashed potato, saucepans full of seemingly inedible cabbage, jugs of custard, bowl after bowl full of wobbly pink blancmange: nothing was too much trouble for Monica. And as she ate one could almost see it visibly adding to her enormous bulk. A little more padding on the thighs, one more ripple on the tummy, another chin, perhaps. She, and she alone, could lay claim to the epithet, 'A legend in her own lunch-hour'.

'That was glandular,' I muttered. My spoon was

dangerously close and getting closer by the moment.

'OK, OK, your new tartan trousers from Kenzo.' The spoon wobbled like a jelly. 'The ones that cost over a hundred and fifty pounds,' she went on ruthlessly.

Oh that was cruel, very cruel. I'd hardly been able to squeeze into them in the fitting room, but I'd bought them anyway in the hope that a week or two of concentrated dieting would do the trick. I racked my brains for a way out of this one. Of course! The summer was coming, tartan trousers would be much too hot, they'd been a big mistake.

Nothing could stop me now, the green light was on as far as I was concerned. I dug in and scooped up a spoonful of mammoth proportions. Lottie put her hand on my arm as it made its way to my mouth. Good grief, what now? A last-ditch attempt? She stuck her face in front of mine and stared deep into my eyes. 'Think,' she said slowly and carefully, 'think of Caro's long . . . slim . . . legs . . .'

It was done with all the best intentions, but it was the biggest mistake she could have made. I gave a sort of blood-curdling, *Last of the Mohicans* shriek, pushed her hand away, and ladled about two hundred and fifty calories into my mouth. If anything was going to make me eat this, it was the thought of Caro's legs which, coincidentally, were at that very moment strolling nonchalantly through the kitchen door. I eyed them speculatively as they passed by, almost tempted to take a chunk out of one of them with my teeth, but I thought better of it. Not meaty enough.

I tucked in with relish as Caro sat down at the table with us. She looked at the mountain of food with disbelief, and then stared at me in horror as I shovelled it into my willing mouth by the spadeful. She turned to Lottie with eyes like saucepan lids.

'What's she doing?' she asked.

Lottie grimaced. 'Getting her own back.'

'I don't understand . . .' said Caro.

'You wouldn't,' I said, looking at her twenty-two-inch waist.

'It's called comfort food, Caro,' said Lottie.

'But I thought we were having lasagne . . .'

I paused between spoonfuls, ice-cream and chocolate dripping from my chops. 'Change of plan,' I said, spraying her with cream and nuts. 'Not fattening enough.'

Lottie giggled and got a couple of spoons from the drawer. She handed one to Caro and then got stuck in herself. 'If you can't beat 'em, join 'em!' she cried joyfully, tucking in with a vengeance.

'Atta-girl!' I cried back, crunching on the nuts and imagining for a moment that they were Harry's — only for a moment, mind.

Caro got up from the table in disgust. 'Honestly, this is just too silly,' she said pompously. 'I don't think I can bear to watch such a dreadful display of pigging out. That is what you're doing, isn't it? I mean, what's it all in aid of?'

'You,' I said under my breath, but she'd already left the room for the safety of 'Dallas', where she could identify with the skinny-hipped, lettuce-eating glamour pusses at her leisure.

Lottie and I ploughed on, but I'm happy to say were defeated by at least half of my calorific concoction. We chucked it in the bin then sat back in our chairs, giggling and holding our stomachs. Totally replete. Or were we?

'Lasagne?' suggested Lottie mischievously.

'Clever girl!' I replied admiringly.

She went to the oven and brought it out, a little burnt and frayed at the edges, but still eminently edible.

'Caro, supper's ready!' I called.

She appeared at the door. 'You didn't really eat all that, did you?' she said in amazement.

'Certainly we did,' I replied. 'Just a little starter, and now it's time for the main course.'

She sat down, thoroughly bemused, and we ploughed womanfully through the lasagne, which defeated us none too soon. I staggered back to the viewing room again and sank into a sofa, feeling a million times better for my binge, but knowing I'd regret it later. As I heaved my colossal legs up on to the sofa, I suddenly remembered something. Of course! There was just one other thing I needed to do to get even with Harry. I grabbed the mobile phone and took it into my bedroom.

'Who are you ringing?' asked Lottie to my disappearing back.

'I'll tell you when I've done it,' I said mysteriously.

I gathered together a glass of wine, a packet of cigarettes and an ashtray, and shut the bedroom door behind me. Then I sat cross-legged on the bed and lit a cigarette. Should I ring him? I practised a few smoke rings which I've never been able to do, and still couldn't. I took a large gulp of wine and rang the number quickly before I could change my mind. At this stage I didn't really have much to lose, did I?

After only a couple of rings a girl answered. 'Savoy Hotel.'

'Hello, could I speak to Mr Adam Buchanan, please?'

I licked my lips nervously as I heard the telephone ringing in his room.

'Hello?'

'Mr Buchanan?' I decided to keep it formal and businesslike. 'It's Polly McLaren here. You asked me to volunteer my services yesterday.' Oh God! My attempts at formality had led me to sound like a prostitute. 'I mean, um, you asked me to help — you know, find Rachel and that sort of thing.'

From prostitute to blithering idiot. Get a grip, Poll. I took a gulp of wine.

'Hey, yes, of course!' He sounded keen and excited. 'Did you find anything?'

Ah-ha! I had him dangling on the end of my line all right. I paused, enjoying my brief moment of one-upmanship. I have so few, but I was too soft-hearted to tease him for long.

'Well, I've been speaking to a girl who was in the same year as Rachel at school and she told me a couple of things, but the thing is – ' and this had only just occurred to me – 'I thought maybe I should hear the whole story from you before I – you know divulge anything.'

What if she didn't want to be found? What if she hated his guts and was avoiding him like the plague? He saw what I was getting at immediately.

'Of course,' he said quickly, 'I totally understand. Why don't we meet and I'll tell you all about it – tell you what, have dinner with me tomorrow night.'

Tomorrow night? Dinner? I was rather thrown by this suggestion, but not displeased.

'Er, well – tomorrow might be a bit difficult.' One couldn't be too readily available, and tomorrow was Friday, rather an uncool night to be free. 'How about next week, Tuesday perhaps?'

'Tuesday would be fine. Why don't we eat here? The Grill Room's very good, shall I book a table?'

Things were looking up: the Grill Room, no less.

'Why not?' I said in an off-hand way, as if I lived in the Grill Room.

'About eight-thirty?'

'Perfect.'

'OK, I'll look forward to seeing you then. Bye now.'

As I put the phone down I felt breathless and strangely elated. It's not every day I meet strange American men for dinner at the Savoy. I leaped off the bed and ran into the kitchen to tell Lottie. She was scraping burnt lasagne into Wellington's bowl who, not surprisingly, was turning his nose up at it.

'He's a Yorkshireman, Lottie, not a bloody Italian.'

'More's the pity,' said Lottie, putting some Pedigree Chum on top to fool him. 'We could do with some hot-blooded continental talent around here.'

'How about a bit of Yankee talent?' I told her about my date on Tuesday.

'Wow!' Lottie was impressed. 'So he's employed you as his private detective, has he? Paying you in kind with a slap-up meal at the Savoy.'

'Why not? I mean if Harry's out on the tiles every night, why shouldn't I be out with a hunky rich American?'

'Why not indeed?' Lottie narrowed her eyes speculatively. 'How hunky? How rich?'

I laughed. 'If we don't find Rachel, I'll point him in your direction. He's a redhead, not my type, but quite cute, you might like him.'

'Carrots?' she said warily.

'No . . . more, more russety really, like a red setter.'

'Mmmm . . . bring him home in a doggy bag.' We both giggled as Caro drifted in.

'I think I might go home now. I've left your clothes on your bed, Polly. I thought, you know, you might need them.' She avoided my eyes. 'Anyway, they look better on you.'

Good grief, was this her conscience talking? I met her half-way.

'Have them if you like, Caro, I won't miss them for a week or two.'

'Thanks, but it's OK, I think I'll leave them. Bye Polly, bye Lottie.'

She kissed us both, looking rather ashamed of herself. Lottie went to the front door with her. I think they had a little talk. She came back, biting her thumbnail and looking thoughtful.

'Sorry about Caro,' she said gruffly. 'She asked me to

apologise. She's a bit, um, insecure at the moment.'

'S'alright,' I said. 'It's not your fault your sister's a tart.'

We giggled and spent the rest of the evening polishing off the wine.

When I went to bed that night, I was surprised to find that for the first time in ages my thoughts didn't revolve around Harry. Instead, my mind was full of Tuesday night's tête-à-tête with Adam Buchanan.

Chapter Six

The rest of the week passed uneventfully, which was pretty much par for the course in my life, and then eventually Tuesday evening arrived. A taxi dropped me off in the Strand exactly ten minutes late, and in my nervous state I overtipped wildly. I ran my hand down the back of my black dress as I got out of the cab, smoothing out the wrinkles and hoping it hadn't creased too disastrously. Linen was always a nightmare. It was also a bit tight and I probably should have taken my pants off to avoid a knicker line, but Lottie had been horrified when I'd suggested it.

'Suppose he notices!'

'He's hardly likely to, unless he crawls under the table and looks up my skirt.'

'Take it from me, Polly,' she'd said, giving me her wise old sage look. 'Some men can just tell.'

That was enough for me: the knickers stayed put. I fingered my pearls as I walked to the Savoy entrance. Should I take them off? Wasn't a little black dress and pearls just a trifle unimaginative? Probably, but they gave me something to fiddle with when I wasn't smoking. They stayed put too.

First stop was the loo. I nipped in and had a quick look in the mirror. Not too bad at all, considering. My skin was surprisingly clear and my eyes looked almost blue in this light. I put my head down and shook it around to jazz up my curls, then threw it back and gave it a blast of hairspray. I considered the effect. Hey. This could almost be called glamorous. Almost.

Feeling faintly giggly, which might have had something to do with the bottle of wine I'd shared with Lottie for Dutch courage, I pushed through the glass double doors on which 'Grill Room' was written in discreet little gold letters. I remembered the last and only time I'd been here. It was for a sixteenth birthday treat with my parents and two older brothers. I'd been wildly over-excited on that occasion too, and had my first legitimate taste of champagne, my illegitimate tastes being the dregs left behind in the glasses after my parents' drinks parties which I used to quaff with a vengeance. My expensive tastes developed at a tender age.

I strolled in, trying to look nonchalant and hoping to God he was here before me. I had a quick look round, but couldn't see him; mind you, I'm pretty myopic at the best of times. The maître-d' cruised up beside me in an instant.

'Can I help you, madam?' he murmured.

'Yes, I'm dining with Mr Buchanan, perhaps you'd show me to his table?' I murmured back, as if I had a bit part in a 1940s film and this was my big line.

Not one eyelid batted. This was obviously the way most people spoke in here. He ran a finger swiftly down a list. 'Ah yes, follow me, please.'

I followed the ramrod-straight, dinner-jacketed back through a sea of tables as we wove our way across the elegant dining room. With its panelled walls, brass fittings and green velvet seats, it could almost be a gentleman's club.

Out of the corner of my eye I spotted Roger Moore having supper with his wife and children. I resisted the temptation to stare, and, anyway, I'd spotted Adam.

He was wearing a beautifully cut charcoal-grey suit with a pale blue shirt and navy spotted tie, all of which did wonders for toning down the red of his hair and bringing out the delphinium blue in his eyes. Things were looking up. He was sitting in the far corner of the room over by the window, and he instantly stood up as I was led to the table. This was a tricky little manoeuvre, as the table had banquette seating so he couldn't push his chair back and he had to maintain a rather uncomfortable skiing position as we shook hands. I sat down quickly to ease the discomfort and he sank back, relieved.

'Hi. It's good to see you, Miss McLaren.'

Oh God, the forties movie was rolling on apace: my fault, no doubt, for being so pompous on the telephone.

'Polly's fine, really,' I said smiling.

He visibly relaxed and smiled back, eyes crinkling. 'Good. Polly it is. Champagne?'

He gestured towards a bottle cooling in a bucket by our table and, as if by magic, an obsequious little waiter appeared to pour me a glass. I lit a cigarette, the first of many. Christ, this place was so understated it was in danger of not existing at all. A little different from the South Ken wine bars I frequented, where you had to rugby tackle your way to the bar, limbo dance your way to a seat at a table, and have a voice like Pavarotti to stand any chance of being heard. I hoped I wasn't going to get loud and raucous.

Adam was obviously a professional mind-reader. He grinned. 'I know, it is a bit subdued in here, but I thought it would be easier to talk. I guess you're more used to Langan's or something?'

'Er, yes, something like that' — but cheaper, I thought — 'but this is, um, charming.' Oh stop it, Polly, when have you ever, ever, said anything was charming? I must be nervous. I hid my face in the enormous menu and guzzled the champagne greedily.

'Any idea what you're going to have?' asked Adam.

'The Dover sole's pretty good, but feel free to have anything you like.'

'Oh no, I'll have the sole,' I said, relieved that at least one major decision had been made for me. 'I love fish.'

Fish? Was that really the way to describe Dover sole meunière? We're talking bank-breaking seafood here Polly, not cod and chips wrapped in newspaper. Oh dear. I sank into the champagne refuge again.

'Two Dover soles it is then,' he said, snapping the menu shut.

The waiter seemed to sense a decision and reappeared out of thin air. Adam ordered for us both with the assurance of a man who'd ordered more meals than I'd had hot dinners. That done he turned to face me. He put his elbows squarely on the table and fixed me with his steely blues.

'Look, I was thinking, instead of making polite conversation and skirting round the subject for hours, why don't I just tell you all about me and Rachel and get it out of the way? Then we can just forget about it and enjoy the meal, how does that sound?'

I nodded enthusiastically. 'Sounds good to me.' I was all for enjoying myself, whenever, wherever and with whomever – in the nicest possible way, of course.

He sat back, folded his napkin into a neat little square and took a deep breath. 'OK. Well, I could start with how I met her, but I'm going to go back a bit, so bear with me, it'll make sense in the end, you'll see.'

'OK, fire away.'

He leaned forward again. 'Rachel, as you know, was at the same school as you – St Gertrude's, right?'

I nodded. 'Right, poor thing.'

He shrugged. 'Well, funnily enough she rather enjoyed it. Her home life was pretty non-existent, so I think she was glad to be away at boarding school, that's probably why she did so well. She buried herself in her books in the holidays too, as far as I can gather. I guess there was nothing else to do.'

'Ah well, that's obviously why I did so badly at school. My home life was far too happy by half. Too many treats, parties, outings, ponies, friends – all my parents' fault, of course. I have them and them alone to thank for my lack of O-levels.'

Adam laughed and stopped folding his napkin into squares. Good. I may not be the brightest pixie in the forest, but I can perk up an atmosphere at the drop of a joke or two and I wanted to keep this as jolly and lighthearted as possible. His eyes looked a lot less steely.

'At least it sounds as if you had a good time. Unlike Rachel. She just swotted away at school and, consequently I guess, got straight As in all her subjects. By all accounts she was brilliant at music and maths and all set to glide through her A-levels and then go on to music school. But uh, uh, no such luck.'

I grimaced. 'Enter the wicked father.'

Adam looked surprised. 'You know about this?'

I could have bitten my tongue out. I wanted his version, not mine. 'Oh, I heard vague rumblings from someone in her year, but go on.'

'Well, as you say, enter the father. Wicked is probably a little strong, but reactionary, Victorian and bloody-minded will do just as well. Anyway, right out of the blue he arrives at the school and, bold as brass, insists that she packs the whole thing in and comes home with him. Can you believe it?'

'I can't really, I mean why? It's not as if he couldn't afford the fees or something, just to drag her out for no reason seems crazy.'

'He is crazy. In fact I think he's certifiable. Apparently he had some archaic idea about her turning her hand to a little flower-arranging or needlework – crap like that, something feminine and undemanding. Said he didn't

101

want her turning into a hardened career woman and that educating girls was a waste of time anyway because all they did in the end was get married and have babies.'

'Good grief, he's positively Dickensian.'

'Totally. Well, anyway, Rachel may be a bit timid and shy in other respects, but she's pretty passionate about her music and she wasn't going to take this lying down. By all accounts she put up a hell of a fight, as did your headmistress incidently: she was pretty horrified too.'

'I can imagine. It's not as if she had many star pupils,' I said, licking my lips as the most enormous Dover sole I've ever seen was put in front of me.

He paused for a second as silver dishes full of juicy little new potatoes and gleaming, al dente broccoli florets were flourished around. Adam seemed oblivious to the food. He pushed it dreamily around his plate, then started fiddling with his napkin again. I covered the fish's eyes with a piece of lettuce so he couldn't eyeball me, and tucked in with relish while Adam talked.

'Of course, there was no contest really. Old man Marsden was, after all, holding the purse strings, and Rachel's pleadings were like water off a duck's back as far as he was concerned. Let's face it, he's used to dealing with the criminal classes on a daily basis, so a schoolgirl was no match for him. He'd made up his mind and that was that.'

He picked up his fork again and toyed idly with his sole. I wondered if it would be terribly gauche to offer to eat what he didn't want, and decided on balance it would. 'Was she terribly upset?'

'Devastated. Cried and cried for ages, which rather disconcerted her father. I think he thought she'd sulk for a bit and then toe the line; but she shut herself in her room for days on end, refusing even to speak to him.'

'Good for her.' I was attacking bare fish bones now, and he hadn't even started. I played with my broccoli, trying to make it last a bit longer. The champagne was slipping down nicely, thank you very much, and I was beginning to feel rather lightheaded. Thus far, of course, I knew the storyline. It was the next bit I wanted to hear.

'I guess she decided that all she really wanted was to get away from him, so she asked if she could go abroad for a bit. It was the first time she'd said two words to him for days, and he was so nonplussed he just agreed on the spot, on the condition that she didn't just travel around, bumming and rucksacking, but went to stay with my family in Boston.' Adam reached for the bottle and topped up my glass.

'What's the connection?'

'Marsden and Dad were at Oxford together, they go way back and they've always kept in touch. According to Dad, he wasn't such a bad guy in those days, although it's hard to imagine him being anything other than a complete bastard.' He abandoned his sole and lit a cigarette. I watched longingly as a waiter whipped his plate away.

'So that's how you met her?' I lit one myself to keep him company.

'Right. I was staying with my folks at the time, and they asked me to pick her up at the airport.'

'You'd never met her before?'

'Never. It was her first time in America, and I'd never bothered to look her up when I'd been in England. So anyway, off I went to the airport with "Miss Rachel Marsden" written on a little placard, thinking this was all a bit of a bore and I could be getting on with some work or having a drink with the guys or something . . .'

He paused and slowly blew a long line of smoke over my head. His hand was caressing his wine glass. He seemed to be miles away. 'I'll never forget my first glimpse of her . . .' he said softly.

I smiled wryly. Now come along, Mr Buchanan, I thought, you're not going to tell me you were dazzled by her beauty or something, are you? I mean, judging by that photo you showed me she's OK looking, but she's not going to stop the traffic. Do you, perchance, carry a white stick?

If he did, his telepathic powers made up for his bad eyesight. He smiled ruefully. 'OK, OK, I know what you're thinking and you're right, she's no great beauty, but Polly — ' he leaned in earnestly — 'you should have seen her that day. Not beautiful, I grant you, but still pretty enough and so young and innocent-looking as she came through the gate with her baggage. She looked — I don't know, it sounds so corny — lost and wide-eyed, her pale, worried little face searching for a friendly face: she just looked so vulnerable. I knew it was her without even having to hold up my sign. She was wearing her school coat . . .'

I nose-dived into my champagne glass at this — Christ, her school coat? That dreadful old green thing? Did this girl have no sense of style whatsoever? Next he'd be telling me she wasn't wearing any make-up.

' . . . and that ridiculous scarf you all seem to wear. Sounds crazy, I know, but I reckon I fell for her almost immediately.'

'How romantic,' I murmured. I was totally unconvinced, but nonetheless made a mental note to dig out my old school coat and try out the vulnerable look. I couldn't help thinking it would need a good six inches off the hemline and not a lot of clothing underneath to make it anywhere near alluring, though. I was enjoying myself hugely now, lapping up the champagne and the dialogue with a vengeance.

'So you whisked her off her feet there and then?'

'Well, not exactly, but I had some time on my hands so I spent the next week or so showing her round Boston, going to concerts and museums and taking her to my folks' country place by the sea.'

Ah-ha! My ears pricked up. I know all about those

empty little cottages in the country. I had the feeling we were coming to a sexy bit.

'Well, one thing led to another, I suppose . . .' He paused, was that all he was going to say? He looked miles away, he wasn't going to go all misty eyed and withdrawn on me, was he?

'And?' I said, breathlessly and shamelessly.

' . . . and . . . within only a couple of days, we were . . . well, we were lovers.'

'A couple of days!' I squeaked. 'What, of her arriving in Boston? Gosh, you didn't waste much time!'

Adam looked alarmed. 'Hey, look, I didn't push her into it or anything, if that's what you're thinking. She was pretty willing, I assure you.'

Ah-ha. So Rachel was the instigator was she? Fast work, kid, and all achieved with a pale face, mousy hair, and an old school coat. I had to hand it to her.

Adam sighed. 'Look. I know it sounds ridiculously soft and unbelievable considering how long I'd known her, but honestly, Polly, I was already in love with her.' He was desperate for me to believe him and I did. I liked the way he said my name, too. Paully.

'Hell, no, it don't sound soft at all.' Why was I speaking with an American accent all of a sudden? And a deeply southern one at that. I cleared my throat and reverted to Queen's English. 'I think it's wonderful, actually. I only wish that sort of thing happened to me,' I added truthfully.

He grinned. 'Well, it had certainly never happened to me before.'

'So you just stayed there? I mean at the cottage? In a romantic little huddle?'

'For a while; then we went home to Boston and I talked to my mom about it. I'm pretty close to her, and she was great about the whole thing, if a little alarmed at first because Rachel was so young.'

105

'She can't have been more than seventeen!'

'Eighteen, actually, but I agree, still very young, and remember her father had entrusted her into my parents' care.'

'Serve him bloody well right!' I said, waving my champagne glass around. I was more than a trifle pissed. 'You didn't tell him, did you?'

He grimaced. 'Well, given his rather manic disposition, we decided to keep quiet for a while. I didn't particularly want him arriving at Boston airport bearing a meat cleaver with my name on it. Rachel wrote saying what a terrific time she was having—'

'—but not *who* she was having!' I interjected drunkenly, roaring with laughter at my own puerile wit.

He smiled. 'Quite.'

It was rather a polite little 'quite'. Simmer down, Polly old girl, I thought. Lay off the juice for a sec or you'll never get to the end of the story. I laid off for precisely one sec before hoovering up again.

'Anyway, the old boy seemed to soften slightly and wrote back saying she could stay on for a bit. Maybe he was feeling guilty about wrecking her academic career, I don't know. Meanwhile we moved back into the house by the sea in Marblehead. He was none the wiser because my parents sent her mail on.'

'Did they mind?'

'A bit, I suppose, but they knew we wanted to be together and they knew he'd come and get her if he ever found out. Mom and Dad are pretty laid back. Rachel couldn't believe them. D'you know she'd never even been allowed to have a date with a boy, even a boy of her own age. Don't you think that's weird? Maybe that's the English way, but Jeez, in the States the kids are dating at about fifteen!'

'Well, I think that's a little early, but even so . . .' I thought of my own relaxed parents who had generally let me do what I liked at that age, providing they met the boys in question and providing I came in at a reasonable hour. I couldn't begin to count the number of times I'd crept up the stairs after a late party, shoes in hand, always to be greeted by my mother's sleepy voice as I got to the landing, 'That you, darling?'

'Yes,' I'd whisper, 'go back to sleep.'

In the morning she'd come and sit on my bed and quiz me mercilessly, wanting to share it all. Who had been there? What had the girls been wearing? Had I met anyone nice? It was all part of the fun of the night before, and I couldn't imagine it any other way. I'd never had to go behind her back — although I have to say, Daddy would have gone into orbit at the thought of me shacking up with some older guy in America. I drained my glass rather conspicuously and it was instantly refilled.

'Sho you lived together?' I was dimly aware that I was slurring my words slightly.

'Yep.'

'How long for?'

'About a year or so, I guess, and then I asked her to marry me. She said yes and . . .'

'Congratulations!' I cried, swinging my champagne glass towards his own unsuspecting vessel and ricocheting off it with a loud clink. I swayed backwards into my seat rather unsteadily. 'Here's to the bride and groom! The happy couple!' I was flying now, and one or two people on the next table were turning round to look. They smiled, probably thinking we'd just got engaged.

Adam laughed, if a little nervously. 'Er, thanks — shall I go on?'

'Pleash continue!' I slurred, making a magnanimous sweeping gesture with my glass and indicating that the floor was all his.

'Well, we talked about the wedding, where it should be — in England or America, how many people we should

107

have, bridesmaids, flowers, etc, and the more we talked, the more we realised there was no getting away from it. We'd have to tell Rachel's father eventually, so we might as well tell him straight away. We could have gone behind his back and just got married, but Rachel didn't want that, and I agreed. I was also quite prepared to wait a year or so if he thought she was too young.'

Even in my inebriated condition, I could see that Adam was looking pretty miserable now. He hadn't even touched his summer pudding, which was a dead giveaway, and he was busy picking the table decoration of rosebuds to pieces.

'So . . . I put her on a plane to England about two weeks ago. That was the last time I saw her.'

He scattered the petals over the tablecloth, rested his elbows on the table and ran his hands through his hair. I sat quietly, sensing no smart-arse remarks would be welcome.

He sighed and lifted his head. 'I thought she'd ring after a day or so and give me the low-down, and when she didn't I rang her father's place. He just put the phone down on me. I tried again and again, same response each time. I wrote a letter and got no reply. I telegraphed — still nothing. After about a week of this I got on a plane and came over. I was terrified he'd dragged her off to Australia or something.'

He leant back wearily in his seat and still, miraculously, I managed to hold my tongue. I looked down and tried to focus on my hands which, rather alarmingly, seemed to have reproduced. If I wasn't very much mistaken there were about twenty fingers on that tablecloth. I started counting them, to myself you understand, but moving my mouth a lot so I didn't lose count. One, two, three . . .

'I went to his house and he slammed the door on me. I shouted through the letter-box, threw pebbles at the windows, camped outside the house in a hired car. I even

– ' and here he looked rather abashed – 'I even tried to break in one night, but the place is wired up like Fort Knox. But that's how worried I was about her.'

He was worried, I thought, staring at my hands; what about my bloody fingers? How would he like to have twenty-two of the bloody things, or was it twenty-three? They seemed to be fluctuating all the time as they moved in and out of focus. Better have a recount just to be on the safe side. I'd got up to eighteen when the coffee arrived. I took a large gulp. It had a surprisingly dramatic effect. Hot, black and strong, it surged through my furred-up veins and made a quick dash to my brain where, miraculously, it brought a brief moment of lucidity. I took another slug. Yes, this was definitely doing the trick; lo and behold, a few bruised and battered little grey cells were surging into action and making a dramatic comeback. Now what were we talking about? Ah yes, of course, Rachel; we were looking for Rachel.

'But she could be anywhere!' I managed to articulate and, flushed with success, roared on to form yet another sentence. 'She could be, well – in the country, abroad – ' I gestured wildly round the room – 'in here even!' Should we look under the tables, I wondered thoughtfully? Might that not be a start?'

'She's not abroad and she's not in the country,' said Adam decisively. 'She's here in London.'

'She is? How d'you know?'

'Because I've seen her.'

This shock tactic worked better than any black coffee could.

'You've seen her! Where?'

'In a taxi. She was with her father in the back of a taxi in Piccadilly. I was stuck in a jam going in the other direction, so there was nothing I could do – but it was her all right.'

'Did she see you?'

'No, she was looking straight ahead. I just remember how pale and sad she looked.'

'Oh!'

God what a mess. What a complete bastard her father must be. I drank a whole cup of coffee down in one and suddenly felt tolerably sober. I looked at my hands. Ten. What a relief: the offspring had flown.

'So where else have you looked, now you know she's in London?'

'Well, apart from laying siege to their house in London, I've waited outside court to try to speak to her father; but that's impossible, he goes everywhere by chauffeur-driven car, which whisks him away before I can get to him. He never walks anywhere, so there's no chance of tripping him up in the street.'

He rubbed his eyes. He looked tired. 'Two days ago I flew to Paris.'

'To see Sally Lomax?'

'You know her?'

'I don't remember her, but I asked around and found out she was Rachel's best friend.'

'Her only friend really. I was desperate and I thought Rachel might have managed to get a message to her. She hadn't, but she'd written Sally a letter on the plane going over to London, obviously posting it at the airport. Sally gave it to me.' He smiled ruefully. 'She said it was more mine than hers anyway.'

Adam took his wallet out of his breast pocket and produced a thin sheet of paper that had obviously been smoothed out, read and re-read over and over again. I spread it out on the table and concentrated like mad. I seemed to be focusing reasonably well. It was written in a round, schoolgirlish hand.

Dear Sally,

If my writing's terrible it's because I'm scribbling this

on a rather bumpy plane journey to England, so bear with me. Fabulous news, you'll never guess — Adam's asked me to marry him! I'm so thrilled I can hardly believe it. I've been mad about him from the moment I saw him — when he picked me up at the airport, in fact — and now I'm going to be Mrs Buchanan. Isn't it fantastic? He's so divine, Sally, I know you'll adore him. He loves the same sort of music as me, a real bonus, added to which he's incredibly good looking (well, I think so, but then I'm biased!).

I couldn't help looking up at this point. He caught my eye and grinned sheepishly. I grinned back and read on.

I can't wait for you to meet him; we're actually thinking of coming to Paris for our honeymoon, but before that I want you to come to London and be my bridesmaid. Please say you will. I'll let you know when, but it'll probably be around the end of September.

The only dark cloud on the horizon is the one waiting for me at Heathrow. I'm flying home to ask Daddy for his permission, and you know what he can be like — help! We'll go ahead and get married whatever he says, but it would be so much nicer to have his blessing. Anyway, I'll let you know how it goes. Must dash, the inedible plastic lunch is on its way round. Write soon,

Masses of love, Rachel.

I folded it in half and handed it back to him. 'Well, that's one of the leads I had for you blown. I should have realised you'd know who her best friend was. The only other thing I discovered was that she got on very well with a couple of teachers at school. I could ring them up and see if either of them has heard from her, if you like?'

'If you think it might help, I'd be grateful.'

He paused and looked at me steadily for a good ten seconds. I instinctively put my hand to my face. What? Had my make-up slipped? Did I have eyeshadow on my nose? Lipstick on my teeth? A bogey? What? He leaned forward and kept those steely blues boring into my shifty greens. What! I thought desperately, what is it?

'Polly, would you do something for me?'

'How can I possibly refuse?' I burbled, relieved that he'd finally spoken and feeling decidedly giggly.

'Would you go and see her father for me?'

'What! Me!' I nearly ate my coffee cup. 'Why?'

'Because he might talk to you. You can say you're an old schoolfriend, which is half true, and ask him if he knows where she is. Say you're organising an old girl's reunion or something. He'll never suspect you're anything to do with me.'

He had a point there, but did I really want to get that involved? Up to now it had been a bit of a laugh, but I wasn't sure I wanted to do battle with a crusty old judge with a meat hook.

I hesitated and tried not to look at Adam's eyes, which were pleading with me to say yes. Damn. I looked at them. 'OK,' I said weakly, 'I'll have a go.'

His whole face creased delightedly and his mouth grinned so hugely it almost split his face in half. He gave me such a hearty slap on the back I thought my Dover sole was going to reappear on the plate in front of me.

'You're a hell of a girl, Polly!' he boomed joyfully. 'A hell of a girl!'

Well, aren't I just? He seemed so overwhelmed by my agreement that it occurred to me he probably hadn't reckoned he had a snowball's chance in hell of getting me to do it. Ah yes, but then he'd reckoned without the sucker of all suckers, Miss Polly McLaren. No job too small, no fee too low, all assignments considered. Need a secretary you can really wipe the floor with? I'm your girl. Looking for a girlfriend you can park inside your front door with 'please wipe your boots' printed on her back? Look no further. Got a little problem with an axe-man of a judge? You've come to the right place. Polly McLaren's the name and gullibility's the game.

'This is where he lives,' Adam was saying, eagerly scribbling the scene of my death on a piece of paper. 'You'll obviously stand more chance of finding him in at the weekend or in the evenings . . .' When it's nice and dark, I thought, and when my blood won't show up quite as much on the carpets. 'Just keep your head' – no chance, it'll be rolling around on the floor, severed inexorably from my neck – 'and I know you'll be fantastic. I can't tell you how grateful I am . . . Tell you what, let's celebrate. More champagne!'

God, I had made him happy, hadn't I?

'Oh no, I couldn't possibly.'

' 'Course you could!'

'No no, really, I'm sobering up nicely on this black coffee.'

'Just a couple of glasses.'

'Oh well . . .'

'Waiter!'

The deed was done. He obviously thought I doth protest too much and he was absolutely right. All that making other people happy lark had given me one hell of a thirst. The bottle arrived. The one that would pour the glass too far. The one that would send me tumbling over the edge.

We both relaxed considerably as we quaffed the champagne. He was now doing his damnedest to keep up with me, but I could tell he was an amateur and, anyway, I had a two-bottle start on him. I started to tell him about Harry – trying to make him sound like the best thing since filtered cigarettes, but somehow he ended up sounding like a bit of a jerk. Surely I wasn't experiencing a touch of in vino veritas?

'Sounds like a bit of a jerk to me,' said Adam, echoing my thoughts, which I must say I thought was a bit strong considering he was talking about the father of my unborn children.

'What about the guy you work for,' he said, 'the guy I met on the stairs. He seemed nice enough, and isn't he what you girls would call a hunk?'

'Ah, now you really *are* talking jerks.' I warmed to my favourite subject and gave Adam a thumbnail sketch of Nick, pitching it somewhere between Paul Daniels and Saddam Hussein.

'And he's the boss, is he?' asked Adam.

'Yes, he set the place up about five years ago with a chap called Hugh Waters, but Waters doesn't have much say, he's just a sleeping partner. Apparently we're doing really well, as small agencies go. Nick's pretty bright, but he will spoil it by charging around barking out orders and instructions as if he owned the bloody place.'

'I thought you said he did.'

'Oh. Yes I did, but he doesn't have to show off about it, does he?'

I fumbled for my cigarettes. My fingers had once more gone forth and multiplied, and it was hard to remember which were the ones I usually used to pick things up with.

Adam laughed. 'You English really crack me up. It's considered bad form for anyone to make money and be a success, isn't it? What accounts do you have?'

We took an appropriate commercial break here as I seemed to be hell-bent on massacring cigarettes as they came out of the packet, but third time lucky I managed to extract an unbroken one. Hand-to-mouth coordination was becoming a real problem now, as someone appeared to have moved my mouth. It certainly wasn't in its normal position. Luckily Adam came to the rescue, turning my cigarette the right way round so I didn't light the filter, sticking it in my mouth and lighting it for me. It occurred to me that he could have gone the whole way and smoked it for me too, but I guess that was asking too much. I inhaled deeply. Now what had that last Brain of Britain question been about? Our accounts? Really? At this time of night? God, he really knew how to tax a girl: was he trying to kill me with a mixture of alcohol and Mensa?

I opened my mouth, hoping the words would just come out of their own accord: these accounts were tongue-twisters at the best of times. Nothing happened, so I decided to go the whole hog and recite them in Swedish, or was it Russian?

'Well, wev got Sujuper Roztie Cwoffee, um Lemonjina Sjoft Drinkz, um . . .'

Adam magnanimously let me off the hook. 'OK, OK,' he laughed, 'some other time perhaps. Somehow I think it's time to make a move.'

'You're going to make a move?' I looked alarmed, this guy was indeed a fast worker, and a fickle one at that.

'Home, Polly,' he explained patiently. 'I think it's time we were going.'

Ah yes, going. This was the moment I'd been having mixed feelings about. What remained of my brain definitely knew it was time to leave, but I wasn't sure how my legs were going to take it or, more particularly, my knees. The table was pulled out for us, and I tested them gingerly as Adam instructed the waiter to add the bill to his room tab. The knees weren't too bad, but the top half of my body seemed to have been caught up in a hurricane: it swayed dangerously from side to side. Had someone left a window open in here? I looked around suspiciously. Adam caught me as a particularly strong gust blew me sharply to the left, nearly knocking me over. I clung on to his arm and, slowly, we began the tricky little exercise of navigating our way out of the restaurant. Some bastard had thoughtfully placed an obstacle course in my way, but I rose to the challenge and meandered through a sea of tables, chairs and fellow diners with surprising agility, although I must say Adam's arm was necessary as well as decorative.

This time I couldn't resist cocking an eyebrow at Roger Moore, who didn't cock one back, which I thought was pretty unsporting. I stuck my tongue out at him. Yeh, I can be rude too, you know, I thought.

Just as we were lurching past the penultimate table, I spotted a very familiar figure in black tie walking into the restaurant. I knew him well but couldn't quite place him; nonetheless I greeted him like the old friend he undoubtedly was.

'Hi there!' I shouted, much to my fellow diners' amusement. I waved cheerily.

'Don't tell me, no − don't tell me, it's on the tip of my tongue?' I went on, bashing my forehead for inspiration. 'You're um . . .'

'He's the maître-d',' Adam hissed in my ear.

'May Tradee? May Tradee?' I said loudly. 'No, that's not it, I'd have remembered a sissy name like that. How many men are called May, for God's sake? Don't be ridiculous, Adam.'

'He showed you to the table,' said Adam, forsaking the whisper − what was the point? The whole dining room had laid down their knives and forks with amusement and were damned if they were going to miss anything.

'He showed me a table?' I thought hard. Ah, yes, obviously an assistant from Peter Jones. I was in there so often. 'Adam tells me you once showed me a table!' I cried as I was propelled past him at speed. 'Well, I think that was very sweet of you! Adam wait, I want to thank him, I—'

Somehow I found myself approaching the front entrance. An east wind was whipping around my kidneys as I was escorted from the premises and out on to the street by this burly American. Ah-ha, this was obviously the same wind that had tried to knock me over in the restaurant. Where was it from: Siberia? Were the Russians buggering around with our weather again? Bastards. I wrapped my pearls a little more tightly round my neck for warmth and shivered. A taxi purred up alongside us and Adam swiftly poured me in the back.

'Where do you live, Polly?' he asked.

'Chunder Road.'

He looked taken aback. 'Chunder Road? Are you sure?'

I tried again. 'Chegunder Road.'

'It's all right, mate,' said the taxi driver through his partition. 'That's pissed for Tregunter Road. I'll see she gets home safely.'

Adam grinned and waved me off. I turned round to wave back as the taxi rolled away, and wished I hadn't. The cab lurched round the corner into the Strand and so did my tummy. I clutched the handrail with one hand and my mouth with another. A friend of mine had once thrown up in the back of a taxi after just such an evening, and been forced to sit watching her dinner roll from side to side in the back as the cab lurched round corners with the driver screaming blue murder at her at the top of his voice. I tried not to think about that, nor my brother's joke about a man hailing a taxi and asking the driver if he had room for eight pints of lager and a takeaway curry before throwing up in it. Oh no. I kept my lips tightly pursed as we trundled down the Fulham Road, up Hollywood Road, and finally came to rest in Tregunter Road.

I tumbled out and handed the driver my purse, trusting him not to rob me of all my worldly goods. I certainly couldn't trust myself to try and open the damn thing. He handed it back to me with a grin.

'It's OK, luv, your boyfriend paid.'

Harry? Good Lord, how extraordinary. The taxi driver

waved a cheery goodbye before disappearing over the horizon, leaving me to chew on this dramatic turn of events. Harry? Where on earth had he sprung from, and how uncharacteristically generous. I shook my head in awe and wonder as I staggered up the front steps.

Before long, however, I had an even bigger conundrum to consider. Like how to get the key in the front door. How bizarre. The keyhole was much too small for my key and it also refused to keep still, leaping around all over the place whenever I tried to stab it. Stab stab stab. Move move move. Well this was a bit of a blow to morale. I thought hard. Ah yes, Lottie had obviously changed the locks while I was out. Too many men had been laying siege again, pestering us for dates. I'd have to break in.

I failed, but made so much noise attempting it that the door flew open and Lottie appeared in her nightie brandishing a tennis racket.

'Lottie! Couldn't get in, bloody lock, bloody key . . .' I mumbled, swaying violently. 'Been playing tennis? Little late, isn't it?'

'Get in!' she yelled, dragging me forcibly by the arm. 'I thought you were a bloody burglar! I was just about to bash you over the head!'

She pulled me in, swearing like a trooper and promising all kinds of vile deaths as she pushed me up the stairs, frogmarched me through the sitting room, and propelled me into my bedroom. She deposited me unceremoniously on my bed, where I lay until morning in a deep and blissful coma, boots still firmly on my feet like all good cowboys.

Chapter Seven

When the fire alarm went off the next morning I realised, with a start, that I was dead. More than dead in fact, reincarnated. Because this sure as hell wasn't my body I was lying in. Whoever I'd come back as had got the most enormous tongue: large and furry and much too big for her mouth. At least, I hoped it was a her. All sorts of problems loomed if it wasn't, most of which were either sexual or lavatorial and didn't bear thinking about in my present condition; or, should I say, this body's present condition.

And what a head this person had: full of throbbing, hammering noises which caused the eyes to ricochet around in their sockets quite unnecessarily. I'd have to sort that out when I knew who I was: no doubt there was a little man in Harley Street who could soon put a stop to all this funny business. As for the throat, how could anyone bear to have that amount of sandpaper stuffed down their neck? Or was it birdseed? Whatever it was, it would have to go. This reincarnation lark was a real eye-opener, a real revelation as to how the other half live. The bloody fire alarm was still ringing. The body swung out a hand and knocked it on the head.

An hour later the alarm went off again. Ten past nine, said the clock through blurred vision. My blurred vision. Oh God, I was still alive!

'Jesus!'

I leaped out of bed and instantly regretted it. I groaned and clutched the head that so manifestly belonged to me and sank back down on the bed again. Any form of movement was agony, but move I would have to, unless I was planning on forsaking my present job and swelling the ranks of the unemployed.

I fumbled through to the kitchen, feeling my way along the walls and hanging on to door frames for support. I drank a pint of water, instantly regretted it, and sat down, weak with exhaustion after so much activity, and feeling sure that any second now I was going to be sharing my water with Wellington, who was sitting at my feet looking up at me quizzically, his head on one side. Perhaps he didn't recognise me in my present condition. Let's face it, I'd only just made the connection. God, my head hurt, I must have been drinking for England last night.

I made my way shakily to the bathroom, pausing en route to poke my head into Lottie's room. It looked like the *Marie Celeste*. There was no sign of life but all the lights were on, the radio was blaring, and her curling tongs, I noticed, were just about to burn a hole in the carpet. I switched everything off. She must have left in an almighty hurry; probably overslept after her disturbed night, it occurred to me guiltily.

Ah yes, Lottie. She hadn't been happy had she? Yvonne Goolagong in a winceyette. I giggled. What was it she was going to do to me? Forcibly extract the larger of my intestines – I remember she'd been most precise – string it between two trees and use it as a washing line: a variation on the guts for garters theme, no doubt.

I made it to the bathroom and ran a bath. It was all coming back to me now. Or was it? There were still some pretty huge gaps, whopping great big chasms, in fact, like what happened between seven o'clock and midnight. I remembered a large Dover sole had been involved somewhere along the line – I clutched my mouth, don't even think about Dover sole – and I vaguely remembered promising to see a judge about a daughter, but I could easily extricate myself from that one. I also remembered making very free with Mr Buchanan's champagne bottle, but had I disgraced myself in the process? I racked my addled brain trying to recall any moments of debauchery, indiscretion or indecent exposure, none of which, I hasten to add, usually feature in my repertoire – well, not all at once. I thought hard. Nah. Not a sausage. I lowered myself gingerly into the bath. I'd obviously behaved impeccably, bringing not one iota of shame upon either myself or mein host. What a relief.

The warm Radoxy waters were behaving almost as they'd promised in the advertisement, refreshing the parts I didn't even know I had, or could reach – or was that called mixing my commercials? Anyway, after a brief soak I climbed out, feeling reasonably human and strong enough to face up to clothes and make-up. I pottered into the bedroom.

But not so fast. On closer inspection every single pair of tights I possessed had a ladder in them, and both pairs of trousers were at the cleaners (I didn't count the leopard-skin ones with the chains hanging from them, as I didn't think Nick would find them as amusing as I did). It would have to be jeans. I retrieved them from the bottom of the heap on the floor, pulled them on quickly, and added a black silk shirt that wasn't too disgustingly creased. This clothing lark had taken longer than I'd envisaged. No time for make-up now: it would have to be the natural look.

I grabbed my coat and bag, but as I was running like stink down the passageway to the front door, I was unlucky enough to catch a glimpse of myself in the hall mirror en passant. I dug my heels in and skidded to a halt, almost singeing a hole in the carpet. Backtracking slowly, I reaffirmed my suspicions with another peek. Oh-oh, just as I'd thought. So natural that no one would recognise me;

121

in fact I might even frighten some timid soul.

I hastily applied some muck to my face, but no sooner had I put it on than it was sucked down into the parched and arid depths as my poor dehydrated skin acted like a demented sponge. No matter, it would have to do: I was seriously late now.

On the shelf next to the mirror sat the telephone, and for one crazy moment my hand hovered over the receiver. Should I pick it up and call in sick, or dead, or dead-grannyed, or something? I dithered, then happily thought better of it. Four times in three weeks might well be construed as taking the piss, and since I'd already killed off most of the geriatric members of my family, I'd have to start on the more immediate members, which I couldn't quite bring myself to do.

Instead, like a brave little soldier, I tottered stoically off to Earls Court tube, feeling incredibly virtuous and quite forgetting my delicate condition was entirely self induced. Once there, I found the nearest pillar and hugged it gratefully. I couldn't even summon up the strength to buy the *Daily Mail*. I just snuggled up to my pillar, breathing heavily and feeling slightly dazed.

As I stood there, basking in the gloomy April drizzle, I felt something soft and warm nestling against my foot. It wasn't an altogether unpleasant sensation, in fact it was rather comforting, but I thought I'd better take a look down in case it was a furry little rat that had decided to curl up and die on my foot. I was close. Because there, poking out of the end of my jeans and about to fall on to the platform, were my knickers.

They were instantly recognisable as mine because of the crumbling elastic and the uniform grey colour that all my knickers go when they've been lucky enough to join in with the sock wash. Blushing furiously, I grabbed them and stuffed them quickly into my handbag.

Thus deposited, I kept my face well down, concentrating

like mad on my shoes as I felt my blush spreading to my fingers, toes, buttocks: you name it, it spread there. Still staring platformwards, I vowed furiously that never again would I take my jeans and knickers off in one fell swoop, thereby leaving myself open to just this sort of embarrassing predicament whereby I not only take them off together but put them on again together too. Furthermore, I vowed that I would eliminate all forms of sluttish and disgusting behaviour from my life once and for all. Thus resolved, I deemed it safe to look up.

I peered under my fringe. OK left, no one seemed to have noticed. Good. I rather over-confidently swivelled my eyes to the right, only to encounter a sadistic little pinstriped chappie grinning at me from behind his *Financial Times*. Mortified, I instantly turned my back and was about to walk away when the tube came in.

I managed at least to get into a different carriage, but as I stepped on I looked down the platform and saw him winking at me. Bastard. It could have been worse, though. It could have happened at work with Nick there to witness it. I shuddered. At least I'd been lucky enough to have a premature ejaculation at Earls Court tube.

Pippa, of course, was the picture of sobriety, good health and secretarial efficiency when I finally arrived at the agency. She was in the middle of greeting a telephone caller in the correct manner – 'Good morning, Penhalligan and Waters, how can I help you?' – when I lurched in clutching the furniture. Her highly polished shoes, nails and telephone manner were almost too much to bear; but, bless her, she had the decency to put the phone down on the prospective client as she caught sight of my miserable condition.

'Coffee?' she asked anxiously, sensing my distress.

'Please,' I bleated feebly, lowering myself thankfully into position. As I did so, a mound of correspondence rose up to greet me from my in-tray. I rested my head thankfully on this thoughtfully placed, snowy-white, A4 pillow.

'Polly, can I give you a list of things I'd like done this morning, please?'

My head shot up from its resting place and I opened my eyes wide, smiling in a bright and alert manner. God it hurt.

Nick was towering above me in his coat. I'd obviously beaten him by seconds, although it was a pretty pyrrhic victory as my last venue had been bed whereas his had been a client meeting on the other side of London. With any luck he wouldn't realise I'd only just arrived.

'Have you just arrived?' he demanded.

'Er, no, I've been here ages,' I lied.

He put his hands on my desk and bent down to have a look at me. He frowned. 'Are you all right?'

'Yes, why?' I said between a smile and clenched teeth, not wanting to breathe on him.

'You look a bit sort of . . . odd, that's all.'

'Oh, do I?' He was getting closer now, peering at me under my fringe; and what's more, he looked concerned.

'Are you cold?'

'No, why?'

'Well you've still got your coat on.'

'Have I? Oh, how extraordinary. I was so busy I didn't notice.' I wriggled out of it.

'And your eyes look like something out of an Ordnance Survey map.'

'Thanks very much,' I muttered, dropping the bright and alert look. 'I've probably been overdoing it a bit lately.'

'Oh I see, it's like that, is it?' He in turn dropped the concerned look. 'Burning the midnight oil while you brush up on your shorthand, I expect,' he said dryly.

'Something like that,' I said, gritting my teeth. What the hell did it have to do with him how I spent my evenings?

'Right, well since there's obviously nothing wrong with you apart from a touch of alcohol poisoning, let's get on with some work, shall we?' he snapped. 'I'd like this document copied eight times and then bound, neatly please. All this correspondence needs typing, as you're probably aware, although I fail to see that you've made any inroads into it so far, and I'd like these two big call reports corrected. If Jason thinks that that's the budget the client agreed to, he and I were clearly in completely different meetings. Although I must confess,' he added wearily, 'sometimes I think he's just on a completely different planet.'

I giggled. Poor Jason was a young account exec, terrifically keen but very green and nervous. He couldn't even pour the coffee in meetings without scalding a couple of clients along the way.

'So change the budget from two million to two thousand, and could I have tea and coffee for six in my meeting at eleven, please? Yes?' This last bark was directed at a caller who'd been put through to him on my telephone. It was the hapless Jason phoning from a meeting at a production company, obviously completely out of his depth. As Nick patiently explained the difference between a double head and a rough cut to the poor boy, I took the opportunity to examine this man-mountain in front of me. From my low-vantage point, I had to admit he was a pretty impressive sight.

Beneath the shock of dark hair his rugged features jutted out at some pretty acute, and even cute angles, and what a gigantic scale it was on. Imagine throwing the rope around that Roman nose and scaling the rolling chest before perching on the dizzy heights of those broad shoulders. It must be quite a view from up there. I giggled. Good grief, that champagne must have been quite something to give me a hallucinogenic hangover: I'd be seeing him in psychedelic technicolour next.

Unfortunately, whilst I'd been tripping merrily, Nick had replaced the receiver and was busy issuing yet another instruction which I appeared to have missed. He hissed through his teeth as he repeated it, ending with the ominous threat, 'And if I were you I'd get this done as soon as possible. You're on thin ice, Polly, thin ice.'

With that he swept off into his office in search of something better to do than torment me, and I rattled away at the word processor feeling decidedly rough.

As soon as he'd gone, Joss and Ron, our only creative team — art director and copy writer respectively — emerged from their office. They sat on my desk to inspect my hangover, for they were, after all, the experts.

'Undercooked fried egg sandwich, Polly?' suggested Ron.

'Nice glass of dog piss?' ventured Joss.

Ron put his hand on my thigh, supposedly to test my reactions. I swept it away, giggling.

'Hmmm . . . a little slower than usual, darling,' he reflected.

Joss and Ron were a pair of ageing hippies who couldn't quite believe that the sixties had really gone forever. They were forty-three going on twenty-three, and both had long greying hair which curled over their collars, and even shoulders in Ron's case. They'd met many years ago at college in Scotland, come down to the smoke together, and twenty years on still behaved like a couple of likely lads who'd just discovered Carnaby Street. Their life-support system consisted of a series of free lunches, one-night stands and piss-ups, and they didn't give a toss about anything. Luckily, the ad racket provided them with all the ingredients they needed to live a debauched and happy life, but they led a precarious existence, treading a fine line between taking four-hour lunch breaks and doing just enough layouts, scripts and headlines to avoid a P45. If they stepped over the line once too often, which, let's face it, wasn't hard, and failed to return from lunch more than, say, ten times in a month, they were invariably fired from whichever agency they happened to be freeloading on at the time.

Once unemployed, a period of austere sobriety would ensue. The boys (for that is what they were at heart) would stay sober for at least a week, carefully comb their greying locks, rearrange their portfolios, adding their latest commercials – and pinching one or two along the way – before sallying forth to seek re-employment. After a few false starts they would invariably land on their feet through an endearing mixture of charm, experience (these boys were drinking in Charlotte Street while Charles and Maurice were still barmitzvahing) and, it has to be said, talent. Once their designer trainers were firmly planted under new desks, they'd rattle off a couple of ads before, worn out and thirsty, they'd be off to check out the nearest hostelry, feeling they'd earned their money for that month.

Every so often, nervous young account executives like Jason would dare to enter their office. Pale, trembling, sweaty with fear and clutching long overdue briefs in their hot little hands, they would approach the sleeping/ drinking/hungover couple only to be told like Oliver Twist:

'*More*! You want *more* work? Fock me, laddie, it'll have to be Kettner's first!'

A table would be duly booked and Jason would have sleepless nights wondering how to explain yet another expense-account lunch to Nick. Once ensconced in their favourite watering hole, the boys would ignore Jason and greet all their creative friends – of which there were many for, remember, these boys had been around – who were also being wined and dined by anxious, timid souls in suits. Towards the end of lunch (about five p.m.) Ron and Joss, who were not unkind, would take pity on young Jason and languidly scribble a couple of layouts on the paper tablecloths so thoughtfully provided by Kettner's, which they would then rip off and hand to the young boy.

'There you go, lad. Now run along and don't lose it. That's an award-winner there if ever I saw one!' they would declare, beaming graciously at him.

Jason, flushing scarlet with relief and clutching the precious paper to his chest as if it were a signed Picasso, would thank them profusely before rushing to the loo to have a long, relaxing, well overdue pee.

Work completed, the boys would sidle off and steadily work their way through the bars of Soho in hot pursuit of chicks, as they still called them. They were childishly obvious in their methods. Joss thought nothing of accidentally spilling beer on a blouse in order to rub it off again, and Ron was forever dropping coins to look up skirts. It landed them in all sorts of trouble, and once back at the agency they were constantly ducking phone calls from irate wives/mistresses/chicks/ships-in-the-night, all of whom were demanding to know what the hell was going on. It would be at this point, when they were well and truly hemmed in, backs against the wall, chips down, that they'd look at each other, shake their old grey heads and declare, sadly, that there was no such thing as a free bonk.

Of course, once a mixture of cajoling and downright lying had been used to extricate themselves from a potentially hazardous situation, the larks would continue apace, but it was all so bad and so obvious you simply couldn't take offence. Everyone in the agency adored them, including Nick who, although he refused to be twisted round their little fingers, recognised a creative talent he couldn't begin to imitate.

On this particular morning, Ron and Joss, having completed a series of headlines and layouts the week before, were going through one of their resting periods. I typed away, trying to ignore them. This was hard, as Ron was stroking my cheek and Joss was staring deep into my eyes.

'What colour are they, darling?' he asked thoughtfully.

'Blue.'

'Really? Blue knickers? How nice.'

I giggled, it was all so predictable. Then I paused for a moment and told them about the knickers-on-the-station episode, knowing it was right up their alley. They cried with laughter.

'Oh God, Polly,' said Joss, wiping away a tear, 'I always thought you were the sort of girl who'd drop 'em at a moment's notice.'

Just then Ron's phone rang. He pressed the requisite number and picked it up at my desk. It was the wife. Her indoors. His back went rigid and he held up his hand for complete silence. We all obeyed, listening in with bated breath. Unlike Joss who was on wife number four, Ron was still married to his first wife, but only by the skin of his teeth. She was a teacher, and apparently he was terrified of her.

'Yes, my sweet? . . . no, no, never too busy . . . Oh, a PTA meeting? What a shame . . . you quite forgot. Well, not to worry . . . No, no, I'll get my own supper . . . Sausages will be fine . . . and baked beans yes . . . Apple pie in the fridge, I'll find it . . . Yes, my sweet . . . No, my sweet . . . No no, don't rush, I'll be fine . . . Have a good meeting then . . . bye bye.'

He put the phone down and looked at Joss, eyes shining with excitement. He rubbed his hands together gleefully. 'Oh joy! Joy! A PTA meeting! Ron, my boy, there'll be bevy and rooty-tooty for us tonight!'

Joss shook him warmly by the hand, and there was much back slapping and jubilation, at which point Nick's head appeared round his door as if it were on a stick. He cast his eye around the room, taking in this happy, unprofessional scene.

Pippa had her feet up on her desk, mine was occupied by Joss and Ron, and Jason, who was back from his meeting, was sitting on top of a filing cabinet, giggling away at the big boys showing off. Nick's face darkened. Jason disappeared behind the filing cabinet and Joss and Ron slipped off my desk in a trice. They tiptoed into their office and closed the door quietly. They could spot a harassed, overworked boss at fifty paces.

Nick turned to me wearily. 'Polly, if you're not too busy — ' was that sarcastic or what? — 'could you get me something to eat, please?'

'Sure, what d'you want?' I was dying to ring Adam to thank him for last night and apologise for any outrageous behaviour. At this rate I wasn't going to have a moment.

'Oh, just a couple of sandwiches, tuna and um, peanut butter will do.'

I ambled off to the sandwich bar, wondering if Harry would ring today. He sometimes did mid-week if only to tell me what a fantastic weekend he was about to have and how sorry he was not to be seeing me.

At Giovanni's takeaway café I had my usual first-form Italian lesson with my friends the proprietors — 'Ciao, bella. Come stai?' on their part and, 'Sì sì bene!' on mine — before sauntering back to the agency.

Nick was scribbling away at his desk when I delivered his lunch. 'Thanks, poppet,' he mumbled, miles away no doubt, as I put them down. You could have knocked me down with an iron girder.

He looked up and came back to reality. This was no poppet, this was the woman whose effigy he stuck pins into every night. He looked flustered. 'Oh, er, Polly, sorry, thanks a lot, what do I owe you?' he unwrapped his sandwich.

'Oh, about one-eighty, but have it on me, you can buy me one next time.' I was still staggered by the endearment, and I always throw my money around when people are nice to me.

He smiled and looked surprised. 'Thanks, I'll do that.'

Suddenly he made a face like he was going to throw up. Perhaps he was. I looked around desperately for the wastepaper bin. He stared at the sandwich in disbelief. 'What's this?'

'What you asked for, tuna and peanut butter.'

He groaned. 'Not together, Polly,' and then he went on in the voice he reserved for morons and retards. 'You see, they don't really *go* together.'

'Oh! Oh gosh, sorry, I wasn't thinking, I'll get you some more.'

He waved me out of his sight. 'No, never mind, never mind,' he said wearily, chucking the disgusting concoction in the bin. 'Just go and finish that pile of typing. I'll get something later.'

I walked out miserably. Why did I have to cock it up, just when we were making progress? Pippa was going out so she offered to get some more sandwiches. I decided to ring Adam. I needed to talk to a man who could bear the sight of me. The switchboard at the Savoy put me through in a second, and all at once I was being soothed by his dulcet, laid-back, North American tones.

'Hi, Polly, how's it going?'

'Badly. I've just been balled out by my pig of a boss.'

Nick's back stiffened behind his glass door. Christ! How much could he hear in there?

'Listen,' I went on, 'I wanted to thank you for last night. It was brilliant.'

'My pleasure, I had a ball!'

'Really? I thought I might have been a bit, you know, tipsy?'

'Hell, Polly, you were flying!'

I laughed. 'Oh dear, I'm afraid that doesn't come as too much of a surprise. Look, Adam, about this judge

131

business . . .' I wondered how I was going to get out of this. I should have thought it through before I picked up the phone.

'The judge? Will you see him tonight?'

'Um, well no, perhaps not tonight, you see I was wondering—'

'Oh sure, sure, tomorrow will do, don't you worry.'

'Oh, well . . .'

'Yeh, yeh that's fine, it'll keep a day or two, but be sure and ring me the moment you get back to tell me how it went. I'm counting on you, OK?'

'Er, yes but—'

'Great. Listen, I gotta go, I'm meeting some guy from back home downstairs in the bar. I'll hear from you soon though, OK? And listen – look after that hangover. Hair of the dog's what you need! Bye now.' He put down the phone.

You berk. You complete and utter moron. You completely cocked it up. Now you'll just bloody well have to go, won't you?

As I sat there feeling sorry for myself, Pippa arrived back with the sandwiches, closely followed by a stunning-looking girl in the most beautiful Armani jacket. I'd clocked it in their window last week, but it was beyond even my wildest overdraft.

She had the sort of cropped, blonde, boyish hair that you can only get away with if you're very young or very beautiful. She was both. She was as slim as a piece of macaroni, had perfect, regular features, and her slanting green eyes did parallel lines with her cheekbones. Aside from the covetable Armani jacket, she was wearing – just – a tiny black lycra skirt which showed off her incredibly long slim legs, clad as they were in dark opaque tights, black suede pumps and a silky yellow polo shirt. The effect was breathtaking. She was beautiful, but also somewhat familiar.

'Can I help you?' I asked in awe.

'Yes, I've come to see Nick — don't I know you?' It dawned on us both at more or less the same time.

'Of course!' she cried. 'You're the girl in the freezer!' and off she went into peals of tinkly laughter.

Ah yes, and you, I thought grimly, are the girl who stood watching me. Famous film star, raving beauty, and Nick's girlfriend all rolled into one. Serena Montgomery. The incessant tinkling was getting on my nerves.

'That's right,' I said breezily, 'I was doing a spot of research for one of our clients with a frozen food product. He wanted to find out what temperature the freezers are kept at. It's to do with shelf life, that kind of thing, but I don't suppose that would mean much to you.' I smiled, but with my mouth only. 'I like to throw myself into my job, you see.'

'Yes, you certainly do, don't you!' she chortled, and went tinkling off into peals of laughter again, obviously under the mistaken impression that she'd made the pun.

Out of the corner of my eye I saw two faces squashed against a glass door. Joss and Ron had heard a mating cry and were instantly alerted, tails up, sniffing around.

I raised my eyebrows efficiently. 'Is Nick expecting you?' I asked, as if he were the chairman of ICI.

'Er, no, but I just thought I'd drop by and take him out to lunch. I just can't tell you how funny you looked in that freezer. You—'

'Then please don't try,' I interrupted smoothly. 'If you'll just wait here, please, I'll see if Nick's available. And you are?'

'Sorry?'

'Who exactly are you?' I asked, giving her a sickly smile as I walked towards Nick's door.

'Serena Montgomery,' she snapped.

'Thank you so much,' I purred. 'I won't keep you a moment.'

I went into Nick's office and leaned against the door. Bitch. But why should I hate her? I probably had looked pretty ridiculous. I sighed, feeling rather tired of life.

Nick looked up expectantly. 'Did you want me?'

'Serena's here to see you.'

He looked alarmed. 'Here?'

'Yes, she's outside, she wants to take you to lunch. Just as well you didn't have a sandwich after all.'

He put down his pen wearily. 'Ask her to come in, would you?'

I opened the door and purred in my best Miss Moneypenny voice, 'Miss Montgomery? Mr Penhalligan will see you now.'

Nick looked at me in amazement and I detected the ghost of a smile on his lips as Serena marched past, glaring at me. I smiled sweetly and shut the door.

A few minutes later she was out again, looking extremely sulky as Nick steered her gently across the room towards the stairs.

'I do think you're being a bore, Nick. I've booked a table at Bibendum, and Justin's waiting for us,' she said.

'Well, I'm sorry,' we heard him say as they clattered downstairs, 'really I am, but I'm absolutely rushed off my feet. I've got a million things to do today. Give Justin my regards and apologise but—'

The rest was out of earshot, but Pippa, Joss, Ron and I rushed to the window and looked down in time to see him guide her around a Mercedes convertible and deposit her in the driving seat with a peck on the cheek. She pouted but looked slightly mollified.

'Wow. He's quite a coolie, isn't he?' breathed Pippa, steaming up the window. 'Not many men would turn down Serena Montgomery, Bibendum and a Mercedes convertible all in one lunch hour.'

'Mmmm . . . Ice coolie,' I agreed reluctantly.

Joss and Ron were speechless with admiration and

incredulity. 'The mon's a fockin' nutcase,' Joss managed eventually, shaking his head.

Ron just looked shattered, and they retired hurt to their office, lost in wonder at a fellow man's totally inexplicable behaviour.

Suddenly I realised that Serena would undoubtedly spill the beans on the freezer episode to Nick, probably later tonight, in bed or something. I saw the two heads, one dark and one blonde, sharing a pillow, and I could imagine him roaring with laughter saying, 'But that's just so typical of Polly. She's a complete head-case!'

Footsteps could be heard on the stairs, and Pippa and I jumped back into our seats just as Nick came marching through the room.

'Polly, Pippa, I'm going to write a presentation now, so no telephone calls and no more interruptions, OK?'

'OK, Nick!' We said in unison, grinning from ear to ear like a couple of schoolgirls.

He grinned back and shut himself in his room.

'*Very* sexy when he smiles,' whispered Pippa.

'Oh, Pippa. Anything in trousers.' But I had to agree, the odd flashes of humanity in Nick were quite agreeable.

My hangover seemed to get worse and worse as the day wore on, and once or twice I reached such a low ebb that I was tempted to ring Harry.

Pippa talked me out of it. 'Once he starts treating you like a girlfriend and less like a rabid dog, I'll let you ring him.'

'But I miss him,' I wailed feebly.

'Tough,' she retorted.

I sighed. She was right, and I knew the rules. I eventually went home and crawled straight into bed with *Tatler*, a Big Mac and a hot water bottle. To be quite honest, I really don't think I could have raised the necessary energy even if Harry had crawled in next to me, added to which, George Michael was becoming unbearably prickly, and I'm not at all sure that he, or should I say she, would have thanked me for submitting to any funny business.

Chapter Eight

The next morning I got up early and rang the school. It was a Saturday, so there wouldn't be many people around, but as far as I could remember, Mrs Compton took a tutorial on a Saturday morning. Miss Arnold, the school secretary, answered, and for a moment I could have been fifteen years old again, with a too-short skirt and ten Number Six hidden in my pocket. I automatically twiddled a strand of hair around my finger, a nervous adolescent habit I'd almost grown out of, but as her belligerent, argumentative voice came resounding down the line, I instantly regressed.

'Yes? St Gertrude's school,' she barked. 'Yes? Speak up, I can't hear you!'

I hadn't said a word. 'Hello, may I speak to Mrs Compton, please?'

'MRS COMPTON!' she bellowed incredulously, as if I'd said Ark Angel Gabriel. 'Mrs Compton is taking a TUTORIAL, she can't POSSIBLY be disturbed.'

'Oh, I see, well could I leave a message for her, please? Perhaps you'd be kind enough to ask her to ring Polly McLaren? My number is 723-1982, I'm an old girl, she'll remember me.'

'Don't bank on it!' she snorted — the charm-school department of St Gertrude's had really rubbed off on her — 'we can't be expected to remember all the gels that pass through these gates, you know, especially those who didn't exactly distinguish themselves, eh?'

I smiled. She remembered me all right.

'Thank you so much, Miss Arnold, and please remember me to your charming sister.'

'Humrph!'

She put the phone down. Her sister had been the matron, an equally nasty piece of work. One icy glance from her had been enough to cut off the blood supply to your heart. She didn't believe in illness. You had to be dying from cholera before she'd grudgingly admit you to the san, and even then you'd rather just die quietly at your desk, thank you very much.

I was quietly burning some toast, mulling over old school days and wondering what one wore when one made house calls to judges, when the telephone rang. It was Mrs Compton.

Now Mrs Compton was a rare breed amongst the teachers at St Gertrude's. Not only was she a wife and a mother, but she was also totally devoid of warts, bunions, hairy legs, varicose veins, bad breath or BO. She was relatively young, most certainly pretty and God knows what she was doing there.

'Hello, Polly, I gather you rang. Don't tell me you've decided to brush up on your algebra at this late stage?'

'Not likely, I can still count to twenty with a packet of cigarettes to help me; that's enough, isn't it?'

She laughed. 'Obviously. OK, so what can I do for you?'

'Well, I was wondering if you'd heard anything from Rachel Marsden. I tried to look her up the other day but she seems to have vanished.'

'Rachel? Hardly the lipstick and disco brigade, was she?'

I laughed. 'No, I suppose not, it's just that a few of us thought we'd get together and somebody suggested Rachel . . .' I trailed off lamely.

'Well, the last I saw of her was when her father took her

out of school. Shame, such a clever girl, but no, I haven't heard a dicky bird from her since.'

'What about Mr Saunders. He taught her too, didn't he?'

'Oh, yes, they got on very well, because of course she was a brilliant musician, but he moved to another school in Sussex quite a while ago. I don't suppose he's spoken to her since, but I could give you his number if you like?'

'No, don't worry, I'm sure I'll find her through some of the other old girls. Thanks very much, anyway.'

'Not at all, give her my love when you find her, won't you? And take care of yourself, Polly, try to keep out of mischief. I seem to remember you had rather a penchant for it!'

I laughed. 'I'll try. It was nice to talk to you.' I put the receiver down.

Well, that had proved to be a dead end, as I'd rather suspected it would. There was nothing else for it. I'd have to go and face Judge Marsden. Once again the eternal question loomed large. What on earth was I going to wear?

I abandoned my toast and ransacked my drawers, hoping for a solution. Quite by chance I found one nestling in the bottom drawer. A kilt. I shook it out and held it up for inspection. How eminently suitable; I'd forgotten I even possessed one. OK, it was a bit short, and the tartan was Fiorucci rather than Black Watch, but what the hell? I put it on, adding navy blue tights and lace-up shoes, which was perhaps taking things a little too far, but I do like to look the part. I wrapped my school scarf around my neck, and tied my hair up in a pony tail. All I need now is a satchel and an apple for the judge, I thought, as I bounced down the passageway into the kitchen, singing the school song at the top of my voice.

Lottie was huddled at the kitchen table in her dressing gown, her nose oscillating between her cornflakes and the *Daily Mail*. She looked up in disbelief. 'Don't tell me.

Harry's into schoolgirls and you're going off for a good caning. He gets to wear the gown and mortar board.'

'Wrong, it's all for the judge. I'm supposed to be an old buddy of Rachel's, remember? And she is a few years younger than me. What d'you think?' I asked, giving her a twirl.

'Oh yes, very Lolita. I hope you've got your navy blue knickers on, he's bound to check.'

I laughed and ran out of the flat feeling unaccountably excited. It was obviously the underhand nature of my mission that was appealing to me and prompting all this adrenalin to whoosh around. Perhaps I should have been a spy.

Adrenalin abounded in the garden too. It was a beautiful early spring morning and the bulbs in the tiny patch at the front of the house were responding eagerly to the call. It was as if they sensed that spring had come rather late this year, and were now doing their damnedest to catch up. A dozen or so slim green tongues were pointing straight up to the sky, like a row of little green soldiers standing to attention, straining to make themselves as tall as possible on the parade ground. Up in the sky a gentle breeze was playfully buffeting a few clouds around, but other than that it was a clear, bright blue morning.

I jumped into my old Renault Five – previously known affectionately as 'Rusty' owing to his chronic problem around the wheel arches, but now just plain old 'car' since Harry had told me that giving a car a name was about the twee-est thing imaginable. And I'd had no idea! You see I was learning all the time. Going out with Harry was really quite an education.

I jammed on my seatbelt, turned the key in the ignition, and shut my eyes as I prayed fervently to God, Allah and Buddha, thus wildly hedging my bets. Miraculously it started first time. I kissed the battered old steering wheel passionately and hurtled off to Kensington, still singing the old school song at the top of my voice.

The Honourable Mr Justice Marsden lived in just the sort of house you'd imagine a man in his position would inhabit. A tall, inscrutable white number with an elegant little square of garden at the front. It was just the sort of garden I wanted to mess up, actually. I had a violent urge to rush around emptying packets of seeds all over it, planting lots of bright vulgar flowers like marigolds and nasturtiums just to break up the tedious tastefulness of it all. A few off-white daffodils were nodding their discreet little heads in the breeze, and even the carefully pruned magnolia tree placed, just so, in the centre of the lawn seemed on the brink of budding. Odd how rich people's flowers even seem to come out first. Do they have the monopoly on sunshine, do you suppose?

I stared up at the house for a moment. Naturally I was looking for clues, like any good private detective worth her free meal at the Savoy would. Ah-ha. Up on the third floor, an Austrian blind in a dotty pink Laura Ashley fabric suggested a young girl's bedroom. Was she there? And if so, was it any of my business?

I could feel my courage running off down the street, and I wanted to run after it. The school song seemed to be stuck in my throat; I warbled middle C just to keep my pecker up. What on earth was I doing here? Did I have a death wish or something?

I tiptoed up the front path, hoping my shoes weren't making too much of a mess on the immaculate gravel path, and stopped at the bottom of the marble steps which led, inexorably, up to the front door. They looked about as steep and uninviting as the ones going up the pyramids in Egypt, and at the top was a large, forbidding, black front door. There was still time to turn and run, but for some crazy reason, I didn't. I climbed those steps – although how I managed it without a few crampons and a length of heavy-duty rope, I'll never know. The air was decidedly thin at the top, but I took a deep breath, pressed the brass bell, and then feverishly rubbed off the dirty fingerprint with my sleeve.

I cleared my throat and murmured, 'Good morning' to myself a few times to see if my voice still worked. After a while, I heard the steady click-click of heels on a polished wooden floor. They came to a halt at the door, and there was a pause as someone obviously had a look through the spy-hole. I tossed my pony tail in the breeze and struck an attitude of frozen gaiety. The door opened a crack but the safety chain was still firmly in place.

'Yes?' inquired a woman's voice.

'Oh, hello,' I said brightly, 'I was wondering if Rachel could come out to pl—was at home, if she was at home.' Christ, get a grip, Polly.

'Who are you?'

'Oh, I'm just an old school chum of hers.' I resisted the temptation to verify this by doing a merry jig on the step, and wondered briefly how this 'chum' word had mysteriously entered my vocabulary.

I had a quick peek around the two-inch gap and caught a glimpse of the owner of the voice: a middle-aged woman with steely-grey hair drawn tightly back from her face in a no-nonsense bun. She had a pointy little face and a pointy little red nose which almost certainly had a dew drop hanging from it. She was wearing a white housecoat, which obviously placed her firmly in the lower orders. Ah yes, this would be Mrs Danvers, the loyal but insane housekeeper.

'Just a moment,' she said.

I grinned in a 'Bunty has fun in the Lower Fourth' sort of way, and she shut the door in my face. Charming. A moment later the door flew wide open and I stepped back in surprise, a sure sign of guilt, I thought later.

I was confronted by a very tall man, at least six foot

142

four, thin as a reed and with a shock of thick white hair swept back from his forehead. His head was slightly bowed, and he reminded me somewhat of one of his daffodils in the garden. He was elderly without being ancient, and was wearing a patched old cardigan over a checked Vyella shirt, tatty old corduroys, and a pair of carpet slippers. He was not an intimidating sight. In fact the only thing that made him look vaguely judicial were the half-moon spectacles perched on his nose. He smiled and peered over them benignly.

'My housekeeper tells me you're looking for Rachel.'

'Yes, I am actually,' I said rather breathlessly.

'Won't you come in?'

'In?'

'Yes, do, come in.'

'Oh!' I nervously crossed the threshold. Even in my most pessimistic moments I'd imagined that when I was being bludgeoned to death with the blunt instrument I'd still be outside on the doorstep. It never occurred to me I'd have to go inside. I made a mental note to put my fees up and hold out for dinner at Annabel's next time.

I followed the carpet slippers into a beautiful pale yellow drawing room full of books and pictures and dominated by a baby grand piano. A roaring fire was crackling away in the grate and the mantel above it was stiff with invitations. Well, he was obviously popular. Shafts of light were streaming in from the large bay window at one end of the room and the open french doors at the other. One or two sunbeams lay across a pile of legal-looking papers and textbooks on a desk in the corner. The wages of sin, I thought grimly. An ancient golden retriever lay stretched out in front of the fire. He watched my progress across the room and thumped his heavy tail on the floor, apologising for being too old to get up and greet me properly. There were lots of silver-framed photographs dotted around and quite a few of Rachel. Any minute now, I thought, she'll walk in and I'll just yell, 'Adam's at the Savoy!' and run for my life through the french windows.

Mr Marsden motioned for me to sit down in a blue Colefax armchair. I perched nervously on the edge. He sank down in a comfortable old chair opposite me with his back to the window.

'And you are?' he asked, getting a pipe out of his cardigan pocket and stuffing it with tobacco. Hardly a murderous gesture.

'Oh, my name's Polly McLaren, I'm an old schoolfriend of Rachel's.'

'Oh really?' he smiled, patting his cardigan pockets for his matches. 'You were one of the St Gertrude gang, were you?' His eyes were friendly and encouraging; in fact I'd go so far as to say they twinkled.

I relaxed. 'That's right,' I said, gaily throwing one end of the scarf around my neck as if I never took it off, even in bed. 'Gosh, we had such fun there!'

He smiled and lit the pipe. 'Well, you know what they say: best years of your life, supposedly, although I was never totally convinced myself. All I remember from my school days are cold showers, fagging, and a great deal of unpleasant food.'

'Ah, yes. Well the food hasn't changed much, they still put putty in the custard, but you'll be pleased to hear that warming up the loo seat for the prefects has gone out of fashion.' Perhaps a little risqué, Polly? You only introduced yourself a second ago, and already you're getting lavatorial.

Luckily he threw his head back and laughed, obviously appreciating my fine line in scatological humour. Plenty more where that came from, your honour, I thought, warming to his merry eyes.

'Well I'm very glad to hear it,' he said. 'Would you like a cup of coffee? I was just going to have one.'

'I won't, thanks awfully, I can't stay long.'

'Ah. Oh well, never mind.' He looked disappointed. Poor old boy, perhaps he didn't get many visitors. After all, it probably wasn't every day he got to reminisce about his school days and engage in witty repartee with a pretty young gel like me. I was so relaxed now I felt I could almost put my feet up on the table and turn the telly on.

'I drink too much coffee anyway,' he was saying, as he puffed away at his pipe. 'Keeps me awake at night.'

The dog ambled over for a pat and he stroked his head. I eyed the impressive array of spirits and bottles on the Georgian cabinet in the corner and wondered idly what time the judiciary limbered up to Bloody Mary's of a Saturday morning. It was getting on for midday. He caught my eye, and my drift.

'What about a glass of sherry, then?' he ventured eagerly, raising his eyebrows and sensing a kindred spirit. He consulted his watch. 'I think we could declare an early drinks time, don't you?' he added naughtily.

'Oh, I don't see why not! As my father always says, it's got to be twelve o'clock somewhere in the world!' I bandied back, resisting the temptation to wink. The old rogue, that was quite a sparkle he had in his watery old eye.

He rubbed his hands together like a mischievous little boy and jumped up with alacrity. He was over to the drinks cupboard in a moment, busily picking out beautiful crystal glasses, holding them up to the light, checking for smears, etc. He turned and peered over his specs. 'Sherry all right, or would you prefer something else?'

'No no, sherry would be lovely.'

There was a satisfying glug-glug-glug noise as the golden liquid left the decanter. It wasn't strictly my tipple, but I could certainly rise to the occasion. He handed me an extremely large drink.

'Thanks, gosh, I'll have to get the bus home!' I quipped.

He laughed. 'Leave it if it's too much: I'm told I'm

rather heavy-handed when it comes to pouring sherry.' He sat down in his armchair again. 'Were you a special friend of Rachel's?' he asked in a distracted way as he wiped the rim of his glass with a rather dirty-looking spotted hanky. He held the glass up to the light, peering critically at it.

'Oh well, perhaps not special, I don't suppose she'd have mentioned me, but then she had so many friends.'

He looked surprised. Well done, Polly, first boob of the morning.

'You were in the same year?'

'Er, no, not quite. I was a couple of years above her.'

'Same house?'

'Er, no . . . but we both um − ' my eyes roved wildly round the room and lit on the baby grand − 'we both played the piano, you see.' I said, sitting firmly on my stubby, highly unmusical hands.

'Ah, another musician.' He smiled and looked at the piano. Christ, there was no way he could ask me to rattle off a little sonata to prove it was there?

'Er, yes, but I'm not in Rachel's league at all,' I said quickly.

'Oh come now, I'm sure you're very accomplished. It's just a question of practice really, isn't it? At least, that's what Rachel tells me. Can't play a note myself, I'm all fingers and thumbs. Anyway, I'm rambling on and you're probably very busy. You'd like to get in touch with her, is that it?'

'That's right,' I said brightly. 'Thought it was time we got together again, maybe play a few symphonies together or something.'

He looked surprised. 'Symphonies? You play with an orchestra?'

'Er no, not symphonies, I mean − well, you know, duets, that kind of thing. Anyway, I just thought it would be nice to see her again really,' I gabbled, desperate to get away from all this musicality.

'Ah.' He nodded, sucking hard on his pipe which had clearly gone out. He tutted with annoyance and started the pocket-patting routine again.

'Your matches are on the little table,' I said kindly. This old buffer was more like a benign and scatty professor than Hanging Judge Jeffreys.

'Ah! Thank you. Damn thing goes out all the time. Terrible habit, you know. Can't seem to give it up, though.'

'Oh, I know, I'm the same with cigarettes,' I said soothingly.

'Any particular reason?'

'Oh, just something to do with my hands, I suppose. Mind you, I'm pretty addicted to nicotine now. I gather there's a nicotine chewing gum you can buy that's supposed to make you give up, but I thought I might just buy some to chew when I'm not smoking. I rather like the idea of constant nicot—'

'No, no,' he broke in. 'Sorry, I meant any particular reason why you want to see her again?'

'Oh!' I was rather taken aback. 'Oh well yes, actually. You see I'm organising an old girl's reunion.'

'Really?' He smiled encouragingly, but the next question came zooming out of nowhere like a ballistic missile.

'Whereabouts?'

'Er, well, I'm not quite sure yet, um . . . my flat maybe, or, or, a restaurant.'

'I see, and when is it likely to be?'

'When?' I was beginning to feel a little hemmed in here as I dodged these quickfire questions. 'Well, quite soon really. Er, probably within the next couple of weeks if I can get everyone together by then.'

'Everyone? Sounds like quite a big gathering. Who have you got lined up so far?' He crossed his legs, rested his head back, and puffed away at his pipe, but it seemed to me he also fixed me with a pair of rather steely-grey eyes

147

over some equally steely-grey bifocals.

I could feel my fringe begin to curl as it always does when it gets wet. My forehead must be getting sweaty. It was awfully hot in here, too hot for a fire. I thought hard of people Rachel might know.

'Well let me see, there's Sophie Steward-Jones, and er, Caro Hamilton and um . . . oh yes!' I cried suddenly inspired, 'Sally Lomax is coming!'

'Sally Lomax? From Paris?'

'Yes, from Paris!' I smiled happily. What a triumph!

'Really? Good Lord.'

Mr Marsden stood up and walked slowly towards his desk, then he paused, drumming his fingers thoughtfully on the blotter. He picked up a heavy leather-bound legal tome and blew some dust off the spine. He opened it and flicked through a few pages, occasionally running his finger down the margin. Evidently he'd just thought of some vital piece of law which was pertinent to his next case. Well fine, don't mind me, I thought, taking a slug of sherry from my basin.

Then he started to hum. The book was still open but, good Lord, he wasn't reading at all, he was staring into space. What on earth was he doing? I studied his profile, he seemed to have almost forgotten that I was in the room. Of course! Yes, of course, he was about to take me into his confidence, and he was wondering how to go about it. Yes, that was it. My playing the Sally Lomax card had worked a treat. He was about to tell me exactly where his daughter was: locked in the basement, living on a Kibbutz in Katmandu, dancing with the Tiller Girls – I couldn't have cared less; what mattered was that he was working himself up to tell me. Obviously he was agonising over how he should go about asking me to keep it to myself. How could he explain that it was a deadly secret and that on no account should I divulge her whereabouts to any living soul? I gripped my sherry tightly, intent on his response.

148

Suddenly he turned to me and smiled. 'How nice,' he murmured softly, 'I'm very fond of Sally, I had no idea she was coming over. She must of course stay here, Rachel will insist.'

'Oh well, er, yes, I expect she'd love to.'

'Unless of course she's staying with you?'

'No, no, not to my knowledge — I mean, no, she isn't.'

'Good. Then we're agreed that she stays with us.'

'Sure, no problem.' I said, nodding in agreement. I couldn't really care less about Sally's sleeping arrangements, and I was rather unsure where all this was getting us. It was getting us rather neatly over to an address book and a telephone.

'I may as well ring her now and let her know there's a bed for her here. Don't want her doing anything foolish like booking a hotel. In a couple of weeks, you say?'

The crafty old bugger. He flipped through a large flowery address book written in a feminine hand, and his wise old finger came to rest in the 'L' department. My forehead was dripping now and my fringe was frizzing with activity. He found the requisite number and reached for the telephone. He began to dial.

'No!' I jumped up in alarm and started towards him.

Slowly he replaced the receiver. Then he turned to face me. 'No? Why ever not, Polly?' This sudden, rather menacing use of my Christian name chilled me to the marrow. I tightened my grip around my bowl of sherry and stared up at him. The sweet, kindly old man had vanished for ever, and in his place was a wicked, bitter, twisted old judge with murder on his mind. He didn't take his eyes off me.

'Why ever not?' he said again.

'Well, because, um because — you were right after all, you see, she is staying with me. I'd just forgotten! Momentarily forgotten!' I jabbered.

I abandoned my drink to a little tripod table and took a

couple of steps backwards in the direction of the door. I had my eyes firmly on the judge, so I very nearly tripped over the dog who yelped and hid under the sofa. I yelped too and considered joining him.

'Miss McLaren, if that is indeed your name,' said the judge quietly, in the voice he no doubt usually reserved for terrorists and serial killers, 'I'm afraid to say that I think you've come into my house under false pretences. In fact, I would go so far as to say that I believe you to be a liar and a fraud. Now what do you have to say to that?'

'I-I say, I say, I say,' I bleated shrilly in true joke-telling music-hall style, only this wasn't funny. Oh God, no. This was bloody frightening. I didn't know what to say.

'I don't believe you know my daughter at all. Neither do I believe you went to school with her. You certainly don't have her best interests at heart. You thought you could trick me, didn't you? You thought all you needed to do was wrap a borrowed scarf around your neck, adopt a silly schoolgirl manner, reel off the names of a few old girls and I'd lead you straight to Rachel. That's what you thought, isn't it?'

The judge was advancing towards me slowly. Where were my twelve men good and true? Where was my defending counsel? This wasn't the English legal system I'd come to know and respect, was it? I kept going backwards in the direction of the front door and the free world.

The judge had finished his summing up and was about to pass sentence. 'You are an evil woman, Miss McLaren — ' Christ! Bit strong wasn't it? — 'and you're obviously in cahoots with a certain American gentleman who, as I've made perfectly clear, will simply NOT BE TOLERATED!'

This was bellowed at about twenty million decibels. The dog yelped again and tried to dig a hole in the floorboards.

I stammered something incoherent like, please don't kill me, and backed even further away, scared out of my few remaining wits. He was still bearing down on me as I backed round the drawing-room door and down the hallway, the once friendly, kindly eyes flashing angrily now. How could I ever have thought he was as mild and reassuring? He was about as mild and reassuring as a Rottweiler. All this over an unsuitable boyfriend? The man was absolutely barking.

'I want you out of my house,' he said softly but dangerously. I was whimpering like a demented kitten now, and my hair had gone completely Afro as a result of the downpour erupting from my forehead.

'I'm going, don't worry, I'm going,' I whispered, as I backed up in terror, trapping myself like a fool against the front door. I felt behind me, desperate for the door handle, frantic to twist a friendly little knob. It was at that moment that he raised his hand to deal the death blow.

'Please don't hurt me!' I screamed, covering my head with my hands and sinking to my knees like the lily-livered coward I am.

His raised hand reached beyond my cowering head and found the door knob. As he swung the door open he almost knocked me flying, and I actually had to advance towards him in order to creep out around the door. Once out, I ran like hell. I took off down those marble steps, half expecting a carpet slipper in my backside as I went, but I was spared that indignity.

'And don't come back!' he yelled after me, at which point a million neighbouring curtains, or drapes as they were probably called in this area, seemed to twitch in unison as a whimpering Afro-haired, overgrown schoolgirl hurled herself down a mountain of steps.

I scrambled to my feet at the bottom and ran down the path, leaping the garden wall and charging across the road to my car. I can run when I feel like it, and I really felt like it.

I wrenched the door open and flung myself into the

driving seat, then with a desperately shaky hand turned the key in the ignition. Nothing.

'Oh come on, come on!' I shrieked. 'Don't desert me now, Rusty!'

In my despair I reverted to his pet name, but there was zilch reaction. Not a sausage. My temperamental little car was having a siesta, and nothing in the world would stir him, except, for I know my car of old, a wait of say ten or fifteen minutes.

I bashed my head on the steering wheel two or three times. Oh God, I wanted to get out of this place so badly! I wanted to get away from that axe-man of a judge who was no doubt sharpening his weapon as I sat here trapped like a rat in a rust-heap.

'Help!' I shrieked, and looked frantically up at the house, expecting the door to fly open at any second. There was no sign of him. And he didn't even seem to be watching from the window. But he'd be out here in a minute, wouldn't he? Out here, axe in hand, demanding to know why I was still sitting in his road, practically outside his house. I wondered if I should rig up a sign or something, write a message in lipstick on my windscreen perhaps. 'I'd really love to be going, I hate you as much as you hate me, but unfortunately, my car's broken down.'

I looked at my hands. I was shaking, really shaking. As far as I was aware this had never happened to me before, and I sat watching my trembling fingers with a morbid fascination. It reminded me of an accident I'd seen when I was young. A man had been knocked over by a car in the middle of the road and was shaking so much that somebody had covered him with a blanket. My mother had propelled me past as the ambulance arrived.

'Why was he so cold?' I'd asked.

'He wasn't cold, he was in shock, darling, that's all,' she'd murmured as I stared wide-eyed.

I eyed my hands rather proudly. Oh yes, I was definitely

152

in shock, no doubt about it. So where was my blanket? Or my mummy, for that matter?

Experience dictated that I had to wait a bit longer before I could try the car again, so I lit a shaky cigarette which seemed to have something of a blanket/mummy effect and calmed down just enough to contemplate for a moment the awfulness of Judge Marsden.

I blew a stream of smoke at the windscreen. The man was certifiable, no doubt about it. I didn't fancy Adam's chances at all. In fact, if I were Adam I wouldn't fancy Rachel either. Who'd want to end up with a father-in-law like that? I'd have to tell Adam the whole story. There'd be no need to embellish it with additional graphic detail: it was graphic enough as it was. He wouldn't be too happy with the outcome, but after all, I'd done my best, hadn't I? I certainly wasn't bloody well doing any more, that was for sure.

The cigarette was helping enormously. I took nice long drags right down to my boots and looked at my watch. Another couple of minutes and this old heap of a wagon might just about start. I looked in my rear-view mirror. What a sight. Coils of frizzy hair stuck out like bedsprings from my pale little face. I found a lipstick on the dashboard and added shocking pink to my quivering blue lips, so that they ended up deep purple. Yuck. I rubbed it off. I looked at my watch again. One more minute and I'd try again. I bit the skin around my thumbnail and thought about Rachel. Poor, poor Rachel. Was she locked in the attic or something? Was she manacled in chains in the cellar with just a bowl of water and the rats for company?

I looked up at the house, half expecting to see a little white face at the third-floor window mouthing, 'Help me'. Instead I saw the front door opening. Jesus Christ, he was after me again! I fumbled for the key and turned it quickly. There was an initial splutter, then a rumble — it started! I looked up as I revved the engine and crunched the gears, half expecting to see him bearing down on the bonnet, but to my surprise I realised it wasn't the judge at all who was coming down the front steps, it was the housekeeper.

She was wearing an old tweed coat and a green felt hat and was half carrying, half dragging, a rather battered old suitcase. It was bulging fit to burst. Was she leaving? Had she handed in her notice in disgust after witnessing the most unpleasant scene imaginable between her bullying employer and a sweet, fresh-faced young girl?

Intrigued, I shunted back into neutral and sat and watched as she made her way slowly down the front steps. The case was small, but was obviously quite heavy, as she was clearly having problems lifting it. She dragged it along the gravel path, then bumped it down on to the pavement. All this activity was too much for the old case. It flew open and spewed its contents over the pavement. I seriously considered helping her, but was understandably wary of going anywhere near that house again, so I stayed put.

She huffed and puffed with growing irritation as she stooped to gather up her clothes, throwing them back in again and muttering away to herself. But hang on a moment. Black Levis? A leotard? Leggings? I looked at the old tweed coat and felt hat. Surely not? She reached for something that had fallen in the gutter. A Walkman? Good grief, was this woman a funky dude in disguise? Was she taking advantage of her day off to go and get on down? Or did all this groovy gear . . . belong to someone else? Of course it did. Of course. I felt a sense of excitement growing within me. It belonged to a young girl. It must belong to Rachel.

Chapter Nine

I kept my head well down as she bundled the suitcase back together again, forcing it to close and snapping it shut. She heaved it towards a battered old Mini parked right in front of the house and opened the boot. It was a strain, but she managed to haul it in. I slid right down in my seat and covered my face with my hands, peeping through my fingers as she walked around the car and got into the driver's seat. My heart was thumping with excitement. Her mission was obvious. To take a change of clothes to the prisoner. Make no mistake about it, this woman was Rachel-bound and I had to follow her.

By rights, of course, I shouldn't have witnessed this little scene. They obviously thought I was long gone, and so I would have been if it hadn't been for trusty old Rusty failing me so magnificently. I mentally patted his battered old bonnet affectionately, keeping my eyes firmly on the action on the opposite side of the road.

The aged Mini was objecting to being woken from its slumber under the trees, and there were one or two false starts before the engine grudgingly turned over and spluttered into action. Luckily my own vintage car was still quietly shuddering away, and as she pulled out in the direction of Church Street, I followed at a discreet distance.

As we trundled down the hill, I opened the glove compartment and fumbled around amongst the sweet wrappers until my hand closed upon my Ray Bans. I rammed them on my nose, pulled at my pony tail letting my hair fall over my face, and wrenched the school scarf from my neck. If she was anything like me, she wouldn't use her rear-view mirror too assiduously, but it was as well to make sure that, if she did, she didn't recognise me. To this end, as we slowly wound our way down Church Street, I had a quick look over my shoulder, surveying the back seat for further disguise. I always travel heavy, and there are usually quite a few props lying around amongst the cigarette packets, plastic bags and general debris that seems to collect there. Today most of it seemed to be seduction paraphernalia − high-heeled shoes, low-necked tops, etc − but, nestling underneath a leather skirt and an empty beer can (not guilty, incidentally), was my father's old brown felt hat. I jammed it over the wayward curls and pulled the brim down over my eyes. I looked in the mirror: shady and incognito. I didn't even recognise myself, so she didn't stand a chance.

I gripped the steering wheel hard as buckets of adrenalin whooshed around my body. I'd already used up a tankful today, and I only hoped I'd kept enough in reserve for this little escapade. We turned left and motored off towards Kensington Gardens, my nose practically pressed against the windscreen due to chronic shortsightedness and the night-time driving conditions foisted upon me by my incredibly dark glasses.

On we cruised, up the hill and on past the immensely phallic Albert Memorial which usually brings a wry smile to my lips. Victoria must have reckoned he was a helluva guy to have had that enormous great thing erected in his memory, and bang in the middle of the park, if you please, for all the world to wonder at. You'd think she'd have parked it somewhere private, like outside her bedroom window or something. This morning, however, my mind was on even weightier things than Albert's member, and I didn't give it a second glance as we swept towards a surprisingly uncongested Knightsbridge.

As we cruised through two sets of green lights together, my hands became sweaty with excitement and the old heart hammered away somewhere in the region of my oesophagus. Where on earth were we going? I had a quick look at my petrol gauge and hoped to God we weren't setting off for a day in the country. I had about a gallon at the most. I cursed my false economy of only putting in a couple of pounds-worth at a time.

We manoeuvred Hyde Park Corner, which proved to be quite a challenge as she caught the tail end of each set of lights and I had to jump a couple to stick with her. I have to say I was enjoying myself enormously now, and just wished she'd put her foot down a bit so I could really show off. We crawled along at a couple of miles an hour. This lady was no speed merchant, and I had trouble keeping down with her but I curbed my Miami Vice-like instincts and rounded every single corner in second, steadfastly resisting handbrake turns.

The Palace was crawling with tourists, and the traffic had come to a standstill as the massed bands of the Coldstream Guards strutted their stirring stuff in the middle of the road. Boom Boom Boom went the kettle drums, and Boom Boom Boom went my heart. Please God, don't let me lose her here, I thought as we waited: it wouldn't be difficult. The band played on as one guard left and another one took its place. Come on boys, hurry it up, I murmured as the soldiers marched past. I couldn't help noticing that the officer in charge looked rather attractive, as far as one could tell under that bearskin. Oh well, not now Polly. At last the guard was well and truly changed, and our little Mini and Renault convoy was waved through by a benevolent policeman. We crawled off towards Parliament Square.

By now I was almost lying on the floor. All this stopping

and starting had provoked even me to look in my mirror once or twice, and I was praying she hadn't glanced behind once too often and wondered why a dirty blue Renault was sticking to her like chewing gum on a jumper.

As we turned left along the Embankment, a rather nasty feeling stirred in my waters. We were getting closer and closer to the river entrance of the Savoy. What was going on? Was this some kind of weird, elaborate joke? It was something of a relief when we sailed past the hotel towards the city and – oh God, yes, of course – the East End! Poor Rachel was obviously holed up in some dirty little attic room above a launderette or a chip shop, chained to a rusty iron bed, no doubt, with nothing to eat or drink. Never fear, fellow old Gertrudian: help is on its way!

I wiped my by now damp hands on my skirt and felt a rousing mixture of guts, determination, and the old Dunkirk spirit stirring in my soul. In my excitement I inadvertently gave the accelerator a bit of welly which almost blew my cover: I damn nearly went up the back of her as we turned left – left? What here? – through some enormous black iron gates that I didn't even know existed. And I thought I was a girl about town. Where the hell were we?

I followed blindly as we drove under an arch and then up a narrow lane with ancient stone buildings towering above it on either side. I nearly bumped my head on the car roof as we crunched over a couple of sleeping policemen and then turned sharp right under another arch and into a courtyard.

To the right of the courtyard was a beautiful garden surrounded by iron railings. An immaculate lawn was laid out like an enormous green tablecloth, and all around it were well-tended flower beds full of mature shrubs, rose bushes, lilac and crocuses. Opposite the garden was a large brick building that looked like a hall and – hang on a minute, this all looked vaguely familiar. Wasn't this where all those barrister chappies had their offices – or chambers? My suspicions were confirmed as a couple of young men rounded the corner and ambled past. They were dressed in their weekend mufti of cord trousers and tweed jackets, but under their arms they clutched bundles of papers tied up with pink ribbons and, if I wasn't very much mistaken, those papers were otherwise known as briefs. Ah-ha, nicely deduced, Polly.

I also had a vague and distant memory of a vague and distant cousin who, having bagged herself a particularly attractive young barrister, clinched the deal in a church not a million miles from here – Temple church, that was it. And of course, if this was the Temple, as I believed it was, Marsden would undoubtedly have chambers here. Things were looking up!

Far from being deserted as one might expect on a Saturday there were quite a few cars dotted around the car park. There were also one or two tourists who were wandering around, snapping their cameras at the Dickensian backdrop complete with old-fashioned gas lamps.

I hung well back and tucked myself in behind a Range Rover as the housekeeper parked her car in the bottom right-hand corner of the courtyard. I switched my engine off.

Mrs Danvers, as she'd become in my mind, got out of the Mini, walked round to the back of the car, opened up the boot and dragged the case out. She carried it with some effort and made her way to . . . now, let's see – yes, the very last doorway on that side. Number . . . forty-one? Was that it? Yes, forty-one! I kept my eyes fixed firmly on that doorway as she disappeared inside. My eyes were watering under the strain of staring wide-eyed for so long, but after what seemed like an hour but was probably more like two minutes, she appeared again, minus the case.

She got back into the Mini and started the engine. I slid

right down on to the floor and peered over the dashboard as she performed an immaculate three-point turn and drove up towards me. She must have passed right by me, but by now my knees were in my ears and I was inspecting the brake pedal. I counted to sixty then crawled up on to the seat and looked around. All clear.

Tingling with excitement, I wondered how I should go about covering the ground between my car and number forty-one without anyone taking too much notice of me. Should I stroll casually down to the door as if I had nothing better to do than mooch around the Temple of a Saturday morning, or should I run like the blazes and get it over and done with? In the end I compromised and did the most conspicuous thing of all: an incredibly guilty running tiptoe incorporating a few deft little zig-zag turns – which I felt were important – as if I were under fire. All I needed was the Sundance Kid giving me cover from behind and I could really have drawn attention to myself.

I ran up the stone steps to the open doorway and peered inside. There was a small flagstone hallway with steps leading up to the next floor. On my right was a black door with a list of names printed on it: Mr Michael Nelson, Mr Charles Morgan-Browne, Mr Richard Solmes, and so on and so on. I gingerly turned the handle. Locked. These were obviously chambers. I ran upstairs and on the next landing found a similar black door with yet another list of names. I quickly ran through them. There was no mention of Marsden. I tried the handle – locked again. The staircase seemed to go on and on, so I followed it up to the next landing.

As I rounded the corner to the third floor, I was confronted by yet another black door, but instead of a list of names, there was just the one. Above the door in gold letters about four inches high was written: SIR EDWARD MARSDEN. If this had been a movie the gold letters would have flashed in and out of focus and the orchestral score would have risen to an almighty great crescendo. As it was I had to clap my hand over my mouth to force my own crescendo down into my throat. Sir Edward Marsden! This was *it*! I'd *found* it! There was absolutely no doubt about it, Rachel Marsden was behind that door!

But what a door. I stood back and surveyed it. Unlike the ones I'd encountered downstairs which had glass panels and brass handles, this one was completely solid and seemed to be made from half a tree. It had no handle to speak of, and no less than three large keyholes: it was like something out of the Tower of London. I couldn't begin to get her out of there on my own. I needed help. I needed a man, or preferably men and — yes, of course, I needed Adam!

There was no doubt about it, I had to get Adam over here immediately. There was no point in trying to break that door down on my own, I'd just end up in hospital. I was just about to batter on the door, shout Rachel's name and tell her I was off to telephone for help, when I suddenly had a thought. What if she weren't alone? Suppose there was someone in there with her, a guard of some sort? Yes, suppose she was being watched over by a heavy? Suppose, as I bashed on the door, he came out and boffed me over the head? Tempted though I was to reveal myself as her rescuer, I decided that the mature thing to do would be to wait until I'd collected a little more muscle in the shape of Adam and perhaps even the police.

I charged down the staircase, bubbling over with excitement. I had to find a phone-box. As I ran, I imagined myself telling Adam and hearing first the disbelief, then the astonishment, and then the joy in his voice as I broke the news. I gave a yelp of delight as I jumped the last few steps and scampered out into the sunshine.

Of course, Rachel and Adam would feel indebted to me for ever, I thought, as I ran in the direction of an exit to the courtyard. Once we'd released her and they'd done their preliminary hugs and kisses, they'd clasp hands, look at me with dewy eyes, and say things like, 'Oh Polly, how can we ever repay you?' Then they'd try to shower me with all kinds of presents — jewellery, money, blank cheques, that kind of thing — but I'd be so magnanimous. I'd smile modestly and refuse everything, saying that all I really wanted was to see them happily married.

Ah yes, the wedding. Naturally, I would be the guest of honour, mentioned in the speeches — mentioned? Good grief, there'd be a whole speech devoted to me, delivered by Adam, of course. I'd blush prettily as a hushed audience listened to him recounting tales of my tenacity, my bravery, my undiluted courage — what was the name of that film about the resistance fighter? *Carve Her Name with Pride*, that was it; that would be a good theme for the speech, wouldn't it? I'd suggest it to him, discreetly, of course.

I dashed out into one of the little sidestreets that led from the Temple and encountered a row of tatty old warehouses, a few decidedly closed pubs and not a lot else. Somewhat lost now, I tried desperately hard to remember the A-Z, and hung a left in what I imagined was the direction of Fleet Street. It was a successful gamble, and I was rewarded by a glimpse of a red bus flashing past and what looked like a shopping parade.

As I hurried on, my mind scurried back to the wedding reception. People would be clamouring to meet me and pointing me out to each other. 'That's her,' they'd say, 'that's the girl who risked her life to bring them together. Isn't she wonderful?' They'd all want to hear the story and I'd repeat it over and over again — probably embellishing it very slightly to include me dodging a few blows to the head from the mad judge — oh, and of course I'd speed up the bit about me following the housekeeper, making that more of a life-threatening car chase. Everyone would be incredibly impressed and all the good-looking men would ask for my telephone number and Harry — God yes, Harry would have to be there, I wanted him to witness all this — yes, Harry would be looking on with pride, casting furious looks at all the predatory men and I'd overhear him saying things like: 'Yes very proud . . . oh I agree, terrifically brave.'

I spotted a phone-box in Fleet Street and fairly skipped into it. I never seem to carry any change, but today God had placed a whole ten pence piece in my purse. I dialled the Savoy's number which I knew off by heart now and rammed in my coin.

'Adam Buchanan please, room twenty-four.'

'One moment please,' said a man's voice.

I heard the telephone ring in his room. I heard it ring, and ring and ring. Oh God Adam, come on, come on.

'I'm sorry, Mr Buchanan doesn't appear to be in.'

'Could you try again?' I asked desperately. 'He might be in the bathroom or something.'

We tried again. 'I'm sorry, he's still not answering. Would you like to leave a message?'

Damn! Where the bloody hell was he? He knew I was due to see the judge today; he should have been sitting by the phone waiting for me to call. My heart sank deep into my lace-ups.

'Could you please just make sure he hasn't left a message for me? He really would have been expecting me to ring. My name's Polly McLaren.'

'Just a moment please, I'll look.'

I drummed my fingers impatiently on the receiver.

'Yes, madam, there is a message for you.' My heart made a quick dash up to my blue-stockinged knees. 'It says he's just popped out for a quick lunch and will be back at about one-thirty.'

One-thirty! I looked at my watch, it was nearly one o'clock. That wasn't too bad.

'In that case, I'd like to leave him a message, and it's

very important that he receives it the moment he comes in. Do you understand?'

'Yes, madam, I understand,' said a rather tight-lipped voice.

'Please could you say that I've found Rachel.'

'You've found Rachel.'

'Yes, she's at number forty-one, Queens Bench Walk in the Temple. Oh – and please could you direct him to the Temple and tell him I'll be there waiting for him? Could you read that back to me, please?'

'She's at forty-one, Queens Bench Walk in the Temple, and you'll meet him there.'

'You'll be sure he gets it?'

'Yes, madam.'

'The moment he comes in?'

'Madam, I'll make a point of personally tripping him up the second he steps through the door,' said the voice dryly.

'Thank you so much.'

I put the receiver down and raced back to the scene of the crime. I wish I'd thought to mention that if Adam could lay his hands on an axe it would come in handy, but no doubt we'd improvise when he arrived.

I took the stone steps two at a time and arrived at the third floor panting and breathless. The big black door loomed up before me again. I looked at the name again. *Sir* Edward Marsden, no less and I'd called him Mister. Good job too. Suddenly all reserve and restraint failed me. That poor girl had been cooped up in there for weeks now, and the least I could do was let her know that help was on its way. If she was being guarded, which in retrospect I somewhat doubted, it would do the thug good to know that I was out here – probably put the wind up him a bit. Thus decided, I really let that door have it. I hammered with both fists making a terrific racket, shouting at the top of my voice:

'RACHEL! RACHEL! IT'S OK! WE'RE GOING TO

GET YOU OUT OF THERE!' I paused for a second, then pounded some more, yelling even more loudly: 'RACHEL! RACHEL! WE'VE COME TO TAKE YOU AWAY, IT'S GOING TO BE ALL RIGHT! YOU WON'T HAVE TO STAY THERE MUCH LONGER, WE'RE GOING TO GET YOU OUT OF THERE!'

Just as I was working myself up into a nice little frenzy, the door swung open and Rachel stood there staring at me in amazement. My fists were flailing around in mid-air and I damn nearly punched her in the eye.

She looked terribly pale and thin and her little heart-shaped face was drained of all colour, totally washed out. She was wearing an equally washed-out blue T-shirt over grey leggings which had gone baggy at the knees. Her mouse-blonde hair looked greasy and bedraggled: she obviously hadn't been able to wash it for weeks, poor thing. Her pale blue eyes blinked nervously, obviously unaccustomed to daylight.

I stepped back in surprise. 'Rachel!'

'Er, yes?' she said doubtfully.

'Thank God! I was so worried you might be dead or something — how did you manage to open the door? Did the housekeeper leave it unlocked by mistake or something, how extraordinary! How ironic, just think you could have *walked* out! You could have just opened the door and actually *walked out of here*!' I gabbled.

'Um . . . yes, I suppose I could.'

'Gosh, you look dreadful you poor thing, absolutely dreadful, so thin and pale, and those ghastly filthy clothes. I bet you don't even know what day it is, do you? Well, it's Sa-tur-day.' I said it slowly in case she had trouble dealing with this, she'd probably been scratching little marks on the wall to keep abreast of the days and I hoped this coincided with her calculations. 'Did you know it was Saturday?' I asked anxiously.

Rachel's mouth was hanging open and her eyes were

wide with wonder, 'I'm . . . I'm sorry, do I know you?'

'Oh!' I whipped off my hat and glasses. 'Of course, you wouldn't have recognised me, but you see I had to wear a heavy disguise just to be on the safe side. Good, isn't it?'

She blinked. 'Er, yes, very good, I'm sorry I still don't . . .'

'Polly McLaren, at your service, I was at school with you, remember? St Gertrude's?'

'Well . . . yes, vaguely.'

Vaguely? She vaguely remembered me – a bit of a schoolgirl legend if I say so myself – or she vaguely remembered St Gertrude's? Either way it was worrying. I peered at her anxiously, scanning her face for evidence of cuts or bruising, bumps on the head and suchlike. None were apparent, but she looked decidedly vacant. Drugged perhaps?

'Are you all right?' I asked anxiously.

'Yes, very well thanks, and you? Would you like to come in?'

Would I like to come in? Do you ask the Seventh Cavalry if they'd like to come in? Or the SAS? Or Bodie and Doyle? Very well thanks, and you? Is that what the Scarlet Pimpernel had to contend with when he flung open the cell doors for the French aristocracy? Oh, hi there, Pimpernel. Yes, very well thanks, and you? I admired her sang-froid, but really.

I shook my head in disbelief and followed her dumbly into the drawing room. The drawing room? Hang on a minute, this was supposed to be some sort of chambers, and yet here we were in a beautiful eau-de-Nil room with large shuttered windows overlooking the courtyard. The neck-rickingly high ceiling sported an enormous chandelier and on Persian carpet level there were quite a few spindly-legged antiques dotted around, plus two enormous powder-blue sofas that looked as if they'd swallow you up whole if you so much as perched on the edge of them.

Hardly what you might call cell-like. More what you might call lap of luxury-like.

'What's this?' I said, not bothering to close my mouth when I'd finished my utterance.

'What's what?' she asked politely.

'This place, I mean it looks like a flat or something.'

'It is,' she said patiently. 'It belongs to my father: quite a few judges have them.'

'Bet they don't keep their daughters locked up in them, though, eh? Boy, I bet you're glad to see me, aren't you!'

She didn't seem to know quite what to say to this, and instead of throwing herself on my bosom and sobbing out her heartfelt gratitude, she perched on the edge of a powder-blue sofa and narrowed her eyes at me in a confused manner. Then it came to me. Oh God, had they brainwashed her or something? Was that it?

'Rachel . . .' I knelt down in front of her and peered earnestly into her pale blue eyes. She looked even more confused at this; in fact she looked downright bloody bewildered, poor kid. I spoke very slowly and carefully.

' . . . Rachel, can you hear me?'

'Er . . . yes.'

'Listen to me, Rachel, have they hurt you in any way? The housekeeper? Your father? Did they swing gold watches in front of your nose? Try to hypnotise you or anything? Can you remember?'

She frowned and looked annoyed. 'Now look here—'

'All right, it's OK.' I took her hand and spoke soothingly. 'We don't have to talk about it now if you don't want to. Some other time. Have you had anything to eat at all?'

She wriggled her hand away from mine and moved nervously along the sofa. 'Yes, I've just had lunch, actually. Look here, what's this all about?'

'About? What's it about? I've come to get you out of here, of course!' Christ, talk about ingratitude, but then, I thought kindly, she's probably still in shock. I sat down next to her and put my arm around her, resting my hand reassuringly on her shoulder. She sat bolt upright and looked at the hand on her shoulder in disbelief, then she looked up at me, her eyes like saucers.

I gave her a bit of a squeeze. 'Rachel, I've been looking for you for a while now,' I said quietly.

'Christ!' She leaped off the sofa in alarm, holding her arm where I'd touched her as if I'd singed her with a cigarette. 'You have? But I don't even know you, why?' Her eyes were flying saucers now.

'Oh, not just me, of course!' OK, I thought, I'll sock it to her now; watch her face light up like a Belisha beacon. I licked my lips with anticipation. 'Your boyfriend's been looking for you too!'

'My boyfriend?' Her face, if anything, darkened.

'Yes, your boyfriend,' I said impatiently. I was getting rather tired of all this playing hard-to-get nonsense. I also had the distinct impression that, far from showering me with jewellery and presents, even a simple thank-you might be out of the question. 'Adam of course, Adam Buchanan.'

I waited for the hug, the tears, the emotion. Instead she backed away from me, her face ashen. Her hand leaped to her mouth. 'Adam? Adam's coming here?' she whispered.

'Yes, Adam's coming here.' Why did she have to repeat everything I said? It made conversation so long-winded, and she'd got me doing it now.

'Oh my God!' Her voice cracked. 'When?'

I consulted my watch. 'Oh, in about ten minutes I should think!' I said jauntily. 'You've just got time to put a spot of make-up on,' I added, eyeing her peaky little face. She wouldn't want him to see her looking like that. I rummaged in my handbag and produced a leaky mascara and my favourite hot pink lipstick. I wasn't entirely sure

168

her face could take hot pink, but it was better than nothing.

'Here, borrow mine,' I said, offering them up generously.

'Oh God!' This came out as a sort of strangled cry, as if someone had got her by the throat, and she rushed out of the room, one hand still clasped to her mouth.

I sat on the sofa, still proffering my make-up and feeling more than a little confused. I frowned and put the lipstick away. Somehow this scenario wasn't going quite as I'd envisaged it would. I bit my lip and wondered where I'd gone wrong. Had it all been too much of a surprise for her? Too much of a shock? She did play the piano, after all, and they were terribly sensitive these artistic types. Perhaps I should have broken the news a little more gently?

An awful lot of banging around was coming from a room down the hall. I cocked an ear in the direction of the noise and then got up, wondering what on earth I should do. There was certainly a lot of frenzied activity going on in that room. Was she doing some kind of happy-clappy dance to celebrate Adam's return? As I've said before, she was very musical.

I crept tentatively down the passageway and poked my head around the bedroom door. Rachel was opening drawers and cupboards, grabbing armfuls of clothes and throwing them on the bed. Ah-ha! Now this was a scene I recognised, this was straight out of Tregunter Road! Of course – she was wondering what on earth to wear for this momentous occasion. I stepped forward eagerly, wondering if I could be of assistance – convinced, in fact, that I could: this was after all my specialised subject. I was just about to offer my services when I noticed that the clothes on the bed were now being stuffed into a red hold-all. I frowned. They were going to get awfully creased in there, and what was the point? Skirts and jumpers were flying in,

vests, vests? So small? A teddy, another teddy – Good
Lord, how many teddies did a girl need – and, heavens,
what on earth was that dreadful wailing noise?

I followed the wail to the end of the bed and there, lying
in a carry-cot and peeping out from beneath a pale blue
blanket was a little ginger head. A baby! A real live baby.

Everything on my face was as open as it could be now:
eyes, mouth, even my nostrils gaped.

'It's a baby!' I cried moronically.

Rachel carried on stuffing the bag as if I didn't exist.
Still slack-jawed with disbelief, I watched as Rachel
grabbed the carry-cot by the handles and barged past me
into the kitchen. I followed blindly. She grabbed bottles
from shelves and jars of baby food from cupboards and
rammed them in the bag, hissing and snarling as she went.
As she flung yet another lorry-load of bottles in, she swung
around to face me. Her face was white with loathing and
her mouth had curled up into a terrifying snarl.

'You stupid cow,' she hissed. 'You stupid, interfering
cow!'

My jaw was still hanging from its hinges, and I tried to
form a sentence or two, but could find neither wind nor
words. One thing was becoming remarkably clear though.
I'd made a major miscalculation somewhere along the line.
Rachel was kind enough to fill me in on what it was.

'He wants the baby, you dickhead!' Her voice was rising
to an hysterical level. 'Don't you understand? HE
WANTS MY BABY!' She screamed straight into my face,
her nose about two inches from mine.

In retrospect I'm glad she pitched it thus, because
somehow the proximity of her distorted face and the
volume at which this staggering piece of news was
imparted did actually have the effect of passing through
my thick skull and into my brain. I recoiled from her
in shock. Adam wanted the baby. He didn't want the
girl, he wanted the baby. I'd led him to the girl, therefore

170

I'd led him to the baby. I felt sick.

'Oh my God!' Now it was my turn to rise to fever pitch. 'He'll be here any minute, you've got to hurry, *hurry*!'

I grabbed her bag but, not very surprisingly, she grabbed it back and pushed me forcibly back against the wall. Flattened against the eau-de-Nil, I watched in despair as she hauled the bag over her shoulder and picked up the carry-cot which was equally heavy. Puffing and panting, she heaved her load out of the front door and began the tricky matter of descending the stone stairs with half a hundredweight of layette in her hands. It would take for ever. Ignoring her snarls and protests, I snatched the red bag from her and lugged it down the steps ahead of her.

'You've got to believe me!' I shrieked as I pulled the bag down on its bottom, my head swivelling back like a periscope as I pleaded with her, 'I had no idea! Absolutely no idea! He used me; he told me this long story about how you wanted to marry him and your father wouldn't let you. He said he was devastated, he said *you* were devastated, he never even *mentioned* a baby, I swear it. Honestly, Rachel, I had no idea. Please, *please* believe me!'

She staggered down behind me, tight-lipped and word-less, concentrating like mad on not tipping up the baby.

'I know I'm a stupid, interfering fool, I know I am, but I'll make it up to you, I swear I will. Honestly, I would never have got involved had I known, but − but he seemed so honest, so believable − well, you must know what he's like, how persuasive he can be, I just had no idea!'

She didn't look in the least convinced, but some of my hysterical ranting must have had some effect, because when we eventually arrived at the bottom, blinking and sweating in the sunlight, she looked one way, then the other, and then, in sheer desperation, at me.

'You absolutely swear it?' she hissed. 'You didn't know?'

171

Almost on my knees I swore on my life, my mother's life, my grandmother's grave, my dog — I thought desperately of other precious things — Harry, Harry's parents who I'd never met but who were obviously precious to him and therefore precious to me, Harry's dog — but she interrupted me.

'*Shut up, will you*!' I shut. 'Quick, where's your car?'

'Over here!'

We ran to the car, sharing the burden of the carry-cot. The little redhead looked up in surprise as we raced him over the cobblestones. Rachel's breath was coming in hysterical sobs now as we flung the carry-cot on the back seat and leaped in the front. I fumbled with the keys, terrified that any minute now Adam's face would appear at the window and a large freckled hand would reach in and close firmly over mine. The car started first time and I made a mental note to treat it to a service one day as a mark of my eternal gratitude.

We shot out of that car park in true Hollywood style, and flew over the ramps in Middle Temple Lane like Freebie and the Bean before coming to a screeching halt at the Embankment. The traffic was roaring in both directions, but at the merest hint of a gap I shut my eyes and put my foot down. A lorry swerved violently and slipped behind my tail, missing me by millimetres, honking his horn and shaking his fist. I swung into the stream of traffic on the other side of the road amidst more honking and fist-shaking and various allusions to my anatomy, but I cared not. We revved and roared and lane-hopped and light-jumped our way towards central London.

Neither of us spoke for a while. Out of the corner of my eye I noticed that Rachel's face was the same colour as her leggings and she was doing a great deal of blinking and lip-quivering out of the window.

I dug deep and found a very small voice. 'I'm so sorry, Rachel, I really am.'

Her chin began to tremble and a tear trickled down the side of her nose. She brushed it away furiously. 'Why couldn't you just mind your own bloody business?' she hissed savagely.

Yes, why couldn't I? I'd never felt so awful in my life. Apart from that time at junior school when I'd trodden on the school hamster in front of the whole class. By mistake, of course: he escaped and I went to catch him. Yes, quite dead. But this was all my fault, I'd screwed up quite comprehensively. I'd fallen for everything Adam had said without even considering Rachel's position. Off I'd shot like an unguided missile, tearing round to her father's house, who, I now realised, had simply been protecting his daughter and grandson and then, not satisfied with upsetting him, I'd charged off again and exposed her quite brilliant hiding place. It had been brilliant, too. How many people would have the faintest idea that those flats existed? Not many Londoners, and certainly not an American.

I still couldn't quite get my mind round all this, though. Rachel had a baby. Adam had a baby. They both had a baby and they both wanted it. What they didn't want — yes, yes, I was getting there slowly — what they *didn't* want was each other. Brilliant Polly. I would have liked to have known why, why they'd fallen out, what had gone wrong in the idyllic house by the sea in America, but I had a shrewd suspicion that now was not the time to ask.

I took another sideways glance and assessed the damage to her face. She seemed to be under control now. In a second or two we might have a bash at a conversation and try to determine the best place for her to go. But then of course she wouldn't have any idea, why should she? I'd only ousted her from her flat ten minutes ago, and she was hardly likely to have yet another brilliant hidey hole up her sleeve. I had to come up with something, and fast. I called upon my under-worked brain to perform some kind of miracle for me. Let me see, let me see, we couldn't go to her father's — God, what a nasty piece of work he must have thought me, I'd dwell on that later — and we couldn't go to my flat because Adam knew where I lived. Did she perhaps have any friends in London?

'Do you have any friends in London?' I ventured timidly.

She shook her head, and either this sad admission or the violence of the shake provoked another fresh trickle of tears down her nose. God I felt a heel. I plunged into my mental file of my two hundred closest friends and went straight to the top. There was really very little competition for this job. It was a position that had to be filled by someone with a big enough heart and a big enough flat to house a distressed girl and a baby. There was only one person who was unlucky enough to qualify, and that was Pippa. Big heart, even bigger house. Pippa it was.

By now, Rachel seemed to have abdicated all responsibility, and didn't even bat an eyelid as we did a U-turn in the middle of the road and headed off to Kensington. She did look up as we approached the bottom of Church Street though.

'Not to my father's,' she said in alarm, 'that's the first place he'll look!'

'I know, I know, don't worry. We're going to a friend's house.'

We dodgemed our way down Kensington High Street, turned left by the cinema and then right into Pippa's road. We came to an abrupt halt outside her house and my head dropped like a stone on to the steering wheel. Thank God that journey was over, I'd aged about a year in ten minutes. My hands, released from their position on the wheel, now began to shake like a couple of pink blancmanges. They'd been getting a lot of exercise in that respect today.

I raised my head and looked at Rachel squarely. It was an effort because her eyes were still understandably hostile, but I felt it was the least I could do.

'I'm so sorry, but believe me, you'll be all right. I promise I'm going to look after you and see that he doesn't find you. I absolutely promise.'

She nodded dumbly. What else could she do? She was in my extremely incapable hands. But I meant what I said. One way or another, I'd see this one through until she and the baby were safe, and well away from the clutches of Adam Buchanan. For once in my life, I, Polly McLaren, would not screw up.

Chapter Ten

When Pippa eventually answered the door it was obvious she wasn't alone. Her usually sleek blonde hair was somewhat tousled, her face was flushed and her eyes were far too bright. She was wearing a short white towelling dressing gown and not a lot else. She pulled the dressing gown closer around her as she peered round the door at her visitors, brushing the hair out of her eyes. 'Polly! What a lovely surprise!'

It clearly wasn't, but I was desperate. 'Pippa, this is Rachel,' I said, pushing a wordless Rachel ahead of me into the house.

'Oh, hi Rachel, um, come in.'

She was in, I'd seen to that, and I was right behind her with the carry-cot. This didn't escape Pippa.

'You've got a baby!'

'He's Rachel's,' I replied, staggering in. God, what did she feed him on?

'Well, I'm glad to hear he's not yours. He's lovely though, isn't he?' she said, bending down to do a bit of cooing. 'How old is he?'

'Five months,' muttered Rachel.

'Oh, he's divine. Is he really yours? You lucky thing.' She straightened up and peered at Rachel. 'Oh gosh, hang on − you're not *the* Rachel, are you?'

'How d'you mean?'

Pippa turned to me. 'The Rachel you've been looking for? Adam's Rachel?'

'Er, yes, but you see the thing is, Pippa, she didn't actually want—'

'Oh! Oh, how exciting!' She turned to Rachel and gripped her arm enthusiastically. 'But that's brilliant, isn't it! She found you, the clever old thing found you! Aren't you thrilled? You must be! Gosh, you look worn out, you poor thing. Have you been hidden away for ages? Yes — yes, how silly of me, I can see that you have, you look simply ghastly. I expect you're dying to have a wash and get out of those filthy clothes, aren't you? I can lend you some things if—'

'I'm perfectly all right, thank you. I had a wash this morning, my clothes are quite clean and no, I'm not remotely thrilled she found me!' Rachel hissed, shaking her arm free. She grabbed the carry-cot and stalked into the sitting room.

Pippa looked bewildered. She raised her eyebrows at me. 'What did I say?' she whispered.

'I'll tell you in a minute. Oh, it's awful, Pippa, you've *got* to help us!' My voice cracked; I was on the verge of tears.

'Yes, but Polly, the thing is I've got—'

'In a minute, Pippa, I'll explain in a minute, come on.'

I grabbed her arm and pushed her into her own drawing room. For a moment I thought she'd been burgled. Every conceivable square inch of carpet was covered in debris, mostly of the clothing kind, but there was also quite a lot of pizza around. The coffee table was on its side, all the large sofa cushions were on the floor, and full ashtrays and empty bottles abounded. Even Pippa looked slightly nonplussed, she obviously hadn't ventured downstairs since the night before.

'Oh, er — sorry about the mess, we had a bit of a raucous evening last night.' She jerked her head meaningfully in the direction of the stairs and rolled her eyes dramatically. I got her drift but pretended I hadn't: I needed her much more than he did, whoever he was.

Rachel was picking her way across the room to a chair. She turned it the right way up, and with forefinger and thumb removed a rather dirty bra before sitting down with the baby in her arms. She turned away from us and stared out of the window into the garden as if she'd temporarily vacated her body.

'I was um, just about to make some coffee,' said Pippa. 'Would you like a cup?' Rachel didn't respond.

'I'd love some,' I said quickly, 'I'll help you make it.'

We escaped to the kitchen and she shut the door. 'What the hell's going on?' she said in a hoarse whisper. 'Is she demented or something? Few sandwiches short of a picnic? She doesn't look all there.' She wiggled her finger around on her temple.

'I'll explain in a minute, Pippa, but listen, promise you'll help us. We're in real trouble.'

'Polly, do you have any idea who I've got upstairs?' hissed Pippa as if she'd trapped a wild animal.

'Who?'

'Only Charles Stanley!'

'No! Charles Stanley? Really?' In spite of my predicament I gasped in admiration. I'd never met the man, but I'd heard him talked of in hushed and hallowed tones by Pippa and various other girlfriends of mine, and was clued up enough to know that in terms of finds he was something of a Holy Grail.

'Exactly, Charles Stanley. I've been after him for *months*, Polly, as you well know. You just can't *do* this to me, in fact you're not going to do this to me, so why don't you just quickly tell me what the bloody hell's going on so I can tell you to bog off and get back to him.'

I groaned. 'Oh no, Pippa, please don't do that, I really need you. Couldn't you just have a tiny word with him and say — say something earth-shatteringly important's come up and you'll see him very soon? Please do, please,' I begged.

Pippa gasped. 'Get rid of him? Now?'

'Oh, I'm sorry, I know I shouldn't ask you, but I'm desperate, really *desperate*!'

'Polly, you must be mad!'

I certainly must have looked it, because she stared at me for a few seconds then shrugged her shoulders in despair. She threw a few mugs on a tray and threw in the towel at the same time.

'All right. But it had better be good. Bloody good. You make the coffee and I'll go and have a word with Charles.' She rammed the Nescafé into my hand and made to go upstairs.

I fell on her arm with relief. 'Oh thank you, Pippa, thank you! Listen — you could meet him later, it's just we must talk to you now, and um — borrow a bit of your house.'

'Oh really?' Her eyebrows shot into her fringe. 'Oh yes, well, please feel free. Which bit would you like: my bedroom perhaps?'

I didn't laugh, in fact I was just about to cry. She sensed it and gave my arm a squeeze. 'Look, don't panic, Polly. Just make the coffee and I'll go and square it with Charles. Tell me all about it in a moment, OK?'

'OK,' I whispered shakily as she ran off up the stairs, dressing gown flapping.

I wondered if my blancmange-like fingers were capable of getting boiling water from the kettle to mugs without giving myself third-degree burns. I just about managed it, and was on my way back to the drawing room with the tray when Pippa reappeared down the stairs followed by one of the most beautiful men I've ever seen. He was tall and long-legged with dark wavy hair which was currently attractively tousled, slanty green eyes, and a huge, lazy,

180

sexy grin which I had the feeling was pretty permanent. He extended the grin even further towards his ears when he saw me.

'Hi, you must be the desperate friend,' he said, tucking his shirt into his jeans.

'I'm terribly sorry—' I began, but he'd already turned to Pippa, taken her in his arms, and was in the midst of giving her the most thorough kissing I've ever seen outside the cinema. I stood there like an usherette with my tray of coffee as he finished the scene.

'Bye, angel,' he whispered as he held her face in his hands. 'I'll see you later.' Pippa whispered something back and opened the door for him. I was impressed. I'd never seen Pippa in action before.

'Right! In here,' said Pippa in a businesslike manner when she'd shut the door. She shepherded me into the drawing room. I put the coffee down and flopped on to the sofa. The white-faced girl in the corner didn't appear to have moved an inch.

'Now, what's this all about?' said Pippa, looking at me. 'I am right, aren't I? This is the Rachel that chap Adam whatshisname was looking for? The guy who took you to the Savoy for din—'

'Yes, yes,' I said, interrupting her hurriedly. I didn't want my free meal at the Savoy to feature too heavily in my tale of courageous – albeit misguided – fortitude. 'This is Rachel, only – oh well . . .' I took a deep breath and dived in, gabbling away about judges, housekeepers, disguises and car chases, but trailing off miserably when I got to the bit about bursting into Rachel's sanctuary.

Pippa turned to Rachel. 'So that's how she found you?' Rachel didn't respond. Pippa turned to me. 'So that's how you found her? She was in the flat all the time?'

'Yes, but you see—'

'Well, so what's the problem then?' said Pippa staunchly. 'It seems to me you've been absolutely brilliant!

I mean, you went to all that trouble just to unite a couple of complete strangers. You've been absolutely marvellous.' She turned to Rachel sternly. 'You've got a lot to thank Polly for, you know. There aren't many people who'd put themselves out to that extent, most people wouldn't have bothered to do anything. I think she's been tremendous, absolutely tremendous. Selfless, spirited, enterprising and—'

'Er, hang on, Pippa' I interrupted nervously. 'I haven't finished yet. You see, the thing is—'

'The thing is,' Rachel's head suddenly turned one hundred and eighty degrees to face us. It was a bit like something out of the *Exorcist*; any minute now we'd be in for a bit of projectile vomiting. Her face was grim, and her eyes almost disappeared into her face they were so screwed up with bitterness. 'The thing is that I didn't want her to find me at all. She's just a stupid, interfering old cow.'

'Oh now, look here!' said Pippa warmly. 'Talk about ungrateful. I mean—'

'No, Pippa. Listen to me,' I burst in. 'Adam wasn't looking for Rachel at all, he was looking for Jamie.'

'For Jamie?'

'Yes, for Jamie, the baby – this baby.' I jabbed my finger babywards. '*Their* baby.'

Pippa's eyes grew wide. 'Oh!'

I sighed. 'Exactly.'

'Oh! Oh gosh, how awful! You mean he just pretended . . . You mean he tricked you into . . . Oh!' She turned back to Rachel. 'So you didn't want to be found at all!'

Rachel declined to answer this, and gave her a look of such withering magnitude that most people would have been silenced for life, but Pippa was determined to get things straight in her head. 'So – so hang on a minute,' she persisted. 'This is like a tug-of-love thing, is it? You know, with the baby in the middle? The kind of thing you read about in the papers, is that it?'

Again this was deemed to be unworthy of response, and Rachel resumed her contemplation of the cherry tree in the garden.

Pippa looked at me, all rolling eyes and raised eyebrows. Oh my God, she mouthed. I nodded back miserably, agreeing wholeheartedly. Yes, oh my God.

'What are you going to do?' she whispered to me.

'I don't know,' I whispered back.

There was a profound silence. I looked at Jamie, who was sleeping peacefully in his carry-cot, oblivious to all the fuss and confusion surrounding him. He really was quite divine: all pink and white and chubby-cheeked with lovely little creases round his neck. Shame about the red hair, but if he turned out to be as good looking as his father, he'd be all right.

As for the mother – I sneaked a quick look at her grim profile – well, I had to say I still didn't remember her. She had a fluffy cloud of fair hair which not only needed a wash but, to my practised eye, could have done with about forty pounds-worth of highlights; a pale, heart-shaped face with pointed features; and small, bluey-grey eyes with those rather unattractive blonde eyelashes. She was, I decided charitably, sweetly pretty in a little-girl-lost sort of way, but next to Pippa, who admittedly had a head start with the just-got-out-of-a-hot-bed-of-lust-look, she scored about minus six on sex appeal. The big grey cardigan didn't help, because you couldn't really tell what sort of a figure she had, but I supposed she had a certain helpless attraction and would appeal to men of the caring and protecting persuasion. I had a sneaky suspicion she was pretty damn tough underneath that oversized cardigan, though: she was certainly toughing this silence out.

'So what's your sto . . . I mean, what's the real story then?' I said as sympathetically as I could. I was beginning to feel a trifle irritated. After all, I'd tried my damnedest

183

to help her. OK, I'd got it completely wrapped round my neck, but the least she could do was shed a bit of light on things instead of sitting there in supercilious silence like something out of a Botticelli madonna and child portrait.

'Rachel?' I raised my voice slightly. Still nothing.

Pippa coughed nervously. 'Well, of course you're welcome to stay here for a bit if that's what you'd like. I mean, I know it's not ideal but, um . . .'

Rachel continued to stare at the cherry tree and the tongue stayed hinged. Pippa looked at me and raised her eyebrows. I licked my incredibly dry lips.

'Well, Pippa, that's terribly kind. I think we'll say yes please, if that's all right with you and if, um, Rachel agrees . . .'

Suddenly Rachel turned towards us, she opened her mouth and – yes – she appeared to be contemplating a sentence. I for one was on the edge of my seat.

'Do you have anything stronger to drink besides coffee?' she asked. Wow! Not just a sentence, but a show-stopper of a sentence.

Pippa leaped up off her chair as if she'd been goosed, and was instantly hospitality itself. 'Gosh yes, of course. What would you like?'

'Could I have a gin and tonic?' It was getting better and better. In fact it was the first sensible thing she'd said since I'd met her.

Pippa raced off to the fridge and came back brandishing a frozen ice-tray, which she banged on the upturned coffee table spraying ice everywhere. Meanwhile, I poured three whopping great gins, adding a soupçon of tonic. We gulped them down thankfully and lit cigarettes. All at once a slightly less frosty, more conspiratorial atmosphere seemed to prevail.

Rachel put the sleeping Jamie in his carry-cot, crossed her legs and rested her chin in her hand. She sighed. 'OK.

I'll tell you how I got into this mess.' Pippa and I leant forwards in unison, anxious not to miss a syllable.

'As you probably know, my father dragged me out of school just before my A-levels.'

'Gosh, how awful, why did he—' began Pippa.

'Sshhh.' I nudged her. For God's sake, she'd started, let her finish. 'Go on, Rachel.'

'Well, I was desperately upset, in fact when we got home I couldn't even bring myself to talk to him. I just locked myself in my room and refused to come out. I think that really shook him, so much so that when I asked if I could go abroad for a bit, amazingly he agreed, on the condition that I stayed with some friends of his in Boston. Well I went, and that's how I met Adam, their son.'

So far so good, I thought.

She hesitated and took a long drag of her cigarette. 'Adam was – is, ten years older than me, good looking and very charming. I was incredibly unhappy, still rather shell-shocked, I suppose, and in dire need of a shoulder to cry on.' She shrugged. 'His was the obvious one: he offered it and I took it.' She paused for a moment and took another glug of gin. 'He was kind and sympathetic and, actually, great fun to be with. He made me feel a hell of a lot better, and we began to see each other practically all the time. Inevitably, of course, we ended up in bed.' She shook her head. 'God, when I look back now . . . you see I was so ridiculously innocent, he was the first person I'd ever slept with, and I was so clueless that I didn't even think about contraception. I mean, I knew all about it, but I just didn't think.' She sighed. 'I got pregnant almost immediately.'

Let that be a lesson to you, Polly my girl, I thought. Keep taking those pills.

Rachel took another huge gulp of gin and continued. 'I didn't tell him for a while because I was frightened of what he might say, but when I really couldn't squeeze into my jeans any longer, I did. He couldn't have been nicer. At one time I'd thought about having an abortion but was too much of a coward to go through with it, and Adam was appalled that I'd even considered it. To tell you the truth, he was thrilled about the baby, and determined we should keep it and get married.'

'Well, that's not so terrible!' I said. I imagined Harry's reaction to fatherhood would be to frogmarch me off to Harley Street where he no doubt knew of an obliging little clinic.

'No, I agree, and for a while things were great. We lived in his parents' house in Marblehead and I got bigger and bigger and felt reasonably happy about it. When I was about seven months pregnant, we rang my father and broke the news.'

'What!' I gasped. 'Didn't he go ballistic?'

Rachel smiled. 'He's not nearly as bad as you seem to think, you know.'

You could have fooled me, I thought.

'I mean sure, he wasn't exactly thrilled to bits, but he came round eventually and, anyway, what could he do? I was due to have the baby in two months. Anyway, he came out to see me in America, met Adam properly, and everyone agreed that we should get married. Everyone, that is, except me.'

'Why on earth not?' said Pippa.

'Because – ' Rachel struggled to explain – 'because I wasn't really in love with him.' She bit her lip and stared beyond us, almost as if she were thinking the whole thing through again as she spoke. 'I'd fallen for Adam when I was at a very low ebb, you see. I was depressed, miserable and lonely. I needed someone to turn to, and he just happened to be that someone. Looking back, I suppose it could have been anyone, within reason of course. D'you know, I think that even then, even right at the beginning when I was sleeping with him, in the back of my mind, I knew that I wasn't in love with him.' She looked up. 'Does that sound terrible?'

Pippa and I shook our heads vigorously.

'No, of course not!'

'God no.'

Oh yes, we'd both been there. We'd both had a few — ahem — liaisons shall we say, with individuals who didn't altogether make our hearts beat faster.

'So you can see why I couldn't marry him?'

We nodded, but less vigorously this time. This was slightly trickier, since neither Pippa nor I had ever been on the receiving end of a marriage proposal. We would have liked to have been, but somehow those four little words had never cropped up in our earshot, and it was hard to say what our response would have been. Nonetheless, we agreed wholeheartedly with the sentiment.

'Oh absolutely,' said Pippa.

'Oh God, I agree. Couldn't marry someone I didn't love,' I added. Unless, I thought privately, he was very *very* rich.

'Anyway,' Rachel went on, 'I prevaricated for a bit and said I'd rather wait for the baby to be born. After all, I was pretty enormous, and I pretended I wanted a proper white wedding.'

'Just playing for time,' said Pippa.

'Exactly. So two months later Jamie arrived, and actually we were OK for a while; I remember feeling reasonably happy. Then Adam started pestering me to marry him again. I put him off and put him off and we began to argue quite a bit. I was also desperate to get back to my music, I wanted to study some more — go back to college and get a nanny for Jamie. Adam was horrified — he thought I should stay at home; but eventually I persuaded him and in fact in the end he stayed and looked after Jamie because he could work from home. But things got worse and worse.'

Rachel rubbed her eyes with the back of her hand. She looked all in. 'Adam became incredibly possessive, questioning me endlessly about the boys at college, refusing to let me go for a quick drink after school with anyone; in fact he took to waiting at the college gates in the car just to make sure I didn't. I even caught him reading my diary once. It was ghastly. I began to really resent him, and then of course, I began to hate him.' She smiled sardonically. 'You know what it's like. A little irritation can easily turn into full-blooded hatred.'

'Perhaps you should have gone on holiday together or something, just the two of you, without Jamie, tried to fall in love again?' said Pippa, who read lots of agony columns.

'But you see I never really *was* in love with him, that was the root of the problem.' Rachel sighed and ground her cigarette out in the ashtray. 'One night we had an absolutely furious row, a real hum-dinger, and the next morning I decided I'd just had enough. Adam had gone to Boston for a meeting, so I booked myself on a flight to London, packed a bag, left a note and went, taking Jamie with me.'

Pippa and I looked rather shocked.

'I *had* to do it like that,' she said emphatically, 'or I'd never have got away. You don't know Adam, he's just so determined.'

I did know Adam, vaguely, and I took her point. If she'd so much as suggested a separation she'd never have got across the doormat, let alone to the airport. I looked across at Pippa who was gripped, her mouth hanging open and about two inches of ash hanging from the cigarette in her hand. I grabbed an ashtray and held it underneath. Too late.

'So you went home to your father's?' she said, ignoring the pile of ash on the carpet.

'I had nowhere else to go. He was pretty shocked and

tried to make me go back and patch things up, but once I'd sat down and talked it through with him, he came round, and in fact he said that in retrospect it was a good thing we'd never got married. The next day Adam telephoned, extremely drunk and extremely belligerent.' She sighed and took out another cigarette. 'He called me all sorts of names, threatened me with all kinds of hideous things, and said he'd never let me have Jamie. That happened about three times. He also threatened my father and said he was coming over to take Jamie back. I didn't consider it an idle threat either, because I know what he's like when he wants something. That's when Daddy and I decided I should go and live at his flat in the Temple. He's had that place for years, but he hardly ever uses it, and I don't suppose anyone even knows he's got it.' She lit her cigarette, blew the match out and crushed it in her hand. 'I liked it there. I felt safe.'

I looked down at my shoes and wondered which part of my body she'd imagined she was breaking into little bits when she savaged the matchstick. I had the feeling another apology might be in order at this point.

'I'm really sorry, Rachel,' I began. 'I had no idea—' but she interrupted me.

'It's OK. I dare say I was living in a fool's paradise anyway. He probably would have found me sooner or later.' I privately rather agreed with this, especially since her father's name was written in six-inch gold letters above the door.

'But surely,' said Pippa, 'surely with your father being a judge and everything, you could have held on to Jamie legally. I mean, couldn't you have got a court order or something?'

'Oh yes, legally, and that's what I intend to do; but that still doesn't stop Adam snatching him back and just getting on a plane to the States, does it?'

'Well what about,' Pippa went on, feeling her way

189

carefully, 'what about if you had some kind of custody agreement, you know: you have him for a while, and then Adam has him for a bit?'

'What, so Jamie spends his whole time to-ing and fro-ing across the Atlantic?' snorted Rachel. 'No thanks. Anyway, once Adam had him out there he'd never give him back, I know him too well.'

I couldn't think of anything to say. I'd been well and truly hoodwinked. And yet he'd seemed so straightforward, so . . . in love. Suddenly I plucked a thought from my brain.

'But there was a letter! A letter to Sally Lomax from you, saying what a terrific guy he was and how mad about him you were. Where did that come from?'

'Oh, come on,' scoffed Rachel, 'pretty easy to forge something like that, isn't it? I mean, do you know what my handwriting looks like?'

'No. No, I suppose not.'

Was I stupid or what? I'd sat at the Savoy making a complete prat of myself. I dug my nails into my hands in embarrassment. What a fool I'd been, and what a con man he was. I couldn't help remembering that bit in the letter about him being so good looking: he'd got quite a nerve to write that about himself, hadn't he? Quite a nerve. I stared into space, contemplating the magnitude of his gall.

Just then, Jamie decided it was time to wake up and exercise his vocal chords. He gave us the benefit of his extremely healthy lungs and — SCREAMED. I had no idea babies could cry quite so loudly. Pippa and I clustered round and bent down for a closer look as Rachel gathered him up in her arms. He stopped crying and Pippa held her arms out for a hold, but Rachel pretended not to notice. She obviously wasn't letting him out of her arms, let alone her sight.

Pippa straightened up and tied her minuscule dressing gown around her in a businesslike manner. 'You'd better stay here for a while, Rachel.' I could have hugged her. 'He's hardly likely to come looking for you here, I mean I don't know him from — oh well, you know.' She giggled, Rachel didn't. 'So you can have the whole of the top floor if you like: there are two tiny bedrooms and a bathroom. It's not particularly spacious, but it's clean and reasonably tidy and, er, oh!'

Whilst Pippa had still been in mid-flow, Rachel had walked straight past us, into the hall and up the stairs. I felt hot with embarrassment. She was beginning to annoy me, a small thank-you here and there wouldn't go amiss. I waited until she was out of earshot.

'Thanks so much, Pippa, you're an angel. Sorry about that ungrateful cow. I mean, honestly, she's probably safer here than she was in the Temple.'

'It's OK. She's probably still upset,' said the ultra-tolerant Pippa, picking up the sofa cushions from the floor and gathering together what looked like a crateful of empty bottles. 'Oh, and you'd better stay too, of course.'

'Me? Why?' I said in surprise, gathering clothes from the floor and folding them up on a chair.

'Because, dick brain, what's the first thing Adam's going to do?'

I turned a pair of jeans the right way out and gave it some thought. 'Go to Judge Marsden's flat?'

'Right, and then?'

I dropped a full ashtray on the floor in horror. 'Go to my flat!'

'Exactly, employing whatever bully-boy tactics he feels are appropriate to pick your brains.'

'Oh my God!' I felt like Salman Rushdie. I was being persecuted — I needed police protection! I reached for my felt hat and pulled it down over my eyes, ramming my Ray Bans on my nose with my other trembling hand. I was not a very brave girl.

'What shall I do?' I whispered, sliding down into a

chair. My knees felt rather weak.

'Just stay here and lie low for a bit.'

Oh, I would. I would lie very low. I would lie under that sofa if necessary, or, or down in the cellar where it was very low, I'd be so low you'd have to rip up the floorboards to find me.

I ran off to the hall to telephone Lottie. I told her the whole horrendous story and explained that she might have a visitor in the shape of one large ginger-haired Adam Buchanan ready and willing to wrench out teeth, hair and entrails in his search for his son. Lottie was totally unfazed by all this: her streak of yellow wasn't nearly as wide as mine. She said she'd pop over later with some clothes for me. All at once I knew who my friends were.

'Oh, and Lottie!' I screamed as she was about to put the phone down. 'Don't drop them all over the pavement, will you? Don't use a case, use a black binliner or something and – and look behind you to make sure you're not being followed. Remember whoever it is could be in disguise and, and – just be bloody careful!' I squeaked into the receiver, thinking of my own skin of course rather than hers.

When Pippa and I had tidied up and she'd shed her dressing gown for something more suitable, we all trooped off for a rather strange and subdued lunch in the Scarsdale. We were an unlikely bunch in the pub that afternoon: Pippa, Charles Stanley, Rachel – with Jamie asleep in a sling – and me.

We couldn't possibly tell Charles the whole story, but you could see his brain was working overtime as he wondered what this dolly mixture of girls was all about. Who was that white-faced one in the corner with the baby? And why did she and the one in the brown hat and dark glasses leap up and down every time someone came into the pub? Were they being followed? These and other unanswered questions clearly ran through his mind, but

Charles, who was a good chap, said nothing and coped wonderfully – entertaining us, feeding us, plying us with drinks, and resisting all offers of payment.

It was rather as if Pippa had suddenly sprung a large and motley family upon him which he was expected to provide for, no questions asked. And wasn't he just taking it all in his giant stride, I thought, as I watched this long-legged hunk of man gaze adoringly at Pippa over his Guinness.

How would Harry have reacted, I wondered? He always enjoyed Pippa's company because she was so pretty, but I wasn't quite sure how he'd have coped with the anaemic waif and baby. I realised with a jolt that I hadn't thought about Harry for at least a day. Seeing Pippa and Charles so happy together made me miss him with an almighty great pang. I'd ring him later. Yes I would. Bet you anything he was wondering how I was. I was almost as good at lying to myself as I was to other people. Had he been trying to ring me, I wondered? At least he could reach me at the agency. I went cold. So could Adam.

'Pippa!' I squeaked, rudely interrupting Charles who was deep in the finer nuances of the latest French film at the Curzon, 'Pippa, he knows where I work! He'll be bashing down the agency door on Monday!' Pools of blood were swimming before my eyes as I imagined the nasty stains on the agency carpet.

'Yes, I was wondering about that,' said the altogether unflappable Pippa, obviously alive to the possibility before it had even filtered through my own fuddled brain. 'You'd better take the day off tomorrow and stay at home with Rachel. If he puts in an appearance, we'll say you've taken some leave: gone to stay with friends in the country for a couple of weeks or something.'

'Suppose he doesn't believe you!' I wailed.

'So what? What can he do? He might well believe it anyway; I mean it's quite likely really, considering he's after you.'

After me! Great Scott, someone was after me! I sank back in my chair in despair, nursing my gin and tonic. Perhaps I should change my identity completely, steal a passport, become a nun or something, emigrate to Australia perhaps.

Out of the corner of my eye I could see that Charles was looking more and more mystified. This latest outburst from the maniac in the hat had really got the cogs whirring in his brain. Ah yes, I was obviously on the run from my drunken, wife-beating husband — he looked at the empty ring finger on my left hand — common-law husband. He switched his gaze to Pippa. Pippa was obviously sheltering me, perhaps she ran a home for battered wives or something, or perhaps — yes — that was it, she was working for the Samaritans. He took her hand tenderly. That would explain the white-faced single parent in the corner. Perhaps white face was also a drug addict or a prostitute and Pippa had generously taken us all under her wing. He stroked her hand and his eyes shone with love and admiration. I drained my glass. Well, one good thing had come out of this saga. We were obviously doing wonders for Pippa's big-hearted image.

That evening, back at Pippa's, I weakened and rang Harry.

'Hi Polyester, how's it going? I've been looking for you everywhere, where have you been hiding?'

My knees buckled and I sat down very hard on the wooden chair by the telephone. A vase of flowers on the table next to it wobbled perilously. Harry had been looking for me?

'Well, I'm staying at Pippa's for a few days,' I replied in a somewhat dazed voice.

'Ah, so that's where you've been. I tried to ring you at lunchtime to see if you wanted a drink, but there was no answer from the flat.'

This time I had difficulty staying on the chair, in fact I

had to grab hold of the banisters. 'You did?'

'Yes, I fancied a pint.'

'Oh! Well, what about tonight?'

'Oh God, I'd love to, darling – ' Darling? – 'but I'm tied up now, I've got to work.'

It didn't matter, nothing mattered, he'd wanted to have lunch with me, he'd actively looked for me, no – no, he'd *searched* for me, oh joy!

'Listen,' he went on, 'I'm up to my eyeballs revising for this bloody stockbroking exam on Monday. I'll ring you in the week, shall I?'

Was he asking my permission? 'Yes, yes, fine!' I said, unable to keep the ecstasy from my voice.

'OK, take care.'

'And you . . .' I hesitated, dug deep for courage, and chanced it ' . . . darling.'

I waited for the snort of derision; none came. 'Bye then.'

'Bye!'

I replaced the receiver and leaned weakly against the front door. Harry had actually phoned me on a normal, common-or-garden Saturday. He'd picked up the telephone and dialled my number because he wanted to see me. No, no, correction. He'd *missed* me. I salivated and tried to recreate the scene – yes, yes, that was it. First he'd missed me (Oh Polly, oh miss miss miss, oh where are you, Polly? Oh, I miss you so), and then, *then* he'd picked up the telephone (rush to telephone, must see Polly, must see Polly now) in order to ask me, to *ask* me (please Polly, please? If you're not too busy?) to meet him for lunch. Nothing mattered now, nothing at all. The whole ghastly Rachel and Adam business faded into insignificance.

With a shriek of joy I leaped two feet off the ground and skipped off down the hall, whooping and thumping the air as if I'd just won an Olympic gold. I ran slap-bang into Rachel who'd been changing Jamie's nappy in the downstairs loo.

'Oops, sorry Rachel! Didn't see you there!' I couldn't wipe the silly grin from my face.

She ignored me and pushed past, taking Jamie upstairs for his bath. Oh God, she must think me a complete cold-hearted bitch, messing up her life and then whooping with pleasure. I went in search of Pippa who was in the kitchen. She was pleased for me, but not as impressed.

'Well, he damn well should ring you at weekends,' she said, shaking a wet lettuce round the kitchen. 'He should ring you every day, come to that.'

But nothing could dampen my spirits now. After a jolly supper with Pippa, minus Rachel who said she wasn't hungry, I went to bed feeling absurdly happy and hugging my happiness to myself.

Later on that night I was awakened by Jamie crying for a bottle, and much much later on I was woken again. Only this time it wasn't Jamie's crying I could hear, it was Rachel's.

Chapter Eleven

When Monday morning arrived it was beautifully sunny. I drew the curtains and hopped back into bed, pulling the duvet up around my chin. I lay there, staring out of the window at the Kensington chimney pots set against a bright blue sky, and watched the plane trees swaying in the breeze. I could hear Pippa banging around in her bedroom next door getting ready for work, and for the first time in my life I actually felt jealous. What the hell was I going to do all day alone in the house with Rachel? Sit next to her in uncompanionable silence?

I would have helped her with Jamie, but she rejected all offers, and in fact positively discouraged me from having any sort of contact with him, which was irritating as well as insulting. It wasn't often I had the chance to get my hands on a real live baby, and I was just getting to the stage in my life when they were becoming vaguely interesting. Only vaguely. I had an idea that it would be rather pleasant to bounce one or two Harry look-alikes around on my knee, help them with their finger painting (or did that come later on?), and watch the little darlings in the nursery school nativity, dressed up as angels or shepherds (later still perhaps?).

Anyway, I liked the whole concept of babies; what I wasn't so sure about was the having of them. This worried me. I'd even taken to prowling round Sainsbury's, browsing around amongst the frozen turkeys looking at the eight- or nine-pounders. They were big bastards those nine-pounders, I can tell you. And that was the size of an average baby? And that had to come out of — well. It took my breath away just thinking about it; no wonder you had to go to classes and learn to breathe all over again. I really took my hat off to my mother and all the other mothers I knew. Talk about the camel going through the eye of the needle: knowing my luck, I'd probably have something about the size of a camel.

I'd read in a magazine somewhere that one of the Mitford sisters had been plagued by similar misgivings, and had asked her mother what it had felt like to give birth. 'Well,' her mother had said, frowning with concentration as she tried to remember, 'it was rather like having an orange pulled out of your nostril.' This awesome simile had stayed with me for a long time afterwards, and I crossed my legs and winced every time I thought of it.

I would have liked to have asked Rachel for her views on the subject, since she had first-hand experience, but she wasn't really the sort of girl you could sit down with for a cosy labour and contractions chat. She wasn't actually the sort of girl you could sit down with for a cosy anything chat, I thought, as she stomped moodily into the kitchen in a full-length vyella nightie to give Jamie his breakfast.

'Morning!' I ventured cheerily, clocking the vyella with amazement.

'Oh, uh, morning,' she mumbled back, as one might mumble to a slug.

'AY AY AY AAAAAY!' chirped Jamie, giving me a great big beaming smile. Now that was more like it!

'Woo Woo, Jamie!' I waved back and made a funny face; he laughed delightedly. Shame he seemed to be on permanent send at both ends though, I thought, as a rather unpleasant smell began to pervade the kitchen. How could a baby as small as that produce smells so monumentally vile? Rachel shovelled Weetabix into his mouth, but he seemed more concerned with spitting it out than getting it in and – oh God, what was he doing now? Pushing it up his nose? Perhaps I'd take a rain check on babies, or maybe I'd adopt one when it had got past this rather messy stage. Pop down to the orphanage and pick out a clean one. When did they become clean I wondered; round about three? Or more like ten, perhaps?

Pippa appeared dressed for work and began spooning what looked like sawdust and milk into her mouth in her latest desperate bid to open up the bowels, an on-going problem that occupied most of her waking hours.

'Still no luck?' I asked. Like most constipation sufferers, she liked to talk about it.

'It's been five sodding days now,' she mumbled back through the sawdust.

'Oh well, never mind, it's probably all that sex.'

'What d'you mean?' she spluttered, spraying me with milk.

'Well, it's bound to bung you up, isn't it?'

'Is it? Christ, so celibacy's the only answer, is it? The only way I'm going to get regular is to make sure I don't get it regularly?'

I giggled. 'Exactly, and the reason you have to eat so much bran is that you get too much oats.'

'God, imagine being a nun, you'd be on the bog all day, wouldn't you?'

We giggled. Rachel looked totally unamused.

'What will you tell Nick?' I asked, as another megaton of fibre found its way in.

'I'll just say you're sick,' she munched.

'Oh, OK. Just hope he doesn't ring the flat, that's all.'

'He won't – why should he? And if he does you can just say you were asleep and didn't hear the phone, I mean, that's what you normally say when you skive, isn't it? Anyway, must go, bye.' She flung her spoon down and replaced it with her handbag.

'Bye,' I said dismally. 'Have a good day at the office.' I felt like the bored housewife already.

It wasn't as if it was high summer and I could lie in the sun all day, and it wasn't as if I had any money to go and play with. I shoved some toast in the toaster. Window shopping was no good. I just ended up feeling poor and envious, and then I had to indulge in a spot of retail therapy to make me feel better. That meant buying something cheap and cheerful and then realising on the bus on the way home that a purple mini-skirt was a big mistake and wouldn't go with any of my other clothes. Then, of course, I'd have to spend the whole of the following lunch hour taking the wretched garment back to the shop. That involved endless imaginative lies about how I'd been high on valium at the time of purchase on account of severe depression following a close relative's death and therefore not in my right mind, or else I'd go through the rigmarole of putting a curtain ring on my finger and saying my husband didn't like me in purple (actually I got a vicarious kick out of this one), and then I'd have to spout out the same stories all over again when the dreary shop assistant called the manager.

'I'm not really supposed to do refunds, you'll have to speak to Mrs Meekins. Mrs Meekins, there's a lady here who says her husband's got a thing about purple . . .'

Some boot-faced old bat would appear and, together with dreary, she'd inspect the garment thoroughly amid loud cries of, 'I hope it hasn't been worn, madam, only it seems rather *soiled*. I see a little stain here!'

'No, no, I think you'll find that's just the sheen of the cloth,' I'd say and – oh God, so it went on. An exhausting waste of time that could easily take up two whole days with absolutely nothing to show for it at the end.

No, shopping was definitely out. I'd just have to watch soap operas all day. I was on my way to the viewing room, wondering if nine-thirty wasn't perhaps a little previous for even the most bored of housewives, when the telephone rang.

'Hello?' I said gloomily into the mouthpiece en passant.

'Hi, Polly? It's Lottie.'

'Lottie! Hi, how are you getting on without me?'

'Oh I'll manage. Listen, I rang the agency and gathered from Pippa you were lolling around doing nothing, so are you free for lunch?'

'Free? I've never been so free in my life, that's a brilliant idea! I'll come to the City shall I?'

'Why not. I'll meet you in Corks at about twelve-thirty. OK?'

'Great! See you then, bye.'

I put down the phone. Things were looking decidedly upward. In fact, when I saw Rachel's stony face advancing towards me down the corridor, I felt as if I'd discovered the wooden horse. My escape was taking shape. Freedom was on the cards. I gave my face a look of friendly concern.

'Will you be all right on your own here if I pop out for a while at lunchtime?' I asked her.

'Of course.'

'Sure? Only I don't want to leave you if you feel nervous. I should lock all the doors, oh, and probably best not to answer the door, or even the phone.'

She didn't bother to reply and gave me a look of utter contempt. Who was I to tell her about safety?

I ran out of the house at eleven-thirty, and leaped the little wall at the front of the garden as if it were Colditz barbed wire. It was ridiculously early, but if I caught a bus it would take ages to get there, and I liked sitting on the top deck at the front. There's nothing nicer than taking a bus through London if you've got bags of time and nothing worse if you're late and desperate to get somewhere.

The number eleven chugged and spluttered its way

slowly through the West End and out towards the City. As we trundled past the Bank of England and then rounded the corner, we passed Harry's office, as I knew we would. I peered in through the dark grey smoky windows on the off-chance that I might get a glimpse. Poor Harry. He was probably scribbling away at his exam at this very moment.

I arrived at Corks at bang on twelve-thirty, and sauntered down the stone steps to the cellar. The place was packed already, heaving with bankers and brokers braying loudly at each other and 'haw-hawing' with laughter. I began pushing my way past a million pinstriped backs, knowing Lottie would be late and arrive looking hot and bothered with tales of ghastly clients wanting advice who had kept her talking on the phone. I peered around the gloom of the dark cellar bar looking hopefully for a table that didn't already have a dozen city types jostling for position around it, and was surprised to see Lottie over in the corner, already in possession of this very rare commodity. What's more, she had a full bottle of wine in front of her. She looked pale and utterly worn out. Overworked and underpaid, I thought sympathetically: she should have stuck to shorthand and short hours like me.

'Hi! What's with the bottle of wine? I thought you people with proper jobs didn't drink at lunchtime?'

'I don't normally, but I thought we might need it under the circumstances,' she said a trifle grimly.

'Oh really?' I kissed her and sat down. Gosh, she really did look all in. Whatever was the matter? Lottie only cracked under the severest of pressure, unlike me, who needed a drink after a typing error. I peered at her through the candlelight.

'Are you OK? You look terrible, if you don't mind me saying so.'

'Had a bit of bad news,' she said, taking a swig of wine. Oh poor Lottie, whatever could it be? Her home life minus a mother wasn't the happiest of places anyway. I hoped nothing had happened to her father, or Caro perhaps?

'What is it, Lottie, what's happened? Is something wrong?'

'Yes, it is actually, and in the absence of anyone else coming forward to tell you about it, it seems to have fallen to me to be messenger boy.'

I felt an Arctic chill pass through my shoulderblades and down my spine. I knew at once that it wasn't her, it was me. I sat very still.

Lottie looked me in the eyes for the first time. She took a drag of her cigarette. 'Pour yourself a drink, Polly,' she said gently.

'In a minute. Go on, Lottie, just tell me.'

Lottie sighed. 'OK. Harry is seeing Caro.'

I let this bombshell of a sentence whistle through my ears, cruise into my brain, and crash into my heart. It exploded on impact and all my blood seemed to drain downwards into my feet. I found my tongue and licked my lips, except they didn't feel like my lips.

'He can't be,' I whispered.

'He is,' said Lottie brutally, knowing full well that brutal was what she would have to be.

'I don't believe it.'

She put her hand over mine and moved her face closer. 'Believe it, Polly, he is, I know he is.'

'But – but, he phoned me yesterday, he called me darling, he wanted to see me, he *asked* if he could ring me later – he *can't* be, Lottie, he just *can't* be!'

'Guilt?' said Lottie simply. Suddenly I knew she was right.

Lottie let me get used to the idea for a second. She poured me a glass of wine. I took a large gulp.

'Define seeing,' I whispered.

She looked down at the red-and-white checked tablecloth and picked a bit of candlewax off it with her fingernail. 'She spent Saturday night there and she was there last night too.'

I gasped in amazement. Somehow, what struck me more than anything was the luxury of two nights in a row. I'd never been afforded that privilege, not even in the early days. Harry was seeing Caro. Harry was *sleeping* with Caro. My guts seemed to be knotting themselves into a fierce ball of anguish. I clenched my fists and tried not to scream. It was a small wine bar and Lottie's local: it wouldn't look good. Try as I might I couldn't resist imagining the scene. It was vivid. I saw Harry launching himself in all his golden glory from the diving board; I saw a giggling, squirming Caro, her perfect body naked on the Conran sheets, her perfect hair spread all over the pillow. My sheets. My pillow. My hand flew to my mouth. I wasn't going to scream, I was going to be sick. I gulped down the nausea and took deep breaths of musty, smoky air. He'd only met her in the flat about a week ago and already . . . I moaned softly.

'How long have you known?' I asked, keeping my sentences to the minimum. A certain amount of puke might well escape if I kept my mouth open for too long.

'Not long.'

'How long?'

'A couple of days.'

'How did you find out?' Details were important.

Lottie sighed. She looked wretched. 'Harry phoned me at work on Thursday for Caro's number.'

I stared at her, dumb with disbelief.

She squirmed and continued bravely. 'It's true Polly, that's how much of a bastard he is. He telephoned *me*, your *best friend* for Caro's *number*.' She spoke slowly, using TV presenter *emphasis* to try to ram the idea home.

'What did you say?'

'I told him to sod off. And I didn't tell you in case he'd

just had one too many at lunchtime and thought better of it later. I rang Caro this morning. I wasn't going to mention Harry but I wondered if she would. She did. She was full of it, bubbling over, couldn't tell me quickly enough in fact,' she said bitterly.

I felt a brief pang for Lottie. Divided loyalties were awful, and she must be feeling ghastly, but it was only a very brief pang. Most of all I felt sorry for me because I was hurting like hell. If someone had whacked me round the head with a cricket bat I couldn't be more stunned. This must be how a man felt when he'd been kicked in the balls. I wouldn't mind kicking some at this very moment, actually. I looked around murderously for a spare pair of wandering balls; any pair would do, as long as they were male and firmly attached. I wondered if it would be possible to kill someone like that. I hoped so. I returned slowly from my homicidal depths and emerged with a raging thirst. I wanted more wine and I wanted it *now* and I wanted more details too. I wanted to cram my head full to bursting with Harry and Caro's indecent exposure and as many nasty, sordid facts as my head had room for, and then I wanted to take a deep breath and explode with self-pity. And boy, would I explode. I drained my full glass and filled it up again, hoping the cellars here could cope with my sudden insatiable thirst.

'I want to know everything, Lottie.'

She sighed. 'Not much to tell, really. Apparently he eventually got her number from those friends they were discussing the other day, the people in Hampshire. Then he rang her up, took her out to supper—'

'Where?' It was important.

'Er, well, Le Caprice, I think,' said poor Lottie.

'*Le Caprice*!' Ouch! I caught that one right in the stomach. It fair doubled me up with pain. Never in my wildest dreams, and let me tell you, there had been some pretty wild ones – including holidays in Mustique, a clothing allowance at Chanel, and sapphire eternity rings – but never, *never*, had I ever dreamed that Harry might take me to Le Caprice. He'd always been dead against fancy – or should I say expensive – restaurants on principle. All that money for a carrot cut into a flower? And all those ridiculous service charges just because we're sitting in Mayfair? Of course I'd been right behind him, thinking there were much more important things for us to spend his money on – like diamonds, for instance. Le Caprice! I recovered from the body blow and lit a shaky cigarette.

'Go on,' I gasped.

'Oh Polly, you don't want to know. I mean, it's obvious really, isn't it? Dinner, coffee, back to his place . . .' She tailed off miserably.

'But they definitely did it?'

'Of course they did it,' she said crossly. 'What, you think they might have played Scrabble until dawn or something? Of course they did it.'

All at once a little ray of hope scuttled across the dark horizon. 'Well – well, maybe it's just a quick fling? Perhaps he just fancied her rotten and felt like a spot of how's-your-father? Because – because of course I haven't been around much recently, you know, Lottie, I've been very busy. In fact he tried to ring me at the flat yesterday, but I wasn't there, but perhaps – perhaps now I'm back he'll drop her like a cup of cold sick and – and come running back to me? Maybe he just couldn't help himself? Some men are like that, aren't they? What d'you think?'

Lottie narrowed her eyes as she blew smoke across the table. 'Maybe.'

'You don't think so.'

She ground her cigarette out and sighed. She leaned forward, perhaps imagining that the closer she got to me the easier it would be to drum some sense into my skull.

'Look Polly, did he ever treat *you* as anything more

than a quick fling? I mean, I know you wasted nearly a year of your life on him, but how many times did you see him? About twenty? Thirty? Think about it, did you ever see him at weekends? Did you ever meet his parents? Did you ever go away together, even for a day or two, let alone a holiday? Did he ever give you anything — flowers, a birthday present, security, happiness, love, anything?'

I was shrinking down in my seat under this rain of bullets, each one hitting the spot. She saw my tortured face and stopped, although there was more.

'I'm sorry, Polly, I don't want to make it worse, but you've *got* to believe it. You can't keep hanging on to someone who was never even there in the first place and hope that this nobody is going to come back in order to give you precisely nothing. Think about it, please.'

I couldn't. All I could think about was Harry and how much I loved him, had always loved him, in fact, from the moment I'd first set eyes on him. I vaguely remembered someone else saying that to me recently. Of course, it was Adam, waxing lyrical on the grim-faced Rachel at Boston airport. My heart went out to him for a millisecond. I drained my glass again and tried to get my head round this nightmare. Harry and I were no more. Harry was seeing someone else. I'd been dumped. His future no longer contained me.

We drank the bottle and ordered another, Lottie drinking much less than me. An hour later I swayed out into the sunshine, blinking hard against the bright light, hoping I'd dulled the pain but knowing I hadn't. Lottie hugged me and shepherded me to a bus stop. She waited until a bus came along then hugged me again and put me on it, handing me sixty pence for my fare as if I were a child. I clutched the coins and walked shakily up to the top deck. I walked down the aisle very carefully, holding myself together like a piece of broken china. If I let go I might spill out all over the place. I made my way to the front and sat down.

London was still bathed in sunshine as we headed back West. Once again we passed Harry's office. I wondered how the exam had gone, and then remembered that it had been a lie. He'd been in bed with Caro. I got out my purse to pay my fare, forgetting that I was already clutching it. Harry's photograph stared at me from the credit card section. I took it out and rubbed some dust off with my finger. It wasn't even one that I'd taken: I'd found it lying around in a drawer in his flat and stolen it. He was lying on his tummy on a Greek beach, squinting slightly from the sun, laughing into the camera, brown and sandy and beautiful.

The tears began to fall. They started slowly at first, just a few trickles down the nose brushed hastily away with the back of my hand, and the odd catch in the throat that could be contained and might well be passed off as a touch of hay fever. But then the tears stopped being individual and became continuous rivers which flowed and flowed. I couldn't stop them, they got faster and faster and my hay fever got louder and louder until there was nothing I could do to control it. I was doing proper shoulder-shaking sobs now, heaving and gasping as I limbered up to reach fever pitch.

'Oooooohhhhhh . . . hagh-hagh-hagh . . . oooohhhh-hoooo . . . hagh-hagh-hagh . . . ohohoooooooo . . .'

The top deck was full, but I didn't care. I let them have it, every single anguish-ridden decibel. The conductor avoided taking my fare, and I kept on shaking and sobbing all the way to Hyde Park Corner. Eventually a fat lady in a furry hat and tweed coat could bear it no longer. She came bustling down the gangway and plonked herself down next to me in the seat that no one else wanted. People were sitting on each other's laps, heads, feet – anything to avoid that seat.

She patted my hand and passed me a tissue. 'There, there, dear, it's all right, it's all right. You have a good cry.'

That's what I was doing, wasn't it? Christ, I was positively in overdrive, what on earth did she call a good cry? I was also at the talking-through-the-sobs stage now, wanting to share my grief with complete strangers, that kind of thing. It was lucky she'd volunteered to sit next to me, actually, otherwise I might have grabbed just anyone, like that terrified-looking teenager in the seat opposite, or the man next to him with his face hidden studiously in the newspaper. They could have been innocent victims.

'I-I-It's – hu hu, my bo-o-y frie – nd – hu hu, he's – hu hu hu hu hu he's—' I sobbed to tweedy lady, wondering if she could possibly stay on as far as my stop and then come home for tea.

'Your boyfriend, is it? There, there, dear, don't worry. He'll be all right, don't take on so,' said the lady, no doubt imagining horrific motorbike accidents or worse. 'Really now, he'll be fine, they can do marvellous things these days, what with medical science and that, don't you worry.'

Oh yes, he'd be fine, he'd be fine and dandy. But it wasn't him we had to worry about, was it? It was me. Would I make tomorrow? She rummaged in her oversized handbag and pulled out a crumpled paper bag.

'Here now, have one of these.'

She passed me a rather sticky peardrop. I took it, and as I sucked, my sobs seemed to subside slightly, rather like Jamie's did when he got to grips with his dummy. It was strangely soothing. I stared out of the window and she patted my hand saying, 'There, there, it's all right,' every now and then, which again was very comforting. They should employ ladies like this to tour the hospitals with their peardrops and their tweedy coats, patting the hands of people with real problems, like relatives of accident victims, girls whose boyfriends really had come off their motorbikes. Women like this should be available on the National Health.

When we reached my stop I stumbled blindly down the aisle to the steps and realised that about forty pairs of eyes were trained eagerly upon me. This must be a little like getting married. A little. Except that this particular congregation were craning their necks to get a better look at the girl who'd had the screaming heeby-jeebies on the bus. I imagined the scenes all over London tonight, in pubs with friends, at home with mum and dad, in the kitchen with hubby. 'Cor, bloody hell, there was this girl on our bus today who had a *fit*, a real *fit*, she did, all shoulder shaking and 'ysterical-like. Ooooh, it was *awful*.' I reckoned I'd done my bit for street theatre.

As I walked home I realised I was heading for Tregunter Road by mistake. So what? I simply turned round and headed for Kensington. It would take about an hour but what the hell? I had the rest of my life to fill, didn't I? The rest of my life without Harry. I looked at my watch, it was only three o'clock. I'd be hard pressed to make it through the rest of the afternoon, let alone a lifetime.

I walked up the Fulham Road, looking at the shops but not seeing anything. On and on I walked, until the shops gave way to tree-lined avenues, the sort of avenues Harry and I were to have lived in. How crazy I'd been, living on dreams. How idiotic of me, and how presumptuous to think that I could have held him. As I walked past a garden square, I noticed the gate was open. I went in and walked around it three or four times. The wind rustled through the trees overhead, and the sun was streaming down through the leaves making a dappled pattern on the grass. I thought of all the times we'd had together; they seemed to be illuminated by the sunlight. I'd never hear his footsteps pounding up the stairs to the flat again, I'd never roar off to supper in his car, I'd never feel that excitement, that passion. But I'd hear about him. Oh yes, I was sure of that. I'd hear about his exploits with Caro, or whoever came after Caro. I'd hear about the parties he'd been to, the fun he'd been having, and I'd want to hear because that way I'd feel I was still a part of his life. I'd want to torture myself.

I walked round the garden one more time, then headed off to Kensington. It was a warm spring day and I'd walked for miles but I felt very cold.

When I reached Pippa's house, I realised I didn't have a key. I rang the bell and Rachel opened the door. She stared at my ashen, tear-stained face in astonishment. I ignored her and walked slowly upstairs. I lay on my bed with my jacket on for about an hour, not really thinking about anything in particular, just staring at the ceiling. I heard the clock down the road strike four o'clock; a few seconds later another one struck. Odd how church clocks could never seem to get it together.

After a while there was a tentative knock on the door. It was Rachel with a cup of tea. She didn't say anything, didn't even ask what the matter was. She just sat on my bed while I drank it and then took the cup downstairs again. People could be kind, I thought, as I turned my face to the wall. The wallpaper was cream with a light green trellis pattern around which roses grew. I stared at the roses winding themselves around the trellis. My eyelids felt heavy. I didn't think I'd sleep, but I dropped off almost immediately, absolutely exhausted.

Chapter Twelve

I arrived for work the next morning looking like I'd just gone fifteen rounds with Mike Tyson. My eyes were like a couple of jam doughnuts – little red holes in bloated puffs, my lips had swollen out of all proportion, and my cheekbones had risen a good three inches. Pippa marched me in like a boxing manager with a prize fighter, glaring at everyone and daring them to comment. She needn't have bothered, it was rather like the parting of the Red Sea the way everyone ran for cover – disappearing behind doors, filing cabinets and photocopiers like frightened rabbits, anxious not to get involved. Of course, as the morning wore on their curiosity got the better of them, and they crept out, sidling up to my desk to borrow a paperclip or a stapler, bending low and sneaking what they imagined was a surreptitious look at my distorted face. I felt like the bearded lady at the fairground, and rummaged in my bag for the trusty sunglasses.

Joss and Ron were among the first to slide their bottoms on to my desk. They could smell boy trouble at fifty paces.

Joss took my hand and stroked it. 'Poor Polly.'

Ron found my knee and stroked that. 'Poor poor Polly,' he echoed, 'but we did warn you, darling, didn't we?'

'Oh indeed we did,' agreed the other half, 'we warned you time and again. We said, whatever you do, Polly, don't play with boys, they're very dangerous. We did say that, didn't we?'

I nodded miserably.

'And do you know why they're so dangerous, my darling?' persisted Ron.

I shook my head wearily.

'Well, I'll tell you. It's on account of the one-eyed trouser snake. Are you with me, Poll?'

I sighed and smiled weakly.

'Ay yes, I think you are, and I think you've been playing with one, haven't you? And we all know what happens to little girls who play with trouser snakes, don't we?'

Joss nodded sagely. 'They get bitten.'

'How right you are, Joss my boy, they get bitten. Best to leave well alone.'

'Become a nun,' suggested Joss. 'I like you in black.'

'Or a lesbian?' ventured Ron eagerly, seeing himself perhaps in the role of managing voyeur.

'Either will do,' agreed Joss, 'but that's all by the by. What you need right now, of course, is some nice casual sex with no strings attached.'

'In a hotel of your choice.'

'My choice,' corrected Joss.

'Not Sussex Gardens again?'

'Why not? Very discreet, sheets are clean, a Teasmade in the bedroom, what more could a girl ask for?'

'A little bit of style, Ronnie boy, that's what! Dear oh dear, we're not talking about one of your regular scrubbers, you know. Polly's got class, she's probably even been finished off at one of those flower-arranging places in Switzerland — Mummy does good works you know, Daddy plays bridge; she's not going to drop her drawers just anywhere!'

Ron held my other hand as I eventually shook him off my knee. 'Don't you listen to him, darling. He's got no idea, and you'd never get your rocks off anyway, you'd be up all night waiting for the earth to move and it wouldn't even shudder. He's all gong and no dinner, that one. No,

no, you come with me. Ronnie boy knows the ropes. We'll
sneak off after lunch for a bit of afternoon delight — I
know a nice little flat in Tregunter Road, actually. About
four o'clock suit you?'

I smiled weakly; they were doing their best to cheer me
up. 'Thanks boys, some other time perhaps.'

'I've never had any complaints, you know,' said Joss in
a mock injured tone. 'I may not be as young as your
Harry, but I'm just as athletic, and I can always be relied
on to rise to the occasion.'

My face crumpled slightly at the mention of his name.
Joss noticed and quickly lit a cigarette for me before
putting it in my mouth. 'Breathe deeply,' he commanded. I
sucked gratefully. 'Drink?' he offered, taking a hip-flask
out of his pocket. I shook my head, that really was the
slippery slope.

'Bit of a lad, that Harry, wasn't he?' mused Joss,
lighting one for himself and taking a quick swig of whisky.
He had a faraway look in his eye and I detected a touch of
admiration in his voice. 'Still, bit rotten of him to roger
your flatmate. Too close to home.' I could tell he was
deeply impressed. I sighed, Chinese whispers had started
already.

'Not my flatmate, her sister.'

'Really? Oh, well that's all right then.' He sounded
disappointed. 'Fair dinkum. What's she like?'

'Oh, you know, pretty, young, sexy, glamorous, big tits,
nothing special,' I said bitterly.

Their eyes lit up. 'Really?' said Joss. Ron whistled
softly. I looked up sharply. 'What a bastard,' he added
quickly, shaking his head.

Nick strode through on his way to his office. 'James
Hutchinson's coming in at twelve o'clock, so clear this
place up, please. It looks like a pigsty.'

Joss and Ron raised their arms in Nazi-style salutes and
goose-stepped back into their office. Nick reached his own

door, then paused and came back to my desk. He took my sunglasses off and peered into the jam doughnuts.

'Jesus, not again, Polly. What have you been up to this time?'

'Gastric flu,' I said, snuffling hard and hastily replacing my glasses.

'Really? Gastric flu? Not alcohol-induced?'

I shook my head. My face wobbled violently: it seemed to be full of liquid. 'No,' I whispered.

'Well, shouldn't you be in bed then?' His voice was soft now, his face kind. Oh God, don't be nice to me, please don't be nice to me, I thought desperately.

'I'll struggle on,' I said bravely, digging my nails into my hand to stop myself from crying and wishing he'd revert to his usual SS tactics.

'I really think you should go home, you look awful. Shall I order a taxi?'

I couldn't reply to this without sobbing loudly and doing the nose trick all over the document in front of me, so I shook my head violently and hoped he wouldn't notice the tear, goddamnit, that had somehow escaped and was even now peeking out from behind my glasses and travelling down my cheek.

He noticed it. 'Harry?' he said simply.

I nodded briefly, surprised that he even knew his name, and not really feeling up to any more lying. I also hoped this would put an end to all the kindly concern and cause a few fuses to blow. It didn't. Instead he did something that reduced me to a shivering mass of jelly. He took a lovely clean white hanky out of his pocket, and wiped my tear away before handing it to me. 'Here.'

This sweet touch of humanity damn nearly did for me. I breathed deeply but it was no good: the inhaling part of the exercise was too shuddery. Great shaking sobs were building up in my breast and I clutched the side of the desk in horror. I must not break down, I must not break down!

I thought hard about unemotional things like the Chancellor of the Exchequer and the Hanger Lane Gyratory System and — and the Middle Ages; anything, in fact, that would help to keep the waterworks at bay. Nick began to look rather alarmed at the prospect himself: the odd tear, fine, but a full-scale flood was clearly a different matter.

He straightened up quickly and sensibly wiped the concern off his face. 'All I really need today is a working lunch for my meeting. D'you think you're up to arranging that?' he asked briskly.

'Oh yes, of course,' I gasped between shudders, glad to be back to normal office-speak and glad to have something to do. 'I'm um, feeling much better already actually.' I managed a wobbly smile. I'd feel even better if he could see his way clear to calling me a lazy good-for-nothing slut, but I supposed that was out of the question in his present mood.

'Good.' He nodded briefly and turned to go back to his office. He paused, and swept his hand around the room. 'Oh, and don't forget to do something about this hell hole.'

I breathed a sigh of relief. That was more like it, although a few more expletives here and there wouldn't have gone amiss. It was as if the hanky episode had never happened. This was the Nick I knew and — I hesitated. For some reason, 'hated' was too strong a word. I buried myself in my typing, wishing I'd never grown out of the dolls and ponies stage. Men were still such a mystery.

Mr Hutchinson arrived dead on twelve, looking even more rat-like than usual. He was panting slightly from climbing the stairs, but as I watched his mousy little chest palpitating up and down, I couldn't help wondering if he hadn't in fact just been for a nice little pedal in his wheel. His beady eyes darted around taking everything in, especially, it seemed, my battered face. His whiskery nose twitched with excitement, and he actually stood on tiptoe to peer over my glasses. I straightened up to my full five foot three inches, which seemed to be more than he had to offer, and he lowered his heels admitting defeat.

'You're looking very mysterious today, Polly. Not trying to hide from me, are you?'

'Of course not, Mr Hutchinson,' I said, taking his paw which he'd held out for a shake. 'I'm just getting over the flu and my eyes are still a bit sensitive.'

Did one's eyes get sensitive? I always enjoyed such rude health I could never quite remember which symptoms went with what ailment, but Ratty didn't seem to want to query this. I relieved him of his grey coat, grey scarf and grey umbrella, and wondered briefly if his underpants were grey too. At least I didn't have to relieve him of those. Suddenly I felt a bit peculiar and wished I hadn't thought about that. I showed him into Nick's office.

'Would you like some tea?' I asked as the two men shook hands.

'Naughty, naughty Polly!' he remonstrated, waving a little claw in my face. 'You know I only drink coffee, don't you!'

'Oh yes, sorry. I'm afraid we're out of filter, though. We've only got instant muck at the moment. Is that OK?'

Mr Hutchinson's face froze. Behind him, Nick shook his head in despair before putting it in his hands. The rat's eyes were narrowing.

'Well I'd better have some instant muck then, hadn't I?' he said nastily.

I groaned and clutched my mouth. 'Oh gosh! No, sorry – um, no – I didn't mean Special Roasty, that's not muck, that's delicious, no – I – I meant something else, something really horrid that's been sitting in the cupboard for ages – I'll get you some Special Roasty right now.'

I disappeared in confusion. When I returned with the tray I didn't look at either of them. I set it down on the desk and scurried away. After all, I didn't really have to look: I could feel Nick's icy glare freezing into the very marrow of my bones.

'Well, I've lost my boyfriend, I might as well lose my job,' I said gloomily to Pippa as we arranged the cold roast beef for lunch on a plate in the tiny galley kitchen.

'Never. He's much too fond of you,' said Pippa, throwing a salad together.

'Fond of me? Don't be ridiculous,' I scoffed, although a white linen hanky did make a brief, fluttery appearance in my mind's eye.

'It's true, he thinks you're wild and wacky.'

'Oh terrific.'

'What's wrong with that? It probably makes a refreshing change from all those sophisticated models and actresses he usually hangs around with.'

'Thanks very much,' I said dryly. 'You mean he thinks I'm gauche and stupid.'

'Something like that . . . Where's the knife to cut this cheesecake with?'

I rummaged in the drawer. 'We've got about a million spoons and forks and no knives — here, use this.' I handed her Ron's scalpel which he used for cutting up layouts.

'Polly, that's hardly hygienic—'

'Oh don't be silly.' I ran it under the tap. 'Here, give it to me.'

She handed me the cake and I cut it into slices.

We deposited the lunch in Nick's office amid deep and turgid discussions about brand shares and meal figures, whatever they were. Once again I thanked my lucky stars that I hadn't been born bright enough to be a career girl. I perched on Pippa's desk and cut the split ends off my hair, wondering if I'd ever be happy again.

'Oh, by the way, Adam was here yesterday,' said Pippa absent-mindedly as she typed away.

I gasped and dropped the scissors. 'No! Was he? What here, in the agency? Pippa, why didn't you tell me?'

'I'm telling you now. You've been a bit preoccupied, you know.'

'What happened? Where was he, was he waiting outside? Pippa, stop typing and bloody well tell me what happened. It's all right for you; it's not your blood he's after!'

Pippa paused and swivelled round in her chair. 'Yes, he was waiting outside; well, pacing actually, stomping up and down like a caged animal, shaking that mane of red hair – incidentally, he's not my type at all, you know, you always get much redder pubes than you think you're going to with—'

'Go *on*, Pippa,' I urged. God, she always got so sidetracked.

'Anyway, he was pacing up and down, and – and shaking his head about like this – ' she shook violently all over her word processor – 'like a rabid dog, in fact, and mouthing obscenities – well, what I assumed were obscenities. Honestly, Polly, if you ask me he's seriously disturbed. In fact he reminded me of a friend of my brother's who went really loopy when he came to stay with us one summer, started talking to himself and—'

'Pippa! What happened?'

'Oh well, eventually Mummy rang the hospital and the little men in white coats came to—'

'*No*! With Adam?'

'Oh. Oh, well the moment I arrived he pounced. He'd obviously pounced on everyone else as well, but he grabbed my arm like this – ' she demonstrated with a sharp pincer grip on my arm; I suppressed a scream – 'and asked me if I worked with you. I said I did and funnily enough I'd spoken to you only last night. I said you'd telephoned to say that you wouldn't be in for a couple of weeks because you'd gone to stay with friends in the country.'

'Good girl. What did he say to that?'

220

'He grabbed my other arm like this — ' more demonstrations — 'and asked me who the friends were and where they lived. When I said I didn't know, he said perhaps I was lying and secretly shielding you. I tell you, it wasn't very pleasant. Anyway, just as he was about to draw the silken cord from his pocket and wrap it around my throat, Nick came flying to my rescue.'

'Seriously, was Adam getting aggressive?'

'Well, maybe not aggressive,' said Pippa grudgingly, 'but I must admit I was jolly glad when Nick appeared. Adam had a pretty loony look in his eye — that guy is definitely barking, Polly. Nick thought so too.'

'OK, OK,' I waved aside Pippa's amateur psychoanalysis. 'So what did Nick say?'

'Well of course he was slightly taken aback when he heard about your sudden departure to the country leaving him secretary-less.'

I groaned. 'Oh no!'

'But it was OK, he rose to the occasion beautifully and said how he wasn't really surprised because you'd been looking so tired recently and you probably needed a break—'

'Knowing it was a pack of lies?'

'I suppose so. I mean he didn't look surprised to see you this morning, did he? Anyway, he was brilliant, he even said Adam could sit in reception and wait for you if he liked, but he'd be waiting there for a couple of weeks. Of course Adam lapped it all up, coming as it did from a fellow man in a suit with a proper job rather tHan a mere secretary. I mean, talk about gullible. Anyway, he came up here just to make sure, had a good poke around, in fact,' she giggled, 'he even looked under your desk. Then eventually he sloped off, probably to slit his wrists; he looked capable of it.'

'Poor Adam. Did you tell Nick what it was all about?'

'Not really, I just said this guy was hounding you

because he thought you were hiding his girlfriend.'

'What did he say?'

'He shook his head and sighed and said, "You know, it really wouldn't surprise me," in a kind of resigned voice.'

'Oh God. He thinks I'm mad,' I said miserably, tapping Ron's scalpel on the desk.

'Probably, anyway then—'

'Pippa, look at this.'

'What?'

'The scalpel, look!'

She looked and grabbed it from me. 'The blade's missing!'

'Exactly.'

We stared at each other for a few seconds.

'It must have fallen off when you cut up the cheesecake,' she said slowly.

'So where is it now?'

I jumped off the desk and bolted to the kitchen. I ran my hand over the work surface looking for a small, but potentially lethal, razor-sharp blade.

Pippa peered into the sink. 'It could have gone down the plughole, couldn't it?'

'Unlikely,' I said, feverishly shaking out tea towels and dish cloths. We faced each other again, at the same time facing the awful truth.

'It must be in the cake!' I gasped.

We ran as one, as if we were tied together in a three-legged race, to Nick's door, and pressed our noses up against the small square of glass. Luckily Mr Hutchinson had his back to us. Nick spotted us and frowned but carried on talking, no doubt trying to pretend that it was quite normal for us to take such a keen interest in client meetings.

The roast beef had been demolished, as had the salad, but the cheesecake was still mercifully intact. But not for long. Still talking, Nick handed Mr Hutchinson a side plate, and then pushed the cheesecake towards him.

'Say no, say no,' I breathed. But how silly, of course he'd want some, after all, it was cheese, wasn't it? The little claw came shooting out cake-wards, but then, miraculously, paused in mid-plunge. It waggled around a bit as Mr Hutchinson no doubt decided it was time to put Nick straight on some highly important point, like how he was the client and it was his money so what he said went. Nick conceded, making a Prince Charles gesture with his hands and nodding his head. Mr Hutchinson sat back in his chair, pleased with his point, probably believing it was his superior intellect that had secured his victory rather than his dosh; at any rate, the cake was forgotten.

We breathed again, steaming up the glass somewhat. But too soon! Seconds later those ratty little taste-buds were reasserting themselves and, with a swift dart of the paw, Mr Hutchinson lunged forward and helped himself to the largest slice of the cake. It was too much for me. I flung open the door and in an equally swift movement removed both the cake from the table and the slice from Mr Hutchinson's hand. It was the work of a moment. Both men stared at me in astonishment, the client blinking away as if his life depended on it.

I laughed nervously. 'I'm so sorry, but it's off.'

'Off?' said Nick.

'Yes, it's bad, you know, gone off. Just had a call from the cake shop.'

Nick looked deadly. 'Polly, what on earth is going on?'

'It's past its sell-by date, you see — way past, in fact — months, years past. They forgot to tell me when I bought it, but they rang just now to let me know. So sorry! I'll take it back.'

'It can't be . . .' began Mr Hutchinson.

'It is, though. Weird, isn't it?' I gave him a synthetic little smile and fled, cake in hand.

Mr Hutchinson's voice trailed me. 'But it looks so delicious . . .'

I closed the door on him. OK, Nick was furious, but I'd rather incur his wrath than kill a client – just. I could see the headlines in *Campaign* next week. 'Secretary kills client – razor in cake.' I shuddered and ran into the kitchen, where Pippa and I inspected each slice like a couple of forensic scientists. We picked them over one by one and, sure enough, the last slice yielded a small, sharp, deadly blade.

'Thank God!' I cried, holding up Exhibit A in my fingers.

Just then the kitchen went dark. I looked up to see Nick's large frame filling the doorway. I instantly dropped the blade in the sink.

'Have you gone quite mad?' he barked, striding over to me. I pressed the cake back into his hands, thus keeping a cake plate's distance between us. It was still too close for comfort. The glare from those eyes was enough to make me want to reach for my sunglasses again.

'Oh Nick, it was all a terrible mistake!' I blurted out. 'The cake shop just rang to say it wasn't our cake that was stale at all, it was somebody else's! They'd got it wrong, isn't that marvellous? So we can eat it after all!' I grabbed a piece and crammed it into my mouth. 'MMmmmmmmm, oh yesh, mmmmm, delishious!' I said, spitting crumbs all over the place and rolling my eyes to demonstrate its delectability.

Nick stared at me in disbelief, but I did wonder if around the mouth region there wasn't just the hint of a flicker of a ghost of a – no, perhaps not.

'I'll speak to you later, Polly,' he snapped. He turned on his heel, cake in hand, and marched back into his office closing the door very firmly behind him.

I staggered back into the pit and fell reeling into my seat. I felt like I'd gone through a mangle. This was all I needed, today of all days. I hadn't even had much time to indulge in some serious self-pity it had been so chaotic. Maybe I should take advantage of Nick's earlier suggestion and go home, stopping off en route to jump in the Thames. At least if I were dead he'd have to think of some nice things to say about me to my parents at the funeral. I sighed. I didn't really want to die, I just wanted to press a fast forward button and be about two months, or two years, hence. I couldn't really go home, anyway: Nick was going away for two weeks on Thursday and there was still masses to do before he went. At least then I could have a break.

I switched on to autopilot and bashed away at the keyboard, wishing it was Caro's face. Perhaps I should have kept my suntan going? Had a few sunbeds? I'd been so brown when I'd met Harry, he'd liked that. Did Caro have an all-over tan, perhaps? I bet she did. I snarled and thumped the keys viciously, well on the way to giving her severe brain damage. I tried to look on the bright side. No need to have my hair highlighted quite so often, ease up on the leg waxing too, I thought. At least I'd be marginally richer – and marginally darker haired and hairier legged too. Yes, really attractive, Polly, just the right combination to catch a new man. But whatever was I thinking of? New man? Good Lord, no, I was in mourning. Odd though, how in the very, very back of my mind – and we're talking archives here – there was just the remotest, almost non-existent feeling of, how shall I put it – relief? Now why was that? Because I didn't have to jump every time the telephone went? Because I didn't have to arrange my life in such a way that everything could be cancelled at the last minute in case he called? No, surely not, it was – good grief, what on earth was that noise?

I looked up from the battering I was giving Caro and cocked my ear in the direction of reception. There was the most almighty commotion going on out there. Probably Josie the receptionist arguing with yet another salesman, I thought. I thought wrong. Because at that moment the door flew open and in strode Adam, looking, as Pippa had so rightly put it, seriously disturbed.

Josie appeared behind him, red in the face and flustered, her glasses slipping off her nose. 'I'm sorry, Polly, I couldn't stop him!'

Adam was terribly pale and hollow-eyed and his lips were thin and bloodless. It made quite a contrast with the red hair. He was almost unrecognisable as the healthy, sparkly-eyed, all-American jock of a week or so ago. A muscle in his cheek was pulsating away at an alarming rate, and I instinctively rose from my chair, realising that a little fast running might well be in order.

He was over to my desk in a second. 'Where is she?' he said in a dangerously quiet voice.

'I — I don't know.' I whispered back, equally quietly, but not in a dangerous way, more in a bloody terrified way.

Adam slammed two large, freckled hands the size of meat plates down on my desk. It seemed to me that on the back of one hand was written the word 'Polly's' and on the other 'neck'. The fingernails were white with pressure, the same pressure which would soon, no doubt, be transferred to my swan-like. He was just limbering up. Pressure applied, my head would come popping off like an easy blackhead — one of those really ripe ones that's been brewing up nicely for a couple of days — just a little bit of a squeeze and — pop! Off it would come, highlights and all, and over the desk it would fly before landing neatly in that conveniently open filing cabinet over there — plop!

I sensibly backed away, self-preservation high on my list of priorities now, all previous ideas about throwing myself in the Thames long forgotten. I wanted to live. I forced my eyes up from the freckly, murderous hands to the cold bloodless lips.

'You bitch,' he breathed.

'Now don't be like that, Adam,' I muttered.

'You're going to tell me where she is, Polly. I know you know, and you're damn well going to tell me, because if you don't I'm going to break your fucking *neck*!'

I knew it, I just knew it would be my neck. I was frightened, bloody frightened. He had a clenched calmness about him that terrified me. I was also dimly aware that I should try and talk him out of anything untoward, that was the received wisdom on dealing with rapists and murderers, wasn't it?

'Now look here,' I squeaked, 'killing me won't solve anything you know. It's − it's pointless and futile and − and totally counter-productive, it's been proved many times and, and − well, it just won't get you anywhere!'

Adam's eyes glazed over. The thought had obviously not occurred to him as yet, but now it was right up there amongst the grey cells where I'd so thoughtfully lobbed it. Hmmm . . . murder, yes of course, that was undoubtedly the answer; thanks, Polly. To this end, one of the freckled meat plates inched forward on the desk and closed slowly round a rather sharp-looking paper-knife that I'd been careless enough to leave lying around. I whimpered. Oh God, yes − that was for my heart. Any minute now he'd raise it above his head and then plunge it into my breast with a Tomahawk screech − HAYACK!! I wondered how far the blood would spurt, over to the photocopier perhaps? As far as the window? And who would clear it up afterwards, Pippa? Josie? Probably Pippa I decided, sobbing wildly.

Knife in hand, Adam took two slow steps to the left, advancing round the desk. I mimicked him perfectly, but cannily took my two steps in the opposite direction, thereby keeping the desk well and truly between us. He took another to the left, I jumped to the right. We occupied diagonal corners now. He paused, then − three to the right! Off I went to the left! Then two to the left! I hopped to the right! Left! Right! Right! Left! I was squeaking with terror but keeping in step like a sort of manic Ginger Rogers. He was dancing up a storm, but I was with him every step of the way, my heart banging away like a demented dinner gong.

A small corner of my terrified mind wondered how the rest of the agency were taking this drama. A quick peek was enough to ascertain that they were taking it 'from behind'. Pippa and Josie were 'behind' the photocopier, Jason was 'behind' a large potted cheeseplant, and Ron and Joss were peering out from 'behind' their door. They could smell the blood all right but, understandably, didn't particularly want to get it on their hands. Thanks, guys, I thought grimly.

Adam and I paused briefly as we once again occupied diagonal corners of the desk. I licked my lips and addressed myself bravely to his steely stare, totally devoid of any of the old Savoy sparkle.

'Look Adam, can't we talk about this sensibly? I mean, it's crazy to behave like wild animals, anyone would think we were— Aaaah!'

I screamed as a mighty great hand came crashing down on the desk, sending papers flying and my fellow members of staff running for even more cover.

'CUT THE CRAP POLLY AND JUST TELL ME WHERE SHE IS! OK? JUST TELL ME!' he bellowed at the top of his voice.

'I – I don't know, I really don't,' I yelped, experiencing a curious loss of confidence in the leg department: they were decidedly wobbly and I hoped fervently that all the dancing was over for today. I was also acutely aware that my deodorant wasn't all it was cracked up to be.

Adam leaned across the desk. 'You do know,' he said, softly now – I infinitely preferred the bellowing – 'and you're damn well going to tell me, because if you don't, I'm going to kill you. Do you understand?'

'She's — she's at her father's,' I lied.

'DON'T LIE!' Christ, he was quick, but then I've never claimed to be a good liar, just a prolific one.

'Well, OK, yes — yes, you're right. I just sort of said that really, she's not at her father's at all, she's er, she's er . . .' Yes, that was it, I'd just carry on saying 'she's er' and something would eventually crop up. He'd get bored, it would be time to go home, the phone would ring, the police would arrive, the building would collapse. 'She's er, she's er,' I muttered — and something did happen. He lunged across the desk towards me and grabbed hold of my hair, yanking my face towards him.

'AAAAAAHHHHHHHH!!' I screamed with terror, loud and shrill, and as I did so, Nick's door flew open. There he stood, a veritable God of War in a Savile Row suit. If anything he looked even more terrifying than Adam. I fervently hoped I'd die of shock and wouldn't have to experience the next ten minutes.

'WHAT THE HELL IS GOING ON?' he thundered.

Adam dropped my hair for a split second, but it was just split enough for me. I seized my chance and legged it, scuttling off in the direction of Nick's broad back. I just wanted to run up those grey flannelled legs, duck under the jacket, and scurry across the blue-and-white striped shirt until I got to the armpit where I would adopt the foetal position and snuggle down with my thumb in my mouth for the next hour or so. Instead I shot around the un-Adamed side of him and cowered behind his beautiful, broad, oh so welcome, grey suited back. And there I stayed not glued, but welded.

'Please leave,' he said to Adam, in what would appear to an innocent bystander to be a reasonable voice, but which was in fact his most lethal. He walked forward. I walked too, shadowing his every move, although why we were going forwards rather than backwards was a mystery to me. He clenched his fists, I clenched mine — you see I'd lost my identity. We were one and the same now, Nick and Polly. A Nolly.

'Come on,' he said, jerking his head towards the door, 'out you go.'

'Not until I've talked to Polly,' said Adam, advancing towards us.

'PLEASE LEAVE THE BUILDING NOW OR I'LL CALL THE POLICE!' Nick strode towards the telephone, I strode too, it was poetry in motion, and as I went I admired the exquisite tailoring at the back of his jacket; anything to keep my eyes off Adam. I was riveted, never have I seen such stitching. Nick had his hand on the phone. There was an eerie silence. Eventually I dragged my eyes away from the grey flannel and took a peek at Adam.

His face was crumpled and wretched. He caught my eye. 'Polly, please!' he said, stretching out a hand and changing tactics dramatically. 'Please, just let me talk to you for a minute, just for a minute. I promise I won't hurt you,' he pleaded.

I felt for him, really I did, but what could I do? I had to stand by Rachel and, besides, I was yellow through and through. I averted my eyes, and in doing so caught a glimpse of the rat, peering out of Nick's office. His little nose was twitching away and his glasses were steaming up with excitement. This was probably the closest he'd ever got to a thrill in his whole life.

Nick picked up the receiver. 'I'm going to give you ten seconds to leave this office and then I'm calling the police. One, two, three, four—'

'OK, OK.' Adam raised his hands in defeat. 'I'm going. But you haven't heard the last of this, oh God no. I'll be back, Polly, you can be sure of that. I'll find my son, don't you worry, I'll find him whatever it takes!' His voice cracked with emotion.

He turned to go, raising his hands again in a despairing gesture. They fell limply to his sides. He looked utterly destroyed. I counted to ten before looking again, and was just in time to see his back disappearing out of the door. It slammed behind him.

A tense silence fell. Nick eventually broke it. He turned to Mr Hutchinson and smiled. 'I'm sorry about that, James. As you can see, Polly has an extremely persistent suitor on her hands, but I'm sure he's got the message now. Shall we continue?' he said, motioning him back into his office with his hand.

Mr Hutchinson reluctantly sidled back into the room looking hugely disappointed. No rape, no blood, no murder – shame. He'd have to revert to slowing down on motorways to view the accidents.

The two men disappeared but, as the door was about to close, Nick stuck his head around it and gave me a meaningful look. 'When I've finished my meeting, Polly, I want to talk to you.' With that he shut the door.

I clutched my desk, lowering myself carefully into my chair. Oh God, that was awful, truly awful. I felt positively ill.

My colleagues gathered around me now, like bees at a honey pot: exclaiming, commiserating, wondering, shrieking, gabbling; glad of a chance to tell me now how they'd been right behind me all the way, straining to hold themselves back from leaping to my defence. Indeed, it was a mystery to most of them how they'd managed to control themselves. I listened to their excited chatter in silence, taking the occasional swig of whisky from a hip flask and dragging a whole cigarette down in one. I wondered if I'd ever be the same again.

Josie was the first to mention the unmentionable. 'Do you think he'll sack you now, Polly?' she said, wide-eyed behind her specs. 'Do you think you've really done it this time?'

'I'd say it's probably a safe bet, Josie,' I said weakly. 'I wouldn't open a book on it, put it, that way.'

'I mean, this is probably the worst thing that's ever happened to you here, isn't it?' she persisted, eyeing my desk somewhat covetously, 'and in front of Mr Hutchinson too!'

I sighed. 'Yes, Josie, I think you're probably right — and rest assured, you'll be the first to hear about it should my position become vacant.'

Eventually they drifted away and I sat out the rest of the afternoon in a daze while Pippa did all my typing for me in silence. It was bad news when she couldn't think of anything comforting to say.

At about four-thirty I showed Mr Hutchinson to the door, dressing him up once again in the grey ensemble. He lingered, keen to discuss the afternoon's events, but I shook him firmly by the paw and practically bundled him down the stairs. Then I walked meekly into Nick's office, head bowed, poised thus for the guillotine to fall.

Through the glass in the door I could see the gang assembling at my desk as they waited for the verdict. Ron had even rustled up a few bottles of red wine. Presumably this bevy was intended to soften the blow, but they appeared to be cracking into it already. Josie had brought her knitting along; she sat in my chair, legs crossed, glasses slipping down her nose, clicking away like a true tricoteuse.

I sat down on one end of the sofa and stared at my shoes. Nick got up from his usual position behind his desk and sat down next to me, obviously favouring the softly-softly approach. He scratched his head and sighed, no doubt wondering how to phrase this without provoking a fresh flood of tears. He looked at his watch. 'Look, Polly, I haven't really got time to talk to you now because I'm supposed to be in a meeting outside the agency in a few minutes, but I'll tell you what. Book a table for lunch somewhere tomorrow and we'll talk about it then, OK?'

I looked up in surprise. 'Oh no, it's OK, that's not

necessary, really. Just do it now and I'll go, really, it's no problem.'

'Do what?'

'Well, you know, aren't you going to fire me?'

He looked exasperated. 'No, I'm not going to fire you. Not yet, anyway – don't tempt me. But what I would like to know is why you arrive at work looking like you've been beaten up, tell our most important client his product is shit, try to kill him with a razor blade in a cake, and then encourage some bulging biceped American to throw his weight around in here, frightening the life out of my staff, not to mention my clients!'

I opened my mouth to begin some form of convoluted explanation (oh God, he'd spotted the scalpel blade), but he held his hand up and shut his eyes firmly, staunching the inevitable flow.

'Not now! Not now. Please, Polly.' He opened one eye cautiously. 'Not now. Tomorrow, at lunch. Book a table somewhere.'

'But Nick—'

'Just do it, will you?' he said desperately, getting to his feet. 'For once in your life could you please just do as I say?'

I stared at him, totally at a loss. A table? Lunch? Was this a stay of execution? And was the interview truly over? Had I somehow survived? I obviously had. Nick raced around the room grabbing documents, files, a pen, his coat, then he departed in a flurry of tweed, briefcase flying, leaving me sitting there to ponder my good fortune.

We were to have lunch tomorrow. Just the two of us, me and the man who loathed taking clients out to expense-account lunches, let alone members of staff. To talk things over, he had said, not to hand me my P45. I breathed again and, in a fit of gratitude, slipped off the black leather sofa and went down on my knees on the grey flecked carpet. I shut my eyes tight.

'Oh please God,' I whispered passionately, hoping He remembered me, 'please don't let me cock it up. Please let me get my story straight, don't let me get it all arse about tit as usual. I've lost my boyfriend – that's Harry,' I added quickly, in case He'd missed his brief appearances – 'but please, oh please, don't let me lose my job too. It's all I've got!'

There was a loud click as the door handle went down and I looked up from my position on my knees to see Nick's startled face peering round the door. He slipped his hand in, grabbed his umbrella from the hat stand, clocked the born-again Christian but, wisely, made no comment. Then he disappeared, shutting the door quietly behind him.

I sighed, got to my feet, and went in search of some communion wine.

Chapter Thirteen

That night I paid a brief visit to my own flat and gathered together everything Harry had ever given me. Needless to say, it didn't take long. Theoretically I was going to throw everything associated with Harry straight in the bin, thereby exorcising him from my heart for ever – a cathartic exercise. Practically, of course, I didn't quite have the guts to go through with it, so instead I decided to parcel everything up, hide it away somewhere and completely forget about it. Then, one day in the far distant future, I'd be turning the flat upside down looking for something like my birth certificate – I'd probably need it to get married or something – and while I was searching I'd chance upon the Harry bundle and have a good old chuckle as I recalled my silly, love-struck, misspent youth. That would be in about one hundred and fifty years' time. Right now, before I hid it away, I was going to have a good old blub over my pathetic little pile of memorabilia, and even I had to admit that 'little' was the word.

First, I dripped copious tears over the two paperbacks he'd given me for Christmas, stroking their covers and marvelling at the vast number of pages – he really could be quite generous. One was called *Cookery for Morons* which I'd thought a huge joke, but which Lottie had insisted was about as subtle as an air-raid and the other was *The Vogue Book of Beauty Tips*, which on reflection wasn't much better, especially since he'd inscribed the inside front cover with, 'Happy Christmas, Polly, Read, learn and have a go, especially Chapter Eleven! Love Harry xxx.' Chapter Eleven was entitled, 'Say Goodbye to Cellulite'. Charming. I sighed, placed the books neatly in the cardboard shoebox I'd enlisted to act as the coffin, and turned my attention to my one and only love letter.

This treasured missive had been hastily scrawled on a scrap of paper and slipped under the flat door one evening when I was out. It was short, but very sweet. It read: 'Called round on the off chance, sorry to have missed you, love Harry.' Now I have to admit that, as love letters go, it wouldn't stand up to too much scrutiny in an Oxford anthology, if there is such a thing, but as with most pieces of literature, there were two ways of looking at it. Oh yes. On the one hand you could read it straight, as I have just demonstrated; but the subtle, more imaginative way, was to fold it in half, thus eliminating the first nine words. This revealed something altogether more romantic, namely, 'missed you, love Harry', and since this was of course the deep, implicit meaning behind the note anyway, it really wasn't cheating at all. Funnily enough, this was my favourite interpretation, so much so that the note was in danger of falling apart, so often had I creased it down the middle.

I smoothed it out now and placed it on top of the books, remembering how Lottie had snorted with laughter when I'd seized it on our way in from the pub, jumping around the flat with excitement, the evidence of my man's love waving around in my hot little hand.

'On the off-chance of what?' she'd scoffed. 'On the off-chance that you might be on for a quick one?'

I sighed. Poor Lottie. She really did have a very cynical outlook. It must be something to do with being a solicitor.

I turned to my next piece of correspondence from Harry — golly, I'd quite forgotten what a prolific letter writer he'd been — a carefully chosen scenic postcard featuring a mountain range complete with chairlift. It read: 'Pissed again on the piste, chalet girls are brilliant . . . cooks! Love Harry.' Gosh he was funny. How I'd laughed when I'd received that. I placed it a trifle grimly on my motley pile, deciding on balance that the letter under the door was far more touching and much more – well much more *Harry* really.

Then I turned to the jewellery collection. Surprised? Oh yes, Harry had given me jewels. The choice had been a little unfortunate, I admit, since the silver (hallmarked, I checked) earrings had in fact been designed to go through pierced ears, which I do not possess. Tainting the earrings even more was the faintly disturbing but highly unreliable piece of gossip that these very same baubles had once dangled from the pierced lobes of a previous girlfriend, which suggested to some people – but not to me – that the ex had left them behind in Harry's flat and he'd simply recycled them. The very idea! More unbridled cynicism. No, no, these earrings had been chosen for me, by Harry, with me and me alone in mind. OK, I couldn't wear them, but I could polish them, couldn't I? I gave them a quick rub on my jumper to prove it and placed them carefully in the box.

To this now burgeoning treasure trove I added the butt of the cigarette he'd smoked when we'd first made love – I'd retrieved it from the ashtray the next morning – and a cutting from his Busy Lizzie plant, which unfortunately had failed to re-root. OK, it had died, only I'd never liked to think of it in such bald terms before, in case it had been symbolic in some way; but what did it matter now? It had been lovingly pressed for posterity, and I laid it like a wreath on top of the correspondence.

Now there was, I'm ashamed to say, one last memento to add to this collection. A pickled kidney stone. Harry had passed it in acute agony in the loo at his flat about two months ago, amid rather a lot of unmanly screaming. I hadn't really thought about it at the time, but I thought about it now and, my God, he'd screamed. Anyway, once he'd passed it, he'd fished it out, washed it, and together we'd inspected it, marvelling at how such a small thing could cause such pain. He'd been about to throw it down the loo again when I'd piped up with the idea of keeping it, well – actually with the idea of *me* keeping it. He'd found the concept hugely amusing, but had graciously handed it over, and even gone to the lengths of providing me with an old jam jar and some vinegar to pickle it in. Unfortunately, within a matter of days it had gone rather a funny colour, what you might call diarrhoea yellow, and had disintegrated slightly. Perhaps I should have held out on the pickling front until I'd got home and used white wine vinegar instead of Sarson's malt. I hadn't liked to suggest it at the time for fear of sounding like a vinegar snob. I placed the jar carefully in the box.

Now that the collection was complete, I put the lid on and tied a red ribbon around it, sobbing quietly. Actually, my tears made a rather nice effect on the cardboard, and I squeezed out a few more, admiring the distressed – literally – look I'd achieved. Eat your heart out Jocasta Innes, I thought as I placed it tenderly at the very back of my wardrobe under a pile of dirty washing. I was quite sure I wouldn't stumble upon it there for a very long time.

Now for the gallery. This consisted of five, or was it six? Yes, six enlarged photographs of guess who, arranged in a haphazard manner on the ceiling above my bed – it had been my way of kidding myself that I woke up with him every morning. There was Harry smiling, Harry pouting, Harry laughing, Harry working, Harry frowning (sexily), and Harry looking moody. I ruthlessly dragged them down, taking care not to damage any part of his gorgeous anatomy, and shoved them unceremoniously under the bed. I also removed the large black-and-white portrait photo from my bedside table and, devil that I am, even managed to flick a rather half-hearted two fingers at it before hurling it under the bed. I instantly regretted it and dragged it back out, pressing my face ardently to his and whispering – didn't mean it, didn't mean it, didn't mean it – before pushing it back under the bed again.

Safely back at Pippa's an hour later, I crawled into bed feeling exhausted. I'm ashamed to report that, during the night, I was ambushed by tears yet again. I tried to beat them back and failed, but at the end of the day it was no bad thing, because I woke up feeling so ghastly I resolved never to shed a tear over a man ever again. So when Jamie had a sobbing fit at the breakfast table and threw his marmite fingers around the room, I sympathised, but didn't automatically feel like joining in as I had yesterday. A major step forward.

Buoyed up by my new attitude, I set off for work feeling a weeny bit tougher. Positive thinking was definitely the answer. One just had to think happy. Mind over matter.

Unfortunately, I was so engrossed in my positive thoughts that I clean forgot to book a table for lunch. It wasn't until twelve o'clock that I remembered and spent a frantic ten minutes ringing round all the local watering holes, desperate for a table. The only place that would agree grudgingly to squeeze us in was San Frediano's in the Fulham Road. Great fun though this teeming joint is, it's hardly conducive to impressing one's boss and hanging on to one's job, but it was the last resort, so I took it.

'What's this place like?' asked Nick as we walked down the Fulham Road twenty minutes later.

'Oh it's great, the food's good and it's got plenty of, um – ' I groped for the right word – 'atmosphere.'

In fact the atmosphere greeted us right around the next bend, before we'd even set foot in the place. A taxi screeched to a halt outside and the driver flung open the door with a flourish, glad to be shot of his cargo of four or five half-cut secretaries, who tumbled out on to the pavement, shrieking with laughter. They pushed past us and poured through the restaurant door. Nick stood aside and raised his eyebrows, but didn't say a word.

He held the door open for me and a terrific barrage of noise hit us full in the face. 'Are you sure you booked, Polly?' he shouted, pitting his voice against the braying and shouting. 'This place looks full to bursting.'

'Oh, definitely,' I yelled back, grabbing the nearest laughing cavalier waiter, complete with whiskers, by the arm.

'McLaren,' I yelled, 'table for two!'

He knew better than to waste his breath and compete with the noise level, but nodded and grinned widely before showing us to a table about the size of a postage stamp, right next to the very same typing-pool party we'd encountered in the street.

Nick lost his patience. 'Don't you have anything quieter?' he barked.

The cavalier grinned even more widely, and threw his arm demonstratively around the gobbling, gabbling throng, as if we might somehow have overlooked the crowd scene. 'So sorry, signor, fully booked!' he beamed, glowing with pride, lira signs shining in his eyes. 'But,' he added, tapping his nose conspiratorially, 'for young lovers — '. I cringed deeply — 'I find more room. I find somewhere more private!'

With that he took a firm hold on our postage stamp and moved it a good nine inches away from the hen party. 'There!' he said, standing back and admiring his handiwork as if he'd miraculously discovered a private room. 'Now you have plenny room to tell her how much you love her!'

I cringed some more and Nick sat down, resigned. 'Really, Polly, couldn't you have booked somewhere a little less "atmospheric", or do you have to live your life in a permanent disco?'

'Sorry,' I mumbled. 'I left it a bit late.'

I crunched maniacally on a bread stick like a demented rabbit. Not a very auspicious start. I also realised that I was unaccountably nervous, sitting here in what one might call a social setting, with my knees about a millimetre away from my incredibly anti-social boss's. I tried to remember if we'd ever had a conversation that didn't begin with something like, 'Dear Sir, Please find enclosed . . .'

Nick's face was only about a foot away from mine, and suddenly I wished I was looking a bit more presentable. I bore a startling resemblance to Chairman Mao, what with the slitty eyes, puffy cheeks and greasy hair plastered attractively to my head: I hadn't washed it since Black Monday – what was the point?

I ran my hand through the limp curls, trying to fluff a bit of life into them, and knocked over our table arrangement with my elbow. A glass vase containing a solitary carnation smashed noisily on the floor. The hen party freeze-framed for a second, then burst into hysterical giggles, pointing and whispering.

The cavalier arrived and brushed it away, instantly replacing it with another. 'You nervous!' he whispered in my ear. 'Ees OK, he love you!'

I blushed hotly and made a mental note never to patronise this restaurant again. Luckily Nick had missed this little aside, but he was beginning to look irritated. 'Polly, just relax, will you? What on earth's wrong with you? You're jumping around like a frog in a bucket.'

'Sorry.'

'And stop apologising all the time.'

'Sorry.'

He shook his head in bewilderment and addressed himself to the menu as the waiter arrived. I ordered the cheapest salad available, not wanting to look like a lunch tart.

'Are you sure that's all you want? Just a salad?'

'Yes, thank you.'

'Well, I'll have a rare fillet steak please, with french fries, and we'll have a bottle of house red.' He handed back the menu.

'Now then.' He folded his arms on the table and leaned forward, which wasn't easy given the limited surface area. His brown eyes bore into mine, but they were kind and encouraging. 'Suppose you tell me what's been going on recently?'

I was afraid we might get around to this, but hadn't envisaged getting around to it quite so quickly. Couldn't we limber up with a bit of friendly repartee first, just to remind ourselves how it was done? Christ, I hadn't even got a glass of wine to slurp on.

'Oh, nothing really,' I said, shifting around miserably in my seat and doing a spot of origami with the paper napkin. What did he want to hear? And in my view that was all that mattered. It was no good getting all honest if it was going to backfire me down to the dole queue.

'Come on, Polly, I'm not that much of an ogre, am I?' I looked up from the shredded napkin and thought I hadn't seen a kinder face in a good long time. But it was no good. He was my boss, and we'd never enjoyed a think-of-me-as-a-normal-human-being sort of relationship, so how the hell did he expect me to start now? I shifted about a bit more, but the brown eyes held their unwavering beam and I knew he wouldn't be easily deterred. I reached for my comfort pack, lit one, and took a deep breath of nicotine.

'OK, where would you like me to start?' I ventured, thinking birth might not be a bad idea if he wanted a catalogue of disasters.

'How about starting with the obsessive redhead?'

Oh yes, him. Nick was obviously still under the impression that Adam was hounding me for my body. I suppose he was, in a way, except that he wanted to cut it up into little pieces and scatter them around the countryside. I could at least put him straight on that score.

I embarked on the Rachel and Adam saga, telling it exactly how is was with no exaggerations or embellishments or what other people call lies.

Nick listened intently, chewing thoughtfully on his steak. When I'd finished he paused and pushed a few peas around before looking up at me. 'That's quite a story, Polly.'

'But it's true!' I said indignantly.

'Oh, I believe you, don't worry.' He wiped his mouth with his napkin. 'Not even a consummate liar like yourself could make up something as outrageous as that. And don't look so miserable, it's not totally your fault, you acted with the best intentions. How were you to know there was a baby involved?'

'Exactly!' Whew. One tiny Brownie point.

'Bloody stupid to get mixed up in all this in the first place, though.' He had to spoil it, didn't he? 'Why couldn't you have left him to sort his love life out for himself? Did you fancy him or something?'

'Certainly not!' I said, bristling. 'I felt sorry for him, he struck me as — as an innocent abroad,' I added piously.

Nick threw back his head and roared with laughter. 'Oh God, Polly, you're so theatrical! An innocent abroad? That guy looked about as innocent as Crippen. Didn't you notice the murderous glint in his eye or the mean and twisted mouth? I suppose those little details escaped you at the time: no doubt you were quaffing buckets of champagne down at the Savoy, were you?'

'The champagne had nothing to do with it!' I said hotly. 'If you must know I hardly touched a drop. I — I just helped him out of the goodness of my heart.'

'Ah I see, just another of your philanthropic gestures.' He grinned. 'OK, Polly, don't get in a bate, I'm just mobbing you up. So what are you going to do now?'

'Do? What d'you mean?' Was there still *more* I had to

243

do? Why was it always *me* who had to do the doing? Couldn't someone else do something for a change?

'Well, she can't stay at Pippa's for ever, and neither can you. How long do you imagine that arrangement can tick along for?'

I sighed. 'I don't know, really. As long as Pippa will put up with us, I suppose. She's being very good about it, but it's playing havoc with her love life.' I thought of poor Charles.

'Doesn't Rachel have any plans?'

'Well, her latest idea is to go and live in Paris.'

'Why Paris?'

'Because that's where her friend Sally Lomax lives, the one I was telling you about who was supposed to have written the letter. Of course, she can't actually stay with Sally, because Adam knows where she lives, but she's asked her to find a flat for her.'

'That sounds like quite a good plan, but who would finance all this? Has she got money?'

'Oh, that's no problem, her father's loaded and she's an only child. Thing is, though, finding a spare flat in Paris takes time; people kill for accommodation over there. I could have her on my hands for weeks.'

'And the idea is to stay at Pippa's till then?'

'It's not ideal, I agree.'

'It certainly isn't. He's only got to follow you home one night, and you've had it.'

I didn't care for the macabre way this was put. Did he mean 'had it' in the sense that dead meat has had it?

'Have you got any better suggestions?' I snapped, irritated that all he'd done so far was put the fear of God into me.

Nick wiped his mouth with his napkin and stared into space, well, not space actually, more like the top of my head where I'm sure my dark roots were flourishing wildly, springing wantonly from my head, untouched by human

244

hairdresser's hands for many a long month.

'Hmmm . . . I'm not sure,' he mused thoughtfully. I waited meekly for the oracle to speak. I fidgeted a bit. He was taking his time and I can only be meek for so long.

'Look, Nick, it's nice of you to take an interest, but the fact is it's my problem and I'll have to deal with it. I'm sure I—'

'Hang on, hang on, you're always so bloody impatient. If you must know, I do have an idea. I'm just trying to work out how to orchestrate it.'

'Oh, really? What is it then?'

Nick finally dragged his eyes away from my roots and fixed me with his piercing beam.

'You know I have a house in Cornwall, don't you?'

Christ, what did this have to do with anything – and no, I didn't know actually, was I supposed to? Was it in my job description or something: always keep a tally of the number of houses your employer owns. How the hell *should* I know, when he played his cards so close to his chest?

'Oh yes,' I mumbled, nodding inanely.

He went a bit misty-eyed. 'I grew up there, it's been in my family for years. It's nothing special really, just a rambling old farmhouse by the sea, probably in imminent danger of falling into the sea it's so run-down, but I love it . . .'

He stared into his wine and I shifted about again. I mean, I was very pleased for him and all that, but what the hell did his idyllic Cornish childhood have to do with keeping wolf-man from the door?

'Tim, my brother, lives there during the week with his girlfriend, and I go down at weekends to make sure the farm's ticking over.'

'The farm?'

'Yes, I said it was a farmhouse, didn't I?'

'Yes, but I thought you meant a sort of converted one. I

didn't imagine it had a proper farm attached.'

'Oh yes, in full working order. In fact, you're looking at the farmer.'

I gagged on my lettuce. 'You! A farmer? You must be joking!' Nick was about the most unlikely farmer I'd ever seen. I tried to imagine him leaning over five-barred gates sizing up the cattle, straw in mouth, briefcase in hand . . . I stuffed my napkin in my mouth to stifle a guffaw.

He grinned. 'I suppose that is quite hard to believe, seeing as you've only ever seen me in a suit at work; but I can assure you, I'm far more at home delivering a calf than I am sweet-talking old rat-face Hutchinson.'

I grinned. So Nick thought he was a rat too, eh? That was promising. 'But – but what's all this got to do with Rachel?'

Nick looked surprised. 'Oh, didn't I say? I thought she could go down there for a while. As I said, it's a big place, she'd have plenty of room and still be out of Tim's way, and this Adam character wouldn't dream of going down to Cornwall to look for her so she'd be perfectly safe. What d'you think?' he calmly folded his napkin.

I sat there, bug-eyed with amazement. Nick would accommodate Rachel in Cornwall? In his house? I struggled to find my voice.

'Bloody hell, Nick, that's a marvellous idea, but we couldn't possibly, it's – it's much too much of an imposition. I mean, you don't know her or anything.'

'You didn't know Adam, but you got involved – and who knows,' he grinned, 'she might even be my type.'

'Highly unlikely, but Nick, why should you? I mean, it's terribly kind, but I just feel it's too much to ask.'

'You didn't ask, I offered.'

'Yes but—'

'Look, Polly,' Nick leaned forward. Suddenly he looked remarkably serious. 'I've been joking about this, but the fact is you're in a hell of a mess, to put it mildly. I saw that guy's face yesterday, and he's not going to stop hounding you until he finds his child. So far he's gone slightly mad in the process. You and Pippa are protecting the mother, which is all very fine and laudable but, frankly, dangerous. For one thing he knows where you work, and is quite likely to turn up every day to terrorise you and pick fights with anyone else who gets in his way. Paris is a good idea but, as you say, it could take a few weeks to get it together. Now, it's no skin off my nose to have her to stay in Cornwall. It's a big house, so I probably won't even see much of her. I'm planning to go down for a couple of weeks as from Thursday, so I can at least keep an eye on her. Now, what I suggest is that you come down with her and stay the weekend so she's not completely fazed by a crowd of strangers, help her to settle in, and then, when she's found her feet, just leave her to have a peaceful few weeks by the sea until the flat in Paris is organised. Now, does that sound reasonable?'

He drained his glass of wine, sat back and lit a cigarette. My eyes and mouth were wide. Reasonable? It was the sanest thing I'd heard in days; it made complete sense. It was also incredibly kind. As for me going too, the idea of staying with Nick at his house initially filled me with horror, but on reflection, as I studied my employer over the table, I almost warmed to the idea. What bliss to get away from all the horrors London held for me – Adam, Harry, everything. I'd been to Cornwall before in the spring and it had been heavenly – brimming over with primroses and early daffodils. I turned the idea over in my mind, and the more I turned it, the more attractive it became.

'Will the daffodils be out yet?' I asked dreamily.

He laughed. 'Would you like me to ring and check before you make a decision?'

I grinned. 'No. No, the more I think about it, the more I think it's an absolutely brilliant idea. I just don't know how to thank you enough, really it's—'

'Not at all,' he said briskly, cutting me off in mid-gush. 'Of course Rachel will have to agree.'

I groaned. 'That's a point, grumpy old cow, I'd forgotten about her.' I had. I'd been skipping through the daffodil fields singing a happy tune, not a sulky face in sight.

'Well, give me a ring at home tonight and let me know,' Nick was saying, filling up my glass, 'because if she agrees, I suggest we set off tomorrow morning instead of waiting for Thursday. No point in hanging around waiting for the mad axe-man to strike.'

'But what about work, haven't you got meetings tomorrow?'

'Only one, and Jason can handle that. It's about time he earned his keep.'

I giggled. Poor Jason was wildly intelligent in the academic sense, but totally useless in any other sense. Client meetings would send him into paroxysms of fear, his glasses would steam up with embarrassment, and he became paralysed with shyness, visibly palpitating whenever it was his turn to utter a few words. Occasionally a sentence would emerge, but when it did it would take him completely by surprise and he'd almost jump out of his skin, looking around wildly as if he half expected someone else to take the credit for saying it. Nick despaired, but was too soft to fire him.

'He'll cope better without you there. You frighten people.' By now my tongue was totally unhinged by alcohol.

Nick raised his eyebrows in surprise. 'Me? Frighten people? Don't be ridiculous; I don't frighten you, do I?'

'Well, no,' I said, thinking well, yes, and we're talking living daylights actually, 'no, not frighten exactly.' I wriggled uncomfortably and felt my colour rising. 'But you can be rather, you know, intimidating.'

'I'm sorry.' He looked genuinely surprised and even a little hurt. 'I don't mean to be.'

'Oh no, it doesn't matter,' I said quickly. 'It's quite nice really in a − in a forceful sort of way.' Christ, what was I saying? Forceful? I'd be on to thrusting next.

Nick looked even more surprised but hugely amused. I went about the colour of the tomato on my plate.

'Forceful, eh?' he said, grinning. 'Is that how you like your men?'

Now in my normal line of work I can take any amount of sexy banter and always come back with a witty riposte, but this was different, this was Nick, for God's sake. What on earth was he playing at? I squirmed about on my seat, gushing from every conceivable pore and wishing I was somewhere else, like in the Ladies'.

He watched me wriggle, then laughed and let me off the hook. 'All right, we won't go into your love life. I have a feeling that's an even bigger can of worms.'

No, just the one, I thought miserably, and even he's buggered off to a new mate. Happily the waiter appeared with the coffee, so I was spared making a reply. As I stirred my cappuccino it occurred to me that Nick had his own love life too.

'What about Serena, won't she be coming down?'

'No, she won't,' he said shortly. Too shortly. I was intrigued as well as relieved; I didn't particularly want to look at her gorgeous face all weekend.

I ploughed on nosily. 'Doesn't she normally go to Cornwall with you at the weekend?'

It was his turn to shift about a bit. He lit another cigarette. 'She's not mad about the place, to tell you the truth; more of a London girl, I suppose. Anyway she's filming this weekend.'

'She must be quite busy − I mean, as an actress?'

'Yes, quite.'

'So I suppose if you go to Cornwall every weekend,

you don't see that much of her?'

'I suppose.'

'And of course you work so late during the week, that must put a strain on—'

'Polly, shall we just stick to sorting your life out for the time being?'

I grinned, mentally notching up marks for trying. Still, it was odd. They obviously didn't see a great deal of each other; perhaps he was still playing hard to get. She was quite a catch, after all.

Nick paid the bill and we left the still throbbing restaurant. Of course I'd drunk too much as usual, and the cold air hit me like a fridge door in the face. I felt a bit unsteady on my feet, and had a sudden desire to put my arm through Nick's strong, dependable tweedy one. I giggled and resisted it. Instead I shivered and pulled my ineffectual bum-freezer of a leather jacket around me. It was pretty damn cool in both senses of the word.

Nick regarded me dubiously as we started up the Fulham Road. 'D'you want my coat?'

'No, it's OK thanks,' I said between chattering teeth. Meanwhile he'd flagged down a passing taxi and I found myself being bundled, protesting, into the back.

'But we're only going up the road!'

'Never mind. I don't particularly want an invalid with pneumonia on my hands in Cornwall.' He pressed the heater button. 'And why don't you eat more? That rabbit food you eat won't warm you up. You're not dieting or something stupid, are you?'

'No.' I sulked in the corner. God, he was such a bully. What business was it of his whether I froze or starved to death? As it happened, for once in my life I wasn't dieting. I just didn't feel much like eating and my clothes were falling off me. It was the only compensation for having a broken heart, I thought wretchedly.

That night, I tackled Rachel on the subject of Cornwall.

I picked my moment, waiting until she'd bathed Jamie, read him a story, put him to bed, made up his bottles for the following day, and eventually had a firm grip on a gin and tonic and normality. I topped the gin up for her and sat down beside her on the sofa. I explained about Nick's house, phrasing the plan carefully so she wouldn't think I was pushing her into it.

'Oh Polly, that's a marvellous idea, but won't he mind?' She turned to me with such eagerness it made me jump.

'Not at all, in fact he suggested we go tomorrow, if you don't think that's too much of a rush?'

'Of course not, the sooner the better, I can't wait to get out of London.' She leaped up from the sofa with hitherto unimagined alacrity. 'I'd better ring my father and let him know, then I'll pack a few things. Thanks, Polly!'

Thanks, Polly! Good Lord, had I found favour? Suddenly I felt a sharp stab of pity for her. I'd been so busy with my own private tragedies I'd forgotten about hers, which were, after all, on a much grander scale. Perhaps she'd been scared stiff on her own here every day, just waiting for Adam to swing through an upstairs window with a knife in his teeth. How awful not to have anyone at all to turn to. There were plenty of friends in the country to whom I could have escaped, but she didn't seem to have access to any. Some uncharitable little notions about how, if she made herself a tad more pleasant and accommodating she might have more friends, were bubbling under in my brain, but I hastened them back down again.

I listened to Rachel's excited voice coming from the hall. ' . . . It'll take a little while to get the court injunction served, won't it? And you know I've always loved Cornwall. It'll be so good for Jamie to get a breath of fresh air, and now I know Adam's in London I can't wait to get away!'

Perhaps the judge didn't feel so murderously inclined to

me now. Well for once, Polly old girl, I thought, you've hit the jackpot. You've actually managed to get something right – or rather, I conceded magnanimously, Nick had. I waited until Rachel had finished and then dialled his number. I'd never spoken to him at home before, and the thought filled me with ridiculous nervous dread.

I practised a bit while it rang. Don't say hi, say hello; remember not to say, 'It's me'; try to sound intelligent. A girl answered, which completely floored me.

'Hello?'

Serena.

'Oh, um hi – er, is Nick there, please?'

'Who is it?' She sounded cross.

'Um, it's Polly – from work,' I said quickly, nearly adding, 'just a boring little secretary with dark roots; no competition at all.'

'Hold on,' she said tersely. Charming telephone manner, suppose I'd been Franco Zeffirelli in disguise, ringing up to offer her a part in his new film?

A second later Nick came to the phone and I told him we'd love to come. We agreed he'd pick us up in the morning at about nine a.m.

I put the phone down slowly and wondered what they were like together. Did they snuggle up on the sofa and watch TV? Did he run his fingers through her white-blonde hair and kiss her pert little nose? Did she trace his rugged features with her finger, a tantalising little smile playing about her luscious lips? Did they walk upstairs together, arm in arm, giggling and kissing the while? Did they get undressed first, or did they still rip each other's clothes off and fall in a tangled shrieking heap on to the bed? Did they gaze into each other's eyes as they lay there, dark and blonde on the pillow before he reached out and gently stroked her – Polly, stop it! I thought, alarmed at the pornographic lengths my imagination could stretch to: what business is it of yours?

That night I dreamed I was drifting through a daffodil field, one hand brushing lightly against the nodding yellow heads, the other clasped tightly in darling Harry's hand. He smiled tenderly and bent down to pick me a flower, but when he straightened up, I realised it wasn't Harry at all, it was Nick. He raised the flower above his head and I looked up, just in time to see the daffodil turn into a meat cleaver. I glanced down at him in surprise but the eyes I encountered were not brown but blue, blue with cold and blue with hate. Adam. The meat cleaver was being raised higher and higher, the music from the shower scene in *Psycho* was screeching in the background, and with an Anthony Perkins' maniacal smile on his face, he plunged it downwards, homing in on the small square inch of brow between my eyes.

I sat bolt upright in bed, shrieking like a Banshee and soaking wet. Christ Almighty, what the hell was happening to me! I flopped down on the pillow, my heart hammering around in my quivering ribcage. For God's sake, I thought miserably, reality was bad enough, couldn't I at least have some pleasant dreams?

Chapter Fourteen

The next morning, at nine a.m. sharp, the doorbell rang, piercing its way through my slumbering eardrums. I shot out of bed like a lunatic and ran, stark naked, to the open window. Without thinking, and still half asleep, I leaned out and peered down just as Nick was peering up. Our eyes met and he hastily averted his: more, I decided, backing away and looking in the dressing-table mirror, out of horror than decency. My hair was standing on end and my face was a riot of blotches and bags. Faced with such an obvious paper-bag job, he'd clearly been put off examining the bodywork.

As I slunk behind the curtain, I watched him on the pavement below, his hands thrust deep into his trouser pockets, his foot tapping away on the pavement as he gave his shoes a great deal of embarrassed consideration.

I dragged my dressing gown around me and stumbled out on to the landing in time to see Rachel appearing from her bedroom looking smug. She was not only washed and dressed, but packed — suitcase in one hand, baby in the other — and ready for the off. Why the hell couldn't she have given me a shout? Pippa put a tousled head round her bedroom door. She was wearing a T-shirt that just about covered the basics, but only just.

She rubbed her eyes and yawned. 'Nick's here,' she said sleepily. 'We overslept.'

Through the gap in the door I caught a glimpse of a

naked Charles, stumbling round the room, picking up bras and pink knickers and dropping them again, in a vain attempt to find his own underpants.

'I know, tell him I'm just coming, will you?' I said as she stumbled downstairs to answer the door.

I raced around the bedroom, throwing on a skirt and a jumper and raking a comb through my knotted hair. There wasn't time for a shower, so I doused myself in Diorissimo instead, hoping it would drown, or at the very least compete, with any unpleasant odours. It had been a stressful night.

I thundered downstairs, rubbing blusher on my pale, wan cheeks, feeling late and foolish as usual. In the kitchen, Pippa was cooking bacon for Charles and Nick, and you could clearly see two inches of bum sticking out at the bottom of her T-shirt as she stood with her back to them at the stove, frying away. Every so often she'd give the pan a vigorous little shake, which had the knock-on effect of making other things shake vigorously too. The boys were chatting away amiably enough over mugs of coffee, but without ever looking at each other: both had their eyes firmly on the chef's behind, and Charles seemed to have no qualms about sharing the spectacle with Nick.

Rachel wandered in and declined breakfast on the grounds that she'd had hers much, much earlier — one got the impression we were talking dawn here. She went to sit in the drawing room, her case at her feet as if she were merely killing time as she waited for her chauffeur to finish his breakfast in the servants' quarters.

I grabbed a piece of bacon from the pan and sandwiched it between some stale Mother's Pride, then sat down and munched away, trying desperately to wake up. Every so often I shot a sneaky glance at Nick, who was laughing and joking with Charles and Pippa.

He looked a different man in mufti. His faded cords and baggy navy sweater gave him an altogether softer, younger

256

look. His dark hair flopped into his eyes from time to time, and he pushed it away as he threw back his head and laughed at Charles's jokes. Without the granite grey suit to augment them, his craggy features looked blunter some-how, as if he'd taken a file to them, rubbing off the sharp edges. He was all smiles this morning, too, quite different from the snarling workaholic I usually encountered first thing in the morning.

He caught me staring and flashed a smile. I flushed unattractively and started clearing up the breakfast things to cover my confusion. What the bloody hell was he up to, smiling at me like that? Anyone would think he was human. But then, perhaps he was, I thought miserably, as I stood at the sink rinsing bacon grease off my plate; perhaps it was me. Pippa certainly didn't have any hang-ups about him, I reflected, as I watched her larking around, pulling blonde hairs off his jumper and holding them up in evidence. They were all shrieking with laughter now.

It must be me, I thought, as I dried my plate, stacking it in the cupboard above. I obviously took this employer-employee thing far too seriously. But we weren't at work now, were we? Hell no, this was supposed to be a break — a holiday even. I'd have to stop running around, doffing my cap at every conceivable opportunity, like some sort of secretarial Uriah Heep, if we were going to spend the weekend together. Yes, I'd be my own person, call a few shots even.

I turned round from the sink, put my hands on my hips and smiled confidently. 'Right, let's go then, shall we?' I said briskly, in my new, assertive voice.

Too assertive. The others broke off from their friendly chatter and looked up in surprise. Nick hurriedly shoved half a bacon sandwich in his mouth and stood up, abandoning his mug of coffee.

'Sure,' he said agreeably from the corner of a bulging

257

mouth, 'I'm ready. Sorry, I hadn't realised you were waiting.'

Oh God, now I was just being a bossy old cow. What was the matter with me?

I traipsed miserably down the hall after him as he strode off to the car. We loaded it up together as Rachel stood watching. Most of the luggage seemed to consist of baby paraphernalia, which she was keen to have aboard but not too keen to touch.

As we drove away, Charles and Pippa stood at the front door with their arms around each other. They waved us off looking like something out of a soap opera, except that Pippa still didn't have any knickers on, and when she raised her hand to wave, her T-shirt rose a good six inches. Nick swivelled his head around one hundred and eighty degrees to get a better look, and narrowly missed colliding with the milkman.

When we'd negotiated most of London and were heading out to the motorway, Nick looked at Rachel in his rear-view mirror and smiled. 'So how old is Jamie, Rachel?' he asked.

'Just over five months,' she mumbled inaudibly.

'Sorry? Did you say five months?'

'Mmmm.'

'Ah. And, is he — you know, good? Is he a good baby?'

'Yes, quite.'

'Doesn't cry too much?'

'Not really.'

'Oh well, that's a relief, he won't keep us up all night then!'

'No.'

'Good, good . . . I must say, he's a nice looking little chap; solid, too: he'll be playing rugby for England soon, by the look of him — what d'you reckon, full back?'

'Sorry?'

'Full back — it's a rugby position!'

'Oh . . . oh right.'

At this point Nick gave up. A lesser man would have baled out sentences ago. Rachel's No Entry sign was firmly in position, and she sat in the back staring out of the window, pretending she couldn't really hear. It must take a certain self-confidence, I thought, to care so little about what people thought of you.

As we negotiated the final roundabout and roared off on to the motorway, I took over the role of question master.

'So how long have you had this house, then?'

'Oh, about three hundred years.'

I gasped. 'How come?'

He laughed. 'That's how long it's been in the family. Various generations of increasingly penniless Penhalligans have lived there since about 1790.'

'And now it belongs to you?'

'Yes, although my younger brother lives there at the moment while I'm in London.'

'So what about your parents, where do they live?'

'Well my father's dead and Mum moved out when he died. Said it was much too big for her to live there on her own, and I think she found it rather spooky without Dad. Too many memories and that sort of thing.'

'Oh I can imagine, how sad. So where does she live now?'

'Just outside a village called Gweek, which is about four miles away. She's converted an old barn there: we'll go and see her if you like. You'd like her,' he laughed. 'She's pretty batty!'

I gave this some thought. 'And is that why you think I'll like her? Because I'm batty too?'

He took his eyes off the road for a moment and grinned at me. 'I'd say you've got a lot of potential, although women only go truly batty at about forty. There's always a chance you'll be a bit previous though — say thirty-five?'

I grinned back, but secretly made up my mind to be a

very late developer in the bats department. I thought of Serena. Serene Serena. That's how I would be all weekend. Very sophisticated, very elegant, very cool. If I had to laugh I would tinkle rather than guffaw, and if I smiled it would be with the minimum of teeth and gum.

I crossed my legs, which were splayed out in front of me at an oafishly obtuse angle, and surreptitiously spat my chewing gum into my hand, noticing as I did so that I had a rather dirty plaster on my thumb which must have been there for at least a week. I deftly pulled it off and wrapped it round the chewing gum before depositing the nasty little bundle in . . . now, where on earth should I put it – ashtray? No, he might find it – ah yes, my handbag. As I snapped the bag shut, I looked up to encounter Nick looking hugely amused, having witnessed the whole operation. Bugger. Better laugh it off. I tried out my new tinkle.

'Cut myself while I was making supper last night – lobster thermidor actually! He-ya! He-ya!'

'What's the matter?'

'Sorry?'

'What was that noise?'

'What noise?'

'Just then, like a horse.'

'Oh! I was just laughing.'

'Really? Sounded very odd, like you had a pain in the tubes or something.'

I groaned inwardly. Christ, I couldn't win. I swiftly changed the subject. 'So who looks after the farm while you're away?'

'Oh, I've got a brilliant farm manager who runs the whole show, he's got a cottage on the estate.'

Estate! Bloody hell where was I going, Balmoral?

He saw my look and smiled. 'Oh, don't worry, it's not smart at all, very much a working farm.'

I wasn't worried. I liked the idea of Balmoral. I mentally

unpacked my suitcase — did I have the right gear? I thought on balance, yes, although I might need to do a little bit of light-fingering in Balmoral's cloakroom; a Barbour here, a pair of green wellies there — all country houses seemed to have enough to camouflage an army.

'But why keep it if you're never going to live there?'

'Who says I'm never going to live there?'

'Well, surely if you carry on running Penhalligan and Waters, you'll never actually live in Cornwall, will you?'

'Which is precisely why I'm selling the agency.'

My jaw hit my chest and my monosyllable was loaded with incredulity. '*No!*'

'Oh yes, definitely.'

'But why? Why on earth would you want to sell, it's going so well!'

'Exactly, and because it's going so well I should get quite a bit of money for it. It was only ever a means to an end, Polly. I needed the money to sort the house out and get the farm running smoothly. You've no idea how expensive it is to run a big house — the roof's caving in; we've got galloping dry rot, and wet rot too I shouldn't wonder; the heating system is archaic; the windows are all falling apart — it takes a lot of dosh to put these things right, you know. I'm just making a fast buck so I can pay for it all.'

'But — but you're so good at it!' I gasped. 'Won't you miss it? Don't you enjoy it?'

Nick threw his head back and laughed. 'Enjoy it? You must be mad. Enjoy entertaining revolting, slimy little toads like James Hutchinson, smarming up to him to make him feel important for five minutes, helping him to off-load his rotten coffee beans on to an unsuspecting public? No, I don't enjoy it, in fact the more I consider what we do every day, the more I hate it. Think about it, Polly: we spend our time filling people's television screens with false images full of happy loving couples and perfect children, we make people believe that's how the other half live, with

261

their big houses and their cars and their holidays, and we hold our hands up in horror when someone breaks into the local hi-fi shop and steals a video because they've seen it on the telly and think they have a perfect right to own one. Advertising stinks, Polly, and the more I see of it, the more I want to get out.'

'But — but what will happen to the agency?' I stammered. 'I mean, you run the place, it'll fall apart if you leave.'

'Course it won't,' scoffed Nick. 'And anyway, I'm not going to sell you all down the river; you'll all keep your jobs. I'm just going to sell out to Waters. I daresay he'll just employ another managing director to lick you all into shape.' He grinned. 'Who knows, he might take you to a few shoots, maybe even treat you to expense account lunches!'

I smiled weakly. For some reason I felt unaccountably sick. 'So — when will all this happen?' I asked in a rather small voice.

'Oh, in about six months, I should think. Hopefully we'll win that dog food pitch, which will add about half a million to our billings, and then I'll be off.'

He flashed his lights at a slow moving truck in the fast lane; it moved over to let him by and he sped past.

I stared at the rather clean bit of thumb where my plaster had been and picked miserably at the few remaining bits of dirty, sticky thread with my fingernail. Whatever he said, the place just wouldn't be the same without him. He was the whole energy behind it, the driving force. If he went, everyone else would just go to the pub. As it was, I shouldn't think many people had gone to work today. Pippa had certainly looked as if she was heading straight back to the bedroom with Charles, and Joss and Ron were no doubt already stalking their prey in a South Ken wine bar.

I looked at the combination of square jaw, Roman nose,

and straightforward eyes sitting beside me. It was all very well saying we'd be OK, but not everyone had that sort of determination or strength of character. Mention a drink, or a day off, or a long lunch, and we were anybody's. He was deserting us, leaving us to our own loose morals and weak characters. I felt absurdly upset.

'Well if you think advertising's so immoral and the people so ghastly, why did you decide to make your millions in it?' I snapped petulantly.

'I haven't made millions, and I didn't say all the people were ghastly: just James Hutchinson and one or two others like him. I know I sound like a hypocrite, and it's easy to take the high moral ground now I'm leaving, but I promise you, when I joined I didn't realise quite how much I'd hate it.' He turned and grinned. 'Which might explain why I'm so bad tempered in the office.'

'Oh I wouldn't say—'

'Polly, I'm well aware that I'm a complete bastard to work for, and I apologise, but it's because I loathe what I'm doing. I've only stayed this long because I realised how much money I could make from it, and I'm not so high-minded that I wasn't going to turn down the money for my new roof, or all the farm equipment we so badly need. All I'm saying is, I don't want to do it for ever.'

I sat in sullen silence. Well, for that matter neither did I, but what choice did I have? I didn't have a convenient farm to inherit. Everyone seemed to have plans except me – what about my life? What was I supposed to do? Hadn't anybody thought of that? I choked down the lump in my throat and tried not to feel too sorry for myself. I tried a different tack.

'Won't you miss London?'

'Not a bit. What should I miss – the traffic? The crowds? The underground? The carbon monoxide? The stress? The ultimate ulcer? Or are you perhaps referring to the gay social whirl?'

'Well, something like that,' I said uncomfortably. 'Yes, I suppose I am.'

Nick paused for a minute as he pulled over to let a Porsche go steaming by us at a million miles an hour. 'I honestly wouldn't care if I never went to another London drinks party ever again. All that tedious standing around, clutching a glass of fizzy white wine, talking to complete strangers about their dreary lives when you really couldn't care less because you know you'll never see them again. No thanks.'

'Surely there are people you like in London? Don't you have any friends?' I added maliciously.

'Oh sure, plenty, and I like seeing them for a drink after work or for supper, but what I don't like is spending an hour in a traffic jam trying to get to their bloody houses, and then coming out a few hours later to find my car's been broken into. Wait till you see what I'm swapping it all for, Polly: it might even make a city slicker like yourself want to head for the wide open spaces.'

'I doubt it,' I snapped. 'I don't suppose Armani has opened a branch in Helford yet.'

He roared with laughter. 'No, but then I don't have much use for Armani — I'd look pretty silly wading through the manure in a designer suit.'

I stared sulkily out of the window thinking life was a bitch. Speaking of which . . . 'What about Serena?'

Nick didn't answer, he stared straight ahead and a little muscle twitched in his cheek. Aha! I'd got him at last! Not so self-assured on that little point, eh, Mr Cool Dude? Mr I-Know-Where-I'm-Going?

'You said she doesn't like Cornwall!' I persisted eagerly.

'No, she's not too keen.' He narrowed his eyes and put his foot down somewhat.

'So will you stay together, d'you think?' Still no answer, but that didn't deter me. 'What d'you think?'

He laughed. 'God, you're like a battering ram. Quiz me

on something else, Polly, this isn't really my best subject.'

Now what the hell did that mean? He wasn't good at talking about it or it wasn't going very well?

I stared out of the window and watched the fields and hedges flash by. Cows and sheep, cows and sheep. We ate up the miles and Phil Collins ate his heart out on the cassette recorder. 'And now we're living, se-ep-arate lives', he crooned. I gulped again. Separate lives. Me and Harry. Another gulp and a blink too. I was definitely upset. About Harry? Perhaps, or about Nick leaving? Perhaps it was just the general feeling of rejection? Yes, maybe I didn't like being deserted on such a regular basis by one and all. I felt about five years old and back in the playground again – quick, run away, Polly's coming!

Nick's voice broke into my misery. 'I know it's a little late, but I thought we might stop somewhere for lunch. Is that OK?'

'Sure.'

It had been a good few hours since that bacon sandwich, and my tummy was doing a sensational job at accompanying Phil on the drum rolls.

We turned off the main road at Wincanton and tootled down a country lane, which led in turn to a series of increasingly smaller lanes until we seemed to be almost on a dirt track. I looked at Nick in surprise.

'I hope you know where you're going.'

'Don't worry, I've been here masses of times.'

The bumpy track, which was producing grunts of indignation from Jamie in the back, eventually came to a completely dead end. As I peered out of the window, I saw that we'd come to rest outside a very ancient-looking pub. It was thatched with pretty bay windows and, surprisingly enough – seeing as it was in the middle of nowhere – there were quite a few cars parked outside.

'Where are we?' I opened the door dubiously and looked around nervously for cow pats and puddles before I ventured forth in my oh so casual, but oh so expensive, navy blue loafers.

'Welcome to the Dog and Duck. It belongs to a friend of mine.' And so saying he whipped round to open Rachel's door. She yawned and stretched as Nick wrestled with the baby's car-seat.

As we ducked our heads to avoid the low-slung beam over the main entrance – yes, myself included – Nick turned to the left and led the way into a cosy little bar with dark, mahogany-panelled walls and an enormous fire roaring away in the inglenook fireplace.

Rachel and I made for it immediately, and stood toasting our bottoms while we looked around the room. The carpets and curtains were a lovely old rose pink, and the panelled walls were dotted with sporting prints. There was a comfortable old chintz sofa, and one or two ancient leather chairs which were sprouting horsehair at the seams, plus a few wooden tables and chairs. It was an effortlessly comfortable room, and looked as if it had been this way for ever, but I had a shrewd suspicion that a great deal of thought and consideration had gone into its well-worn antiquity. As I stared out of the leaded windows to the fields beyond, a shriek went up from my left.

'Nick!'

I swung round to see a ravishingly pretty girl framed in the doorway. She was small and as slim as a blade, with dark shiny hair cut in a bob, large almond-shaped eyes, and a wide sexy mouth which almost split her face in half as it spread into a smile of true pleasure. She squealed with delight and threw herself with gusto into Nick's welcoming arms. He swung her round in a massive bear hug, lifting her clean off her feet. Why did I feel just the tiniest bit proprietorial as she gave him a series of resounding kisses, two – no three on his cheeks – followed by a severe hair ruffle? He held on to her, laughing as she squealed to be

266

put down, before eventually setting her back on her feet again.

'Nick!' she spluttered breathlessly, 'you old goat, what the hell are you doing here!'

'Thought I'd surprise you — catch you out and see what mischief you've been up to. I must say you're looking pretty damn fit Pen. Being a country bumpkin obviously suits you!'

'You're looking pretty tasty yourself for an advertising executive — but why the hell didn't you tell me you were coming? It might have been my day off, and I'd have killed you if I'd missed you.'

'Well I had a feeling you'd be here — you know, watching for my car, waiting by the door . . .'

She squealed with mock rage and went to hit him as he ducked and pinned her arm down. He turned to us, laughing. 'This is Penny the publican! She runs this place with irritating efficiency and alarming success. Penny, meet Polly, Rachel and Jamie.'

We all smiled and said hi, it was impossible not to take to her immediately, she was so full of fun and life. I instantly recognised a kindred spirit, with her merry eyes and naughty smile; just the sort of girl who would go down extremely well in my neck of the woods.

Penny bent down to coo over Jamie, breaking off now and again to throw questions out to Nick. How was so-and-so? What were they doing now? Who was doing what to whom? How was the agency going? They obviously knew each other extremely well. How well, I wondered?

After we'd toasted our bums a bit and they'd done the preliminary chat, we followed her through into a pretty olive-green dining room, streaky with sunlight which streamed in from the bay windows. It was surprisingly crowded, and as we sat down at the only remaining table, I was surprised to see a fair amount of silver and a crisp linen tablecloth. This was no ordinary pub.

Penny declined to eat with us on the grounds that she was far too busy, but served us herself, pausing to chat as she piled our plates high with rare roast beef, baby sweetcorn, mange tout and the tiniest, sweetest little new potatoes I'd ever tasted. It was all absolutely delicious and I told her so.

She smiled. 'Well that's all down to Tim, Nick's brother. He grows organic vegetables and delivers them here whenever he can. I must say I adore them, they really do taste quite different, don't they?'

They certainly did, and so did the summer pudding with great dollops of clotted cream which followed. I sat back, full to bursting, as she brought our coffee and pulled up a chair to join us.

I studied her carefully as I sipped the piping hot coffee. This was no country bumpkin. What on earth was a beautiful girl like this doing running a little country restaurant, albeit a very attractive and obviously successful restaurant, in the middle of nowhere? Shouldn't she be charging down Sloane Street looking for that elusive but crucial little black number to wear to some crumpet-filled Chelsea drinks party tonight?

Nick and Penny chatted about old friends and old times, all of which meant nothing to me, but I listened carefully, waiting for interesting snippets to fall by the wayside.

'So how are you and Serena?' asked Penny, dropping me the very snippet I was looking for. 'Still throwing plates and gin bottles at each other?'

I tried to look casual as I stirred my coffee, but my ears felt like Mr Spock's, pricked to distraction.

Nick smiled, lit a cigarette – funny how the mention of her name made him do that – and blew the smoke out thoughtfully. 'Well, let's just say we've reached a stage of armed neutrality.'

Curiouser and curiouser, what the hell did that mean?

'You mean you're both standing by your guns but you're not using them?'

'Something like that.'

'So whose guns are the biggest?'

Nick laughed. 'Ah well, that would be telling!'

Well, we wouldn't want to do that, would we? Hell, no. Would someone please tell me what they were talking about? I love gossip – thrive on it actually – especially, I thought, looking at Nick, in this case.

Nick expertly manoeuvred the conversation away from his love life and round to the restaurant, giving advice when she asked for it, and praising her for everything she'd done. Rachel and I joined in with equally effusive praise. When lunch was over, we wandered back through the rickety corridor and out under the low beam of the front door into the sunshine.

Nick and Penny kissed each other goodbye with, to my practised eye, a great deal of unnecessary hugging, and we all piled back into the car. She stood at the door, smiling and waving until we were out of sight.

I was burning with curiosity, but managed to hold myself back until we'd at least negotiated the bumpy track and were whizzing down the country lanes again.

'So how d'you know Penny?' I asked casually.

'Oh, she's just an old friend.'

'Looked like a pretty good one to me.'

He grinned. 'OK, a pretty good, old friend.'

'Why on earth is she running a pub out here in the middle of nowhere?'

'She likes it, I suppose.'

'But it's so . . . quiet.'

He smiled. 'That's why she likes it.' He turned on the cassette recorder but I wasn't dissuaded that easily.

'Have you known her long?' I persisted.

Nick caved in. 'Penny's an old girlfriend. We went out together, years ago. It was just after I came down from

269

Cambridge. I was living in Cornwall at the time, and she lived there with me. When we split up, she went back to London and found she couldn't bear living in the city any more; she really missed the country. I scouted around in this area and helped her find the pub. She'd been left a bit of money, and the rest she borrowed, and she's been here ever since making a very decent living. Her boyfriend owns the antique shop in the village and, as far as I know, she's extremely happy – is that so strange?'

It was to me. 'No, no, not at all!' I lied, thinking I'd go stark raving mad stuck out here in the country, miles from anywhere. So Penny was an ex-girlfriend, eh? That explained all the kissing and cuddling.

'Are you on such good terms with all your exes?'

He laughed. 'I suppose I am, although there haven't really been that many, only Penny and—' He broke off and pretended to look at a signpost, although he must have known the way blindfolded. And who? Who couldn't he bring himself to talk about? God, he was mysterious.

I resigned myself to the fact that no more blood was going to come out of this particular stone at present, and contented myself with staring out of the window, watching the countryside slip by.

Little by little the scenery was changing. The fields seemed to be getting smaller, the hedges taller, the hills steeper and the lanes narrower. The hedgerows at the side of these tiny lanes had gone quite berserk; primroses and bluebells were jockeying for position on the steep banks, and all the flowers seemed to have the same death wish as their heads were inevitably knocked off by cars as they swept past.

The lanes were so thin that there came a point when we seemed to go backwards more than forwards, as we reversed to let other cars, or more often tractors, pass in the opposite direction. It was impossible to see into some of the fields now, the hedges were so high, but every so often I caught a glimpse of a beautiful lush green meadow, or saw a flash of yellow as a field full of glorious daffodils shot by.

I sat up eagerly, like a child waiting to see the sea. Now and again a village – or perhaps even a hamlet, they were so small it was hard to tell – would whizz by. If you blinked you'd miss the irregular smattering of low, whitewashed cottages, their heavy thatched eyebrows frowning over tiny latticed windows, all clustered around a small, mouse-grey church. I opened the window and leaned right out, shutting my eyes and letting the wind sweep through my hair.

Nick laughed. 'What are you doing?'

'Giving my diseased lungs a taste of this wonderful country air – you're right, it is lovely here.'

A broad grin spread across his face. I'd pleased him. How touching to be so proud of a little patch of England. I couldn't quite imagine feeling the same way about Esher. Even Rachel, who'd been asleep, was now sitting up in the back, pointing out cows and sheep to Jamie who was gurgling appreciatively. Suddenly I felt almost happy. There was a definite holiday atmosphere in the car, a real sense of adventure and camaraderie – any minute now I'd break into a spirited rendition of 'Green Grow the Rushes Oh'.

As we hurtled down a particularly narrow lane at breakneck speed, with Rachel and I squealing in mock terror, Nick suddenly changed dramatically from fourth to second gear and swung the car left through some crumbling white gates. We trundled over a cattle grid and down a narrow, pitted drive. It was long and windy with woods on either side, through which the sun flashed intermittently, as if someone were shining an almighty great flashlight at us. Seconds later, the woods parted, and a sweep of lawn rose up before us. Straight ahead, looking out proprietorially on to this sylvan scene, was a large and ancient grey stone house.

It was long and low, with large sash windows at the front and an imposing arched front door surrounded by a sweep of grey stone. Covering almost half of the house was a giant wistaria, which looked about as old as the house itself and, as we drew nearer, I could see what looked like a stable block behind, with a bell tower peeping out over the rooftops.

I caught my breath with delight. 'Oh Nick,' I breathed. 'It's beautiful!'

'Isn't it just!' echoed Rachel.

Nick beamed with pleasure, looking like the Cheshire Cat. 'It is rather a decent-looking place but, unfortunately, as you'll see on closer inspection, it's falling to bits.'

We got out of the car and wandered up – and I did see. The brickwork was literally crumbling to the touch in places, and most of the windows were rotten, hanging in their frames at precarious angles.

Nick strode ahead and pushed through the giant wooden door, leading us into a large creamy hall which looked remarkably like the National Gallery. The walls were crawling with ancestors, and a very gloomy crowd they looked too. Most had piggy brown eyes and big noses, and were swathed in what looked like velvet and ermine. They also appeared to be sporting quite a few sizeable baubles, notably around the head and neck region. What was going on here: was Nick related to royalty or something? Was I in fact in the presence of a young pretender, the last of the Cornish Plantagenets, perhaps? One of the old codgers on the wall certainly bore an unnerving resemblance to that king with the hunchback and the dodgy leg who does a lot of Shakespeare. He gave me the creeps and I decided to keep well clear of him. I could do without being followed around by those piercing, judgemental eyes.

'Tim? Where are you!' yelled Nick. 'It's me!'

I heard voices coming from behind the double doors

opposite, and a shout of recognition went up. Nick pushed open the doors and, as he strode through, a smaller, thinner version of Nick leaped up from an armchair, scattering pieces of *The Independent*, and sending an ashtray flying.

'Nick!' he vaulted over a sofa to get to us. 'What the devil are you doing here? I didn't expect you till tomorrow!'

He slapped Nick on the back, who slapped him back, grinning, and then they slapped each other a bit more, as men seem to do.

While the Morris Dancing was going on, I noticed a pretty girl with curly brown hair and freckles get up from a chair in the corner. She put down her book and took her glasses off, smiling shyly. Nick took two giant strides to get to her and kissed her smartly on both cheeks.

'Sarah! It's good to see you. How are the stables? Still up to your knees in it?'

She laughed. 'They're fine, thank you, and you'll be pleased to hear I change my jeans when I come over here, so no more manure jokes, please.'

'Glad to hear it, especially if you're sitting on my chairs . . . Oh, this is Polly, and Rachel, and Jamie. Sarah Mansfield, Tim's — revolting word — fiancée.'

She grimaced. 'Isn't it just, but I suppose that's what I am. Hello.' She turned to Rachel. 'What a beautiful baby, can I hold him?'

Jamie was duly bundled into her arms with a smile from Rachel. Sarah cooed and tickled him, and I wondered if she'd been briefed — be nice to the scared-looking one with the baby who looks like she's just got out of Belsen. Jamie took hold of her finger and squeezed it in his fierce little grip.

'Oh! Aren't you sweet!' she cooed. 'I've got a little nephew just like you, but not nearly so good looking!'

Rachel looked proud, and they knelt down by the fire

talking babies. Rachel looked positively happy. I supposed this must feel rather like reaching Switzerland after escaping from Colditz. Nick offered to show me the house and, as we were on our way out, Rachel turned to him, eyes shining.

'Thanks, Nick!' she blushed. 'I mean for driving me here, and – and everything.'

'No problem,' said Nick, 'just make yourself at home. I thought you and Jamie could have the pink room at the top. It's got its own bathroom. Tim will show you where it is.'

Tim nodded, 'Sure.' He was staring at her intently as she sat huddled by the fire in her outsized grey cardigan, thinking, I'm sure, what most people think when they meet her for the first time: how small and lost and vulnerable she looked. He poured her a large drink, and Nick and I disappeared to look around the house.

As we wandered from one vast, high-ceilinged room to the next, I realised why Nick was so desperate to keep it. It was just as pretty inside as it was out, but again, in a precarious way. I felt that a sudden gust of wind breezing through an open window could sweep all the fragile pieces of china off their shelves, whisk the soft silky curtains from their few remaining threads, and break the legs on all the spindly little pieces of antique furniture. Everything was beautifully pale and washed out, too, rather as if someone had turned down the colour on the telly. The floors were very pale oak, the Persian carpets were so faded you could hardly see the pattern, and the walls had lost most of their original colour and were those lovely soft, muted shades that paint manufacturers would kill to recreate. It was indeed beautiful, and it occurred to me, as I ran my amateurish, *Antiques Roadshow* viewer's eye over it, that it all looked rather valuable too.

I casually picked up a pretty blue and white plate which weighed about half an ounce, and put it down hastily as I realised how eminently breakable it was.

'Couldn't you sell some of this?' I ventured timidly, gesturing around at the treasures. 'I mean, if the house is costing so much to repair, surely you could get quite a bit for the furniture and, um – china?' Was china the right word? Somehow it sounded too much like the ground floor of Peter Jones.

'I could, I suppose. I daresay the porcelain – ' the very word I'd been groping for – 'would fetch quite a bit at auction, but I don't want to. I grew up with all these things – they're like family to me. Anyway,' he grimaced, 'it wouldn't be enough. Holes in roofs make pretty enormous holes in pockets.'

We wandered into the dining room and encountered a vast mahogany table, heaving with silver. An enormous candelabra stood in the middle, surrounded by lots of little silver animals: pheasants, foxes, ducks . . . I picked up a little hare and turned it over in my hand.

'Oh! How pretty!' I exclaimed. 'Where did you get them from?'

'I'm not sure,' said Nick, scratching his head. 'They've always been here. I suppose Mum would know, but they were probably here when she arrived on the scene too.'

Of course, how stupid of me, people like Nick didn't buy their own silver. I wondered how many more cringe-makingly naff remarks would fall from my lips during the course of the weekend. Any minute now I'd be demanding to know why there wasn't a fluffy little mat on the loo seat, or how come the front door bell didn't play 'Jingle Bells' when you pressed it.

Nick showed me the rest of the house. I smiled a lot and nodded admiringly whenever I deemed it appropriate, but said little. Surely smiling and nodding couldn't be wrong?

As we went back through the hall, though, I couldn't help enthusing about a dear little walnut table which stood at the foot of the stairs. It was terribly delicate and intricately inlaid, just the sort of thing I'd kill to have by my bed one day. On it stood a tiny bowl of primroses which were just dropping a few of their petals on to its smooth walnut veneer.

'Oh look!' I breathed. 'Isn't it divine? What a beautiful little table!' I ran my finger over its smooth, highly polished surface.

'It's pretty, isn't it? It was a Christmas present, actually.'

'Really? How incredibly generous. Who from?'

Nick looked slightly uncomfortable. 'From Serena.'

'Serena? Gosh!' I recalled my own, I'd thought, incredibly generous Christmas present to Harry – one navy blue cashmere scarf – and realised I was well out of my depth here.

'How kind,' I muttered.

'Wasn't it?' agreed Nick. He stooped and picked up a few rose petals that had fallen just by my feet. His hand accidentally brushed my shoe. He straightened up and smiled. 'Nice legs.'

I flushed with pleasure, thrilled that he'd noticed one of my undoubted assets, set off, rather attractively today, by black lycra tights. I lowered my eyelids and smiled coquettishly.

'Yes, I love the way they bow, ever so slightly, at the bottom,' he went on.

I gasped with horror. Who was he calling bow-legged! Bloody hell! I intercepted his gaze and followed it back to the walnut table – oh! Oh, yes I see, OK. I nodded vigorously, hoping he hadn't noticed my flaming face.

'Oh I agree, I um – I like them like that, sort of – curvy.' I followed him meekly back into the drawing room, feeling decidedly disappointed. Tim and Rachel were sitting by the fire, chatting away in what I have to admit was quite an animated fashion. I even heard Rachel laugh once or twice, and at one stage I could have sworn she came close to completing a paragraph.

Tim was listening intently, egging her on and encouraging her to reveal yet more of her wildly attractive personality. He seemed intrigued by her, willing to spend time and energy coaxing words to flow from her mouth. And flow they did, albeit in a somewhat jerky fashion. Perhaps a combination of these kind, friendly people and the country air was getting to her, and perhaps now, finally, we could all relax a bit, I thought, flopping down thankfully into a nice squashy sofa.

Sarah had gone back to the local riding stables which, I gathered from Tim, she ran practically single-handed. It sounded like a pretty labour-intensive job, and not one I particularly envied. I always like to slip into a nice tight pair of breeches and some black leather boots if there's anyone around to admire the effect, but I'm damned if I want to get near the beastly creatures, and as for working in a stables – imagine the pong! But Sarah returned a couple of hours later looking flushed and happy, and reeking, not of manure, but of job satisfaction.

'Two new pupils today!' she said cheerfully, helping herself to a glass of wine. 'And they've both signed on for a course of ten lessons!'

'Excellent!' beamed Tim. 'If you keep going at this rate, I can retire! Keep at it, work harder!' he cried, cracking an imaginary whip. 'What's for supper, by the way?'

She threw a cushion at him, laughing. 'You'll be getting it yourself if you're not careful, but since you ask, beef bourguignonne. I'll just go and see how it's doing.'

And so saying, this capable girl whizzed off to the kitchen to put the finishing touches to her dish, wisely waving aside my feeble offers of help – for feeble is what they would have been. Beef bourguignonne was the sort of thing I ordered in restaurants: I'd certainly never attempt to recreate it.

Supper that night was a happy and relaxed affair. After

Tim and Nick had dispensed with the preliminary farm chat, with Nick asking questions about crop yields and lambing, and Tim prefixing his answers with words like 'high', 'excellent', and 'bloody good considering', all of which made Nick beam with pleasure, we got down to the interesting bits, like me asking who owned what – surreptitiously, of course.

The house and most of the land apparently belonged to Nick, who had obviously inherited the lion's share, but Tim owned a certain amount of acreage adjacent to Nick's estate, which he also farmed, but in a purely organic way. There was apparently a cottage on the land, too, which Tim and Sarah were painstakingly restoring so they could eventually live there.

'Probably in about the year 2000 at the rate we're going!' said Sarah, laughing; but she looked pretty happy about it, and Tim blew her a kiss over the table.

'Don't you worry, I'll be struggling over the threshold with you long before that!'

'Oh!' I said breathlessly, seizing on a subject that was close to my heart. 'When are you getting married?'

'Next year,' said Sarah happily, 'at the church in Manaccan. It's so pretty, you must come and have a look at it.'

'I'd love to!' I said, jumping at the chance to talk flowers and bridesmaids' dresses and wedding lists. I wondered if the London stores would take on a wedding list this far away? No doubt it was a problem she'd already wrestled with, but I supposed there were obvious compensations attached to a country wedding: a picturesque setting; off to the reception in a pony and trap; perhaps a dance in a marquee in the evening . . . I sighed wistfully.

We laughed a lot that night. The beef bourguignonne was ambrosial, the claret flowed, and Nick showed the sort of form I wouldn't previously have thought possible. He and Tim had us in stitches as they played a couple of

Cornish yokels, affecting deep country burrs and clowning around in a ridiculous manner, egged on by the shrieks of laughter from us girls. As I watched him larking around with his brother, he turned suddenly and caught my eye, smiling, and raising his eyebrows inquiringly. 'All right?' he mouthed. I nodded and smiled back, hoping he wouldn't notice that there were tears in my eyes. Recently I wasn't used to anyone bothering to find out if I were happy or not.

That night, I left the curtains open and pulled the bedclothes high up under my chin as I stared out at the vast black sky. An owl hooted way off in the distance. A lamb bleated for its mother, then there was quiet. I breathed deeply, savouring the cool night air. I smiled. How comforting it was to know that in the morning I'd wake up – not to an alarm clock, followed by a rushed breakfast, followed by the underground – but to those enormous oak trees swaying in the breeze outside my window, and a field full of sheep with their spring lambs. I snuggled down further in the bed and closed my eyes, letting the dark night wash over me. This was the nearest I'd come to happiness in a good many days.

Chapter Fifteen

At breakfast the next morning, over great platefuls of bacon and eggs, expertly cooked by Tim, Nick suggested we all had a look at the farm. My heart sank deep into my Docksiders. I had visions of myself, up to my designer-jeaned knees in cow pats and manure, miserably swatting flies with my handbag.

'Sorry, I'm far too busy, got to get the beans in today,' said Tim, helping himself to more toast and mopping up his fried egg. He grinned at his brother. 'Some of us have to work, you know!'

'Well, you're lucky you can do it down here rather than in London. How about the wife-to-be, or are you keeping her nose to the grindstone, too?'

''Fraid so,' said Sarah. 'I've got a new pony arriving at about ten o'clock. Maybe I'll catch up with you later, though.'

'Rachel?'

She sighed. 'I'd love to, but unfortunately Jamie will have to have another sleep in about an hour, so I'd better stay here with him.'

Nick made a face. 'God, I'd no idea this mothering lark was such hard work. Having you and Jamie around certainly makes me think twice about throwing myself into parenthood.'

'Ah yes, but you'd only be a father, wouldn't you? That doesn't come with quite so many occupational 'hazards,' said Rachel darkly.

That's pretty rich, I thought, considering Adam's moving heaven and earth to take on those hazards, but I wisely held my tongue.

Nick turned to me with a smile. 'Looks like we're on our own, then – how about it?'

For some reason, my heart stopped lurking sulkily in my shoes and rocketed swiftly back into position again. 'Yes, I'd love to see the farm.'

'Sure? You don't have to be polite, you know, you can do what you like.'

'I should think the last thing she wants to do is trail round a smelly old farm,' said Tim. 'If I were you, Polly, I'd catch a bus into town and check out the only boutique in Helston.'

'Don't be silly, there's nothing in that ghastly little shop that would interest Polly. Why don't you come to the stables with me?' suggested Sarah. 'I'm only doing half a day today, we could go and have some lunch in a pub when I've finished.'

'Oh no, that's very kind, but I'm not desperately fond of horses and, anyway, I'd really like to go with Nick!' I said eagerly. Far too eagerly. The phrase 'really like to go with Nick!' seemed to hang, echoing in the air. I felt it needed a little explaining. 'You see,' I stammered, 'I'm . . . I'm terribly interested in farming!'

'Really?' Nick looked up from his bacon and eggs in surprise. 'Polly, I had no idea!'

No, neither did I, and hopefully he'd forget I'd said that, but he showed no signs of doing so just yet.

'Which particular areas are you interested in?' he asked.

'Um, d'you mean – which particular areas, in particular?' I faltered, playing with some crumbs on the tablecloth.

Nick looked confused. 'Well, yes, I suppose I do mean that.'

'Oh. Oh well, all sorts really.'

'All sorts?'

'Yes, but, um, if you want to get specific, I'd say particularly animal, vegetable and, er – mineral.'

By now Tim, Sarah and Rachel had all put their knives and forks down and were looking at me in astonishment.

'Animal, vegetable and mineral?' inquired Nick, his mouth twitching slightly.

'Yes, you know, cows, sheep, er – hay, straw . . .' I racked my brains. What else did they have in these bloody places? One of Jamie's animal books sprung helpfully to mind. 'Oh yes, and chickens, horses, zebras—'

'Zebras!' cried Sarah in astonishment.

'Oh, er – did I say zebras? Oh well, perhaps not in this country, but certainly in Africa. Yes, there are a hell of a lot of zebras out there, and of course I'm interested in farming on a very global scale – you know, global farming.' I seized this concept gratefully.

Tim snorted with derision. 'But zebras are wild, they charge around on game reserves. People don't farm them!'

'Oh you'd be surprised, Tim,' I said, nodding sagely and wishing I too was safely charging around on a game reserve in darkest Africa. 'Some of those tribesmen will stop at nothing.'

'Have you spent a lot of time in Africa then?' asked Sarah in wonder.

'Well, perhaps not a lot, but certainly a bit, yes, I'd say a fair bit.'

'Really? Whereabouts?'

'Whereabouts? Oh, all over really, but mostly – mostly East, you know, East Africa.'

'What – Tanzania? Kenya? Or further up?'

'Mmmm . . . yes, mostly – I say, I love that jumper. Did you buy it locally?' I snatched desperately at the first handy distraction to catch my eye.

'What, this old thing?' said Sarah dubiously, staring

down at what indeed was a very old thing, a sort of dirty grey Shetland wool affair with bobbles of wool where it had been rubbed and patches on the elbows. She gazed at me incredulously. 'This is the one I wear to the stables. D'you like it?'

'Very much.' I nodded vigorously, chewing hard on my bacon and staring at the truly repulsive jumper which had absolutely nothing to recommend it. I waved my fork in its general direction. 'Everyone's wearing them like that in London. It's quite the thing this season, especially with the elbows patched. Goes with the ripped jeans, you see. Rachel's got one, haven't you?'

'Have I?' asked Rachel, wide-eyed.

'Yes, except it's not quite a jumper is it? More of a cardigan, really, that lovely baggy grey thing you wear all the — quite a lot.'

'Oh that! God, I wasn't aware it was fashionable.'

'Oh, very, very,' I said, still nodding furiously, lips pursed, and I have to admit, warming wickedly to my theme. 'I know girls who'd kill for a cardigan like that — kill. You can't move for them in the King's Road at the moment.'

Out of the corner of my eye I caught a glimpse of Nick, who seemed to be stuffing the tablecloth into his mouth and making strange hiccuppy noises.

'Really?' Sarah looked dumbfounded. 'I had no idea that sort of thing was trendy, but then it's so long since I've been to London — oh well, I've got hundreds more like this. In fact there's a mauve one upstairs which is so threadbare it's unreal. You can borrow it if you like. I'll run and get it.' She put down her napkin and made to go upstairs.

'Oh er, no, Sarah, it's OK,' I said, polishing off my bacon and eggs in one huge mouthful and jumping down from the table. 'I don't think I'll wear a jumper today. I find it frightfully warm for the time of year, don't you?'

I fanned my face with my napkin, which was suitably flushed with the exertion of so many verbal gymnastics, and beat a hasty retreat upstairs to the safety of my bedroom and my beautifully smooth, unbobbly lambswool jumpers.

I threw myself thankfully on the bed. I felt exhausted already, and it was only half-past nine. Why did I have such a propensity to dig whopping great holes for myself and then proceed to clamber inexpertly out of them in front of a vast audience? Ah well, never mind, at least the agenda for today was looking good. A whole day on the farm with Nick – now why was that such a treat? I declined to answer, afraid of all the mighty implications it could throw up.

'Don't think about it,' I instructed myself, jumping off the bed. I opened my suitcase and pulled out a whole heap of clothes, throwing them into a huge colourful pile on the bed.

Now, for someone who's more at home in South Ken than South Cornwall, 'A Day on the Farm' was a tricky brief, but I rose gleefully to the challenge. What it called for, I decided, was something that would ease me gently into the part without looking too contrived. In the end I settled on a pair of brown corduroy jodphurs, a yellow and red checked shirt which leant on the lumberjack side, and a pair of brown leather riding boots which were serious but sexy. I studied the overall effect in the mirror. Hmmm. Whilst not exactly looking at one with nature, at least I didn't look as if I'd been born in a wine bar.

As I bounced downstairs in a jaunty, country girl manner, I saw Nick waiting patiently for me at the bottom. He was leaning against the hall table reading an old copy of *Country Life*. He looked up and smiled as I came down. I smiled winningly back and skipped on down; then, warming to my jaunty theme, decided to jump the last few steps to display a certain amount of fresh-faced athleticism. A huge error. As I took off I realised – too

285

late — that five steps and a shiny wooden floor as a landing pad was, to say the least, ambitious. As I plummeted through the air, I had just enough time to catch the look of alarm on Nick's face as I hurtled towards him. Nine-and-a-half stone of blonde lumberjack cannoned into him and sent him crashing to the ground.

'Oooof!'

'Sorry!' I gasped.

'Christ, steady!' he cried in alarm, as he was sent sliding towards the front door, pinned to his ancestral floorboards by my tremendous weight. As we shuddered to a halt, perilously close to Serena's fragile little table, he struggled desperately — too desperately, I felt — to free himself from my bone-crushing bulk.

'Sorry!' I gasped again, as I clambered to my knees. 'Lost my balance!'

Nick was on his feet before I was and he pulled me up. 'So it seems. What were you trying to do, kill yourself? Or kill me, perhaps. Are you OK?'

'Fine,' I lied, wincing from a shooting pain in my ankle and the embarrassment of it all. What must he think of me? Did he think I was being incredibly forward or something? Did he imagine I was literally flinging myself at him? I blushed to my dyed roots.

'Sure you're all right?' he asked with concern, still holding my arm as I gingerly tried my ankle. 'Can you walk on it?'

I hobbled around. 'Yes, honestly, I'm fine, sorry about that.'

'It's OK. Just warn me next time you're feeling energetic, and I'll lay on some trampolines or something . . . Christ — what's that terrible pong?' He sniffed the air suspiciously.

'What pong?'

'That funny smell, like rotting cabbages or something.'

'Oh that,' I cringed deeply. 'It's called Country Girl.

Just something I put on to make the cows feel at home.'

'You mean you bought it? In a bottle?'

'It didn't smell too bad in Boots,' I muttered.

'Jesus. Well let's hope it doesn't knock the cows out. Come on, let's go.'

He marched off, farmyard bound, and I hobbled along after him, nursing my pride and my ankle.

As it turned out, the farm was immaculate: hardly a cow pat to be seen, and certainly not a pebble out of place in the cobbled yard. The barns were spotless, and everything that could shine did, in fact the milking equipment looked like it had been on the receiving end of a passionate love affair between Mrs Mopp and Mr Sheen. I half expected doormats as we inspected the outbuildings.

'Hope my shoes are clean,' I muttered as we entered a huge Dutch barn, 'I had no idea farmers were so houseproud.'

Nick laughed. 'It's just been cleaned up, actually, but I agree, we keep the farm in better nick than the house. Sometimes I think it would be more comfortable to sleep in the haybarn than in my bedroom, where the windows don't fit and the plaster's falling off the walls. The thing is, though, the farm's always got to come first. It's our livelihood.'

Our livelihood? I wondered who he was planning on sharing it with.

We looked in on the cows in their five-star accommodation. It was cool and dark in the shed, and the cows stood in a long row, pulling at hay nets and stamping their feet. They turned their heads briefly and stared at me insolently before going back to their rhythmical munching, swaying their heads and rotating their jaws. I felt as if I'd interrupted some kind of religious sect chanting a mantra. I patted one gingerly on the bottom. She stamped her foot and swished her tail around in irritation. I backed off smartly.

287

'Sorry,' I muttered.

'They're waiting to be milked,' explained Nick. 'They get a bit jumpy with strangers.'

One of Nick's farm hands appeared and started to fix them up to milking machines, so we left him to it, emerging out into the sunshine again, blinking against the bright light.

Just then a hearty male voice hailed us. 'Hello, hello! I can't believe you're the new cow girl, but if you are, things are looking up!'

I swung around to see a rather attractive man smiling at me from the other side of the post and rail fence. Although he was the wrong side of forty, he had obviously been extremely good looking once, but was now steadily going to seed. His bright blue eyes sported terrific bags, and his handsome face was lined and ruddy; the result, I suspected, of a combination of fresh air and too much alcohol.

'Good Lord, Nick, how did you manage to entice such a delightful creature into your barns. D'you think she'd like to look at mine too?'

Nick grinned. 'Polly, this is Jack Crawley: neighbour, stud farmer, womaniser and piss artist.'

'Come now, dear boy – "bon viveur" is much more to my liking . . . Enchanted, my dear!'

He grasped my hand and put it to his lips. I smiled delightedly, keen to make the acquaintance of someone who would flatter me rotten in front of Nick. He ran his rather sexy, bloodshot eyes over me appraisingly, and held on to my hand for a second longer than was absolutely necessary.

'Been showing you the equivalent of his etchings, has he? Want to see mine?'

I grinned. 'Are they up to scratch?'

Jack roared with laughter and, as he opened a gate to let us through, took my arm and whispered in my ear, 'So I've been led to believe, but who am I to say? Women tell such terrible whoppers. Come and see the horses anyway and then we might find time for a little mid-morning tipple . . . Got time, Nick, or shall I take her myself?'

'I think I can spare a couple of minutes,' said Nick with a grin. 'You're incorrigible, Jack.'

We followed the delightful Jack through his lush green fields towards the stable block in the distance. Over by the far gate were a few brood mares with their foals. The foals frolicked around in the sun, bucking and kicking, trying out their spindly new legs. Every so often they would return to their mothers for a reassuring nuzzle before shying off to test-drive their legs again. The mares, meanwhile, munched contentedly at the grass, or just stood staring into space, basking in the early spring sunshine, resting a back leg and swishing the occasional fly away with their tails. It looked a peaceful sort of life.

One elegant bay mare trotted over, and I stroked her velvety nose as she blew warm, sweet air into my face. She seemed to like me, so it was with a new enthusiasm for horses that I went to the yard to meet Sorcha, Jack's prize stallion.

There were quite a few boxes in the yard, most of which were unoccupied, but there was a great deal of stamping and snorting coming from the one in the corner. I wandered over and leaned over the stable door, peering in to see what all the fuss was about. Suddenly Sorcha's enormous chestnut head came looming out of the darkness, eyes rolling, teeth bared, like Jaws emerging from the depths.

I yelped and jumped backwards, dodging the teeth as they went to take a chunk out of my nose. He'd obviously got a whiff of Country Girl and couldn't believe his nostrils, but I must say I was mildly insulted.

'Jesus, he's a bit wild, isn't he?'

'It's nothing personal,' laughed Jack, 'he's just a

dreadful old misogynist, I'm afraid.' He patted his nose, and Sorcha nuzzled his hand like a pussycat.

'Doesn't bode well for the brood mares, does it?' I said doubtfully.

'Oh, he's keen enough when it comes to sex, he just can't be doing with the social niceties.'

'Hmmm, I've known a few like that,' I muttered darkly.

Jack laughed. 'Oh, the mares don't mind, they've been so revved up by the teaser he could pick his nose while he was on the job for all they cared.'

'What's the teaser?' I asked, wondering if it was some kind of sexual aid for horses, an Anne Summers equine tickler perhaps.

'Here's the teaser,' said Jack, indicating a small and rather scruffy looking grey in a nearby stable. He was circling round and round, neighing his head off in a demented manner. 'Meet Roger.'

'Poor old thing,' said Nick, patting his neck. 'His only role in life is to sniff around the mares and make sure they're in season. He gets them thoroughly sexed up and, just when he thinks he's going to get his wicked way, the mare will be led away for the likes of Sorcha or one of the other stallions to service.'

'So he never actually gets to do the business himself?'

' 'Fraid not, poor old Roger.'

'That's a singularly inappropriate name, isn't it?'

Nick laughed. 'It's Jack's warped sense of humour, I'm afraid.'

I watched, fascinated, as Roger was indeed led out to inspect a mare. He sniffed and snorted and rolled his eyes, prancing around her in a provocative manner and evidently pronouncing her to be not only in season but ready for anything. After a great deal of flirting and circling and, just as the poor old boy thought he was getting somewhere, the by now thoroughly over-excited mare was abruptly led away to the covering yard for bigger and better things.

At this point Sorcha was led out of his box by a stable boy. He strolled casually over to the covering yard, looking, I have to admit, devastatingly attractive: tall, dark, and not a hair out of place on his gleaming chestnut coat. His muscles rippled, he tossed his arrogant head, and the poor, mystified grey mare went weak at the knees, all thoughts of Randy Roger completely forgotten.

It reminded me of a haunt of mine in the King's Road, a nightclub where quite a few pretty girls go to dance round their handbags and get picked up. Invariably some spotty no-hoper of a guy would do just that. Having made contact with a girl, he'd ply her with drinks, dance his little socks off, shouting above the disco to make himself heard and, just as he'd be about to pounce, lo and behold, his good looking coolie friend − six foot two and not a spot on his chiselled, smouldering face − would stroll up and take over. Coolie would claim just one dance − usually a slow one − before disappearing into the night with her, leaving spotty no-hoper to gnash his teeth and chew the dashboard of his second-hand Mini.

Like a lot of these cool Chelsea guys, Sorcha had no manners whatsoever and didn't know the meaning of foreplay. He walked nonchalantly around the back of the mare, and heaved himself on board without so much as a friendly neigh in her general direction. Having said that, I have to admit he did his stuff with one of the most impressive pieces of kit I've ever seen. It was enough to make your eyes water, and the little grey mare looked pretty impressed too, if her eyes bulging out of their sockets were anything to go by.

'Make sure it's in deep, for God's sake!' yelled Jack to the stable boy, who had the mammoth task of guiding Sorcha in.

At this point I had a violent attack of schoolgirl giggles, and had to move away, stuffing a hankie in my mouth to muffle the snorts. The whole thing was titillating enough anyway, but somehow, standing next to Nick made it even worse. I felt ridiculously embarrassed.

I went off to comfort Roger, who was thrashing around in his stable looking thoroughly pissed off, chewing anything he could get his teeth into: stable door, bucket, manger – anything to relieve the frustration. I hastily moved away, just in case he decided it was time to bury those enormous yellow teeth into harmless human flesh.

When Sorcha had finished and the mare had been led away to recover and ponder her good fortune, Nick and Jack wandered over.

Jack rubbed his hands together. 'Well, hopefully that's another prize winning foal in the bag. Where did you get to, Polly, you missed the best bit!'

'Didn't want to put him off his stride. I thought he might perform better without too much of a gallery.'

'Don't you believe it, old Sorcha likes an audience. Got time for a swift one back at the house, you two?'

'Some other time, Jack,' said Nick. 'I promised to show Polly the rest of the farm, and then I really must get down to some work.'

'Ah, that's your excuse, is it? Fair enough, I know a couple of love birds when I see them. Run along and frolic in the cornfields then. See if I care!'

Nick laughed. 'You've got a one-track mind, Jack. See you tomorrow, possibly – come up to the house.'

'Will do. Bye, Polly.' He winked. 'Watch him now, he's one hundred per cent pure beef, like the rest of his herd!'

By now my face was puce pink, but I laughed gaily and shook hands, rather unaccountably at a loss to know how to react to this sexy banter. The natural thing would be to tell Jack he'd got the wrong end of the stick, but on the other hand . . .

Nick and I climbed the fence and strolled back towards his farm again. It has to be said there was rather a telling silence. I'm not very good at silences, telling or otherwise.

'He seems like a nice chap,' I said lamely.

'Jack? Oh he's great fun. Got a brain the size of a pea, though and he keeps it between his legs.'

I laughed. 'Yes, he did seem a little – obsessed.'

Nick opened the gate to his yard. 'Well, let's face it, he runs a stud farm, so it's all he ever thinks about. He lives and breathes sex, does Jack . . . Jump in, I'm just going to check on the cows.' He indicated an open-topped Land Rover standing in the corner of the yard.

I obeyed, quietly relieved. My shiny brown boots were already caked with mud, and my legs were beginning to ache from all this exertion. A minute later, Nick jumped in beside me. Now you're talking, I thought, as we zoomed off, my hair streaming away from my face like corn in the breeze, or so I liked to think. This was much more my scene.

As we charged around the farm, Nick pointed out his woods and fields and, in the very, very far-flung distance, boundaries where neighbouring farms began. He seemed to own half of Cornwall, and it occurred to me to wonder whether he wasn't in fact Prince Charles in disguise. That would certainly explain all the regal looking portraits in the hall.

We roared off down a particularly bumpy track, which seemed to be going nowhere. All I could see in the distance was bright blue sky. The bumps were getting larger, and I folded my arms protectively across my chest, fervently wishing I'd had the nous to invest in a sports bra before embarking on an all-action weekend like this. All of a sudden, Nick slowed right down and we came to a shuddering halt. He turned the engine off.

I wondered why we'd stopped, there didn't seem a great deal to see, but I got out obligingly. We were at the very edge of a cornfield and, as I walked to the edge, I caught my breath. The cornfield sloped away to green fields below, and below that, to what I'd originally perceived to be the sky, but which was in fact a great expanse of sea. I stared down at the sparkling chasm that had opened up in front of me. It was dotted with tiny boats which bobbed jauntily around, their sails fluttering in the breeze. The water was as smooth as a mirror, just tilting now and then to offer up a different angle for the sun to reflect. Far away, on the opposite shore, I could make out a cluster of tiny white cottages basking in the sunshine.

I turned to Nick in amazement. 'This is absolutely beautiful. I had no idea we were by the sea!'

He laughed. 'Really? Well, I suppose technically we're not. This is a river, actually. It runs up to Gweek which is a few miles in that direction, and out to sea the other way. Over there is Frenchman's Creek — see?' He pointed out a dark and narrow inlet overhung with trees and heavy foliage.

'Oh yes — is it really? How romantic!' It was one of the few books I'd read, and I could quite imagine the dashing young Frenchman snaking up there in his boat to treat his aristocratic lady friend to a bit of *je ne sais quoi* behind some ancient oak tree.

'The village you can see over there is Helford,' said Nick pointing to the white cluster in the distance. 'If you like we'll take the boat over there tomorrow and I'll show you around. It's really pretty.'

'You have a boat?' Was there anything this man didn't have?

He laughed. 'Well, it would be pretty silly to live here and not have one. Do you sail?'

Now I don't actually 'do' anything that one is supposed to do, like ride, ski, sail, hunt, or even cook, and the only time I can answer a 'do you?' question in the affirmative is when the next word is either drink or smoke; but having come up against quite a few of these tricky little inquiries in my time, I go armed with a set of stock replies. I smiled up at him. 'No, but I'm very good at lying around in a bikini waiting for the sun to pass over the yard-arm.'

He laughed. 'I bet you are, but I'm afraid there's no deck to speak of on this little dinghy. It's more of a ropes and reef-knots affair. What are your knots like?'

'Oh I do a lovely sheep shag,' I said with a smile, and then realised that wasn't quite what I'd meant at all.

Nick roared with laughter. 'Well you've come to the right place for that. There's a whole flock in the next field who'd be only to pleased to oblige! Perhaps I'd better let you off the actual sailing part, though. You can just sit at the back and look decorative. I must say I like the sound of the bikini.'

He gazed down at me speculatively from his dizzy heights. I met his eye fleetingly, but instantly looked down and dug up an ear of corn with my toe. Good Lord, was he flirting with me? Surely not. I looked up again and saw the brown eyes still twinkling away in my direction. A smile played around at the corners of his mouth. I immediately returned to my ear of corn. Christ, he was, and what's more the shock had completely taken the wind out of my normally flirty little sails. This was most out of character for both parties. Surely he should have warned me? Sent me a memo or something?

To Polly: Just to inform you that on Saturday 12 April there may be a brief and uncharacteristic flirtation on my part in the large cornfield overlooking the Helford River. Please be ready to anticipate just such an eventuality and respond accordingly. Nick.

Yes, that would have been much more in keeping. As it was, I was struggling to remember just one of the well-honed lines that would normally trip straight off my tongue in this sort of situation, and which had ensnared the likes of Harry Lloyd-Roberts and plenty more before him. I bit my lip.

295

'Wind . . . that's your problem,' Nick muttered.

I gasped with horror, wind? Christ! Had I, in my nervous confusion, inadvertently expelled some vile and evil-smelling gases? How unspeakably ghastly!

I looked up in alarm, but he wasn't looking at me any more. In fact he seemed to have totally forgotten about my existence. I followed his gaze out to sea. He was watching an unfortunate windsurfer who was struggling to stay on his board, collapsing repeatedly into the water.

'You've got to have a bit of wind to keep the thing upright,' he went on, shading his eyes against the sun and monitoring the sailor's progress. 'It's absolutely hopeless in this sort of weather, can't think why he's even bothering.'

'Oh! Oh yes, crazy . . . on a day like this,' I managed.

I tried to pull myself together. I realised now of course that Nick's reference to the delights of my bikini had just been small-talk. Yes, that was it. A casual pleasantry designed to please and perhaps even flatter, but nothing more than that. I, of course, had overreacted as usual, and had taken it to mean that he couldn't wait to take me in his arms and bowl me over in the cornfield.

I breathed deeply. How hugely disappointing. Hang on a minute – hugely what? Disappointing? Good grief, whatever was happening to me! Wasn't I supposed to be heartbroken? Hadn't I more or less decided that, since I couldn't have Harry, I was through with men and would probably remain celibate for the rest of my life? What on earth was I thinking of? I had a quick mental flick through my file of Harry pictures and found the pre-launch diving board one, an old favourite. I studied it carefully. Good gracious. How extraordinary. Surely his eyes hadn't always been that close together? And wasn't that mouth just a tad on the pinched side, and was it possible that his hairline was – heavens above – receding?

Shocked to the core, I filed the picture away again and

looked up at the one beside me. Wide-apart eyes, generous mouth, plenty of hair. Oh no. This could not be happening to me. My toes twitched nervously in my boots.

Of course, I reasoned, it's bloody hard to be cool and objective when you're up to your knees in corn, gazing out at just about the most beautiful sylvan scene in Christendom, and standing next to the dashing young owner of all that the eye can see. Confused? Who wouldn't be?

The windsurfer eventually called it a day, and swam back to shore dragging his board behind him. The sun disappeared behind a cloud. I shivered. Suddenly the sylvan scene didn't seem quite so peaceful and serene. In fact it seemed full of danger.

'Cold?' asked Nick, noticing my shiver.

'Mm, a bit chilly.'

Nick looked at the sky. 'I have a feeling it's going to rain, actually, which would be no bad thing. We could do with the water. Come on, let's go back, I could do with something to eat, apart from anything else.'

We climbed back into the jeep and sped off across country again. As we bumped along by the side of the field, I surreptitiously studied Mr Many-Acres sitting beside me. One arm was resting on the door, the other was casually guiding the wheel, his shirtsleeves rolled up to the elbows exposing already brown, muscly forearms. He hadn't shaved that morning, but that did nothing to detract from the strong chin and the classic jawline.

I looked away, wondering how many other girls had fallen for his rural charms down here: not that I had of course – yet – I mean at all, and nor would I, but I just wondered. It was, after all, interesting to muse, wasn't it? How many others, exactly? According to him, not many. Penny I discounted on the grounds that she was a historical figure and very much a mate now, but Serena. Ah Serena, she was a different matter. She was not only very current but very beautiful. I bet she looked great, flat on her back in a cornfield. For some reason my teeth seemed to grind together when I thought of this, and my top lip curled in an unattractive manner.

Where was she at the moment? Ah yes, filming. Dangerous job filming. All sorts of accidents occur, so I'm told; falling lights, masonry, scaffolding, that kind of thing. I wondered if anything untoward would befall her this weekend. Not that I wanted it to – dear me, no, nothing serious anyway. But perhaps if a piece of scenery did collapse – not too heavy mind, just a tree or something – and if she were to suffer, not a permanent injury, but something that would put her out of action for a while, briefly incapacitating her for, say, a couple of months? A broken leg maybe? And perhaps an arm too? Oh, and a touch of facial bruising, I added quickly, thinking she'd still look darned attractive lying in a hospital bed in plaster unless the face was, temporarily of course, disfigured. Well then, that would clear the way a bit, wouldn't it? Give me a bit of time. For what, Polly? What exactly did you have in mind? Goodness, I thought, shaking myself, sometimes I even managed to shock myself.

Chapter Sixteen

As Nick had promised, we spent the following day in true Enid Blyton style. Five Go Sailing on the Helford River: Nick, Tim, Rachel, Jamie and me. It was a fine, blustery morning, and we seemed to rocket across the river in record time. I'd always imagined sailing was a slow, rather sedate form of travel, but both Nick and Tim seemed to be speed merchants when it came to boating, doing their damnedest to get as much wind into the sail, and leaning right out over the side on a frighteningly dangerous rope affair, appropriately called a trapeze. I forced a jolly smile on to my rather green face, but was secretly extremely glad when we hit terra firma. I had a feeling it would take me a while to find my sea legs; if, indeed, I had any to be found.

We tied up the boat − or moored, as I'd come to call it, by the jetty on the Helford side and strolled up to the conveniently placed pub which overlooked the water. We laughed and chatted as we went, and I relished the prospect of crab sandwiches and ice-cold lager. This place was having a curious effect on me: I seemed to be permanently hungry. As we walked in, we greedily surveyed the list of goodies chalked up on the blackboard, licking our lips at the prospect of a boozy, slap-up lunch − at least, three of us did. Once we'd secured a table outside and sat down, Rachel declared that she wasn't in the least bit hungry, and was going for a walk with Jamie. 'Sometimes,' she announced, with more than a touch of the Greta Garbo's,

'I just want to be on my own – you know, to think things through a bit.'

She bit her lip and stared wistfully out to sea. Greta was now playing *The French Lieutenant's Woman*; all she needed was a hooded black cloak.

She sighed mournfully and turned back to us, 'I don't want to be rude, it's just – well, I've got so much on my mind at the moment. I just need a little time alone.'

Don't we all, darling, don't we all? But we don't make a big song and dance about it, do we? We don't sell tickets. We just creep off when no one's looking and lick our wounds in private, and when we return to the fold, we fervently hope that nobody noticed our absence, and if they did, we pretend we got stuck in the loo or something. But not our Rachel.

'It's just that – well, it all gets a bit much sometimes, and I have to get away,' she whispered, clutching Jamie to her breast, a pained expression on her peaky little face.

'Of course you do,' said Nick, looking concerned. He stood up and put a protective hand on her shoulder. 'You've been through a hell of a lot recently. I don't know how you've coped.'

Rachel sniffed a bit.

'Poor you, it must be awful,' agreed Tim. 'Shall we look after Jamie for you?'

'No, no,' she clung to him, chin up now, a brave little soldier look on her face. 'I'll carry him in his sling. I – I hope you don't mind, though, me going off like this?' Her eyes were wide and anxious.

'Not at all, not at all!' I chirped. 'Bye!'

'But will you be all right on your own?' asked Tim.

Would she be all right? For Christ's sake, she was going for a walk, not a bungee jump off the nearest suspension bridge – more's the pity. Of course she'd be all right.

Rachel bit her lip and nodded furiously, as if she didn't quite trust herself to speak.

I certainly didn't trust myself. Over the last couple of days it hadn't escaped my notice that, in her own quiet way, Rachel Marsden was one hell of a drama queen. She spent most of her time having long and meaningful discussions with Tim, the majority of which were conducted in huddled whispers by the drawing-room fire. He would gently prod and probe, asking her questions about Jamie, Adam, her father, and she would stare into space, twiddling a piece of hair around her finger before eventually muttering a monosyllable which you needed a hearing aid to catch.

This scintillating repartee would come to an abrupt halt if anyone was foolish enough to also want to sit by the only fire in this large and freezing-cold house. She would break off in the middle of one of her riveting replies such as, 'Um, I'm not sure,' or, 'Yes, perhaps,' and stare moodily into the flames, until the offending intruder got the hint and tiptoed off into another, colder room, at which point she would resume the halting discussion, pausing now and then to look up at Tim shyly from beneath her eyelashes.

It made me want to run to the nearest loo and stick my fingers down my throat, it all seemed so unbelievably phoney, but I wisely kept my counsel, not wanting to appear the arch bitch.

Tim found her fascinating and delighted in 'bringing her out of her shell', as he called it. He was patience itself, and regarded every muttered utterance on her part as a major breakthrough. Nick told me that Tim had always been brilliant in this respect, particularly with animals. I'd guffawed at the time, thinking this was a bit rich even with regard to Rachel, but I knew what he meant. He had a way of coaxing the timid and the shy, and Rachel certainly seemed to be opening up to him, but it occurred to me to wonder what Sarah thought about all this opening up while she slogged her guts out at the stables.

So here was our tragic heroine once again, standing on

301

the sea front, baby clasped to bosom. 'See you a bit later,' she whispered, and off she drooped, cardigan flapping in the breeze, hair straggling down her shoulders, head bowed against the elements.

'Bye-ee!' I trilled.

'Poor little thing,' muttered Nick.

'She just seems so . . .' Tim struggled for the right word. If it turned out to be 'vulnerable', I decided I'd have the screaming heebie-jeebies and throw myself headlong into the river, tearing my hair out en route.

' . . . defenceless,' he finished.

This was almost as bad. I ground my teeth together to stop them from seizing Tim's arm and shaking it like a dog.

'Hardly defenceless,' I said in what I hoped was a cool and level voice, but which I suspected had a touch of madness in it, 'I mean she's got you two socking great lads running round in circles, ready to defend her at a moment's notice.'

'Well, if she needed us of course we'd be there,' Tim agreed staunchly, failing to notice the shovel-load of irony I thought I'd piled on.

He folded his arms and leaned towards me over his pint. 'I must admit I find her fascinating. How well d'you know her, Polly?'

I sighed. 'Not well at all, she wasn't a friend of mine at school or anything.'

'So you only got to know her because of all this Adam and Jamie business?'

'Yes, and I'm quite sure our paths wouldn't have crossed otherwise,' I said with feeling.

Tim shook his head and looked thoughtful. 'You know, I get the feeling there's a lot more to Rachel than meets the eye. She's obviously extremely intelligent and very highly strung. I'd like to find out more about her, but it's so difficult to get her to talk, although I must say she's certainly started to chat a bit more since — Jack!'

He broke off in mid sentence to jump up and slap Jack Crawley on the back. Jack, by some miraculous stroke of good fortune, had appeared at our table, grinning from ear to ear and swaying violently. He was definitely the worse for a gin and tonic or six. I'd been groaning inwardly as Tim had opened up yet more discussion on the topic of the fascinating Rachel, so I was immensely pleased to see him.

'Hello there, one and all!' he boomed, clutching the table for support.

'Jack! What the devil are you doing here!' Nick quickly slipped a chair beneath his bottom as it headed floorwards.

Jack sat down heavily. 'Oops! Thanks, old man — just been to a drinks party at the yacht club, hell of a good do, you know, can't think why you weren't there. Christ, they make a mean Bloody Mary, though; nearly blew my socks off. Thought I'd pop in here on the way home and see if you reprobates were propping up the bar as usual, and here you are! I say, it's the gorgeous Polly again!'

He slipped a lecherous hand on to my knee, and leered into my eyes. I giggled and brushed him off.

'Been showing you round the haybarns again, has he?' he asked with a grin, winking towards Nick. 'Can't see what a sophisticated girl like you sees in a chap like that. You'd be much better off with me, you know!'

The hand reappeared on my knee, and the other one went around my shoulder. 'How about a little drinkie over at my place tonight? Slip into something a bit more comfortable, preferably diaph-, diaphan-, diaphanous — oops! Bit of a tongue-twister that one, when you've had a few. Anyway, you know what I mean, black netting, or chiffon or something, and come round at about, ooh, nine o'clock? That suit you?'

I giggled. 'That's way past my bedtime, Jack.'

'Splendid, splendid! Couldn't be better! S'way past mine, too, so that's where I'll be, in the bedroom — you can't miss it, top of the stairs, second on the left. I'll be the wildly attractive one lying on the square flat thing in the corner with not a lot on, now what d'you say? Eh?'

And so he went on, flirting outrageously, falling over his words and making us scream with laughter as he recounted what I suspected were mostly apocryphal tales of his love affairs with what seemed like the entire female population of Helford.

It only took Nick or Tim to prompt him with, 'And what about that blonde one, Jack?' or, 'Whatever happened to Sue?' and Jack would be weeping with laughter into his pint as he recounted yet another romp in the hay, the back of the Land Rover, the stable, or even — so he claimed — the covering yard.

We spent an entirely happy hour or so, laughing and joking and trying unsuccessfully to stop Jack pouring yet more drink down his throat. Eventually he admitted defeat and got unsteadily to his feet.

'S'no good, y'know, I can't sit here all day chatting to the likes of you lot. Some of us have got work to do. Some of us have got mares to service!'

Just then Rachel appeared around the corner.

'And speaking of mares, here's another pretty filly!'

Tim got up quickly and gave her his seat. 'Rachel, this is Jack Crawley, a neighbour of ours. Jack, Rachel.'

Jack took Rachel's hand and held it to his lips, as was his wont. 'Enchanted,' he murmured in his practised manner.

Rachel frowned and pulled her hand away as soon as was politely possible.

'Rachel's staying with us for a while, with young Jamie here,' Tim explained as she sat down.

Jack chivalrously pushed her chair in for her and made an exaggerated sweeping bow. He lost his balance and staggered slightly on the way up. 'Delighted to hear it. The more girls the merrier, I always say!'

Not in this case, I thought grimly.

Rachel smiled thinly, looking at his bloodshot eyes with distaste, clearly deciding he wasn't worth even the briefest of hellos.

'So this must be young Jamie!' Jack roared, undeterred by the chilly reception he was getting. 'I say, what a fine-looking chap, look at those rosy little cheeks! How are you, young fella?'

He leaned, or even lurched across the table to tickle his face, and no doubt poor Jamie got covered in an entire brewery's worth of fumes, but Rachel's reaction was, nonetheless, unforgivable.

She swept Jamie away out of Jack's reach and turned to him with a look of utter loathing. 'Keep your hands off my baby, you disgusting old drunk!' she hissed.

Jack drew back in alarm, retrieving his hand as if he'd been burned, his mouth wide with disbelief.

There was a moment's shocked silence as this gratuitous attack was digested. Rachel, pink with fury, stared defiantly at Jack, who was rooted to the spot. It was probably the stillest he'd managed to stand all lunchtime.

Nick leaped in quickly and put his arm round Rachel's shoulder. 'Jack didn't mean any harm, Rachel, he's a friend of ours, he wouldn't hurt Jamie!'

' 'Course he bloody wouldn't!' I added staunchly, rage pouring from my nostrils.

'I say, certainly not,' muttered Jack, puce with embarrassment. 'Most awfully sorry and all that, didn't mean to frighten you or anything.'

Tim looked at her kindly. 'I'll get you a drink, shall I? You're just a bit overwrought, that's all.'

Rachel looked at the shocked faces assembled around the table and burst into tears. 'I'm sorry,' she sobbed. 'It's just — I have to be so careful, I hate anyone coming near him, I'm so sorry!'

'There now, it's all right,' soothed Tim. His hand

305

covered hers on the table. 'Of course you feel like that, it's only natural after what you've been through, but old Jack here wouldn't hurt a fly, you know.'

Old Jack was doing a good job at catching them, though, as he stood facing her, wide-mouthed and incredulous. 'Lord, no, 'course not!' he mumbled.

'I know, and I'm so sorry, I do apologise, I totally overreacted,' managed Rachel at last, between sniffles. She looked up at him. 'I'm — I'm just a bit nervous about anyone touching my baby at the moment, you see.' She blew her nose noisily into a hankie.

'Quite understand, quite understand,' said Jack, who clearly didn't. He shook his head vigorously. 'Can't be too careful these days, can you? Best forgotten now though, eh?'

Rachel nodded and smiled briefly. 'Yes, absolutely.' She turned to Tim. 'I think I will have that drink now, Tim, if you don't mind.'

'Sure,' he got to his feet. 'Gin and tonic?'

'Please. I'll just go and wash my face. Rachel got up and headed towards the Ladies'.

Jack turned to me and raised his eyebrows. 'I say, what about that?' he said quietly. 'I don't mind drunk, or even disgusting, but old!' He looked at me in horror and I giggled.

Jack polished off his pint. 'Might just slip off, though. Don't want to catch the sharp end of that one's tongue again. One always knows the women one can and can't charm, and I couldn't charm the shoes off that one, let alone the pants. Bye all!' and with that he donned his flat cap and hastily withdrew.

Rachel returned looking composed but, I was pleased to see, slightly shamefaced. As she sat down there was an awkward silence, and I for one was determined not to break it. I hoped it was killing her.

Tim took pity and smiled, handing her her drink.

'Before Jack arrived, I was about to ask Polly how you two knew each other. I gather you didn't bump into each other much at school?'

Rachel took a sip of her gin and visibly relaxed. 'No, Polly was a few years above me, but I knew of her of course. Everyone at school had heard of Polly, she had quite a reputation!' She smiled at me and I tried not to fall off my stool.

Heavens! Could this be for real? Was Rachel paying me a compliment? I beamed graciously at her. Ah yes, it was true, of course, I had been a bit of a lad. A bit of a one for the dastardly deeds – shimmying down knotted sheets from dormitory windows, putting salt in the headmistress's tea – all pretty mundane stuff in retrospect, but jolly daring at the time.

'Oh yes,' Rachel went on, warming to her theme, 'there are so many stories about Polly I hardly know where to begin!'

I was keen for her to begin wherever she felt like it, if it was going to make me look terrific.

'Most of them apocryphal, I'm sure,' I said bashfully, lowering my eyes and playing with a beer mat to keep me from rubbing my hands together with glee, 'or, at least, exaggerated,' I added quickly, lest anyone should think the daredevil stunts Rachel was about to recount were entirely make-believe.

'What sort of things?' asked Nick, intrigued.

Yes, what sort of things Rachel? I was on the edge of my seat. I was vaguely aware that I'd been regarded as a bit of a coolie by the lower forms, but I'd no idea I'd gone down in the annals of schoolgirl history as some kind of wild and abandoned folk heroine. A sort of Joan of Arc of the Upper Fifth.

'Well, let me think now . . .' Rachel frowned as she tried to remember some of the more hilarious anecdotes.

I leaned forward eagerly, wishing I could prompt her,

but realising that might look a bit keen.

'Oh yes, I know!' she said.

Oh goodie!

'What about that time you were caught handing out drugs to everyone. D'you remember that, Polly?' Rachel turned to me with wide, innocent eyes.

Drugs! The word hit me hard in the face and seemed to stick there, slap in the middle of my forehead, written up in red. I caught Nick's rather shocked face out of the corner of my eye, and nearly gagged on a slice of gin-soaked lemon as my elbow went into overdrive, chucking it down my throat. Christ! What the bloody hell was she up to? I retrieved the lemon from my tonsils and brushed the gin off my chin in what I hoped was a nonchalant manner.

'Oh well, hardly drugs eh, Rachel?' I said lightly, cranking up a smile. 'I mean a few magic mushrooms mixed with the leaves of what I thought was a marijuana plant, but which in fact turned out to be an Aspidistra — I mean that hardly constitutes hard drugs does it? No one's going to mainline on Aspidistra leaves and mushrooms, are they?'

Nick and Tim roared with laughter. Phew. What a relief.

'Oh God, Polly,' said Nick. 'I can just see you chopping up Aspidistra leaves and cramming them furtively into little plastic bags!'

'Was that all it was?' Rachel looked disappointed. 'Oh, I'd heard there was more to it than that. I thought the police were called in and—'

'Good Lord, no!' I cut in hastily, 'No, no — nothing like that!'

There had, admittedly, been a brief interview with the headmistress in her study on account of the wooziness of one or two faint hearts in my dorm, and yes, this particular interview had in fact taken place in the presence of one Police Constable Moore from the local constabulary, but one piddly little village constable hardly amounts to calling in the police, does it? I mean, come on, Miss Marsden, we're not talking Miami Vice here, are we? And anyway, once I'd explained that I'd merely been attempting to make some herbal tea and had distributed it around the dorm on the grounds that it might be a soothing bedtime relaxant, all had been forgiven and forgotten, as I sincerely hoped it would be now.

'You see, that's how these little stories get exaggerated!' I cried, laughing nervously and taking a slug more gin: my throat was inexplicably dry. Come on, Rachel, get off the subject of drugs and police and on to some of my more amusing escapades, like the time I streaked naked through the village for a bet, or what about when I—

'Oh yes!' she announced, raising her index finger.

Oh good, I thought with relief. But it was oh bad.

'What about that dreadful business when you were caught cheating in your history O-level — looking at someone else's paper or something. D'you remember that, Polly?'

I did, and I didn't like the taste of sawdust in my mouth or the nasty glint in her eye. This was most definitely below the belt; so far below that I felt my knees sag in my leggings.

Of course I hadn't cheated. The very idea. No, it was all perfectly simple. Sophie Maxwell, sitting next to me, had dropped her paper and I'd merely picked it up, pausing, of course, to glance at it and to check that — well, to check that her name was at the top of the paper and that it was in fact hers, before handing it back to her. Wouldn't anyone? Anyone, it appeared, except the ghastly invigilator who hauled me out of the exam room and accused me of nicking Sophie's dates. The historical kind of course.

I narrowed my eyes at my new accuser. 'That was all a big misunderstanding,' I said slowly, sounding, I hoped, rather like Margaret Thatcher, 'a total misunderstanding which was cleared up very quickly. There was a full inquiry, and I'm pleased to say I was fully vindicated.'

'Ah,' said Rachel thoughtfully, 'I wondered. I mean, after all, you didn't pass, did you? So it wasn't as if you even benefited. Am I right in thinking you were the only girl to leave St Gertrude's with absolutely no qualifications whatsoever? What a scream!'

Not nearly as much of a scream as you'll make when I get my hands round your throat, I thought savagely.

'But am I right?' persisted Rachel. 'Did you get any?'

I ground my fingernails into my rather damp palms, thinking that it must surely be time Rachel went for another walk, along the clifftops perhaps, perilously close to the edge.

Nick looked confused. 'Oh no, no, that can't be right, can it, Polly? Because on your CV it says you got six O-levels, I distinctly remember.'

Which in turn distinctly reminded me of something I'd temporarily forgotten. This was my boss we were talking to, or rather, Rachel was talking to. Surely there were rules about this sort of thing? Unions to complain to, punishments to hand out. Surely she couldn't get away with it without a life sentence to contend with?

'It was six, wasn't it?' repeated Nick.

My eyes glazed over and my mouth opened bravely. What on earth would come out of it? I marvelled at its courage. What form of words would it deem appropriate? I sat waiting, as they did too, for my lips and tongue to surge into action.

'That's right, six. I took them at a Crammer,' I spluttered. Brilliant! Absolutely bloody brilliant! Who needs O-levels when your mouth can say things like that, eh?

'Which one?' piped up Rachel, but she was fighting a losing battle. No one was terribly interested in which Crammer I'd gone to.

'Which one? Oh, one in Oxford,' I said vaguely, 'can't remember the name of it. Would anyone like another drink?'

'No thanks,' said Tim, draining his glass. 'We'd better be getting back, I've got work to do.'

And so have I, I thought savagely as we sailed across the river ten minutes later. It was called murdering a fellow house-guest in cold blood without anyone noticing. If only I'd read more Agatha Christie. Perhaps I could just slip her over the side? I peered into the water. It looked pretty deep and cold, eminently suitable, but this was a very small boat and I didn't think I could subtly up-end her into the murky depths without drawing attention to my actions and ending up in deep water myself. I would bide my time, I thought, grinding my teeth to pulp. Revenge, they say, is a meal best eaten cold.

I was still quietly seething when we got back to the house. Nick disappeared to tend to his sheep, so I made for the only warm chair in the house, the one Rachel usually bagged by the fire. I found a little footstool for my feet, and arranged the intelligent bits of the Sunday papers decoratively around me, although of course in reality I was shaping up to an hour or two's uninterrupted kip.

Rachel curled up on the rug by my feet. I shut my eyes and thought how amusing it would be if my leg had one of those involuntary spasms that sometimes occur when you're almost dropping off to sleep, and I inadvertently kicked her in the teeth. My foot twitched eagerly but I held it back. It might, after all, look a little too obvious.

I drifted off into a glorious dream in which I was quite the heroine of the hour as I singlehandedly delivered twin lambs. It was late at night and Nick was in the Dutch barn, where he'd been struggling for hours with a heavily pregnant ewe who was groaning in agony as she tried to give birth. Alerted by all the noise, I appeared in a rather fetching little nightie, and because my arm was thinner

311

than his, was about to stick it up the sheep's whatsit and deliver the lambs. (I knew, of course, that in reality this would have been absolutely impossible because at the merest hint of blood I'd have been heaving and chucking all over the place, but happily, of course, in dreams, one can ride roughshod over little details like that.) Anyway, suffice to say, Nick was absolutely delighted, beaming at me and showering me with compliments and praises, in fact – yes, that's right, he was hugging me, giving me a great big bear hug when, all of a sudden, Tim's voice piped up in the distance.

'Come on, Rachel!'

I opened one eye. He was over by the grand piano, patting the stool in an encouraging manner. 'Come on, come and give us a tune, it's about time we heard you play!'

I groaned softly. Oh God, we were bringing out Rachel again. I shut the eye and snored softly, hoping to suggest that I for one did not relish the prospect of being hauled from the Land of Nod by Rachel doing her party piece.

'Oh no, I couldn't,' said Rachel.

I couldn't resist a peep. She was huddled by the fire, smiling shyly and twiddling her hair.

'Oh come on,' urged Tim. 'We'd all love to hear you!'

Speak for yourself, I thought grimly.

'Oh no, really, not now . . .'

'Oh please do,' said Sarah, who had just arrived back from the stables. 'No one ever plays that piano unless it's to bash out "chopsticks" or something.'

'Oh no, I don't think I could.'

'Oh, please.'

'No, really.'

Just as I was about to rise up from my chair like a woman possessed, charge across the room and single-handedly ram the entire grand piano into her mouth, she demurred.

'Oh well, OK. I'll just play a bit of Bach.'

She shuffled over to the piano and sat down. I braced myself. She flexed her fingers around a bit, and then she played. And I have to say it brought a lump even to my cynical throat. As the music filled the room, full of sadness and heartbreak and loss, I listened and stared, mesmerised. She certainly had a gift, a real talent. It was almost as if she'd become a different person. I blinked. That surely wasn't Rachel Marsden over there, venting all that passion and emotion, was it?

It was a long piece, but we were all on the edge of our seats, and when she finished, there was a moment's silence. Then we all clapped like mad, even me, which I thought was big of me.

'Bravo! Bravo!' shouted Tim.

Rachel smiled shyly. 'Thanks,' she whispered, looking down at her hands. 'It really wasn't awfully good, you know.'

She slipped off the stool and slunk over to the fire again to resume her hunched, gnome-like position once again. All emotion had gone, all passion was spent. Rachel, the tight-lipped little mouse was back *in situ* again.

Tim was in raptures, falling over himself to praise her. 'But that was fantastic, Rachel! I've never heard anyone play like that and, honestly, I may strike you as a philistine, but I have been to quite a few piano recitals. You really should take it up professionally, you know, I'm quite sure you're good enough. I honestly think you could be a concert pianist or something.'

'Oh well, one day maybe,' murmured Rachel.

'You really should try, you know, you've got so much talent. Don't you think so, Polly?'

'Definitely,' I muttered.

After this, of course, there was no stopping her, and with more encouragement from Tim, she performed for Nick when he arrived back from the farm. All the pieces she played were serious and melancholy, and marvellous though it all was, I felt ready to slit my wrists at the end of it. I also realised, with a dull thud of my heart, that it was time to go home.

I sighed and pulled a train timetable out of the bookcase, flipping through it miserably. I looked at the clock. God, at this rate I'd be back in London at about three a.m; I really must go and pack and get someone to take me to the station. The idea of leaving Cornwall filled me with doom and gloom. Who would have thought I'd want to swap the bright lights for cow pats so quickly? Of course, that wasn't the whole story, it had more to do with finding a different set of bright lights, namely the ones shining in those dark eyes over there. They met mine as I looked up from the timetable, and advanced towards me. I gulped as Nick sat on the sofa beside me and instinctively lifted my thighs up a bit to make them look thinner.

He took the book from my hands and snapped it shut. 'Is there any real need to go back tonight?'

Oh heavens, he was going to be all masterful. My knees began to wobble with excitement, and I had to abandon the raised thigh position.

'Well, no, I suppose I could go back in the morning — but I'd be a bit late for work.'

'And who would be there to care?'

I took his point, but wanted to appear conscientious. I frowned. 'There's quite a lot to do you know,' I said piously, 'all the scripts for the Din-Din's Dog Food pitch have to be typed up, not to mention the entire presentation.'

'Well, I've yet to write it, so it can hardly be typed.'

'Even so, the work will be piling up.'

'Rubbish. I'm not there so why should you be? You might just as well stay here for a while.'

For a while? My heart did a backward flip-flap and danced merrily around in my ribcage. He wanted me to stay! He really wanted me to stay – or, to put it another way, he simply didn't want me to leave him! Of course. Yes, it was obvious. Over the last two days he'd become totally besotted with me, and whereas previously he couldn't bear to have me *in* his sight, he now couldn't bear to have me *out* of it. What a funny old world. I tried my voice.

'I'd – I'd love to . . .' too high. I coughed and tried again. 'I'd really love to stay, I – I really would, I just love it here, it's all so beautiful – the countryside, the house, the animals and oh – just everything. I haven't been as happy as this for ages!' I gushed.

Steady Polly steady, don't overdo it. I took a few deep breaths and tried to calm myself.

'Good!' He tossed the timetable over the back of the sofa. 'That settles it, then. To be honest I really can't be fagged to drive you to the station.' He grinned.

I winced, but managed to smile back as I caught the body blow. Ouch. It had hurt quite a bit actually, but not enough to entirely dampen my spirits. If you really wanted someone to leave you'd move heaven and earth to get them to the station, wouldn't you? I mean, if someone was really getting on your tits, a little forty minute car ride would be a breeze, wouldn't it? Absolutely. I realised, though, that I might have to review his besottedness in the light of this comment. Later. Much later. For the moment I was happy just sitting here on the sofa, close to him – really quite close to him indeed. I'd say there was no less than, what – three inches between our respective buttocks?

He flung his arm along the back of the sofa, fixed me with his liquid brown's and talked about the farm. I sighed happily and thought about the farmer. Blissikins.

'Sorry, am I boring you?'

'What? No of course not! Why?'

'I thought you yawned.'

'Did I? Oh! No just a sigh. I was just thinking – well, I was just thinking how nice it is to be staying on, um, for a bit – not long of course, just a bit.'

'Stay as long as you want,' he replied with a dazzling smile.

'Thank you,' I whispered, staring into his glorious deep brown eyes and wondering if we were talking weeks, or months or even . . . No, don't be silly, Polly. I gave myself a little shake and listened attentively as he spoke of crop yields and lambing figures, nodding intelligently and asking pertinent questions, as any good farmer's wife, I mean, secretary should.

Chapter Seventeen

The next few days flew past. Rachel and Jamie stayed mostly at the house, and Tim and Sarah went back to work, which left Nick and me. We walked for miles, sat in quiet little pubs eating crab sandwiches and treacle tart and talked endlessly. When we weren't walking, talking or eating, we were either rowing or sailing – depending on the wind – up and down the river.

On one particularly sunny morning, as we drifted slowly up Frenchman's Creek, I lay back in the boat and pulled my straw hat down over my face. Through the holes in the straw I could peer at Nick without being observed. His black hair was tousled and his face, if not brown, was certainly ruddy after just a few days in this early April sunshine. All week his increasingly tanned forearms had stuck out of an array of denim shirts and baggy jumpers, and today it was the turn of a rather countrified checked number to expose him to the elbows.

I stared at his strong hands as they gripped the oars tightly, expertly guiding the boat around rocks and overhanging branches, and tried to remember what they'd looked like when they'd held documents and files and protruded from the sleeves of a pinstriped suit in an office in South Kensington. Then I tried to imagine all of him back in South Kensington. Funny, it seemed like another world, and one that he didn't belong to at all. Did I belong? Where was my world?

I shut my eyes and imagined for a moment that it was here. And not just in a small way, but in a mighty big way — so big, in fact, that within a twinkling I was mistress of Trewarren, wife to Mr Nicholas Penhalligan and mother of his — ooh, let's see, five, no — six children. It was the work of a moment. And within another moment, I'd pictured myself in Trewarren's kitchen, up to my elbows in cake mixture, singing away tunefully as I baked a cake for tea.

Now and again I'd smile down indulgently as my black-haired, brown-eyed babies frolicked around at my feet, happy with their finger paints and their Play-doh, and with none of that unnecessary shouting and screaming that seems to accompany most children's games. They were certainly the most angelic of babies, and one or two of them — or perhaps even all of them — were capable of changing their own nappies, had done so since birth, in fact; and they'd never been sick in their lives. But I digress.

As I poured my Victoria Sponge mixture into a baking tin, the kitchen door opened, and who should appear, fresh from the fields, with the smell of corn in his hair and a special kind of wife-hungry light in his eyes, but my husband, the farmer. I wiped my floury hands on my apron, and greeted him with a tender kiss. Filled with a passion that hadn't wavered for a moment during four wonderful years of marriage — hang on, how many children did I say? Well some of them were obviously twins, er — yes, all of them, actually, three sets of twins — anyway, filled with this passion, he seized me firmly around the waist and pulled me, quite roughly really, towards him.

Under his coarse, tweed jacket which tickled my face, I could feel his hard, muscly body rippling against me, simply aching to take me upstairs, or perhaps — yes, that was it, what he really wanted to do was to ravish me right here and now on the kitchen table.

318

'How about it?' his eyes seemed to say. I glanced down at the children. 'Not now,' my own eyes seemed to say, a smile playing around my luscious lips, 'later.'

Panting hard, but somehow managing to control himself, he gazed deep into my sapphire eyes and planted a long lingering kiss on my full, rosy lips, marvelling, for the umpteenth time, at his supreme good fortune in finding himself such a terrific wife, who was not only effortlessly capable and ran the house with sizzling efficiency, but was also devastatingly attractive and downright saucy in the bedroom.

I frowned under my hat. Would the capable and efficient bit be a problem? I scratched my chin thoughtfully. I dare say I could learn, but – wait a minute, why bother? Why on earth should I be immersed in cake mixture? Surely I'd have a cook? Yes, of course. I wouldn't be in the kitchen at all, I'd be in the morning room!

Quick as a flash there was a speedy scene change and I was transported to the morning room, seated at my writing desk with the sun streaming in behind me through the huge bay window. Now what was I doing? Ah yes, planning the menu for a forthcoming dinner party. Such a bore, but one must entertain the locals occasionally: the Master of the Hunt, the neighbouring farmers etc; they expected it, and of course I did it so well.

I took off my diamond bracelet – a wedding present from my husband, but so incredibly heavy it made writing difficult – and jotted down the courses: watercress soup, followed by salmon en croute, followed by raspberries and cream. There, that should do it. Oh, and I must remind Jenkins to get the appropriate wine from the cellar – or would Nick do that? I wasn't sure.

Anyway, I got up from my desk, pausing only to smooth a few wrinkles out of the wonderfully understated navy blue Armani dress I was wearing, and adjusted my pearl

319

choker – another wedding, no, anniversary present from my husband. I caught a glimpse of myself in the mirror. The pearls looked so good around my throat, gleaming away against my Christmas-in-the-Caribbean suntan.

As I passed by the window I spotted my delicious children being either pushed in prams or carried around the immaculate gardens by a tribe of uniformed Norland nannies. I opened the window and blew them all a kiss – 'Co-ee darlings!' They waved back adoringly.

I drifted on into the kitchen in search of my cook, Mrs Bridges – no all right, too obvious – Mrs, um, Smith.

'Ah, Mrs Smith there you are. You'll be pleased to hear I've finally decided on tomorrow night's menu.' And so saying, I'd sink languidly into the large wheelback chair by the Aga and cross my slim, silk-stockinged legs.

'Very good, M'am,' she'd say, wiping her floury hands on her apron (*her* floury hands, note – not mine), and giving me her undivided attention. Would she curtsey? No, of course not, don't be stupid, Polly.

I leaned forward and fixed her with my capable, efficient eye. 'Now, as you know, Mr Penhalligan is very partial to watercress soup so I thought—' Just then, just as I was in the middle of briefing my cook, the door flew open and in strode my husband – fresh from the fields, smell of corn in hair, wife-hungry look in eye, etc, etc. Without pausing for a moment, he strode over to the chair, took me in his arms and – oh, just *before* he took me in his arms, Mrs Smith suddenly got an urgent telephone call from the butchers, saying the joint she'd ordered was ready and would she please come and pick it up *immediately* because, um – because otherwise it would go off. So off she rushed, and as soon as the door had closed behind her, he strode over to the chair, corn in hair, wife-hungry look, and took me in his arms. His breath was roaring away in my ears. 'Oh my darling!' he murmured, 'I want you so badly!' He kissed me hungrily, then he lifted me into his arms and strode to the table where he set me down, and roughly but gently, but firmly but roughly, he—

'What on earth are you doing?' My hat flew off my face at the very best bit and I looked up to see Nick, my boss – friend at most, but certainly not my husband – staring down at me, a puzzled look on his face.

'Are you all right?'

I sat up guiltily. 'What? Yes, of course. Sorry what was I doing?'

'Well, you've been muttering and sort of squirming and wriggling. At one point you started moaning, quite loudly actually, about watercress. I thought perhaps you were having a nightmare, except you seemed to be rather enjoying it.'

'Ah! Yes – well, you're right, you see I was dreaming! I fell asleep and – and had this awful feeling that great clumps of watercress were bearing down on me, like – like the Triffids. It all came rising up out of the river and got me round the neck, like this!' I demonstrated, clasping my throat hard. I shivered. 'Phew, lucky you woke me when you did. That was no joke, I can tell you!'

'You look rather hot, your face is terribly red.'

'Is it?' I fanned my flaming face with my hat. 'That's probably because I thought I was being strangled, all the blood probably went to my face.'

'Are they always so vivid?'

'What?'

'Your dreams.'

'Oh! Oh yes, always. God, sometimes I cry out and . . . and thrash around. Once I even got up and walked downstairs. I've got such a terrific imagination you see, and it all seems so real. I'm hell to sleep with.'

'Really?' Nick raised his eyebrows.

I fanned my face even harder as it got hotter and hotter. 'Well, no, having said that, no I'm not, I'm pretty easy to

321

sleep with actually — easy in the sense that, well in the sense that I'm not difficult . . . I mean, no one's actually ever complained — not that there have been many who would — complain I mean, simply because there really haven't been that many, if you see what I mean.' Things were getting decidedly out of hand here.

Nick roared with laughter. 'Polly, you are hysterical. I really couldn't care less how many people you've slept with or whether or not they've complained. It's none of my business.'

'Well I haven't,' I said crossly, indignant now, and keen to set the record straight, 'slept with many, that is, and the few that I have haven't complained either, so there.'

I childishly turned my back on him and stared down into the water, furious with myself for behaving like an idiot, and furious with him for not wanting it to be any of his business. I could feel my face heating up the river. God I was a moron.

Nick rowed on, and I couldn't see his face but I was sure he was laughing at me. Determined not to turn around, I let my hand drift along in the water, grabbing at reeds and bulrushes and pretending I was thoroughly absorbed by the ripples.

The silence was deafening but I wasn't going to break it, he would just jolly well have to be nice to me for a change, and he'd have to make a real effort. How dare he laugh at me like that and — and how dare he be so rude? He needn't think he could get round me with a couple of glasses of cider and a ploughman's lunch either, oh no, he'd have to do better than that.

'Polly?' said Nick after a while.

'Hmm?' I responded sulkily. Whatever he wanted, the answer was no.

'I thought I might go to Gweek this afternoon. It's about time I looked in on Mum; she'll think I'm avoiding her. D'you want to come?'

'Oh yes please!' I spun around eagerly. 'I'd love to come!'

'Good. I'll give her a ring when we get back.'

Sulk? What sulk. It was high time I met my mother-in-law.

And so it was that a few hours later I found myself being driven off to meet Mrs Penhalligan. I mean surely. Come on. He could quite easily have gone on his own, couldn't he? It would have been much more natural to say, 'Hope you don't mind, but I must go and see my mother, can you amuse yourself this afternoon?' But no. No, it was important that I came too.

As we whizzed along in the Land Rover, I unclenched my nervous hands and smoothed out the skirt of my Laura Ashley dress.

Nick had looked highly amused when I'd waltzed down the stairs in this particular number, but there was no doubt in my mind that it was absolutely perfect. To capture the essence of this dress, one really has to refer to it as a 'frock', a sort of spriggy cotton muslin affair with daisies and an itsy-bitsy collar and a flouncy skirt. Twee, I grant you, but it's only ever worn on 'meet the parents' outings, and it's never failed me yet. Eminently suitable.

I tucked a little lace hanky into the sleeve for good measure, and gave Country Girl just one more chance, restricting it this time to wrists only and not backs of knees, neck, or other assorted pulse points.

Now. Chocolates? Flowers? Daffodils would be a little like coals to Newcastle, I decided, so I settled for chocolates and ordered Nick to stop at the village shop. He obeyed, and looked even more amused when I reappeared bearing a large box of fudge.

'Who's that for?'

'Your mother, of course.'

He exploded with laughter at the wheel.

'What's so funny?'

'Nothing, it's just that that's what all the plebby tourists buy to take back to Purley or Dagenham. Look at the label.'

I turned it over and saw, 'A present from Cornwall' in olde-worlde writing surrounded by gnomes and fairies. I sighed and tossed it into the back seat. I knew I should have gone for the clotted cream.

As we rounded the corner into Gweek, I was pleasantly surprised to see that it had a rather refreshing, businesslike air about it. Helford was undoubtedly prettier, but it was very much a holiday homes and cream teas village. Gweek, on the other hand, was a village where real people lived and worked. No cutesy cottages here; in fact the only one I saw was right on the edge of the village, perched on the top of a hill. It was whitewashed and thatched with honeysuckle rampaging around the front door and clematis winding its way around the windows. A large tabby cat sat sunning herself on the doorstep.

'That's Mum's place,' said Nick as we sped past.

'Oh! How pretty!' I nearly twisted my head off in an effort to catch a glimpse. 'But why aren't we stopping?'

An icy hand gripped my heart. Had he got cold feet? Had second thoughts? Couldn't bring himself to introduce someone as gauche and stupid as me to his undoubtedly highly sophisticated, elegant mother?

'Because she won't be there, she'll be in here.'

We rounded a corner and scrunched to a halt on the gravel drive of a pub just outside the village.

'Oh!' I was deeply shocked. You wouldn't catch my mother in the Fox and Hounds in Esher High Street on a Thursday afternoon. The Conservative Party Bring-and-Buy sale, perhaps, but not the Fox and Hounds.

'Has she got a problem?'

My vision of the immaculate Mrs Penhalligan, dressed in twinset and pearls and deftly arranging chrysanthemums in a crystal vase in her drawing room, was plummeting fast in the direction of a whisky swilling bag lady, pub-crawling her way round southern Cornwall.

Nick laughed. 'Good God, no, I mean she certainly likes a drink, but it's not a problem.' He held open the door for me.

'So what's she doing in here in the middle of the afternoon?' I asked suspiciously as I ducked to avoid a low beam.

'This is where she gets her inspiration.'

'Inspiration? For what?'

'You'll see.'

My eyes took a while to adjust from the bright sunshine outside to the near darkness of the saloon bar, but when they did, Hetty Penhalligan was the very first person I saw.

She was sitting in the corner by an open window which shot the only beam of light into the gloomy room, surrounding her in a faint halo-like gleam and lighting up the unmistakable Penhalligan features.

Although I recognised her instantly, she was totally unexpected. I'd somehow assumed that the boys had inherited the Roman nose and square, determined jaw from their father, but in fact they sat very well on her strong, chiselled face. Her black hair, now streaked with grey, was cut in a sharp, geometric bob which complemented her striking features. She was a handsome woman.

I fluffed up my skirt and set my face in a sweet girlie smile as I followed Nick over to her but, as we got closer, my sweet smile froze and I had a violent urge to tear my frock from my back and run to the nearest Oxfam shop.

For that is undoubtedly where Mrs Penhalligan bought her clothes. Over a pair of baggy blue mechanic's overalls – or was it a boiler suit? Yes, it was a boiler suit – anyway, over this she was sporting a man's tweed jacket with the sleeves rolled up to her elbows. Around her neck was a spotty red handkerchief and on her feet were a pair of what looked like hobnailed Doc Marten boots. The whole ensemble was splattered with paint as if someone had systematically flicked the entire contents of a Dulux factory at her.

She didn't look up as we approached, but kept her eyes firmly on an old man sitting opposite her, staring at him in a peculiarly penetrating way. His eyes were staring equally fixedly into his pint.

As the penny dropped it activated my jaw which swung open with surprise. A painter! Propped up in front of her was a canvas, to which she added a couple of quick daubs, and, to her left, a glass of white wine which was rather an odd colour. It became apparent why, when she absentmindedly dipped her paint brush in it, mistaking it for the water.

'Damn!' she bellowed, 'I keep *doing* that! Barney, get me another drink, will you? This one's gone Prussian blue again.'

She waved the offending glass at the barman, and then caught sight of Nick. 'Darling!' she cried, in a crackly, gin-soaked voice, 'what a lovely surprise!'

Nick kissed her. 'Hi Mum, thought I might find you in here.'

He settled himself down next to her.

'And who's this charming little flower?' she asked, her eyes roaming over the itsy-bitsy frock.

'Oh this is Polly McLaren, a friend of mine.'

'Hello Mrs Penhalligan,' I said, holding out my hand and smiling.

'You must call me Hetty, everybody does,' she said, taking my hand. 'Oh look, how silly of me, now you've got paint all over you. Here,' she handed me a piece of oily rag and I wiped my hand.

I felt absurdly self-conscious in my frock, and faintly irritated that Nick hadn't warned me. It wasn't as if I couldn't have looked the part, too: I had a whole collection of arty-farty clothes back at the house just aching for an outing. There was that lovely French peasant's smock and the pedal-pushers and, oh, all manner of bohemian gear. I whipped the lace hanky out of my sleeve and hitched the ghastly skirt up a bit when I sat down.

'Barney, for Christ's sake!' she roared, making me jump out of my skin. 'It's like the bloody Gobi desert in here. Line up three gin and tonics, will you, there's a love.'

Barney grinned good humouredly from behind the bar, put down the glass he'd been wiping, and hastened to oblige his customer. It had to be worth his while, she was a pretty colourful asset for any pub — cheaper than buying a fruit machine, I thought to myself.

'So how's it going, then?' asked Nick, straddling a stool next to his mother and peering over her shoulder at the picture. 'Been discovered yet?'

' 'Course I bloody haven't,' she boomed — this seemed to be the only volume her voice could manage — 'the philistines around here wouldn't know a decent canvas if they stuck their heads through it. All they want is chocolate-boxy pastoral scenes or little children with tears running down their cheeks. Ugh. No, I'm afraid I'm just going to have to kill myself. Nothing like a dead artist to send prices soaring through the roof.'

'Or cut your ear off?' I suggested tentatively.

'Might work,' she agreed, 'bit messy though.'

I looked at the painting. It was a riot of blotches and blobs and I could quite see why the locals weren't too enamoured. I thought it was dreadful. But I also knew, from my experiences at private views in London, that what I thought were unspeakably bad pictures were usually deemed to be extremely good.

'It's awfully good,' I lied creepily.

Nick guffawed loudly. 'Looks like someone's been sick!'

Hetty ignored her son and addressed herself to me

327

instead. 'Thank you, my dear. Yes, it is rather, isn't it?' she agreed calmly. 'But then it helps to have a sitter as ugly as Arthur here. Bags of character.'

I glanced quickly at poor Arthur and hoped he was deaf as well as ugly. Hetty's voice had a certain resonance about it which made it hard to miss. Luckily he appeared to be not only deaf but brain dead too, as he sank further and further into his pint.

'Thank you, Arthur!' she yelled at the top of her voice, prodding him in the arm. 'That will be all for today!'

He waggled a bony hand in acknowledgement and raised his watery old eyes briefly from his beer.

I smiled at him. Sweet old man. It took me a few seconds to realise that he wasn't a sweet old man at all. He leered nastily at me and, rolling over on to his left buttock, let rip with a fart of such asphyxiating intensity it left me positively reeling. I gasped. Something had obviously crawled up and died inside him.

Hetty fixed him with her steely glare. 'I said thank you, Arthur, that will be all.'

But Arthur seemed unwilling to leave the cosy little gathering and join the rest of his cronies in the public bar. He sat resolutely still, leering into his pint.

Hetty sighed and got to her feet. 'Let's go and sit in the garden. It's much too stuffy in here anyway.'

Stuffy was the mildest possible way to describe the putrefied atmosphere that prevailed, courtesy of Arthur, and I followed her with alacrity as she headed off through the back door.

She stuck her head round the bar as we left. 'Oh, and Barney, we'll have three rounds of sandwiches and some of Mabel's lovely bread-and-butter pudding, please, when you've got a moment!'

This command was greeted with much mock forelock-touching amongst the bar staff, and one of them caught my eye and winked. I giggled.

'Your mother's very imperious,' I whispered as Hetty strode on ahead.

Nick grinned. 'That's nothing, you should see her when she's feeling bossy!'

We walked through the garden carrying our drinks. It was no more than a field really, the grass was long and full of wild flowers, and strewn here and there were one or two rugs for the customers to sit on. We found a sunny spot and sank down happily amongst the flowers.

Hetty sat next to me. 'Aah . . . that's better, I can't bear being inside that smelly old pub for too long. Have to get out in the fresh air.' She turned to me. 'Are you a country girl, Polly?'

'Oh yes! Well, I mean, at heart I am. I live in London but my parents live in Esh . . . in the country.' I knew from experience that not a lot of people considered Esher to be the country.

Hetty took hold of my chin and turned my face at an angle. 'Hmm . . . you've certainly got a fresh, country look about you.'

I wasn't quite sure how to take this. Did she mean in the bumpkin sense, I wondered?

But Hetty was nodding appreciatively now as she turned my head this way and that. 'Marvellous profile . . .' she muttered. 'Love to paint you some day.'

Thrilled to bits, I sucked my chin in and lowered my eyelids. This was definitely to be encouraged. I let her manhandle my face for a while, hoping it would give Nick a chance to stare long and hard and realise just what it was I'd got that Serena hadn't. And just what was that? I wondered, recalling Serena's Helen of Troy-like perfection. I also recalled that Hetty had found Arthur's profile pretty marvellous too. Laughing nervously, I rescued my face from her vice-like grip on the pretext of lighting a cigarette.

'Terrible habit,' said Hetty, getting one out herself.

'You'll end up with lungs like mine, shot to bits I shouldn't wonder. I keep telling the boys to lay off the ciggies but they won't listen to me: they don't listen to anything I say these days.' She turned to Nick. 'How's the farm going? Did you interview that chappie I told you about? The one I said would make a good farm manager? I suppose you didn't take my advice on that score either.'

'Tony? Oh no, I hired him. You were right, actually, he seems pretty good. I had a long chat with him the other day and we appear to be doing much better than we were this time last year. I think he's quite shrewd, but time will tell.'

'You see!' Hetty was pleased. 'I told you he was all right. Old Bob Hawkins said he was a marvellous manager. So you do listen to your old mother occasionally! Got to keep an eye on him though, it's no good letting him have his head too much. Remember all the trouble Dad had with that dreadful chap – whatsisname – Reg Parker – remember?'

She reached out suddenly and touched my arm. 'Sorry, farm talk. Boring for you, I know, but I do like to keep in touch.'

I smiled. 'Oh no, don't worry about me, I'm perfectly happy.' I lay back on the rug. 'I'll catch up on my suntan while you catch up on the farm.'

I shut my eyes and they chattered on. Every so often I'd catch a sentence or two, but it wasn't long before I was back playing dinner parties in the blue Armani dress. Except that I'd progressed to a rather beautiful pink silk Versace number now, and I wasn't hosting a dinner party I was opening the local fête, or – yes, agricultural show. Well, they were bound to ask me, weren't they? I was, after all, the modern equivalent of the squire's wife.

I frowned. If I had to cut a ribbon or two I would probably need quite a selection of hats, and hats were always a problem. I had quite a big head and they never seemed to fit properly. Ah yes, of course, I'd have them specially made; silly of me not to think of it before. I'd whisk up to Herbert Johnson to be measured or − no, I'd go to Paris! Yes, one or two trips to Paris every year would be a very good idea. I mean the country is undoubtedly lovely, but one wouldn't want to take root, would one?

Yes, I'd spend a couple of weeks every year viewing the collections. I rather fancied the idea of perching on one of those spindly little gilt chairs in the front row of a fashion show, with − oh, I don't know, Princess Caroline on one side and Jackie Onassis on the other? I'd probably saunter in a bit late, and of course a million heads would turn and then the whole place would be buzzing.

'Who's that?' they'd whisper.

'Don't you know? It's Nicholas Penhalligan's wife.'

'Ah . . . I'd heard she was a beauty, but I had no idea . . .'

'They say he's absolutely besotted, hates to let her out of his sight for even a moment.'

'Well, I can imagine . . .'

And so it went on, getting more and more outrageous and out of hand. I was just agonising over what I was going to wear to dinner at Kensington Palace, and wondering how I would manage without a cigarette between courses because of course Diana is very anti, when I heard a snippet of real-life conversation that made me open my eyes and sit up.

'How's Tim, married Sarah yet?' Hetty was asking.

Ah ha. Cows and sheep were off the agenda and marriage was on. This was just my tipple.

Nick laughed. 'Don't you think the news might have filtered down your way if he had? I mean, I know he plays his cards close to his chest, but I think he might tell his own mother.'

'Can't think why he's hanging around till next year,'

grumbled Hetty. 'Why not do it now? Seize the moment, go for it. He's so bloody prudent it's ridiculous. All this talk about money and where they're going to live − what does it matter? Why don't they just go and shack up in a rented flat or something? A lovely girl like Sarah will be pinched from right under his nose if he's not careful.'

Atta-girl, Hetty! I mentally applauded like mad. This was fighting talk and I was right behind her. Why pussyfoot around when you're in love? This woman certainly had her heart in the right place. She obviously wasn't the sort of mother who couldn't bear for her sons to let go of her apron strings either. All of this boded well for the future.

'Well, you tell him, then. It's no good talking to me about it!' laughed Nick.

'I will,' promised Hetty, 'and while we're on the subject, what about that uppity little actress bit you were seeing. I hope the emergence of young Polly here means that that's all over and done with.'

She put a friendly arm around my shoulders and raised her eyebrows quizzically at Nick. 'Am I, perhaps, sitting next to your latest girlfriend?'

I sat bolt upright, rigid with delight, hardly daring to breath, and the little bit of breath that did escape was well bated, I can tell you. Yes, Hetty, I thought gleefully, are you perhaps? I resisted the temptation to raise my eyebrows too.

He laughed, obviously quite used to her blatant nosiness. 'Mind your own bloody business, Hetty,' was his disappointing answer.

Hetty sighed. 'They're both the same, I'm afraid, these boys of mine. They won't tell me a thing. I should have had a daughter, they're much more forthcoming.'

It was on the tip of my tongue to venture that a daughter-in-law might do just as well, but decided that, even with Hetty's obvious penchant for straight talking, it might be considered a little previous.

'So tell me, my dear,' asked Hetty turning her beady brown eyes on me. 'What do you do? You don't throw yourself about half naked on film sets do you?'

'Certainly not,' I said priggishly. 'I'm a production assistant.'

Nick's eyebrows shot into orbit. 'You're a what?'

I was so used to lying about my job I'd forgotten for a moment just who was listening in. 'Oh, er – I mean a personal assistant,' I said quickly. Nick's eyebrows lowered very slightly.

'Well actually,' I said humbly, coming completely clean. 'I suppose I'm just a secretary really.'

'Oh no, I'd say you were definitely a personal assistant,' said Nick, grinning.

I grinned back. Just then a young girl walked through the field towards us armed with great platefuls of sandwiches and bread-and-butter pudding. She set them down in front of us; my mouth watered greedily.

'A secretary, eh? So what's your boss like?' asked Hetty, passing me a sandwich.

'A bastard to work for, but totally divine out of the office.' I gave Nick a huge smile, what did I have to lose? He had the grace to blush.

'Just like you, I bet!' said Hetty, prodding Nick's arm with a bony finger. 'I'd hate to have to work for you, I bet you're thoroughly bad tempered.'

'He is,' I said truthfully. 'You see, it's Nick I work for.'

'There you are, what did I say!' She threw back her head and roared with laughter. 'So I was spot on! How hysterical. Well, don't you take any nonsense from him, Polly. Lick him into shape. He needs a firm hand, you know.'

'I'll see that he gets it!' I said gleefully.

'Must be difficult, though,' said Hetty, tucking into an enormous roast beef sandwich. 'I mean, with the baby. I suppose you have a nanny, do you, or does it go to a childminder or something?'

She sounded so sure of herself that for a moment I wondered if perhaps I did have a baby and had temporarily forgotten about it, tucked it away in a drawer or something. I am incredibly absent-minded, but not normally on such a mammoth scale. I was pretty sure I'd remember giving birth, too. It was, by all accounts, pretty bloody painful. I racked my brains. No, I definitely hadn't given birth.

'I don't have a baby,' I said carefully.

'You don't?'

'No.'

'Oh.' Hetty frowned and looked perplexed. Was this a problem, I wondered? Did she like her future daughters-in-law to come complete with babies? Was there a breeding problem with the Penhalligans?

She turned to Nick, winking broadly. 'Darling!' she drawled, 'What a hectic life you lead.'

'Come on, Mum,' said Nick, getting cross. 'What the bloody hell are you babbling on about?'

Hetty finished her sandwich and got out a cigarette. She lit it and puffed the smoke out thoughtfully. 'Well, I thought Polly here was someone else, you see, another of your female friends.'

'Who?' he said impatiently.

'I don't know, do I? I've obviously never met her, whoever she is.'

'Christ, Mum, what are you on about?'

'Well you see, yesterday I was sitting in the pub painting, when this chap came in and asked at the bar for Mrs Penhalligan. I popped up my hand and he came over. We chatted away for a bit, he said he'd seen one of my pictures in London and had really liked it and because he was on holiday down here, thought he'd seek me out − load of bullshit, of course, but you know me,

334

I'm a sucker for compliments.'

'Oh, do you show your paintings in London then?' I asked.

'Er, well, no, I don't actually, not yet anyway.'

'Exactly,' said Nick grimly, 'go on.'

'Anyway, he bought me a drink and said he knew you,' she nodded at Nick, 'said he saw quite a lot of you in London, and that he was in advertising too and that's how you'd met. Then he asked if you were down here at the moment, and if so did you have a girl with you, with a baby. I said I had no idea, because if you were here you certainly hadn't managed to stagger down to Gweek to see your old mum and, anyway, I never really knew whether you were in London or Cornwall. Well, that's why, when you walked in here with Polly, I assumed she was the girl he was talking about.'

She put her hand on my shoulder, 'Especially in that dress, my dear. It's the sort of thing you wear when you've just had a baby.' She smiled kindly and patted her tummy. 'Hides the paunch.'

I tried to answer, but my mouth was so dry it felt as if someone had just given it the once over with a hairdryer.

'Who was this friend, exactly?' said Nick quietly. 'Did he say?'

'Oh no, I've no idea what his name was, darling. He might have said, but you know me and names. He was quite a big chap, though, burly, with red hair. American, I think, rather cute actually.'

Chapter Eighteen

My first reaction was one of horror. Nick and I exchanged
shell-shocked glances in the wake of this exploding missile.
Christ Almighty, he'd found us already! I reached for my
tongue, but it was sensibly staying put on the roof of my
mouth, glued on with a mixture of terror and bread-and-
butter pudding. I left it there and abandoned myself to my
second reaction which was, I'm ashamed to say, fury.
Bloody Adam and bloody Rachel − damn them! Here I
was having a half decent holiday for the first time in
months, with a thoroughly decent man, and they were
doing their best to ruin it for me. I was tempted to suggest
we simply reunite the surly mother with the aggressive
father and push them out to sea in a leaky boat, hoping
they'd sink without trace, but I could see that Nick was
determined to take a more conscientious line.

He was questioning his mother closely. 'When exactly
did you see him?'

'I told you, yesterday.'

'Yes, but what time of day?'

'Around lunchtime, I suppose, yes, about twelve
o'clock. He said he'd been over to the house earlier and
there was no one there.'

'We were all out yesterday, thank goodness, but you
didn't actually say I was in Cornwall?'

'No darling, why should I? I didn't know you were here,
you never let me know what your movements are. In fact I

distinctly remember telling him that, since I hadn't heard from you, I imagined you were probably in London.'

I relaxed slightly. That was something, surely? Maybe Adam had somehow heard that Nick had a house in Cornwall and had come down purely on the off-chance, just to check it out? And, on finding it empty, he'd headed back to London? But how on earth had he rumbled the fact that Nick was even remotely involved? Just a hunch? Or was he slightly better informed? None of this boded well.

Nick chewed his bottom lip thoughtfully. 'I don't suppose you have any idea where he's staying, Mum?'

'I do actually, he's renting one of Mrs Green's cottages in Manaccan, that little white terraced one in the middle of the village, I think. I've got her telephone number in my address book if you want it.'

Oh Christ, renting. That sounded a bit too permanent for my liking, but there weren't, I supposed, too many five-star hotels around these parts, and a bed and breakfast would be a bit infra dig for our Adam.

'So you definitely didn't say we were here, or were expected down soon, or anything like that?' persisted Nick.

'Darling, do stop banging on, I told you, I simply said I had absolutely no idea where you were,' said Hetty petulantly, her eyes wandering somewhat: she'd got rather bored with this interrogation. 'Oh look there's Arthur!'

Sure enough, out of the back door came Arthur, roaring along on his Zimmer frame.

'Darlings, may I leave you to fend for yourselves now? Only I must finish Arthur this afternoon, I fear he's not long for this world. Arthur! Co-ee! Arthur, you're not going home yet, are you? Where are you off to?'

Arthur pointed to the outside loo and made an obscene gesture to indicate his intention on reaching it.

Hetty sighed. 'He's quite repulsive, of course, but what

can I do? He's such a marvellous sitter, so still and corpse-like. Honestly, the sacrifices I make for art's sake. I'll intercept him on his way out – must fly!' She gathered her cigarettes and lighter together and got up to go.

Nick grabbed her arm. 'OK, Mum, but listen, if you see this guy again, don't mention you've seen us, will you? Oh, and hang on, the phone number.' Nick pushed a scrap of paper and a pencil under her nose and she jotted it down.

'Bye, my darlings!' She blew us a kiss. 'Have fun – oh, and if you fancy another little drinky-poo, just tell Barney to put it on my slate, all right?' And with that she disappeared.

I felt my insides curdling. 'Will we have to go back to London?' I whispered miserably, selfishly thinking of my own happiness as usual.

Nick was staring into space, eyes narrowed. He didn't answer for a moment. 'No . . .' he eventually said, slowly, 'I don't think so. In fact, the more I think about it, the more I think we'll just stay exactly where we are. In fact . . . yes, I want him to know that we're down here.'

'But you just told Hetty not to say anything if—'

'I know,' he said impatiently, 'but I've changed my mind. We'll face him head on this time. I'm not being ousted from my own house by one lousy American, nor am I going to run around England like a fox with the bloody hounds behind me.'

'What – so we just stay put and wait for him to pay us a visit? I mean, he will find us Nick, there's no doubt about that, and he's not going to politely knock at the front door either. He'll probably smash his way through the french windows – or, or through my bedroom window most likely!' I gabbled, frightened out of my cowardly little mind. It was all very well, but Adam definitely hated me more than anyone else in the whole world. I was number

339

one on his hit list without a shadow of a doubt. Nick was silent.

'Well?' I squeaked.

'Hang on, Polly, I'm thinking.'

'But you've seen what he's like, he's a nutter! In fact he's probably clinically insane by now, he'll stop at nothing – and – and anyway, what about Rachel and Jamie?' I added charitably but desperately.

'Don't worry, I'm not abandoning them at this stage, although God knows, sometimes I think Rachel deserves all she gets. No, we'll just have to think of a way around this.'

'But what if—'

'Polly, for God's sake shut up, will you? I'm trying to think!' he snapped.

Ah. I pursed my lips and sat back, folding my arms. I recognised a flash of the old Nick there: hadn't taken long to surface, had it? Nevertheless, I obediently shut up and waited for my next order. I didn't wait long.

'Come on, hurry up.' Nick got to his feet and drained his pint.

'Where are we going?' I scrambled around, looking for my handbag.

'Back to the house, of course. Thank God Tim and Rachel have gone into Helston this afternoon.' He strode off.

'Oh! Right, hang on, just coming.' I drained my glass, scooped the last of the bread-and-butter pudding into my mouth, and ran after him.

Nick was already half-way across the garden. 'Bring the glasses will you, Polly?' he yelled over his shoulder.

I dashed back meekly to pick them up. Odd how in a crisis we'd suddenly reverted to our more usual roles of servant and master.

I panted back down the garden after him. 'In a couple of weeks we'd have been shot of her, she'd have been in Paris and we could have told him to sod off. Oh, why did he have to come now?' I grumbled breathlessly, running to keep up as he strode round the side of the pub to the car park.

He didn't answer but, without pausing to open the door, vaulted neatly into the open-topped Land Rover and revved up the engine. It was a cool, effortless move straight out of the movies.

Suddenly I felt a little twinge of excitement. After all, here we were, bang in the middle of what the tabloids would call a tug-of-love scenario, protecting the mother, and ducking and weaving from the vengeful father: we were a team, a duo — yes, we were partners. We moved as one, we thought as one, we stood up for justice, we protected the weak, we leaped into jeeps — I took a little run up, grabbed the top of the door and jumped — about two inches off the ground. Nowhere near. I tried again, run and — hup! Gosh, how on earth did he do it? Panting with exertion, but determined to crack it, I stepped back for another try. I charged towards the door just as he, simultaneously, leaned across and swung it open to let me in. It caught me full in the stomach.

'Ooooffff . . .' With a loud, yob-like moan I fell back on to the gravel, bent double and clutching myself like a footballer who's been kneed in the privates. As I lay there, moaning and rolling around in a heap of Laura Ashley, he came running round to retrieve me.

'Gosh, I'm really sorry, I had no idea you were still leaping around out there. Are you OK?' He helped me up.

'Sure,' I croaked, staggering to my feet and clutching what was left of my stomach. 'My fault, really, showing off as usual.'

Would I ever be able to have all those babies now, I wondered? Wasn't that where all the important tubes were? I nursed what remained of my abdomen, wincing and gingerly feeling around for signs of blood. None, unfortunately.

Nick heaved me bodily into the jeep, slammed the door and ran round the other side. With a screech of tyres and a great deal of flying gravel, we shot out of the drive.

We sped off in silence, and I was loathe to break it, knowing from experience that whatever I said would be wrong. He was either hatching a master plan, or so pissed off he couldn't speak. At last he did.

'Right . . .' he said slowly, 'now listen, Polly, this is what we're going to do.'

'Yes?' I whispered. Surely yes couldn't be wrong?

'First of all, we're going to send Rachel and Jamie away, get them as far away as possible from the action, somewhere safe.'

'Like where?'

'Like Penny's. Tim can take them, he often goes to deliver vegetables anyway. He's pretty quiet on the farm at the moment, so he could probably stay a few days and surreptitiously play bodyguard, make sure they're OK. There's no way Adam will find them there.'

Don't be too sure, I thought grimly, he found us here; but I had to agree, it wasn't a bad plan.

'Will Penny mind?'

'Not a bit, she's got bags of room at this time of year, and she's always glad of some company.'

'OK, and meanwhile?'

'Meanwhile, I'll telephone Adam and invite him over for a drink.'

'You'll what!'

'I'll ask him over for a drink.'

I was bug-eyed with amazement. 'Well, don't mind me, but I'll just be down at the nearest travel agent negotiating a one-way ticket to Australia!'

'Listen, Polly, if we seize the initiative we might just get away with it. I'm not prepared to sit around and wait for him, and I think it makes sense to catch him off-guard. The last thing he'll expect is a friendly telephone call.'

'Well I'm not crazy about being a sitting duck, either, but what happens when he accepts our offer and turns up keen to stage the Cornish Chainsaw Massacre?'

Nick paused as he slammed down a gear and negotiated a tricky hairpin bend. 'We tell him a little story,' he said softly.

'Oh really? And what might that be?'

'We tell him that the strain of being caught in the middle of this ghastly situation – you know, looking after Rachel, leaving your flat, and not being able to come to work, not to mention splitting up with your boyfriend – left you feeling absolutely exhausted.'

'Too right,' I said with feeling.

'You were totally drained, emotionally and physically, so much so that you almost became ill – basically you were in dire need of a break.'

'Dire. Dire need.' I nodded emphatically.

'So, I suggested that a little holiday in Cornwall might do the trick. You agreed, and here we are.'

'What, just the two of us?'

'Why not? After all,' he took his eyes off the road for a second and gave me a most dazzling smile, 'we are having an affair, aren't we?'

I gulped, getting my oesophagus in a serious twist. 'An – an affair?' I stammered, through twisted tubes.

He grinned. 'Yes, an office romance – you know, dipping the pen in the company ink and all that. Goes on all the time. But of course, it couldn't be conducted in London for all the agency to witness, so we came down here for a bit of peace and quiet.'

'I – I see,' I faltered, recognising a somewhat familiar fantasy here, 'and what about Rachel?'

'We have absolutely no idea where she is now, neither do we care. The last we saw of her was when we dropped her off at her father's house.'

'Oh come on, that's very weak. Adam will have been

watching the house in Kensington like a hawk. He'll know she's not there.'

'Exactly, he'll know we're lying, and he'll pounce on that immediately. That's when we deliver the red herring. Under extreme pressure – and I mean extreme pressure, let him stamp around a bit and flex his muscles, maybe even exert a few bully-boy tactics – you eventually admit that you heard her on the telephone inquiring about homes for unmarried mothers.'

'Christ, we'll have him breaking down every hostel door in London!'

'So what? They're quite used to lunatic fathers raising merry hell, they'll just get the police on to him. Good thing too.'

'Suppose he doesn't believe us?' I quaked.

'Well, what does it matter? He won't find them if he decides to search the house, and then what can he do – kill us? He a frustrated father, Polly, not a mass murderer.'

'Don't be so sure,' I muttered nervously, recalling those giant freckled paws, which in my mind's eye had already grown Mr Hyde-like claws. 'So do we tell Rachel all this?'

'Christ no, she'll be terrified if she knows he's down here, we don't want her panicking all over the place. I'll have a quiet word with Tim, explain the whole story, and get him to ask her if she'd like to go up to Penny's for a few days.'

'She'll smell a rat though, won't she? I mean, why should she go to Penny's?'

'Because Tim will tell her we want to be alone to conduct our illicit affair in private.'

'Oh God, you mean she's going to get the story about us having a ding-dong too?'

'Why not? He'll tell her we're both feeling rather self-conscious and we'd like a little time to ourselves, just a couple of days, of course. Once we've seen Adam and we think the coast is relatively clear, they can come back,' he grinned, 'to the hotbed of lust and passion!' He threw his head back and laughed, no doubt at the sheer outrageousness of it all.

'Oh yes, I see, very good!' I said faintly. I threw back my own head and added a merry little chuckle of my own, but it was awfully hollow, principally because I couldn't quite see the joke. What was so side-splittingly funny about us being lovers, I wondered? He was still guffawing loudly. Was he going to be sick?

As he coughed and spluttered over the steering wheel, I considered the joke from Nick's point of view. Good-looking, successful, loaded young blade, with beautiful, highly desirable actress girlfriend, risks all to nip down to Cornwall for a bit of how's your father with gauche, dyed blonde, overweight secretary. I squirmed uncomfortably. Yes, well, put like that I could see wherein lay the mirth.

I stared miserably out of the window. The hedgerows reared up and waved at me as we flew past; grasses and flowers waggled their heads knowingly: it was as if they were laughing, mocking me, and who could blame them? I'd been living in a dream world these last few days. Nick would no more fall in love with me than sell the farm and become managing director of ICI. And why should he? He had a perfectly good girlfriend back in London. I stared out of the window. Yes, she was all the way . . . back in London.

I was feeling low, very low, but not low enough for this last, indisputable fact to escape me. The girlfriend was, indeed, a long way away, and I was, indeed, right here. She was three hundred miles up the M4, while I was all of three inches. She was over six hours from his presence, while I was half a moment. What's more, we were to be alone.

A small window of opportunity presented itself. It was about the size of a cat-flap with about as much visibility, but still, it was there. I mean, there's a great deal to be said for being on the spot, isn't there? If only in the sense that it's better than not being on the spot. I gave myself a little inward shake. Atta-girl, Polly, where's that famous McLaren spirit? Rally it fast, please.

It wasn't as if I'd really turned on the charm yet either — OK, yes, I'd been trying, but not very hard, not as hard as I could. I hadn't, for example, fixed him to any of my smouldering hot looks, I hadn't got as far as the come-hither eyes or the sexy suggestive smiles, and I hadn't even begun to turn him on with my wardrobe. And my golly, I had some pretty lethal gear with me one way and another: the leather mini-skirt, the clinging cross-over top, the blue silk shirt with most of the buttons undone, the tight black leggings — he didn't stand a chance. And of course, once I'd hooked him, winding him in would be the work of a moment. I smiled smugly, secure in the knowledge that I may be a talentless little secretary, but at least my snogs were up to scratch.

As we turned the corner and swept through the gates of Trewarren, I felt a little better. So you think it's all a big joke do you, Mr Penhalligan? Well, we'll soon see about that.

As soon as we got back to the house, Nick buttonholed Tim in the cow shed. I left him to it, unwilling to be deafened by the bellows of laughter, or to witness the side-holding and thigh-slapping that would undoubtedly occur when the incredible Nick-and-Polly fantasy was raised.

It had already been decided that Tim, of the famous animals-and-oddballs touch, would speak to Rachel but, until he'd done so, I couldn't let her out of my sight. Odd, I thought, that I could be so allergic to Rachel but still not want to see her baby wrenched from her arms. I shadowed her around to the extent of following her into the tiny downstairs loo while she changed Jamie's nappy.

She frowned up at me as she knelt on the floor, a half-dressed baby wriggling around between her knees. 'Did you want something, Polly?'

'Noo, noo nothing,' I laughed nervously, 'just interested really. Oh, I see, those disposable things just have sticky tape at the front, do they? No pins?'

'Polly, you've seen me do this millions of times.'

'Have I? Oh well, I must have forgotten. Anyway, I might have a baby of my own one day, so I need all the practical demonstrations I can get.'

'What, you look after a baby? Do me a favour.' She snorted with derision.

'And why not?' I said hotly. 'I'll have you know I'm extremely maternal; I'd be a brilliant mother.'

'You might be maternal, but you're hardly responsible, are you? Babies are one hell of a commitment, you know, you can't just look after number one all the time.'

I fumed silently, steam pouring from all orifices. Ungrateful cow, if only she knew. She was one hell of a responsibility, and I was shouldering her pretty well at the moment. I waited until most of the steam had subsided. No point having a row with her now.

I shrugged. 'I suppose I'm just a bit bored, really.'

'Well d'you think you could move slightly to the right, only I need to spread this plastic mat out?'

'Oh yes, right.'

There wasn't much room, so I put the lid down on the loo and stood on that instead.

Rachel looked up at me in alarm. 'Are you sure you're OK?'

'Fine, fine . . .' I gave my face a vacant expression and stared up at the cracks on the ceiling, biting my thumbnail, swaying slightly and humming to myself. Hopefully she'd just think I'd gone a bit mad and ignore me. I was making Jamie laugh, anyway. I rolled my eyes and pulled faces as he gurgled up at me.

'Rachel?' Tim shouted from the corridor.

'In here! Come in, everyone else has.'

Tim poked his head around the door. He looked up at

347

me in wonder. 'Don't tell me — number of people in a downstairs loo? *Guinness Book of Records*?' He leaped up beside me. 'Three! Four with Jamie!'

I giggled and jumped down, closing the door behind me. No, I thought grimly, bodyguard to the sulky and undeserving. I wandered off to the kitchen in search of calories. Instead I found Nick, prowling around, locking doors and windows.

'Don't do that!' he snapped, as I opened the larder and made for the light switch. I jumped and snatched my hand back.

'Sorry!' Was he possessive about his chocolate biscuits? I knew the feeling. 'Just felt a bit peckish,' I stammered guiltily.

'Fine, go ahead, but don't turn the light on!' He came over and put a hand on my shoulder. 'Sorry, didn't mean to snap, it's just that while Rachel and Jamie are still here we've got to be so careful. If Adam is prowling around outside, we don't want him to think there's anyone here. When they've gone, which hopefully will be soon, it doesn't matter, but just for the moment let's keep all the doors and windows locked, turn the lights off and keep away from the windows, OK?'

'OK,' I whispered. Anything was OK if he kept his hand on my shoulder like that. I'd creep around on all fours if he liked.

'Did you speak to Tim?' I asked, trying to keep him talking, trying to keep the hand on the shoulder and prolong the ecstasy.

'Yes I did, he's talking to her now. I hope they're going to leave as soon as possible. Tim was planning on delivering some vegetables tomorrow, anyway, so it's worked out quite well.'

Footsteps approached the kitchen. The hand disappeared like lightning.

'Well!' said Tim, rubbing his hands together and smiling

348

as he came in. 'Rachel thinks it's a great idea, don't you?'

Rachel was right behind him. 'Yes, I'd love to go. It'll be a nice change and, of course, it'll give you a break, Polly.'

Her mouth twisted into an unattractive little smirk as our eyes met. Ah yes, of course, she'd heard about the Polly-and-Nick affair, the one that was so unspeakably sordid it needed acres of space in which to be conducted. It couldn't come within miles of another living soul, so shameful was it. She obviously thought I was a right little tart, too. Only a few days ago she'd dished out tea and sympathy as I'd lain prostrate on my bed, distraught at Harry's desertion, and now here I was throwing myself at Nick.

Well for your information, *dear*, I thought glaring at her, it's all an elaborate hoax laid on for your benefit, purely to save your anaemic little skin. I conveniently forgot that it would be fine by me if the fantasy we'd cooked up turned into reality; for the moment I was concerned only with her deeply hypocritical smugness. I mean, didn't she just take the biscuit? It was only because of her little indiscretion with a man she didn't love that we were all running round in circles now. Oh yes, it's all very well taking the high moral ground with me, Miss Marsden, but if you hadn't jumped into bed with Adam, we wouldn't be going through with this idiotic charade now. I glared back at her.

'Er, good!' beamed Nick, ignoring the sparks that were so obviously flying between the women. 'That's settled then. You'll enjoy staying with Penny, Rachel, the food's infinitely better than it is here, and you get room service thrown in too. I must say I envy you, I could do with a few days of being waited on hand and foot!'

'Oh, I'm sure you'll survive,' purred Rachel. 'After all, you've got Polly to look after you.'

Nick blushed. 'Oh, er – yes, well of course. Um – tell you what, let's all have a quick drink before you go. It had

349

better be a quick one, though, because I expect you'll want to get off while it's still light.'

'Oh there's no rush is there?' said Rachel. 'I thought we might go after supper. It only takes a couple of hours to get there, doesn't it?'

'Er, yes, but Penny might be expecting you for supper — oh God, that's a point, I'd better ring and tell her you're coming!'

Rachel looked puzzled. 'She doesn't know? But I thought she invited us?'

'Oh! Yes, she did! Rang this morning actually. No, what I meant was, I'll just let her know when you're leaving.'

'So she can have some supper ready,' I added soothingly.

'But — but I thought you said she was expecting us for supper?'

'Oh she is, she is!' said Tim quickly. 'But it's always as well to remind Penny, she's so absent-minded, we don't want to turn up and find she's closed the restaurant, do we!'

'It's hardly likely, it's only five o'clock now!'

God, she would go on, wouldn't she?

'Is that all!' Tim looked at his watch. 'I had no idea it was so early — to tell you the truth, Rachel, I'm absolutely starving, and I just want to get to Penny's as soon as possible so I can get stuck into some decent food! A man could die of starvation in this place.'

'Oh, right.' She looked reasonably convinced. 'Oh well, I'll just go and pack. I won't have a drink thanks, I'll just get my things and organise Jamie.'

She shuffled off to her room and the three of us headed thirstily for the drawing room where the gin bottle beckoned.

'Christ!' Nick flopped down on to a sofa nursing his drink. 'All this lying is really taking it out of me. I didn't realise it was such hard work. I must say, you're awfully good at it, Polly.'

'Years of practise,' I said without thinking. 'Er − well, you know, I've been in one or two tight spots before.'

'I can believe it.' He twinkled knowingly at me.

I squirmed uneasily. Now what was that supposed to mean? As I sipped my drink I brooded on its implications.

A few minutes later, Rachel reappeared laden down with baby gear. The boys sprang up to help her. Tim drove the car round to the back door where there was more privacy. They loaded the car, sat Jamie in his car seat, Tim and Rachel climbed in the front, and with a scrunch of tyres on the gravel, the Wincanton party sped off.

Nick and I watched from the window, peering out from behind a curtain. I for one heaved a huge sigh of relief. Thank God. I'd just about had it up to here with that ungrateful little hussy, and was very much in need of a sabbatical.

As the car reached the end of the back drive and turned the corner out of sight, I gazed out at the view. It was a beautiful afternoon. The sun was still bright but it was quite low on the horizon, and the countryside was bathed in a golden, soupy glow. The trees that lined the drive cast long skinny shadows across it at intervals, like an erratic railway track. Up in the sky, a few clouds raced along in the blue, as if they'd been separated from the rest and were dashing to catch up. Just outside the window, the daffodils were bobbing around like billy-o, trying to keep their heads up in the breeze. I sighed dreamily. This was England at its very best, at its most beautiful. And I was alone with Nick.

He was standing next to me by the window, holding the curtain open a crack. Our shoulders were close. I turned to him and gave him one of my most turning-on smiles.

'So what shall we do now they've gone?' I murmured. 'It's such a beautiful evening, why don't we take the boat out on the river? Or go for a walk along the cliffs?'

'We'll do neither,' he said grimly. 'We'll ring Adam Buchanan.' He turned on his heel and made for the telephone in the hall.

'Oh.' My heart sank down into my espadrilles. 'Yes, I'd forgotten about that.'

He turned and looked at me in amazement. He shook his head. 'Sometimes, Polly, I wonder what planet you're on.'

He marched on, telephone-bound. I trudged meekly after him. Well, I thought gloomily, I'd like to be on a wildly uplifting planet, or even over the moon perhaps, but unfortunately someone keeps bringing me right back down to earth.

Chapter Nineteen

I sat down at the bottom of the stairs, hunched up and hugging my knees like a little gnome. Any minute now, Adam would be on the other end of that telephone. I shivered. Suddenly there seemed to be a nasty east wind whistling through the very marrow of my bones, and yet it was such a beautifully warm day. These old houses were unbelievably draughty. I pulled my jumper right down over my hunched-up knees as Nick picked up the telephone.

'Shall I go away?' I asked. 'Would you be better on your own?'

'No, stay,' he licked his lips nervously, 'I need moral support.'

Any time, I thought dreamily, studying his Docksiders as I sat at his feet; moral support, physical support – my eye was roving up his blue-jeaned legs – surgical support . . .

Nick took a crumpled piece of paper out of his back pocket. He telephoned Mrs Green and got the number of the cottage in Manaccan.

'Right,' he said replacing the receiver, 'ready?'

'As ready as I'll ever be to invite a mad-man for a drink.'

He grinned. 'Courage, Polly, courage!'

He dialled the number. There was a long pause as it rang at the other end. Please God, please let him be out – my huge yellow streak was well to the fore as usual – please let him be out and I promise I'll go to church when I get back to London; Matins, Evensong, confession, happy-clappy tambourine time – you name it, I'll be there. God had heard it all before. Adam was in.

'Mr Buchanan?' Nick raised his eyebrows, I held my breath. 'It's Nicholas Penhalligan here, I saw my mother this afternoon, she said you were looking for me, is that right . . . ? Yes, of course, no problem, but I can't help you much, I'm afraid. I gather you're looking for Rachel and Jamie . . . No, no, they're not . . . No, I've no idea where they are, I'm afraid . . . Polly? Well no, she's not in London, she's down here with me . . . Yes, staying here. She's sitting right next to me, actually.'

He glanced down and winked. My hands started to sweat, I dug my nails into my palms.

'Well, let's not go into that right now, shall we? Why don't you come over for a drink, then we can all have a civilised chat about it . . . Yes, why not? . . . Seven o'clock? . . . Fine, we'll see you then . . . Goodbye.'

He replaced the receiver. I wiped my sweaty hands on the stair carpet and looked up anxiously. 'Well?'

'That's it. He took the bait, and he's coming over.'

'How did he sound?'

'Perfectly normal.'

Perfectly normal. That's how people always sound when they're about to do something perfectly atrocious. Everyone always says so afterwards: the neighbours, the greengrocer, the stunned and weeping mother. 'Oh, he seemed perfectly normal that day, right as rain. He was always such a good boy, such a comfort to me, I can't think why he suddenly took it into his head to let loose with a Kalishnikov and mow down two innocent people in cold blood.' Yes, it was always thus. Suddenly I felt awfully scared.

'Could I perhaps stay in another room while you speak

to him?' I ventured timidly. 'I mean there's no need for me to see him, is there? Three's rather a crowd, isn't it? You could tell him our little story and I could be getting on with something useful upstairs. Maybe I could clean out the attic or something? Would that be a help?'

He laughed and kicked his shoes off, changing into one of the many pairs of wellingtons that lay in a jumble in the hall. 'Polly, it's all going to be fine, stop worrying. He's just coming for a friendly chat.'

'But – but I might say the wrong thing, cramp your style, you know.'

'I wasn't aware that I had a style. Anyway, you don't have to say anything much if you don't want to.'

'But – but what are you going to tell him? Shouldn't we get our story straight? Synchronise watches? That kind of thing?'

'Don't worry about me, I'll just wing it!' He grinned, grabbed his Barbour from the banisters and headed for the front door. Where the hell did he think he was going? I grabbed his arm in alarm.

'Where are you going?' I squeaked, hanging on like a limpet, feet almost off the floor. 'Take me with you!'

'I'm just going to check on the cows.'

'I'll come with you,' I gasped. 'The dear, darling cows, haven't seen them for ages!'

'Don't be silly, it's getting dark so you won't see much, and anyway they don't like to be disturbed. I won't be long. Pour yourself a nice big drink and turn on the telly. This will all be over before you know it.'

He patted my hand abstractedly, then prised the fingers one by one from his arm before wandering off to the relative calm and comfort of the cow shed.

It's all very well for you, I thought miserably, dragging my feet back to the drawing room; you've got your ruddy cows, what have I got?

I curled up on the sofa and tried to watch the television,

maniacally switching from channel to channel and staring blindly at the flickering cathode rays. I seemed to be sucking a cushion. I started to play 'what if?' with myself. What if he didn't believe us? What if he turned nasty? What if he had a knife? I stuffed the cushion further into my mouth and nearly gagged on the tassel. It was quite conceivable though, wasn't it? I mean, OK, I had Nick to protect me, but what if Adam was armed: there wasn't an awful lot Nick could do against a sub-machine gun, for instance, was there? And Americans carried guns as a matter of course these days, didn't they; it was in the constitution or something. In fact, I had a feeling it was compulsory for all American males over the age of twenty-one to carry a gun.

Suddenly I knew what I had to do. I reached for my handbag, pulled out a pencil and rummaged around for a piece of paper. I found my bank statement, which I never open and which therefore always serves as a handy notepad. On the back I began, in a shaky hand, to pen my final instructions.

Dear Lottie,
In case I never see you again, I want you to know that I leave you my compact-disc machine and all the cassettes. Please also take whichever clothes you fancy and offer the rest to Pippa. I'd be grateful if you didn't give any to Caro. My legit jewellery had better go back to my parents, but by all means make free with the Butler and Wilson. I want you to know that you've always been a terrific friend and ally over the years, please think of me fondly from time to time, your dear, most probably dead friend, Polly.
    PS. Please ensure that Harry hears of my demise and gets an invite to the funeral.

Ah yes, the funeral. Death does have its compensations

356

doesn't it? I sucked my pencil thoughtfully. I wondered where it would be. Probably in that nice little church off Pont Street, yes, that would be quite smart, quite – you know, social. Handy for a wake in the Admiral Codderington afterwards. Funny how my fantasies always seemed to revolve around churches. I'd been up and down this particular aisle on a number of occasions – vertical, of course, and dressed in white. This time I'd be horizontal and dressed in, well, in a shroud, I supposed. Were they white too?

I could see my coffin, laden with flowers as it proceeded slowly down the aisle. The church was packed – naturally – so much so that some people had to stand outside. Harry was a pall-bearer, as was Nick (if he wasn't dead too, of course), and there they stood, side by side in their dark suits, heads bowed, breasts heaving with emotion, united in their grief. They stared down at my coffin which lay at the front of the church.

'There'll never be anyone quite like Polly,' whispered Harry between sobs, hanky dabbing wet eyes. 'How could I have been such a fool? My own little Polyester – gone for ever!'

Nick simply couldn't speak, his face was contorted with emotion, he wrestled with pent-up tears. Eventually, of course, his grief got the better of him and he broke down, flinging himself at my coffin, beating on the lid with his fists and crying, no – better still, shrieking – 'Polly, Polly! My only true love, come back to me, don't leave me! I can't bear to go on without you! I just can't bear it!' I sucked my pencil thoughtfully. Was that too over the top? Too – you know, nancy-boyish? I hesitated. Nah, for God's sake, I was dead, wasn't I? He was entitled to be over the top.

Anyway, eventually he was prised from the mahogany by other mourners who tried to calm him, but he pushed them all away and stumbled outside, blinded by tears, unable to face the rest of the service; unable, in fact, to face the rest of his life.

At the bottom of the church steps was Serena, looking remarkably unattractive for her, actually: greasy hair, one or two spots, bags under the eyes. 'Nick – darling!' she called out, but Nick brushed her aside, quite roughly, before staggering off under the weight of so much emotion, to be alone with his memories. Or, wait a minute – yes, perhaps Serena should look absolutely stunning and *still* he brushes her aside. Yes, that would be even better.

I doodled on the envelope. Should I jot down a couple of hymns in case Lottie didn't know any real tear-jerkers? I wanted nice dreary ones to set the mood and get the weeping under way. I was just wavering between 'The Lord's My Shepherd' and 'I Vow to Thee My Country', when Nick walked in. I stuffed the letter in my handbag. No doubt the police would find it there later and pass it on to Lottie, and I dare say I could trust her with the order of service. She had, after all, been to a convent.

Nick looked calm and relaxed. 'OK?' he queried, raising his eyebrows.

'Sure, fine actually,' I bleated, with a brave little smile. 'Much better in fact.'

'Good girl.' God he was gullible. He sank down in front of the television with a sigh. 'God, I'm knackered.' Then he sat up a bit. 'Oh great, "Dad's Army" – it still makes me laugh, even after all these years.'

And laugh he did, quite a lot actually, was this man human? I had a go, just to show willing, but it sounded like a pregnant hen being strangled. He looked at me in alarm.

'It's going to be fine Polly, really. Don't worry about it.'

I nodded dumbly, feeling very sick all of a sudden. My tummy was churning and rather a lot of bile was rising up from it en route to my throat. Just at that moment the doorbell went. Coincidentally I completely lost my bottle. I shrieked and ran out of the room.

'I really don't think I can cope with this, Nick, please don't make me!' I pleaded from behind the door. 'I've got this terrible pain in my tummy, I really think I ought to go and lie down, I've had it before and if I don't lie down I'm generally sick all over the carpet!'

'Don't be silly.' Nick dragged me out from behind the door. I dug my heels in but he was too strong for me. I slid along the shiny floorboards.

'Would you just sit down and relax? Here.' He steered me, like a professional ice-skater with a beginner for a partner, towards the sofa. 'Now stay there while I let him in.'

I looked doubtfully at the sofa. He gave me a little push. 'Sit.'

My knees creaked as they bent unwillingly into it, my buttocks clenched with terror as they sank down towards it.

'It'll be an absolute breeze, I promise,' he lied, and with that he sallied forth to answer the door.

'I whimpered quietly as I heard Adam's unmistakable trans-Atlantic drawl getting closer and closer. A moment later, Nick was ushering him into the room. He seemed to fill it. Everywhere I looked there was a piece of Adam — an arm here, a leg there; I'd forgotten how big he was, and how red. I cowered back in terror, watching his enormous shadow lurk along the curtains.

'Hello, Polly,' he said in a strained but civil voice.

'Hello,' I whispered.

'Drink?' asked Nick.

'Please. Whisky and soda, if you've got one.'

He sat down at the other end of the sofa, but I felt as if he'd sat on my lap. Christ, there were plenty of other chairs in the room, weren't there? I scrambled right into the corner, holding on tight to the arm. Adam crossed his legs and leaned back, flinging his arm along the back of the sofa. I flinched as his freckly hand landed inches from my head. Bastard. He grinned, rather menacingly I thought.

'Don't worry, Polly, I'm not going to bite you.'

'That's what I keep telling her,' said Nick over his shoulder from the drinks cupboard, 'but she won't have it. She thinks you've come round to bump her off.'

Adam grinned. 'Not unless I'm severely provoked!'

'Don't provoke him, Polly,' warned Nick. 'I don't want to have to pick up the pieces. Ice?' he asked Adam.

'Please.'

Oh terrific, I thought grimly, glaring at Nick. Gang up on me now, won't you? Be Adam's buddy boy, laugh at silly old Polly. Well wait till he chases you round the table with six inches of cold steel at your throat, because he undoubtedly will: see how funny you find that. I looked furtively at Adam's jacket, looking for bulges that might indicate a jack-knife or a gun. Nothing was glaringly obvious. Perhaps in his socks; people often kept knives in their socks, didn't they . . . I dropped my cigarette packet and bent down to pick it up, meanwhile scrutinising his footwear.

'I'm not armed, if that's what you're wondering,' said a sarcastic voice in my ear.

I breathed in sharply and jerked upright to find ice-cool blue eyes boring into mine. Of course, he was telepathic, I'd quite forgotten. Somehow this was more frightening than any arsenal he might have secreted in his socks. I scrambled back to the relative safety of my corner again, bringing my knees up to deflect any body blows.

'Just dropped my cigarettes,' I mumbled, taking one out of the pack with a shaky hand.

A gold Cartier lighter flicked silently into action under my nose. The flame was bright and steady. I dipped my trembling cigarette into it and sucked hard.

'Thanks,' I muttered.

'How are you finding Cornwall?' asked Nick as he handed Adam a whisky.

Adam's eyes narrowed. 'Look, I'm not about to beat the shit out of anyone, but let's cut the crap, shall we? Cornwall's fine, but I didn't come here to pick wild flowers, I came to get my son.'

'Well, in that case I'm sorry, but I'm afraid you've come all this way on a wild goose chase. It seems you had too much faith in Polly's sense of responsibility. Jamie's in London with Rachel, we left them up there. They're fending for themselves now.'

'So you said on the telephone,' said Adam grimly, 'but I'm not entirely convinced, I'm afraid.'

'Look.' Nick sat down opposite Adam. 'D'you mind if we look at this from our point of view for a minute? Get things into perspective a little?'

'Sure, if you must.'

'I must, because you don't seem to realise that you're not the only one in a tight spot here. Polly feels very guilty about the mess she got Rachel into—'

'You mean the mess she got *me* into,' interrupted Adam fiercely, jabbing his chest with his finger, no doubt to indicate the size of his massive pectorals which were soon to partake in the dismembering of my body. He glared at me. I whimpered and threw more gin down my throat and, oddly enough, my jumper.

'All right, all right, the mess she got you into, have it your own way,' sighed Nick. 'I'm not prepared to go into whose side she should have been on, because the point is that she shouldn't have been put in the position of having to pick sides in the first place. I mean, none of this whole ridiculous business had anything to do with her, did it?' He turned to me. 'In fact, it still beats me why you ever got involved in all this in the first place.' He shook his head with genuine incredulity. I hung mine in shame.

'Anyway,' he went on, 'that's another story, and we

361

won't go into Polly's inability to mind her own business right now; but believe me, when she told me all about it my immediate reaction was one of absolute horror. I couldn't believe she'd got mixed up in all this. I told her in no uncertain terms that she should extricate herself from the whole affair, tell the pair of you to bugger off, and let you fight it out between yourselves. As far as I was concerned, there was no reason why she should dig herself in any deeper − I mean, it's not as if she even knew either of you, for God's sake. It's one thing to help out old friends, but complete strangers? Come on. She'd done more than enough.'

Too right. I rather enjoyed that little speech, it had a nice protective ring about it. Adam looked thoughtful. He cradled his whisky in his fingers and swirled it around a bit. He didn't say anything.

Nick leaned forward. 'The whole situation was becoming totally absurd. She couldn't go home to her own flat in case you were waiting for her there, she couldn't come to work in case you followed her and attacked her—'

'Oh come on!' said Adam. 'You make me sound like an animal. I had no intention of attacking her—'

'Oh really? Well that wasn't the impression we got. You come charging into our office, brandishing knives and scaring the pants off everyone − what are we supposed to think?'

Adam shrugged, he looked a little shame-faced. 'OK, OK, I admit I acted a little crazy that day, but I was − well, I was desperate. I'm sorry, I apologise for all that, it's totally unlike me, I hate violence − really, but I've been under a hell of a lot of strain lately, as you can probably imagine. I guess I just lost my rag.'

Nick shrugged. 'Well, fair enough, it happens, but you can see my point. We weren't to know that you'd just temporarily "lost your rag". Polly really thought her number was up.'

Adam shook his head and sighed. 'This is crazy, you know. I'm not trying to hurt anyone, or even frighten anyone. I just want to find my son.'

'Fine, I realise that, but all I'm saying is that, at the time, we weren't to know that your threats were idle. Polly was scared out of her wits, and I was pretty worried myself, I can tell you. Anyway, that's why I suggested – ' he paused and let a hint of a smile play around his lips – 'with, I have to admit, something of an ulterior motive, that she come down here and stay with me for a while. To get away from it all and to – well, to have a holiday.' He grinned. 'I've been trying to drag her down here for some time, actually. In a way this was the perfect excuse.' He shot Adam a quick, half embarrassed, half cocky look, and then turned to look out of the window, letting this sink in.

I was impressed. Talk about the gifted amateur, this was the work of a seasoned liar, not a total beginner. Perhaps he'd been taking notes from me.

Faced with Nick's back, Adam swung round to me for confirmation. I'd done nothing but look permanently shifty for the last five minutes, and it was a demeanour which suited this revelation right down to the ground. I shifted some more.

Adam's top lip curled into a knowing sneer. 'Well, well, what do you know? Looks like I've stumbled in on a bit of a love nest here, doesn't it? Well congratulations, you guys, I hope you'll be very happy together,' he drawled.

'Thanks very much,' said Nick with a grin. 'I'm sure we will.' He got up to pour himself another drink, and paused en route to take my hand. He gave it a quick squeeze; it instantly broke out into a muck sweat. He looked casually at Adam. 'Another drink?'

'Sure, why not?'

'Polly?'

'Mmmm!' I nodded furiously, and gulped hard, hoping

363

nobody was expecting me to say anything more than that. Just breathing and drinking were proving to be enough of a struggle at the moment.

'Well, Polly,' smirked Adam, 'you've certainly changed your tune, haven't you?'

'What d'you mean?' I said quickly. Too quickly. As usual my mouth had responded before my brain had had time to engage. I didn't want him to tell me what he meant at all.

'Well, as I recall, a little over a week ago, Nick here was not exactly your favourite guy. And certainly not what you might call dream-boat material. In fact, if I remember rightly, you went so far as to write him off as a total jerk, am I right?'

I tried hard to erect a dam at the top of my neck to stop the red hot blush from spreading on to my face, but it was no good. 'Don't be ridiculous!' I spluttered. 'I would never say anything so − so absurd!'

'Ah, but you did!' said Adam, enjoying himself. 'In fact, I remember your very words. You called him − not a jerk, but that marvellously English insult − a git!'

Nick threw back his head and hooted with laughter. 'Well, thank you, my darling. A git, eh? That's not what you said last night!' He tapped me playfully on the nose as he handed me my drink.

I fumed at Adam, puce with embarrassment. What must Nick think? 'How dare you! It − it's outrageous of you to repeat a private conversation. I remember now that I'd had a bad day at work and was feeling a bit miffed with Nick over something silly, I don't remember what, and − and I might have said something to you in the heat of the moment about how I was a bit, um, irritated with him, but I certainly wouldn't have called him a git!' I gabbled.

Adam and Nick were both grinning widely. Nick sat on the arm of the sofa, threw an arm around my shoulders and hugged me towards him.

'Don't worry, darling, he's teasing you. Anyway, I know what you used to say about me, I dare say I've said a few uncharitable things about you in the past, too, but that's all forgotten now, isn't it? And of course you know what they say: there's a very thin line between love and hate!'

'Yes — yes, they do say that, don't they? D-darling,' I stammered. I was positively dripping with perspiration, and we hadn't even got to the difficult bit. Perhaps I could go and clean the attic now? The only consolation was that Adam had loosened up a bit, obviously enjoying my discomfort.

He smiled sadistically. 'Well, hey, I'm sorry if I've put a spanner in the works. I guess you'll have fun kissing and making up when I've gone, though. I must say it's fascinating to hear yet another chapter in Polly's somewhat chequered love life.'

'Chequered?' I spluttered. 'There's nothing chequered about it. I'll have you know it's always been extremely straightforward!'

He laughed and held up his hands. 'OK, OK, I'll take your word for it. Anyway. We digress. Let's not get too sidetracked by your incredibly "straightforward" love life, shall we? We don't want to lose sight of the point of my little visit.'

He swilled his whisky around in his glass. For a moment I'd completely forgotten what the point was. He hadn't.

'Polly, where's Rachel?' he asked, in a soft but deadly voice, raising his eyebrows at me.

I shrank back. Did I say he'd loosened up? I felt the blood drain away from my face. Victoria plum to sheet white in less than five seconds; quite an achievement, really. My eyes caught on his like Velcro.

'I really don't know,' I whispered.

Nick strengthened his grip on my shoulders. 'Look, Adam, we haven't a clue where she is now, but there's no harm in telling you that we dropped Rachel off at her father's house before we came down here.'

'Oh, come on, d'you really expect me to believe that? There's no one at that house except the judge and the housekeeper. D'you think I haven't been watching?'

'Well, maybe she's not there now, but I can tell you, we dropped her off there last Wednesday morning, plus Jamie and half a ton of baby gear. That's the last we saw of them, and we haven't heard from Rachel since.'

Adam shook his head. 'No way.'

'Take it from me, it's true. Maybe they were only there for an hour or so, perhaps they moved on almost immediately, I don't know. I'm just telling you that that's where we bow out of the story. That's where we left them.'

Nick looked Adam straight in the eye. Adam hesitated. My toes were creaking with suspense. He must have heard them, he turned to me.

'You spent a few days with Rachel, Polly, you must have talked to her. Did she give any clues as to what she was going to do? You must have discussed it with her. What were her plans?'

'I really don't know, she didn't say.'

'Oh come on, she must have said something!'

'She didn't — really, she kept very much to herself.'

'You know, you really shouldn't tell lies, Polly.'

'But it's true! Honestly, it's true, she — she didn't say a word!' I stammered nervously, no acting required.

Adam stared at me for a moment, then he rubbed his eyes and sighed deeply. He scratched his head. He didn't look in the least bit menacing now, he just looked tired.

'Look. I can quite understand why you don't want anything more to do with this business, but just listen to me for a minute, the pair of you, will you?'

I nodded dumbly. Did we have any choice?

'I'm not going to try to snatch Jamie away from Rachel.'

I looked at him suspiciously. 'You're not?'

He shook his head. 'No. Now I admit that originally I was so incensed that all I wanted to do was to find the pair of them, grab Jamie, and take him back to the States with me; but I've had a lot of time to think recently.' He leaned forward and rested his forehead in his hands, staring at his shoes. 'I've sat in quite a few hotel rooms, or rented houses, staring at walls trying to get things straight in my mind, and I've come to the conclusion that in the long run, it wouldn't get me very far. Rachel and her old man would have the police on to me in seconds. I'd just spend the whole time running and hiding. It would be pretty horrific for Jamie, too.'

'It certainly would,' agreed Nick.

'Yeh, yeh, I know, don't worry, I've worked it all through now. I know I'm on a hiding to nothing. All I want to do is find Rachel, talk to her, and see if we can't sort something out like a couple of sensible adults. There must be some kind of custodial agreement we can come to without going through the courts.'

'But she's too frightened to see you now, she won't speak to you,' I said.

Adam held out his hands in despair. 'But why? For God's sake, why won't she speak to me? There's no rhyme or reason why she should be scared. OK, in the heat of the moment when I was absolutely furious — and blind drunk incidentally — I made a couple of stupid telephone calls to her father's house, but she knows me well enough to know that I'd never hurt her, or Jamie. She's making out that I'm some kind of maniac, some kind of homicidal nut-case — it's crazy! What have I ever done to her, apart from love her, have a child with her, and ask her to marry me? Is that so terrible? Well, apparently it is, because d'you know what she did? Without any warning whatsoever, without even giving me an inkling of what was on her mind, she just up and left one day taking our son with her. She left a little itsy-bitsy note — about three lines long, it was — on the kitchen table and, cool as anything, walked out. Can you believe that? She just packed a bag, tucked Jamie under her arm, and got on a plane to England. And now she won't even speak to me — don't you think that's a little strange after all we've been through together? Wouldn't it drive you a little crazy if you were in my position? My whole world has collapsed and everyone's acting like I'm the lunatic, like I'm the one who's acting irrationally!' He shook his head in disbelief.

'Look, Adam . . .' began Nick softly, but Adam went on as if he hadn't even heard him. It was as if we weren't even in the room.

'But you know what? D'you want to know the craziest thing of all? In spite of all she's done, I still love her. I'd marry her tomorrow if she'd have me. We had a child together, my son, who I love more than anything in the world. That's what's important. That's what I keep hanging on to.'

He paused and ran his fingers through his hair. He looked terribly tired. Nobody spoke for a moment. At length, Adam continued. His voice had a crack in it.

'Now, I realise she doesn't feel the same way about me. I'm coming to terms with that, and I daresay one day I'll even accept it. People fall out of love all the time, and I just happen to be the injured party, that's all. OK, fine, but Christ, she owes me some sort of an explanation, doesn't she? Jesus, just to get on a plane and take off to another country like that without a word, taking Jamie with her.' His voice all but collapsed here; he fought to control it. 'I mean, whatever you think of me, you've got to admit, she owes me some kind of access to my son. She owes me the right to see him from time to time, doesn't she? Am I asking so much of her?'

I stared out of the window. I was surprised to discover I had tears in my eyes. I blinked. The curtains hadn't been drawn, and while we'd been talking it had got quite dark. A black, starless sky hung over us. The wind had dropped completely and all was still and quiet. There wasn't even a rustle in the trees, or a distant bleat of a lamb.

Of course he wasn't asking too much. She did owe it to him, and she owed him a lot more besides. I tried to imagine what it must be like to come home from work one day and find that your family has disappeared. We were well and truly caught in the middle here, and more and more I realised where my sympathies lay. I wanted to tell him where she was. I wanted to blurt it out — say that he'd find her holed up at a little pub called the Dog and Duck just off the Wincanton Road. All the same, I knew I couldn't. I was supposed to be feeding him the unmarried mothers line. I looked in desperation at Nick. He too looked pained, and shifted about uncomfortably on the arm of the chair. I wondered if he was thinking the same thing as me.

'Nick?' I whispered.

Adam pounced, misinterpreting my appeal. 'Nick, is there anything you can tell me? Something you know?'

Nick hesitated. 'No — no, not really . . .'

'For pity's sake, please!' Adam urged him.

'Well — well, actually she did mention something . . .'

'Yes! Yes — go on.'

'No Nick, don't,' I said softly.

He put a hand on my arm, 'I think we should, Polly.' I gulped and stared at the carpet. This was going to be more convincing than we could have possibly imagined, and I couldn't bear it. I couldn't look at Adam's eager face.

'Go on?' he leaned forward eagerly.

Nick sighed. 'Well, it's just that, while the girls were staying with Pippa, before they came down here, Polly overheard Rachel on the telephone.'

'Yes?'

'Well, she got through to one of those hostels, a

369

home for unmarried mothers . . .'

A light seemed to go on inside Adam's tired, dull eyes. I turned away. 'A home? You mean like a shelter, that kind of thing?'

'That's it. I don't suppose she was thinking of staying there on a permanent basis, perhaps for a week or two, I don't know, and I'm afraid I've no idea which one.'

Adam shot me a look. I shook my head vigorously. 'No,' I whispered, 'no, she didn't say.'

He stood up slowly. 'An unmarried mothers' home. Yeh, we have those in the States, I know what you mean.' He walked to the window and looked out at the black night.

'You won't get in,' I said quickly – somehow I couldn't bear to think of him beating his way into these places to no avail – 'and – and they'll just get the police on to you if you try.'

Unwittingly I'd managed to seal it. He drained his whisky. 'Will they indeed?' he said grimly. 'Just let them try.'

He turned to face us. His freckles stood out harshly on his pale, determined face. His eyes were wide and staring now. He put his glass down on a table.

'Thanks for the drink,' he said curtly. He nodded to us and turned to go. As he got to the door, he hesitated, his hand on the handle. He turned back. 'Thanks. I realise you didn't have to tell me that. I'm grateful. Thanks, Nick. I guess you can understand a little of how I feel.' With that he opened the door and walked out.

Nick and I sat in silence. I heard the front door close behind him, then I heard a car door slam. An engine turned over and roared into life. There was a crunch of gravel as the tyres spun on the drive, a familiar rattle as the car crossed over the cattle grid, and finally a distant roar as it sped off, no doubt heading for the London road. Still neither of us spoke.

Chapter Twenty

Eventually Nick sighed heavily and got to his feet. He crossed over to the fire and kicked one of the logs savagely, sending sparks flying on to the hearth. I felt like kicking something myself, but I'd had so much to drink I didn't think I was capable of standing up, let alone raising one leg off the ground and taking aim. Instead I sat in a booze-sodden heap feeling seriously depressed. Nick threw a couple more logs on the fire, and stood brooding down into the flames. Then he turned, warming the backs of his legs. He saw my dejected face and shook his head.

'It's no good looking like that, Polly. We did what we had to do.'

I sighed. 'I know. It just seems so unfair, though. Why do we have to take her side?'

Nick shrugged. 'Why do we have to take any side? It's a bloody ridiculous situation. Here we are, being forced to manipulate the lives of two people we hardly know, sending one off on a wild goose chase, and playing bodyguard to the other.' He shook his head grimly. 'I tell you, the sooner this is all over, the better.'

He turned back to the fire. We watched the flames for a while.

'Poor Adam,' I said eventually. 'He'll be banging on all the hostel doors in London tonight.'

Nick turned on me angrily. 'Well, that was what you

371

wanted, wasn't it? It's no good saying "poor Adam" now!'

'I know, I know, but – well, I just feel so awful, I almost wish we'd told him where she is!' I blurted out, feeling close to tears.

Nick looked at me, exasperated. 'God, Polly, sometimes I just don't believe you! What did you expect me to do, for God's sake? Dig out a road-map and trace a route for him from here to the Dog and Duck? Wave him on his way and let him charge up the motorway and go storming into the pub without giving Tim, Penny or Rachel any warning? Is that what you wanted?'

'No but—'

'Well, what then? And anyway, who's to say that he's telling the truth? Who's to say that he wouldn't just grab Jamie and take him back to America: how would you feel then? You'd be saying "poor Rachel" then, wouldn't you? Well, wouldn't you?' he demanded angrily.

'Yes, I suppose so,' I whispered.

I blinked hard. It had been a tough evening, and I really didn't think I could cope with anyone else having a go at me. Tears were literally poised on the precipice. I bit a very wobbly lip and looked away, but he saw the wobble and immediately sat down next to me, contrite and full of remorse.

'Oh Polly, I'm sorry, don't cry. It's not your fault, I'm just letting off steam. I know I shouldn't take it out on you, but to tell you the truth, I'm fed up with being in such a bloody awful position. It's really beginning to get me down.'

My chin wiggled dramatically as I fought with the waterworks. He sighed and ran his fingers through his hair.

'And I know why I'm angry. Because for what it's worth I feel the same way you do now. The more I hear about this saga, the more I think that Rachel acted abysmally, but that's not the point, is it? The point is, we promised we'd look after her, and we can't just abandon her now. You do see that, don't you?'

I gulped. 'Yes, I do, and I know you're right but – but it just seems so rough on Adam. He's not such a bad chap really, is he? A little impulsive, I grant you, but who wouldn't be under the circumstances?'

He laughed dryly. 'I must say you've changed your tune. Half an hour ago he was public enemy number one.'

'I know, but everything looks different now. He's been so hurt, and for what? I mean, as he says, all he's ever been guilty of is falling in love with a girl, getting her pregnant, wanting to marry her, and wanting to look after her and the baby. That's not so terrible, is it?' I gritted my teeth and clenched my fists. 'If you ask me, Rachel Marsden is a complete and utter bitch!'

Nick grinned. 'Feel better for that, do you?'

'I do, actually.'

'Polly, I agree with you, and the whole thing is very frustrating, but there's nothing we can do about it. Let's just try and forget it. We've got rid of Adam, and in a few days we'll get rid of Rachel, too. Then it'll all be over and you can relax. OK?'

I smiled weakly. 'OK.'

'In the meantime,' his voice softened considerably, 'why don't we just forget the pair of them and try to enjoy what's left of this little holiday?'

Now I know a seductive tone of voice when I hear one, in fact I can detect one at twenty paces, and I could have sworn I'd just heard one. I looked up in surprise. Nick smiled, and – good gracious, yes – the brown eyes were most definitely soft and encouraging. Like two deliciously gooey chocolates, they seemed to be beckoning me on.

'Oh yes, please,' I whispered greedily. 'I mean, yes please, let's enjoy ourselves. I'm all for enjoyment, aren't you?'

I gave him what I hoped was my most smouldering, sexy smile, but which could well have been taken for a pissed leer. He smiled back. Suddenly everything was so still, I could hear my heart beating. I waited, rigid with excitement. *Something* was definitely going on here, *something* was about to happen. I held my breath and sat quietly. Nick's smile turned into a steady gaze which seemed to envelope me completely. I bathed in it wantonly, not daring to move.

Overhead, a lone seagull wailed mournfully as it circled the house; the long case clock ticked away steadily in the corner; the fire crackled cosily in the grate. Other than that, there was just a highly charged silence. It was killing me, and so, for that matter, was my head. An intoxicating mixture of gin and desire was sending it into something more usually associated with the final spin-dry of a washing machine. How maddeningly inconvenient. I shut my eyes briefly in an attempt to arrest the cycle. A fatal mistake. Even though I was sitting down, I swayed violently. I opened them immediately.

'Are you all right?' asked Nick, whose come-hither gaze had turned to one of concern.

'Fine, fine, really. What were we saying?'

He smiled warmly. 'Something about enjoying ourselves.'

'Ah yes,' I murmured, and smiled back, even more warmly.

The washing machine abated slightly as every conceivable nook and cranny in my body tingled with anticipation. My heart went into overdrive, thumping away as it sent red-hot blood steaming around my body, pumping it into places that didn't normally require it. Even my toenails seemed to be throbbing, charged up to the cuticles with the stuff. Please hurry, I willed him silently, please hurry *up*!

But still he sat there, silent and watchful. Eventually,

after what seemed like a century but was probably three seconds, he turned his body in towards me slightly and rested his hand on the sofa behind my head. Yes, yes, *yes*, I urged silently, go for it. GO FOR IT! He didn't take his eyes off me. His hand rested softly on the back of my head. He stroked my hair gently and smiled.

I met his gaze, but was aware that my nostrils were flaring dramatically. I seemed to have far too much breath, I didn't know what to do with it. Out it came in short, chuggy bursts, and then in went gallons more. Where did it all come from? The more I tried to disguise it, the more I chugged and snorted. Now his hand was on the back of my neck, stroking it gently, making my hair stand up on end, making goose pimples break out in the oddest places, and all the while, he fixed me with those deep brown eyes.

I wasn't used to such slick, subtle moves. Most of the men I'd had close encounters of the sexy kind with would have had their tongue round my tonsils by now and be grappling with my bra strap. This hair-stroking lark was a new one on me, but it certainly sent the pulse rate soaring.

I chugged and snorted a bit more. We were close, but not that close. About twelve to eighteen inches of Colefax and Fowler chintz upholstery was still most definitely between us. There was no doubt that either a quick lunge or a surreptitious sidle would have to be made by somebody. But not you, I told myself sternly. Don't be fast and vulgar. For once in your life, be slow and tasteful. Just concentrate on sitting very still and he'll do the rest.

But when? He stroked and smiled, and stroked and smiled, and suddenly I could bear it no longer. Slow and tasteful be damned, I'd be dead soon. In one swift, jet-propelled move, I launched myself across the eighteen inches of sofa and flew into his arms.

He ricocheted slightly on impact, and out of the corner of my eye I caught a hint of a raised eyebrow, but no matter. Hating myself for my highly previous nature, but unable to control it, I lifted my face and – yes, he was lowering his. In an instant we were locked in the most divine, the most passionate, the most, oh so exquisite kiss I'd ever experienced. On and on it went, getting sweeter and sweeter, and deeper and deeper by the moment. I could have stayed there for ever, but breathing difficulties were becoming apparent on his part, and so at last, like a couple of deep-sea divers, we came up for air. Locked in his arms, I gazed up to see what effect all this passion was having on the geometric features. They'd softened considerably. He looked pleased, if a little surprised.

'Well, well, well,' he said softly, gently tracing my mouth with his finger. 'Who would have thought . . .'

'Yes, who would have thought!' I whispered back breathlessly.

Who would have thought what? That I could be such a brazen hussy? That he could have lowered himself to the depths of snogging his secretary? Or that it could all be so deeply wonderful? Who would have thought what? I longed to know but, more than that, I longed for more. Unfortunately my head was against it. Once more it had switched into spin-dry mode, and I had to steady myself on his shoulder to stop the room from spinning round.

I held on tight and breathed deeply. It was important to take very deep breaths and on no account to shut my eyes. I concentrated like mad on the fire, I watched the flames as they licked greedily around the logs, and then, when I deemed it safe to move my head, I looked up. Nick frowned down at me as I span.

'All right?' he inquired.

All right? What – the kiss? Was he asking me? 'Oh yes! Fantastic! One of the best – the best in fact!'

Nick seemed to find this a puzzling response. He frowned some more. What a thoroughly sexy frown, I thought dreamily as it swam in and out of focus. What can he be thinking about? Whatever it was obviously required a great deal of thought. Ah yes! I know, he's wondering where we should go from here! Only literally, of course, we know in theory where we're going, but where should the action take place?

Was he the kind of man who had to do it in a bed? Or would that mouth-wateringly appetising Persian rug in front of the fire do just as well? Still he frowned. The location was obviously not to be chosen lightly. Of course! He was probably considering the hay barn! Hadn't he mentioned only the other day that he'd like to sleep in it? Now if that isn't a broad hint, I don't know what is! I helped him along.

'Are you thinking about the barn?' I whispered.

'Sorry?'

'The barn, is that what you're thinking about? Because if you are, I want you to know that I think it's a very good idea, very – you know, rustic!' I gently nudged his gloriously hunky shoulder with my head and winked in a knowing fashion.

Nick looked even more puzzled. Then suddenly he disentangled himself and got up. He went over to the fire, crouched down and poked it thoughtfully. I sat up. Gracious, this seemed to me to be an entirely retrograde step, what on earth was going on? It didn't take that much thought, did it?

'Only joking about the barn,' I mumbled. 'I'm easy.' God, that sounded awful. 'About – about where we go, I mean.' Even worse. I flushed and looked down at my hands.

More frowning, and more fire maintenance followed these brazen confessions. I bit my lip. I felt decidedly out of my depth here. These decorous periods of inactivity might be highly civilised, but they puzzled the hell out of me. After all, the first kiss had been planted, intent had been established, action should be taking place. Shouldn't we even now be thundering upstairs, tearing each other's clothes off, and launching ourselves at the double bed in a frenzy of excitement? Even the restrained hair-stroking was preferable to this malarkey. I thought hard. No Polly, no, you're wrong as usual. This was obviously how civilised people made love. Of course! How silly of me: fire-poking was probably the ultimate in erotic symbolism. After all, he had been to Cambridge, hadn't he? And I hadn't been exposed to such high-minded love-making before. Up to now it had all been very – well, very red-brick. Even polytechnic at times.

I watched eagerly as he rooted away in the grate, excitement growing within me – oh yes, I see, I see! The more he poked, the more excited I got, I was really catching on now – God, this was thrilling! But how should I respond? Join him at the fireside? Throw on a lump of coal? This was all new to me; how taxing it was!

I racked my brains. Come on, Polly, think, think. Suddenly it came to me. I would dance towards him. Yes, of course, a dance – what could be more erotically symbolic than that? And I was a good dancer too.

'Nick?' I whispered eagerly.

'Yes?' he turned around.

'Ready?'

'Er . . . yes.'

I got unsteadily to my feet, pulled a lock of hair over one eye, and fixed him with a sexy, penetrating gaze. I put my hands on my hips and wiggled them seductively. Then I rotated my shoulders, slowly. Next I concentrated on the wrists, twirling them around, seven veils-fashion, stretching out the fingers – oops, there went an ashtray, crashing to the floor, spilling ash everywhere – no matter, I was well away now. I really began to move. I swayed towards him, flashing my eyes from under their lashes, and giving the sexy smouldering smile yet another outing. Atta-girl, I thought to myself, atta-girl! This will rock his socks off.

He watched, in wonder and in a little too much amazement, as I shimmied towards him, hips snaking, arms twisting. The more I shimmied, the wider his eyes grew: he was totally captivated. I was right above him now as he sat crouched, a trifle nervously perhaps, by the fireside. I really let him have it. I threw back my head and twirled and snaked and twisted and writhed and –

'Oops!' – tripped over the rug, toppling headlong towards the fire.

'Watch out!' yelled Nick as he grabbed me, rugby-tackling me away from the flames.

'Oof, sorry!' I landed, rather heavily it has to be said, in his arms. OK, so it wasn't the most graceful of landings, but there I was, where I most wanted to be. I smiled up at him dreamily as both of his rather fuzzy heads separated for a moment and then came together again. All I had to do was lie here and wait. Any minute now he'd pull me roughly towards him, and envelope me in the most passionate embrace, kissing me madly the while. I shut my eyes in an ecstasy of anticipation.

Nick cleared his throat. 'Right. Bedtime I think.'

He just couldn't wait, could he? 'Oooh, yes please!' I wriggled gleefully, then reached up and pulled his head down towards mine, lips parted, eyes shut – one for the road, eh?

Lip contact was never made. I opened my eyes. Nick seemed to be disentangling my arms from around his neck. 'No, Polly, separate bedtime.'

He stood up, hoisted me to my feet, turned me around and pointed me in the direction of the door. 'Go on,' he said softly. 'I'll see you in the morning.'

I stood there, swaying incredulously. My mouth opened wide, my eyes boggled. I turned back. 'Separate beds?' I echoed dumbly.

'Separate,' he affirmed decisively.

My insides curdled, my jaw slackened. I was amazed,

incredulous, uncomprehending. Separate beds? That's what he'd said all right, but was he serious? And if so, what did it mean? That I'd got it all wrong? That I'd read his signs wrong? Surely not.

I frowned, pondering the mighty implications of it all. Then, quite suddenly, it dawned on me, crashing over me in a tidal wave of shame and embarrassment. Oh my God. Of course! I'd failed the kiss test.

Now, I freely admit to having failed a lot of tests in my time. Scores of O-levels, a smattering of A-levels, Grade Three piano, cycling proficiency and life saving, to name but a few, but never, *never*, have I failed the kiss test. Let's face it, I've had too much practice. In fact, without wishing to sound immodest, I generally pass with flying colours and leave the lucky recipient begging for more. But to fail! I hung my head and felt my face flame. How deeply shameful.

What could it be, I wondered? Galloping halitosis? Or something more sinister like a nasty little cold sore at the corner of the mouth? I put up a tentative hand and felt around gingerly. Nothing seemed to be glaringly apparent; it must be lurking nastily beneath the surface.

But, on the other hand, maybe it wasn't that at all. Maybe – and this was a real shaker – maybe he just didn't fancy me. Perhaps he'd thought it might be quite fun, a bit of a laugh, but when it came to the crunch he'd found it – well – rather nauseous; repulsive even. After all, he already had a girlfriend, didn't he? And a jolly pretty one at that: why should he mess around with the likes of me? I was mortified. How could I have been such a fool? I felt a bit of a lip tremble coming on. I stiffened it instantly. Bear up, Polly, bear up. We'll have none of that, thank you.

I raised my head and met his eye. 'Right-o then!' I said in a cracked little voice, desperately trying to force a hockey stick into it. 'I'll be off to bed. You're right, I am rather tired actually – cheerio! See you in the morning!'

Smiling bravely, I turned and crossed the room in a reasonably straight line, although I have to admit, I lurched the final yard or two and had to grab hold of the door frame to steady myself. Every moment in this room was unbearable now.

I was aware that he was following me. I could feel his eyes on my back as I made it through the hall to the bottom of the stairs, albeit with a bit of wall-hanging along the way.

'Are you OK?' he asked anxiously as I began, gingerly, to mount the stairs.

'Sure!' I croaked, raising my hand in a backward wave to reassure him, and quickly replacing it on the banister as I nearly lost my balance. Sure. Only about eighteen inches tall now and getting smaller by the minute, but other than that, fine, just dandy.

The stairs seemed to go up and up for ever; higher and higher they went, like something out of a 1940s Hollywood musical set, and all the time he would keep standing at the bottom watching my unsteady progress. I looked back. Yes, he was still there – Christ, what a long way down! I grabbed the banister as I stumbled: how extraordinary, I seemed to be suffering from vertigo.

I bit my quivering lip. Don't cry, I thought with rising panic. Don't cry yet. Not yet. And don't, whatever you do, look down. I climbed the last step, turned left, realised my mistake in an instant – lightning reflexes – and turned right instead. I stumbled blindly down the dark passage-way, feeling my way in the dark.

At last I reached the right door. Now you can cry, I thought as I stumbled in. I shut the bedroom door behind me and leaned heavily against it. Now you can cry all you like. I threw myself on my bed and buried my face in my pillow. The floodgates opened. I sobbed and sobbed, for about – oh, a couple of minutes probably. Because after that the strangest thing happened. Instead of sobbing long and hard, and on and on, into the small hours, as I'd rather imagined I would, almost immediately, I fell fast asleep.

Chapter Twenty-one

When I awoke the next morning I was almost blinded by the light. The window and the curtains were wide open and a sixty-watt bulb was glaring down at me above my head. I blinked and rubbed my eyes. How very odd. Why on earth was the light on? Had it been on all night? I raised myself up on to my elbows. A huge mistake. A wave of fresh spring air surged through the open window and hit me full in the face. I moaned low and sank down on to the pillow again.

I felt awful, really awful. I lay still for a minute as I tried to get the measure of this. Something deeply unpleasant was going on here, mostly in the head region. My brain seemed to have expanded overnight and was fighting for accommodation, bashing away against my skull in a painful, frenzied fashion. My tongue had swollen out of all proportion and had grown fur, like some ghastly Caliban festering in its cave. What on earth had I been up to last night to surface in this sorry condition?

I frowned and cast my mind back a few hours. Slowly, the penny started to drop. It landed with a resounding clatter and the whole horror of the night before slotted into place. I stuffed the sheet into my mouth. Oh my God! I'd tried to seduce him! I'd leaped into his arms! I'd — I'd, oh horror of horrors, I'd danced! Had I really? Yes I had! I pulled the sheet right over my head and groaned. Suddenly I went cold. Had I — and here I had trouble even suggesting the notion to myself — had I, perchance, danced naked?

I sat up, terror-struck, and had a swift glance round the room. Happily, most of my clothes could be accounted for. There was my skirt on the lampshade, my shirt on the bookcase, my jumper hanging out of the window, my bra — where was my bra? I glanced down. Oh. How odd. I frowned at my chest. I seemed to be wearing it. Oh well, at least it hadn't come off; but what other face-flushing atrocities had I committed?

With a heavy sigh I lay down again and turned on to my side. As I did so, I realised there was something wrong with my feet. I couldn't move my toes. I tried to wiggle them, it was quite an effort. Ah yes, of course, I was obviously paralysed. I'd heard of people being paralysed with embarrassment before; clearly it had happened to me. Paralysed from the — let me see, I tried an unsuccessful ankle wiggle — yes, from the knees downwards. What a shame, I was rather fond of walking. I peeped warily under the bedclothes and spotted my cowboy boots still clinging to my person. Ah. That explained it. How peculiar, I usually remembered to take my shoes off.

At least that was all of my clothing accounted for, except — except my knickers! Where the hell were they? Draped over a lampshade in the drawing room? Hanging over an ancestral portrait in the hall? Decorating the banisters perhaps?

I jumped out of bed, clad fetchingly in a bra and cowboy boots like something out of a Soho sleaze joint, and stared wildly round the room. Ah! Thank goodness. There they were in the washbasin. I fell on them gratefully and hugged them to my bosom. At this point I experienced a certain amount of head rush and had to steady myself on the washbasin. I shouldn't have leaped out of bed so quickly. I took a deep breath, counted to ten, then crawled back to bed and shut my eyes tight.

After about half an hour I realised, with a glance at my clock, that it was already ten o'clock and if I left it any longer *someone* might breeze in full of pity and find me in this hideously unattractive state. Some sort of repair job would have to be done on the face before such an eventuality. Apart from that, a raging thirst was beginning to get the better of me. I had to get up.

I staggered to the washbasin and glugged desperately at a running tap, wet hair streaming down the plughole, but it was no good. A hosepipe turned on full blast was needed to quench this sort of thirst.

I gazed in the mirror above the basin. How strange. Someone rather like me but much uglier was gazing back. Same shaped face and same hair, but with tiny, slitty little eyes which were only being kept open by the weight of a huge pair of pendulous bags which dragged the bottom lids down. The complexion was pasty and pallid and the mouth enormously swollen. Swollen heart, too, I thought mournfully as I brushed two inches of fur off my teeth. That was the worst of it, and something I could only just bring myself to contemplate. He didn't want me. He'd rejected me. If I was the last woman on this earth he'd emigrate to Mars. And I loved him.

It hit me full in the face like a runaway train. I loved him. The ugly face in the mirror began to quiver perilously and the piggy little eyes looked alarmingly moist. Don't cry! I commanded the face sternly. It shuddered obediently to a halt and the eyes blinked back their tears. For God's sake. You're ugly enough as it is, don't make things worse.

I showered long and hard and dressed slowly. Then I spent about half an hour on my make-up, to no avail. It was quite clear that on this particular morning I had the choice of looking like a prostitute or a battered wife. Initially I went for the prostitute look, then got half-way down stairs and ran back to wash it all off again. If I looked like a tart it might remind him that I was one. No.

Bare-faced cheek was the order of the day.

With freshly scrubbed cheeks I crept down into the kitchen. There was no one about. Nick had obviously breakfasted long ago, up at five with the cows, no doubt. I opened the fridge and greeted the orange juice like a long-lost friend. The muesli was a different matter. I toyed with it limply and stared out of the window. Where was he? Hiding in a barn? Ringing Tim and Rachel, begging them to come back and rescue him from the hands of a nymphomaniac who'd taken the whole charade seriously and had tried — unsuccessfully, mind — to get into his jeans? I groaned. Oh, the shame.

The muesli was making me retch so I poured it down the sink, clogging up the plughole. Suddenly I looked up — I could hear footsteps on the path outside. Oh God, it was him, and before I even had time to decide what sort of an expression I would have on my face, he was opening the back door.

'Hi!' he greeted me cheerily, looking fresh-faced and windswept. His hair was tousled, his eyes were shining, and he looked utterly divine. How could I ever have thought he'd be mine?

'Hi!' I managed to gasp in response. The expression my face had chosen for me was of the timid, cowering, puke-making variety. I hovered by the Aga; should I stay? It would be too rude to leave immediately, and yet I couldn't bear to make small-talk with him.

'Had some breakfast?' he asked conversationally as he sat down and pulled his boots off.

'Oh, yes thanks.'

There was a silence. I cast around desperately for something interesting to say.

'Have you?' Pathetic, Polly. Truly pathetic.

'Yes, I had mine hours ago. Been up since six.'

'Ah.'

It was so hard to talk, and yet recently it had been so

easy. I stared miserably at the kitchen floor.

'What have you – um, been doing then? I mean this morning?' I faltered.

'Oh this and that, been out with the sheep mostly. Oh, incidentally, I telephoned Mrs Green.'

'Oh yes?' I tried to sound interested, but really I couldn't have cared less. I was fed up with other people's lives.

'And she said that Adam left last night. Just paid the rent, packed his bags and shot off, saying he was going back to London. He was in quite a hurry apparently.'

'Oh well, that's good. Gosh, that's good. What a relief!' I said unconvincingly. I stared at my fingernails. I must go on saying ordinary things.

'Everything – um, all right on the farm front, then?'

'Yes, fine, one of the ewes had twins which is always a bonus. I'd got her down as a singleton, but she popped two little ones out first thing this morning.'

'Oh good.'

'Yup, and they both seem to be doing well. Oh, and the lamb whose mother died seems to have been fairly successfully adopted by another ewe who lost a lamb, so things are looking up.'

'Great!'

A silence ensued. It had to be filled. I felt myself blushing. The whole room seemed hot.

'And – and the cows?' I faltered.

He grinned. 'The cows are fine, thank you, and I'm sure they'll be pleased to hear you've been asking after them. Shall I give them your best?'

He was laughing at me. I bit my lip. I could feel tears gathering behind my eyes. I turned away and lifted the top of the Aga, putting the kettle on to boil. It boiled almost immediately and I poured myself a coffee. Still I couldn't bear the silence. I had to fill it, however clumsily, however stupidly. I must seize new, harmless topics.

'I wonder how — how they're getting on back at the agency! Without us, I mean — well, without you.'

Nick looked at his watch. 'Oh, I should think they're probably all in the pub by now, don't you? I mean it is ten-thirty. That's where you all normally congregate when I'm away, isn't it?'

'Er, well, not always, now and again, I suppose. Yes, we do have the odd drink.'

He grinned, 'Well, why not? It's different when you're working for yourself, of course. Time spent in the pub is money lost as far as I'm concerned.'

'Yes, yes, I suppose it is.'

Another silence. This was gruesome, truly gruesome, I'd never felt so uncomfortable with anyone in my whole life. I had to get away. I sidled towards the door clutching my coffee. Nick struggled to pull his second boot off, threw it on the floor and grinned up at me just as I'd reached the door.

'So how are you feeling?'

I turned. 'Me? Oh fine, fine.'

'Really?'

'Really. Well, no all right, ghastly actually. Got a bit of a headache.'

He laughed. 'I'm not surprised! You were drinking for England last night!'

'Was I? Oh, yes, well perhaps I did have a bit too much.'

'A bit? Polly, you could hardly stand!'

Really, this was hardly chivalrous, was it? To remind a girl the following morning of a totally uncharacteristic over-indulgence the night before?

'Well, yes, perhaps I didn't — you know, pace myself very well.'

Nick got up and went to the sink to wash his hands, but it was full of muesli. Without a word, he scooped it out by the handful and threw it in the bin. I stared at his back as he rinsed his hands. It was no good. At some point I would have to make reference to last night, and I might as well do it now while I had the advantage of addressing his back rather than his face.

I took a deep breath. 'Nick, I'm sorry about last night,' I burst out.

He grabbed a towel to dry his hands and turned to face me. 'What d'you mean?'

Oh God, this was too much. What did he want me to do, rewind last night's spool and run through it again for him?

I blushed. 'Oh well, you know. Throwing myself at you and all that. Can't think what got into me.'

'A litre of gin, perhaps?'

I grinned. 'You're right, I was a bit pickled.'

He sat down at the kitchen table and looked at me as I hovered by the door. 'Polly?'

I met his eyes.

He held out his hand. 'Come here,' he said softly.

'What?'

He beckoned me over. 'Come over here.'

I sidled gingerly across to the table. 'What, right over here?'

He grabbed my arm and pulled me down on to his lap. 'Yes, right over here!'

'No, I'm too heavy!' I squeaked. I kept one foot firmly on the floor, hoping it would take most of the weight. What was this — corporal punishment time? Was he going to put me over his knee and spank me for my outrageous behaviour last night?

'Now listen to me. There's no need to apologise for anything you did last night. I loved it.' He grinned. 'Especially the dance!'

I hung my head in shame.

'But you were so pissed, so unbelievably steaming, I just had to send you up to bed on your own. I honestly think you would have passed out if we'd risked any funny business, either that or thrown up. I mean, you probably 'don't remember this, Polly, but at one stage you were rambling on about barns. You kept talking about wanting to go to a barn, d'you remember that?'

'Um, vaguely,' I muttered. I flushed to my toes.

'At that point I thought you'd got serious alcohol poisoning.'

'Sorry,' I mumbled.

'Don't be sorry, it doesn't matter. God, we've all been in that state. I just didn't want to respond too eagerly in case I got my face slapped in the morning.'

I struggled to make sense of this earth-shattering turn of events. 'Oh! So you mean — you weren't necessarily that adverse to my, um — you know, advances?'

He smiled. 'Not necessarily that adverse, no.'

'Oh! So, so — oh. So . . .' I stumbled on, vainly trying to get my dehydrated grey matter around this revelation, and wondering what it signified. 'So, what you're saying is, that in a way, you almost liked them. My advances, I mean.'

He threw back his head and roared with laughter. 'Yes, I think we could safely say that I almost liked them, most certainly, Polly, yes.' He stopped laughing and just smiled, rather tenderly in fact. 'To tell you the truth, I've been thinking about them for some time now.'

I gulped. He looked utterly serious.

'Really?' I breathed.

'Really.'

I wanted to say I'd spent every waking moment thinking about his advances too, but that would have sounded silly. I sat as still as I possibly could on his knee. A silence enveloped us, but I couldn't fill the gaps any more, couldn't think of any words. I just felt dumb with longing.

In the event, no words were necessary. Nick gazed into my red-rimmed eyes which must have looked remarkably like road maps. I held my breath. He cupped my face in his hand and tilted it towards him. And then he kissed me.

Softly and gently. At length, we parted, and as I breathed again I realised I'd been kissed like that once before. Of course, last night. As he held me tightly against him, I was relieved to hear his breath roaring in my ear. At least this time I wasn't the only one with respiratory problems.

'So,' he whispered, puffing a bit, 'shall we go upstairs?'

I opened my mouth to answer, thought better of it, and nodded. Surely if I just stuck to nodding I couldn't cock it up too comprehensively?

We climbed the stairs hand in hand. Those stairs had seen a lot of action one way and another. Twelve hours ago they'd borne me up in the depths of despair, now they bore me up in ecstasy. I felt as if any minute now someone might appear from behind a curtain, snap a clapperboard in front of my nose and cry, 'Right! Take three, Miss McLaren, let's try those stairs one more time, but this time we'll do the despair again, shall we?'

But no. We reached the top and walked hand in hand down the passageway that led inevitably to his bedroom.

But once inside I hesitated. I felt suddenly shy and awkward. My face was a mess and I had none of the gung-ho, alcohol-induced courage of the night before. I looked at him apprehensively. I did hope he wasn't just being kind. Charitable even.

'Nick, I do hope we're doing the right thing. I mean, it would be a shame to spoil our – you know – our friendship and everything, shouldn't we—'

But my heart wasn't in it, and anyway, whatever else I'd been going to say was lost as he took me in his arms and kissed me very firmly on the mouth.

'For once in your life, would you just shut up?' he asked reasonably.

What was a girl to do? I demurred, and let him kiss me again.

We were just inside the bedroom door. Still we kissed. Filled with a sudden desperate greed, and impatient as ever, it occurred to me that we still had a lot of floor space to cover before we were to make contact with the double bed and enjoy the pleasures of the horizontal, but I needn't have worried, Nick was alive to this. He wisely rejected carrying me, but steered me gently towards the bed. Still locked in each other's arms, and indulging in yet more passionate lip contact, we sank down on to the duvet with awesome choreography. This was obviously meant to be. As he went on to address my ear, my mouth and my neck and ultimately of course, my buttons, he whispered tenderly in my ear.

'Sorry if I smell of cow shit.'

I giggled, delighted that someone else was feeling disadvantaged on account of their slovenly ways.

'Couldn't matter less. Sorry about the bloodshot eyes, the dog breath, the sweaty palms . . .'

'I love it . . . all of it,' he muttered back.

It was quite some time before we muttered again. When we did, he was lying on his back, one arm around my shoulder, and I was nestled up against him, my head resting on his bare chest and my arm thrown across it.

'Happy?' he murmured.

'Delirious,' I muttered back.

He smiled and stroked my hair. I studied his chest as it rose gently up and down, centimetres from my eyeballs. It was a pale, biscuity-brown colour with a discreet little smattering of dark hairs growing in a clump in the middle. I wondered how well I would get to know that clump. My eyes travelled up along his neck, and came to rest on his chin, which jutted out dramatically above me. It looked like the Rock of Gibraltar from my vantage point. I traced round it with my finger and smiled, 'Well, who would have thought.'

'Who would have thought what?'

'Exactly.' I grinned and shifted up on to my elbow to look at him. 'You don't remember, do you? That's what you said to me last night and that was exactly my reaction. Who would have thought what?'

He laughed. 'I suppose I must have meant, who would have thought this could finally happen.'

'Are you happy about it?' I asked tentatively, not wanting to spoil anything, but needing to know that it hadn't been a horrible mistake on his part and that he wasn't even now plotting how to get me on the next train to London.

He reached up and pulled me down towards him. 'You bet I am.' He kissed my nose. 'You're beautiful, Polly.'

I smiled, hugging the words to myself. I wasn't beautiful. I was rather overweight, my features were not desperately regular, and this morning did not find me at my best, but if he said it, I could feel it. He went on staring at me and, oddly enough, instead of squirming away and hiding behind my hair, the more he looked, the better I felt.

We lay there, locked in each other's arms, and would no doubt have embarked on a stream of tender pillow-talk for the next hour or two if my tummy hadn't decided it was time to register a protest. It had, of course, rejected the muesli some time earlier on the grounds that it might not have stayed put, but now it was rumbling noisily and clamouring to be given a second chance.

Nick laughed. 'Something tells me you need some blotting paper to mop up last night's excesses.'

I smiled ruefully. 'I suppose I am a bit hungry, but I'll survive.'

There was no way food was coming between me and pillow-talk. I snuggled up to him. My tummy had other ideas. Mount Vesuvius eat your heart out, I thought, as it rumbled again.

Nick laughed. 'Bloody hell, you'll erupt in a minute . . . Come on, let's eat, you're in danger of wasting away.'

'That'll be the day. I always used to wish for anorexia at

Christmas when I got the wishbone.' I sighed. 'But you're right, I'm starving. I'll get up and get us some breakfast — or lunch even.' I glanced at his bedside clock. It seemed to be twelve-thirty.

He kissed my shoulder. 'Let's have it in bed.'

'Oh yes, let's!'

How unlike Harry he was, who had always wanted to get up as quickly as possible and get on with the important things in life, which had never included me.

I threw back the covers and climbed out of bed. He pulled me back down again. 'I'll get it, you stay here. I want to come back and find you exactly as you are.'

I sank back down on to the pillows again. My whole body seemed to be wreathed in smiles. Oh joy! A man who actually wanted to do things for me! I was totally unused to this; it was a long time since I'd been out with anyone who wasn't a complete and utter bastard.

Nick got up and I was treated to a quick glimpse of his broad brown back before he pulled on his jeans and a shirt. He smiled down at me as he tucked the shirt into his jeans.

'You look fabulously wild and dishevelled. Don't move an inch. Just stay exactly like that and I'll be back in five minutes complete with tea and toast.'

'I won't move a muscle,' I said in a ventriloquist's voice, without moving my lips.

He grinned and leaned down to plant a kiss on my forehead. 'Peanut butter or Marmite?' he murmured.

'Peanut butter.'

And off he went, thundering noisily down the stone stairs. I heard him singing along to the radio as he clattered around in the kitchen, getting out mugs, boiling the kettle, making toast. I stretched luxuriously, feeling like the cat who's not only got the cream but the whole dairy too. I couldn't have been happier. He thought I was beautiful. Wild and dishevelled, eh? If only he knew how easy it was to look like that; it was sophisticated and elegant that caused the problems.

How wild, I wondered? I nipped out of bed and stole across to the oval mirror propped up on a chest of drawers. My face was quite attractively flushed and my eyes had widened considerably; there was a definite sparkle about them, too. Not bad, I thought appraisingly, not too bad at all considering the very raw material of first thing this morning. My hair was all over the place, but that apparently was no bad thing, and thank God I'd washed all that make-up off. It would be decorating his pillows by now.

I hopped back into bed and drew the sheets up under my chin. My feet took it upon themselves to do a little jig of joy under the duvet. So. Here I was at last. In Nick's bedroom. I took a good look around the room. It was perfect. Not like Harry's with its silly futon and oh-so-tasteful minimalist bits and pieces, but cluttered and lived in and – yes, welcoming.

The walls were Wedgwood blue with an indistinct criss-cross pattern, and the carpet a darker blue and very worn, with a series of reddish Persian rugs strewn over it, probably hiding a few holes. The bookcase underneath the window was crammed with books, which jostled each other for space and spewed out on to the floor, and the drawers in the huge chest on which the mirror sat were mostly open, with clothes falling out of them. A series of hunting prints covered one wall, and on another there were a few old maps. Above the bed was a rather modern, and quite good, painting of the house.

The room was untidy, but not massively so. Of course it had nothing on my sluttish tendencies, but it definitely showed promise. The bedside table, for instance, was covered with a thin film of dust, and in one corner of the room a pair of dirty jeans, some old socks, and a jumper lay festering in a heap. A nice touch, I thought. There were no photos either. Good. I liked a man who didn't wear his heart in his picture frames.

Balancing on top of the curtain pelmet were a few old Airfix planes. They brought a lump to my throat. He really had grown up in here. I wondered if he'd made the planes with his father. I wondered what he'd been like. Suddenly I wanted to know everything about him, about his parents, his childhood – everything. That was the joy of it all. We were at the beginning, with so much to find out about each other. I smiled to myself. Happiness flooded through every vein.

I plumped up the pillows and arranged myself decoratively upon them, with my hair spread out like a fan around my face. Then I set about my cleavage with a vengeance, draping the duvet seductively so it just covered my boobs but left quite a lot protruding voluptuously over the top. I positioned my arms to wedge the duvet in position, but made sure they didn't actually touch my sides or they'd look fat. I looked down. All was in order. Thus arranged, I waited. He'd been gone at least five minutes now, hadn't he? What was he doing, making the bread? Picking the tea? I smiled to myself. No. He was probably doing something terribly sweet like picking flowers for the tray. I'd pretend to be really surprised. 'Nick! Daffodils, how gorgeous!' I'd cry as he pressed a large bunch into my arms.

But wait a minute? What was that? Was that Nick's voice? Yes, it was, who on earth was he talking to? I frowned. There was another voice down there too. Female at that. Rachel? Surely she wasn't back already! No, it couldn't be Rachel, it must be – yes, of course, it must be Sarah! Sarah, over from the stables for a break and a cup of coffee. Of course. Hopefully Nick would get rid of her, tactfully. We could always ring her later of course, ask her over for a cup of tea. If we weren't indulging in a spot of afternoon delight, that is. I allowed myself a quiet little squeak of excitement — eeeeek! It really was all too thrilling!

The next minute I heard heavy footsteps bounding up the stairs. Goody-goody! I gave the duvet a last-minute adjustment and smiled eagerly. The door flew open and Nick came in. He stood in the doorway. His face was pale and drawn and the muscle in his cheek was bobbing up and down. The sweet, tender look of ten minutes ago was nowhere to be seen. He didn't say anything for a moment.

'What is it? What's happened?' I whispered in alarm.

Nick came over and sat down on the edge of the bed. He ran his hands through his hair. He looked shattered. 'I'm afraid we'll have to postpone our lunch, Polly, we've got a visitor.'

'Why? Who is it?'

He looked down at the duvet. There was a terrible silence. I felt my heart pause in mid-beat, then it started hammering away somewhere in the vicinity of my mouth. What on earth was going on?

'Nick, who is it? Who's downstairs?'

Funnily enough I knew the moment I'd said it. Nick merely confirmed my fears. He looked up and met my eyes.

'It's Serena,' he said quietly.

Chapter Twenty-two

'Serena!' I sat bolt upright.

Nick looked wretched. 'She's just arrived, I'm afraid. Look, Polly, I'll try and explain—'

'Darling? Darling, are you upstairs?' A strange bird-like trill interrupted us, warbling up from below, shrieking down the passageway, careering round the bedroom door, and hitting me full in the face like a runaway train. Those were Serena's dulcet tones, all right.

'You'd better go,' I whispered, suddenly filled with panic at the thought of her venturing upstairs and appearing at the door in all her Armani glory to witness this sordid little scene. 'Go on, quick. She might come up!'

Nick looked at my stricken face and took my hand, giving it a reassuring little squeeze. 'I'll explain everything later, Polly. It's just that — well, she's terribly vulnerable at the moment, and I really don't want to hurt her if it's at all possible. You do understand, don't you?'

He looked at me beseechingly and I nodded bravely, understanding precisely nothing. Hurt her? How about hurting me? Vulnerable, eh? Yes well, if you must know, I felt about as vulnerable as an open wound. An open wound that's just been on the receiving end of a Bruce Lee Kung-Fu kick, one of those flashy sideways ones that comes at you out of nowhere — ha-ya-ho! — and leaves you doubled up on the floor, spluttering and gasping for breath.

'Dar-*ling*!' There it was again, that voice; shrill, clear and confident, ricocheting off the bedroom walls.

Nick dropped my hand hurriedly and disappeared.

I lay there for a second feeling numb. Then I crawled slowly out of bed and fumbled around for my jeans and jumper. A tear dropped on to the Persian rug as I sat down to pull on my socks. I blinked hard. You silly little fool, I thought savagely, did you really think you were meant to be that happy? Don't you know the story of your life by now? What made you think you could start rewriting it at this late stage?

I found a comb and pulled it through my hair, looking in the mirror. The same mirror that moments earlier had revealed a flushed, excited, happy Polly. Now it revealed a white-faced, scared little creature with wet eyes and a trembling jaw.

I faced my reflection and addressed it sternly in a stage whisper. 'Pull yourself together, will you? OK, so the girlfriend who you'd both conveniently forgotten has arrived – it had to happen some time, didn't it? And just remember this, he's very, very fond of you. No one, *no one*, could have pretended like that back there – I eyed the crumpled sheets meaningfully – without being very, very, well, fond.' Ghastly word. One could be fond of a hamster, but one wouldn't necessarily want to spend the rest of one's life with it. I revised my adjective. 'Special, then. You're very special, OK?' I commanded my reflection. Somehow it didn't look convinced. What seemed to me to be more convincing was the blatant truth, but could I take it?

I eyed myself menacingly. 'OK, try this one for size, wobble-jaw. Nick Penhalligan is madly in love with the extraordinarily beautiful actress Serena Montgomery, who, unfortunately, is too busy attending to her glittering career to be with him for much of the time, so out of sheer frustration, and on the spur of a mad and lecherous moment, he bonks his secretary, Polly McLaren, of whom he is reasonably fond.'

I gulped hard. It certainly rang true. My reflection nodded back dumbly. Yes, that seemed to be much more like it. In which case, where did that leave me now? I felt panic rising within me. What was I doing upstairs? Tidying the airing cupboard? Dusting the bedrooms? Just making myself useful? What did concubines do, I wondered?

I buried my face in my hands, but only for a second. Then I shook myself. No, there was no doubt about it, she had to be faced, but this time – I flew out of Nick's room and ran down the passageway to mine – with war paint on and guns blazing.

Feverishly, I slapped on a protective coating of blusher, eyeliner, mascara and lipstick, then, suitably masked, I marched downstairs, summoning up as much of the old Dunkirk spirit as I could possibly muster. OK, I was going down, of that there was no doubt, but I wasn't going down without a fight.

However, all ideas of fighting Serena on the beaches disappeared in a little puff of smoke as I walked into the drawing room. My guns gave a brief splutter, a windy little fart, and died. She was sitting, or should I say, reclining, on the sofa, armed up to the eyeballs with beauty, poise and, what's more, a glass of white wine and a cigarette. Here she had me at an immediate disadvantage – what I wouldn't do for a cigarette, I thought, eyeing her pack enviously – but it was her staggering beauty that had me disadvantaged in a much more serious manner. We're talking crippled, actually.

How could her eyes be as green and sparkling as that? And did those cheekbones seriously shoot off into her temples in such a breathtaking manner? And was her complexion really so clear and peachy? What the devil was Nick up to, playing around with a flaky old yobbo like me when he had this devastating creature in tow? Was he insane? Or blind? Or perhaps her beauty intimidated him? It certainly intimidated the hell out of me.

As I came in, she ran a hand through her ash-blonde hair and stood up; not, you understand, out of any sense of politeness, but purely to give me the benefit of her devastating figure. The long, long legs seemed to take an eternity to unfurl and straighten and, as they sauntered towards me, clad in brown suede and topped with a cream silk shirt, I realised that, whereas I in my pancake make-up and tight jeans looked just wrong, she, on the other hand, looked just right. Not too glamorous for the country, but stunning enough to put anyone else to shame. In fact, come to think of it, she reminded me of a beautiful young filly: long-limbed, beautifully groomed, and gleaming to perfection, even down to her shiny little feet, shod as they were in expensive Italian leather and gleaming like newly oiled hooves.

There was simply no competition. I know when I'm beaten. This was Nick's girlfriend all right, she had it written all over her.

I shuffled towards her, forcing a smile and feeling like somebody's mother. 'Hi,' was all I could manage.

'Well, hello,' she said, raising her eyebrows as she extended an icy white hand complete with immaculate red nails.

I took it gingerly, then dropped it hurriedly as Nick appeared in the doorway with a tray full of coffee. I wasn't standing next to her for comparison, no siree. I shuffled off to my basket in the corner and curled up on a cushion. I knew my place, and it was low, very low. Definitely floor level.

Serena evidently knew her place, too, and it seemed to be reclining on the arm of the sofa, head back, legs crossed, arm flung out along the back of the sofa with all her assets to the fore. If truth be told it was an old trick of mine, but one she did with a lot more style.

Nick set the coffee down and had the grace to look sheepish. He turned to Serena. 'You remember Polly, don't you?'

'Of course I do.' She swivelled the green headlamps in my direction and smiled benignly. 'Goodness only knows where you'll turn up next, though! One minute you're behind a typewriter, then you're floundering around in a freezer, and now you're lolling around down here! I mean, really, whatever next?' She gave her silly, tinkly little laugh.

'Yes, that's me,' I muttered darkly. 'Ubiquitous.'

She frowned. 'What did you call me?'

'When?'

'Just then, you said you – something-or-other, what was it?' she sounded angry.

'Ubiquitous. It's a noun, not an insult.'

'Oh.' She frowned again and I saw Nick suppress a smile.

Actually, an insult was what I really would have liked to have hurled at her, along with some incredibly heavy pieces of furniture, like that mahogany chest over there, or those thumping great fire irons in the grate. I didn't like her sneering manner, nor did I like the freezer reference or the secretary tag. I flexed my not so much bitten as tapered nails, feeling well out of practice, and looked searchingly at her as if her face temporarily escaped me.

' . . . and it's um, Selina, isn't it?'

She looked taken aback for a moment, then her eyes narrowed and the lips tightened. 'Serena,' she hissed. 'Serena Montgomery!'

'Ah yes, of course, sorry.'

I smiled sweetly and wondered what my next mode of attack should be, but my heart wasn't in it and I felt weary already. Cat fights weren't really my scene; I didn't have the nails for it. Anyway, let's face it, why shouldn't she be angry, if not livid? She was, after all, the incumbent girlfriend – although let's not mention that: she might think I was suggesting she had bandy legs – and here was I, a usurper, lolling around, as she so eloquently put it, her boyfriend's house. Sorry, seat. Well, yes, that too.

'So how long will you be with us for, Polly?' she inquired, neatly ramming home the fact that she and Nick were very much an 'us', a couple, and since three was surely a crowd, should I not perhaps be thinking about boarding the very next train back to London?

'Oh, I don't know really, not very long. Haven't really thought,' I muttered miserably, thinking – just as soon as I've stolen your cigarettes.

'Sweet of Nick to ask you down; he said you needed a break. I do hope you're feeling better?'

I glanced at Nick, but he had his back to me as he poured the coffee. So that's what he'd said by way of explanation. The benevolent employer was treating one of his menials from the workhouse to a holiday. Some poor deserving wretch, who did nothing but bash away at a word processor all day until her hands were red and raw, and who had eventually fallen on her screen in a state of nervous exhaustion, had been magnanimously rescued by her big-hearted boss, who'd whisked her away to breathe some clean, country air at his stately home. Services to shorthand no doubt. I glanced beseechingly at the back of Nick's head. Couldn't he just turn around for a second? Give me a little look to say, Don't worry, Polly, everything's going to be OK? Apparently not.

'Yes,' I sighed. 'Very good of him.'

At that moment there was a tap on the window. One of Nick's farm hands was standing outside. Nick went over and opened it.

'Sorry to disturb you, Nick,' he said, sticking his head through, 'but there's a ewe out here I'd like you to have a look at. She's cut herself quite badly on some wire. It's a pretty nasty wound, we might need the vet.'

'Damn.' Nick set his coffee down. 'There's too much of that bloody wire around; I thought I'd asked you to clear it all. All right, Larry, I'm coming.' He took a cigarette from Serena's pack and swept out through the french doors.

I watched him go. He strode purposefully through the garden, smartly vaulted the fence, and marched off towards his sheep in the far field. Well, thanks a bunch, I thought bitterly. When the going gets tough, the tough go shepherding. It briefly crossed my mind to follow suit and head for the wide open spaces myself, leaving Serena to bitch away to the fireplace on her own, but as usual my nerve failed and I stayed rooted to the floorboards, looking up at her expectantly like a subservient first former waiting to see if the head girl would be handing out detention today.

'You're bound to feel better soon,' she tinkled on. 'This place is such a marvellous tonic. I always come down when I'm feeling a bit — you know, rough.'

What was I supposed to be, a drug addict going through cold turkey? A drying-out alcoholic? What sort of garbage had Nick been feeding her?

'Actually, I'm perfectly all right,' I said in a level voice, adding, with an uncharacteristic show of spirit, 'in fact, there's nothing wrong with me at all, never has been. Nick just invited me down for a holiday.'

She ignored me and carried on as if I hadn't spoken. 'The sea air will do wonders for your complexion, of course. You must get Nick to take you sailing: he has a darling little boat, and Frenchman's Creek is absolutely magical at this time of year.'

All my complexion needed was a day or two off the juice and eight or nine hours uninterrupted sleep, thank you very much, and anyway, on closer inspection I decided that a great deal of hers was out of a bottle. I also realised that she wasn't quite as young as I'd originally supposed; she definitely had three or four years on me. I revised my previous description from filly to mare and felt about a millimetre better.

I wondered if I could slip away now, run upstairs to my bedroom and hide under the duvet, or slink off to the stables for a chat with Sarah, but as I tentatively tried to raise myself up from the floor, Serena fixed me with her beady eye and warbled off in her stagey voice again. I fell, winded, pinned, and gasping beneath the weight of her mighty RADA monologue.

' . . . Yes, I come down here whenever I can, I simply love it, it makes me feel human again. People just don't realise how bloody hard acting is, they really don't. The hours are simply appalling for a start, up at dawn for make-up, and then shooting all day, usually in the blistering heat of some sub-tropical jungle or desert. I mean, people think it's glamorous, but it really isn't. They see us scampering around in foreign locations and think, Wow! What a fantastic life; but what they don't realise is that I'm sweltering away under the weight of some ghastly seventeenth-century costume and positively dripping under my make-up and those hellish lights. And the people! Ugh, I can't tell you. Sometimes I'm convinced I'm doomed to be surrounded by morons, you know.' (Here she gave me a searching look and I wondered if perhaps I'd just become chief moron, a walk-on part only, of course; chief, spear-carrying moron.) ' . . . If it's not some idiot of a director telling me how to read my lines, it's some goon of a lighting cameraman − usually foreign because our ridiculous union rules dictate that we have to employ a certain amount of natives − telling me where he wants me to stand, as if I don't know by now. Some of them don't even speak English, you know! I can't tell you how frustrating that is. It happened to me in Delhi just the other day. Some cretin of a native tried to tell me my job, and he couldn't even speak the lingo! I mean, really. They say travel broadens the mind, but as far as I'm concerned it just reinforces prejudices, d'you know what I mean?'

I'd been staring fixedly at a matchstick that was wedged between a gap in the floorboards. I pushed it down with my fingernail and it slipped through, down to the bowels of the earth. I longed to slip down with it, but I managed to raise my aching eyes and murmur, 'Oh, yes, quite, absolutely.'

'No no, give me good old England any day,' she warbled on gaily. 'You know, sometimes I literally have to just close my eyes and − as the expression goes − think of England. I do, really I do. I'll be playing some ghastly love scene with some revolting ham actor with bad breath, and I try to imagine I'm back here on the farm with Nick. I imagine I'm helping with the baby lambs, or − or that we're drifting up the river together, lying back in the boat in the sunshine, my hand skimming along in the water as we row quietly up and down. It's my way of preserving my sanity, do you see?'

I nodded. I was wilting steadily and I had a nasty sicky feeling in my stomach. I had a shrewd idea she was playing a very clever game.

'I picture we're gently floating up Frenchman's Creek. I see the glistening water, the overhanging willow trees, I hear the sound of the seagulls circling overhead—'

'Yes, I've been actually.' I said, with a sudden flash of bravado.

'Oh, really?'

'With − with Tim and Sarah,' I added, coward that I am.

'Ah yes, you'll know all about it then. It is utterly divine, isn't it?'

'Oh yes, utterly,' I mumbled, this RADA lark was catching, but I couldn't help wondering where the eulogy on Frenchman's Creek was getting us. She didn't keep me in suspense for long, bless her.

'I simply adore it, it's quite my most special place.' She

put her head on one side and gave me what I can only describe as a Dame Edna smile. 'Of course, you know why, don't you?'

'Er, no.' I felt like a rat in a trap.

The eyebrows shot up. 'You mean, he didn't tell you?'

'Tell me what?'

'That that's where he proposed to me, of course! In Frenchman's Creek!'

I gasped audibly. 'Proposed!'

'Yes, didn't you know?' There was a nasty glint in her eye and she glowed with triumph. 'In his dear little boat. Down on one knee he went. God, I remember it so clearly, we were wobbling around all over the place, in fact we nearly capsized – I promise you it was priceless!'

Her tinkly laugh homed in on my nerve centre and it seemed to me that I was being slowly but surely electrocuted.

'He was so sweet, I'll never forget how he asked me. He didn't say, "Will you marry me", or anything boring like that, he said, "Serena, would you do me the honour of becoming my wife?" – isn't that just too divine? Of course I spoiled the dignity of the whole occasion by leaping up and crying, "Yes! Yes! Yes!" I was so excited! Then I just fell on him, simply covering him with kisses, and then of course the whole thing got totally out of hand and we ended up in a tangled heap at the bottom of the boat, giggling hysterically as the boat rocked perilously from side to side – I tell you, we were lucky not to go in!'

I wondered if I could just quietly be sick in that potted begonia without her noticing – or perhaps, yes, perhaps the coal bucket by the fire would stand up to my projections a little better. There might be rather a lot of it. I nodded, biting back the bile.

'Anyway, when we'd, you know, straightened ourselves out a bit – because actually the river isn't *all* that private and you never know *who's* going to cruise up beside you;

there are all kinds of nosy parkers around — anyway, that's when he produced the most darling little ring from his pocket — look!'

She thrust her hand under my nose and wiggled her finger around. A very pretty antique gold ring with a jade stone winked up at me.

I gulped. 'V-very pretty.'

'Of course, it's only a makeshift ring, until I find something more suitable — you know, diamonds or sapphires maybe, but I think I'll always wear it anyway. It's charming, isn't it?'

'It certainly is,' I managed.

'He said he bought it because it matched my eyes.'

'Yes, yes it does,' I whispered, clutching a handy Queen Anne chair leg for support.

'Lord knows when we'll find time to get married, though. We're both just so busy. I've got this new film coming up, and Nick's got to tie up the agency — you know he's selling out, don't you?'

'Yes, yes I know.' This at least was one piece of news that didn't come as a total shock.

'So anyway, it could be a while, but at least we've made the commitment. I think that's so important, don't you? So many people these days don't make that commitment, and I think it's a mistake, I really do.'

I mumbled a suitable response. I'd collapsed in a little heap now, and the more I paled and wilted, the more Serena seemed to exult and billow and triumph.

She lit yet another precious cigarette, put her gleaming blonde head on one side, and smiled that caring little smile again. 'I do hope you won't take this the wrong way, Polly?'

I gulped. All sorts of things seemed to be going down the wrong way, one more surely wouldn't make much difference.

'Fire away,' I said bravely, and didn't she just.

'It's just that, well, I met Jack Crawley on the way over here, and he said you'd been making a bit of a fool of yourself, one way and another.'

I gasped. 'What d'you mean?'

Serena held up her hand to stop me. 'Now, there's no need to explain, really. I can quite understand how it happened. I know that Nick is a very attractive man, and I don't blame you for falling for him, but the point is that — well, he's finding it all just a teensy bit embarrassing.'

'That's not true!' I could feel myself going scarlet.

'Oh, I can assure you it is,' she said in a steely voice. 'Why d'you think he rushed off to deal with his sheep like that? Larry was quite capable of sorting out that little problem, but Nick was just glad of an excuse to get away. He's fearfully embarrassed about the whole thing. You really do moon around after him, you know.'

'I do not moon around!' I flushed angrily.

'Oh, but you do, everyone's noticed it. Why, Jack told me you follow Nick around like a little dog. Honestly, Polly, I'm only telling you this so you don't make a complete idiot of yourself. It was wrong of Nick not to tell you we're engaged, but perhaps he thought you wouldn't be able to take it.'

I stared down at my shoes, wishing I was a million miles away. I wanted to tell her where we'd been when she'd arrived, what we'd been doing, but I hadn't the nerve.

I licked my lips. 'Has Nick said anything?'

'I'm afraid he has. Of course he blames himself, he knows he should never have been so weak, but I am away an awful lot and it's terribly difficult for a man when a girl — well, when she throws herself at him, d'you know what I mean? Especially when he's been — well, doing without it for a while. One can understand how he might just — you know, go for it.'

I caught my breath. The bastard, how could he? I didn't trust myself to speak, and carried on staring at the fascinating top stitching on my shoes.

'Now, Polly, don't look so glum. You know as well as I do that boys will be boys. The poor dears find it so frightfully difficult to control themselves, and when the cat's away — ' she shrugged — 'well, look what happens. Now, I'm not suggesting he's totally blameless, but I think you'll admit that most men would find it pretty hard to resist when it's handed to them on a plate like that.'

Please, could I just die quietly now? Don't let me live any longer God, please! Had he really told her? Or was she just guessing wildly? I daren't look up. There was a long pause. My face was flaming as it faced the carpet. Any minute now it would surely just melt and drip steadily through that rug into the floorboards.

'Anyway,' she said at length, ' I don't want to make a big thing of it, I just want you to know that I'm not a fool and I know what you're up to, OK?'

My eyes remained glued to my shoes.

'And I don't want to be brutal, but you must realise that hanging around here is doing you no good at all. You're just making everyone feel uncomfortable: Nick, me, all of us. You do see that, don't you?'

I nodded miserably.

'The trains to London are pretty frequent, you know. I could give you a lift to the station if you just wanted to slip off quietly? There's no rush, of course.'

I met her eye with difficulty. 'Don't worry. I won't be hanging around making things uncomfortable for you. I'll be off just as soon as I've packed — and I'd rather walk to the station, thank you very much.'

She smirked, 'You'll find it's rather a long way, I'm afraid, but as you wish.'

She ground her cigarette out in an ashtray, and brushed her hands together lightly as if that little piece of business had been successfully concluded. Having made mincemeat of me, she turned her attention to the house. She got up

411

and glided round the room, pausing here and there to wipe dust from a picture frame or rearrange a piece of china. Her eye swept around proprietorially.

'I really must do something about this room. Honestly, when I'm not here the place just goes to rack and ruin. These ghastly covers are finally falling to bits: a blessing in disguise, I think; perhaps Nick will finally get some new ones.' She fingered the lovely faded old chintz on the sofa. 'And as for these dirty old rugs, they've been here for ever.'

I was tempted to suggest that this was entirely their charm, but decided against it as she kicked the beautiful Persian rug with her expensive Italian boot. I didn't want to be on the receiving end of that toe-cap. No doubt in her mind's eye she already had the whole place carpeted wall to-wall in off-white shag-pile.

She strolled towards me and I shrank back in terror, wondering what adjustments she had in mind – a biff on the nose perhaps, or a nice black eye – but no, she was making for the begonia. She fingered the soil in the pot and I fervently wished that I'd stuck to plan A and thrown up in it. She shook her head, tutting loudly.

'You see, no one even bothers to water the plants. If I'm not here to do it, they just keel over and die. I must talk to Nick about getting someone to help out here: a daily or, even better, someone to live in. This place needs a good seeing-to. If we're going to live here when we're married, I won't be able to see to it all on my own; I'm simply not used to that sort of thing. I must have some staff.'

She looked down at me, curled up as I was in a pathetic, squirming little bundle at her feet. She put her head on one side and eyed me speculatively. Good grief, was she sizing me up as a potential cleaner? Was she wondering if I wouldn't in fact do nicely? Why not? I was already on the pay roll, I could just change my position. From secretary to char in one swift little demotion. I had a sudden, powerful urge to grab her elegant little ankles, rugby tackle her to the floor and kick her smartly in the teeth. Unfortunately I controlled it and, instead, in a totally shameless manner, blurted out my most overpowering need.

'D'you think I could possibly have one of your cigarettes?' It couldn't be helped. Unless I got some nicotine into these gasping lungs, they'd seize up.

She was all concern and benevolence. 'Of course!' she purred, pressing the packet into my hand like Maundy money. 'Take the packet. Goodness, your hand's shaking, you poor thing.'

'I don't want the packet,' I said petulantly. 'I've got some somewhere, I just can't remember where I've put them, that's all.'

'Of course you can't,' she said consolingly, 'you must be in a terrible muddle at the moment. I bet you don't know if you're coming or going!'

'Oh, I've got a pretty shrewd idea I'm going,' I muttered darkly, 'but don't worry about me. I'm fine,' I said, grabbing a box of matches and lighting the cigarette. It wasn't easy, as the match wobbled alarmingly in my hand. I sucked the nectar down to my boots.

'Really? Are you sure you're all right?' She glided over and sat down next to me in the Queen Anne, crossing her elegant ankles. 'Only, I hope you don't mind me mentioning it, but I hear Nick's not the only man you've fallen for recently. You've got rather a tangled love life at the moment, haven't you? Mmmm?'

'What d'you mean!' What on earth did she have up her sleeve now? A jack-knife? An anaconda? An Exocet missile? I kept a tight hold on my cigarette in case I needed to jab her in the eye with it.

'Well, I hear your last boyfriend gave you a rather rough ride. It was Harry Lloyd-Roberts, wasn't it?'

My jaw dropped. 'How on earth did you know about that?'

'Oh, everyone in London knows Harry, he's part of the scene. In fact I even had a bit of a dalliance with him myself once, but he bored me after a while. He was frightfully upset when I dropped him, kept turning up at the studios uninvited making a fool of himself; then he used to sit outside my flat in his car for days on end, just waiting for me to come out. He's dreamy looking, of course, but there's absolutely nothing at all between the ears. No substance whatsoever. You're much better off without him, you know.'

Was there no end to her charm? Would she just go on and on like this until someone put a bullet through her brain? Please could it be me? I'd heard about girls like this, read about them in the problem pages of women's magazines, real live bitches who took pleasure in pouring salt in wounds. Well, now I'd met one. Only this time, I thought with a small degree of satisfaction, she was wasting her time. She wasn't hurting me at all. I couldn't give a damn if she and Harry had bonked for Britain. The very thought was registering absolutely zero on my Richter scale of pain. Not a pang, not a twinge, not a sausage. Sorry Serena.

I felt just a weeny bit stronger, but not enough to stand up, so when the telephone rang it was Serena who strolled off to answer it. Well anyway, it was her phone, wasn't it? I lay down on the floor and gasped, glad of the chance to catch my breath. When she came back she looked rather annoyed.

'It's Tim. He wants to speak to you or Nick.'

'I'll take it,' I said, sprinting past her, desperate to talk to a normal human being. I grabbed the telephone.

'Tim?'

'Hi, Polly, how are you?'

'Oh er, OK. You?'

'Yes, I suppose so.'

'What's wrong? You sound a bit down.'

'So do you, come to that.'

'Well . . . I s'pose I am a bit.' Riveting stuff, eh?

'Listen . . .' he said, coming slowly to the point. 'Rachel and I thought we might come back, if the coast's clear, that is.'

'Oh yes, well clear. We saw Adam last night — ' was it only last night? It felt about a year ago — 'and he swallowed the whole story. We did it rather well, actually. Nick checked with Mrs Green yesterday, and apparently he shot off back to London pretty sharpish.'

'Oh good, we'll come back then.' He sounded relieved. Was there a problem? Had Svengali and his pupil fallen out already? It wouldn't be hard, I admit, her sulky moods would try the patience of a saint; but Tim really was a bit of a saint on the quiet, and he'd been so keen to bring her out. Perhaps he'd just discovered there was nothing worth exposing.

'See you later then.'

'Yeh, see you, bye.'

I took the scenic route back to the drawing room, pausing en route to spend a couple of hours lying down on my bed. I was too upset to cry. Despair overwhelmed me. I just lay there looking at the ceiling, listening to my clock ticking. He was engaged to her. Engaged to be married, and I'd had no idea. I'd done it again, picked another bastard, and once more it was too late to do anything about it, I was head over heels in love with him. Oh God, what was I going to do? Go home pretty damn quick, that was for sure, either to London or to my parents, as long as it was far away. As soon as I'd got my strength up. I shut my eyes. To think I'd been presumptuous enough to imagine anyone in Nick's class could fall for someone as gauche and stupid as me when he had Serena — first-class bitch, granted, but beautiful and famous nonetheless —

hanging on to his arm. How could I have been so ludicrous?

Chapter Twenty-three

I lay like that for an hour or more. Not crying, just staring into space, looking at the cracks in the ceiling. I could feel myself shaking a bit, so I pulled the duvet over me and hugged the pillow for comfort, burying my face in it. In actual fact I felt rather numb. I couldn't quite believe it was all true. I shut my eyes to block out the misery, and I suppose I must have dropped off, God knows I was tired enough, because the next thing I knew, I was opening my eyes and someone was knocking loudly on the door.

I reached out my hand and grabbed the clock by the bed. Ten past three. I must have been up here for ages. Who was at the door? Was it Nick? Had he come to find me? I sat up eagerly.

'Come in!'

Tim's head appeared around the door, followed by his body.

'Oh hi, Tim, you're back.' I tried not to sound disappointed.

'Yep, just arrived. I came to tell you lunch is ready. It's gone three o'clock, but no one seems to have eaten, so Sarah's rustled up a fish pie.'

'Thanks, I'll come down.'

Damn, I couldn't escape now. I'd have to put in an appearance at what would undoubtedly be one of the most grisly meals of my life. Tim turned to go, but lingered at the door, fiddling with the handle. He didn't look quite

417

right somehow, his normally jolly, open face was pinched and haggard. He turned back. We both spoke at once.

'Are you all right?' we said in unison.

He laughed and I mustered a smile. He came over and sat on the side of the bed. I sat up and hugged my knees.

'What's wrong?' he said, peering into my face. 'You look absolutely terrible.'

Men never seem to learn that, even if we girls feel like death, we don't like to be told we look like it.

I grimaced. 'Oh, nothing.'

'Come on, what is it?'

Could I tell him? Right now I needed a friend extremely badly, but Nick's brother? And for all I knew he might be Serena's number one fan.

'I've just got a horrendous hangover, that's all. Totally self-inflicted. How about you?'

'Oh, er – well, yes the same.' He looked shifty.

'Really? But you don't even drink, not properly, anyway.'

'Well, perhaps that's why I got so plastered, not used to it, you see.' He avoided my eyes and studied the wallpaper. Being such an accomplished liar myself, I can spot a porky pie a mile off. I reached out and put a hand on his arm.

'Tim? What is it? Is it Rachel?'

His face puckered up when I said her name, and I knew I'd hit the spot. They'd obviously fallen out in a big way.

'Have you had a row? Is that it?'

'Oh no,' he shook his head, 'nothing like that. Quite the . . . quite the reverse, really.'

The reverse? Quite the reverse of having a row? Well, what the devil was that then? They'd got on too well? Impossible. They'd got on so well that something untoward had happened? They'd got on so well that they'd ended up . . .

'Oh my goodness, Tim!'

Tim's shoulders sagged. He ran his hands through his

hair and put his head in his hands. A guilty man if ever I saw one. I was staggered.

'Tim, you mean?'

Tim nodded into his hands, still avoiding my eye.

'Oh my God. You and Rachel? I just don't believe it!'

'Neither do I, now,' he whispered. 'I really can't believe it happened. But I promise you, Polly, at the time I felt absolutely powerless. I simply couldn't resist her. She was so . . .' he shook his head as he struggled to find the words, as well he might. 'Well, she was just so – so captivating, so, I don't know – irresistible, I suppose. And it all happened so quickly. One minute we were sitting downstairs chatting, and the next minute – the next minute we were in my bedroom. It was extraordinary, I just – I just couldn't help myself.'

Rachel? Captivating? Irresistible? Hang on a moment, did we have the same girl in mind here? Frumpy old, miserable old, bag lady Rachel? I struggled to get my mind around this one. Was he trying to tell me that that grumpy little heap of mouse droppings had, in the space of just one night, lured him away from his lovely, sparky, pretty girlfriend and succeeded in bewitching him to such an extent that he'd – had he?

'Did you?'

'What?'

'You know . . .'

He ran his hands through his hair and nodded. 'Yes, of course.' He'd ended up compromising himself wildly. Well, blow me, you had to hand it to her, didn't you? And here he was now, this handsome hunk of a man, reduced to a shivering pulp, eaten up with what I fervently hoped was remorse and not more desire.

'Do you regret it now?'

He wrenched his head out of his hands and groaned. 'Of course I bloody do, it was a stupid, irresponsible, idiotic thing to do, but I promise you, Polly, I just didn't stand a

chance! I was putty in her hands, you can't imagine how —
well, how downright sexy she was!'

I tried. I tried really hard, but no, he was right, I just
couldn't imagine. It made you think though, didn't it? I
mean, all these years I'd been dousing myself in Chanel,
pulling my necklines down, hitching my skirts up,
endlessly crossing and uncrossing my legs, throwing back
my hair, pulling it over one eye, practising smouldering
looks in the mirror, cultivating a sexy voice, and do you
know what I should really have been doing? I should have
been taking piano lessons, twiddling my hair round my
finger, sitting in a heap in a nasty grey cardigan and
occasionally, for extra sensuality, donning a pair of
tortoiseshell National Health spectacles. And there was I
thinking that those spectacles were just another form of
birth control, along with acne and bad breath. Ah well, we
live and learn.

I was woken from this mind-boggling reverie by Tim,
who was up to his elbows in confession. Once he'd started,
he was determined to finish, as Magnus would say. He was
over by the window, staring out at the fields, frantically
unburdening himself to the sheep, the cows, the trees —
anyone and anything that would listen.

'And yes, OK, I suppose I'd had a couple of glasses of
wine, three maybe, which is more than I'd normally have,
but that's no excuse, I certainly wasn't pissed. It just
seemed so right, so natural. There we were, having supper
in Penny's candlelit dining room which, as you can
imagine, is pretty conducive to a little dinner à deux . . .'

Now this I could imagine. Penny's dining room would
be magical in the evening, with its dark green walls
smothered with oil paintings, and its cosy little alcove
tables laden with silver; little hideaway places where two
people could sit in relative privacy, their faces flickering in
the candlelight, a cosy log fire crackling away in the grate
beside them . . . Yes, I could imagine it would make quite

420

a seduction scene. In fact, I made a mental note to reserve a table the next time an eligible young man wanted to take me out to a little country – oh well, forget that. There was never going to be a next time. It was the nunnery for me.

'Are you listening to me, Polly, because I can tell you this isn't the easiest story to tell.'

'Sorry, go on.'

'Over dinner, she started to tell me a bit about herself. I was really pleased, because you know how shy and withdrawn she can be, don't you?'

I ground my teeth together, dug my nails hard into the palm of my hand and nodded.

'She told me all about her mother dying when she was young, and how she grew up with just a father and a housekeeper, not even any brothers and sisters, and d'you know she wasn't even allowed to go out or have friends round?' Tim shook his head. 'Terrible. Then, of course, this Adam chap appeared on the scene. Just what she didn't need; I mean, he just sounds like a complete head-case. As far as I can gather the man's completely barking. He was incredibly possessive, followed her around the whole time, wouldn't let her make her own friends – rather like her father actually. You know, one way and another, she's had a really hard time, Polly.'

'I know, I know, just get to the point,' I said quickly. 'Then what happened?'

I wanted to move this monologue on apace, I really didn't think I could stomach any more of Rachel's hard times on top of my own heartache and hangover.

'Well, we chatted on and on for ages. It's a long time since I've had a good chinwag, I'm always so bloody busy. She seemed really interested in me, asked lots of questions, and I told her all about Dad dying, something I realised I hadn't talked about for years. She was really sweet and sympathetic; well, she'd lost her mother, of course, so she knew how I felt. Then I told her all about the farm, and how I was determined to make it work, even though everyone assures me that organic farming is an economic disaster area, and she didn't say that. She was really supportive and encouraging.'

Well, she would be, wouldn't she? And come to that, wasn't Sarah too, who slogged away on his farm at the weekends after a gruelling week at the stables? Or was it only candlelit support that mattered? I bit my tongue.

Tim sighed. 'Well I suppose after a while we'd exhausted nearly every channel of conversation, and we just ended up looking at each other. You know how it is, Polly.'

I nodded, a woman of the world of wine bars. 'You exchanged a few meaningful looks?'

He sighed, 'Yes.'

'She looked down shyly, then up into your eyes again?'

'Well, yes.'

'She put her hand on the table?'

'Er, yes.'

'You covered it with yours?'

He looked surprised. 'Yes.'

'Your eyes met again, and this time you both held the gaze for a fraction longer than was absolutely necessary?'

'How on earth did you know that?'

I sighed. God he was naïve. 'Let's just say I recognise the signs. Then you paid the bill in silence while Rachel sat gazing at you, elbows on the table, her face cupped in her hands. You both got up slowly from the table, she took your hand, you walked out of the restaurant and, without another word, went upstairs?'

Tim looked miserable. 'I had no idea it was all so predictable.'

'Only thus far. It's the next bit that intrigues me. I mean, it could all have ended with a reasonably chaste, albeit lingering kiss on the lips at her bedroom door, after which she smiles sweetly, thanks you for a lovely evening, and slips into her room and then into her winceyette. On the other hand . . .'

'Er, yes, on the other hand?'

'You tell me, Tim.'

'Must I? You do it so well.' He sighed. 'OK, we did go upstairs, and we did, you know, pause at her bedroom door because – well – I wanted to give her the opportunity to get rid of me if she wanted to. I even said goodnight.'

I nodded.

'And she didn't. Get rid of me I mean. She just strode on past, still holding my hand, until we got to my door. Then she took the key out of my trouser pocket – which was a hell of a turn on in itself, I can tell you – opened the door, and, well, naturally, in we went.'

I raised my eyebrows. 'Naturally.'

'Oh no, Polly, she wasn't pushy at all, it was so obviously going to happen anyway.'

'Maybe, but notice how it's Rachel who takes not only the initiative, but your hand, and the key to the door.'

My goodness she was a smart cookie. She'd had her eye on him right from the word go, and nobody, certainly not Tim, had even suspected it. She'd had him for breakfast.

'How d'you feel about her now?' I asked.

He shrugged. 'Oh, I'm fond of her, of course,' I flinched at that word, 'but if truth be told it was just a one-night stand really, probably from her point of view, too. Don't get me wrong, it was great at the time; yes, it was really – ' his eyes glazed over – 'great.'

I coughed.

'Oh, er, sorry, what I mean is, it was fun, but it didn't really mean anything, not in the heart department anyway. For goodness' sake, let's be grown-up about this, these things happen, don't they? Well, you'd know all about that, wouldn't you, Polly?'

'Thanks,' I said grimly

'Oh God, I didn't mean it like that, what I meant was, you're not stupid. You know as well as I do that it's easy to get carried away, or rather, you know how easy it is for men to get carried away.'

Don't I just? I tried to banish his equally errant brother from my mind and listen to what he was saying.

'The problem is, I feel so wretched about Sarah. I wouldn't dream of hurting her, and there's no way anyone could ever take her place.'

'Well, that's a relief. Look Tim, the best thing you can do now is just forget it ever happened. Don't, for God's sake, decide to purge yourself and run off confessing to Sarah. Believe me, she may not be quite so reasonable about it.'

Tim scratched his head. 'The only problem is, Sarah might find out.'

'Why?'

'Because Penny came into my room the next morning with a cup of tea. '

'Oh no! What did she do?'

'Well, she looked pretty shocked and left, of course, but she slammed the door behind her. She and Sarah are very close.'

'How did Rachel react?'

'Pretty calmly. I leaped out of bed in a complete panic and started throwing my clothes into a bag, but she just sort of lay there smiling to herself.'

I bet she did.

'Well, then I rang you to say we were coming back. I couldn't bear to stay there a moment longer. I didn't see Penny again, not that I actively tried to find her. She was probably avoiding me, too. Polly, d'you think she'll tell Sarah?'

I sighed. 'Hard to say really, Tim. Female loyalty's a funny thing. Whereas boys probably wouldn't dream of spilling the beans, we girls tend to think it wouldn't be fair to let a friend go on believing that her man is whiter than white. Stupid really. On the other hand . . .' I hesitated. Lottie had told me about Harry's indiscretion, and in the long run I was glad she had, but then Harry was a louse. Tim, on the other hand, wasn't, and it would certainly be better if Sarah wasn't told.

'I think you should ring Penny and ask her not to say anything. Tell her you were drunk out of your mind, it was a huge mistake, and you're still absolutely bonkers about Sarah.'

Tim brightened considerably. 'D'you think that would work?'

'It might. On the other hand, it might not. She might insist you tell Sarah yourself.'

Tim banged his fist on the bedside table in fury. 'Women! Christ, you're all so bloody smug, aren't you? Do this, do that, don't do anything naughty because if you do we'll tie you up in knots before you can even apologise. It's almost like they're lying in wait for you. I mean, it was just a quick bonk, for Christ's sake, can't we leave it at that? Apparently not, no, we have to pick it all over, examine my motives, make me feel a complete and utter bastard, and where does that get us? I mean, what is the point?'

He was feeling nice and sorry for himself. A quick bonk, eh? This, from the lips of sensitive, caring, organically and politically correct Tim. Perhaps he'd thought a quick bonk would bring her out? Perhaps he'd thought he was behaving in a social, caring manner? Ah yes, that must be it.

'Well, I can't help you then, Tim,' I said quietly. 'I've told you what I think you should do. If you don't want to take my advice, you can sort it out for yourself.'

Tim blushed and looked at his shoes, instantly contrite. 'Sorry, Polly. That was infantile of me. It's all this guilt creeping out, I'm afraid.'

I looked at his shoes, too, half expecting to see the guilt seeping out all over the carpet. I wondered if Nick was leaking as well. As we watched his shoes glumly, both lost in our own private misery, Serena threw her best operatic voice upstairs.

'Lunch-is-rea-d-y!'

Neither of us moved.

Up it came again. 'Yoo-hoo, lunch-is-rea-dy!'

Tim sighed. 'We'd better go down. Thanks for listening, Polly, sorry I've been such a pig. I do feel a bit better actually.'

Terrific, I thought gloomily, as I dragged myself out from under the covers. I'm glad somebody does.

Chapter Twenty-four

It goes without saying that lunch was an unmitigated disaster. Sarah was the only one in high spirits, which in itself was unbearable. She'd heard that Tim had come back early, and had immediately dropped everything and raced over from the stables. In the space of about ten minutes, she'd thrown together a delicious lunch for us all and was obviously hoping for a jolly reunion party. She smelled outrageous, and I was longing to shower her in Dior to overcome the horsy fumes, but she couldn't have cared less. As she rushed around, helping us all to enormous platefuls of fish pie, she positively bubbled over with enthusiasm and happiness, chattering away, and not seeming to notice that no one really uttered back.

I couldn't bear to look at her, and I couldn't bear to look at Tim. Come to that, I couldn't bear to look at Rachel, and I certainly wasn't going to look at Nick. As for Serena, she was totally out of the question. That left Jamie. Luckily I was next to him. This was generally regarded as a bad seat, but today I was thankful. I gave him my undivided attention and concentrated on catering to his every whim; picking up his spoon whenever he dropped it; smiling gamely when he poked his sticky little fingers in my eyes, and indulging in fascinating lunch party repartee which involved lots of enthusiastic nods and smiles on my part and lots of shrieking and food-spitting on his.

Only Serena and Sarah were capable of eating the fish pie; the rest of us pushed it round our plates in a desultory manner. I toyed limply with a prawn, and Rachel stared dreamily into space. Occasionally she would flash a knowing look at Tim, who would flush guiltily and look away before shredding his napkin, apparently unaware that it was cotton and not paper.

Nick glowered into his wine glass, as if the answer to all his problems were somehow floating in a sea of Frascati.

Only Serena seemed equal to the situation. She sat at the head of the table and presided over lunch like the officious table monitor she had once so obviously been. She suffocated any attempts anyone else might have had at conversation by regurgitating a ceaseless flow of drivel about her latest film. It appeared to have a cast of thousands, and all concerned had their names dropped at regular intervals.

' . . . and as I said to Anthony when we were in make-up the other day—'

'Anthony who?' asked Sarah, right on cue.

'Andrews, darling,' came back the delighted reply, and then, in case anyone had failed to link up the Christian name with the surname, 'Anthony Andrews,' and then, in case anyone had been living in a cave in Outer Mongolia for the last ten years, 'he was in "Brideshead", remember?'

'Yes, yes, we know who you mean,' said Tim, 'get on with it.'

'Well, it's just that he was saying how glad he was that he still had a base in England, and I couldn't agree more. You see, it's terribly tempting just to up sticks and go and live in Hollywood. I mean, let's face it, that's where all the work is, so that's where all the money is, but is it worth it? I mean, OK, it's great fun, what with the parties and the fantastic weather and everyone paying you so much attention all the time; but really, there's more to life than that, isn't there? I mean, yes, sure, I've been tempted to stay: I remember one particular occasion when an absolutely divine director offered me the most amazing part — God I was tempted — but it was a long TV series which would have taken for ever to film, and at the end of the day I just had to turn him down. No, I said, no, Roman, I'm sorry, but I'm going home, right? England is my home and home, as they say, is where the heart is, right? Well, of course he was flabbergasted, but what could he do? I mean, after all, it's my life, isn't it? I'm the one that's got to live it, right?'

She finished this string of platitudes with a triumphant flourish of the fork, and looked around expectantly as if awaiting applause. Most people appeared to be contemplating the table-mats, but someone must have raised their aching eyes for a moment and murmured an assent, because she ploughed on.

'I mean, sure, yes, LA is very exciting — it's fast, it's glamorous — but you know what? It's artificial. No, really, it is.' She nodded sagely as if perhaps we didn't believe her. 'Whereas,' she went on, waving her fork, 'whereas here, in dear old England, everything is — well, it's so *real*, isn't it? D'you know what I mean?' She cocked her head on one side. 'Hmmm? And you know, there's so much I miss when I'm in the States. Oh, I could bang on for ever about the countryside and the history and everything, but you know what I really miss? Hmmm? People. Because when all's said and done, it's people that count, isn't it? And there are so many characters here. In LA everyone seems to be out of the same mould, they're all — well, they're plastic, right? Yes, lots of little plastic people!'

Her tinkly laugh rang around the dining room, and then her green eyes fell proprietorially on Nick, who was sitting next to her looking slightly mad about the eyes. He was maniacally smearing fish pie around his plate.

She leaned in close and ruffled his hair. 'I know what you're thinking, darling, and no, I haven't forgotten you. It goes without saying that when I'm away I miss you most of all,' she purred. She took his chin in her hand and turned his face towards her, going on in a baby voice, 'and I don't think you'd have been very happy in LA, would you Pusskins?' she murmured, rubbing a bright red nail down his cheek. 'Hmmm? Not your scene at all really, is it?'

'Hardly,' said Nick grimly, jerking his head away and resuming his contemplation of his fish-smeared plate.

She turned back to her audience. 'Let's face it,' she said, as if some of us had been having difficulty, 'it's a fantastic place, but only in small doses, right? I know it's hard to believe, but one can get terribly bored with the rather self-indulgent lifestyle.'

'I don't find it hard to believe at all. I think it sounds a perfectly dreadful place and I know I'd be terribly homesick,' said Sarah defiantly, desperately attempting to embark on some sort of discussion to rescue us all from this weighty, oppressive, cliché-ridden, minor-movie-star monologue. Alas, to no avail.

'Oh it's not *dreadful*, darling, it's great fun! But it is rather fast, and yes, if all you want to do is muck out stables, then you'd probably hate it. But I will say one thing,' she said, waving her fork around again and not entirely shutting her mouth as she masticated the fish pie. 'If you're not careful, you can end up losing your identity, d'you know what I mean?'

'Not entirely.' Sarah looked puzzled, as well she might.

'Well, you know how it is, darling, one's constantly being entertained and fêted and flattered, but some people make the great mistake of believing all that crap. You mustn't. You must stand still for a second, stand back from the whole scene and say – hey, now hang on a minute, what's going on here? Who am I – you know? I

430

mean, what's it all about? Who are all these people? Are they for real?'

Well you certainly aren't, I thought, pushing half a ton of potato around my plate. I'd never met anyone so utterly phoney in my whole life.

'Don't you agree, darling?' She nudged Nick, who'd got bored long ago and was discussing crop rotation with Tim who was on his left.

'What? Oh yes, definitely.' He turned back to his brother.

'So that's why I decided to come home,' she concluded with a triumphant smile, as if anyone had been wondering. 'I just got fed up. I woke up one morning, packed my bags, and got a taxi to the airport.' She scraped her plate clean, put down her fork, and delicately patted her perfect cherry lips with a napkin. 'And here I am.' She turned to Sarah. 'Incidentally, Sarah, that fish pie was very good, but just a teensy word of advice. I always put a bit of parsley in mine: it makes all the difference. And perhaps a little less milk in the potato, it was slightly on the mushy side, wasn't it? I know you won't mind me mentioning it, because if you're anything like me, you'll welcome constructive criticism, right?'

Not only phoney, but poisonous too, I thought, almost with relief. What on earth does he see in her?

She leaned towards Nick and rested her head on his shoulder, although actually it was more like his back, because he'd almost completely turned around to talk to Tim.

She nuzzled into him as best she could. 'You couldn't believe it when I rang to say I was getting on the next plane back, could you, darling? Darling?'

'What?' Nick broke off his conversation.

'Honey, when I'm talking to you, you might at least listen. I can't talk to your back.'

'Sorry.' He resumed his discussion with Tim.

Serena turned back to address the rest of her equally unwilling audience. 'Anyway, apart from anything else, I just knew I had to come back to sort this place out. It needs so much attention. The roof is full of holes, for a start, and that's going to cost a fortune. Darling, did you speak to anyone about the roof? Darling? *Nick!*'

'Sorry, what?' He sounded irritated.

'I said,' began Serena, hissing through her teeth, 'did you talk to anyone about mending the roof?'

'No, I didn't, I'll get round to that when I've got some more money, all right? Sorry Tim, what did you say?'

'Well, you know, that might just be too late; those holes aren't going to get any smaller. You really must get someone to give you an estimate. Apparently there's quite a good chap in Helston. He's just started up, so he might be glad of the work and give you a good price. And the windows are a disgrace, they're just falling off their hinges. I mean look at that one!'

She flung her arm dramatically towards the dining-room window. We all turned our heads obediently, except Nick and Tim who were drawing diagrams on the back of an envelope now, their dark heads bent together.

'I mean, that just isn't going to survive another winter, is it? It's completely rotten, and if we get any more rain, it'll just crumble. We'll have water coming in and the carpets will be ruined. Not that there's much to ruin – look at this old thing – but Nick, you must get hold of a carpenter, really you must. Nick? Nick?'

She stared at the broad back that faced her. Still the brothers conferred. There was a terrible pause.

'NICK!' Serena flung down her napkin, scraped back her chair, and stood up. Everyone looked up at her; even Nick and Tim paused from their calculations.

'WILL YOU LISTEN TO ME!' she shrieked. Her face was white and she was shaking slightly. Suddenly she picked up her empty plate, raised her arm, and sent it

432

crashing to the ground where it broke into a thousand tiny pieces. Then, with a stifled sob, she ran from the room.

There was a startled silence. Eventually Nick sighed, got up from the table, and with a look of resignation went after her.

We all looked down at our laps. I fiddled with my napkin. Rachel sniggered nastily.

At length, Sarah spoke up hesitantly. 'Don't take her too seriously. She can be — well, rather theatrical at times, I'm afraid.'

'Artistic temperament and all that,' muttered Tim, looking embarrassed.

'And I think,' went on Sarah, 'well, I think she's rather unhappy at the moment.' She looked at me briefly, not in an accusing way, but I flushed to my dyed roots nonetheless.

'Ah well, that gives her a perfect right to behave badly, doesn't it?' said Rachel sarcastically.

There was an embarrassed silence.

'I really must get back to the stables,' said Sarah, slipping down from her chair. 'I'm late already.'

'I'll come with you,' said Tim, throwing down his napkin and following her hastily. That left Rachel and me.

'Acting, of course,' said Rachel, licking her fork. 'She's just a spoilt little brat.'

It's hard to believe, but at that moment I felt a certain amount of sympathy for Serena, mainly because I felt such loathing for Rachel. I looked at her smug, self-righteous little face and felt myself coming up to the boil.

'And who are you to talk about behaving badly, Rachel?' I asked quietly.

She looked surprised. 'What do you mean?'

'Well, who exactly is behaving badly around here, eh? Answer me that one.'

'What are you driving at, Polly?' She narrowed her eyes warily.

'Tell me, do you feel even the slightest twinge of guilt when you sit next to Sarah? I mean, you are boffing her boyfriend, aren't you? So do you feel just the slightest bit uneasy about passing the time of day with her and eating her food, or does that hypocritical stuff come naturally to you? I assume you know they're getting married? How easy is the old adultery lark, do tell?'

She narrowed her eyes even more until they were just two little grey slits. 'I don't know, Polly, you tell me. You're the expert.'

I sat back in surprise. 'What d'you mean?'

'Well, how easy do you find it to sit next to dear Serena? After all, you're "boffing" – as you so elegantly put it – her fiancé, aren't you?'

I gasped in horror.

Rachel smiled. 'Spot on. Well, that was a shrewd guess, wasn't it?'

I gulped.

'Oh, don't look so surprised, it's quite obvious to anyone with half a brain cell. You haven't been able to take your eyes off him all lunchtime and he looks absolutely racked with guilt and remorse. So tell me, how do *you* sleep at night? When you're not with him, I mean?'

I bit my lip and looked away.

'Nothing to say, Polly?' she said quietly. 'Try taking the plank out of your own eye before you start complaining about the splinters in other people's.'

I took a large slug of wine and lit a cigarette with a shaking hand. Of course, to anyone but the educationally subnormal, the similarities between Rachel and myself would have been obvious long ago. But recognising the obvious, especially the painfully obvious, has never been my forte, and when my brain is addled up with wine, lack of sleep and heartache, it's even more difficult. However, Rachel's acute observation pierced through the fog and left me reeling.

I licked my lips and tried to think of something to say. But what was there to say? She was right. I was no better than her, no better than Caro, and no better than any other cheap little slimeball who went around stealing other people's men. Serena and Nick were engaged to be married. I listened to her sobs coming from the kitchen and, not for the first time that day, felt sick. But this time with myself. Why shouldn't she rush down here to warn me off, waving her little green ring under my nose? Why shouldn't she point out the structural changes which were to occur under the forthcoming Mrs Serena Penhalligan regime? Of course she wanted to know when I was going: she wanted my claws out of Nick and back in London as soon as possible.

And what, after all, did I mean to Nick? Much the same as Rachel meant to his brother? A one-night stand? It was becoming more and more apparent that our one and only morning of passion had been a rather amusing indiscretion – perhaps even a charitable act – on his part.

I heard Nick's voice coming from the kitchen, soothing her, comforting her. Gradually her sobs subsided and there was quiet. No doubt he was kissing the tears away.

Not before time, I too slipped down from the table. I didn't look at Rachel, because I knew the sort of smile she'd have on her face. I just ran. At least I could do that. I could run away.

Upstairs, I tore around the bedroom like a lunatic, throwing things into a suitcase. Red shirt, leather skirt, little black dress, riding boots – all those well thought-out outfits had done the trick all right, but where had the trick got me? In one hell of a mess, that's where.

The tears were streaming down my face by now, and I made no effort to check them, I just bunged on my sunglasses. I loved him so much, but I mustn't think about that because I'd go mad. The best thing I could do would be to slip away quietly and let him breathe a huge sigh of relief when he discovered the empty bedroom.

The only problem was, I couldn't do my case up. As always, I seemed to have twice as many clothes as when I'd arrived. I sat on the blasted thing and bounced up and down, but even my colossal weight couldn't close it. Eventually, in desperation, I took out a couple of jumpers and a pair of shoes and shoved them under the bed. I just had to get away.

I stole downstairs as quietly as one can steal with a two-ton case in tow, looking around feverishly for any sign of life. No one seemed to be about. Nick and Serena were probably still in the kitchen at the back of the house, Rachel and Jamie were no doubt up in her bedroom by now, and Sarah and Tim were at the stables.

I tiptoed quietly across the great hall, dragging my case, which luckily had those nifty little wheels at the back. I was just about to heave the solid oak front door open, when the telephone rang.

Christ! I dropped my case and ran to it in a frenzy, terrified that someone else would hear and come running. I managed to grab the receiver just after the first ring. I put my hand over my mouth to muffle my voice.

'Yes?' I whispered.

'Hello?'

'Yes, hello, who is it?' I hissed rudely.

'Oh, er, sorry to disturb you. I was just wondering, is Polly McLaren staying with you by any chance?'

I sat down heavily on the bottom step. I'd know that voice anywhere.

'This is Polly,' I said quietly.

'Is it? Polly! God, it didn't sound like you at all. It's Harry!'

'I know.'

'You sound a bit odd, are you all right?'

'I'm fine. Fine. Hang on a minute.' Harry! It was no good, I had to have a cigarette. I dropped the receiver for a second, ran to the door, dragged my case back and punched it open. I rummaged desperately, flinging clothes out all over the parquet floor, found my ciggies, lit one, and inhaled deeply. Harry. Harry ringing here, looking for me. No wonder my hand was shaking. I picked up the receiver again. 'Hello?'

'You still there? I thought you'd done a bunk!'

'Er, no, I'm still here. What d'you want, Harry?'

'I rang to apologise, Poll.'

'Oh yes?'

'Yes, and to, well, to tell you I miss you.'

'Oh!' I was shocked to the core. I took another drag of nicotine and found my voice. 'But what about Caro, Harry? Isn't she keeping you company?'

'Oh Polly, don't be like that, I can explain, really I can. I just − well, I just got carried away, and I didn't think you'd find out, which I know is an awful thing to say and no excuse at all but − honestly, Poll, Caro was just a flash in the pan; ships in the night and all that, you know? I can't tell you how much I regret it now. When I heard you'd buggered off like that, I just didn't know what to do. Honestly I was tearing my hair out. Please forgive me, darling, please!'

My mouth was open. I didn't know what to say. I didn't know what to think.

'Say something, please Polly!'

'I . . . don't know what to say, Harry.'

'Oh, Polly, don't be like that, you sound so cold and hostile. Please don't go all hostile on me, just tell me you understand, I promise you it'll never happen again.'

'Oh, really?'

'Oh God, you're really pissed off, aren't you? Are you pissed off?'

I sighed. 'I honestly don't know.'

'Don't be, please don't be. It was such a mistake, such a ghastly, never-to-be repeated mistake. For what it's worth, it only happened once. She's so childish, she drove me up the pole after just one day. I know that doesn't make it any better, but I promise I've been regretting it ever since. I'm sorry, really I am, I can't tell you how awful I feel about it now. I've been all this time trying to trace you, none of your friends would tell me where you were.'

'So – so how did you find me?' I stuttered in disbelief.

'I worked on Pippa and she cracked eventually. Polly, I've got something very important to say to you.'

'Oh yes,' I croaked.

'It's not easy, because to be honest I've never said it before, but I've done a lot of thinking while you've been away, and I've come to a pretty staggering conclusion. You see, I reckon I'm in love with you.'

I gasped and reeled back against the stairs, grabbing the banisters for support. The receiver slipped from my nervous grasp. I fumbled to retrieve it.

'Hello? Hello? Polly, are you still there?'

'Y-yes, I'm here.'

'Look, I know this must come as a bit of a surprise. I mean, I know I wasn't exactly the model boyfriend, and I didn't treat you particularly well, but – well, I just took you for granted in London. You were always there. It was only when you went tearing off to Cornwall that I really began to miss you. And once I'd started I couldn't stop. Please come back. I really need to see you.'

I couldn't believe this was happening. Harry missed me? Harry needed to see me? Harry – hang on, brace yourself for this one girls – Harry *loved* me? I gaped into the receiver.

'Polly . . . ? Polly . . . ? This must be a really bad line, I can hardly hear you.'

'It's OK, Harry, I can hear you. Look, the thing is, I'm on my way back right now actually.'

'You are? Great! That's terrific! What train are you catching, shall I meet you?'

'Er, no, it's OK, I'll get a taxi. I'm not sure what time the trains are.'

'Oh, OK. Well, when you get to London, why don't you get the taxi straight round here.'

'Straight round where?' I said stupidly.

'Here, to my place. We could grab something to eat and then well, you know,' he laughed. 'Get to know each other again!'

I stared into the mouthpiece. He shouldn't have said that. He really should not have said that. It was a big mistake. It not only made my skin creep, it made my toes curl up in their boots. Get to know each other again? Me and Harry? The diving board and futon nonsense all over again? In bed? With no clothes on? Embarking on a sexual marathon? With perhaps a little short back and sides thrown in for good measure? The very idea repulsed me. Oh no, I couldn't go back to that, not when I'd tasted the real thing. I thought of Nick. No, I could never go back to Harry.

I leaned back on the stairs, relief flooding over me. A colossal weight seemed to be lifting from my shoulders. I was shaking off my chains, I was free, and it was the most wonderful feeling. He meant nothing to me. Harry Lloyd-Roberts was history. Hoo-bleeding-ray.

'Polly, I think I'd better ring you back, I can't hear a word you're saying.'

'That's because I'm not saying anything, but I'm going to say something now, Harry. Are you ready?'

'Er, ready,' he said uncertainly.

'You're absolutely right.'

'I am?'

'Absolutely. You did take me for granted in London, and you're right, there is no excuse. Not only weren't you the model boyfriend, you weren't even a boyfriend. Far from it. If you really want to know, you were a pig. And I've been doing some thinking too. I've been thinking that

I've actually got along quite well without you down here. I'm sorry, Harry, but our few days apart have obviously brought us to entirely different conclusions. You see, I'm over you. I hate to be brutal, but I'm afraid you're just too late. Sorry and all that.'

I heard a few distant splutterings at the end of the line. Without waiting for a reply, I gently replaced the receiver. Then I gathered my clothes up from the parquet floor, stuffed them back into my case, sat on it, snapped it shut, and dragged it over to the door again. With an almighty heave, I lugged my belongings over the threshold and staggered off down the drive towards the Helford Road.

Chapter Twenty-five

As I panted down the sweep of gravel to the gate, dragging my case behind me, I went over the extraordinary conversation again in my mind. It was incredible, what on earth had brought about this sudden change of heart? A little over a week ago he'd been indifference itself, now he was all over me. Did people change their minds as dramatically as that? I suppose they did. I mean, look at me, a couple of weeks ago I'd have flown back into his arms and been the happiest girl in the world, but not now. Not after Nick.

Nick. He'd changed too, hadn't he? And even more rapidly, come to that. Only this morning he'd told me — well, what had he told me, after all? Nothing very much when I came to think about it — that I was beautiful, yes, but that was just pillow-talk; he hadn't said anything truly heartfelt, had he? My own heart lurched as I thought of what he was telling Serena now. That he loved her? That he wanted to marry her more than anything in the world? That I'd been nothing more than a — what had Harry said about Caro — a ghastly mistake?

I sobbed audibly, and dragged the wretched case over the cattle grid at the gate, tears streaming down my face. It didn't help matters that I had three-inch heels on: I'd changed my shoes before lunch in a desperate attempt to make myself look a bit taller and perhaps even to come up to Serena's tummy button. I cursed my black crumpetcatchers now as I wobbled around precariously on them, tottering off in the direction of the river.

I had to get the ferry across to Helford before I could even begin the epic journey to Helston, and I had no idea when there'd be a boat. Did one just sit and wait, or did I have to hail one like a taxi? I struggled along the bumpy road feeling none too dry under the arms, and then turned off left and lugged the case down the bumpy track to the river. It bounced along behind me, steadily gaining momentum down the steep slope, forcing me to go faster and faster, so that when we eventually arrived at the bottom I was running pretty fast and very much out of control. Luckily I careered into some white railings on the jetty, which saved me from going in the water, and I sank down gratefully in a crumpled heap to wait for the boat, glad of a chance to get my breath back.

'You hopping on luv, or what?' said a voice.

I looked up. A little boat was bobbing around in front of me, packed full of people. They all seemed to be staring at me.

'Sorry?'

'I said are you hopping on?' said the voice again. It appeared to belong to a man with a blue cap and a wide grin. ' 'Cos if you are, you'd better get a move on, we're leaving any minute.'

I stared at the little boat. 'Oh! Is this the ferry?' Somehow I'd been expecting something much bigger, something more like the cross-channel jobbies that go over to France. This was just a little dinghy.

He grinned again. ' 'Tis as far as I know – and I should, I've been ferryin' it there and back for more 'un twenty years now!'

I jumped up with alacrity. 'Oh! Oh well, yes please, don't go without me.'

'Give me that, luv.' He reached over and took my case. Someone else stretched out a friendly hand and helped me

442

aboard. I sank down gratefully into the last available seat and, with a shrill whistle and a little blast of steam, we chugged off.

We were packed in like sardines, and I was jammed between two large women with enormous tweedy bottoms that cushioned me nicely on either side. It was really quite comfortable. I studied my fellow travellers. They were mostly sensible-looking women with empty shopping bags, off to do the weekly shop, no doubt. Their brown, wrinkled faces viewed me with interest and their kindly eyes twinkled. I tried hard to twinkle back but my face seemed to be locked into the forces of gravity which continually pulled it downwards. I'd twinkle later, I decided, when I needed to ask them the quickest way into town.

By now my feet were killing me. I decided to risk it and swap the ridiculous heels for a pair of espadrilles. My case was at my feet and I snapped it open, threw in the accursed shoes, and pulled on some heavenly flat ones. I crammed the lid down again, but of course once opened, the damn case wouldn't shut again, at least not with a pair of bulky high heels inside it. I got up from my seat and sat on the case. I bounced up and down, but it would hardly close, let alone shut. Tears of rage and self-pity were welling up in my eyes now.

'It's not goin' to shut, is it lover!' ventured the tweedy woman next to me. She cackled in a friendly manner. 'Reckon you've got too much in there, you see!'

'Certainly looks like it, doesn't it,' I mumbled back, aware that my voice had a wobble in it.

I had one last bounce, but to no avail. Suddenly I could bear it no longer. With a squeal of rage I grabbed the stilettoes and threw them overboard. They hit the water with a satisfying plop! and then sank slowly down into the murky depths, never to be seen again. With a gleeful little shriek, I jumped on the case and snapped it shut.

I heaved a sigh of relief and grinned around at my neighbours. 'I never liked those shoes anyway!' I said to one and all.

Eight or nine horrified pairs of eyes met mine. Their good, honest, hard-working faces were aghast. No one smiled, no one spoke. They just stared. There was a terrible silence. Yes, in one reckless flick of the wrist I'd succeeded in alienating the good folk of Helford and Manaccan. The very people on whom I'd hoped one day to bestow prizes graciously at the village fête were open-mouthed with horror and disbelief. One by one they turned away, and a whispered muttering rose up around me. I caught the eye of the friendly captain. He looked away. I stared at the floor, hot-blooded shame filling my face.

How could I have been so stupid? Those shoes probably cost, oh, let's see, about as much as it took to feed a family for a week — God, a month even! Most of these people probably thought themselves lucky even to own one pair of shoes; their children probably ran around barefoot. I mean, they did in the country, didn't they?

I stared down miserably, not daring to look up. Eight or nine pairs of shoes met my gaze. That confirmed it. All the shoes looked like museum pieces. They were at least a hundred years old, no doubt handed down from gene-ration to generation, from grandmother to mother to daughter, lovingly cared-for and restored — no, cobbled, that was it — over the years.

As we chugged across the water and then into the quay on the Helford side, I braced myself to look up. It was true, my fears were confirmed. Distrust and suspicion had replaced any kindly interest that might previously have helped me to secure a lift into Helston. Take those labourers, for example. Now normally I have a good working relationship with labourers. I saunter past, they whistle, I look coy, they make obscene gestures, I toss my head — everyone's satisfied. But not today, oh no. I tried a timid smile as they got off the ferry, but they instantly looked away, jumping into a waiting Land Rover and speeding off without so much as a, 'Cor, 'ello darlin'!' in my general direction.

As everyone else scattered, I realised I was the only one left standing on the quay. Feeling nice and sorry for myself, I took hold of my case, put my head down, and trudged down the lane in search of a bus. Get real, Polly, a bus? It took me half an hour before I could find anything that even remotely resembled a bus stop, and even then I wasn't sure. The little red symbol looked remarkably like a cattle truck to me. Oh well, I could hardly walk all the way to Helston. I sat down heavily on my evil case and waited. And waited. And waited.

After what must have been a good half-hour, I decided to take my life in my hands and hitch a lift. I rummaged around in my handbag and, right at the bottom, my hand closed gratefully on an enormous pearl that was stuck in the lining. I pulled it out. Ah yes, there it was, my giant-sized hat-pin. On the odd occasion when I'm forced to hitch a lift, I like to keep it to hand. Lord knows where I imagine I'm going to stick it: somewhere soft, certainly, but I've never got more specific than that, it just comforts me to know it's there. I stood up and struck a pose at the side of the road. I stuck my thumb out purposefully; it was erect and jaunty.

Twenty minutes later, my thumb was wilting sadly. Alas, word had spread about, above and beyond. The good people of Helford had clearly been forewarned: do not, on any account, pick up an overweight blonde girl dragging a case. She's a profligate hussy with more shoes than sense. Not one car even slowed down, let alone stopped.

Eventually though, a little old lady came waddling towards me with an empty basket. Now she must be going into town, I thought, and surely someone of her age and stature — she was wider than she was tall — wouldn't walk all that way, now would they? I watched her approach with mounting excitement. It was like something out of Monty Python. Any minute now I expected a bus to career round the corner, whereupon she'd stick out her foot and trip it up. No such luck. She waddled straight past me.

'Excuse me!' I shouted desperately.

She stopped, turned around, and stared at me with curiosity. 'D'you happen to know if there's a bus into Helston today?'

She cackled with laughter. 'Oh, so that's what you're waiting for, is it? No, not today, lover. Tuesdays and Thursdays, yes, but not today.'

She cackled a bit more and made as if to walk on. Not so fast, Grandma, I thought. I persisted, somewhat nosily.

'Well, how are you getting into town then?'

'Me? Oh I've got a lift comin', don't you worry about me!'

Her use of the personal pronoun was distressing enough, but just as I was about to disregard it and suggest I shared her transport, sure enough, it appeared around the corner. A milk float. With room enough for one.

'Af'ernoon, Dolly!' hailed the cheery milkman.

' 'Tis for some!' she cackled back as he heaved her aboard by the arm. She plumped herself down beside him and, with a cheery backward wave, they rattled off into the distance.

Well, that did it. That really did it. Without any more ado, I put my head in my hands and sobbed. And not just the whining, snuffling nonsense that I'd been doing for the last couple of hours, oh no, this was a good, honest-to-goodness sob.

I worked my way through a repertoire of gasping, spluttering, moaning and case-kicking, and was just building up to a nice shoulder-shaking crescendo, when I became aware of a car engine purring away in front of me.

Pausing for a moment from my gasps and heaves, I peered through the deluge and made out an orange Golf convertible, fully converted. It had stopped right in front of me and was humming away quietly. An electric window slid silently down.

'I thought it was you!' A familiar voice foghorned out. 'What on earth are you doing sitting there in the road?'

As the mist and rain clouding my vision cleared slightly, I made out the shadowy figure of Hetty Penhalligan at the wheel. I banged on my Ray-Bans and sprang to my feet, relief and alarm alternating within me. She might at least take me into Helston, but what on earth was I going to say to her by way of explanation?

'Are you trying to get to Helston?' she asked.

'Yes!' I yelped joyfully.

'Well that's where I'm going. Hop in, and throw your case in the boot.'

I had the suitcase in the boot and my seatbelt clunk-clicked before she'd even blinked.

'Are you all right, my dear?' She peered anxiously over my glasses. 'Only you look absolutely terrible. Why on earth were you sitting by the side of the road like a little gnome?'

'I was trying to get to Helston and I thought there might be a bus, you see. I didn't realise they only ran about once a year down here.'

'D'you mean to say you've walked all this way with that heavy case? How perfectly ghastly!'

She crunched into first gear and we shot off, achieving nought to sixty in about ten seconds. I caught my breath, recovering from what felt like whiplash in my neck, and hung on for dear life as we hurtled round the lanes at a spectacular speed.

'Why on earth didn't Nick bring you?' she shouted above the roar of the engine.

'It was an emergency and Nick wasn't at the house!' I shouted back.

'Oh? Where is he?'

'He's um – he's gone to market!' Wasn't that where farmers went?

'Market? Today? How extraordinary,' she mused. 'It's usually on a Monday.'

'Er, yes, that's right, so he said, but apparently they changed the day because, um, a lot of the farmers couldn't make it last Monday.'

She looked at me as if I had two heads. 'What on earth do you mean, couldn't make it?'

Yes, what on earth did I mean? I struggled to make sense of myself. 'Well, you see a lot of them were away last Monday, on holiday – well, long weekends. You know, because of the good weather and all that. They took an extra day. So the people who organise the market, the, the er, market organisers, decided that since so many of them had missed it, they'd have it today instead!'

Hetty threw her head back and roared with laughter. 'Is that what he told you! Good Lord, that's a good one. Long weekends, eh? Ha ha! Polly, I'm afraid you've been had; he's obviously up to no good. Farmers don't even have weekends, let alone long ones!'

'Oh, really? Yes, well I must say I thought it was a bit odd, I expect it was a little white lie then – ha ha!' It made a nice change to blame my lies on someone else, I don't know why I hadn't thought of it before.

'So what's the emergency?' she yelled, as we took another bend at death-defying speed. I hung on to the door handle and shut my eyes hoping to God it was locked.

'What?' I yelled back, playing for time.

'The emergency, why are you rushing back?'

'Oh! Oh well, I've just heard that my mother's ill.'

'Oh dear, I'm so sorry, what's wrong with her?'

I gripped the dashboard as we shot over a humpbacked

bridge, taking off from all four wheels and landing with a smack on the tarmac. Hetty obviously thought we were in Monaco rather than Manaccan. She also had an unnerving habit of leaning over to one side as she took her corners, as if she were on a motorbike. For some reason I felt myself leaning with her. It was quite hard to concentrate on my poor mother when I'd become the indispensable second half of a bobsleigh team.

'What's wrong with her?' she shrieked again.

'Malaria!' I shrieked back wildly.

Suddenly a traffic light loomed. It was red. I shut my eyes and offered my soul to the Almighty, plus anything else he considered worth taking. We screeched to a halt.

Hetty peered at me, full of concern. 'Malaria? How perfectly dreadful, has she been abroad lately?'

'Er, no, I don't think so, why?'

'Well, because one doesn't usually catch it in England.'

'Oh, abroad! Sorry, I wasn't quite with you. Yes, yes, she has been abroad. She went to, let me see – yes, France! She was in France last week, only you see she goes so often I sort of forget that it's abroad really. We've got a house out there, so it's rather like a second home.'

Hetty raised her eyebrows. 'She caught malaria in France? How frightfully unlucky. Especially in April.' She looked doubtful. 'Surely not mosquitoes?'

Damn. Of course, how stupid of me. Malaria was one of those nasty tropical diseases, wasn't it? You could only pick it up if you were spearing crocodiles in the Congo, or going native down the Nile. Why hadn't I picked something average, something close to home, something you could pick up in your local supermarket if you felt like it? Flu, for example, that would have done very nicely. Why did I have to be so ambitious?

'Er, no, you're right, it wasn't mosquitoes. The doctor thought perhaps it was something in the water. She was, after all, very deep in the deep South of France.'

I lowered my voice dramatically in an effort to suggest that my intrepid mother had ventured where perhaps no white man had gone before; certainly no white, middle-aged housewife.

'I mean,' I went on desperately, 'to be honest, we're talking Spain really.'

Happily, this struck a chord with Hetty, who obviously thought anything south of Paris was third world.

'Ah well, that explains it. Spain. Yes, of course. Never trust the Spics.' She shook her head violently. 'Never! The sneaky bastards, I wouldn't put it past them at all!'

I leaned back with relief as we sped off from the lights. At least we'd sorted that one out, but I was nonetheless confused. Was Hetty suggesting that these untrustworthy Spics had actually put something in my mother's water? I'd always imagined the water just became contaminated naturally, from the archaic water system, or the sewers perhaps. I had no idea that the locals actually went around slipping evil potions into glasses of aqua con gas which were then served up to unsuspecting tourists. How appalling! Someone should be told! I shuddered, and it was with some relief that I realised that my mother was not, in fact, lying prostrate in a hospital bed, but was safely at home in Esher, and probably even now absent-mindedly putting Pedigree Chum into the shepherd's pie and giving half a pound of minced beef to the dog.

We hurtled around another hairpin bend, and I once more adopted the obligatory Barry Sheen position. A lorry swung away from us in alarm as we occupied far more of our share of the road than was strictly fair, and the driver shook his fist at us as we passed. Hetty waved back cheerily. Another bend and yet another lorry loomed, this time with two tons of hay on its back. My knuckles were white with fear as they gripped the dashboard, and my foot pumped away at an imaginary brake.

'Look out!' I screeched, as it missed us by inches.

Hetty looked at me in surprise. 'Am I making you nervous, my dear?'

'No, no, not at all!' I lied, as we roared dangerously into a village and slithered to a halt at another welcome set of lights. My heart was pounding wildly. 'I'm just not used to these twisty little lanes, that's all.'

'Oh don't worry, I know them like the back of my hand. You're quite safe.' She patted my rather sweaty hand.

I smiled but doubted it. In fact I was convinced I was going to die in this car. But on the other hand, I thought brightly, as I looked around at the little village we'd stopped in, if I was so concerned about dying, I must feel I had something to live for, right? Otherwise it wouldn't bother me, right? Right. But what?

I stared dreamily out of the window at the row of cottages we'd pulled up next to. They were all thatched, but each one was different and achingly pretty in its own way. Their pink, blue and white faces basked peacefully in the afternoon sun, their leaded windows sparkling as they caught the light. They were heaven. Crawling with honeysuckle and early roses which were already trying to bud, they had tiny cottage gardens at the front, and were flanked at the back by long stretches of lawn which swept up the hill beyond. The gardens backed on to fields where clusters of little creamy lambs danced and played, butting their patient mothers and snatching at the bright spring grass. I sighed. How beautiful it all was, and how unfortunate for me that I'd not only fallen in love with Nick, but also with Cornwall.

I bit my lip as the eyes welled. That way madness lies, I told myself fiercely, don't even think about it. Instead I stared out of the window fixedly, and concentrated like billy-o on a green Volvo that had just drawn up in front of one of the cottages. I studied the hub caps fiercely. Don't think about Nick and don't think about Cornwall, or you'll flood the car, and then what will Hetty say? I suppose I could have blamed the sudden emotion on my mother's malaria, but I didn't really want to get embroiled in that little malarkey again.

I blinked hard and concentrated on the Volvo. The door was opening and a cloth cap was emerging. It belonged to a young man who was getting out of the driving seat. He slammed the door behind him, not bothering to lock it. Well, why should he? We weren't in thieving Fulham now, were we? I sighed despondently as I realised that I very soon would be. The young man strode up the path towards the pink cottage, taking a key out of his hip pocket as he went. What an idyllic place to live, I thought, as he put the key in the door. I bet it was full of quarry tiles and oak beams.

The lights began to change. Hetty, keen as mustard for a Le Mans start, slammed into first and revved up the engine. The young man opened his front door and made to go in. Funnily enough, although I hadn't seen his face, he struck me as being rather familiar. He had a certain gait which reminded me of someone . . . Yes, it was definitely the way he walked, and, yes, something about those broad shoulders, that hair sticking out from under his cap . . . that . . . red hair.

My hand flew to my mouth. 'Oh my God!' I shrieked from the open-topped car.

He swung around instantly. Our eyes met. I ducked down, and at that moment Hetty saw green and roared off, but it was too late.

'What?' she yelled at me over the engine. 'Oh my God, what?'

'It's him!' I wailed, wringing my hands. 'It's bloody him again, isn't it!'

Chapter Twenty-six

I swivelled round in my seat. Adam was standing stock-still, half-way up the garden path, staring after us. We hadn't fooled him at all, he was still here! Not in Mannacan, of course — having an iota of intelligence, he'd probably realised we'd check that out — no, he'd simply switched villages. How stupid of us to be so sure of ourselves, so arrogant, so complacent! I swung back into my seat again, panic rising within me.

Think, Polly, think. I thought. I gripped the upholstery. Oh my God, if he had any sense he'd act fast! Let's face it, he didn't have much choice now that he knew I'd seen him. In fact, at this very moment he was probably sprinting down the path to his car, revving it up and speeding off to Trewarren to snatch Jamie back before I raised the alarm. Then he'd whisk him off to the nearest port and from there, back to America. I imagined little Jamie, wide-eyed and trusting, bundled up in his blue blanket, hurried on to boats, planes, through customs. My heart lurched. Oh poor little baby! I bit my lip. It was no good. I couldn't possibly go to London now. There was only one thing to do.

'Stop the car!' I yelled at the top of my voice.

Even though we were at that precise moment negotiating an immensely tricky hairpin bend, Hetty accepted the challenge. She shot me a quick sideways glance, just to ascertain that I was serious, and, having satisfied herself, slammed on the brakes and executed a surprisingly immaculate emergency stop.

'Quick, quick! Turn around!' I urged.

'But why?' she began, 'Why have we—'

'Never mind, never mind, I'll explain in a minute, but please hurry, we must be quick!'

Wide-eyed but unprotesting, she acquiesced, throwing herself into this impromptu driving test with gusto. With a great deal of revving up and sheep-frightening, we performed a five- or six-point turn in the middle of the snake-like lane. Hetty was enjoying herself now. She was keen to please. She leaned forward, gripping the wheel, looking up at me expectantly, eagerly awaiting her next instruction. What she really wanted to hear was, 'Follow that tractor!' or some such other Miami Vice-like instruction, suitably adapted to our rural surroundings.

'Quick, quick!' I squeaked. 'Back to Trewarren!'

Crouched over the wheel like a bird of prey and with her mouth set in a determined line, she rose gleefully to the occasion. I had the distinct impression she'd been waiting for this moment for years. With a little whoop of pleasure, she let out the clutch and we shot off in the direction of Trewarren.

My mind was in overdrive now. Of course he hadn't believed us, what fools we'd been to think he would! As we hurtled back past the row of pretty cottages in the other direction, I noticed that the green Volvo had gone. He hadn't wasted any time, but if we hurried, we might just catch up with him.

'Hurry, hurry,' I muttered softly under my breath, but not softly enough for Hetty's keen ears. Her eyes widened and glinted with pleasure as she caught the magic words and the accelerator hit the floor. I gripped the dashboard and prayed hard as an amber light greeted us around the next bend. We screeched through on red, a cloud of dust shimmering in our wake.

Only now, as we zipped along a fairly open stretch of road, did Hetty allow herself to question the abrupt curtailment of her weekly shopping trip to Helston.

'Why the hell are we going to Trewarren?' she yelled above the roar of the engine.

'Because of the baby!' I shrieked back, forgetting for a moment that she didn't know the full story.

'The baby?' she looked at me quizzically.

She was one of those drivers who has to look at you while she's talking to you, unnerving for any passenger, but especially a nervous one travelling at the speed of light. I had to think quickly. The Rachel/Jamie/Adam story was much too long and complicated to go into right now, and Hetty would feel obliged to look at me throughout, which was not conducive to staying alive. I rooted around for a suitable lie.

Hetty helped me out. 'You mean we're going back for the baby?'

'Yes, that's it!' I agreed, grateful to her for providing me with such a marvellous explanation, and so simple a one too. 'I've forgotten the baby!'

'Oh!' Hetty's eyes were off the road and on my face in an instant.

'Yes, you see you were quite right. He is my baby, after all, I was just a bit embarrassed about it when you asked me before. I thought you'd disapprove, you know, unmarried mothers and all that — but he really is mine and the awful thing is, I've forgotten to bring him with me! I only realised, just back there, that he's probably still lying in his cot in Trewarren. I completely forgot about him, can you believe it!'

Hetty obviously couldn't, and was staring at me in a rather horrified manner. We were also slowing down quite dramatically. I licked my lips and realised — too late — that this story wasn't as simple as I'd hoped, and I had quite a lot of explaining to do. Hetty looked scatty enough, and was no doubt capable of leaving all sorts of things lying around – her purse, her car keys, her glasses – but a baby? Who forgets a baby? The speedometer was dropping by the second. Forty, thirty, twenty – she wasn't happy. I struggled to defend myself.

'It's – it's this damn post-natal depression, you see!'

'Ah!'

Was that a look of sympathy? Had I struck a chord?

'Yes,' I went on. 'I went into a complete decline after he was born: couldn't eat, couldn't sleep, and couldn't really believe I'd had a baby at all! I kept thinking he must be someone else's. And – and the terrible thing is that, even though I'm much better now, I still forget occasionally that I'm a mother, and I leave him lying around in the most awful places!'

'My poor child!' She put her hand on my arm in consternation.

Buoyed up by her concern, I warmed to my subject. 'Yes, I left him in Peter Jones once.'

Hetty shook her head and tutted sympathetically. 'Easily done,' she muttered. 'China and glassware?'

' 'Fraid so. Oh, and once I left him outside the post office, and in the greengrocer's, and the cinema—'

'You take him to the cinema?' Hetty looked alarmed.

Oh Christ, didn't babies go to the cinema? Probably not – wouldn't it have been easier to go into the Adam and Rachel saga? Too late. I struggled valiantly on.

'Oh well, it helps him go to sleep, you see, and I don't take him to see anything sexy or violent, just love stories and that sort of thing, or nature films, you know, anything soporific.'

'Oh, right.' Hetty still looked dubious. 'Was it a terrible birth then?'

'Oooh shocking, shocking! Went on for weeks!'

'Weeks!' Hetty gaped at me and we almost came to a

standstill, she was rooting in the glove compartment for a cigarette.

Oh, hell! If only I knew more about birth. What a pity Rachel hadn't been more forthcoming, but surely I'd heard that some women were in labour for ages?

'Er – well, no, not weeks, it just felt like weeks, but certainly days, about, um four or five anyway.'

Hetty looked horrified. 'You poor thing!'

'I know, it was ghastly, all the doctors said it was quite the most appalling birth they'd ever come across. It took five of them to deliver me: they needed forceps, ropes, pulleys, all sorts of things. I made medical history, there's a bit in a textbook about it now. It crops up in exams, and someone even wrote a thesis on it. Anyway, that's why I get so depressed and, well, you know, forget about him occasionally.'

'Well of course, of course.' Hetty shook her head. 'Goodness me, we must get you some help,' she muttered, looking grave.

Happily though, she seemed satisfied with my bizarre explanation, and the speedometer climbed again. I watched it like a hawk. Within seconds we were well into the fifties. It occurred to me that Hetty might consider popping me into the local police station for some routine questioning on child abuse, or stopping at a telephone box to report me to the NSPCC or the Esther Rantzen Childline, but no. Thankfully she was obviously of the opinion that a child's place was with its mother, no matter how hopelessly deranged that mother happened to be.

No more was said, and eventually we rounded the bend that led to Trewarren. We swung through the gates, fairly flew over the cattle grid and, with a spray of gravel, came to an abrupt halt in front of the house.

I was out of that car and leaping up the stone steps to the front door in a trice. Knowing what superhuman strength it took to force the door open, I ran at it, ramming it with my shoulder. Unfortunately it was already deceptively ajar, so I burst in a little faster than I'd anticipated. I careered across the hall like an unguided missile, and cannoned into Nick who was coming out of the drawing room.

'Hey! Whoa, steady on!' he said, grabbing my shoulders as I headbutted him in the chest. 'Ooof! Polly, it's you!'

He obviously recognised me by my entrance. I thought he looked slightly relieved, if a little winded. However, if it was relief, it was very momentary, and it very soon turned to anger.

'Where the bloody hell have you been? I've been looking everywhere for you, why did you just take off like that?' He spotted Hetty behind me. 'Mum! What are you doing here?'

Hetty was still glowing from the after-effects of having just broken the land speed record. She fanned her rather flushed face.

'Hello darling, isn't this a surprise? I simply must have a large drinky. I'm absolutely pooped! We've just had the most terrifically exciting car journey, and Polly's been simply fascinating company. Honestly, the things she's been through, you just wouldn't believe it. First the baby, and now her poor mother . . .' She collapsed on a chair in the hall. 'Darling, hurry up with that gin, I'll expire in a minute.'

Nick jerked his head towards the drawing room. 'Help yourself, Mum, would you? Usual place.'

Hetty got up, and thankfully disappeared in the direction of the drinks cupboard before she had time to elucidate further on my fascinating career.

Nick still had my shoulders in a vice-like grip. 'Polly, just what the hell is going on here?'

'Where are Rachel and Jamie?' I blurted out.

'As far as I know, Rachel's reading in the garden, and I think Jamie's asleep upstairs. Why?'

I wriggled out of his hands, pushed past him, and leaped up the stairs two at a time. As I reached the landing, I heard Rachel's voice coming up from the hall below. I glanced down quickly. She was wandering in from the kitchen, book in hand. No Jamie.

She frowned. 'What's going on?' she asked, as she watched me scramble up the stairs like a neurotic mountain goat.

Nick shrugged and leaped up the stairs after me. 'Search me. Polly, what are you up to?'

'Jamie,' I muttered as I flew down the corridor to his bedroom.

The door was open. I raced over to the cot and looked down. A much-sucked teddy bear looked back at me with beady black eyes. The pale blue blanket was pushed back to reveal a white sheet sprinkled with yellow buttercups. A little blue rabbit was half squashed through the bars. Other than that the cot was empty. Somehow, although I'd been expecting it, I wasn't prepared for the reality.

My hand flew to my mouth. 'Oh Nick, he's gone!'

Nick raced in behind me. 'Oh well, hang on a minute, I may be wrong. He may have been in the garden with Rachel, or—'

Rachel was in the room in an instant. She rushed, white-faced, to the cot and looked down. Then she screamed. She gripped the side of the cot and just screamed and screamed as if she would never stop. It wasn't a sound I'd ever heard a human being make before: it sounded more like the shriek of a snared animal, an eerie, primeval sound that tore at the heart and froze the blood.

'He's gone! My baby's gone! He's taken my baby – oh my GOD!' She covered her face with her hands and screamed again.

Then she turned on me, her face drained and bloodless. 'Where is he? Where is he! You saw him, didn't you, you saw him! Tell me where he is!'

She ran at me, beating me with her fists, shaking my shoulders, her white, distorted face inches from mine.

'This is all your fault!' she shrieked. 'Tell me where he is!'

I was terrified. Nick was over in an instant, pulling her off. She gave a moan and collapsed on to him. He held her tightly as she shook violently in his arms.

'It's Adam!' I gasped, shaking quite a bit myself. 'I saw him coming out of that little row of cottages in New Town, he didn't go to London at all − and he knew I'd seen him, so he obviously rushed over here and − and just took him while he still had the chance!'

Rachel moaned again and put her head in her hands.

'Shit!' hissed Nick through clenched teeth. He sat Rachel down on a chair and knelt beside her. She was sobbing and shaking uncontrollably. He took her hands.

'Now listen to me Rachel. It's OK, it's going to be all right. We'll get him back in no time, don't you worry, he can't be far away − minutes at the most. Everything's going to be fine.' He straightened up and shot me a look. 'Look after her,' he muttered, as he rushed from the room.

'Where are you going?' I ran after him.

'To ring the police.'

I bounded downstairs behind him. By the time I'd got to the bottom he was already dialling the number.

'Green Volvo!' I breathed.

'Good. Anything else? Registration?'

'Didn't see, but it was a big one, an estate.'

He got hold of the local police and briefed them in a controlled and lucid manner. A baby had been snatched from its mother at Trewarren. A tall, red-headed American, about thirty, driving a green Volvo. Could well be making for the London road, or possibly a port. Hurry.

'Wearing a cap!' I prompted.

Nick gave me a withering look and refrained from imparting this vital piece of evidence. Then he slammed the receiver down and made for the door, grabbing his car keys from the hall table.

'Where are you going now?' I cried, running after him.

'He can't be far away, I'm going to look for him.'

'I'm coming with you!'

'No, stay with Rachel,' he ordered.

'Not likely,' I muttered, throwing myself down the front steps after him.

He jumped into the Land Rover. 'For God's sake, who's going to look after her?' he growled as I jumped in beside him.

'Your mother,' I said, slamming the door, 'she's brilliant with distraught young mothers, I know that from experience. Now come on!'

We reversed, and the tyres spun on the gravel drive as we took off. Nick swung the Land Rover around the side of the house, and we sped off down the back drive, bouncing all over the place on the un-made-up, rock-strewn road.

'Where are we going?' I gasped, steadying myself on the window as we roller-coasted down towards the back gate.

'We'll head for the London road,' said Nick. 'We'll just have to take a chance on him going that way. He obviously didn't go back towards Helston or you'd have seen him. I know a short-cut to the main road so we might be able to cut him off.'

'If he's smart he'll ditch the car, he knows I've seen it.'

'What, and charge about on foot? Come on, Polly, a redheaded man carrying a baby for miles is pretty conspicuous, and it would take him for ever to get to the main road and hitch a lift.'

'He might get a train.'

'The police will be on the look-out at Helston station, and that's the only main line around here.'

We paused for a second at the bottom of the drive, before swinging round left into the lane. He flashed me a look. 'What the hell were you doing in New Town anyway?'

I stared out of the window. 'Going back to London.'

'Idiot,' he muttered, but made no further comment, as we tore off down the road.

We raced around a sharp bend, taking half the hedge with us, and I hastily withdrew my elbow from the open window. Nick had obviously learned to drive at his mother's knee, I recognised the style. If I wasn't very much mistaken, this was a former pupil of the Hetty Penhalligan Kamikaze School of Motoring. At least I'd been on a trial run once already today, so I knew the ropes. I planted my feet firmly on the dashboard to act as shock absorbers, and gripped the upholstery with my nails. The tyres screeched around on the tarmac, reminding me abruptly of Rachel's screams. I shivered.

'D'you think we'll find him?'

'I just don't know.'

'How far away d'you think he is by now?'

Nick, thankfully, didn't have his mother's penchant for eyeball contact. He stared straight ahead. 'Hard to say, a mile maybe, perhaps two if he's really motoring.'

He obviously wasn't feeling chatty so I kept quiet. Well, at least for a couple of seconds, anyway.

'What are we going to do if we do see him?' I ventured timidly.

'Follow him of course.'

We lurched sideways as we swerved to avoid an old man on a quivering bicycle.

'Yes, but then what?'

In my mind's eye, I saw us drawing up alongside the Volvo and gesturing for Adam to pull in, whereupon he'd shoot us a villainous sideways glance, snarl, and go even faster — but he'd be no match for us. We'd be right by his side, tearing along through the twisty-turny lanes, neck and neck, until eventually we'd ram him and force him

462

into a ditch. Nick would leap out, drag him from the car, and spreadeagle him over the bonnet in a half-nelson, and I'd be right beside him, frisking him and reading him his rights: 'You have the right to remain silent, but anything you do say . . .'

'Use the car phone to telephone the police and give them his exact position. They'll have a squad of cars after him in no time,' answered Nick calmly.

'Oh. Oh yes, of course, good idea.' I was rather disappointed.

As we rounded the next bend, we nearly went straight up the back of a little red post office van which was tootling along at a leisurely thirty miles per hour. Nick sat on the horn, but the van stood its ground, which happened to be most of the road.

'Oh, come on, you berk! Move over!' I cried, banging the dashboard in frustration and willing Postman Pat into the nearest ditch. He was damned if he was moving over, but eventually the lane widened slightly, albeit on a horrifically blind corner, and Nick shunted down a gear and roared up beside him, forcing him into the hedge. As we shot past I caught a glimpse of a little purple-faced man, waving his fist and shouting obscenities. Blood pressure was clearly a problem, and a heart attack looked imminent, but I had no sympathy. He'd cost us vital seconds.

The next thing I knew, we'd hung a sharp left into a ploughed field and were bouncing along down the side of it. All four wheels seemed to be leaving the ground at regular intervals. Thank goodness I hadn't managed to make much headway with the fish pie, I thought, as my bottom left the seat and my tummy shot into my oesophagus. I gritted my teeth and clutched my bosoms as we took off from a particularly deep rivet. God, I was getting some exercise on this holiday.

At last the dark furrows came to an end, and we swerved

463

into another field, this time, thankfully, of the green and pleasant variety. My organs slipped back into their rightful slots and I managed to speak, or squeak, 'Where the hell are we going?'

'Short-cut!'

'But won't the farmer mind?' I asked, as hordes of terrified sheep scattered in all directions.

'I am the farmer.'

He slammed on the brakes and we screeched to a halt in front of a huge fence. Oh no! What now? Through it? Over it?

'Open it!' he barked.

Oh Christ, it was a gate! I hurriedly scrambled out and fell flat on my face in some very dubious business.

'Oh God, yucky poo! Sheep shit, all up my nose!' I wailed in disgust as I got slowly to my feet.

'Get on with it!' bellowed Nick, banging the steering wheel.

Nausea was rising within me, but I hurriedly wiped my nose and addressed myself to the gate. It had one of those really complicated catches, with bits of wire and binder-twine all over it — the sort of thing you need a degree from Cirencester to open. My fingers were like sausages as I fumbled nervously around.

'I can't do it!' I wailed pathetically.

'Jesus!' a voice hissed in my ear. Nick was beside me. He swept my inept fingers away and muttered something under his breath, but I couldn't quite catch what he said except it sounded like 'hopeless', 'fucking', and 'prat', but I probably misheard.

He had it open in an instant, then he ran back to the car, revved up, and shot through.

'Now shut it!' he barked from the driving seat.

It was bloody heavy, but I prayed to God and luckily He provided me with some superhuman strength. I rammed it shut.

As I ran back to the car, I suddenly glimpsed a long flash of green through the hedge on the opposite side of the field. The green streak was travelling at speed down the lane at right angles to ours.

'There he is!' I shrieked, 'that's him!' and almost before I was back in my seat, Nick was after him.

We roared up to the crossroads, swung left without stopping to see what was coming, and raced up the lane. There was no sign of the Volvo now, but at least we knew we were on the right road.

'After him! After him!' I squealed, bouncing up and down in my seat with excitement.

'Put your seatbelt on!' ordered Nick as I bounced a bit too hard and nearly cracked my head on the roof. I dragged it across and snapped it into place.

An uncharacteristically long stretch of road opened before us and, right at the very end, just as it was about to disappear over the brow of the hill, we saw the green Volvo.

Nick opened up the throttle and we fairly flew along, all thoughts of ringing the police forgotten in the chase. As we reached the same brow, the road twisted suddenly – then again – and again – and again. Each time we rounded a bend, I saw a tantalising flash of green appear and disappear, all in the space of a millisecond.

'Quick, quick! Faster, faster!'

Nick didn't utter, but his mouth was set in a grim line and his knuckles were white on the steering wheel. We were definitely gaining on him. Nick had the advantage of knowing the lanes backwards, so he anticipated every bend and cornered expertly. I tried the motorbike lean so favoured by his mother, but obviously went a touch too far when I ended up with my nose in his lap.

'For God's sake sit still, will you!' he yelled, and I scrambled dutifully back into my corner, hanging on to the strap above the door as the speedometer approached eighty m.p.h. I'd always wondered what that strap was for, and now I knew. Life-threatening situations. They don't mention that in the glossy brochures though, do they? Added extra – one handy strap for hanging on to when you're looking death in the face.

'D'you think he knows we're behind him?' I yelled above the roar of the engine.

'Doubt it, I shouldn't think he's looked behind him once, he's just driving like a maniac to get the hell out of here!'

We seemed to be gaining on him all the time, but then so, unbeknown to us, was a tractor. Only the tractor was travelling in the opposite direction. It had recently emerged from some fields a mile or two hence, and was trundling back to the farm that bordered on Nick's, just over the hill. It was a large, red, uncompromising vehicle, the old-fashioned variety with huge protruding wheels at the front and a trailer at the back. It was making slow but steady progress down the lane, just as Adam was making fast and unsteady progress up it.

We were far enough behind not to witness the inevitable meeting, but the sickening crunch of metal was unmistakable.

I shrieked and covered my face with my hands. Nick hit the brakes. Within seconds we were skidding around a corner, and then another, before coming to a precarious halt, inches away from a horrifically concertina-ed Volvo.

Its back end was jutting out at right angles to the road. The front was almost totally embedded in the tractor. I couldn't see Adam or the tractor driver.

Nick was out and running before I'd even come to my senses. I stumbled out and raced after him, but as I approached I stopped dead in my tracks and shrank back in horror. Adam's twisted body was draped upside down over the front of the tractor. He'd obviously gone straight through the windscreen and somersaulted down on to his back. Blood was gushing down on to his face, over his eyes, and into his open mouth. His head was slumped forward at a peculiar angle to his crumpled body, and I couldn't see his legs at all. They seemed to be embedded somewhere in the tractor.

Vomit rose up in my throat and I turned away. I threw up on the verge several times. By the time I looked up, which was a good minute or so later, I could see that Nick was crawling precariously over the tangled heap, slowly inching his way towards Adam's immobile body.

'Oh God, he's dead! He's dead, isn't he?' I shrieked.

By now Nick had reached him. 'No he's not, he's still alive – just!' He yelled back. 'For Christ's sake, get Jamie out!'

'Jamie! Oh my God!'

I ran like stink to the back of the car and peered in, bracing myself for what I might find. At first I couldn't see him at all, there was nothing on the back seat. Then I saw him. The carry-cot was on the floor in the back, wedged in between the front and back seats. Jamie's big blue eyes stared up at me. His little mouth was open and getting wider by the minute. The eyes disappeared as they screwed up tight; he took a deep breath.

'WHHAAAAaaaaaa!'

Thank goodness! That sounded healthy. I yanked the door open and dragged the carry-cot out. It was the old-fashioned sturdy sort with rigid sides, and it was completely unharmed; and so, as far as my totally inexpert eye could see, was Jamie. He was bloody cross though. He bellowed in indignation as I grabbed him roughly and held him close, stroking his little back and feeling his warm, comforting weight, heavy against my shoulder.

'Whaaaa . . . whah, whah! Hu, hu, hu . . . whaaa, whaaa, whaaaahhh . . . !'

'Sshhh, shush Jamie, you're all right now, I've got you, you're all right.'

467

His cries gradually subsided, and after a while he made little snuffling sounds as he snuggled happily into my neck, grabbing at my hair and shoving it into his mouth, suddenly oblivious to the drama surrounding him. I was shaking like a wet puppy, but he didn't seem to mind.

I turned back to the mangled car. Nick was perched precariously on the bonnet, crouching down over Adam.

'He's all right!' I yelled, 'Jamie's perfectly all right, not hurt at all!'

'Thank God. Adam's in a pretty bad way, though. Quick, Polly, ring for an ambulance on my car phone.'

'Right!'

I grabbed the carry-cot from the car and, clutching Jamie, raced back to the Land Rover. I put him in his carry-cot on the back seat, then I jumped into the front.

'Car phone, car phone . . .' I muttered as I scrambled around looking for something with familiar dials or buttons on it. I don't even own a portable phone, let alone a car phone, so I was a bit out of my depth here. Where do people keep these things − on the dashboard? Under the seat?

'Oh please let me find it, please . . .' I muttered desperately as I feverishly rooted around in the glove compartment. 'Please, don't let me be a complete and utter moron!'

I emptied every compartment I could find and threw everything on the floor; torches, maps, barley sugars, but no telephone − where the hell was it! I dived down on to the floor and thrust my hand under the seat. Was this where it was kept? Under here?

'Oh where is it, Jamie, help me!'

The door flew open and Nick was behind me.

'I can't find it!' I wailed, wringing my hands from my cringing position on the floor.

'Christ, Polly, you're just the person to rely on in an emergency, aren't you?'

468

I thought this was a bit rich considering all I'd been through, but I kept mum as he leaned over and wrenched open a catch by the handbrake, pulling out a handpiece with buttons on it. He punched out 999.

'I thought that was part of the handbrake!' I whispered.

Without bothering to answer, he barked out instructions to the ambulance service.

I looked in the back seat. Jamie's eyelids were getting heavy. I watched as they closed, his little mouth opened, and his clenched fist unfurled. A second later he was fast asleep. I tiptoed away. Retching violently, I forced myself to go back towards Adam. I crept down the lane with my hand to my mouth. As I tentatively inched closer to the wreckage, I thought I saw his eyelids flicker.

'Adam?' I whispered, from a good ten yards away.

This time the mouth twitched too. I inched a mite closer.

'Adam?'

'What the bloody hell happened?' said a voice out of nowhere.

I jumped about a foot in the air and swung round to see the tractor driver staggering around in the road holding his head. Oh Christ! We'd forgotten about him. He was about seven foot tall and built like an all-in wrestler, a great bear of a man. He looked as if he was pretty much intact, but he was swaying violently, like a tree in a gale, as if he'd completely lost his sense of balance. I ran to steady him.

'Sit down, sit down!' I cried, lugging him towards the grass verge. As I lugged I realised he had the most spectacular BO. I wondered whether it was due to fear, or whether he was always so highly perfumed.

He sat obediently. I sat down next to him, then inched away as the odour shot straight up my nostrils. 'What happened?' he muttered.

'There was a crash, you're obviously in shock,' I informed him at arm's length.

469

He looked at me with bleary eyes. 'And who the hell are you, Florence Nightingale?'

I ignored this smart remark, and peered into his face which was florid and jowly. He had a little cut above his right eye, and a terrific bruise appearing on his chin, but other than that there wasn't a scratch. The tractor was completely open to the elements, so he'd obviously been thrown clear without the added complication of going through a windscreen.

'You don't look too bad,' I ventured. 'Are you all right?'

'No, I'm not sodding all right. I feel bloody awful! I've got a sodding great lump on my head and a pain in my back and my leg's killing me. Who the fuck was that idiot in the Volvo? What the bloody hell was he up to, he must have been doing about ninety miles an hour – ooh, my bloody head!' He swooned a bit.

'Put it between your knees,' I ordered, grabbing hold of the back of his bull-like neck and shoving his face downwards.

'Geddoff, will you?' he protested, pushing away my hand and making as if to scramble to his feet. I couldn't cope with a lumbering man-mountain on the loose.

'Just shut up and sit still,' I ordered. 'I'm a nurse.'

This seemed to do the trick. He looked doubtful for a moment, then lowered his head obediently until his nose was about two inches from the tarmac.

We sat in silence. I looked across at the tangled heap of machinery in front of us. Nick had climbed back to be with Adam again. Adam looked larger than ever, his huge bulk plastered over the front of the tractor like an enormous insect splattered flat by the impact. Blood was pouring out of his head and his shirt was scarlet now as it trickled down his neck to his collar. He was totally motionless. Nick reached out and took his hand. I shivered, hugging my knees to my chest and resting my head on them.

'Oh, please God,' I whispered, 'let Adam be all right. Let him live. I know I haven't prayed for ages, but this isn't for me, it's for Adam and Jamie. I mean, he only wanted his baby, didn't he? Please don't let him die for it.'

I prayed on and on, mumbling into my knees for what seemed like an eternity. I couldn't look at the wreck any more. A great stillness seemed to descend on the scene. After a while I heard voices in the background. Other cars had evidently accumulated behind us: car doors were slamming, people were whispering hoarsely to one another, 'What happened?' 'Is he dead?' Still I didn't look up.

Eventually I heard the distant wail of a siren. I lifted my head from my knees. Flashing lights were appearing around the corner.

A small crowd of concerned but goggle-eyed motorists had gathered, and the police, who had arrived simultaneously, had to organise them all out of the way before the ambulance could even begin to nose its way through. It seemed to take for ever. At last they managed to clear a path. The ambulance pushed its way through, the back door swung open, and a stretcher appeared. A couple of ambulance men inched their way gingerly over the stunted Volvo towards Adam's twisted body. With Nick's help they managed to prise him from the wreckage and lift him on to the stretcher. They covered him in a red blanket and tucked it in around him. At least he looks more comfortable now, I thought, as he was loaded into the ambulance. The tractor driver was also ushered in, grumbling and blaspheming, and the doors slammed behind him.

Nick approached the driver. 'We'd like to follow, if that's all right.'

'You know him?'

'Yes, and we've got his baby here with us. He was in the

car. He seems fine, but he should be checked over at the hospital.'

The driver nodded. 'OK.'

In silence we got back into the car, and for the third time that day I sped off down the lanes. We trailed the solid white ambulance with its siren blaring and lights flashing for about a mile and a half and then, suddenly, without warning, it slowed right down, indicated left, and came to an abrupt halt in a lay-by. The siren and the flashing light stopped. We drew in behind it.

The driver opened his door and jumped down. Nick wound down his window. With head bowed the driver walked back to us and crouched down at the open window. He took his cap off and scratched his head.

'I'm sorry, sir, I thought I ought to stop and tell you. His injuries were just too severe and he'd lost too much blood. There was nothing we could do. I'm afraid he's dead.'

Chapter Twenty-seven

There were forms to be filled in at the hospital and questions to be answered by the police who arrived to grill us, but eventually, after a gruelling hour and a half, we were allowed to go home. I'd telephoned Rachel from the hospital to let her know Jamie was safe and well. I didn't mention Adam and she didn't ask.

We drove home in silence and, as we rounded the corner to Trewarren and swept up the drive, I saw a little hunched figure in a grey cardigan sitting on the top of the steps by the front door. She stood up as we scrunched to a halt and ran down to meet us.

I was holding Jamie in the back seat. Rachel opened the door and I passed him to her. She buried her face in his tiny body, tears streaming down her cheeks.

'He's OK,' I said wearily. 'They checked him over at the hospital. Luckily his carry-cot was wedged on the floor in the back of the car and that saved him.'

She nodded, but couldn't speak. I put my arm around her shoulders, but she shook it off violently and turned on her heel.

I sighed and slowly climbed up the steps behind her into the house. She disappeared into the kitchen. I made for the drawing room, helped myself to a stiff gin, and flopped down into the nearest armchair. There was no sign of Hetty; perhaps she'd gone home, or resumed her shopping trip in Helston.

I was exhausted. I felt as if I'd aged dramatically in the last few hours. But then death did have that effect on one, didn't it? It was rather a sobering experience, watching someone die; made you grow up a bit. And Adam was definitely dead. I still couldn't quite get used to that fact, but he was.

Nick appeared and sank down on the sofa opposite me. He rubbed his eyes vigorously with the heels of his hands as only men do, girls being too aware of smudgeable mascara, and yawned widely. I wondered if I looked as tired as he did. His face was drawn and haggard.

There was something I had to ask him. I leaned forward. 'Nick, you don't think,' I began timidly, 'you don't think we chased him into that tractor, do you? It's just I'd hate to think that we somehow caused him to speed up or—'

Nick shook his head. 'Polly, don't even think about it. As I said to you at the time, he probably wasn't even aware that there was someone on his tail. He had to go at that speed because he must have known the first thing we'd do would be to alert the police. He had to put his foot down whether he knew we were there or not. No, it wasn't our fault, although God knows, that doesn't make it any better.' He rubbed his weary eyes again. 'I just wish there was something we could have done to save him. I felt so helpless, I just didn't know what to do apart from be with him, hold his hand, talk to him. I was so terrified of moving him . . .'

'You did all you could,' I said soothingly. 'God, I was hopeless, I couldn't get within inches of him. You did plenty.'

'Well, it wasn't enough, was it?'

He slumped forward and stared miserably at the carpet. I wanted to reach out and touch him, in fact my hand ventured forth in his direction for a moment, then I remembered Serena and I snatched it back.

It occurred to me briefly that there was no sign of the

lovely Serena. In fact, now I came to think about it more than briefly, she hadn't been around when I'd arrived back with Hetty. Probably down in Helston choosing curtain material for the dining room, I thought bitterly. I didn't like to ask. For once my own problems seemed somewhat eclipsed by recent events. I'd never experienced death before and it made me feel mighty peculiar. I shivered.

Nick noticed. He leaned forward. 'Are you OK, Polly?' he asked gently.

'Yes, fine,' I said, 'just a bit cold.'

'It's probably the shock – here, have this.' He whipped off his jumper and threw it over to me. I put it on and snuggled into its woolly warmth. It smelled delicious. I wondered if he'd notice if I stole it.

Rachel appeared from the kitchen with a bottle in one hand and Jamie astride her hip. She sat down on the rug in front of the fire and propped him up on her knee. She offered him the teat and he latched on to it enthusiastically, sucking greedily. We sat in silence, watching him drink, his eyes half shut, his podgy little hands clutching the bottle eagerly as he gulped away. So small and vulnerable, thank goodness he was all right. He drained the bottle in minutes. Rachel sat him up and rubbed his back to wind him. He let rip with the most enormous belch. We all laughed, breaking the silence.

Then Nick got up and stood by the fire next to Rachel. He licked his lips. 'Rachel?'

It seemed as if she'd never be able to tear her eyes from her baby, but eventually she looked up at him.

'Yes?'

'Adam died in the car crash.'

She stared at him for a second, then a ghost of a smile flickered on her lips. I felt sick.

'Yes,' she said, 'I thought as much.' She quickly looked down at Jamie again.

Nick was taken aback. 'I'd um – I'd like to be able to

tell you he didn't suffer much, but I'm not too sure about that . . . I'm pretty sure he was unconscious most of the time though . . .'

Rachel didn't even look up.

Nick soldiered on, braving her stony silence. 'Look, I was thinking, we'll have to contact his parents . . .'

Rachel raised her head. 'I'll deal with that,' she said coolly.

There was a silence. I stared at her. On the one hand I rather admired her lack of hypocrisy – at least she wasn't pretending to be upset – but, none the less, her cold-blooded attitude unnerved me. She had, after all, been in love with the guy at one time – about to marry him, in fact, and he was also Jamie's father.

I suddenly felt an urge to speak up for Adam. 'Don't you feel anything at all, Rachel?' I blurted out.

She slowly lifted her head and looked at me. Her eyes narrowed. 'Why should I?'

'Oh, er, well I don't know really,' I faltered, back-tracking like mad; Rachel rather frightened me these days. 'It's just that, well I can't help thinking—'

'What can't you help thinking?'

'I don't know . . . I can't help thinking you're being very calm about all this, that's all.'

'Really?' she sneered. 'And what did you expect, tears? Hysterics?'

I had a feeling I was well out of my depth here, but I dug deep for courage and ploughed on regardless. 'No, of course not, but – I mean, you were going to marry him at one time and, after all, he was Jamie's father and all he really wanted—'

'Was he?' she cut in, silencing me.

I frowned, puzzled. 'Was he what?'

'Jamie's father?' she said in a cold, flat voice.

'Well – well, yes, of course he was, well, wasn't he?' I blustered.

476

She looked me straight in the eye and her thin little mouth all but disappeared. 'No, he wasn't,' she said shortly.

I gasped. Nick and I exchanged shell-shocked looks.

'Well, for Christ's sake!' blustered Nick. 'What's this all been about then? Why was he so obsessed with taking Jamie? Why have we been chasing him all over Cornwall? What the hell are you talking about, Rachel?'

Rachel tied a bib around Jamie's neck and took a jar of baby food out of a bag. She unscrewed it and, without a word, calmly began feeding him as if Nick hadn't even uttered. Nick wasn't having that. He crouched down on the rug next to her and took her chin in his hand, jerking her head towards him, forcing her to look at him.

'Rachel, a man has died today. Come to that, Polly and I damn nearly died trying to get your baby back. Now what's going on here? If Adam isn't the father, who the hell is?'

Rachel stared at Nick for a second, her face inches from his, then she brushed his hand away contemptuously. She drew herself up and took a deep breath as if she were about to make a speech.

'If you must know,' she said briskly, 'and to be honest I can't see that it's any of your business, Jamie's father is a man called David Saunders.' She turned to me, 'You'd probably remember him better as Mr Saunders.'

I stared at her. I hadn't the vaguest idea what she was talking about.

'Mr Saunders?' I echoed dumbly.

'From school.'

From school. My God. It came to me. It hit me like a flying grand piano. My jaw dropped, my eyes boggled, I spat the dummy. Jesus Christ, Mr Saunders the music teacher!

'Mr Saunders the music teacher?' I gasped in disbelief.

'That's right,' she affirmed calmly.

Then I remembered. Of course. Mrs Compton had mentioned him when I'd telephoned the school; said Rachel had got on particularly well with him. I'd thought nothing of it, why should I? Jesus. Mr Saunders. Mr Saunders with the . . . ginger hair. I looked at Jamie's red tufts, which had previously made him so obviously Adam's son. But Adam didn't have the monopoly on carrots, and Rachel clearly just had a penchant for it. Well, would you believe it: Rachel Marsden, the brilliant music student with her mind on more than treble clefs. Base clefts, more like. But of all people, Mr Saunders . . . Nausea rose within me. It wasn't the fact that he was a teacher that stunned me – although that in itself was pretty breathtaking – it was more the physical attributes of the teacher in question that had me reaching for the sick bag. We're talking yuck-a-roony here. I gagged quietly.

'Now just hang on a minute,' said Nick. 'This chap Saunders is Jamie's father? Not Adam? Did Adam know that?'

Rachel sighed. 'I tried to tell him, but he wouldn't believe me. Look, Nick, if you don't mind, I really don't want to go into all this right now. It's personal, I'm very tired, and it's a long story.'

She tucked Jamie under her arm, got to her feet, and made as if to go. Nick grabbed her arm and pulled her down on the floor. I've seen him look pretty furious in my time, but nothing like as incensed as this.

'Tell it, Rachel,' he hissed grimly. 'Tell the story in all its sordid personal details because, believe me, we need to know. Polly and I really need to know.'

Even Rachel looked taken aback. She looked warily at Nick's grim, determined face and bit her lip. She sat down again.

'Well, all right, if you must know, I'll tell you,' she said sullenly. 'It's just hard to know where to begin.'

'The beginning will do nicely,' said Nick, still staring grimly at her, 'try starting there.'

Rachel sighed. 'All right,' she said at length. She held Jamie in one arm and twiddled her hair with her other hand. 'David was a teacher at our school. You remember him, don't you, Polly?'

I cast my mind back a few years. Sure. I remembered him all right. Mr Saunders. I could see him now, with his thin white face, his wispy ginger hair, his John Lennon glasses and his goaty little beard which he'd twiddle round his finger whenever he was nervous, which was most of the time. He was totally unsuited to teaching, and had no idea how to control a class full of bored sixteen-year-olds, whose minds were always on boys and pop music and never on Debussy.

I could hear him now. 'Girls! Girls, settle down please!' he'd plead in his thin reedy voice, visibly palpitating behind his glasses. 'Let's have a little hush, shall we?'

This pathetic appeal would only serve to augment the noise, and more desk-banging, rubber-throwing and shrieking would ensue, whereupon, in desperation, he'd put Beethoven's Fifth on at full volume in an attempt to drown the noise and to make it appear to any casual passing teacher that he was in full control. Then he'd slump down at his desk in a deep depression, miserably aware he was an unmitigated disaster.

His shoulders were constantly hunched: weighed down, no doubt, by his sense of failure; but also, I suspected, by the constant avalanche of dandruff which landed in drifts on his musty tweed jacket. Little white flakes would float down, gather, and be brushed off surreptitiously, only for more to land not a moment later. As a bored-out-of-my-skull teenager, it made fascinating viewing.

But dandruff was the least of Mr Saunders' personal problems. The biggest cross this unfortunate man had to bear was undoubtedly his dampness. His nose and forehead were permanently wet and, try as he would to wipe the beads of sweat away with a variety of spotted hankies, the drips would automatically reappear. His hands were obviously in the same state, as he was constantly wiping them on his trousers, and his little horn-rimmed glasses steamed up on a regular basis. Again, it made compulsive viewing, and we girls did a lot of sniggering and mock puking behind his back as we speculated on the probable state of his armpits. In fact, 'snuggling up to Saunders' gushing pits', was one of our 'Fates Worse Than Death', alongside licking Matron's corns and squeezing Dorothy McAlistair's spots. We would dream up these revolting forfeits in the dorm at night, and then stuff our duvets in our mouths and squeal with horror at the thought of executing them. And to think Rachel had done more than snuggle . . . I drifted out of my reverie and stared at her in disbelief.

'Yes — yes, I remember him,' I whispered.

Rachel laughed. 'You probably fancied him yourself, didn't you, Polly!'

I stared at her in horror, choking down the bile. I shook my head dumbly. 'Er, no, not as such, no.'

'Oh come on, we all fancied at least one of the male teachers. Who did you have your eye on then?'

Now this was perfectly true. It has to be said that most of us girls had formidable crushes on the very few men who flitted in and out of our sheltered lives at school. Monsieur Ferout, French master and ultra-smooth froggy dude, had reputedly received no less than fifty-two valentine cards one year, and I'm ashamed to say mine was amongst them. Clive, the gardener, was constantly finding bunches of half-dead wild flowers placed lovingly in his potting shed, and even Billy, the odd-job boy, had apparently been propositioned behind the guinea-pig hutches by a desperate fifth former, but never, *never* Mr Saunders.

480

I licked my lips and stared at her glassy-eyed. How could she? 'Oh well, you know, er, no one in particular. I kept an open mind.'

'I bet you did! Kept your options open, eh?' she smiled nastily.

I was about to rise furiously to the bait, when Nick interrupted sarcastically. 'Fascinating though this tale of unrequited schoolgirl passion is, can we get back to the point? You had an affair with this Saunders chappie, then?' he asked Rachel.

'David and I were in love,' she said simply.

I had a bit of trouble taking this concept on board, but somehow managed to turn an incredulous guffaw into a hacking cough. She looked at me suspiciously as I snorted into a hankie.

'How long had it been going on for?' asked Nick.

Rachel stared into the fire. 'About three months, I suppose. It all started when he organised a trip to a concert at the Festival Hall. He put a notice up on the board in the common room, and I was the only one to put my name down. It was all strictly above board, of course, in fact he even press-ganged another girl into coming too, but she didn't turn up. Anyway, because it was just the two of us, we went for something to eat afterwards. Nothing happened then, of course, but we talked for hours and hours, we got on so well. I felt as if he was the first person in my life who'd ever understood me.'

The flames lit up her face as she remembered. For a moment she looked quite pretty, quite transformed. She smiled. 'We just couldn't find out enough about each other, in fact I remember now we very nearly missed the last train back, we were so absorbed. I think we both knew then that this was the start of something. That there was no going back.'

She turned away from the fire and back to us. The soft, dreamy look suddenly disappeared. 'Anyway, that's how it all started. After that, we'd meet in the town whenever I could slip out of school. Our so-called affair was really just an endless and frustrating stream of cups of coffee or walks in the park; all pretty tame, really.'

'But how did you manage to keep it so quiet?' I felt a certain grudging admiration. If I so much as put a toe out of bounds, I was invariably hauled back by the scruff of the neck and severely punished. The idea of conducting a clandestine affair, tame or otherwise, with a member of staff, filled me with horror.

'We were very careful. It meant a hell of a lot to both of us, and we were determined not to be found out. Occasionally we'd get daring and go to an evening concert or a play together, but that was about it. Until of course — well, until we just couldn't bear it any longer, couldn't control it.' She smiled wryly. 'And naturally, that was the one time we were discovered.'

'What — you mean . . . Where were you?' I faltered.

'In bed, of course. Well, not literally, but certainly figuratively.'

I gasped. 'Good grief, you mean you were actually — you know, doing it — when someone . . . Who found you?'

Rachel gave a wry smile. 'Miss Fisher.'

'Miss Fisher!' I gagged on my tonsils. It couldn't have been worse. Miss Fisher, the deputy head, of the razor-sharp tongue, the biting wit and the fine line in sneering sarcasm. Even now, years later, I cringed at the thought of her.

Nick grinned. 'So where were you when she found you, his place or your dorm?'

'Actually, we were in a deserted boat-house by the river,' she turned to me. 'Remember that funny old place by the broken bridge?'

I gulped again and nodded; by now grudging admiration had developed into unreserved hero-worship. The boat-house had been so totally and categorically out of bounds, it was considered dangerous to come within feet of it unless you had an overwhelming desire to be expelled. It was a beautiful old weather-boarded place, surrounded by reeds and bulrushes and flanked by an enormous old weeping willow which wept all over the roof. It was apparently falling down, and its collapse was always said by the staff to be imminent, but countless girls had dreamed of a romantic tryst in there; it was the perfect setting. It was permanently locked, but I imagined 'David' would have had access to a key. I tried to imagine Miss Fisher's face at finding them there.

'Was she furious?'

Rachel grinned. 'Speechless, literally. She appeared in the doorway, a vision in red flannel and rollers, flashing a torch around. We were lying on a pile of rugs in the corner without a stitch on. We just looked at her and she kept opening and shutting her mouth and nothing came out.'

I gaped. 'God, I wish I'd been a fly on the wall. What did she do?'

'Well, of course it was the middle of the night, and anyone with any sense would have left it until the morning, but oh no, she insisted on marching us back to the school and parading us in front of Miss Harper there and then. She telephoned Harpie, and we sat in the study for ages waiting for her to come down, whilst Miss Fisher breathed fire and paced up and down. Eventually, poor old Harpie appeared in her dressing gown looking bleary-eyed and pissed off, and told us to go back to bed, saying she'd deal with it in the morning.'

I grinned. I could imagine our laid-back headmistress being more than a little irritated at being woken up in the middle of the night.

'Anyway, the next morning I filed back in to see her, and after a brief discussion was unceremoniously expelled. Daddy was summoned to take me away.'

I nodded. 'I remember that. Everyone thought he was dragging you out of school for no good reason. We thought it was terribly bad form just before your A-levels.'

'That was the story that was put around to keep you lot off the scent.'

I had to hand it to old Rachel. There was I, thinking I was a real Jack the Lass for organising the occasional cider knees-up in the dorm, and discussing what 'doing it' might be like with my virginal comrades, and grilling Rebecca Crocker over and over again because she'd come close to 'doing it' on a skiing holiday, and all the time Rachel, the quiet, mousy scholar was shagging the life out of one of the teachers in the strictly out-of-bounds boat house. Impressed? I was prostrate at her feet in awe and wonder.

'So what happened to David?' asked Nick.

Rachel looked sad. 'I never saw him again. He wrote to me from a school in Kent where he'd managed to get a position. Evidently Miss Harper had told him that if he left without a fuss his family wouldn't be told.'

'Family?'

'He had a wife and two children,' said Rachel calmly. 'Apparently he told his wife he'd been dismissed due to musical differences with Miss Harper. Ridiculous really. Harpie wouldn't know F sharp from B flat, but anyway, she swallowed the story and off they went to Kent.'

'But why was it all kept so quiet?' asked Nick. 'Surely he should have been hauled over the coals by the board of governors and all that sort of thing, made an example of?'

'Very probably, but you see my father was one of the governors and he had a lot of sway. In his position as a judge he just didn't want the publicity – I mean, you can just see the tabloids, can't you: "Teacher in Love Nest with High Court Judge's Daughter".' Rachel smiled wryly. 'Oh yes, Daddy made sure it was all hushed up.'

'So then what, he packed you off to America?' I asked.

'Yep, Daddy arranged it all. He was terrified I might try

to get in touch with David, which of course I would have done, so he arranged for me to go and stay with friends of his in Boston. I didn't know at the time that I was pregnant, had no idea. For what it's worth, David and I had only slept together that one time, so I really didn't even consider it. Anyway, by the time I'd missed two periods, Adam was well on the scene, both as a shoulder to cry on and − well, as a lover, to take my mind off things. I was just so miserable. I knew I didn't love him, but I allowed myself to go along with it, hoping a steamy affair would cure me of David. Of course it didn't. Anyway, by the time I was obviously pregnant, everyone naturally assumed it was Adam's, including Adam.'

'But couldn't it have been his after all?' asked Nick.

Rachel shook her head. 'Definitely not. I know that for a fact, because my dates worked out exactly to that one night with David. I'm glad too.' Rachel held Jamie close. 'I wanted his child. I wouldn't have wanted Adam's.'

'So as far as everyone else was concerned, Jamie was just a bit earlier than expected?' said Nick

'Exactly. Jamie arrived a month early and I pretended to be as surprised as anyone.'

'And they all believed you?'

'Why shouldn't they? No one knew about David.'

'Except your father,' I said.

'Yes, except Daddy, and I dare say he had his suspicions when he found out I was pregnant; but of course when Jamie arrived with red hair, he promptly breathed a sigh of relief. He'd never met David, so he wasn't to know there was another source.'

Nick straightened up from where he'd been crouching beside her and looked down at her thoughtfully. 'OK fine, that all makes sense, but just tell me one thing, Rachel. When you realised you didn't love Adam, and you wanted to get away and bring Jamie to England, why in heaven's name didn't you tell him he wasn't the father? I know it's brutal, but you could have avoided all this aggro.'

Rachel smiled up at him and shook her head sadly. 'D'you think I didn't try? Of course I did. I told him the day before I got on that plane. We had a fearful row, but he just wouldn't believe me. Then when I got to England I wrote to him, spelling it all out, telling him the whole story about me and David. He still didn't believe it, and he categorically refused to have a blood test, saying it was ridiculous to have to go to such lengths to prove Jamie was his son when it was so palpably obvious. You see, he didn't want to believe it. Yet there must have been a smidgen of doubt in his mind, don't you think? Otherwise, why not do the test?'

'So he just decided to come over here and snatch him back,' said Nick.

Rachel nodded. 'Exactly. He obviously decided not to try to gain access through the courts because he'd have to do a blood test to prove he was the father, so he just planned to grab him. And I knew how single-minded he'd be about it, too. He'd stop at nothing. I'd have spent my whole life looking over my shoulder, always running and hiding and shielding Jamie, never knowing whether he was trailing us or watching us, waiting to snatch him away.'

She stroked Jamie's downy red head, smoothing down his wispy curls. She turned to me. 'You asked me if I felt anything about Adam's death. Well, I do. I feel relief. I feel as if an enormous great boulder has been lifted off my shoulders, because now Jamie and I can relax and try to have a normal life.' She looked at me earnestly. 'You can understand that, can't you? I mean, in my position, you'd feel the same way, wouldn't you?'

It was almost a plea, an entreaty, the first time she'd ever shown a truly vulnerable side, a need to be understood and vindicated − liked, even. I looked at Jamie, asleep in her arms now, traces of milk still on his little pink lips, his head thrown back, one pudgy hand still wrapped around

486

her finger. Yes, I understood. I could never like her, but I understood.

I nodded. 'Yes.'

Rachel gave the tiniest of grateful smiles.

A silence enveloped us all. I looked outside. The window was full of inky black night now. One or two stars were winking away up there. I shivered and turned back to the fire which crackled away in the grate. I stared into the embers.

At length, Rachel spoke. She looked down at her baby. 'Bedtime for you, little boy,' she whispered. 'You've had rather a busy day, one way and another.'

She gathered him up in her arms and slowly got to her feet. Nick picked up his favourite blue blanket, which was lying on the sofa, and draped it over him.

'Sleep well, Jamie,' he said, stroking his hand. 'At least you haven't got the faintest idea what's been going on here.'

Rachel turned to go but, before she got to door, she stopped and turned back to us. 'Oh, I almost forgot,' she said sheepishly. 'I meant to say thank you. Thanks for getting him back, that is.'

Nick nodded and gave a half smile. 'I'd like to say, "It was nothing", but that wouldn't be quite true.'

She smiled briefly and nodded. 'I'll be going back to London first thing in the morning and I won't be troubling any of you ever again. Say goodbye to Tim for me, would you?' With that, she disappeared upstairs.

Chapter Twenty-eight

I sank back on the sofa and shut my eyes, more than a little tired. So it was all over. Adam was dead, and he hadn't even been the father. Perhaps he'd known all along, as Rachel had said. It hadn't stopped him loving Jamie, though, had it? It hadn't stopped him wanting him. And what of Jamie? I wondered which parent he would have been better off with. I wondered what sort of a mother Rachel would turn out to be. How would all this affect the way she brought Jamie up? What would she say to him when he was old enough to ask about his father? Would she tell him the truth, I wondered? Somehow I doubted it.

I opened my eyes and gave myself a little inward shake. What business was it of mine what she told him? It was about time I stopped interfering in other people's lives. The only reason I'd got involved at all in the first place was because I couldn't mind my own business. Well, it was time I learned.

Goodness, what was this, a smidgen of wisdom creeping into my soul? It was more like weariness, actually. And a growing awareness that there were some things that just couldn't be changed, and it was foolish and time-consuming even to try. All I could do was live my own life and forget about everyone else's.

I looked up and saw Nick, in a by now familiar position, standing with his back to me looking out of the window. My heart, from its already sunken position somewhere in my nether regions, plummeted even further down into my boots. The trouble with living my own life, I reflected, was that it categorically refused to go according to plan. Here, for example, was the man who held the key to my future happiness. The man on whom my hopes depended and my dreams pivoted. And what was he doing? He was counting his sheep.

I sighed and got to my feet. Of course. It was time I left. Silly of me to have stayed so long. For a moment I'd almost forgotten I didn't belong here. Another minute more and I'd have been swinging my legs over the arm of the chair, picking up the telly guide, sinking my teeth into an apple, and asking my boyfriend if he could possibly throw an omelette together because I was too knackered to get supper tonight. Wasn't it lucky I remembered my boyfriend was actually engaged to be married to someone else? He was clearly waiting for me to leave, and politely turning his back in order to let me slip away in a seemly fashion. No fuss, Polly, no hysterics, his back seemed to say. What a gent. Well, leave I would. I got up and crept towards the door. Nick swung round as a floorboard creaked.

'Where are you going?'

I froze in mid-creep, like a child playing grandmother's footsteps. 'Oh, er, well home again, actually,' I faltered guiltily. 'You know, because I was actually on my way when all this − when all this happened.'

He stared at me. Then at length he said, 'Polly, you really do amaze me. After all we've just been through − Adam's death, this whole ghastly business − it's had absolutely no effect on you whatsoever, has it? You just carry on as normal, don't you? Pick up where you left off before you were so rudely interrupted by a snatched baby, a distraught mother, a car chase and a dead man. That's about it, isn't it?'

'No, of course not! I'm absolutely shattered by what's

happened, but I've still got to go, haven't I? I mean it doesn't change anything!'

'So what were you going to do – sneak off without saying goodbye again?' He shook his head wearily. 'Go on then, off you go. Back to Harry, no doubt.'

I gaped at him in amazement. At length I found my voice. 'Back to Harry? Don't be ridiculous, of course not!'

He didn't answer, but he gave me a strange, penetrating look before turning back to the window. I stared at his back. For a moment I felt chastened. Guilt-ridden even. Then I bridled. Why? Why should I feel guilty? How dare he? How dare he talk to me like that! I was only going to make things easier for him! Suddenly all guilt and humility left me and I felt my colour rising. I rounded on him, pink with indignation. 'You've got a sodding nerve!' I blurted out.

He turned back, raising his eyebrows. 'Oh? And why's that? For pointing out your propensity to bugger off when the going gets a little tough?'

'A little tough? *A little tough*? You call what happened this morning a little tough?' I squeaked.

'Look, if you're talking about Serena pitching up here, as I said at the time, I'm sorry, but there was nothing I could do about it, I had no idea she was coming. I also said everything would be all right if you could just be patient, but patience isn't in your repertoire, is it, Polly? You like everything to be tickety-boo instantly and if it isn't, if there are one or two slight complications, then you really can't cope, can you? You just wait until my back is turned and sneak off like – like some sort of criminal.'

'How dare you!' I exploded. I marched over to him and prodded him in the chest with my finger. 'How dare you speak to me like that! *You're* the one who goes limping off across the fields to see your sheep the moment your girlfriend arrives on the scene, leaving me at the mercy of her unfortunate personality disorder! *You're* the one who refuses to acknowledge me in her presence and lets her prattle on to me about living here as lady muck of the manor!'

'Now just a minute!' Nick grabbed my finger as I prodded away, but I shook him off, well and truly unstoppable now.

'LET ME FINISH!' I bellowed, punctuating each word with more piercing prods to his chest. 'And *you're* the one who led me to believe you even vaguely fancied me, so that against my better judgement – and totally out of character for me I might say – I allowed myself to submit to some *very* amateur love-making on your part! And all the time – yes, all the time that shameful act was taking place, *you* were thinking how safe you were because of course the *real* love of your life, girl of your dreams, bitch in a million, call her what you will, was waiting patiently for you in London!'

'Polly, wait—'

'Oh yes, you thought it was quite all right to give good old Polly a quick bonk, didn't think there was any question of being found out, did you? Thought knobbing the secretary was an acceptable perk of the job! But you got a bit rattled when the wife-to-be arrived on the scene, didn't you? That was a little inconvenient, wasn't it? And yes, that's what *really* bugs me, if you must know, the fact that you didn't even have the *guts* to tell me you were engaged! And now you have the – the, *nerve* to tell me – to tell me-ee . . .'

I ground to a shuddering halt as I realised my head was in danger of wobbling off my neck. My shoulders were being shaken really quite hard.

'Polly, will you shut up a minute!' Nick was yelling into my face. 'For Christ's sake, shut up!'

I shut, panting with the exertion of stringing so many words together in one go.

Nick stared at me. 'What are you talking about? Wife?

Engaged? What the hell are you banging on about, for Christ's sake?'

'Oh, don't try and pretend!' I spat with renewed vigour, now I'd shaken off his hands and reclaimed my neck and head. 'Don't come the innocent with me. I know all about it, even down to the dear little boat you proposed in. I was even lucky enough to have the dear little ring stuffed up my nose – or down my throat – as she outlined her wedding plans to me, which will of course be carried out just as soon as you've both compared Filofaxes and found a gap in your oh-so-busy schedules.'

Nick stared at me incredulously. His mouth was open but he didn't utter. I stood panting up at him, face flushed, hands clenched, well fired up now and ready to embark on any number of new accusations at a moment's notice. Just let him try and defend himself, just let him try!

At length he ran his hands through his hair and groaned. 'Oh Christ. God, I had no idea!' He shook his head despairingly. 'But I suppose I should have known.'

He turned away and sat down slowly on the arm of the sofa. He looked shattered. All of a sudden I felt as if I were floundering around in the dark again, a feeling I really should have been getting used to, as it was not uncommon these days. This wasn't quite the reaction I'd had in mind.

'What? Known what?'

He looked up at me. 'What she was capable of.' He stood up and took my shoulders again. 'Polly, listen to me. The whole thing is a fabrication.'

I felt more than a little confused. 'A fabri— A what?' For some extraordinary reason a roll of chintzy curtain material sprang to my fuddled mind.

He gave my shoulders a little shake. 'A lie, a load of rubbish, a figment of her imagination. Crap, if you will. I've never asked Serena to marry me, never did, never would, never shall.'

I stared at him in disbelief. 'Are you sure?'

'What d'you mean, am I sure — of course I'm sure! Proposing marriage is not the sort of thing you forget about in a hurry, is it! It's not the sort of thing you run around doing every day!' He sighed and shook his head. 'I suppose I should have guessed she might do something like this . . .'

'So — so what's going on? She's still your girlfriend, but you're not getting married? Or — or she thinks you're getting married, but you're not sure, or — or what?' Any number of alarming permutations ran through my crazed mind.

Nick sighed. 'Oh God, what an idiot I've been.'

I was inclined to agree, but I let it pass, if he would just tell me what was going on. 'Nick, please . . .'

He shook his head. 'She really is quite unbelievable. Quite unbelievable. Sit down, Polly. I think I'd better tell you a little bit about Serena.'

He motioned me into the sofa and I sat, dumbly. Nick perched on the arm. He licked his lips thoughtfully and stared into space somewhere above my head.

'When I first met Serena,' he said slowly, 'I don't mind telling you I was absolutely knocked out by her. I thought she was the most stunningly attractive girl I'd ever seen.' He paused and looked down at me. 'Well, you've got to admit, she's bloody pretty.'

I ground my teeth, grimaced, and admitted it. 'Bloody pretty,' I muttered. The first word was easier than the second.

Nick looked back over my head towards the fire. He narrowed his eyes. 'I remember I was at this ghastly drinks party, hiding in the kitchen nursing a glass of warm champagne and wondering when I could conceivably escape, when she came in to get a drink. She asked me if there was any orange juice because she was driving, and I remember, I could hardly answer. I just gaped and stuttered something about there possibly being some in the fridge, I was so floored by her. Anyway, she found the orange juice and wandered off again, but later on, I was in the bedroom rooting around for my coat, and she came in for hers. We laughed, and whispered something about it being an awful party and how we couldn't wait to leave, and we got chatting. We talked in the bedroom for a bit, and then of course we both walked downstairs together and out into the street. I was about to say goodbye and walk off when I thought better of it. I found myself asking her what she was doing, if she wanted to get something to eat. I couldn't believe it when she said she'd love to.'

'Fast work for a country boy,' I said dryly.

'Well, why not? I didn't have much to lose. If she'd blown me out, it would have hurt my pride, but that would have been about it. Anyway, we went out for dinner, and over the next few weeks I took her out quite a lot, feeling pretty pleased with myself, I might tell you. We'd walk into one restaurant after another, and a million heads would turn and I'd feel about ten feet tall. Pathetic really, but totally intoxicating.'

I could imagine how good they'd look together. I tried not to, but I could imagine.

'I was mad about her,' he went on, 'absolutely infatuated. The whole film-star bit, the looks — everything. I freely admit I fell for the glamour. Anyway, she seemed to feel the same way about me, and before I knew where I was she'd moved in with me.'

'Really? Just like that? How long had you known her?'

'A couple of months, I suppose.'

'Wow. Not long.'

'No, I know, but I really thought this was it. I actually remember thinking this would be for ever.'

My insides knotted a bit at this. 'Go on.' (Quickly, please.) I was anxious to pass over this lovey-dovey phase and move smartly on to the bit where hopefully it all went wrong.

He sighed. 'Anyway, that's when it all started to go wrong.'

Ah, good.

'At first it was fine, we were still in the first flush of – well, call it what you will – love, passion, I don't know. But then, everything calmed down a bit and we got down to the business of living together. You know – give and take, and who squeezes the toothpaste where and who does the washing up and all that sort of thing. It was a complete disaster. It was quite obvious that Serena had never had to think about anybody but herself in her entire life. She'd been spoilt rotten by everyone up to now – her parents, her boyfriends, her friends; she'd never had to do anything for herself or consider anybody else's feelings. Life had just fallen into her lap; she'd got by solely on her good looks and superficial charm. And that's what she was, superficial. Shallow, even.'

He turned his eyes away from the fire and back on to me. 'I'm sorry if this sounds cruel, Polly, but I want to try and explain exactly what she's like.'

'Noo, nooo, not cruel at all!' I shook my head vigorously, lapping it up. The more cruelty the better, as far as I was concerned.

'Well, to begin with I suppose I let her wipe the floor with me. Honestly, I ran around after her like a bloody servant: cooking meals, tidying up after her, taking her clothes to the cleaners, picking her up from rehearsals, dropping her off at the hairdresser's or the beauty salon – it was ridiculous. Then one day I just stopped. Said I was busy and I couldn't take her shopping at Harrods because I had to work. She was absolutely furious, I don't think anyone had ever crossed her before in her entire life. Well, that was the beginning of the end, really. We had a major row and that set the scene for the next few months. We began to argue quite a bit, like every other day, and to be honest, after a few solid weeks of her petulant, spoilt behaviour, I got to the end of my rope. I seriously began to — sounds awful I know — well, to dislike her.'

'Not awful at all,' I murmured. 'Go on.'

'I'd stay at work later and later, partly because I had to, but partly because I couldn't bear the thought of going home. Then when I did get home, she'd go absolutely berserk. She'd usually downed a couple of bottles of wine by then, and she'd fly at me as I came through the door, ranting and raving about how I avoided her and demanding that I spent more time with her.'

'She sounds like the archetypal bored housewife.'

Nick shrugged. 'Perhaps that's it, perhaps she just didn't have enough to do. Actresses spend a hell of a lot of time "resting" as they call it. Anyway, she'd fly into the most incredible rages, throwing things round the room, cutting my clothes up, chucking the crockery out of the window, and then she'd throw herself on the bed sobbing violently, so I'd have to comfort her and tell her everything was all right, although I was pretty damn certain everything wasn't all right at all. I tell you, it was really getting me down.'

I was surprised. This didn't fit in with my image of the icy-cool, controlled Serena. I frowned. 'But she's so — so cool when you meet her.'

'I know, but remember she's an actress, she can be whoever she wants to be. In reality she's completely mixed up. You saw her at lunch today: she just suddenly snaps and goes bananas.'

'She sounds like a bit of a head-case.'

Nick sighed and shook his head. 'Either that or just incredibly theatrical, I was never really sure. She's so tenacious, too; gets her teeth into something and just won't let go. It was when she started ringing me all day at the agency — you wouldn't have noticed because she had my private number — that's when I knew I had to do something. If I told her I was in a meeting, which I usually was, she'd just ring again two minutes later. It was incredibly embarrassing with clients sitting there listening. Then she started turning up out of the blue to drag me out to lunch.'

'I remember that, Pippa and I were amazed when you turned down a famous film star, a convertible Mercedes and lunch at Bibendum, all in the space of one lunch hour.'

'Well, now you know why.'

'Why didn't you just finish it? Tell her it was over?'

Nick groaned. 'I tried, I tried to end it loads of times, but she just wouldn't listen and she categorically refused to leave the flat. I hadn't the heart to physically throw her out and change the locks, although I had the feeling it would probably come to that one day. The thing is, Polly, she knew it was over months ago but she just couldn't face it. I'm not even convinced she was in love with me, I think she just couldn't bear being dropped.'

I was amazed. 'You mean she just wouldn't go? Even though you said it was over?'

'She just refused. In the end I told her I was going to Cornwall, and I expected her to be gone by the time I got back.'

'That was just before you came down here with me.'

'That's right, the day before. I have to say I didn't think even Serena would have the gall to follow me, and when she turned up I was absolutely flabbergasted. I wanted to keep her from finding out about you and me, because for one thing I didn't want to rub her nose in it, and I also had a shrewd suspicion she'd tear your hair out. It would seem to her as if I'd jumped straight from her bed to yours in the space of a few days, even though, if the truth be told, Serena and I were washed up a long time ago and I'd felt strongly about you for . . . Well, that's another story.'

He broke off here and pulled at a thread in his jumper. I gulped hard and somehow overcame a burning desire to say – oh please, *please* let's get on to the other story! Much as I was enjoying this one, I had an inkling the other one, with me as the heroine, was going to be even better. I was jolly glad he'd asked me to sit down now: my knees were shaking so much from ill-concealed excitement that I doubted if they'd have supported me. I was also dying for a cigarette, but I had an idea that this perhaps wasn't the moment for ashtray breath.

He abandoned his jumper and looked down at me. 'She obviously spun the phantom engagement story when I was out with Larry.'

'Yes, that's right, you were seeing to the sheep. Oh, but hang on,' I thought back, 'what about the ring?'

'What ring?'

'The little green one.'

'Oh that! Yes I did give her that, about two weeks after I'd met her, at the height of my infatuation. It was an impulse buy, I saw it in an antique shop. It reminded me of her eyes.'

'That's what she said,' I said slowly, as everything began to fall into place. 'So – so where is she now?' I looked around nervously, half expecting her to pop up from behind the sofa, machete in hand.

'She's gone. When I found out you'd disappeared, I was livid. I couldn't continue the charade of pretending you meant nothing to me, and I couldn't bear to have her in the house anymore. I went berserk. No more softly-softly, let's tiptoe round Serena's feelings. I let her have it. Should have done it ages ago, it was bloody effective, the only language she understands. And, would you believe it, just as I was getting to the well-worn bit about never wanting to see her again as long as I lived, she gave me a resounding slap round the face, spat in my eye, told me I was a complete and utter jerk and she didn't know what she'd seen in me in the first place. Then she jumped into her Porsche and roared back off to London. Off to snare some other poor bastard, no doubt.'

Relief flooded over me. She'd gone. Thank Christ for that. I leaned back in the cushions. Bliss. Utter bliss. He wasn't going to marry her, he didn't even love her, by all accounts he didn't even like her. And surely, surely he'd more or less hinted that — well, that he liked me quite a lot, hadn't he?

I was suddenly very aware of his presence. He was perched on the arm of the sofa, his leg warm against my arm, close to me. I could feel his eyes upon me, melting over my face. I leaned my head back, half closed my eyes, and parted my lips very slightly. This was surely our moment. The most monumental touchy-feely moment of all time. I could feel the excitement tingling all over me, right down to my toenails. I waited in an ecstasy of anticipation. I waited for what seemed like an inordinate length of time. Nothing seemed to be happening. Eventually I couldn't keep the half closed eyes bit going any longer, my eyelashes were beginning to bat maniacally. I opened them.

He was watching me. 'Polly?'

Jesus. He wasn't looking remotely touchy-feely. 'Er, yes?'

'What about Harry?'

I jumped. 'What about him?'

'Well . . .' He hesitated. 'I need to know how you feel about him. I mean, you were pretty hung up on him in London and — well, I'm almost sure he got in touch with you down here.'

I sat bolt upright. 'How did you know that? Did you hear me on the phone to him?'

He looked uncomfortable. 'No, no I, er, I heard Serena on the phone to him.'

'Serena?'

'Yes, she knows him, you know.'

'Yes, I know, but why on earth would she be ringing him from down here?'

Nick shifted about a bit on the arm of the sofa. 'Well, she asked him to give you a ring.'

'SHE WHAT!'

'She asked him to − well, to lure you back to London. Said you were in her way down here − I heard it all, I was in the bathroom and she was using the phone in my bedroom. He seemed pretty flattered that she'd called him − most people are, of course. From what I could gather, he said he'd do what he could. I'm sorry, Polly, I wouldn't have told you, only I need to know if that's why you went.'

'Nick, what are you saying! Do you mean to tell me Serena actually *asked* Harry to ring up and pretend he was missing me and that he still loved me and all that crap about being the only girl he'd ever − *bloody hell*! Is that what you're saying?'

'I know, I know it's a little hard to believe, but you see she's quite capable—'

'Hard to believe! Hard to believe! It's bloody monstrous! Bloody hell! I mean, who does she think she is? Did she really think she'd get away with it? I mean, did she really think I'd go panting off back to London to see him! Christ!'

I was seething. Seething with fury at her audacity and seething also with hurt pride. So it had all been a ruse, a hoax to get me out of the way! Thank God I hadn't fallen for it.

'So you didn't,' said Nick.

'Didn't what?'

'Go panting off back to London to see him.'

I stared at him, incredulous. 'No, of course not! I told him to get stuffed, if you must know.'

Nick looked relieved. 'Oh! Oh good. Sorry, I had to ask. You see, I knew you'd dashed off out of the blue, and I was pretty sure it was because of Serena, but on the other hand I knew Harry had probably spoken to you, and I wasn't sure — well, to be honest, Polly, I wasn't entirely sure that you weren't still in love with him. And if you were, I wasn't sure that I could handle it.' He looked at me anxiously. 'You're not still in love with him, are you? I hate to be pushy, but I just sort of need to know.'

I looked up at his kind, honest face, his brown eyes searching mine, looking for clues. I smiled. All my anger drifted away. What did it matter? What did Harry matter, what did Serena matter? They were the losers, after all. The winners were sitting right here. My smile seemed to be spreading all over my body, I was positively wreathed in smiles. I felt unbelievably happy. I wanted him to kiss me quite badly now, but at the same time I felt something even more overwhelming than desire sweeping over me.

'No, I'm not in love with him,' I said softly. The feeling seemed to be getting stronger and stronger, surging from my heart, through my body, until eventually it found its way to my lips. 'Actually, I'm in love with you.'

His anxious look disappeared, his face seemed to clear, and he smiled gently. He leaned down, and the kiss that I'd been longing for dropped onto my mouth at last, soft and full.

'I'm surprised,' he murmured at length.

'Why?' I felt alarmed. Oh horrors, what had I done now? Scared him off already?

He slid off the arm of the sofa and knelt down in front of me, his arms around me felt huge and warm and strong. My heart thumped madly as he kissed me on the neck, working his way slowly and beautifully round to my ear. 'Because you don't strike me as the sort of girl who would fall for an amateur love-maker.'

I gasped and sat bold upright, gripping his shoulders hard. 'Oh no, you don't understand!' I pleaded earnestly into his face. 'I just said that to make you angry! I didn't mean it, I — I just said it to get my own back! I didn't think you were amateur at all, in fact I thought − I still think − you're, you're a true professional! Oh no! I mean, not in any awful sense of having been around, but you know, you know what to do and − oh God, I just think you're wonderful!'

He threw back his head and roared with laughter, holding me tightly against him. 'Oh God,' he gasped at length, 'I must say I think you're pretty wonderful too, Polly, but I've never known anyone with quite the propensity to get themselves in such a comprehensive mess!'

I grinned ruefully. 'Well, this is one comprehensive mess I don't mind in the least.'

'I agree,' he said softly. 'In fact, I don't mind it at all, because I believe I'm in love with you too.'

I gasped, which was lucky really, because it meant I took in a great lungful of air which kept me going as he kissed the breath out of me. When we surfaced, moments later, we clung to each other, and I could hear our hearts racing away in tandem. His breath was coming in fast and furious bursts, and I could almost see his ear flapping in the breeze as I hurricaned into his. Love, lust, excitement, and God knows what else, were all contriving to get the better of our breathing apparatuses.

'Now where were we,' he whispered, as he manoeuvred me skilfully down on to the Persian rug, deftly immobilising me beneath him, 'before we were so rudely interrupted some time earlier this morning?'

My tummy, furious at having missed at least three meals by now, rumbled ominously as I lay back on the rug. We giggled. I reached up and took his face in my hands, drawing it down towards me.

'You were making toast,' I murmured.

'I've got other plans now,' he murmured back.

The Real Thing

For Fred, Emily and Sophie

Chapter One

I put the receiver down and felt panic rise. It shot through my body like a turbo-charged lift. My eyes glazed, my insides curdled.

'Jesus!' I breathed.

I glanced quickly at the kitchen clock. One o'clock. One o'clock! Only two hours to go.

'What? What's happened?' demanded Laura, bent at right-angles over my kitchen table, her icing bag poised precariously above the dinosaur's left eyeball.

'Spotty Lottie's got cystitis!' I yelped.

Laura's icing bag quivered nervously and she inadvertently gave Tyrannosaurus Rex a squint. 'Spotty Lottie?' she demanded. 'Who's that – a dog?'

'The entertainer, you fool,' I hissed, running my hands through my hair till it stood on end, and rising from the table like a sea monster coming up from the depths. 'For Clemmie's party! The female equivalent of Paul Daniels for four-year-olds has cancelled – says she can't possibly come, because she's welded to the loo seat. Oh God, Laura, what am I going to do?' My hands left my dark curls and began to wring desperately. 'In precisely two hours' time, seventeen four-year-olds will be thundering through that door,' I pointed a quivering finger, 'demanding white rabbits, puppet shows and hideously twisted balloons, and all I'll have to offer them are some Marmite sandwiches and a few bowls of Hula Hoops. I'll be lynched!'

1

'Oh, is that all?' My sister calmly flicked back her long blonde hair and resumed her icing. 'For a moment I thought something awful had happened. I mean, you don't *have* to have an entertainer, do you? Just play a few jolly games and give them a piece of soggy cake in a napkin like Mum used to. They're only four, for God's sake.'

'Jolly games? Soggy cake?' I gave a hollow laugh and sank back down on my chair again.

I regarded Laura in her casual yet immaculate navy-blue linen ensemble, which somehow reeked of taking the day off from one's PR agency to help at one's niece's party but not sinking to leggings, thank you very much. I shook my head grimly.

'Oh Laura, how little you know. Four-year-olds today are a different *breed*, they're nothing *like* we used to be at that age. For one thing they know their party rights, and those include –' I ticked them off on my fingers '– one large balloon filled with helium and not puff, one party bag containing at least five items – three of which must be edible and bad for teeth – and either one bouncy castle *or* an entertainer, preferably unseen at any other children's party in the neighbourhood within the last three months.'

Laura frowned. 'Sounds rather Draconian to me.'

'Of course it's Draconian!' I shrieked. 'They're monsters! They're manipulative little devils who know exactly how to— Oh, hello, darling!' I broke off breathlessly as Birthday Girl herself pranced into the kitchen dressed in her prohibitively expensive party frock. She gave us a twirl and we clapped dutifully.

'D'you like your cake?' I beamed. 'Isn't Laura doing it beautifully?'

Clemmie inspected it with an eagle eye. 'Very nice,' she concluded finally as she walked round the table, scrutinising the dinosaur from all angles. 'I'm glad you're making it, Laura,' she said. 'Even Hugo couldn't eat the one Mummy made last year. Is Edward coming to my party too?'

Laura crouched down to Clemmie's level, beaming at this reference to her latest man. She smoothed her niece's smocked dress. 'No, poppet, he's at work. Why, would you like him to come?'

Clemmie wrinkled her nose. 'Not if he's still sad.'

Laura frowned. 'What d'you mean?'

'Mummy said he was a sad little man to Daddy last night. Didn't you, Mummy?' She turned to me.

'No, no, darling,' I said quickly, flushing horribly. 'That was a man Daddy works with, he's called Edward too.'

I turned to Laura who was looking decidedly hostile. 'Honestly, the things children remember. Mention someone they've never even heard of and they remember his blinking shoe size, say "bugger" once and they remember to say it every day, but try to get them to remember to say "thank you" and it completely slips their tiny minds! No, no, this Edward chappie's a barrister – in David's chambers. It's very sad, he lost his—'

'Leg?' offered my sister icily. 'Mind?'

'Er, no, wife. He's lost his wife.'

'How careless.'

'Quite. Now come on, Clemmie,' I hustled her out quickly, 'run and play in the garden, would you? I've got loads to do in here.'

Clemmie dragged her feet slowly to the back door. 'When will Spotty Lottie be here?'

'Soon, darling, soon,' I said weakly, watching as she scuffed her new shoes in the dirt on the way to the sandpit.

I stood at the sink avoiding Laura's eye, and looked out instead across our side passage to the one next door, and beyond to the one next to that . . . So it went on, passage after passage, all leading to fifty-foot gardens behind our terrace of three-storeyed houses with four bedrooms – number four used either as a study for the childless or a nanny's room for the with-child – complete with knocked-through drawing room on top of knocked-through basement kitchen.

There were subtle differences, of course. Some kitchens had the sink at this end, which meant French doors onto the garden, and some had the sink at the other end (no French doors), and some had even knocked the kitchen wall down altogether and built a conservatory, thus eliminating the side passage entirely.

The occupants of these houses were startlingly similar too, chiefly in their respectability. The men tended to be doctors, barristers, accountants, solicitors, surveyors, bankers and Lloyd's brokers, and the women, the same again, but with more of a smattering of media, publishing and the art-world thrown in for good measure. In other words, all fully paid up members of London's professional classes, and all living cheek by jowl in tarted-up Victorian semis in the tarted-up boroughs of Putney, Fulham, Hammersmith, Wandsworth, Clapham, Balham and, at a pinch, Streatham.

And of course, I mused, as I picked a dried fruitgum off my jeans, there were the other women, too. Women like me who didn't work, whose lives revolved around children. Again, there were subtle differences. Like the way we filled our time when the little darlings were away from us at school, or ballet, or tinies' tennis, or yet another tea party. Some supplemented these gaps from child-rearing with charity work, or gardening, some with decorative art courses and some with the gym. I wiped the sticky mark on my jeans with a dishcloth and then dropped it back into the sink. I as yet hadn't decided what my particular supplement would be.

4

I gazed across the sunny, wisteria-clad walls, narrowing my eyes against the sun. None of this sameness bothered me; to be honest I found it rather comforting. Safety in numbers, so to speak. I'd even hazard a guess that some of my neighbours had sensitive, unmarried sisters like mine who lived in flats in smarter parts of town like Chelsea and South Ken and who put up a damn good front but secretly longed to acquire a husband and family and with a huge sigh of relief join their less glamorous sisters in these quieter, more restful, suburban parts of town.

I could sense Laura's eyes on my back now, could feel the offence I'd caused. I just knew how she was sitting, too, at my distressed pine table in my Shaker kitchen, one navy trouser leg crossed over the other, a Gucci shoe wagging nervously, one hand at her neck fingering a French scarf beginning with H (I never dared pronounce it for fear of showing my ignorance), her eyebrows raised, her lips pursed, waiting for me to explain, to dig myself out of yet another hole, to apologise.

I sighed. Suddenly I felt tired, old, and, more than anything, bored. Bored with having to placate, to bolster up, to calm down, to gently ease everyone back into position again. Bored with other people's lives. How come I never got soothed and eased myself? Who was it said: "Never complain, never explain"? I took a deep breath, turned around and gave Laura a dazzling smile.

'Cystitis isn't that serious, is it, Laura?'

Laura blinked, wrong-footed. 'Er, well, I . . .'

'Doesn't it just mean you have to go to the loo all the time?'

'Well, yes, but—'

'Well, she can damn well sit on the loo and do her act there. How dare she cancel at the eleventh hour for something as piddling as bladder control? Good grief,

Clemmie's bladder control is practically non-existent and I still send her to school! No, if she's that incontinent we'll have it in the upstairs bathroom. She can sit on the loo and wear one of my long Monsoon skirts draped over her knees – the children will never know. I'm sure we can squeeze seventeen in there, they're only little, after all. We could get at least four in the bath, one in the basin – Holly Bates can go in there, she's not much bigger than a bar of soap anyway, poor child – a couple on the windowsill, and I'll tie balloons and streamers to the loo chain and—'

'Oh, don't be ridiculous, Tess, you can't possibly have the party in the bathroom. Quite apart from anything else it's unhygienic,' snorted my sister. 'What an idea! Just call Clemmie back, sit her down and tell her gently but firmly exactly what the situation is and just why she can't have an entertainer at her party. She'll understand.'

I looked at my sister. For one so smart she'd been successfully deflected from the 'sad Edward' episode without me even trying. So I could soothe and ease with my eyes shut now, could I? How about that. Laura flicked her hair back confidently as if she were just about to walk into a meeting and advise a client on a slight change of strategy and possibly an increase in his budget.

'I'll talk to her if you like,' she said, giving me a bright smile.

I smiled pityingly and patted her hand kindly. 'No, darling, it's OK. It would take me ages to prise your eyeballs off her little fingers. You just be an angel and carry on icing the cake, and meanwhile I'll get on the phone and offer every magician in London double wages and as much booze as they can drink between three o'clock and five, OK?'

I seized the *Yellow Pages* and thumbed through to the Entertainment section.

Laura shook her head. 'You'll never get anyone at

this late stage,' she said smugly.

'Watch me, everyone has their price,' I said grimly. 'If necessary, I'll throw in some casual sex. My body's pretty casual at the moment.'

'Ah yes, that's it – just mention the Caesarean scars, the stretch-marks, the varicose veins and the saggy boobs, and we'll have the house surrounded by the entire Magic Circle in no time at all.'

'Thank you, Laura,' I muttered, knowing full well she was letting me know she *hadn't* forgotten. 'Thank you for those kind words. Ah, here we are – Magicians. Let's see . . . Funky Frankie – no, can't have him, Clarissa Williams had him last week. What ab-ou-t . . . Magic Malcolm? Oh goodness, no. I forgot, we can't have him either.'

'Why not?'

'Hugo had him for a Christmas party. We were down here with some other parents quaffing champagne when the ceiling started vibrating and plaster started coming off. We rushed upstairs and found this poor chap cowering in a corner surrounded by fifteen seven-year-olds stamping rhythmically and shouting, "*Magic Malcolm's got a tiny willy!*" He didn't work for months after that, and Sally Bateman tells me he's still in therapy. I feel frightfully guilty, but what can I do? Ah! Here's one I don't know – Perky Percy.' I picked up the book and ran to the phone in the hall.

Five minutes later I was back, flushed with success and smiling broadly. 'He's coming,' I announced, 'and guess what, with not just one, but *two* white rabbits!'

'I'm not surprised. With a name like Perky Percy he's probably got ferrets down his trousers, too. What did you offer him, if it's not too much of a personal question?'

'Oh, just a socking great wodge of money,' I said airily.

'You realise you've probably just wrecked some other poor child's birthday party, don't you? I dare say he's cancelling right now, complaining of the male equivalent of cystitis.'

'All's fair in the infant party world,' I said briskly, dropping the *Yellow Pages* on the table with a thud. 'Now shift yourself, Laura, I need that seat for Musical Chairs. Oh – and pop up and get a couple more from my bedroom, would you?'

'God, give us a chance – I'm still doing the cake. Anyway, can't David help out? Where is he, anyway? Why isn't he participating in this joyous event?'

'He's in the garden pretending to prune the roses. Josie's stretched out on the lawn stark naked and he needs an excuse to ogle.'

'Not completely naked, Mummy,' said my son and heir, suddenly appearing at my left elbow. 'She's got something round her middle and up her bottom – look.'

I followed Hugo's ink-stained finger through the French windows – yes, we were lucky enough to have our sink at the *right* end of the kitchen – to where our buxom, bronzed, Australian au pair lay prone amongst the daisies.

'What is that thing anyway?' he asked, staring.

'That thing, my darling, is a thong.'

Hugo was delighted. 'The thing is a thong. A thing-thong! Laura – Josie's got a thing-thong up her bum!'

'Bottom,' corrected Laura. She found my ear. 'How can you let her lie out there like that?' she hissed, peering over my shoulder. 'Look at David, he's going absolutely *apoplectic* with desire. He's pruning that rose like a thing possessed – he'll dig it up in a minute!'

We watched as my usually calm, not to say languid husband, who normally wouldn't be seen dead in the garden unless it was to read Kierkegaard in a Panama hat under the apple tree, launched a frenzied attack on Madame Grégoire, at the same time keeping both eyes firmly on Josie's bronzed backside. Every so often he'd pause to flick a strand of blond, rather Heseltinian hair back from his high – and these days increasingly higher – forehead. He paused again, straightened up to his full six foot four, flicked another strand of hair away, and this time, adjusted his trousers too.

'Adds a new dimension to the term "prune hard", doesn't it?' I murmured.

Laura giggled and frowned in Hugo's direction, but as we were constantly being reminded by his school reports, Hugo had a low boredom threshold and had already wandered off in search of something more stimulating like Power Ranger News.

'But don't you care?' she persisted. 'I mean, talk about putting temptation in his way! Why did you *hire* someone like that? There must be ugly nannies, surely?'

I sighed. 'I hired her because the agency sent her and I was too desperate to send her back.' I giggled. 'I must say, when I saw her staggeringly long legs – she had to practically limbo dance through the front door – it did occur to me we might have problems with David's blood pressure – not to mention the roses,' I added watching him lop off yet another of my prize blooms. I banged on the window.

'Hey, David. Stop it!'

David swung round alarmed, immediately got the wrong end of the stick, averted his eyes from the luscious Josie and began attacking Madame Grégoire with renewed vigour. I groaned as he eventually hacked her off at her ankles.

'There goes another fifteen quid at the Garden Centre! God, sometimes I wish he'd just throw down his secateurs, whip off his trousers, stride over there and get on with it, just so long as he left my roses alone!'

'Tessa!'

'Well, why not? It would let me off the hook for a while, wouldn't it? Think of all that precious sleep I'd

9

catch up on. I mean, that's what concubines were for, wasn't it? To let the poor, worn-out, child-encumbered wife have a lie-in on a Saturday morning . . . Jolly good idea, if you ask me.'

'Tess, you are joking, aren't you?' asked my younger, less child-worn sister anxiously. 'You'd be horrified if anything really did happen, wouldn't you?'

'Well I don't know, Laura,' I mused, shaking my head thoughtfully. 'Sarah Hooper's husband had a fling with the nanny and Sarah said it was wonderful. The poor man was absolutely dripping with guilt and kept the house permanently stuffed with fresh flowers – couldn't even buy petrol by all accounts without adding a cellophaned springtime-selection to the Access card – practically *fought* her to unload the dishwasher, and Sarah said she only had to mention Sainsbury's and he was in there, trolleying around like a lunatic. She said it was absolutely marvellous.'

'Tess, you can't be serious!'

I patted her shoulder and gave a wry smile. 'No, of course I'm not. But . . .' I hesitated. 'Just don't expect too much, that's all.'

'Of what?'

'Oh, you know, marriage, everything.'

I turned and looked back out of the window again. Josie, bored with the sun, had pulled on a T-shirt and was loping back up the garden, her long legs covering it in about three strides. Hopefully she'd make a few sandwiches now, but since she wasn't actually on duty for another half an hour I didn't like to suggest it. She strode past us through the kitchen.

'Hi there,' she drawled to Laura in her relaxed Australian brogue.

'Oh, hello!' chirruped Laura, in her uptight English one.

I smiled. Back in the garden, it seemed to me David

had almost heaved a sigh of relief. He dropped his secateurs, picked up his hat, staggered across to the other side of the garden and flopped down in a deckchair, his hand reaching down instinctively for his book, his comfort blanket. He put it on his lap, folded his hands on top of it and tipped the brim of his hat down over his eyes, visibly relaxed. I smiled. Even after seven years he was still quite an attractive sight. Tall, still lean, fairhaired – albeit veering towards grey – and with really rather noble features. He could be Lord Many-Acres sitting there contemplating his land, instead of an overworked barrister contemplating his garden fence. His eyes, pale blue, but flecked with brown like a gull's egg, slowly began to close, worn out by all that ogling, no doubt.

'I wasn't actually planning on marrying Edward,' said Laura, rather hesitantly. 'I mean, it's not that serious.'

I swung round. 'Really? Oh, excellent! That's terrific! I mean—' I quickly tried to temper my enthusiasm. 'Excellent that you're not thinking of marriage yet. Much too early. Plenty of time for all that.'

I turned back to the garden again. I heard Laura scrape her chair back from the table behind me as she came to join me at the window. David's mouth was open now. I couldn't hear him, but ten to one he was snoring.

'Tess, you'd never leave him, would you?' she asked tentatively.

I threw my head back and laughed out loud. 'Leave him? No, of *course* not!' I swung round to face her. 'I'm talking about *marriage*, Laura, not David. God, he's the same as any other husband – tired, jaded, stressed out, getting older, thinking ruefully of his far too guided youth and how he wished he'd misspent it a bit more when he had the chance . . . No, no, they're all the same. Why on earth would I want to leave him? And what would I swap him for – the same again? God, at least we get on. You should see some couples we know, like the Bartletts or the Frazers. Sniping away at each other at dinner parties, constantly at each other's throats . . . At least we like each other; at least we have a laugh. All I'm saying is—' I hesitated. 'Oh, forget it.'

'But do you ever think . . . Do you ever sort of wonder . . .'

'What?' I sighed. Laura, like most unmarried women, constantly wanted to talk about relationships, chew them over, discuss them. What she didn't realise was that most married women were exhausted enough living them, without constantly analysing them too.

'Do you ever wonder if you'd have married him if you hadn't been pregnant?' she blurted out.

Uh oh. This old chestnut. 'Laura, you've asked me this a million times,' I said wearily. God, she did like to dredge everything up, didn't she? She was like a tabloid newspaper sometimes, or worse, *Titbits*.

'Yes,' I said patiently, 'I'm sure I would. I know I would.'

There was a pause. 'He is a lovely man, you know,' she said softly.

I screeched inwardly and contemplated reaching for the saucepan on the draining board to bash her over the head with. 'Yes, I *know* he's a lovely man, I wouldn't have married a jerk, would I? Some sad little git with a toupée or something?' Then, realising I'd said 'sad' again and that – oh damn it, Edward didn't have much hair either – I rushed on hurriedly: 'All I'm saying is you can't expect passion to continue on a grand scale for ever, that's all.'

Laura shook her head. 'I don't believe that,' she said firmly. 'I want someone who's going to light my fire every day till I'm ninety.'

I wiped the draining board down with the dishcloth and threw it back in the sink. 'Take my advice and settle for someone who turns your heater on twice a month,' I

12

said drily. 'And if he'll take the children to the park on a Saturday morning too, you're laughing. Now if you'll excuse me, I've got some serious negotiating to do with my daughter on the subject of magicians.' I pushed past her, rolling up my sleeves. 'I tell you, I don't know why they don't just send a posse of mothers to the Bosnian talks, all we do is negotiate peace, I bet I could teach those politicians a thing or two.' And with that I marched off to hold a summit meeting in the sandpit.

Clemmie was busy burying one of Hugo's prized Action Men as deep as she possibly could and patting the sand down neatly so there was no sign of his grave. I made a mental note to retrieve it later. I sat down and began my spiel. Clemmie listened carefully to my terms, her dark, silky head on one side.

'Has he got a rabbit?'

'Two.'

'Funny balloons?'

'Hysterical.'

'Tricks up his sleeves?'

'Possibly even up his trousers.'

She thought for a second. 'OK, but I want a party bag too, all right? Not just the guests, and I want –' she thought wildly for a minute, then got realistic – 'seven things in it.'

I smiled and stuck out my hand. 'Done.'

We shook on it. No flies on Clemmie, I thought proudly as I heaved myself out of the sandpit, she'd be OK. She was no pushover. David, however, was less convinced. He lifted the brim of his hat.

'Perky Percy?' he murmured from his deckchair. 'Sounds a bit suspect to me.'

'David,' I said, exasperated, realising he'd been feigning sleep for the last ten minutes to get out of party preparations, 'no one in their right mind is going to make a career out of entertaining four-year-olds unless they

13

are indeed a bit suspect. Just keep your back to the wall and you'll be fine, OK?' I glanced at my watch. Two-thirty. Christ! 'And now that you've finished wrecking my roses, perhaps you'd be good enough to sort out the seats for Musical Chairs. There's a hell of a lot to do today, you know. We can't all sit around admiring the scenery!'

David looked surprised. 'All right, all right.' He put his book down and made to get up. 'You only have to ask.'

'Well, I shouldn't *have* to, should I? That's the whole point. It should be perfectly bleeding obvious, shouldn't it!'

I marched back into the kitchen ahead of him, slamming the door shut behind me. It shuddered in its frame. Laura jumped in alarm. I ignored her and pulled open the kitchen drawer, ransacking it for cake candles. Hugo popped his head round the door, saw my face and popped out again. I ground my teeth as paper napkins, cocktail sticks etc. fell to the floor.

'Oh God! Why is it I can never *find* anything!' I stared down at the chaotic drawer. 'Well, there just aren't any, are there, so now I'll have to go to the shops. Great. Where's my purse? Where's my blinking *purse*?' I lurched around the kitchen, picking up bundles of newspapers, scattering children's drawings and piles of discarded clothes.

'Jesus!' I shrieked. 'Why is it that in order to get anything done in this house you have to split the bloody atom first?'

Laura slipped silently through the kitchen door to the garden. Through the window I saw her make a face to David. She jerked her head back in my direction and raised her eyes to heaven. David made a resigned face in response, shrugged his shoulders and slowly made his way up the garden path.

I picked my purse out of the fruit bowl on the dresser, wiped a bit of rotten pear off it, and sighed. At what stage in my career, I wondered, had I turned into this mini domestic tyrant? Last year? The year before? Five years ago? I hadn't always been like this, surely? I seemed to remember being a rather sweet, good-natured girl once. I shook my head and made for the back door, just as David was coming through it.

'I blame other people!' I snapped in his face.

Chapter Two

In the event, the party passed off smoothly enough. Perky Percy arrived complete with full make-up, ginger wig and manic smile and was instantly deemed too perky to be exposed to David. I hustled him into the playroom with a gin and tonic until his big moment. Then the first child arrived on the doorstep, accompanied by her rather perplexed mother.

'Um, the balloons on the door . . .' she faltered, flushing slightly.

'Yes, they're to show there's a party here,' I explained with a bright smile. 'It helps people find the right house.' I enunciated this slowly and carefully. Poor woman, too much day-time TV, clearly.

'Yes, it's just that— Well, look.'

I popped my head round and looked.

'HUGO!' I roared up the stairs. 'GET DOWN HERE IMMEDIATELY! I'm so sorry,' I murmured back to the mother. 'It's my son's idea of a joke.'

Hugo was duly cuffed and instructed to remove the pink phallic ensemble complete with two small round and one long pendulous, *now* please, and replace them with something more tasteful. Then the party went off without a hitch.

No one vomited after Musical Bumps, Josie managed to keep her clothes on for five minutes and hand around the jellies, and Hugo gave us ten minutes of perfect peace as he invigilated Dead Lions, striding amongst eighteen supine, motionless four-year-old girls with a menacing look on his face and a plastic sword in his hand. It was only when one little girl started to go purple that we realised he'd told them no moving or *breathing* was allowed and we frantically lunged amongst them, shaking shoulders and shouting, 'BREATHE DAMN YOU, BREATHE!' not relishing the prospect of explaining to seventeen sets of parents that their children had passed away on the party floor. The rest of the games were then supervised by me, and it was only when two Sophies had a fist-fight over which Sophie was the true recipient of the final pass, that Pass the Parcel degenerated into Pass the Valium.

Finally, when all the children had been dispatched with bags and balloons and Josie had been sent upstairs to supervise the baths and bedding down of two hysterical, over-excited children, I ordered David to the off-licence.

'Wine – quickly – now!' I gasped, but he'd already gone, needing it even more badly than I did.

Laura and I collapsed on the sofa.

'Never again,' I groaned.

'You say that every year.'

'Ah, but this time I mean it. Next year it'll be a pantomime and McDonald's with David at the helm.' I kicked my shoes off, swung my legs round and plonked them on her lap. I shut my eyes.

'God, I've never needed a break so badly,' I muttered. 'I can't *wait* for Scotland.'

Laura pulled a face. 'Hardly a break for you though, is it? I mean, you still have the children and you still have to cook.'

'I know, but at least I've talked Josie into coming. I couldn't bear it without some help.'

Laura sat up. 'But Tess, she's appalling. She never *does* anything. All she did at the party was fanny around with a few jellies!'

18

'She's not paid to do any more than fanny around with jellies, Laura, she's a thirty-quid-a-week au pair, not a two-hundred-quid uniformed Norland nanny. Now please don't upset her, I couldn't contemplate life without her at the moment. Apart from anything else she keeps me from murdering the children. I'm much nicer to them when she's around *and* she keeps David permanently busy. It's amazing. Whatever room she's in, he's there too, on some spurious errand like cupboard-sorting-out or shelf-putting-up, and all so he can stare at her bum. He fixed every single appliance in the kitchen last week.' I shut my eyes again. 'And apart from anything else, Clemmie adores her.'

'Hugo doesn't.'

'Yes, but that's because he's at a boys' prep school now, they programme them to be misogynists from Day One. It's nothing personal.'

Laura sighed. 'Oh well, it's not my problem if she comes. I shall just lie by the river and ignore her.'

She clasped her hands behind her head and shut her eyes. I propped myself up a bit and looked at her. As sisters we presented quite a startling contrast. Her, small, sleekly blonde, blue-eyed and with fine petite features, and me, tall and long-limbed with dark curly hair, large grey eyes and a wide mouth. The only thing we had in common was our classic English pearshape, inherited from our mother – reasonably slim at a glance but on closer inspection, not much up top and quite a lot down the bottom, thank you very much, Mother. I pulled David's M&S jumper down over my jeans wondering how she always managed to camouflage it better than I did.

I watched as she yawned, quite prettily really, showing perfect white teeth. Laura definitely won the looks competition, always had done, which made it all the more surprising that I'd had such an easy time with men and she'd made such a hash of it. Half the problem, in my opinion, was that she went for such total nonentities. It was no wonder she got bored with them after five minutes. I sometimes wondered if she wasn't afraid of competing, afraid of going out with a chap as attractive and personable as herself in case he dumped her, so she stuck to safe, mousy little men who adored her and whom she ditched after a couple of months. This latest teacher chappie, Edward, was a classic example. He had 'Destined for Laura's Rubbish Heap' written all over him. Still, I thought, I really must try harder to like one or two of them.

She looked up and I gave her what I hoped was a conciliatory smile. 'Is Edward coming to the Tarn with you?' I asked.

She frowned. 'Not sure.'

'Why?'

'Well, it's all a bit *en famille*, isn't it? Mum, Dad, Penny and Piers and everyone, I don't want him to get the wrong idea. Don't want him to think he's meeting the in-laws.'

'Ah. So . . . it's not that serious, then?' I asked as innocently as possible.

'No, it's not that serious,' she snapped, 'and don't pretend you're disappointed. I think I might be going off him a bit actually.' She frowned and chewed the skin around her thumb. I kept quiet, knowing anything I said would be totally wrong.

'And also,' she went on, 'I'm a bit worried about Daddy. You know what he can be like, picking holes in people, making them look stupid. I'm not sure how Edward would fare under that sort of pressure.'

Pretty diabolically, I thought privately, but I tried to look non-committal. 'Well,' I hazarded, 'you never know, they might get on brilliantly. Daddy likes the strangest people.' God, why did I *say* that? Thankfully it didn't seem to have registered with Laura. She was looking at me and had a sly grin on her face. She sat up a bit, and suddenly I knew what was coming.

'Of course, you know who *is* going to be there, don't you?'

I sighed. 'Yes, Laura, Patrick Cameron. And if you really think you're the first person to bring me that piece of news, you're mistaken. Penny was on the phone a week ago, gleefully informing me of it, then Mummy rang yesterday to tell me exactly the same thing, and even David asked me the other day if I knew Patrick was going to be there. Then he watched my face really carefully to see my reaction. I couldn't believe it.'

'Really? Did he seem worried?'

'I don't know about worried but certainly apprehensive, and I just think it's such a huge overreaction on everyone's part. So what if he's going to be there?'

Laura raised her eyebrows and rolled her eyes expressively. 'Well let's face it, Tess, you did have one hell of a fling with him and this is the first time you've seen him since, isn't it?'

'Yes, so what?'

'So it's only natural that David might feel a bit – well, as you say, apprehensive.'

'You mean in case Patrick gallops up to me at the river on his white charger and our eyes meet and some gigantic arrow pierces me in the heart and I drop my fishing rod and my cheese roll and stagger over to him in my wellies, heave myself up behind him in the saddle and disappear over the horizon with him?'

'I don't know about that, but—'

'Well, what then? I mean what d'you think I am, Laura? Some bored Putney housewife with seven-year-itch who's just ripe for bumping into her glamorous ex-boyfriend on holiday, ditching her nice, safe, comfortable husband

21

and embarking on a steamy affair with him? And all in the name of *finding* myself, or something? Needing my own space? This isn't one of your Aga sagas, you know, this is me, Tessa Hamilton, happily married mother of two, and apart from anything else I went out with Patrick twelve years ago – bloody eons ago! It's like hoicking someone out of your past and saying: "Ay ay, look who's here, it's that spotty boy from down the road who did wheelies on his bike to impress you, or – or Sandy from *Crossroads*, or—"'

'I *never* fancied Sandy from *Crossroads*!'

'Oooh, Laura! What a fib! You *know* you did, you were absolutely hot for him!'

'I was not!'

'You were, I distinctly remember it. You even wrote to ask if you could join his fan club and you got a letter back – probably from Meg – saying Sandy didn't actually *have* a fan club as such, but would be delighted for you to be the founder member.'

'No!' Laura looked shocked.

'It's true. Let's face it, Laura, you've always gone for,' I hesitated, 'well – *sensitive* types, haven't you?'

'Unlike you,' she said nastily.

'David's sensitive,' I said defensively.

'Yes, all right, but Patrick's not, is he? He's completely wild, sex on legs.'

'And I'm not attracted to him,' I said patiently. 'I was once, but I'm not now – OK? In fact, the more I think about it, the more I realise he was never remotely my type.'

'So you've thought about it.'

I ground my teeth. 'Of course I've thought about it – and that's what I've thought, all right?'

We were silent for a moment. Remembering.

'He never married, you know,' said Laura after a while.

I sighed. 'You say that as if it's weird, it's not. He's

still only thirty-something, not an OAP.'

'I know, but I just wonder if, well – if he couldn't. After you.'

'Oh Laura, you're so melodramatic! And if that's the case then I'm doing him a huge favour by going up there, aren't I? He'll take one look at me twelve years on and think – Christ, what a disappointment – and instantly be released from his chains. He'll be down at Invertarn register office with the first wee lassie he can lay his hands on.'

'His father died, you know,' she went on, not really listening to me.

'I *know*,' I said wearily.

'So he's coming back to claim his estate.'

'You're talking about him as if he was some returning Laird, swathed in tartan, surrounded by pipers, coming down the mountain to reclaim his kingdom.'

'And his queen,' she giggled.

'Oh, for heaven's—'

'Who's a queen?' asked David, barging through the door armed with clinking Threshers bags.

'No one – that Perky Percy probably,' I said, jumping up and taking them from him.

'Undoubtedly. Drink, Laura?'

She stood up. 'I won't, actually. I've got to get back and do my packing.' She kissed us both. 'And I'm seeing Edward later. I think. If I decide to ring him, that is.'

'Treating him mean, are we?' asked David with a smile.

'Not intentionally. It just seems to come naturally these days.' She shrugged. 'Not quite sure what to do about him actually.' She started to bite her thumb again. 'Anyway, I must go. See you up there. In Scotland, I mean.'

I let her out of the front door and watched her go down the path. She waved and I shut the door. Poor

Laura. If only she was settled, if only she didn't *expect* so much. If only . . . oh, I don't know. I went back to the drawing room, twiddling a strand of hair.

David stretched out his hand from the sofa. I took it. He gave it a waggle.

'She'll be fine, stop worrying about her.'

'But I do, David, I can't help it.' I flopped down on the sofa next to him. 'She's so mixed up, highly strung, nervy – and everything has to be so damn perfect with her. She's just like Daddy really. I mean, earlier on I just vaguely mentioned that marriage wasn't all hearts and flowers and chocolates and that there was quite a lot of tedium involved, and she instantly asked me if I was thinking of leaving you! She's so unreal, everything's got to be either pitch black or snowy white with her.'

'She's got no stability, that's all. Once she's found the right bloke she'll be fine; she's just twitchy because she hasn't.' He put his arm round my neck. 'Anyway, come here. I'm sick of you worrying about your bloody sister and your mother and the children and God knows who else. Let's worry about you for a change.'

'Me?'

He kissed me firmly on the mouth. 'You.'

'David!' I drew back in surprise.

'What? Can't I kiss my wife?'

'Don't be ridiculous. You know very well there's no such thing as gratuitous kissing in this house. If we kiss it's sex and we can't possibly have sex because Josie's upstairs bathing the children!'

'She'll be ages yet, she's putting them to bed too, isn't she? And we could lock the door.'

I narrowed my eyes. 'You've been looking at that girl's bum too much, haven't you? It's made you all randy and – Oi, get off!' I giggled as he grabbed my hands and pinned them behind my head.

'I love it when you talk dirty,' he murmured, kissing me again.

'I did not!'

'You did – bum, randy – very dirty for you.' He bit my ear.

'David,' I hissed, 'any minute now Josie's going to be back through that door!'

He leaped up, and in two strides had slammed the door shut, locked it, lunged for the curtains and dragged them across the bay. 'There.' He leaped back onto the sofa again with a grin.

'Ow!' I shrieked. 'God, what's got into you? What's all this he-man stuff?'

'Don't know, must be all those jam sandwiches.' He thrust his head into my neck and nibbled my ear.

'Geddoff!' I laughed, pushing him away.

He sat up and narrowed his eyes quizzically at me. 'Am I to deduce, from your somewhat negative body language, that you're not on for this then?'

I stared up at him. He was serious! What – here, now? On the sofa? His eyes were unusually bright and very blue. For a moment he looked almost as young and attractive as when I'd first met him, but attractive or not, this was really most inconvenient. For one thing there was all that washing up to do in the kitchen and I hadn't even looked at the Sunday papers, and there was a new three-part Jane Austen thing on the telly I wanted to watch which started in about – I glanced quickly at my watch – about two minutes. I hesitated.

'Oh, all right, but for God's sake make it a quickie.'

David regarded me for a moment, then gave a wry smile and heaved himself off the sofa.

'Call me old fashioned, but that just about took all the romance out of it.'

I made a contrite face as he went to the windows and pulled the curtains back. 'Oh. Sorry.'

'Doesn't matter.' He found the Review section of the paper on the floor and sauntered off with it into the kitchen.

I reached down, rather too quickly, for the remote control, snuggled back happily into the sofa and switched on the telly. Bliss.

Chapter Three

I first met Patrick Cameron when I was seventeen.

It was the usual family holiday at Kilmarnoch House, way up near Invertarn in the Scottish Highlands and we were the usual contingent. Two families of Fergussons: Aunt Rachel, Uncle Robert and my Cousin Penny; and Mummy, Daddy, Laura and me. Kilmarnoch House stood on the banks of the river Tarn. Daddy and Uncle Robert had grown up there, and when Grandpa died, they'd somehow managed to avoid selling it and kept it as a holiday home. The theory was that we took it for the whole of August and rented it out the rest of the year, but in reality this was fraught with difficulties because Kilmarnoch was a thoroughly uncomfortable, unlovely house and my father spent the whole year literally pressganging friends, acquaintances and anyone he could trip up in the street into renting it and fretting about the loss of income in the months the house stood empty.

From the outside it looked like one vast slab of granite rising up out of the ground; flat, dour and grey, with no distinguishing features at all except for its cold glassy eyes and a network of black drainpipes which snaked frenetically about as if someone had scribbled all over its face. Inside it was huge, cold – even in summer – and dilapidated, and not in a gentrified, quarry-tiled and ancient Persian rug sort of way, but in a lino-floored, motheaten fitted carpets and electric fires sort of way.

To us children though, it was heaven. It was a house to hide in, to run in, to charge through the empty attic rooms shrieking in, to play ping-pong in the cellar in . . . a house so tatty it could accommodate any number of buckets of seaweed and slime being accidentally tipped over it when searching for that crucial shell . . . a house that seemed to absorb sand and mud into its very substructure, leaving absolutely no trace.

Outside it had four acres of overgrown garden to explore, huge oaks to climb, streams to dam and woods to make camps in. At the bottom of the garden was the river. Here we fished, paddled, or in my case, just lazed around sucking blades of grass. I'd lie on my tummy with my nose over the edge, watching the clear water as it rippled over smooth pebbles, dreaming of being beautiful and fanciable and funny and exotic – Russian perhaps, or a Romany gypsy, or maybe even orphaned – anything, really, other than a vicar's daughter from Claygate.

When we were younger we started thinking about Kilmarnoch the moment Christmas was over, and were almost sick with excitement when instead of crossing off the weeks, we began to cross off the days. At seventeen, of course, one had to adopt a slightly more superior attitude to the family holiday, bored – contemptuous even, if possible – but I can still remember the secret rush of excitement as we crossed the border into Scotland, and the not-so-secret shout of, 'There it is!' from the back seat, as Kilmarnoch finally came into view across the valley.

Most of our days were spent standing on the banks sending flies skimming across the water. We'd watch the fly drift downstream, wait for a hint of movement, then with a flick of the wrist, cast again. After a couple of hours we'd throw a few rugs on the bank and stop to eat our piece, then we'd pack up, wander upstream to another pool and cast again. And so it went on. It has to be said that although fish *were* sometimes caught, it was a huge event, and more often than not, they weren't, and if three or four days had gone by without anyone catching a dicky-bird, we children began clamouring for a change of scene, which invariably meant the beach.

The day that I recalled now was a beach day. The sky was pure blue, without a whisker of a cloud, and the three of us, Penny, Laura and I, were stretched out in a row, motionless and silent in our bikinis, as if the stiller and quieter we lay, the browner we'd get. Penny and I were both desperate for tans. Desperate to go home with at least something to show for a holiday spent, not camping with friends in the Dordogne or backpacking round America, but fishing in Scotland with the parents. I was also aware that the cricket club dance was only three days after I got back, and if I was really going to wear that very skimpy yellow T-shirt pulled off the shoulder, I needed to at least get one of my shoulders brown. I lay there, feeling the sun scorching my eyelids, letting the fine dry sand drift through my fingers.

It was Penny who saw him first. I heard her bangles jangle as she sat up beside me.

'Wow! Look at that!' she hissed, digging me in the ribs. I knew from her hormonal tone that she'd found a man.

'Wow!' echoed Laura, who was fourteen.

'Not bad,' muttered Penny under her breath.

'Not bad at all,' agreed Laura, without the faintest idea what she was talking about.

I groaned, turned over and shut my eyes tight. Now I'm the first to admit that I was as obsessed with boys and sex as the next girl, but Penny at sixteen was just one huge walking talking gland. She was also a social barometer for all that was populist. Whichever blond Adonis was plastered on the cover of her teenage

29

magazine was also plastered to her bedroom walls, but only for as long as he was in favour with her fellow glandettes, only for as long as he was *à la mode*. If he wavered in popularity for just an instant, he was ruthlessly ripped down and replaced by someone else. Penny followed the herd religiously, principally because when left to her own devices, her taste was execrable. She had no discernment of the male species whatsoever, which was why, when I finally deigned to take my nose out of the sand and turn my head to take a peek at what was riveting her – some airhead nutting a football, no doubt – I hated myself for being equally riveted.

He was sitting on the sand with his back against a rock, his brown legs crossed, wearing a pair of old white tennis shorts and a faded denim shirt rolled up to his elbows. His hair was dark – black, really – and quite long, curling well over his denim collar, and he was very brown, but somehow, effortlessly so, as if it were merely an occupational hazard. His eyes were dark too, and they were flashing up and down, first down at his lap, then out to sea. Initially I couldn't work out why, then I realised he was drawing. A small pad rested on his bent knee and his hand was moving over it like quicksilver as his eyes captured a fishing boat gently bobbing out there in the water.

I turned my face away and feigned boredom. 'God, you're predictable, Penny,' I muttered. 'Tall, dark and I presume you think handsome, but I have to warn you, he won't be your usual beefcake type.'

'Why?' demanded Penny.

'Well, he's drawing, isn't he? He shows dangerous signs of having a brain, or at least some sensitivity. He may not even play rugby.'

'I don't *have* to go for the rugger-bugger type, you know,' she said huffily. 'Anyway, I'm going to take a look at his etchings.'

30

She stood up, giggled and adjusted the triangles of her bikini so a huge amount of her generous bosom protruded. Then she flicked back her mane of long blonde hair and sauntered off. I sat up in horror.

'Penny, you can't just—'

But with her figure she could and she knew it. Laura, in her navy-blue school costume went giggling in her wake, sticking out her non-existent chest and doing an exaggerated version of Penny's wiggle.

I smiled at Laura's bony, undulating bottom, then lay down on my side to watch as Penny sidled up, smiled and said something no doubt utterly puke-making.

The boy looked up in surprise and flushed, obviously startled as she bent to inspect his drawing. He recovered and allowed her to take the pad, gave a brief glance at her chest which he could hardly miss since it was hanging in his face, then looked away embarrassed. She flicked through the pages slowly, giving him time to look again, but he didn't. When she handed back the pad, she held on to it for a moment, forcing him to look up at her. She gazed at him and her cherry lips parted in a coy smile. I cringed heavily. This was usually the moment for her to wind in her catch, to land him right there on the beach, but for some reason this boy didn't run true to form. He took the book back with a tight smile, nodded his acceptance of her gushing praise and carried on with his drawing. Penny knelt down next to him, bending forward so her blonde hair almost touched his paper, trying to make him talk while he worked, but he just gave the odd curt nod or muttered an occasional monosyllabic response. If he did smile, it was in Laura's direction. My sister was now doing an hysterical impersonation of Penny, wiggling furiously along the shore, hands cupped under imaginary bosoms which were clearly so heavy she was staggering under their weight.

31

Eventually Penny came huffily back, bangles and bosoms jiggling, face red, followed by a giggling Laura. 'He's too boring for words,' she announced sulkily, flopping down beside me again. 'Can't even string a sentence together, let alone manage a conversation. You were certainly wrong about him being intelligent, Tess. I think he's brain dead.'

'Or simply not succumbing to your charms perhaps?' I murmured, eyes shut.

'Don't be ridiculous,' she snapped. 'I wasn't flirting with him, if that's what you mean. I just wanted to look at his drawings.'

I turned my face away from her, back in his direction, watching through half-closed eyes as he carried on sketching, liking him even more for not admiring Penny. Of course, I reasoned, if he didn't fancy Penny who might be a little pneumatic for some people's tastes but was nonetheless a stunner, there was no chance he'd fancy me – unless of course he preferred the very pale and totally uninteresting look. I smiled at this. He smiled back. I froze for a second, then flushed and turned my head away. Christ! He must have thought I was smiling at *him*, being as obvious as Penny. After a while, however, I steeled myself to look back. He glanced over in Penny's direction, raised his eyebrows and grinned again, conspiratorially. This time I gave a huge, village-idiot beam in response.

I kept those smiles to myself all week, rewinding them, playing them back in my head a million times, hugging them to me. I imagined a quiet, sensitive boy, who'd sit by me on the riverbank talking of painting (his) and poetry (mine) – I secretly fancied myself as a bit of a poet. I saw us walking hand in hand having long philosophical discussions, arguments even, and then resolving our intellectual differences behind the gorse bushes in the moonlight, with a passion that knew no bounds.

Actually, it had to know no bounds because I hadn't the faintest idea what it was all about. As a vicar's daughter at an all-girls' school with one sister and one female cousin, where the devil was I expected to meet boys, let alone have sex? In fact my one and only sexual encounter to date had been with a very short boy called Nigel who, to my astonishment, had asked me to dance at some ghastly tennis club disco. Shocked but delighted I'd instantly dropped my hot dog into my friend Melanie's lap and shot onto the floor with him, thinking, Jesus, he may be short but at least I'm *dancing* – when suddenly, in the middle of *Lay Lady Lay*, and à *propos* of absolutely nothing, he stuck his tongue in my mouth. He circled it precisely twice, thrust his hand up my jumper, ferreted round to the front, boldly seized the middle of my bra and hoicked it up – and over. Now I'm sure the whole ghastly First Time business must be as horrific for boys as it is for girls, but excuse me, not even to *bother* to go round the back and attempt the bra strap struck me as not only cowardly but downright churlish. Round and round we went, me, cut in half by M&S underwear, hideously uncomfortable, eyes boggling over his shoulder, and him, all sweaty and trembly, feverishly investigating whatever fall-out he'd managed to squeeze out of the bottom. When the Lady finally Lay across Bob's Big Brass Bed, Nigel walked me, dazed – and I think that went for both of us – back to my chair. He deposited me next to Melanie and my cold hot dog, and as I sat down, he bent to whisper in my ear.

'You were fantastic,' he muttered. Well, let's face it, my sex life could only get better.

Back at Kilmarnoch, eight days went slowly by until finally, my father walked out of the front door one morning, peered up at the cloudless blue sky and deemed the weather bright enough and the fishing poor enough for us to down rods and go to the beach again. Silently whooping with delight I quickly packed up the boot and urged the others to come *on* or the day would be wasted. We all piled in and I sat in the front, willing the car to go faster, willing the boy to be there. At last we arrived and made our habitual slow and motley progress across the dunes, a straggly procession struggling under the weight of too much beach equipment, me at the back gazing around hopefully, my father at the front, striding out and leading the way, bellowing, 'Come on, you lot!' over his shoulder.

My father has never been much of a style guru but in those days he took a hell of a lot of laughing off, particularly when dressed in his leader-of-the-pack beach ensemble. A vision in khaki – shorts to the knee, short-sleeved shirt buttoned to the neck, socks, sandals, and an Australian bush hat – he put his head down and belted along at breakneck speed, carrying an assortment of pots and pans, a kettle, a primus stove, bags of sausages, bread rolls, kitchen utensils, collapsible chairs – anything, in fact, that one would normally find in the kitchen, because yes, we were that family. The one that cooks on the beach.

Now as anyone who has ever attempted a fry-up in a force eight gale on a Scottish beach will testify, one or two windbreaks are crucial. One or two, not seven, as we invariably had. My father was obsessed by windbreaks; he fussed about them all holiday, constantly fretting he wouldn't have enough, and was never really happy until he was totally surrounded by the bloody things and couldn't actually see the sea, the mountains or even the sky, just acres and acres of red and white ticking with all of us huddled in the middle like something out of Custer's last stand. He'd bang the final post in and bawl, 'There! Now can anyone spot a gap?' All heads would shake vehemently. 'No, no gaps, Daddy!' Because of course it fell to us children to carry the bloody things.

'Don't dawdle, Tessa!' he yelled back to me as I brought up the rear, balancing a couple of the wretched things on my head. I ignored him, and stopped at the top of a dune, gazing around, hoping he'd be there. He wasn't. The beach was empty apart from a couple of families with young children over by the rocks and a man walking his dog along the shore. Damn it, just my bloody luck. I swallowed miserably and walked on slowly, looking all around and just praying that any minute now I'd see his dark head peeping up from behind those rocks where it was more sheltered, or maybe over there where—

'Hey! Look out – bugger!'

Suddenly I was flat on my face, nose down in the sand with a windbreak on my head and papers flying all around me. I looked up into his furious dark eyes.

'You stupid bloody – oh!' He stared. 'It's you.'

I sat up. 'Sorry,' I gasped. 'I didn't see you there – oh, I've ruined your drawings!'

I scrambled around after them, covered with sand and embarrassment, vainly snatching at sheets of cartridge paper as they whipped around us in the wind.

He grabbed them from me. 'Leave them. It doesn't matter, they were crap anyway.'

He retrieved a few more then screwed the whole lot up in a big ball and tossed it over his shoulder with a grin. The wind picked the ball up and bounced it along the sand, whipping it further and further away. We watched as it sailed off into the gorse bushes behind and stuck fast.

'That's not bio-degradable, you know,' I said prissily and instantly wished I hadn't.

'If it's crap it is, isn't it?' he countered, raising his eyebrows.

'Actually, it looked rather good to me,' I said timidly, desperately trying to claw my way back in.

35

'Shows how much you know about art then, doesn't it?' he said, but he grinned.

We stood, staring at each other. Out of the corner of my eye I could see that down on the beach, Camp Fergusson had paused during windbreak erection and all eyes were focused on me. Even from this distance I was aware that Penny's mouth was wide with fury.

'Off to frazzle another layer of skin off your body then, are you?' he said.

I drew a circle in the sand with my toe. 'Well, there's not much else to do. The water's freezing and I'm too old for sandpies.'

'I'm going for a walk,' he said suddenly. 'It's too windy to draw. D'you want to come?'

I jumped. 'Um – er, well I'll have to—'

'Ask Mummy?'

I flushed. 'No, put these windbreaks over there with the others, actually.'

'Well, I wasn't suggesting we took them with us. Go on then, hurry up.'

I fled obediently and dumped the windbreaks. My heart was pounding.

'Just going for a walk,' I muttered to my boggling family, surreptitiously taking a rather juvenile ponytail out of my hair.

'With whom?' demanded my father.

'Um, that boy over there. We were just . . . chatting.'

My father peered over my head, frowning. 'But who is he? Do you know him?'

'Well, sort of. I met him with Penny.' I looked desperately at Penny for corroboration, but she was still speechless.

'Oh Ian, she'll be fine,' soothed my darling mother, putting her hand on his arm. 'Stop fussing. Go on Tess, off you go.'

I flashed her a grateful smile and took off back over

the sand, just as my father was saying, 'Well, I do think she might at least introduce us. That's typical of Tess. Why does she have to dash off like that without even—' but whatever else he thought was lost in the wind, and I'd gone, skimming across the sand, back to the dunes, back to Patrick.

He grinned. 'I see you're built for speed, unlike your buxom cousin.'

'How d'you know she's my cousin?' I panted.

'Checked up on you,' he said as he marched off. 'You're Ian Fergusson's daughter, aren't you? He's going to be thrilled when he discovers you've been taking cliff walks with me. He loathes my parents.'

'Daddy? Really?' I scrambled over the dunes after him. 'Who are your parents?'

'The Camerons. We live at Gilduncan. Hasn't he ever mentioned them?'

I shook my head, still panting a bit from my run. 'Don't think so.'

'Oh well, I loathe them too, my father anyway, so I don't really blame him.'

'You loathe your father?' This was a new one on me. I found my father oppressive, domineering, hypercritical and impossible to please, but I'd have trouble forming the word 'loathe' about him. 'Why?'

'Because he's a shit,' he said simply. He turned and grinned. 'Shits do have children, you know, and just because they're our parents we don't have to be blinded to their shittiness. We don't have to like them.'

I stopped and stared at his back for a moment as he strode on. Somehow this wasn't quite the shy, sensitive artistic boy I'd had in mind; this boy was foul-mouthed and angry. I clambered up the cliff after him again, silenced.

He stopped ahead of me and turned back. 'You're off on Saturday, I take it?'

'How d'you know that too?'

We'd reached the top of the cliff. He sat down and lit a cigarette. He offered me one. I glanced quickly down at the beach below. They were a long way away but I could still see my father. I shook my head.

'Because you've been here nearly three weeks. You don't have to be Einstein to figure out you'll be heading back to the comfort of the home counties soon, back to your tennis lessons and your pony and discos at the cricket club, getting on down to Shawaddywaddy on a Saturday night.'

I flushed. 'You're deliberately making it sound tame and suburban.'

'Well, it is tame and suburban compared to this, isn't it?' He swept his hand around at the majestic blue heather mountains behind us, the huge stretch of beach below and the sea that ran out for miles and miles ahead of us.

'Yes, of course,' I said crossly, 'but we can't all live in the Highlands, can we, and if we did it wouldn't look like this, you know. It'd be overrun with Leisure Centres on those hills and municipal swimming pools in the valleys, you wouldn't be able to see the beach for badminton nets, so from your point of view it's probably just as well we're not all up here admiring the heather.'

'Thank God I am,' he muttered, pulling at the rough grass and staring out to sea. 'It's about all that keeps me sane.'

There was a silence. I didn't like to break it and apart from anything else I didn't know what to say. He seemed so strange and – well, haunted almost.

After a while he turned to me and grinned. 'Well that's promising. It's not often you meet a girl who doesn't feel she has to fill the air space.'

'God, you're patronising!' But I couldn't help feeling pleased. 'What did you ask me up here for anyway if you

38

don't want to talk – or did you just want to get up my father's nose?'

'No, I just thought you looked all right. Sort of, approachable, and normal.'

I grinned. 'And I've spent the last seventeen years trying to be extraordinary and mysterious.'

He made a face. 'Mystery's very overrated. Nine times out of ten it's just a front for something very banal and boring.'

'Oh really?' I sucked at a blade of grass. 'You're pretty mysterious, aren't you? All this pent-up aggression and dark brooding looks out to sea and allusions to your sanity – it's all a bit Heathcliff, isn't it? I mean, what's it all about?' He opened his mouth to speak but I interrupted. 'No, no – don't tell me, let me guess. A broken home, terrorised childhood, misunderstood adolescence . . . am I close?'

He stared at me with narrowed eyes, and for a moment I really thought he was going to hit me. Then suddenly his face broke into a grin. 'Not far off, but you forgot to mention under-exposure to suburbia. I'm a seriously deprived child in that respect.'

Suddenly he stood up, seized my wrists and hauled me to my feet. He looked into my eyes. 'And let me amend my last, rather muted compliment, to approachable, normal and really rather extraordinarily smart. Better?'

I grinned. 'For the minute. We'll get on to my finer points later.'

He held my eyes. 'Fine by me.' We stood looking at each other, and for a moment I really thought I was in grave danger of fainting and toppling over the edge of the cliff.

'There's a film I want to see in Brookenhead tonight,' he said abruptly. 'D'you want to come?'

'A – a film?'

'Yes. We have cinemas here as well as heather, you know.'

'I – I'm not sure. It's just that I'm with my family and—'

'OK, fine. Don't.'

He turned and set off back down the cliff path at a cracking pace. I ran after him.

'Hey, hang on a minute. All I meant was I'd have to ask my parents, or is that just too incredibly mundane for you? Would you rather I knotted my sheets together and shimmied out of my bedroom window without telling them where I was going?'

He turned back and laughed. 'You're not afraid to take the piss out of me, are you?'

'Why should I be?'

'No reason. I'll pick you up at seven then, OK?'

'OK.'

Chapter Four

What he didn't know was that it would have been far easier to shin out of that house on knotted sheets. Although part of the blame for my sheltered existence lay with my female-oriented life, it has to be said that the lion's share lay with my father, the Reverend Ian Fergusson. To say he kept an eye on his daughters was like saying the Gestapo kept an eye on the Resistance. Sometimes I felt I couldn't fart without clearing it with him first.

Back at the house at teatime I steeled myself to break the news. Daddy had been holding forth for twenty solid minutes, berating poor Aunt Rachel about the ignominies of the Church of England, telling her precisely why he was still a rector when lesser men had accelerated past him to become bishops. I looked at the clock. Five-thirty, only an hour and a half and he'd be here, and if I wanted to have a bath and iron my shirt . . . I cleared my throat.

'Daddy?'

He didn't even pause for breath. 'You see, what they *really* want, Rachel,' he went on, banging his tea cup down in its saucer and making her jump, 'is some poncy git with a beard and a guitar who's going to *question* the Scriptures, who's going to *doubt* the Virgin Birth and the parting of the Red Sea, or any of the other miracles come to that, entirely missing the point that that's what they bleeding well are! Miracles!'

My mother, sitting over in the window seat, raised

her eyebrows and smiled sympathetically at me over her newspaper. It suddenly occurred to me that she'd guessed I had a lot of ground to break here and had positioned herself quietly in the wings to help me chip away at him. I was always glad of her support. My father ranted on.

'We won again yesterday,' she murmured across him.

'What?' I looked round. She was reading the football results. 'Oh, good.'

My mother was an ardent Chelsea supporter. She followed every match they played and much to my father's horror even went to watch them sometimes. No one quite knew why she supported them with such zeal, but I secretly suspected it had a lot to do with the fact that it wasn't considered a particularly fitting hobby for a vicar's wife. It was my mother's way of rebelling. It amused her to hold sherry parties at the vicarage and discuss the latest new player's transfer fee instead of the verger's rose garden.

She sighed and closed the paper. 'We're away to Liverpool next week, though – that won't be quite so easy.' She nodded over in Daddy's direction. 'Try again, darling.'

I licked my lips. 'Daddy, please can I just ask you—'

'– I mean, Christ, even the bloody *Creed's* under suspicion now,' he stormed. 'I believe in God, the Father Almighty, Maker of heaven and earth – who says so, eh?' He glared at Rachel, who blinked nervously. 'Who says He made heaven and earth? Oh yes, that's what the powers-that-be want to hear, Rachel. They want a bit of lively discussion, because in their ignorance, they think that shows intelligence! And of course what they don't want is faith. Oh no, that's a really dirty word. Faith's not fashionable at all, faith's right out of the window. They don't want any namby pamby *believers* in their churches, they want doubting bloody Thomases!' He

42

paused for breath and to slurp his tea. Alf Garnett in a dog collar. 'And d'you know what else they want – eh?'

Rachel shot me a glance. 'No, Ian, but I think Tess wants to—'

'D'you know what else those bloody bishops want – do you? Just a minute, Tessa, I'm talking. D'you know what else they want, Rachel?'

Rachel sighed. 'No, Ian. Tell me.'

'They want pederasts.'

'Oh Ian, please—'

'Oh yes, yes they do.' He nodded vigorously. 'They want fashionable little pederasts, and it's no good you sighing, Daphne, you know very well it's true. It's not enough these days to be a red-blooded heterosexual family man. What the church wants is a groovy gay vicar – Larry – who introduces his partner – Brian – to the congregation at the church door every Sunday, and if Larry's been done for a spot of indecent exposure in the local park and it's made it into the Sunday papers – well, so much the better! Oh yes, halle-bleeding-lujah, that's wonderful, because then we can all forgive and forget and it'll all be so cuddly and lovely and we'll all pray for Larry and Brian and have happy clappy and join hands with our neighbours and give them a good old snog – kissing's more or less mandatory in churches now, Rachel – and Larry will play his guitar and Brian will sit in the front pew and sway a bit and think how heavenly Larry looks in that long white dress and – yes, Tessa, WHAT IS IT! For heaven's sake stop mumbling and spit it OUT!'

'Daddy, that boy I met today,' I blurted out. 'He's asked me to go to the cinema tonight. Please can I go?'

My father stared at me as if I had two heads. 'Boy? What boy?'

'On the beach, you saw him.'

'To the cinema? When?'

43

'Tonight.'

'Of course you can, darling,' said my mother smoothly. 'You go and get ready.'

'What's his name?' barked my father as my bottom rose from my seat.

'Patrick Cameron.'

My father's tea cup froze midway to his mouth. He put it down slowly. His eyes were like stone. 'It's out of the question.'

'Daddy, please I—'

'Don't argue, young lady, you're not going. That boy is Marcus Cameron's son. He's a reprobate, a layabout, a dropout and most probably a drug addict to boot.'

'Who?' enquired my mother mildly. 'The father, or son?'

'Both probably!' exploded my father. 'Like father like son! Willie tells me that boy was thrown out of Marlborough and Harrow and then sent down from Oxford. All he does now is arse around at the fisheries pretending to work and then drip around drawing wild flowers on his days off!'

'That's not fair,' I protested. 'He's a very talented artist – I've seen his pictures.'

'And that's all you're going to see of him, my girl,' he barked.

I stood up, shaking with rage. 'Oh this is wonderful, this is marvellous, you've been checking up on him haven't you? You've been talking to the gillie about him already and all because I spoke to him on the beach today! And how come Willie knows so much about him?'

'Tessa, the Camerons live at Gilduncan,' he said with studied patience.

'So?'

'So everyone knows their business. The locals always know what goes on at the big house, half of them work there for God's sake, and no one in their right mind would let their daughter touch that boy with a barge-pole!'

'I'm not going to touch him, I'm just going to see a film with him,' I shrieked. 'You're behaving like a bloody Victorian! I'm seventeen years old and—'

'Don't you swear at me, young lady!'

'Tessa, go upstairs.' My mother put her hand on my quivering arm. 'I want to speak to your father in private.'

I turned and fled, tears streaming down my face. Out in the hall Penny and Laura were sitting on the stairs, mouths open, eyes huge, listening intently to the action. I ran past them up the stairs.

Ten minutes later my mother came up. 'Dry your eyes, darling, and get ready.'

I looked up from the wet pillow. 'Are you serious? Am I going?'

'Of course.'

What she said to him I'll never know. No one ever knew how my mother got round him, but once in a while, when the chips were really down, she did, and an hour or so later I was leaping down Kilmarnoch's front steps as the lights from Patrick's red Spitfire lit up the drive.

We didn't go to the cinema in the end, we went to the beach and watched the sun go down. We talked a lot, laughed even more, and at eleven o'clock precisely Patrick drove me back to Kilmarnoch. He bade my father – who was waiting, silhouetted in the open front doorway – a polite good night, and left. The following day the Ian Fergussons piled into the car, waved goodbye to the Robert Fergussons and drove the 600 miles or so back to Kent, and that was the end of that. Or so my parents thought.

What they didn't know was that within minutes of sitting on that cold, windy beach I'd felt that pang. That sharp one that makes your heart stop for a moment and then dance around like mad as you realise this is different, this is real, this is *it*. All the short Nigels, shy Malcolms and reasonably attractive librarians I'd ever vaguely considered in my short and limited career sank into obscurity as my toes curled with excitement in the cold sand. I hugged my knees and pressed my chin into them thinking, this is it, Tessa. This is *it*! Quiet and sensitive he certainly wasn't, but clever, irreverent, original and hilarious he was, and not in a cynical way that made you give a twisted smile and think, Gosh, how clever – but in a throw back your head and laugh out loud sort of way.

It was quite clear he'd had one hell of a childhood, with parents who rowed constantly – and sometimes violently – and a father who far eclipsed mine in ghastliness. Marcus Cameron was a cold, starchy, sneering Dickensian figure who dined in a dinner jacket every night and then proceeded to get as drunk as a Lord and pour scorn on his only son and heir for being such a huge disappointment to him. Mr Cameron's disappointment stemmed chiefly from Patrick's not wanting to either row for Oxford, join the Army, or become a Conservative MP, but to do what came naturally – to paint. What must have been irritating in the extreme for Marcus was that Patrick could have done all these things, and more, but chose not to. He wasn't a chinless wonder living off his trust fund, he'd got a scholarship to Oxford, even though he'd been thrown out of one school and been 'this close' to being thrown out of another – not, incidentally, as my father had snidely suggested, for 'doing drugs', but for what Patrick laughingly referred to as 'kicking against the pricks'.

For someone like me this was still awesome talk. The model daughter, the diligent student who always did her homework and her violin practice, I'd never so much as nudged let alone kicked the pricks he was referring to – teachers, tutors, dons – people in positions of authority, positions which to my mind were not up for debate. But

Patrick debated everything and everyone, questioning things I considered unquestionable, like the validity of having a piece of paper with 'first-class Honours degree, Oxford' written on it.

'What's the point?' he demanded, narrowing his dark eyes at me in the moonlight and dragging on his cigarette, 'when I know I want to paint? What's the point in a degree in history, for God's sake?'

I gazed at him in astonishment, longing as I did with all my heart to go to university, to get away from home. But Patrick was not so easily fobbed off.

'I'm buggered if I'm going somewhere I don't want to go just to get away from somewhere else, and no one, particularly my bloody father, is going to make me.'

I came away from that beach reeling. Not only had he affected my heart but my head, too. For the first time he'd made me think independently of the people who took it upon themselves to guide my cerebral processes. I was still reeling in Kent a week later and when I got back to boarding school two weeks after that. But gradually, as I sat doodling at my desk, or lay staring at the cracked magnolia ceiling in my dorm, the euphoria wore off and grim reality sank in. Here was I, at a girls' boarding school in Dorset, and there was he, working at a salmon farm in Scotland. I had a whole year to get through until I could conceivably see him again, if indeed he even wanted to see me. Would he write, for instance? Every night I said three Hail Marys – I'm not even Catholic – tapped my headboard three times, kissed the Bible twice, crossed myself, turned three small circles, touched the floor for luck, got into bed, and prayed to God that he would.

He did. I went through the whole rigmarole nightly, and amazingly, the following Friday another letter appeared, and then another, and another, until it began to look increasingly likely that whatever it was that had made us sit together on that cold windy beach stood more than a cat's chance in hell of lasting until the following August.

I for one went to crazy, adolescent lengths to make sure it did. Never had a set of A-level exercise books been so elaborately graffitied with hearts, initials and true love arrows. Never had I been so obsessed with art galleries and all things Scottish – the tartans at the local drapery store were fingered lovingly, Campbell's Mulligatawny soup, which I loathed, was supped in gallons. I even, in very lovesick moments, took to lingering in the fishmonger's, gazing fondly into the cold grey eyes of the salmon stretched out on the slab.

All very juvenile, but all crucial for keeping true teenage love alive. And it worked. When I returned to Scotland the following year, I didn't have to worry about re-kindling my fire; my embers were still piping hot. Of Patrick, I wasn't so sure. He was older, had certainly had more experience and must have had many more distractions than me in the past twelve months. He might well have gone right off the boil. It was therefore with a certain amount of trepidation that I prepared to keep our first clandestine meeting at midnight – timed to thwart my father – on the very first night.

I lay in bed, watching the illuminated hands of my alarm clock move slowly round to the twelve. When they'd both almost made it, I pushed back the duvet, pulled on a pair of jeans and a jumper and crept stealthily out of the bedroom I shared with Laura. Shaking with nerves I tiptoed downstairs in the dark, lingering for a moment on the bottom step to make sure no bedroom doors were opening above me. My heart was pounding. No one seemed to be stirring so I crept quietly through the hall, unbolted the huge front door, wincing at every creak and groan the archaic bolts gave, and swung it back. I shut it softly behind me, tiptoed out into the night, and ran down the hill towards the river.

As I crashed through the brambles at the bottom of the garden I came to the clearing where we'd arranged to meet. My heart was galloping around in my throat now; I could hardly breathe for nerves. It was pitch black and I couldn't see him, and for one ghastly moment I wondered if he'd got cold feet, decided not to come. Then suddenly, softly, he called my name.

'Tess!'

I swung around. He was sitting on a low stone wall with his back to the river smoking a cigarette. He was wearing an old blue fisherman's jumper, a pair of jeans and that fatal, devilish, lock-up-your-daughters grin. As he stubbed his cigarette out on the wall, sparks flew everywhere. He jumped down and came towards me and as he got close, he reached out and took my hands.

'Hello.'

'Hello!' I gasped.

I'd envisaged this meeting for a whole year, planned it, rehearsed it, and my God I was going to be so cool and sophisticated and now here I was – damn it – hardly even able to speak.

He smiled, eyeing me closely. 'Well, well. I really wondered if you'd make it.'

'You mean you doubted it?' And there was me doubting him.

'I wasn't sure how your courage had come on in a year, but since you're here I think we can safely say leaps and bounds. Sneaking out at midnight to meet your undesirable boyfriend, eh? Whatever next?'

Boyfriend. He'd said boyfriend. 'Oh, I think I have a pretty shrewd suspicion,' I gulped brazenly, meeting his eye.

For a moment I think this even took the wind out of his billowing sails, then his face broke into a delighted grin. He swooped forward and collected me up in his arms.

'Good heavens, Tess, you want to watch it. You'll lose that nice shiny halo if you're not careful.'

'The sooner the better,' I murmured, burying my face in his jumper. He gave me a squeeze then set me down, gazing at me, exploring my face with his eyes. Then he bent his head and kissed me, beautifully, slowly, deliciously, the second kiss I'd ever experienced and so terribly different from the first.

That night, of course, I lost more than my halo. We walked, talked and made love down by the river, as we did for virtually the next thirty-two nights. And every morning at 4 a.m. I'd sneak back into the house and go to sleep with a smile on my face. No one could understand why I couldn't wake up until about midday and why, when I did eventually drag myself out of bed, I just lay by the river, smiling, dreaming, watching dragonflies, not even bothering to fish much. My whole family were exasperated by me, but still no one knew, nor even suspected. Only Daddy, over lunch on the bank one day, came vaguely close, asking me abruptly, but *sotto voce*, if I'd heard from that damned fellow Patrick. I said no, I hadn't, adding slightly miserably that I thought he'd probably forgotten all about me.

'Well, of course he has,' he barked, not bothering to hide his relief. 'He's probably got a string of women spread all over Scotland!'

No, just the one, I thought quietly, nibbling my cheese roll.

'Probably forgot you the moment you got out of his swanky little car,' he added gleefully.

And my father thought he knew so much about faith. *Oh ye of little . . .*

And so the holiday went on, the days – and nights – going by all too quickly, until around came the one I'd been dreading. The last. Or so I thought. Patrick, it transpired, had other ideas.

'Come to Italy with me,' he said, as we lay on the bank together, staring up at the stars.

I turned my head. 'To Italy?'

'I'm going to go and paint there.'

I sat up. 'You never said!'

'I only decided yesterday. I've got to get away from here for a while. I'm twenty-one next week so I come into a bit of money. Whether my father likes it or not, I can do what the hell I want.'

'Really? You mean you're suddenly going to be loaded or something?'

He grinned. 'Do I detect a sudden spark of interest? No, not loaded exactly, the trustees are pretty mean with their dosh, but certainly I'll have enough to cover our air fares and the rent on a flat somewhere, Florence perhaps, or Siena. Then I'll get a job.'

'As what?'

He shrugged impatiently. 'Oh, I don't know, Tess. Maybe teaching English or working in a bar or something. Perhaps you could waitress at the same place, then we could be together.'

I boggled. 'Blimey. Daddy would have a fit!'

'Of course he would. He'd have a fit if you so much as mentioned my name. You wouldn't be able to *tell* him, you'd just have to get on a plane and come.'

I gulped. My courage may have come on in leaps and bounds but this called for out-and-out rebellion. Patrick had been a rebel all his life and was just doing what came naturally. For me it was different. I was a law-abiding daughter, fond of my parents.

'So what d'you think?' he demanded.

I pulled at some grass on the bank. 'I don't know, Patrick, I mean it's all so sudden, isn't it? And it's all very well for you, but I'm supposed to be going

51

to university in October.'

'Yes, I know, but you don't want to go yet, do you? You said yourself in an ideal world you'd take a year off and travel. It's only your father who wants you instantly locked up and institutionalised again, so why don't you just defer it for a year? I'm not talking about for ever.'

I took a deep breath. 'Patrick, I can't just leave home like that . . .'

He shrugged and threw a pebble into the river. 'Fine, OK, don't. We probably won't see each other again though, will we?'

'That's not fair!' I cried. 'I deliberately chose St Andrews so I could be near you.'

'Oh, so what am I supposed to do – hang around on campus like some love-sick pillock waiting for you to come out of lectures – no, thanks. Look, all you want to do is write anyway, so what's the point of going there in the first place? Just fix yourself up with a pen and an exercise book, and get scribbling! Do you really think a few seminars on Sir Gawain and the Green Knight is going to help you write better poetry?'

'Concentrates the mind,' I muttered lamely.

'Rubbish, it just clouds the issue. Or perhaps it's the social life you're after, is that it? D'you secretly want to be part of Freshers' Week and join the Brass-Rubbing Society and the Drama Club and help organise the Rag Ball? Perhaps you'd like to have a crush on your English professor and cram like mad to get a first to impress him – or maybe it's the college scarf that attracts you, the whole "I'm a student" bit with your Railcard and your good luck gonk for exams and—'

'Oh Patrick,' I said impatiently, 'you're so cynical about anything remotely conventional. University doesn't have to be as squeaky clean as all that.'

'No, but it would be for you, Tess. That's the way you'd do it and you know it. You've been programmed

52

from birth to do the right thing and if no one's there to stop you, you'll revert to type and run around organising every committee under the sun, throwing yourself into lacrosse and basketball and—'

'What's wrong with that?' I snapped.

'Nothing,' he said patiently. 'There's nothing wrong with it at all, if it makes you happy. Oh, it'll certainly make your teachers happy and your father will be ecstatic and everyone will pat you on the back and say "Jolly well done, Tess. Isn't she marvellous?" but what about *you*? What happens if you're standing there three years later with your mortar board on your head, a frozen smile on your face, clutching your bits of paper wondering if you've pleased everyone except yourself?'

I stared at him, unsettled.

He seized my hand abruptly. 'I dare you, Tess, I dare you to be happy. Go on, pack a bag next week, leave a note for your parents and meet me at Heathrow. Yes, your old man will be livid; he may even follow us out and try and take you back, but you're eighteen now, you can do what you like. The point is, Tess, he'll get over it – but if you don't come, will you?'

I squirmed. 'It's . . . the deceit I hate, slipping out, leaving a note. You don't think if I just asked him . . . ?'

'Oh what, that he'd say, "Great idea, Tess, hang on a minute, I'll get my keys and drive you to the airport myself"?'

'N-no, but—' I struggled desperately, looking for loopholes. 'What if it doesn't work out?'

He threw up his hands in despair. 'What if, what if! Look, if it doesn't work out and we hate it, or hate each other, you can still go to St Andrews the following year. You can defer your place, can't you?'

'Y-e-s, I suppose so, but—'

'So do it.'

I stared at him. He stood up and hauled me to my

feet. He grinned. As far as he was concerned, it was settled.

'See you at Terminal One then. I'll get the tickets!'

'Oh, for God's sake, Patrick,' I snapped, exasperated. 'It's not as simple as that.'

He stared at me closely. 'It is if you want it enough. Don't blow it, Tess. You'd be surprised how rare this kind of thing is.'

For 'kind of thing' I suppose he meant love. But how was I to know that? I'd stumbled upon it so quickly and easily, how was I to know some people look for ever and never really find it at all?

I tried to meet him, I really did. Back home in Kent a week later I packed a bag, my tummy raging with butterflies, and left a note under my pillow in my bedroom. Then at the last moment, half an hour before I was going to leave the house, I told Laura. I think in my heart I knew she'd be far too scared to keep such a colossal secret to herself, that she'd tell Daddy. And she did. I sat motionless on the bed, waiting like a condemned prisoner, my bag on my lap, listening to the shout of rage in the kitchen as she spilled the Patrick beans, then the *thud thud thud* of footsteps coming up the stairs. The door flew open. It was late on a Sunday morning and Dad was still dressed in his cassock, his preacher's kit. His face was white with fury. I sat there, gripping the handle of my bag, as he towered above me like an avenging angel.

'Over my dead body!' he thundered.

A very ugly fight ensued and we both said things I'd rather forget, but never will. I'd never seen him so furious, so seething, so venomous. My mother, in a very brave moment, appeared behind him, and suggested that perhaps I should go for a week or two, just for a holiday, and that as a matter of fact she wouldn't mind coming with me as a sort of chaperone, she'd always wanted to see the frescoes – how about it, Ian? As he swung around to face her, I really thought he was going to hit her. He hustled her out and slammed the bedroom door behind them both and I threw myself on the bed and burst into tears. I sobbed into my duvet feeling utterly distraught, miserable and totally powerless, but – I sat up on the bed and blew my nose – if that were so, why was it then that there was just the merest hint of relief stealing over my soul? I stared through my tears at my bookcase, groaning with childish books, old teddies, a few rosettes on the wall above it. Was it because it had actually been too much of a big adventure? And now it was out of my hands? No longer my fault if I didn't make it?

I stayed up in my room all day while my parents talked in hushed tones below. Eventually, the telephone rang. My father called me down. Almost in a daze, I went slowly downstairs. Daddy was standing in the hall, dangling the receiver between his thumb and finger as if it were a piece of dog shit.

'Tell him,' he said, as I took it from him.

He stood over me as I explained, in a quivering voice, that I wouldn't be coming.

'Not ever?' asked Patrick, dumbfounded. 'Can't you meet me there later on, in a week or two? Give him the slip?'

'No,' I said, 'not ever.'

My father nodded, tight-lipped as I handed the phone back to him. I walked slowly upstairs to my room.

The following day I wrote to Patrick's mother and asked where he was living. Amazingly she wrote back and told me. I sent three or four letters to Florence, pleading with him to understand, to consider my position. He didn't reply. I suppose he simply couldn't believe I was so unlike him. So spineless, so timid.

That October I went miserably up to St Andrew's University. The first few weeks were the usual riot of frenetic activity with everyone rushing around joining societies, being personable and witty and madly collecting friends. I couldn't be bothered so I collected few. I withdrew into myself, worked incredibly hard and gained a reputation for being bright, but aloof and unapproachable, whereas in fact I was just plain lonely and miserable. Of course, as time went by I thawed and by the fourth year I'd made a few friends and even had a couple of flings, but nothing serious.

Then right at the end of my final year, I fell in love. I went to a party, met a law student and to my complete amazement, was totally bowled over by him. I sincerely believed lightning couldn't possibly strike twice, but this quiet, gentle man literally snuck up on me and persuaded me otherwise. Perhaps it worked because he was so different from Patrick, so laid back, mellow, kind and screamingly academic and intelligent. Perhaps I was just ready to try again. At the time he was debating whether to go on with his studies and do an MA at Cambridge with a view to becoming a don, or to join the Bar and make some money. Six months later the question was decided for him. I became pregnant and neither of us wanted to get rid of the baby. We married, very happily, and David became a barrister to support his new family.

Chapter Five

'Oh, for God's sake give her some Calpol!' snapped David as we sat in an horrendous traffic jam on the Hammersmith flyover, already an hour into our journey to Scotland and still only half a mile from home. In the back, Josie was sandwiched between our bored and fractious children, one of whom was already threatening to throw up.

'She feels *sick*, David. Calpol's not going to help!'

'No, but at least it'll knock her out and with any luck we'll have a bit of peace.'

'My God you have some strange ideas about bringing up children,' I snapped, thinking it was a bloody brilliant idea and wishing I'd thought of it, and, incidentally, thought to put the blinking stuff in the car rather than in my case in the boot. There was no way I was admitting to such gross inefficiency now though.

'No no,' I said brightly, 'we can't resort to drugging them just yet. I know, let's have a sing-song. After all, we are off on our hols, aren't we?'

David shot me an incredulous look. 'Hols?' he muttered. 'Jesus, you'll be getting out the ginger beer next.'

I ignored him and swung around to my equally incredulous children. 'Now,' I said beaming, 'what about *The Wheels on the Bus*?'

'What about them?' growled Hugo.

'Or *The Happy Wanderer*,' I persisted, ignoring David's

low moan. 'D'you know that one, Josie? Do they have that in Australia?'

She blinked. 'Not to my knowledge, but how about *Kookaburra*? We could do it in rounds.'

David went pale. 'Darling, please, I beg you,' he muttered, 'not *Kookaburra* in rounds. Perhaps past Stirling when we're absolutely desperate, but we haven't even got to the Talgarth Roundabout yet!'

'What do you suggest then?' I said irritably.

'A cup of black coffee and a browse through the *Observer* springs instantly to mind, but failing that, how about one of those God-awful tapes they torment us with sometimes?'

Another bloody brilliant idea and this time I took him up on it. I rifled feverishly through the glove compartment.

'Postman Pat or Funny Bones?' I threw over my shoulder. Fatal. Absolutely fatal, and me an experienced mother.

'Postman Pat!' yelled Clemmie.

'Funny Bones!' yelled Hugo.

'Postman Pat!'

'No, Funny Bones!'

'Postman – Oi! Ow!'

'Well, you thumped my leg! Mummy, she thumped my leg!'

'POSTMAN PAT! POSTMAN – OW! GEDDOFF! MUMMY, HE'S HITTING ME!'

'*All right, that will do!*' I bellowed. 'We'll have Funny Bones first and then Postman Pat, all right?'

But of course it wasn't all right. Hugo crowed and Clemmie cried and a major fist-fight ensued across Josie, with me flinging in a few of my own right hooks from the front. At this point David let out a howl of anguish, performed an astonishingly dangerous U-turn in the middle of the Hammersmith flyover and belted down to

King Street with his awestruck, silenced family around him. He screeched to a halt outside Rumbelows, ran inside, and two minutes later appeared with two personal stereos. He plugged both the children in while I rose to the occasion and shovelled a couple of spoonfuls of Calpol into their mouths – to quell the over-excitement, don't you know – and we crawled back into the jam again, now an hour and a half into our journey, even closer to home, and £75 worse off.

I groaned and slumped down in my seat. 'Happy holidays.'

David smiled and patted my hand. 'This is always the worst bit,' he said reassuringly. 'It'll be fine once we get there. We'll all relax – even you.'

'Don't bank on it,' I said grimly. 'All sorts of things will conspire to get on my nerves, like Penny and Piers for instance.'

David sighed. 'Oh God. Here we go.'

I ignored him. 'I wonder, for instance, just how much money Penny's spent on her house since I saw her last, hmm? What d'you think, David? Four thousand – five? I dare say those hideous gold towel rails have come in for a bit of re-plating, and I should think the shagpile's wearing a bit thin by now, they must have had it at least six months. Oh yes, I imagine the Credit Card Queen has been dealing her way all round Harrods and all because Piers is *such* a successful barrister, the implication being of course that you're not!' I ground my teeth.

'I don't think that's true,' said David mildly. 'You take everything so personally.'

'Because it's *meant* personally – you just never see it. God, last year he even told me, in a quiet and oh-so-frightfully-well-meant way, what an excellent barrister you'd make if you could just find that killer punch. I tell you, he damn nearly found it in his solar plexus right

59

there and then, and *then* he had the audacity to say that he was surprised you had so many briefs!'

David smiled. 'What did you say?'

'I said I was surprised he had so many teeth.'

David threw back his head and shouted with laughter. 'Oh Tess, you do rise to him.'

'I can't help it. I mean, he staggers in every year with a groaning case full of work, never does any of it, of course, just shuffles it around under your nose and sighs over it at the desk periodically – what's he trying to prove?'

'He's just insecure, darling, you know that.'

'And bloody Penny tells me *constantly* how poor Piers is s-o-o busy and has to work every evening and every weekend because he's in such demand, and isn't it nice that you have so much time to relax . . . I mean, bugger off!'

'Barristers always like to appear busy,' said David, calmly overtaking a huge juggernaut in the middle lane. 'They have to talk it up.'

'But you don't, you never do!' I objected exasperated. 'People ask you what sort of work you do and you say – "Oh, crap mostly".'

'Well it is, mostly.'

'But you don't have to say so! Especially not in front of Penny and Piers – for my sake, darling, please.'

David raised his hand in thanks as he was let into the fast lane.

'David?'

'Hmmm?'

'Please, darling, don't talk yourself down in front of them, OK?'

'OK, OK!' he said. 'Stop nagging, Tess.'

'Well, they're so bloody competitive,' I said tetchily. I scratched my neck violently. 'God, she's bringing me out in a rash before I've even got there.'

'She's not that bad,' said David. 'You just handle her badly.'

'And it's not even as if I want to be like her!' I went on. 'I don't want her immaculate tasteless house on the Wentworth bloody estate, I don't want co-ordinating apricot hand towels with a nice gold P in the corner, or a sauna in the basement, or a *fountain*, for heaven's sake, in the conservatory . . . but what bugs me is that she thinks I do!'

'Oh God, Tess,' said David weakly.

'I don't want her homogenised, sanitised, ultra-hygienic home, thank you very much. I don't want to be forever flicking round my ghastly Lalique ornaments and my onyx ashtrays with a feather duster. D'you know, David, I once looked under the pepper-grinder in her kitchen and guess what I found?'

'What?' he said faintly.

'Nothing. Absolutely nothing. David, everyone has pepper under their grinder. She must be the only person in the history of the world who dusts *underneath* it! She is that anal, David.'

'She's your cousin, darling. Look, why don't you save this for the end of the holiday? We've got three weeks to get through yet.'

I sighed, scratching my neck again. 'I know, I know. I just thought maybe if I got it off my chest now I might not be so rude to her when we get there. Incidentally, I've told the children to stop calling them the PPs. I just hope Perfect Child's taken a turn for the worse though, otherwise I might have to flush her head down the loo.'

David frowned in the direction of our less-than-perfect children in the back, who would have loved to have joined me in the disposal of PC – Penny's ultra-cute daughter – but a quick glance over my shoulder told me a soothing mixture of aural stimulation and Calpol was still giving them that lovely, vacant, open-mouthed glazed look. Josie was also tuned into her Walkman, a beatific expression on her lovely bronzed features.

'With any luck she'll have progressed from a perfect three-year-old into a normal, horrible four-year-old,' he soothed.

'Don't you believe it,' I said bitterly. 'If she could recite the whole of *The Owl and the Pussycat* last year while Clemmie was having trouble saying "ball", it's bound to be Keats or at the very least Shakespeare this year. D'you know, on the beach last year she asked me what I thought of John Major, and as I struggled for breath informed me that Guinea Fowl was very over-rated. I nearly nose-dived her into the sand.'

David shook his head resignedly. 'I don't know why you let it get to you, Tess. You know Penny hot-houses that child, force-feeding her flash cards and God knows what else – she probably has her plugged into Civilization cassettes while she's asleep. She'll burn herself out by the time she's six, and you know you don't approve, so why get in such a state about it?'

I sighed. 'I know. Why am I in such a state?'

I looked out of the window and watched the countryside roll by. Penny and Piers had a lot to do with it of course, they always sent my blood pressure rocketing sky high, but there was an added irritation this year. Patrick's reappearance was more than anything else, annoying. I couldn't care less about him being there, but nonetheless I didn't want to bump into him looking like something the cat wouldn't even bother to drag in. It was irritating to think that I might have to bother to wash my hair more than once a week, or put on a dash of lipstick if I went into Invertarn, or even wear uncomfortable support pants, damn it, so that he didn't get the shock of his life when he stood behind me in the queue at the butchers and wondered who the lowslung woman in front wearing her bottom round her knees was, or struggled to recognise the female weight lifter, swearing and cursing as she dragged forty-two cans of baked beans – obligatory holiday fodder for Hugo – out of the grocers.

Yes, there was no doubt about it, twelve years and two children had taken their toll on my body, and if Patrick was going to even recognise me I'd have to walk around sucking in everything I possessed – tummy, bottom, all my chins – as if I had a cucumber up my bottom. Such a blinking *bore*. Or perhaps I shouldn't, I mused, watching the fields flash past. Perhaps that was the answer; perhaps I should wash my hair *less* often, abandon make-up altogether and let everything hang out, that way, he wouldn't recognise me at all. I could walk past him in the street in the perfect knowledge that he wouldn't have a clue who I was. I brightened. Yes, that was it. After all, he would have changed too, wouldn't he? So I might not even recognise him. We could be totally oblivious to each other. I mean, twelve years is twelve years – God, he was probably an accountant or something by now – a bald one, with a paunch. I snuck a look at David. At least one could say he was only vaguely thinning on top and he was still as slim as when I'd met him. I smiled. Comparisons, in this case, might be rather less than odious. I slipped my hand onto his knee and gave it a little squeeze. He slammed on the brakes and a coach damn nearly went up our backside. It honked furiously.

'What was that for?' David yelled.

'What!'

'You squeezed my knee!'

'I know! Affectionately, damn it – can't I do that?'

'Jesus.' David accelerated away from the bus, clearly ruffled. 'You gave me the fright of my life, I thought I'd missed a car pulling out or something.'

'For heaven's sake, David, I was just being friendly!'

'Well, don't – OK? At least not when I'm driving. It's too much out of character for you.'

We drove on. On and on, 582 miles to be precise, until finally, eight hours later, our car crawled slowly into Kilmarnoch's drive and crunched to a halt on the gravel. One by one, the surviving members of the Hamilton family emerged, exhausted, dishevelled, ratty and smelling very distinctly of sick. Clemmie, having threatened us with it for 580 miles, had finally delivered the goods half a mile from Kilmarnoch's front gates, giving us precisely two seconds to find the bucket, the one we'd so thoughtfully got ready just north of Slough but which was now buried beneath a mountain of sweetie papers. We didn't stand a chance. As we lunged hopelessly towards the Quaver packets, Clemmie retched and projected into Josie's – bless her – gallantly cupped hands. Having caught most of it, Josie then turned and threw it through what she thought was an open window, but sadly, wasn't. It was for this reason that at least two of the occupants of the back seat were now emerging from the car looking like a couple of Pizza Hut specials.

As we shuffled sheepishly up the front drive, the door swung back and there stood the Williams family; first (as always, to bag the best bedrooms), clean and tidy (naturally), and refreshed by a sensible overnight stay in York. Huge smiles of greeting were stamped on their well-scrubbed faces, but those smiles froze as they took in the Hamiltons. Then they dropped them altogether.

'Heavens, look at the state of you all!' gasped Penny. 'What happened?'

'I should have thought that was perfectly obvious to anyone with eyes and more particularly nostrils,' I snapped.

'Clemmie was sick,' said David patiently.

'But why didn't you stop?' she asked as Piers

disappeared hurriedly down the hall, wrinkling his nose in horror.

'We thought it was more fun not to,' I said.

'No!'

'No, Penny, there wasn't time,' I said slowly. 'Otherwise, believe me, we would have done. She didn't give us any warning.'

'Well don't just stand there on the doorstep,' she said bossily, 'for goodness sake come in and get out of those clothes.'

The only reason we were standing on the doorstep, I thought gritting my teeth, was because she was barring the way into the house. We followed her in.

'In here, Clemmie – no, not in the drawing room, in the *kitchen*, child,' she shrieked, dragging poor Clemmie down the hall. 'We don't want it all over the carpet, do we? Now, strip off and then it's upstairs for a bath.'

She began with ruthless efficiency to strip Clemmie down to her pants. I sighed. I had to admit that Penny was the first one to give hands-on practical help while Piers was the first to disappear, but her no-nonsense manner always had the effect of reducing my children to tears. I could see Clemmie welling up even now.

Josie saw too and took Clemmie's hand. 'It's OK, Penny. I've got to go and have a bath too, so I'll take Clemmie with me and we'll get in together.'

I gave Josie a grateful smile as she led a sniffing Clemmie gently away.

Penny turned to me. 'Is that your nanny?' she hissed.

'Yes, why?'

'Did I *say* she could call me Penny?'

I groaned. 'Oh, for God's sake, Penny, she calls me Tess, d'you really want to be Mrs Williams all holiday?'

'Well, she might at least *ask*. It's a bit rich just to *assume* isn't it?' She bustled off down the hall. 'Anyway, let's go and get Clemmie some of Leonora's pyjamas, then at least you don't have to unpack.'

I followed her upstairs to the landing, watching as she rifled busily through the airing cupboard. She was just as buxom as she'd always been, but now in a much more matronly way. Her bust no longer rollicked happily around in low-cut blouses, popping out at the slightest provocation, but was strapped firmly into what surely must be a feat of engineering, so that it now resembled a large and sturdy shelf. You felt you could almost use it as a sort of bar, to lean on and chat to her, balance your drink on even, and still not be too rudely close to her face. Her blonde hair was cut to her shoulders now and neatly tied back in a band. The good-time girl with the big tits and long blonde hair was nowhere to be seen. And that was exactly the way Penny wanted it.

Since her introduction to Piers Williams six years ago, Penny had undergone a complete and miraculous personality and image transformation. So successful had it been that Piers – who came from a rather grand and pompous Gloucestershire family – had confided to me at their wedding reception that he was so terribly thrilled to have found such a fresh young gel like Penny, who for this day and age was so remarkably unspoilt and who had no – *ahem* – reputation to speak of – 'if you know what I mean, Tess.'

When I'd finally wiped my mouthful of champagne off his tie and taken my olive out of his top pocket, I nodded furiously, agreeing wholeheartedly that Penny was of course the most unspoilt girl I knew.

'So fresh,' he murmured.

'Couldn't be fresher,' I muttered back, thinking, blimey, so blinking fresh you had to literally tie her down, hold her back, because at the slightest opportunity Penny would *go*. With anyone really – doctors, dentists, builders, merchant bankers, merchant seamen, toy-boys, sugar daddies – I'll say this for her, she had no prejudices and no age limits; if it had a pulse it would do nicely and she just *went*. VROOM! In bedrooms at parties, in ploughed fields behind the wedding marquee with the best man, or the groom – or both – in the back of taxis, in the front of taxis . . . Given a man and an opportunity Penny was in there, rutting away as if her life depended on it.

Now quite how this had bypassed Piers I've no idea since most of London was acquainted with it – let's face it, most of London was acquainted with *her* – but blissfully ignorant he remained, which was all very well for Penny, but jolly taxing for the rest of us. This huge deception was an absolute minefield, and I was forever forgetting and saying things like – 'Oh come on, Penny, you *must* remember Charles, you went *out* with him!'

Penny would look at me sharply, glance quickly at Piers slumbering quietly over his brief, then stare thoughtfully into space, wrinkling her brow as if she were trying to remember.

'Oh y-e-s, Charles,' she'd muse eventually. 'I did once, didn't I – to the cinema, I think.' She'd glare at me through the frozen smile. 'Just a date.'

She was very keen on this 'date' word, conjuring up, as it did, a vision of a fifties-style Penny in a white cardy and gloves swinging her Etam handbag outside the Odeon, pecking her 'date' chastely on the cheek, whereas in truth she'd probably had her mini-skirt up round her ears, swinging her bra round her head whilst she sat firmly astride some bemused bog-brush salesman, joyously riding for England in the back of his Ford Capri.

Occasionally Piers would look up, frown and grunt something like, 'You went on an awful lot of dates, didn't you, darling?'

To which Penny would smile sweetly, lean across and murmur, 'An awful lot of boys were after me, darling,' at which point Hugo would leave the room, ramming two fingers down his throat in mock puke.

I looked at her now in her navy-blue skirt, Laura Ashley piecrust shirt, pearl earrings and velvet hairband with her nose in the airing cupboard, exuding not sex, but efficiency. It was a shame really. I actually much preferred the good-time girl who frolicked in the fields and was far less up-tight and inhibited, but then it was her marriage bed and she had to lie in it. Occasionally, especially on holiday, Penny would have a few drinks and let the mask slip and we'd have quite a laugh, because actually, when she wasn't being a pain in the tubes, Penny could be really good fun. I couldn't see much signs of a slipped mask right now, but as David had pointed out, we had three weeks to get through yet and it was crucial we at least started the holiday on the right foot even if we were at each other's throats by the end of it.

She handed me a pair of pyjamas. 'Here, these should fit her.'

I smiled. 'Thanks. Hey, sorry, Penny, I haven't even said hello properly yet. How are you anyway?' I gave her a hug. She instantly thawed and hugged me back.

'God, sorry Tess, I'm such an old bag I haven't given you a kiss either. I'm fine. A bit tired – I feel as though I've been preparing for this holiday for months now – freezing food and God knows what – but I'm bearing up. Have to, really. Piers hates whingers.'

I followed her back downstairs. 'It's all very well, but he'd whinge if he had to look after a four-year-old all day. These men don't realise how knackering children are.' I said this charitably, secretly thinking what a doddle it must be to have only the one – and Perfect Child at that. 'How is Leonora, by the way? I haven't seen her yet.'

'Oh she's fine, she's asleep.' Penny glowed. 'D'you know, she can count to a hundred already *and* write her full name and address and she's only just four, isn't that amazing?'

'Amazing,' I muttered, following her dispiritedly into the drawing room.

I flopped down into the huge armchair which was still exploding its usual quota of springs and stuffing, put my head back and gazed around. Suddenly I felt much better. Nothing had changed. I smiled.

It was a large room by any standards but the amount of furniture crammed into it was enough to make Crystal Palace seem snug. The two beaten-up old sofas were still either side of the fireplace, a couple of tatty leather armchairs were wedged in between, at least six hard wooden chairs were scattered elsewhere, and any surplus floor space was taken up by various coffee tables. The red threadbare carpet was thinner than ever, as were the rugs that covered the odd hole or stain that was really too disgusting to contemplate clearing up so was better covered. Above the fireplace hung the nondescript watercolour landscape with its unnaturally blue loch in the foreground and outrageously purple mountains behind, and around the other walls – in dire need, incidentally, of their five-yearly slap of magnolia – were those terrible drawings of salmon in various stages of gutting that Daddy had been conned into buying by some local artist years ago.

Down one entire side of the room was a waist-high bookcase, which was doing its usual melodramatic groan under the pressure of an eclectic half-hundredweight of books, all of which had been shoved in totally randomly, so that *Black Beauty* stood next to *Ulysses* which stood next to *A Cricket Pro's Lot* on top of which lay *The Secret Garden*. Just the other side of the room by the window, the huge mahogany cupboard was doing a competitive groan, creaking as it did with its boxes of Monopoly, Trivial Pursuit, Pick-up Sticks, Cribbage, Scrabble, jigsaws – most of which had at least one piece missing – and any number of table tennis bats, tennis rackets and balls. I sighed happily. It was, as David had said, relaxing in its timelessness, its dear familiarity.

At the far end of the room, opposite the fireplace, was a huge bay window with a window seat where Penny, Laura and I, years ago, had sat huddled for hours, clasping our knees, dreaming, plotting, arguing, laughing, and where our children now sat and did the same. The tatty chintz curtains still hung on a rusty rail around the bay. They were never pulled in case the rail collapsed – or the whole window, come to that – but then again, you'd never want to. Because the view from that window was breathtaking. Even now it dragged me up, tired as I was, from the armchair and pulled me across the room.

I rested my hands on the sill and gazed out. The lawn swept down from the house to the woods at the bottom, which in summer screened off most of the river. Just now and again though, you'd catch a glimpse of light, a bluey-grey flash of water. Rising up from the river on the other side was a steep bank, some fields, and then beyond that, the mountains. The light was fading fast now, but I could still make out the faint purple glow of the heather. I threw open the window and breathed deep.

'Aaah . . . that's better.' I turned and smiled at Penny. 'Still does the trick, doesn't it?'

'I'll say,' she said, wandering over, 'although these help too, of course.' She stood next to me and lit a cigarette.

I grinned. Piers was vehemently anti and had no idea his wife still smoked about ten cigarettes a day, another of Penny's little deceptions that gave one an idea of the state of Piers' brain cells and, incidentally, another bloody minefield. Penny was forever hastily handing lit cigarettes over as Piers walked in the room and then one had to go through a ghastly charade of: 'Oh – you mean this, Piers? Yes I had given up but I do have the odd one just now

70

and then . . . yes, very silly I know . . . yes I know Penny's given up, isn't she marvellous?'

Piers obviously wasn't around right now because she was puffing away beside me like Thomas the Tank. I looked around.

'Where is everyone anyway? It's like the *Marie Celeste*.'

'They're all down at the river. First day enthusiasm – they'll probably still be fishing at midnight. Piers and David slipped down to meet the others when you arrived, they took Hugo with them for a breath of fresh air.'

'So who's here then, Mum and Dad?'

'Yep, and Laura and her new man.' She rolled her eyes expressively.

'She brought him – Edward?'

'She certainly did,' Penny said drily.

'Ah.'This didn't sound promising. 'So um, what d'you think?'

Penny tapped her cigarette ash out of the window. 'Well he's all right if you like white mice, I suppose. I mean, God – all I said was "Hello, you must be Edward", and he stepped back into the fire in fright. We had to spend the next five minutes stamping the carpet out. Where does she *find* these wet blankets, Tess?'

My heart sank. I had hoped that this one might perform just a little better than Gormless Martin had last year. 'I don't know,' I admitted. 'I really don't. Still,' I rallied, loyally, 'he might improve. It's only the first day and he's probably just a bit shy.'

'Don't give me that, Tess. You know damn well your sister's got extraordinary taste in men.'

'And your parents?' I went on, swiftly changing the subject. 'Are they here yet?'

'Sadly not,' she said in a small voice.

I looked at her quickly. 'What d'you mean? They are coming, aren't they?'

She shook her head, her eyes suddenly full of water.

'Not this year, I'm afraid. Daddy's taken a turn for the worse.'

She gulped and I threw my arms round her, hugging her hard. My own eyes welled up. I felt terribly, terribly sad. Penny's father, my darling Uncle Robert, had been in remission from cancer for some time. He'd battled against it for fifteen years now, when at the time they'd said he'd be dead in two. But he and Rachel had never given up.

'Is he in hospital?' I whispered.

'No. You know Daddy, he wouldn't hear of it. He's at home.' She blew her nose and laughed shakily. 'Mummy says he's even talking about getting over this little hiccup and joining us for the last week.'

'Well, there you are then!'

Penny blew her nose again noisily and shook her head. 'No,' she said quietly, stuffing her hanky up her sleeve. 'Mummy thinks this is really it now. But it could still be a few months, so they made me come up here. I'd much rather be with them, but for Leonora's sake . . .'

'Of course,' I said staunchly. 'You had to come, and if anything happens – I mean, if he gets worse – they'll ring, won't they?'

She nodded. 'And I'll fly back. I made Mummy promise she'd let me know the moment—' Her face suddenly crumpled. 'Oh God, Tess,' she gasped, 'I'll miss him so much!'

I clutched her close, as she fell into my arms, tears streaming down my face now. So would I. Oh so would I. Lovely, dear, kind Uncle Robert, with his mild manner and gentle ways, who always thought the best of anyone and would never hear the bad. Suddenly I felt frightened. I didn't like change. I wanted everything and everyone to stay just as they were, as they'd always been, like this house. It wouldn't be the same without Robert in it, hearing his voice as he helped Rachel wash up in the kitchen, or mended Hugo's bicycle in the hall. A quiet presence, so unlike my own father who couldn't enter a room without shouting, was preternaturally suspicious and generally thought the worst of everyone until proved otherwise. I jumped suddenly as his voice reached us through the open window. I looked over Penny's shoulder towards the river. I couldn't see anyone, but could hear Daddy's unmistakable tones rising above my son's wails. As I listened it took me sailing back. It could have been me, twenty-five years ago.

'Oh, for heaven's sake, Hugo, it's only a drop of water. Don't be such a ninny! If you're going to cry every time you get your feet wet there's no point in *having* a holiday by a river, is there? You might just as well stay in London!'

Out of the bushes emerged David, carrying a very soggy, tearful Hugo, followed by my father, hectoring away at him from behind.

'Now for goodness sake, brace up!'

I gave Penny a watery smile. 'Well some things never change, do they?'

Chapter Six

Supper that evening was the usual rowdy first night affair. We were down to eight without Robert and Rachel, but still managed to make as much noise and get through the usual staggering quota of Bulgarian Red. Piers brayed and roared and my father thumped the table for random emphasis as they both argued long and hard with David; two arch Conservatives against one rather lapsed, but essentially still socially conscious woolly Liberal.

'But it doesn't state anywhere that He didn't want women to become priests, does it?' persisted David.

'Of course it bloody doesn't!' exploded my father, 'because God never thought in a million years it would blinking well happen! Just as He didn't think it was worth jotting down that perverts can't become priests, or hamsters. I mean, some things just aren't worth wasting the parchment over. Some things you just take for granted! It never occurred to the Almighty that some idiot might one day think ordaining women was a *good* idea, otherwise He'd have put a clause in every bloody Scripture!'

David frowned over his glass. 'It's not the competition that worries you, is it, Ian?' he asked wickedly.

My father had unfortunately just taken a gulp of wine and couldn't answer this for seizing up with an outraged coughing fit.

Piers took up the mantle. 'OK David,' he demanded, 'how would you have felt about being married by a woman? Would that have bothered you?'

'Not in the slightest. In fact Clemmie was jolly nearly christened by a Deaconess in Putney but Ian felt so strongly about it we didn't do it in the end.'

'I'd rather she rotted in hell!' roared the Reverend, regaining his vocal cords and wiping wine off his chin with his napkin. He slapped the table. 'No grandchild of mine is going to be brought into the Christian faith by some jumped-up know-it-all female, because as far as I'm concerned, if she had, she'd still be a bloody heathen!'

Laura and I broke off our weighty debate on the pros and cons of Donna Karan's expensive, but effective, tummy-firming tights to raise our eyebrows at each other. Here we go again. Of course it was all academic because Clemmie was a heathen anyway. I glanced quickly round the table. Penny and Mummy were comparing carrot-cake recipes, Josie had retired early to bed, so that just left Edward who, with no one to talk to, had forged through his plate of roast lamb and was now trying to make a piece of broccoli last the ten minutes it would take everyone else to catch up.

I studied him surreptitiously under my fringe. I'd met him a couple of times before, once when he'd been to our house for a drink before going out to dinner with Laura and once when we'd all been to see a film, but the first time was brief and the second dark, so I'd never really had a chance to scrutinise him properly. He was blinking nervously behind his glasses, his rather sweet, boyish face pale beneath his freckles, his sandy hair flopping over one eye. God, he didn't look much older than Hugo and about a quarter as confident. I rifled around desperately for something to say. I'd already asked him if he enjoyed fishing, to which he'd blushed and replied he'd never done it before in his life, which of course put him at an immediate disadvantage since the rest of us had been flicking out straight lines with Farex on our trousers, and there's nothing quite so unsexy as a fumbling novice trying desperately to hoick his fly out of the gorse bush and then slapping it – *plop* – into the water followed by reams and reams of line flapping around like knitting wool. He caught my eye. I smiled warmly. He palpitated a bit behind the specs and smiled back. I smiled again. He smiled back. God, *say* something, Tess.

'Edward reminds me rather of Peter, that chap at the Chandlery, don't you think, Laura?' I said desperately.

Laura peered at her boyfriend as if she'd never seen him before in her life.

'No.'

'Oh come on, imagine him without the glasses.'

She peered again. Edward blushed and adjusted his glasses apologetically, as if he'd like nothing more than to smash them right there and then in order to look like Peter from the Chandlery. Anything to accommodate.

'No, nothing like.'

'Peter who?' demanded Penny, never letting mantalk pass her by.

'Peter who works at the Chandlery,' I explained patiently. 'I was just saying Edward looks a bit like him.'

Penny frowned at Edward. 'He's nothing like him. Honestly, Tess, you do talk rubbish. That chap's really tall and dark whereas Edward here's really—'

'No, not *that* one,' I said quickly, 'the other one, he works there on a Saturday. He's blondish with blue eyes and—'

'Oh, I know the one you mean,' said Laura suddenly. 'Yes, you *are* rather like him, Edward, around the eyes.' Edward inclined his head graciously, turning all the colours of a tropical sunset now, but clearly delighted Laura was reasonably pleased. 'Yes, he's got the same sort of thin hair as you. Penny, you must remember,

77

you told us he's only got one—'

'More potatoes, Edward?' I said loudly, piling them on his plate and eyeing Laura sternly.

'One what?' asked Piers.

'Finger,' I said quickly. Laura had been about to say ball and I had the feeling Piers would want to know how Penny came by such classified information.

'Only one finger?' said Piers in surprise. Laura giggled. We spoke together.

'Frostbite.'

'Bacon-slicer.'

'Er, yes,' I went on. 'He was a very keen mountaineer and his fingers all got frostbite. They didn't actually drop off but they went a bit stiff and because they were so stiff he accidentally cut them off in the bacon-slicer.'

Piers stared. 'What was he doing with a bacon-slicer?'

'He worked in a butcher's.'

'Good grief. Sounds an odd sort of cove. Did you know this chap, Penny?'

'Not remotely,' Penny growled, looking thunderous. Laura was spluttering into her napkin.

'Plenty more veg, Edward. Here, have some broccoli.' I beamed at what I could see of him behind the huge heap of vegetables I'd piled on his plate.

'Now tell me,' I went on brightly, 'what sort of a school d'you teach at, Edward? Is it one of those rather enlightened ones where you don't have to go to lessons if you don't want to, you just wander off and pick wild flowers and take recreational drugs?'

'Er, no I'm afraid it's a bit more structured than that.'

'Well, I should think from your point of view that's just as well. Imagine trying to round everyone up and detoxify them and—'

'I think I should like to have it off,' interrupted my mother abruptly.

We all looked at her, stunned.

'Mummy!' I gasped.

'I think if it were me, I'd like it off. The finger. So untidy, dangling like that.'

'Don't be silly, Daphne,' said my father. 'Much better to have one than none at all. I'm sure it was very useful, wasn't it, Penny? Who was this chappie, a boyfriend or something?'

Penny couldn't speak but she looked positively murderous now. Laura was crying into her wine as David quietly suggested all the ways in which it might be of use – hailing cabs, bidding at auctions, picking one's nose . . .

'Shut up, you two,' I said quickly. 'I'm asking Edward about his teaching.'

'He's at a comprehensive,' said my father, waving a fork in his general direction. 'I've already asked him,' he added as if Edward wasn't really with us. 'Can't get much out of him but I imagine it's one of those ghastly inner-city ones. Chap's probably a Communist or something, eh Laura?'

He turned to Laura for verification. She stopped spluttering and took a sip of wine. There was a silence. She blushed, as we'd both blushed for my father's blatant rudeness over the years. 'No, he's not,' she said shortly.

'But you're right, it is an inner-city school,' said Edward, rather bravely. 'It's in Tottenham.'

'Tottenham?' enquired my mother. 'And are you a fan?'

'Sorry?'

'Spurs – d'you support them?'

'Er, no.' Edward looked bewildered.

'Good. Bloody cad's game,' said my father. 'Well, that's one point in his favour, eh?'

'But I do support Sheffield Wednesday,' he added, even more bravely.

'Do you indeed?' purred my mother, as if he'd just

said he had £300,000 a year and an estate in Gloucestershire. She gave him a twinkly smile. 'Good for you, Edward.'

My father hurumphed. Piers was peering at Edward as if he'd only just noticed him.

'Is that where your people are?' he asked abruptly.

Edward jumped. 'My . . . people?' He had a dazed look on his face, wondering perhaps if Piers had somehow mistaken him for Big Chief Running Bull who'd left his people behind at the wigwam camp.

'Your family,' put in David kindly. 'Are they from Sheffield?'

'Oh! No, Streatham, mainly.'

'Really?' Piers raised his eyebrows incredulously then inclined his head, mouth twitching. 'Well, I suppose someone has to be,' he murmured.

'Teaching must be jolly hard work,' I went on, shooting Piers a venomous look and really, rather hating my family.

'Oh, er, it has its moments.'

'You must have to have infinite patience,' agreed David, helping me out. 'I'm sure I couldn't do it. I'd lose my rag with those kids in no time at all.'

'Actually you'd be brilliant,' I said, flashing him a grateful look. 'Remember when you wanted to teach? You were going to be a don.'

'That's a lot grander than teaching at a comprehensive,' said Edward, wildly turning his hand to a conversation.

'It may be grander but I should think it's a darn sight easier to teach a few nineteen-year-olds who are eager to learn than twenty rowdy fifteen-year-olds who haven't the slightest interest in anything other than skiving off school and playing football. I take my hat off to you, Edward. I imagine it's damned difficult.'

Edward began to glow under this sudden paean of

praise for his chosen career, and even Laura began to look at him with renewed interest. 'Oh well,' he shrugged modestly, 'it's not too bad.'

'What exactly is it you specialise in?' I asked.

'Art.' He blushed some more. 'I teach art.'

'Really? Laura, you never said!' Laura shrugged, as if surprised it would be of any interest to anyone. 'Did you bring your paints with you? There's some fabulous scenery round here, you know.'

'I did, actually. I was hoping I might find time to do some sketching. Maybe even a few watercolours.'

'Ah well, Tess can show you all the best places for that, can't you, Tess?' said Penny slyly. 'All the etching hot spots?'

'Come on, Penny,' said David sharply. 'Get that port moving or we'll be here all night.'

'I shan't be,' said my mother, declining the port and dabbing her mouth with her napkin. 'I'm going to bed. I've got a lot to do tomorrow, especially if I'm going to find time to call on Madelaine Cameron.' She fumbled around on the floor for her handbag.

'Madelaine Cameron?' I said quickly. I looked at my father who'd gone a bit pale. 'Patrick's mother?'

'Yes,' she said, vaguely searching through the bag. 'Now her dreadful husband's died I thought I'd pop up and see her. Offer my condolences and all that. Now where did I put my reading glasses?' She began patting her cardigan pockets.

I could feel my colour rising. 'But why, Mum?'

'You'll do nothing of the sort, Daphne,' commanded my father suddenly. 'Leave well alone!'

'I certainly shall not,' she said quietly. 'Ah – here they are.' She reached into her skirt pocket, fished out her spectacles and made to leave the table. She smiled at the assembled company. 'Night, all.'

'I didn't know you knew her that well,' I blurted, aware

that quite a few eyes, including David's, were on me.

'Oh yes, very well. We were good friends years ago, when she married that ghastly man, but we lost touch. Madelaine's a very nice woman. I shall ask her to tea next week.'

Daddy went puce. 'Daphne, I absolutely forbid it!'

'Oh, but it's undoubtedly the Christian thing to do, darling,' she said quietly, 'now that the poor woman's all alone.'

Daddy looked thunderous. 'She's *not* alone. She's got that wretched boy with her!'

'Ah, but not for long. I gather he's going back to Italy in a couple of weeks. He's become quite a successful artist over there, apparently. Has quite a following. There now, I think I've got everything. See you in the morning, and don't forget to turn the dishwasher on, will you, Penny dear?' She beamed at her niece.

'But Mummy,' I persisted, putting my hand on her arm as she made to leave the room, 'you can't just run up the hill and be her best friend after all these years!'

'Why not?' she said mildly.

'Because it'll look so . . . odd.'

My mother patted my hand. 'Not at all, dear. I think it's entirely natural to pay one's respects to one's old friends. It would look most odd if I didn't go. Now I'll hear no more about it from anyone, thank you!' And with that she removed my hand from her arm, gave her husband a pointed look and left the room.

A silence fell on the table as she went. Neither Patrick, nor his parents, had been mentioned for years in our family. Even my father was strangely quiet. I caught his eye, and he raised his eyebrows sheepishly. For once we were in agreement; we both knew there was no arguing with her when she was in this sort of mood.

Penny cleared her throat. 'Right, well I'm off too,' she said, getting up and clearing the plates. 'I'm knackered and I need an early night.'

I followed her out to the kitchen, bringing the rest of the plates with me.

'I'll do this, Penny,' I offered. 'You go to bed.'

'Sure?'

'Positive.'

She sighed. 'OK, thanks. I'm bushed, actually. I'll see you in the morning.'

When she'd gone I stacked the dirty plates in a pile by the dishwasher, and was about to put them in when I stopped and stared at them. Suddenly my eyes welled up, and for no reason at all except – oh God, everything really – I found I was fighting back tears. I took a deep breath and gazed out of the window into the dark night, biting my lip. Why did Mum have to go and stir everything up after all these years? To stir me up, more to the point. It was *my* past, the precious little there was of it, why couldn't she leave it alone? If she went to Gilduncan, Madelaine would undoubtedly come here and there was more than a chance I'd bang into Patrick. I'd certainly hear about him, for God's sake. And I didn't want to. Suddenly I felt afraid. I wanted to be back in Putney, tucking my children up in their own beds, to feel safe, secure. I didn't feel safe here. I felt as if someone was rattling my cage. Shaking my nest.

I picked up a plate and scraped it. Slowly I put them one by one in the dishwasher, trying not to think about what Mum had said. Just those few words had been enough to unsettle me. 'He's become quite a successful artist. Has quite a following.' I straightened up and gazed out of the window. So he wasn't an accountant after all. I tried not to, but I wondered what his studio was like. In Florence, overlooking a square perhaps, one of those beautiful old, crumbling, terracotta buildings. High up, I saw Patrick hanging over the balcony, laughing, talking to someone below. It was a huge balcony full of sunlight and trailing bougainvillaea. Behind there were sunny, light rooms, full of friends, laughter, parties, flowing Chianti, pretty girls with long dark hair.

I crouched down and fished around under the sink for the dishwasher powder. The top came off in my hand and some spilled on the floor. Bugger. Still crouching, I stretched my hand up for a dishcloth in the sink and without looking, grabbed it, but the last person to use it hadn't washed it out and it was still covered in Clemmie's sick. I dropped it in disgust then tossed it into the bin. I got a new one out from under the sink, wiped the floor and tossed it back into the sink, not bothering to rinse it myself. I stared at it, lying there covered in dishwasher powder. And this was my lot, I thought, pursing my lips. This was the annual holiday I'd been so looking forward to. The absolute pinnacle of my year, my only release from the tedious routine of everyday life. Three weeks in Scotland with my bickering family who didn't even have the grace to make poor Edward feel welcome. Three weeks with Piers and his arrogant supercilious comments, with my father and his bombastic bullying ways, with Laura already abdicating all responsibility for her new man and hiding behind her silly giggles, Penny with her sly remarks, and now Mummy . . .

I shut the dishwasher door and turned it on. My mother. Most of the time so henpecked and browbeaten but just occasionally, like tonight, a complete law unto herself. An unguided missile that no one, not even my father, could stop. What was she up to? I heaved a great sigh. I for one had no idea. Oh well, only another twenty or so evenings like tonight to go. I bit my lip. Normally I looked forward to this holiday so much . . .

I shook my head as if to physically banish all rogue thoughts. The kitchen was tidy; I could go upstairs now – should go upstairs – but somehow I didn't feel like going to bed yet. Perhaps I could do with some fresh air? I walked slowly to the back door and hesitated. Who was I trying to kid? I knew I wanted to walk by the river in the dark, I also knew exactly where I wanted to go. And I knew why. To reminisce. I took my hand off the handle. No. That really would be madness. I turned back, and was about to switch off the lights and go upstairs when I spotted some ashtrays that needed emptying. I chucked the butts in the bin and took them to the sink, pausing as I did so to stare out of the window at the inky black sky. Perhaps just for a moment. Not right down to the river, just in the garden, and maybe as far as the woods. I quickly rinsed the last ashtray and turned off the tap. Suddenly I felt hands on my waist.

'Shit!' I jumped and dropped the ashtray in the sink. 'David, don't sneak up on me like that!'

'Sorry.' He looked surprised. 'I wasn't sneaking, I just came to find you. Everyone else has gone to bed. What are you doing down here on your own?'

'What does it look like?' I snapped. 'I'm clearing up. Someone has to, it doesn't happen by magic, you know.'

'Well, come on, you've done it now.' He took the ashtray from me, seized a tea towel and dried it. 'Let's go to bed, it's gone midnight.'

'I will in a minute, I just want to wipe this floor. The children brought mud in from the river; it's filthy already – look.' I grabbed a cloth and bent down to wipe it, hiding my face.

'Josie can do that in the morning, can't she?' David put his arms round my waist and pulled me up from behind. He nuzzled into my hair. 'Come on,' he muttered. 'Put the damn dishcloth down and come to bed. We're supposed to be on holiday.'

I pulled my head away roughly. 'Oh, for heaven's sake, David – is that all you ever think about? Sex?'

He dropped his hands from my waist. I turned my

head guiltily and saw his face. He raised his eyebrows, picking up an ancient copy of the *Spectator* from the table.

'Good Lord no,' he said lightly, 'hardly ever. How silly of me, I'd quite forgotten I'd had my quota for this month. I shan't be troubling you again until – oooh, the middle of September, or is that too soon?'

He tucked the *Spectator* under his arm and wandered out, but his back was rigid.

I groaned. 'Oh God, David, I'm sorry. I didn't mean to say that.'

He carried on walking.

'David!'

But he didn't turn back and I didn't go after him. I whirled round to the sink and threw in the dishcloth. Shit. Shit-shit-SHIT! I heard him going upstairs, then his footsteps on the landing above me. A door closed. I stared blankly at some aubergines on the chopping board. Someone had got them out and left them there to make into ratatouille in the morning. Suddenly I seized a large knife from the metallic rack and plunged it into the middle of one. Then I started hacking. I hack-hack-hacked away, spitting and snarling and cursing, until the whole work surface and most of the floor was covered in little bits of aubergine flesh. When I'd finished I felt a lot better. I threw the sad remains guiltily into the bin, wondering if I could blame the cat. Probably not. As I turned the lights off and went upstairs, I decided that if anyone asked, I'd just say I'd felt a bit peckish in the night.

Chapter Seven

Days passed and the holiday settled into its predictable routine. We fished, we ate, we fished some more, we ate some more, we played Scrabble and cards round the fire, we chatted, we went to bed. There was nowhere to go apart from the river or the beach, no television to watch and no dinner parties to attend. It was the perfect antidote to London life, and gradually our brittle urban nerves were soothed and softened as day after day we did little other than gaze into the dear familiar waters of the river Tarn and feel the warm breeze in our faces. We let the world slip by and we learned to relax. At least, most of us did.

For some reason I still felt restless. I felt as if I'd been doing all this for a thousand years and would still be doing it in a thousand years' time. I had a huge sense of here-we-go-again which irritated me because I'd been looking forward to this break. I did quite a lot of sighing and flopping down into chairs, was 'snappy' according to my husband and 'always in a strop' according to my children. Everything seemed to be such a huge effort, and all rather pointless. All that shopping in Invertarn for instance, heaving great bags of groceries home – and then all that cooking – and for what? Just so they could blinking well eat it! And all that washing and ironing and trekking down to the clothes line at the bottom of the garden with basketfuls of wet clothes – and again, for what? So they could wade in the river and frigging well make them dirty again!

When I expressed this sentiment to David, admittedly with a rather wild look in my eye on account of my third pre-dinner sherry, he regarded me over his *Times*, and murmured something about life being like that, really.

'Well perhaps I don't want it to be,' I snapped.

He gave me an odd sort of look and after that I learned to keep my own counsel. I went for a lot of walks and tried not to think too much. When I did think, I attempted to analyse my dissatisfaction and realised the problem was that I felt my life was marching on in a rather monotonous sort of manner. This shocked me a bit – heavens the last thing I wanted was a midlife crisis – so I tried to banish that rogue idea, but it would keep popping back. In the end I decided to consider it rationally. I racked my brains. Perhaps my life had always been monotonous and I'd only just noticed it? I rewound my lifespool back, three years, five years, ten. I sighed. No, I was sure that even then, even though I'd never exactly led a merry dance, I had at least pranced a bit, hadn't I? All right, shuffled. Perhaps not enough? Perhaps if I'd pranced and shuffled a bit more I wouldn't feel this bleak forced march so keenly?

My family, wisely, ignored me during these periods of introspection, and made Mummy's-in-one-of-her-moods faces at each other, presumably hoping I'd snap out of it, as indeed I hoped I would too.

There were other irritations too. In the space of a year Leonora's vocabulary had gone from strength to strength and now included words like *croissant* and *Wiener schnitzel*.

'I knew she'd be speaking French but I didn't expect her to have German under her belt too,' I hissed in a paranoid fashion to David.

In the face of such fierce precociousness, my children instantly dug their heels in, went on strike and reverted to babbling babyhood, so that whilst Leonora was carefully winding spaghetti carbonara onto her fork, doing up all her buttons and saying please-may-I-leave-the-picnic-rug, mine were eating with their fingers, throwing themselves on sweetshop floors and holding their breath until their demands were met, peeing on the bathroom floor and generally acting like Vlad the Impaler.

'Hugo, for God's sake, aim!' I bellowed as I cleared up yet another puddle.

'I did aim,' he informed me. 'I was aiming at Leonora's shoes, but some of it must have leaked out.'

I stared, aghast, at the pair of urine-filled Mary-Jane Startrites, let out a Mohican-style shriek and sent him straight to bed, but nothing I could do or say would make them repent or change their course of action, which was, it transpired, to corrupt Perfect Child.

Hugo, who at eight was deeply anally fixated, would spend hours crouched beside her, furiously trying to teach her to fart, purple in the face from the exertion of demonstrating himself, and doing heaven knows what damage to his own sphincter, but all to no avail. Nature's trumpet would not sound.

'You're not pushing hard enough,' I heard him complain as he monitored her progress. 'I don't think you're even trying.'

'But if I push too hard I'll do a poo,' objected Leonora.

'Even better!' roared my son.

Poor Clemmie didn't fare much better. She wasted the best part of a morning patiently showing her pupil how to go through her mother's make-up bag, put powder on her face and quite a lot on the carpet, try on all the lipsticks and blunt them in the process and smother herself in Chanel No. 5. She then steered her over to Penny's jewellery box, decking her out in all her mother's pearls and losing an earring or two along the way – but Leonora simply refused to learn, and after a while wandered off to read her storybook or cut out paper-chain dollies. She was, it seemed, one of Nature's goody-goodies, a shattering revelation to two of Nature's baddy-baddies. I felt almost sorry for them as they crept into bed with me one morning and told me in shocked, whispered tones, how she didn't even like tomato ketchup, Mummeee, had never had a bag of crisps, didn't have a video and had never even heard of Mrs Goggins. The final straw came when she refused to raid the biscuit tin with them, at which point they gave up in disgust.

'You want to be careful, Penny,' I murmured, as we lay on the riverbank together, feeling the warm sun on our faces and vaguely keeping an eye on my two who were splashing around upstream. 'You'll turn that child into a freak. A social outcast.' I nodded over at Leonora, sitting quietly on her own listening to *Peter and the Wolf* on Hugo's Walkman.

'Nonsense,' snapped Penny. 'I'm teaching her to be an individual, not to slavishly follow the herd, that's all.'

'What does she do at parties then if she doesn't have jelly and ice cream and orange squash? Sit there with half an avocado and a Perrier?'

'She doesn't go to parties yet,' said Penny primly. 'She's only four years old. I'll cross that bridge when I come to it.'

'Doesn't go to parties? Good heavens, she's *already* a social outcast. Clemmie was on the party circuit at eleven months, she's been getting down to Musical Bumps since she could walk!'

'I dare say,' said Penny darkly, 'but then I'm not altogether sure I want a social butterfly for a daughter.'

'Had more of a cardiologist in mind, did you?'

'And why not?' retorted Penny.

'Why not indeed. I'm sure Leonora would make an excellent surgeon, I just can't help thinking if you push children too much they sort of burn themselves out, react against it, know what I mean?'

'Look, Tess, you bring up your children the way you think fit and I'll do the same – and incidentally, I'd be grateful if you'd restrain your son from inflicting his scatological obsessions on my daughter, it's not very—' She broke off in mid-rebuke to stare past me. 'Oh for God's sake look at that. It's pathetic,' she spat.

I sat up and followed her gaze upstream to where her middle-aged husband was teaching Josie and Edward to fish. Ostensibly he'd been teaching them both for the last four days, but in actual fact Edward's tuition had consisted of little more than a few cursory instructions yelled over Piers' shoulder. Josie's tuition, on the other hand, was far more demanding. She needed the full practical. Today her instructor had chosen to stand behind her, arms round her waist, hands gripping hers on the rod as he 'taught her from behind', quite a favoured method of his actually.

'Easy does it now,' we heard him coo as he nestled up close to her, cuddling into her rear. 'Take the rod back . . . gently, gently, and – flick!' The fly came down with a plop in the water followed by reams of tangled line.

'Oh I say, that was awfully good!' brayed Piers.

'Ah sheet! That was terrible!' shrieked Josie, going into peals of laughter.

'No no no! *Au contraire*,' gushed her instructor, 'I think you're definitely getting the wrist action. Now, let's try again, shall we? Only this time . . .' he eagerly clasped her again, legs pressing against her bare brown thighs in their high-cut denim shorts, 'this time, give it a bit more of a – flick!'

The fly came down again, still with a plop, but perhaps not quite so deafening.

'That's it! That's it!' chortled Piers, jumping up and down on the bank, clapping like an overgrown schoolboy.

91

'Absolutely first class!' He gave her a quick congratulatory squeeze round the waist. She shrieked with laughter. He moved in again, perhaps for another playful little hug, but as he did so, he caught the cold eye of his wife further downstream. His hands flinched off Josie's slim young waist as if it were molten lava, and one of them hoisted itself into the air in a nervous wave.

'Hello, darling,' he called.

'Good morning, Piers,' she responded coolly.

He came galloping over with a silly grin on his face, looking distinctly flushed. He flopped down next to us, panting a bit. 'Having a lovely time, my darling? Nice and relaxing?'

'Reasonably relaxing, Piers, but as you can see we do seem to be looking after the children, which wasn't actually the idea since Tess did bring a nanny along for just that purpose.' She smiled thinly. 'But she seems to be otherwise engaged.'

'Ah yes, your nanny!' He turned to me. 'I say, *super* girl, Tess, *super* girl,' he enthused, somehow missing Penny's shovel-load of irony. 'Really – well – *jolly*. So much more fun than that Hungarian shot-putter type you brought last year.'

'Yes, but then the Hungarian shot-putter was frightfully good at other things, like cooking and cleaning and shovelling food in mouths and clearing up sick,' I said sweetly, 'but I do agree, not quite so *jolly*.'

'No, not at all. This new one's a real, well – treasure!' He turned eagerly to his wife. 'You're always banging on about getting some help, aren't you, poppet, and goodness knows, you girlies work so hard you really deserve it. How about asking Josie if she's got any nice friends, hmm?'

'Now don't you worry your head about my domestic arrangements,' purred Penny, patting his hand. 'You leave all that to me. I've got a nice Miss Mason coming back

92

for a second interview when we get home. She's a bit deaf, but sweet, spinsterish. I think you'll like her and after a while you won't even notice her facial warts.'

Piers went a bit green. 'Ah ha ha,' he laughed nervously, scraping back his hair. 'Marvellous, terrific,' he muttered. 'Still, must get on – lots to do. Toodle-oo, my darling!' And he scampered hastily back to his pupil.

'Over my dead body,' said Penny darkly, lying down next to me again. 'Honestly, Tess, you must be mad having that creature in the house. David must walk around with a permanent hard-on.'

I grinned. 'God, you're insecure, Penny. Are you seriously telling me you wouldn't employ a pretty nanny in case Piers fancied her?'

'I certainly wouldn't want Claudia bloody Schiffer mincing down to breakfast in her baby-doll nightie, I can tell you that. I mean, look at her, Tess. A pink vest with no bra on, nipples sticking out like marbles, bottom spilling out of those shorts, it's positively indecent.' She folded her arms behind her head. 'But then I suppose you don't really care any more, do you?'

I frowned and turned my head towards her. 'What d'you mean?'

'Well, you don't really care who David fancies or whether he's frustrated or not. You've lost interest in that side of things, haven't you?'

I sat up, horrified. 'Penny! What on earth makes you say that?'

She shrugged. 'Intuition.' She shaded her eyes against the sun and stared at me. 'It's true, though, isn't it?'

'Of course it's not bloody true,' I spluttered, my eyes darting away from hers. 'David and I have a marvellous sex life, thank you very much.'

'Balls,' scoffed Penny. 'I bet you do it about twice a month, and that's because you feel you have to, just to keep things ticking over.'

'Oh, and I suppose you and Piers are swinging from the rafters every night, are you?'

She considered this. 'No, not every night, but we're still pretty active. Three or four times a week at least.'

'Three or four times a week!' I gasped. 'Good heavens, Penny, what are you on?'

She looked at me sideways. 'Lust. Remember that?'

I threw back my head and laughed hollowly. 'Lust! Crikey, yes, vaguely, somewhere in my dark and distant past. Before I spent my life looking after small children and wiping floors and tables and noses and bottoms and God knows what else. Wasn't it something to do with feeling a strange tingling sensation in your loins which spread all over your body and then doing a lot of panting and not being able to get up the stairs fast enough before you could tear your clothes off?'

'Thought it might ring a bell.'

'Only a very dull and distant one.' I smiled. 'No, Penny, I have to say, lust is fairly low on my list of priorities now. It's quite hard to fit it in between rag-rolling the kitchen, belting off to do the school run and doing battle in Sainsbury's.' I lay down again with a faint smile. So she was still just as keen to get her rooty-tooty, eh? Still got her brain lodged firmly between her legs.

'And you're not planning on experiencing it ever again?'

I looked across at her. 'What?'

'Lust. That's it then, is it? For ever – end of story?'

'Well no,' I blustered. 'We still have sex, we still love each other—'

'Not quite the same though, is it?'

'As what?'

'As it used to be. Bit stale and boring really, isn't it? Bit predictable.'

I stared at her. 'I'm not quite sure I know what you

mean, Penny,' I said carefully.

'Oh, I think you do. But you don't really care. You've written it off. Been there, done that, on to the next thing. Something more grown up, like gardening. Or stencilling. Lust is for adolescents, isn't it?'

'Well, I—'

'You know what you need, don't you, Tess?'

'Penny, I don't know how or why we even embarked on this conversation, but to be honest I really don't want to discuss—'

'You need a damn good affair.'

I sat up and stared at her. 'Oh, don't be ridiculous!' I scoffed.

'Don't pretend it hasn't occurred to you. You blush every time his name is mentioned.'

I blushed obediently. 'Whose name?'

'Patrick's, of course.'

'As usual you're talking total crap,' I muttered.

'Am I?' She sat up next to me. 'Listen, Tess, if you ask me it's just what your marriage needs – a damn good kick in the butt. A bit of extra-curriculum wham-bam would do you the world of good. Let's face it, you've been thinking about him ever since you got here. Why don't you just go and do it, get it out of your system? You'll go back to David feeling amazingly sexy and rejuvenated and so incredibly guilty you'll be plying him with sexual favours, practising all your new techniques. I promise you, he won't know what's got into you but he won't give a damn because he'll think it's so terrific. It'll do you both the world of good.'

I stared at her, fascinated. 'Is that what you do then, Penny, when you're feeling a bit down? When the dusting gets a bit much, or the Hoover breaks down or you've OD'd on pyramid-selling jewellery parties? Go and learn a few new techniques?'

'Oh no,' she smiled smugly. 'I got all that out of my

system long ago. I've had all the men I need; I'm quite satisfied with my husband now. You, on the other hand, have only ever been to bed with two men, haven't you?'

'Oh, for heaven's sake,' I groaned, 'if we're going to start counting conquests we'd better get a ruddy calculator out for you. You're being particularly childish now.'

I shut my eyes, pretending to sleep. I wished she'd be quiet. It was past midday now and the sun was burning. I could feel it hot on my eyelids. I stretched out on the grass and pulled up my skirt, letting it scorch my thighs. I tried not to think about Penny's idiotic ramblings and switched my mind instead to something else, tonight's supper for instance. I wondered if Coronation Chicken might be nice for a change, we hadn't had that yet and there was plenty of cold chicken in the fridge. With a salad.

'Anyway,' she murmured after a while, 'it's not really cheating, is it?'

'What?'

'You've done it with him before so it doesn't count. And you know what actors say – it doesn't count on location either, so there you go, you've escaped on two counts. Added to which, he'll be going back to Italy in a few weeks and you'll be off to London, so you'll never see him again. Perfect!'

I swivelled my head and stared at her. Her eyes were shut; she had a slight smile on her perfectly made-up lips.

'What are you, the devil dressed up as a Wentworth housewife? Talk about stuffing the poisoned apple down my throat!'

She shrugged. 'Just trying to help. Just trying to save your marriage.'

'Penny, there's nothing wrong with my marriage! Just because I'm not salivating behind the front door waiting for David to get home from work so I can wrest his briefcase from his hand, rip open his suit, tear the shirt from his back and savage him on the doormat doesn't mean my blinking marriage is on the rocks!'

'No, not on the rocks, but shallow water I'd say. Sand-banking, perhaps.' She shrugged. 'It's not serious. All you need is to get your eye back on the ball again.' She giggled. 'Get a taste for it again. The problem with you, Tess, is you don't think sex is important. You'd rather be pruning your roses or making a bloody Coronation Chicken or something.'

I blinked. Coronation Chicken . . . Christ, how on earth had she—

'And what you don't realise,' she went on, 'is that those are the incidentals. The fillers-in, the things we're supposed to do to pass the time when we're not making love.'

'Oh, far out Pen, pull up a beanbag, what about giving peace a chance too?'

'Mummy!' Leonora called to her from further along the bank. She was having trouble getting her boots on.

Penny stood up. 'Oh, you can scoff, but you'll see I'm right in the end. You're just papering over the cracks at the moment, but something will give, it's bound to.'

'Oh really? And pray, tell me, when am I supposed to have this tempestuous affair, the one that's going to cement my marriage up like the Great Wall of China? In between making the cheese rolls for lunch and giving the children their bath, perhaps?'

'*Mummy!*'

Penny brushed her skirt off at the back. She smirked. 'Ah, well now you're talking How, and not If, Tess.' She winked. 'I'll leave the logistics to you.' She walked briskly off to help her daughter. 'Coming, darling!'

I stared after her. For a moment I felt a bit dazed, then I shook my head. I smiled. Dear old Penny. Quite the philosopher today, wasn't she? Fancy thinking sex with another man would help my marriage . . . Wasn't that just so typical of her? Who else, I wondered, would come up with a solution like that? As if I even *needed* a solution! There was nothing wrong with my marriage. I was just feeling – well, a bit down, that was all.

I watched as Penny helped Leonora on with her boots. She took her hand, then striding up to where Clemmie and Hugo were fishing with nets, shepherded them both briskly out of the river and sat them all down on a rug to have their lunch. I should have gone over and given her a hand, but somehow, I couldn't face the arguments over who wanted jam and not ham in the sandwiches, and counting who'd had the most biscuits today. Anyway, Josie was around. She could help for a change.

I got up and quietly slunk away in the opposite direction, along the riverbank. I rounded the bend and found a rock to sit on. I drew up my knees and rested my chin on them, smiling to myself as I watched the water rushing past; clear, bright and fast as it hurried over its bed of grey pebbles. Yes, dear old Pen. So naive, so simplistic, so convinced that sex was what made the world go round. She hadn't given a thought to loyalty or love or duty, or honour, or any of those rather more taxing words, but then Penny wasn't one to be taxed unless she had to be, was she? I envied her that in a way. She was a simple creature, at the mercy of her animal instincts. She saw an erotic opportunity and went for it, without considering the repercussions. I threw a pebble in the water and watched the water ring out around it.

What about the lies, the deceit an affair would involve – had she given a thought to that? And then afterwards, the guilt, the regret, the shame. But of course there wouldn't be any of that with Penny, would there? It wouldn't eat away at her afterwards because she had no moral sensibility. But I did. I was – well, I was more complex, I thought smugly, more cerebral if you like, and certainly more moral, and it was because of that that I'd no more have an affair than fly to the moon. I simply couldn't live with myself afterwards.

I pulled up a strand of grass and chewed it. And what about the old marriage vows, eh Pen? Forsaking all others and keeping only unto thee? Good heavens, Penny had never forsaken anyone in her life and she'd kept unto thee, thee and thee as a matter of principle! Before she was married, naturally. I was pretty sure she was telling the truth when she said she didn't indulge now, but as she pointed out, she didn't need to; she'd had her fill. She was full up, as it were.

I frowned and smoothed a bit of rock with my finger, gazing down at the shiny granite. Was there anything in that, I wondered? Was that why I was feeling a bit melancholy these days, because I hadn't indulged myself enough in the past? I stared into the bright water. No, of course not, and I wasn't about to indulge myself now either – and not because I hadn't satiated my appetite in the past like she had but because I didn't *want* to, didn't *need* to have an affair, thank you very much.

Suddenly I flushed. The very idea! Betray my lovely, loyal David, make a cuckold out of him, break my solemn promise, and for what? A quick roll in the hay? And me, a wife, a *mother* no less – what on earth was she thinking of? And she, practically my children's *aunt*, suggesting their mother took a lover! Suddenly I was angry. Angry that she'd even had the nerve to suggest it, had presumed to know what went on in my marriage bed. How dare she? Why had I let her talk to me like that? Instead of laughing it off and thinking 'dear old Pen' I should have told her where to get off, in no uncertain terms. And I would too, I determined, later on tonight. I'd have a quiet word with her in the kitchen, or a noisy one if needs be, and tell her to mind her own bloody business.

It wasn't as if I even *wanted* to go to bed with Patrick Cameron. The whole idea was absurd. I was quite happy going to bed with my own husband, thank you very much.

As if to prove it, I flashed up a quick picture of David and me in bed together, recalling the last time, which would have been – ooh, a couple of weeks ago. Yes, that's right, a Saturday morning while the children were downstairs watching *The Flintstones* and very nice it had been too. A warm glow came over me as I remembered. Hmm, lovely, apart from Clemmie bursting in like that at the last minute and asking me to mend her doll's leg – '*Now* please, Mummy.' Other than that it had been just fine, no complaints whatsoever.

I smiled. I know, just for fun, just for Penny's sake, why not summon up another little snapshot, one of Patrick and me together? Where should we be . . . in a hayloft, perhaps? Would that be rural and tacky enough for her? Lots of tickly straw, was that what she had in mind? We'd both have to be semi-naked, of course, lots of hastily discarded clothing, and I suppose we'd be writhing around a bit, locked in some kind of athletic embrace, skin on skin, bodies hot, wet and – *Wooooosh!* I gasped as a bucketful of adrenaline suddenly shot up the back of my legs. I wobbled and clutched the rock. Crumbs, that had been a bit more than a warm glow, hadn't it? I looked around nervously. Talk about wiping the smile off my face.

I blinked, adjusted my skirt and settled myself on the rock again. Blimey. I wouldn't be trying that again in a hurry . . . or would I? I bit my lip. Perhaps I should take another look, just to make sure I wasn't mistaken, that it hadn't just been my tummy rumbling? My mind needed no further prompting: it fled guiltily, back to the hayloft scene. Ah yes, there was Patrick, lying propped up on one elbow now, his chest bare – I made sure he had his trousers on this time though – and he was smiling down at me, fondly, but not too lecherously. I paused, testing my reactions. OK, Tess? Yes, fine, I was fine, carry on. So – there he was, leaning over me in the hay, pushing a strand of hair out of my eyes, smiling, stroking my face with the back of his hand. His fingers traced slowly down my neck, moving towards my bare shoulder, pausing, slipping downwards, caressing my— God, it was happening again! This time I jumped clean off the rock because as well as all that adrenaline sloshing around I had a tingling sensation in my loins which was spreading to the rest of my body and – heavens, I was *panting*! Any minute now I'd be sticking my tongue out like a dog. I felt hot, flustered and very excited. Unnerved, I sat down abruptly on the grass and listened hard to my body. My heart was thumping away madly now and the dull bell which had rung so faintly recently was suddenly clanging loudly and very persistently indeed. Lust!

Abruptly I swung around and stared at the river. A moorhen was dipping and diving amongst the reeds on the other side. I gazed intently, knowing it was very important to keep that moorhen at the very forefront of my mind. Was it looking for fish, I wondered? Where was its warren, or whatever it was it slept in? What were its mating hab— no! I mean its migratory habits? Gradually my heart stopped pounding and my pulses ceased throbbing. I got unsteadily to my feet.

At *my* age, I thought as I brushed off my skirt. At my age, lust! What was I thinking of? Well, sex, clearly, that's what had done it, but really, after eight years of marriage and two children, it was a little *outré* to get in such a state, wasn't it? I walked on.

Or had I, I wondered after a while. Perhaps the sun had just been a bit much for me . . . It was remarkably warm for the time of year, wasn't it? I felt my forehead –

hot, yes. And I'd had no lunch of course, an empty stomach always made me feel a bit dicky. Silly to think it might have been anything else. And there again Penny's idiotic ramblings hadn't helped much either . . .

As I rounded the next bend I came across the main pool at the top of the river. This was where the real fishermen gathered. Standing on the bank today were my mother, Laura and Willie, son of the old gillie, Hamish, who'd handed over the running of the river to his son a few years ago. Further upstream I spotted Hamish too, a huge, grey-haired old man gazing intently into the river, watching for signs of life. It was Hamish who'd really taught me to fish. Years ago, when Laura and I were children, he'd stood on the bank for hours beside us, watching us cast, quietly instructing us, and whereas my father had always given up with a shout of irritation after we'd tangled our lines for the millionth time, Hamish didn't. He patiently unravelled them and encouraged us to have another go, until eventually we flicked out something resembling a straight line. Although he'd retired now he still came to help out now and again, particularly when us Fergussons were fishing. It was as if he were unable to let the river go, and perhaps my family with it. I crept up quietly and stood behind them. These were serious fishers. I was glad I'd found them; it gave me something to fix on.

I watched Mum and Laura as they stood a few yards apart in the sunshine, even from the back, so alike. The way they stood, one leg resting, the tilt of their heads, both small and yet both so elegant. Mum, with her silver hair pushed up under an old felt hat of Dad's, and Laura, effortlessly stylish in a Barbour but with a baseball hat pulled firmly over her blonde hair, as if to cock a snook at being too green-wellied.

Willie stood next to my mother, looking on approvingly as she cast expertly upstream and let the fly drift down. He towered above both the women, tall, broad and fair. He could only have been in his early thirties, but his face was already weathered by years of working the river, tending the fish, supervising the rods.

'Caught anything?' I whispered.

'Not a sausage,' murmured my mother. 'If you ask me the river's empty although Willie assures me otherwise.' She grinned in his direction.

'Och, there's fish there orright,' he affirmed. 'It's just catching 'em that's the bugger. And this hot weather dinny help much either.' He looked at the sky. 'What we need's a drop o' rain.'

I smiled. Every year since I could remember we'd have this conversation with the gillie and spend the whole of August, when most people were desperate for sun, praying for a drop of rain to swell the river.

'Ah well, if you will work on a spate river, Willie,' I teased.

'I dunno none better,' he retorted, rising to the bait as usual. 'I'd rather work this one than some bloody river where it don't matter what the weather's doing – where's the fun in that?'

'Where indeed,' I agreed, although I secretly thought there might be quite a lot of fun in actually catching a salmon or two now and then. We stood in silence. A dragonfly whirred off in the bulrushes in front of us.

'Children all right?' murmured my mother, after a while.

'Fine. They're with Penny.'

I watched as she cast out again, straight as a die, over to the other bank.

'Mum?'

'Hmmm?'

I kept my eye firmly on her fly. 'Did you ask Madelaine Cameron to tea in the end?'

'Yes – why?'

'Oh, no reason.' I paused, waiting for her to elaborate. She didn't.

'When's she coming?'

'Tomorrow afternoon.'

I watched the fly drift downstream. It got caught in the rushes.

'Damn.' She gave it a tug but it was stuck fast. 'Why, darling?'

'Oh, I just wondered.'

I turned and walked for home.

Chapter Eight

David frowned into his Bran Flakes. 'Tess, I do think at the very least you should check him out. We can't have her tearing around the countryside with any Tom, Dick or Harry.'

'I agree,' said Piers staunchly, stabbing his boiled egg with a soldier.

'David, it's none of our business where Josie goes or who she goes with. She does what she likes in London when she has time off, so what difference does it make up here?'

The men were hurt. Feathers had been ruffled. Josie had met a boy in a pub, a young boy, and by all accounts he was taking her out tonight.

'But a bike boy,' muttered Piers peevishly.

'Vrmmm vrmmm!' I giggled.

'All I'm saying,' said David patiently, 'is that we should meet him first, find out a bit more about him, that's all.'

'Ask him what his intentions are? David, she's your nanny, not your daughter, but I dare say he'll pick her up from here tonight on his Harley-Davidson, you can just flip up his visor and ask him what the devil he thinks he's up to.'

The men flinched at this allusion to the bike, conjuring up as it did visions of youth, freedom, irresponsibility, power throbbing between still-taut thighs, black leather and undoubtedly, more hair.

At that moment, Josie popped her own tumbling

blonde mane round the breakfast-room door and a palpable *frisson* ran through the assembled male company.

'I've dressed the kids, Tess – is there anything else you want me to do? Otherwise I think I'll have a bath.'

At the mention of his goddess, supine and naked in warm water, Piers swooned visibly, swept back his own thinning head of hair and fixed her with mad, lustful eyes.

'No, you go ahead, Josie. I'll clear up here and when you've had your bath perhaps you could give me a hand with the picnic.'

'Sure, no problem.'

'I should think so too,' muttered Penny who was sitting next to me. 'Oh, and Josie . . .' She reached into a Boots carrier bag at her side and handed her a packet. 'On your way up, put these in the upstairs loo, would you?'

Josie stared at them. 'Sure, what are they?'

Penny gave a thin smile. 'Medicated disposable lavatory-seat covers, of course.'

'Penny!' I gasped in horror.

'It's no good looking like that, Tess. You really can't be too careful these days, you know.'

'Oh, for heaven's sake, Penny,' I spluttered, 'we're family!'

'Edward's not, is he,' she hissed, 'and who knows where he's been? Laura has after all had an awful lot of boyfriends and I'm not convinced this one's in the best of health. He does a hell of a lot of scratching and his personal body odour lends itself more to rotting cabbage than— Ah, good morning, Edward. We were just talking about you!'

Edward sidled nervously up to the table scratching his head and dislodging a certain amount of dandruff. It spiralled around in the beam of sunlight coming through the window.

'Morning,' he muttered.

'Morning!' barked Piers and David in unison as a wall of newsprint went up. They didn't like talking at breakfast at the best of times and Edward, in his bobbly Fair-Isle woolly, blinking sheepishly behind his specs wasn't much of a replacement for the fair Josie, it had to be said.

'Good morning, Edward,' I said cheerfully. 'Come and sit down.' I patted a chair beside me.

He slipped in gratefully, smelling, I had to admit, distinctly ripe.

'Now,' I went on, 'there's the usual toast and cereal, or if you can stomach it I made some lumpy porridge earlier. It's over there on the hotplate, but don't feel you have to.'

'Sounds delicious!' He got to his feet eagerly, keen to please, and lunged towards the sideboard where he began to clatter around with bowls and lids.

'Ow!' There was a resounding crash.

'The lid's hot,' I murmured.

'Sorry, dropped it!'

The newsprint didn't flicker for an instant but my mother, nearest the sideboard, slipped out of her chair and got up to give him a hand. She retrieved the lid, put it back and picked up the bowls. Then she took one, filled it with porridge and handed it to him.

'Looking forward to giving you a good thrashing on Saturday, Edward,' she murmured.

Edward leaped as if he'd been stuck in the buttocks with a pin and as he did, the bowl of porridge leaped too, jerking out of his nervous grasp, flying up into the air, somersaulting, then crashing down onto the floor, splattering everywhere.

'Dear dear.' Mummy reached for a cloth.

'What did you say?' he gasped.

'On Saturday. We're playing you at Villa Park in the

League Cup. Don't think you've got a leg to stand on myself.'

I suppressed a giggle as Edward tried to regain his composure. There was porridge on the hotplate, the wall, the window, my mother's shoes, her skirt and all over the floor. At the table, no one even murmured. They might have been a clutch of Trappist monks sworn to silence.

'Oh! Oh yes, right! Er, should be a good game. Gosh, I'm so sorry, Mrs Fergusson. What a mess. Here, let me—' He looked around desperately for another cloth.

'No dear, that's Penny's headscarf.' Mummy quickly seized the square of Gucci silk from his sweaty hand and I felt Penny freeze next to me.

'Here, just take your porridge,' she ordered, 'and eat it while it's hot, there's a good boy. I'll clear this up.' She turned him round by his shoulders like a child and pointed him at his seat, raising her eyebrows at me in despair.

'So Edward,' I began cheerfully as he shuffled in beside me, 'going fishing again today? Looking forward to landing your first salmon?'

He reached forward for the orange juice and emptied the carton into his glass. 'Oh yes, I'd love to,' he said eagerly. 'I'm not sure I'd have the expertise to land it, but – oh!' He peered into the carton. 'Oh I say, I'm awfully sorry, I've taken all the orange juice. Um, would anyone like some – some of mine? Or can I get some more from the kitchen?' His bottom came up once more and hovered over his chair. 'I'll do that then, shall I? I'll just slip out and—'

'Edward, just sit down,' I said exasperated. 'We've all had ours. Now, what about going up to the top pool today, where Laura was yesterday? I'm sure she'll show you where it is. Where is Laura, incidentally?'

'I'm not sure. Actually I was going to ask you.' He blushed.

'Is she up yet?'

'Er . . . to tell you the truth I've no idea.' He blushed some more and spooned away at his porridge.

Oh hell. They clearly weren't even sharing a room now. Had Laura moved out? What was going on?

'She was up early,' muttered Piers from behind the *Telegraph*. 'She's gone fishing with your father.'

'Ah!' exclaimed Edward and I in unison as if we'd hit upon the Holy Grail. 'Oh well,' I went on brightly, 'if she's gone with Dad, how about fishing with me today?'

'Er, well, actually I thought I might take my sketchpad out, do some drawing, if – if that's all right?'

'Marvellous idea,' I said quickly, flooding with relief. 'Lovely day for it.'

Lovely day for sitting on your own having been abandoned by your girlfriend and thrust in the midst of her not particularly friendly family, I thought as I cleared the plates.

As soon as Edward had been dispatched with sandwiches and a flask of coffee like a small boy and the real children organised with buckets and spades to go to the beach with Josie, I hurried off to find Laura. Sure enough, she was at her favourite spot high up at the start of the river. Dad was ten or fifteen yards downstream of her standing right in the middle of the river in his waders. He waved and I waved back. I strode up to my sister.

'Edward's been looking for you.'

'Well, here I am,' she murmured, casting towards the opposite bank. 'He can come and find me, can't he?'

'Oh, that's really friendly, isn't it,' I snapped. '"He can come and find me, can't he." What's the matter with you, Laura? Why are you treating him as if he's got the plague?'

'I told you in London, I've gone off him.'

'Why did you bring him then?' I said, exasperated.

'You always do this, Laura.'

'He wanted to come. Said he'd been looking forward to it. Thought everything would be all right once we got here – once I'd relaxed, as he put it. I knew it wouldn't, I knew it would be worse, but he pleaded, so I let him come.' She calmly drew her line back and cast again.

'So now you've chucked him out of your room?'

'Not at all. I merely suggested he might like to sleep next door.'

'But that's so em*barr*assing for him, Laura. Everyone *knows*. Couldn't you just lie next to him, keep up the pretence?'

'No, I couldn't. I find him physically repulsive. If you must know, I was finding it hard to go to sleep without puking on him.'

'Oh, don't be so melodramatic! You must have fancied him at some stage.'

'I think I must have been drunk.'

'What, permanently? You went out with him for two months, didn't you?'

'Clearly.'

'Clearly what?'

'Clearly I was permanently drunk,' she said lightly.

'Laura, you're being deliberately obtuse. Why do you always *do* this?'

'Do what?'

'This. Bring some poor chap up here and dump him the moment you arrive.'

'I don't *always* do it.'

'Well, you did last year. Remember the cringing chiropodist?'

'He was clinically insane,' she said calmly.

'And before that, Toby with the one eyebrow that went from ear to ear, and Clive the enthusiastic potholer who brought all his kit up thinking the Highlands would be full of holes – oh, and that tubby one, Martin, who laughed before you could even get the joke out, and—'

'Oh, all *right*!' Laura suddenly flung her rod down. 'All *right*, Tess, so I make a mess of my love life. Fine, OK, I admit it – what do you want from me?'

'Nothing, I'm just—'

'Just pointing out my shortcomings in the boyfriend department, my propensity to pick no-hopers, my lack of a proper partner, my inability to find Mr Right – yes, well I know all that, thank you very much, OK?' She glared at me. There were two very bright pink spots in her cheeks.

'Laura,' I said patiently, 'I'm doing nothing of the sort. I'm merely trying—'

'Oh, it's all right for you, isn't it?' she broke in angrily. 'You, who've only ever had two love affairs in your whole life, both of which were the ultimate, both of which were perfect! The first one lodged neatly in your memory for you to look back on fondly and the second one by your side for the rest of your life – well, lucky you! But life's not like that for the rest of us, you know. It's a bloody jungle out there. There are so many predatory bastards trying to lure you back to their lairs it's not true, and while you're tiptoeing past those you get snared by another type, the ones lying low, the ones who've disguised themselves in beards and anoraks, the quiet shy ones who on the surface seem terribly kind and nice but underneath are so horribly weak and insecure they've got even more hang-ups than you have!'

'Oh, come on, Laura, there must be something in between.'

'*Find* me one, Tess, and I'll believe you. You're so bloody sure and smug, you just *find* me one.'

She picked up her rod and wound the line in furiously. She cast again. I watched her.

'Those bastards that you're so terrified of,' I said after a while. 'What are they like?'

'You want me to pick a bastard?'

'No, I'm just saying, since you insist there are only two types of men and you religiously bring home the anorak type which seems to end in tears, what about giving the bastard type a go? You never know, you might find one with a soft centre.'

There was a silence.

'Like Dad, you mean?'

I stared at her. 'What d'you mean, like Dad?'

'Tess, if you think I'm going to let some tyrannical bully boss me around for the rest of my life just because now and again there's a flash of humility, you're wrong. I'm not going to spend my life waiting for the odd flash.'

I groaned. 'God, Laura, I had no idea we had a psychological problem here!'

'We do *not* have a psychological problem and there's no "we" about it. This is my life, thank you very much, and if you don't mind I'll sort it out for myself!'

With that she reeled in her line, seized her fishing bag and stalked off down the river. I chased after her.

'Laura! Laura – wait, don't be so bloody silly!' I caught up with her and grabbed her arm. I swung her around to face me. She had tears in her eyes. She stared past me, over my shoulder.

'It's all right for you,' she sniffed, 'but oh God, Tess, you have no idea! I'm so terrified of getting it wrong. Of making a mistake.'

I put my arms round her and hugged her hard. 'You old silly,' I murmured. 'Why on earth would you do that?'

'Well, Mum has, hasn't she?'

'Has she?' I was shocked. It struck me, not for the first time, that Laura and Mum were very close.

She nodded. 'I think so, and I think she thinks so

too.' She pulled back, fished a hanky out of her pocket and blew her nose. 'Come on, Tess, how would you like to be married to Dad?'

I glanced across at him, legs apart, up to his thighs in water, cap pulled right down over his eyes, mouth set in a determined line. 'Well, no, but – well, he's just our dad, isn't he? We can't change that.'

I'd never really thought about it. It wasn't as if Mum ever complained; she was always so – stoical. Laura clenched her fists.

'But you see, I don't *want* that! I don't want my children to think – he's just our dad – I want them to adore him! I want him to be perfect!'

I shook my head in amazement. 'Laura, this is no way to fall in love. You're not out there choosing a piece of furniture. You don't take a cool, calculated look from all angles and wonder if he's going to make a good husband or a good father. You don't try the drawers, examine the hinges and then say, "Yes, that'll do nicely, I'll take it." You meet someone, the thunderbolt hits you splat between the eyes and wham bam you fall in love!'

Laura gave a hoot of derision. 'Oh, don't make me laugh. In Mills and Boon books, maybe, and maybe even in your life, but take it from me, the majority of us mortals struggle on out there without even feeling half a volt, let alone a thunderbolt.'

'But you won't let it happen, Laura,' I urged. 'You've got to stop tiptoeing around, you've got to be open to the so-called bastards once in a while, just in case. I mean, for God's sake, you're beautiful, you're intelligent, you could have anyone. You can't just keep playing it safe and hanging around with doormats or you'll never fall in love, and apart from anything else it must be so depressing!'

She bent down and started putting her flies away in

her tin. She picked up a rather beautiful one, peacock blue with a gold streak, and stared at it. 'It is,' she said in a small voice.

'Well then, for God's sake be true to yourself! Make yourself available to the hunks, the sexy ones with the chiselled chins and smouldering eyes – so what if he's got a Porsche, a pad in Knightsbridge and a Gold American Express Card – you'll get over it! You'll struggle through the dinners at the Gavroche and the nights out at Annabel's; you'll maybe even get used to the yacht in the Bahamas. I promise, once you get the hang of it, it'll be a breeze!'

She was sniffing again. I bit my lip. Stop it, Tess. She was unhappy and I was getting into my Mickey-taking stride, enjoying the sound of my own acerbic tongue. Why did I always do that? She straightened up and I gave her a guilty hug.

'Sorry,' I muttered.

She sniffed into my hair. 'No, you're right. Someone has to say it. I'm a coward. An emotional coward. A scaredy-cat, as Hugo would say.'

'Sitting on an Edward doormat.' I clapped my hand to my mouth, horrified at the vision. 'Oooh Laura,' I groaned, 'I don't know how you can.'

She gave a wry smile and swung her bag over her shoulder. 'Oh, I just think of it as charity work. Administering to the needy, the less fortunate.'

We wandered back downstream together arm in arm. For a while neither of us said anything. Eventually I broke the silence.

'And have you really never felt anything like I described?' I said tentatively.

She sighed. 'Oh yes. Once.'

I looked up quickly. 'And?' I knew better than to make that, 'Who?'

She shrugged. 'And it wasn't reciprocated.' She smiled

perceptibly. 'I made a complete fool of myself, if you must know.'

I nodded and left it at that. She wouldn't elaborate, I knew. I wondered if Mum would know anything about it? I'd ask her. Sometimes I got so wrapped up in my own life and my own children I forgot about Laura. Except on holiday, of course, when I lectured her. I sighed. More guilt.

'Oh well,' I said brightly, 'at least you know you *can* feel like that – that's a start, surely? I mean, better to have loved and lost than—'

'Oh please, Tess,' she widened her eyes in mock horror, 'spare me *that*!'

I grinned back. At least she was smiling again. 'OK. No clichés, but listen, no more doormats either, all right? Promise me that at least. I'd rather you were celibate than doing charity work with another of those wallys who shake your hand like a piece of jelly.'

She giggled. 'OK. No more wallys.'

'But,' I wagged a finger schoolmarmishly, 'in the meantime you could at least be civil to the wally you've brought on holiday. You don't have to sleep with him but you could at least bare your teeth at him occasionally, toss him a civil word or two. It wouldn't hurt to—'

Laura put her hand on my arm. 'Sshh! Talk of the devil,' she murmured.

I looked up, horrified. Sure enough, just around the next bend, slightly hidden from view amongst the gorse bushes was Edward, perched on a little collapsible stool sketching the mountains. His knees were practically touching his chin on the ridiculous seat and he looked like a little gnome.

'D'you think he heard?' I hissed.

She shook her head. Suddenly he glanced up and saw us. I nudged Laura in the ribs. Her hand shot up in the air.

'Hi there!' she called.

Edward looked surprised, then flushed with pleasure. 'Hi!'

He stood up – too eagerly – and knocked his stool over. As he turned to pick it up he kicked over his open flask. He made a desperate lunge to stop it soaking his sketch pad, but as he did so, his glasses slipped down his nose, off his face and into the drink. He seized them and, clearly not wanting to be at any more of a disadvantage – like blind – rammed them back on again, coffee and all.

'Give me strength,' muttered Laura as it dripped down his face.

'Be *nice*,' I counselled her.

She grinned and galloped gallantly over to help him pick up his things, wipe his glasses and calm his nerves. I watched her raise a hopeful smile from him and even – good grief – a laugh, then I turned and made for home.

It was all very well, I thought to myself as I strode through the woods back to the house, this bossiness, this sorting out of other people's lives, this preaching the word about being true to oneself . . . but how true was I going to be to myself, eh? I strode up the gravel path. Answer me that one, Tess. I didn't, because I had a sneaky feeling that, 'Too true,' was the answer, but at this stage I was damned if I was going to admit it. Least of all, I thought as I pushed open the back door, to myself.

Chapter Nine

'Tess, this is Madelaine Cameron.'

I stopped mid-stride. I was making my way down the hall to the rod room to relieve myself of my wet boots and clothes and had to backtrack a bit to peer through the open drawing-room door. My mother and another woman were sitting either side of the fire drinking coffee.

'Oh!' I stared in surprise. 'I – I thought you were coming for tea.'

Madelaine smiled broadly. 'I was, but at the last minute something came up so your mother invited me to lunch instead.'

'Oh!'

'Darling, don't just stand there dripping water. Go and take your boots off and come and join us,' admonished my mother.

'I will. I'm just . . .' Just staggered by the sheer beauty and elegance of this woman who was absolutely nothing like I'd imagined.

In the first place she wasn't hefty and tweedy, dressed from head to toe in lovat green with a headscarf covered in horsey paraphernalia and a couple of black Labs at her heels, and in the second place she didn't have a commanding thigh-slapping manner and a county accent. This woman was slim, petite, expensively and elegantly dressed in a nut-brown cashmere polo neck and a camel knee-length skirt. Her legs were slim, encased in sheer silk and crossed at the ankle, her ash-grey hair waved softly behind her ears, her skin was almost translucent and her eyes were clear and blue like Patrick's. She looked about forty but must have been more like sixty, but what was even more staggering was that she was clearly French.

'Tess,' said my mother again uncomfortably, as I gaped.

'Yes! Right! I'll be back in a minute.' I hastened to the rod room and was back a moment later.

'Sorry for staring,' I said as I came back in, extending my hand towards her and hoping it wasn't too grubby, 'but you're not a bit like I imagined.' Either I came clean, I'd decided, or she'd forever think I was an open-mouthed, gormless nutter.

Madelaine laughed and shook my hand. 'Ah, I think you were expecting someone a leetle more traditional? A leetle more English, yes?'

I sat down, noticing that Mummy had managed to give her the exploding armchair and that the springs were even now attacking her expensive cashmere arms.

'Well, yes, or Scottish I suppose, but I'm very relieved to find you're not. I should think there are quite enough people round here who can trace themselves back to Bonnie Prince Charlie and permanently reek of haggis. They must regard you as a breath of fresh air.'

She shrugged and grimaced. 'Too fresh, I theenk. You know, unless your ancestors went to school with Macbeth you will always be a stranger in these parts.' She smiled ruefully. 'But of course I didn't discover that until I married.'

At the mention of her marriage I remembered. 'I – was sorry to hear about your husband,' I said quickly.

She inclined her head in acknowledgement. 'Thank you.' She reached down into her handbag and took out a packet of Gauloises. I watched as she lit one and blew a thin line of blue smoke high into the air. I was impressed, having only ever seen cool French adolescents indulge before, but then, Madelaine was, I decided, essentially cool. She uncrossed her slim stockinged legs and regarded me quizzically with her bright blue eyes.

'And you, if I may say so, my dear, are not at all as I imagined either.'

I flushed and instinctively pulled David's fishing jumper down over my thighs. This was the *quid pro quo* of course and I was at a distinct disadvantage. I'd assumed I'd have time to wash and change before she arrived at teatime; as it was, my hair hadn't seen a shampoo bottle for a week and I must reek of the river. I brushed a tangled lock out of my eyes.

'Oh, er, really? In what way?' Knowing, of course, that she could only mean in the unattractive, ungroomed, smelly sort of way.

She frowned. 'I had imagined you would be more of a cringing violet.'

'Oh! Er, d'you mean shrinking?'

'Exactly! You are more forthright, more self-assured. I thought you'd be rather . . .' she searched for a word and tried one '. . . demure?'

Mum laughed. 'I don't think anyone could call Tess demure.'

'I was once,' I said abruptly. I knew what Madelaine was talking about. 'When I was younger. I didn't always have the courage of my convictions.'

'Ah, but sometimes it is more courageous to do the right thing, than rebel and do the wrong thing, you know,' she said softly, meeting my eye.

There was a silence. Her hand slipped towards the coffee table and picked up a photograph. 'We've been looking at your lovely family, Tess.'

I glanced across. Mum had obviously found some pictures of Hugo and Clemmie.

'They're beautiful,' she went on. 'I am very envious

of Daphne having grandchildren anyway, but to have such divine ones is too much.' She shook her head ruefully.

I waited, wondering if this would be the moment for her to bring up Patrick, to rebuke him for not providing her with a daughter-in-law, grandchildren.

'And this is your husband?' she went on, peering closer.

I leaned over to see. Oh, for heaven's sake. David appeared to be asleep in a deckchair with his mouth wide open and Clemmie and Hugo had clearly taken advantage of this to put a half-empty bog-roll in his mouth and an old loo seat round his neck. They were doubled up behind him, holding on to each other, crying with laughter. I cringed.

'Mum,' I hissed. 'Where did you get that from? It's awful!'

'I took it in the garden last summer,' said my mother in surprise. 'I thought it was rather fun.'

'Ah yes it is, it is!' insisted Madelaine. 'Such a feeling of –' she waved her hands expressively – 'of family! Of *joie de vivre*!' She poked a manicured finger at it. 'This ees the picture the designers really want for their perfume ads, the ones with the beautiful people cavorting on beaches with young children, yes? But they never seem to capture the essence! The *esprit*!'

Personally, I wasn't convinced that Giorgio and Calvin would be lining up to trade in their supermodels for an ageing barrister dressed as a lavatory flanked by his guffawing children, but then she was probably just being polite. What must she think of us? I wondered.

I looked across at Mum, who although always elegant was pretty shabbily dressed as usual in an ancient jumper and skirt. When was the last time she'd bought any new clothes? I wondered. I glanced quickly around the room and for the first time saw it for the mess it was. Toys littered the floor, old roses drooped in vases, books lay open everywhere. Madelaine's Parisian chic seemed to highlight everyone and everything. I blushed. Couldn't Mum at least have tidied up a bit? Thrown some of the old newspapers away, emptied a few wine glasses, chucked Barbie and Ken into the toy box and shoved their revolting dream kitchen and chalet-style bungalow behind the door? Madelaine's eyebrows suddenly shot up.

'Ah! Is that them?' She turned eagerly towards the window. 'The children? How enchanting!'

Childish shouts were undoubtedly coming from the garden and I moved quickly towards the window, keen to beat her to it, to shove my bulk between her and anything too enchanting. Would the little darlings be killing the cat perhaps, or Leonora even? I held my breath and peered out nervously. Happily, an unexpectedly tame scene met my eye. Down on the lower lawn, Piers was playing chase with Hugo and Clemmie. The children were shouting with laughter as he ran after them and he'd even blown up some balloons which they were tossing around in the air. Madelaine clapped her hands ecstatically.

'Ah! *Regardez! C'est tellement agréable!*'

I was pleased and very surprised. Piers didn't often play with my two – in fact, I'd go so far as to say never. I watched as he and Hugo raced towards the house.

'Yes, they can be rather sweet,' I agreed indulgently.

Hugo leaped the little box hedge and made it to the terrace. He flashed by our window, grinning from ear to ear and waving a balloon. We smiled and waved back, but suddenly my hand and smile froze, it wasn't a balloon he was waving at all, but an inflated condom. A second later Piers flashed past too, purple in the face, steam pouring from every orifice.

'Come back here, you little bastard!' he roared.

121

Mummy tutted. 'So competitive,' she murmured.

'Er, more coffee, Madelaine?' I said hastily, steering her away from the window and back to the table.

'*Non, merci.* I've had plenty, and a most delicious lunch too. Your mother really is a wonderful cook, Tess. I must get that recipe from you, Daphne, chocolate roulade is so difficult and yours was perfection. And what lovely lilies.' She paused to admire the only vase of surviving flowers in the room.

'Yes, beautiful,' agreed Mummy, 'but not frightfully well arranged, I'm afraid I'm a bit of a plonker.'

Madelaine frowned, perplexed. 'A bit of a – ah! Ian, how lovely!' Suddenly her face cleared, she beamed and we all turned to witness my father tiptoeing past the open door, boots in one hand, rod in the other, obviously hoping to make it to the rod room at the end of the passage without being seen. He froze in mid-creep, foot poised high in the air like a pointer. The foot wavered for a moment, then dropped. He knew he was trapped.

'Madelaine, how delightful!' He gallantly swept his hat off his head and advanced with a fixed smile, hand extended stiffly.

Madelaine took it and also planted an elegant peck on each of his cheeks too. He managed not to cringe or rub them off, but nonetheless stepped smartly back, out of range for any more. His chin jutted out.

'I was um, sorry to hear about Marcus!' he almost shouted, as if he was determined to get it out. He twisted his flat cap round and round nervously in his hands.

Madelaine smiled. 'Thank you, Ian.'

'It um, must be very difficult for you,' he bellowed.

'I'm bearing up.'

'Yes, yes,' he nodded hard. 'My – my sincere condolences. Er, anything we can do, of course, delighted. Don't um –' his hat was spiralling now as if it might take off like a propeller at any minute, 'don't hesitate to er—'

'Thank you, Ian, but I'm fine, really. Daphne has been most kind and cooked me a delicious lunch. I just hope she will come to me next time.'

She reached for a chocolate-brown throw hanging on the back of a chair and swept it round her shoulders. She gave a dazzling smile. 'But now I really must be going.'

'Oh.' I was dismayed. 'So soon?'

'I'm afraid so, my dear. I have to take the car to the garage. Another bleenking gasket has blown or something, that's why I couldn't come at teatime. Such a bore.'

'Ah, yes, cars, too tedious. Well, if you'll excuse me.' Daddy reversed out of the room at top speed, half nodding, half bowing. 'Lovely to see you, Madelaine, delightful,' and he escaped down the hall.

'You too, Ian.' She smiled to herself, then turned to me. 'Tess.' She gazed for a moment, then suddenly leaned forward, resting her hands lightly on my shoulders. She kissed me on both cheeks. 'It was so good to meet you at long, long last.'

I gazed back at her and for a moment couldn't speak. She turned to my mother.

'Daphne, such a treat, thank you so much.' They kissed warmly and walked towards the door together, arm in arm, away from me.

'We must do it again some time.'

'Yes, we must, it's been too long.'

'Far too long. I'll give you a ring and—'

'How's Patrick?' I blurted out suddenly.

They stopped and turned back to me in surprise.

'Oh, he is fine,' said Madelaine. 'Yes, very well.'

Both women were staring at me now. I felt my colour rise. 'Good. Good,' I said faintly, feeling foolish.

Madelaine was charm itself. She came back towards me, carrying the conversation, smiling, letting me recover.

'His painting is going so well now, you know. He is really making quite a name for himself, he's had four or five exhibitions in Florence and one in Rome. I went out to see the one in Rome for myself and my goodness, I felt quite important – the mother of the artist, you know! And in just two weeks' time he 'as a one-man show in London, at the Pierre Boulavère gallery in Cork Street, very prestigious, I believe. But still,' she sighed, shaking her head, 'still he ees not settled. Still he 'as no wife, no family, and he is so secretive, tells me precisely nothing.' She appealed to Mummy. 'Are your girls the same, Daphne, or is it just the boys, you think?'

Mummy had been watching me carefully, but she turned her attention to Madelaine now. 'Laura's certainly secretive,' she admitted. 'She never tells me anything about her love life, about how she really feels anyway.'

'But you meet them, her menfriends? She brings them home?'

'Oh yes, we meet them all right, but they're all,' she struggled, trying not to be disloyal, 'well, a bit dreary, I'm afraid. They're all out of the same mould, the trainspotter type.'

Madelaine was mystified. 'Trainstopper? You mean on the tracks? They throw themselves?'

'Sadly no,' murmured Mummy. 'No, it's a type, Madelaine. It means timid, really.'

'Ah.' She shrugged. 'Ah well, we have to let them find their own way, I suppose.' She turned back to me and smiled. 'The problem with my boy is, I think, that he never really got over you, Tess.'

I stared at her. Gulped. Couldn't speak. She patted my arm. 'So lovely to meet you, my dear.' Then she turned and went.

I managed to wait till she'd left the room, then my hand shot to my mouth, stifling a gasp. She couldn't know, of course. She couldn't know that that was like tossing a sweetie to a child who's been deprived for years, that I would throw myself on those words so hungrily, devour them so voraciously. I watched from the window as Mum saw her to her car. I could almost feel the blood pumping through me, pounding in my fingertips, in my toes. 'The problem with my boy is, I think, that he never got over you.' I savoured the words, rolling them around in my mouth. '*Never got over you.*' My blood surged and my heart beat faster, I glowed with guilt and delight. They were the words I'd been waiting for and I knew it.

I watched Madelaine get into her car, heard it crunch slowly down the drive and as it went, a secret smile spread over my face until I thought the bottom half of it might drop off. For the first time in ages I felt wide awake, alive. Madelaine had unwittingly lit the blue touch paper and my advice to everyone now was: *stand well back.*

On a sudden impulse I slipped out to the hall and ran upstairs before Mum came back through the front door. There was something I wanted to do. I hurried along the landing to our bathroom and as I pushed open the door, almost tripped over a pile of washing. I kicked it, exasperated. It was a bundle David had put out, presumably in the vain hope that if I fell over it, it might get washed. Lying on top was a shirt I'd given him last Christmas. The sleeve was flung out at an angle as if waving at me, flagging me down, reproaching me. I seized it angrily and chucked it in the linen basket. No, I would *not* be reproached, I would *not* be frowned on, and apart from anything else, I thought, slamming the door shut, I hadn't even done anything yet, had I? I refused to feel guilty about a crime I hadn't even committed, and maybe wouldn't commit either! I mean, maybe I just wanted to feel this warm glow for a bit, to fantasise, to know that there was someone out there thinking about me, someone who'd – and I quote – *never got over me*. Yes, that's right, me. I stared at my flushed reflection in the mirror, Tessa Hamilton, mother of two, housewife from Putney.

Quickly I began unbuttoning my shirt and peeled off my clothes. There was no lock on the door, but I was pretty sure nobody was about right now. I got down to my socks and bra and knickers and hopped over the pile of clothes to the full-length mirror in the corner. Hmm, I pursed my lips. Very pop socks and white M&S undies. I took the pop socks off and then whipped off my bra too, throwing it on the floor with a flourish – there! Then I shuffled closer to the mirror and peered in. Good Lord. Where on earth had my boobs gone? Apart from the odd cursory glance in the bath it was ages since I'd inspected these two properly; they seemed to have turned into a couple of small tea-bags. My eye travelled nervously down to my tummy, which far from disappearing had, in the absence of my critical eye, taken the opportunity to spread itself rather luxuriously. Perhaps that's where my boobs were, somewhere in my tummy? Had they relocated without me even realising it? I looked like a duvet that had gone thin at the top and fat at the bottom. I needed to be seized by the ankles and given a damn good shake.

Panic-stricken, I lay down. Perhaps that would help, if I shifted everything around a bit? I swivelled on the cold lino floor and craned my head to look in the mirror. There was a definite improvement in the tummy and thigh department, but my boobs seemed to be pointing the wrong way now. What was the attraction of my armpits, for God's sake? I sat up, alarmed. Would he notice? Would he find me very altered? Well, of course I was altered! I'd given birth twice, breastfed twice, failed to keep up my post-natal exercises twice, cheated on my pelvic floors twice and eaten vast quantities of Jaffa Cakes and abandoned fish fingers every day for the last eight years. All that was bound to take its toll on a girl, but would it matter? Would it put him off?

Suddenly I reached across and grabbed my eyeliner from the bathroom shelf. Ah yes, the pencil test – always the acid test of droopy boobs at school. Could I still pass it, or would I have to go and hang myself from the nearest netball post? I hoicked a tea-bag up and stuck the pencil underneath. It clung like a cling-on. I wiggled around a bit but it stayed resolutely put. Damn. I gazed sorrowfully at my reflection. Oh well, I reasoned, boobs weren't everything, were they? I mean, look at my legs. They were still pretty terrific, weren't they? Still long and thin. I stuck one in the air and waggled it. Not bad. I'd go so far as to say amazing even, except – wasn't there something a bit odd about the consistency of those thighs? Weren't they looking a bit *porridgey*? I poked one and it wobbled violently. Hell's teeth. I slapped my leg smartly to arrest the slipstream and then all of a sudden, rather rudely, it dawned.

The gym. Of course! So *that's* why all my friends went there so religiously, three or four times a week sometimes – toning up, slimming down, doing weights, pumping iron, sweating buckets, charging up and down imaginary steps like lunatics and I'd always thought it such a narcissistic waste of time, such a vain, navel-gazing obsession. I'd always rather smugly claimed to prefer a good book, to be doing something about the bit on the *in*side rather than the bit on the *out*side . . . Why hadn't someone let me in on the secret? That the *real* reason I needed to look after my body was not that I might need it some day, that I'd live longer, feel better for it, have a better quality of life and blah blah blah – no, the *real* reason was that someone *else* might need it some day. Someone *else* might be requiring a toned thigh, a tiny

127

waist, a firm bust, a taut tummy – and we're not talking your ever-loving here either.

I sat up and sighed. Oh well. Too late to do anything about all that now and anyway, I reasoned, there were other, more subtle charms on offer too like, well, arms, for instance. I twirled an undeniably slim one ruefully. Oh, and my smile, of course. I quickly changed the rueful one in the mirror to a seductive one and discovered a tea leaf. I picked it off thoughtfully. Oh – and my laugh – that couldn't have changed much in twelve years, surely? I experimented with a girlish tinkle: 'Ah ha ha ha!' Hey, not bad, and that thrownback head certainly minimises the chins, Tess. Have another go. 'Ah ha ha – shit!'

The door flew open and two heads appeared, David's at the top and Hugo's at the bottom.

'Here she is!' cried Hugo. 'Why are you laughing and why is there a pencil under your bosom? Are you drawing on them? Can I have a go?'

I grabbed a towel. 'No, you bloody well can't.'

'Are you all right?' said David. 'We heard you laughing – you sounded a bit delirious.'

'Yes, of course I'm all right,' I said shortly. 'I was just doing some – some exercises, if you must know! And I was laughing at something –' I thought wildly – 'something Penny said.'

'What?' demanded Penny, pushing the door open and barging in too. 'Oh, there you are, Tess, we've been looking everywhere for you. What did I say?'

'When?'

'You just said I said something funny, I heard you.'

'Yes, what?' demanded Hugo.

'Oh, nothing really,' I said, scrambling to my feet and pulling the towel around me. 'Just something you said down at the river, made me smile, that's all.'

'Laugh,' corrected my son, 'really loudly, and she was

doing exercises in the nudey-wudey.'

'What was it?' persisted Penny with a smile, always keen to imagine she was amusing. 'What did I say, go on, what?'

'Oh, you *know*,' I said, winking and pretending we shared a private joke, desperately trying to think of anything Penny had ever said that was remotely funny.

Penny frowned, then her eyes grew wide. 'Oh, you mean about You Know Who!'

I gasped, suddenly realising what she meant. 'No!' I said quickly. 'No, not that, something else.'

'My goodness, you old devil.' Penny nudged me, eyes shining. 'You're going to do it, aren't you? Exercising in the nude eh, getting yourself in shape – you old dog.'

'May I enquire as to what all the hilarity is about?' asked David who'd been quietly filling the bath for Hugo who was once again soaking wet from the river.

'No, you may not,' I snapped. 'I don't know what Penny's talking about.'

'What?' shrieked Hugo, jumping up and down in his wet clothes. 'What are you going to do, you old dog, WHAT!'

'NOTHING!' I screeched back, grabbing my clothes off the floor and barging past them out of the room. 'God, sometimes I feel like Greta bleeding Garbo!'

'Did she exercise in the nude too?' asked Penny.

'No, but she wanted to be alone!'

I ran down the passageway but Hugo was right on my heels. I flew into the loo at the other end, and locked the door smartly behind me.

'WHAT!' screamed Hugo, hammering on the door. 'What are you going to do, tell me you fat belly farty MUMMEEE!! TELL ME-E-E!'

I sank down on the loo seat knowing I'd have to sit this one out but jumped up smartly as I hit the medicated seat cover. Bugger Penny, bugger her! I'd only just made up my mind to consider this blinking affair, only just allowed the idea to filter into my own consciousness, and now suddenly my whole bloody family wanted to discuss it – Jesus!

I folded my arms and leaned back on the wall, knowing a battle of wits was about to commence out there. I wouldn't move until Hugo moved and he wouldn't move until I did, except – hello, hang on. I put my ear to the door and heard footsteps padding away. Tentatively I placed my hand on the handle, but – no, wait: footsteps were padding back, accompanied by – clink, clink, clink – oh no, a bucket of Lego! I groaned. He was setting up camp out there, I could be in here for *hours*. I tightened my lips and folded the towel around me decisively. Not bloody likely. I turned the key, opened the door and stepped smartly over boy and Lego. Hugo was up in an instant.

'Mummy! Mummy what! What are you going to do, tell me please!'

I rounded on him. 'Go and have your bath immediately!' I thundered.

'But—'

'NOW Hugo!'

'But why? I—'

'Because I am the mother!'

'So?'

'So I outrank you!'

I stormed off, pretending I hadn't heard the muffled, 'Bugger,' behind me. I didn't often pull rank but when I did, it was curiously effective.

I marched into my bedroom, slammed the door and flopped down on my bed pulling the pillow over my head. Damn and blast the lot of them.

I didn't encounter Penny again until I joined her at potato-peeling hour in the kitchen that evening.

'Thanks very much,' I said tartly as I walked in and grabbed a knife from the draining board. I began peeling furiously.

'What?' she giggled. 'I was only—'

'Only suggesting I might commit adultery when my husband and son were both in the room. Yes, thanks a bunch.'

'Well, are you?' she asked eagerly.

I stared at her incredulously, put my knife down. 'No, of *course* not, Penny. I wouldn't dream of it.' I shook my head despairingly and resumed peeling. 'You really do say the most ridiculous things sometimes, you know.'

'Don't fib.'

'I'm not bloody fibbing.'

'You bloody are, Tess. I can tell, you were definitely up to something in there, lolling around on the floor with nothing on and simpering in the mirror. I know when you're guilty, you get all cross and defensive and start swearing a lot. I remember that summer with Patrick, you used to shout "Bollocks" a lot and – God what's that?'

A huge roar happily interrupted her quaint reminiscences, making us both jump. Through the kitchen window we saw an enormous motorbike loom up the drive; it turned and skidded to a halt outside and a spray of gravel hit the window. A youth encased in black leather and a red helmet gave us the benefit of his back, and then a bit more throttle.

I went to the kitchen door. 'Josie!' I yelled up the stairs.

He gave a couple of toots on his horn and sat waiting for her.

'Too cool to knock at the door, I suppose,' snapped Penny, glaring out of the window. 'Who does he think he is, tearing up our drive like that?' Penny did so love to play the Lady of the Manor.

131

Seconds later Josie stuck her head round the kitchen door. 'Bye then, Tess. I've got a key so don't bother to wait up.'

I gazed at her in wonder. She looked terrific. Long blonde hair, a real waist and slim brown legs, a very small proportion of which were encased in a short red skirt, white T-shirt and red jacket. She could knock any model I'd ever seen into a cocked hat. I felt almost proud of her.

I grinned. 'Bye, Josie, you look amazing. Have a good time.'

'Crikey,' muttered Penny, equally awestruck. 'I'd forgotten she wasn't even trying during the day.'

We watched, unashamedly now from the window, like the couple of has-beens we were, clutching our potato-peelers, wanting just a little sniff of the action, wanting to breathe in just a hint of our lost youth. Josie ran out to greet him. She flipped up his visor and kissed him playfully on the nose, then swung a long brown leg over the back of his bike and snuggled up close, clutching him round the waist. He turned back to check she was on properly, and as he did so, I saw his face for the first time. His bright blue eyes met mine and crinkled up in a smile. My jaw dropped, my eyes glazed, my potato-peeler fell with a resounding clatter into the sink. It was Patrick.

Chapter Ten

'Bloody hell!' squawked Penny. 'Did you see who that was?'

I was still staring out of the window as if I'd seen a ghost. I'd lost all control of my vocal cords.

'It was Patrick! Didn't you recognise him, Tess?'

'What the – how did they – where did they—' I floundered. My brain was spinning and I was having huge trouble with basic English.

'Oh, so it must have been *Patrick* she met in the pub,' breathed Penny. 'How extraordinary. Isn't that weird, Tess?'

My mouth was still moving, but no coherent sounds were coming out. Josie and Patrick? Surely not – no, it was too outrageous, it was obscene, it was – suddenly, my mouth connected with my brain.

'It's sick!' The words erupted from my lips like Mount Vesuvius. 'How *dare* she! What the hell does she think she's playing at!'

'What d'you mean?'

'Well, he's *far* too old for her!'

'Well not really, Tess. I mean she's what – twenty-two – and he's early thirties; that's not such a huge age-gap. But I know what you mean,' she mused. 'Because he's our age and she's so young and pretty, it does seem as if she's from a different generation, doesn't it? Well, different *planet*, actually, ha!'

This had the effect of rendering me speechless again

and I damn nearly grappled her to the floor and stabbed my potato-peeler into her throat.

'I don't care what bloody planet she's from,' I spluttered. 'She's my nanny, for God's sake, my employee. I won't have it, I just won't have it!' I leaned heavily on the draining board for support. I was in danger of hyperventilating here.

'And how dare *he*!' I muttered, staring into the sink, my eyes boggling down the plug-hole as the situation became clearer by the minute. 'How dare he roar up our drive and whisk her away like that, right in front of our noses. The cheek! The – the nerve!'

'Do you think he knows she's your nanny, then?' said Penny. 'I suppose he must have gathered by now – he definitely saw us at the window.'

'She's deceived me,' I seethed, 'betrayed me, the little hussy, the little tramp, the little two-bit jumped-up, brainless, braless, knickerless harpy!'

Penny frowned. 'Now hang on a minute, Tess, I'm not her biggest fan, but that's not really fair. She wasn't to know, was she? And anyway, I thought you said at breakfast yesterday she could go out with who she liked?'

'Yes, but within reason,' I spat. 'I don't particularly want her poaching my ex-boyfriends! Did you see her skirt, Penny? Up round her *arse*!'

I was totally out of control now, in the grip of a violent, homicidal rage, my potato-peeler seemed to be stabbing wildly at my chopping board.

'And all that *make-up*!' I brought the knife down savagely, gouging a hole in the wood.

'I don't think she was wearing make-up actually, just a bit of lipstick perhaps, a touch of blusher . . .'

But I wasn't listening. I was in another world – the one Othello no doubt inhabited for a while.

'And as for him,' I ranted on, 'a motorbike! I mean I ask you, at his age – who does he think he is – James sodding Dean? He's thirty-four, for God's sake!'

'Well not all thirty-somethings want a Volvo with a couple of baby-seats in the back, you know. I thought he looked quite cool actually.'

'Cool? Penny, he looked sad. A sad old sugar daddy cradle-snatching a gold-digging bimbo!' My voice rose hysterically. 'The whole thing is repulsive. I won't have it, I won't!' I stamped my foot.

Penny put her arms round my trembling shoulders. 'All right, all right,' she soothed in the kind of voice one reserves for the mentally deranged contemplating a leap off Beachy Head. 'Now you come and sit down here and I'll pour you a nice big drink. You're just upset, that's all.'

'Upset?' I muttered, allowing myself to be led to a chair. 'Who's upset? I'm not upset, don't be ridiculous.'

'Of course you are, and it's understandable. As far as you're concerned he's still your property,' she went on in her caring, counsellor tone, 'and you can't bear to see him with someone else – especially someone as young and beautiful and perfectly formed as Josie because you know you can't compete. It's perfectly natural,' she soothed.

My teeth snapped manically at this and she damn nearly lost her nose, but at the last minute I got a grip and sank them into my hand instead.

'Don't be silly,' I croaked, forcing a laugh, and knocking back the glass of wine she put in front of me. 'I couldn't care less!' I piped in a high, unnatural voice.

She sat next to me. 'Of course you could. You and I both know you secretly entertained hopes of, well, how shall I put it – turning back the clock? Revisiting old pastures, shall we say?'

'No we shall not!' I snapped. 'God, you're revolting, Penny. How can you be so tacky? I had no intention of revisiting anything with Patrick, I'm merely concerned for my nanny's welfare, concerned she doesn't make a fool of herself, the little—' It was no good, the venom was rising again, it was in my throat, my mouth and – 'TART!' I bellowed. 'The little hussy, harlot, painted bloody Jezebel, Judas sodding Iscariot!' I clenched my fists.

Penny refilled my glass. 'Drink,' she ordered.

I swiftly obeyed, knocking it back in one.

'And she's a hopeless nanny,' I spat. 'Hopeless! All she does is sit around on her arse watching spot-the-brain-cell quiz shows and reading bonk-busters all day. She's crap at ironing, hasn't a clue how to sew a button on – God, I even had to teach her how to make oven chips! I'm going to sack her,' I went on in a quiet, mad sort of way, 'tomorrow. No, why wait? Tonight, when she comes back – the moment she sets foot through the front door.'

Penny frowned. 'But I thought you said she was good. I distinctly remember you saying—'

'I don't care what I said, she's going, she's as good as gone. That girl is history, she's on the next train back to London in the morning.'

I turned and seized Penny's arm urgently. 'I can do that, can't I Penny? It's not against the law, the trade's descriptions act or anything? Or do I have to give her notice? What about just a huge wodge of money, hundreds, thousands – I know, what about my gold Rolex, d'you think she'd like that?'

'Tess, you can't sack her just because she's seeing your ex-boyfriend!'

'It's got nothing to do with that,' I hissed. 'I told you, she's going because she's useless and the children hate her.'

My fingers wound round the stem of my empty glass like snakes; any minute now my tongue would fork too.

'Oh, what rot, the children adore her, you know they do.'

As if on cue, Clemmie ran into the kitchen in her pyjamas and picked up the cup of warm milk Penny had put out for her on the table. I seized her wildly.

'Clemmie darling, you hate Josie, don't you? Secretly? Yes? Tell Mummy, she's mean to you, isn't she? Makes you eat your horrid sprouts?'

Clemmie frowned and wriggled free. 'No, Mummy, I love Josie. Mummy, are you still my mummy?'

'She's lying,' I hissed between clenched teeth, letting her go. I gulped my wine.

'Mu-mmy!' Clemmie plucked at my arm. 'Are you still my mummy, only I haven't seen you all day and if you're not careful I might have to divorce you like that boy in the papers did. Will you read to me?'

Where would they go? I wondered. Along the cliffs for a moonlit walk? To the sand dunes?'

'MUMMMEE! Read to me in bed.'

I glanced down. 'Hmmm? Oh no, darling, not tonight. Daddy will read to you, Mummy's tired. Now run along.'

I drained my glass. Or would they go to the river, where we used to go? Lie side by side on the bank?'

'No, you blinking fat MOO!' roared my daughter.

'Clemmie!' I bellowed. 'Don't you speak to me like that. Go up and find Daddy immediately. Go on, up those stairs this instant!'

Rather fortuitously, David appeared at that moment in the doorway, bearing a bundle of washing. Clemmie promptly burst into tears and ran to him. He scooped her up.

'I'll give them their tea, bath them *and* put them to bed then, shall I?' he enquired. 'And then shall I do this pile of washing that's been sitting on the bathroom floor for three days?'

'Oh, for God's sake, David, don't give me that sexist demarcation crap. I'm on holiday too, you know!'

'Of course you are, my darling, and don't we know

it.' He flung the washing down on the floor and marched upstairs with a howling Clemmie in his arms.

'Damn. Damn, damn, damn!' I refilled my glass.

Penny got up from the table, raising her eyebrows at the heavy marital scene and then at the almost-empty wine bottle.

'Um, Tess, I know I said have a drink but d'you think you should drain the thing dry?'

'Yes, I do,' I muttered, clutching the bottle possessively, cuddling it almost.

Penny silently resumed her potato-peeling at the sink. I gazed at her disapproving back. It seemed to be going in and out of focus quite dramatically. One glass was generally enough to make my eyes go squiffy, two tended to make them rotate, how much would it take to drink myself into oblivion, I wondered? I whimpered slightly at this. Oh God, was I hitting the bottle? Here I was experiencing all the repercussions of an extra-marital affair – heavy drinking, neglected children, parental rows, resentful husband – and I hadn't even bloody *had* one!

I heaved a great sigh. Nor would I have, at this rate. I sank back miserably in my chair. The shock was abating slightly but it was being replaced by a tidal wave of self-pity. Where were they now, I wondered. Arm in arm somewhere, staring at the stars? And what would they talk about? This cheered me slightly. Yes, what exactly *would* a grown man talk to a twenty-two-year-old nanny about? Who was doing what to whom in *Neighbours*? Whether or not Take That would ever re-form? I mean, it was hardly likely to be *A La Recherche du Temps Perdu*, was it? I gave a hollow laugh and poured myself another *soupçon* of wine. It had to be a *soupçon* because that was all there was left. Oh yes, I reasoned, having a great body was all well and good, but without the grey matter to back it up . . . I tapped my temple smugly, but suddenly my fingertip froze. *Hang on a minute.* I had a nasty feeling . . . hadn't Josie mentioned something about a degree when I'd first interviewed her? Now what was it? I racked my brains furiously – table tennis, needlework or – oh, hang on, it was coming to me now . . .Yes, that was it: *History of Art.*

My eyes glazed. History of Art! Shit! So they'd be talking paintings, introspection, Impressionists, light formation . . . they'd be snuggling up on the beach together making plans – great galleries we must visit! My chest felt strangely tight. Good God, what had I hired here? Was I out of my mind? I'd only gone and hired Brian bloody Sewell masquerading as Claudia blinking Schiffer! Why hadn't I gone for a Rumanian weight-lifter with enough space in her head to park a brace of caravans? Oh God!

I moaned low, slumped forward onto the table in defeat. I lay there with my head on its cold Formica surface. Penny ignored me and carried on peeling. I groaned again, pitifully. Still she ignored me. I shut my eyes painfully. I could hardly see now and my head seemed to be in the grip of a centrifugal force, but funnily enough, it was strangely comforting. I abandoned myself to the mind-numbing headspin but after a few minutes I heard the back door fly open.

I opened my eyes bleakly. Laura was standing there, grinning from ear to ear and carrying a huge, shiny, dripping salmon.

'Look!' she cried. 'How about that!'

'Oh, well done!' cried Penny. 'That's our first, isn't it?'

'It certainly is,' beamed Laura proudly, 'and what a whopper – eight pounds two ounces. Have you got anything planned for supper, or shall we have it tonight?'

'No, I've only done some vegetables, let's eat it. Oh, you are clever, Laura. Here, let me help you.'

Together they manhandled the salmon over to the work surface and eagerly began cleaning and gutting, chatting away happily as they worked. I watched blearily through my hair, my head feeling like a lead weight on the table. Eventually Laura glanced around. I shut my eyes tight. She whispered something to Penny. Penny whispered back.

'*No!*' I heard Laura gasp. 'Really?'

I peeped and saw Penny nod expressively. Laura glanced over again in my direction. I quickly shut my eyes.

'And is she a bit . . .?' she murmured. 'You know . . . about it?'

'More than a bit,' muttered Penny.

'More than a bit what!' I barked raising my head abruptly. 'You old witch, you old spleen dragon, what vicious lies are you whispering, what filthy muck are you spreading about me now!'

Laura stared at me, astounded.

'Tell me, Penny,' I spat, probably looking rather like that attractive little girl in *The Exorcist* whose head managed a 360-degree turn. 'Tell me exactly what you said or I'll boil your silk pyjamas!'

'I was merely explaining to Laura why it is you're a little upset,' she said soothingly.

'For the last time,' I thundered, 'I am not upset!'

Just at that moment my father came through the back door. 'Laura, Willie tells me you've got a salmon!' He rubbed his hands together gleefully. 'Marvellous news – I was beginning to give up hope.' He crossed the room and gave her a hug. 'I rather thought this might be our first year when we didn't catch a thing, and that was starting to depress me somewhat!'

He laughed, patted Penny on the back, then turned and caught sight of his elder daughter, hair askew, eyes rotating, swaying slightly at the kitchen table, hugging an empty bottle of Chardonnay to her bosom. His smile froze and his eyes went cold.

'What's wrong?' he demanded. 'Why are you drinking, Tessa? What's happened?'

'Oh, for heaven's sake,' I said, stifling a burp, and getting up and making for the back door. 'Making' was about right, since my first attempt landed me in the larder.

'I'm thirty years old,' I said as I fought my way out through baskets of vegetables, skidding on a rogue tomato. 'Can't I even have a drink if I feel like it?' I lurched past them all, eventually finding the back door. 'I'm going for a walk. You can stuff supper!' I blundered out into the garden.

I stumbled down the first lawn, jumped the little hedge, somehow landing on my feet, then ran down the second and plunged into the woods beyond, crashing through them blindly, scratching my face on brambles and tripping over roots. I still felt extremely woozy but the fresh air was reviving me slightly and I didn't stop running until I reached the water's edge. The last thing I wanted to hear was my father's footsteps behind me, his booming voice, catching up with me, seizing my arm and demanding to know what the devil was going on.

I ran and ran, along the river path, over the little bridge, and across into the heather, to the round, clear pool I always liked to sit by. I sank down on the shingle at the water's edge, panting. My heart was hammering in my chest now. I flopped on my back and gazed up at the still blue sky.

A dragonfly, making the most of the last minutes of daylight, whirred around above me and higher still, a pair of swallows swooped in formation back and forth across the water. Suddenly I felt a bit sick. I sat gingerly up. The trees span around me, then stopped, casting their long evening shadows across the water. I grabbed a handful of pebbles and threw them angrily at their reflections. The water peppered, the trees wobbled a bit, then slowly cleared to their still reflection again.

I sighed. Thirty years old. Yes, I was thirty years old. And he was thirty-four. And what a difference, eh? I gave a hollow laugh. Here was I, pissed off, careworn, body a mess, responsible for just about everything and everybody, and there was he charging around on a Harley-Davidson with a babe on the back, not a care in the world and not looking a day older than when I'd first met him. I chucked in another handful of stones. And what a babe. I thought of Josie, stretched out sunbathing in our back garden at home, tiny waist, firm boobs, long athletic legs just the way he liked them; 'built for speed' he'd say. Then I thought of my own sad reflection in the mirror this afternoon. I shuddered. Perhaps after all I'd had a lucky escape? Perhaps I'd spared myself the embarrassment, the look of disbelief on his face as he recoiled from me in horror? I picked up another handful of shingle and threw it savagely in the water.

'Hey! What d'you think you're playing at!' barked a voice behind me.

I swung around quickly. A huge figure loomed from behind a tree, but the low evening sun was right in my eyes and at first I couldn't see who it was. My heart pumped a bit, but then I relaxed.

'Oh God, it's you, Willie. You gave me a shock!'

'Yull be shockin' those fish too, I shouldn't wonder. What are you tryin' to doo, stone them to death? Are you lot that desperate for fish?'

I blushed as he towered over me. 'Sorry.' Disturbing the river was distinctly frowned on. 'Is anyone still fishing?'

He sat down next to me. 'No, but that's ney the point, is it? You're upsetting my charges, disturbin' their beauty sleep!'

He grinned and I tried to grin back but failed. He looked rather thoughtfully at me and I quickly looked away.

Willie leaned back, resting on his elbows, eyes narrowed. There was silence. I knew he was watching the river, he always was, never seemed to take his eyes off it. I observed him out of the corner of my eye, a huge mountain of a man, but so serene, so at ease with himself. But then he had his lifestyle to thank for that, didn't he? Day after day, month in month out, he led a solitary existence, taking care of the river and the wildlife it supported, except for a few months each summer when harassed townies like us would descend on him, desperate for just a couple of weeks of his own particular brand of contentment, for just a small slice of the inaction that he called normal life. What cares did he have? What pressures? I followed his eyes to the opposite bank but couldn't see anything.

'There,' he said quietly, pointing.

I stared. 'Oh yes.'

A young water rat was inching its way cautiously out of a hole, poking its nose out nervously then popping back in, until finally, it decided the coast was clear and slipped like a snake into the shallows.

'Did you see it?'

I nodded. His moss-green eyes crinkled in satisfaction and the wind ruffled his sandy blond hair. His eyes darted along the bank again, looking for other signs of life. I sighed, envying him his peace, his calm. I'd known him since he was a child; we'd all played together. I used to think he was shy but now I knew he just liked his own company. He was sure of himself in the truest sense, which was more than I could say for me. Another mammoth sigh unfolded from my boots.

'So what's up then?' he asked softly, following a dragonfly now.

'What d'you mean?'

'Why are you sitting here on your own throwing stones and sighing like that?'

'Oh, I don't know, Willie. Just life in general, I suppose.'

'Dunny give me that.'

'What?'

He didn't answer.

'What? Don't give you what?'

He shrugged. 'It's none of my business.'

I swallowed hard. 'All right then, more than just life in general. It's something . . . something I thought might happen . . . which won't, now.'

He chucked down his blade of chewed grass and picked another one. 'Oh ay? Somethin' you'd been looking forward to, like?'

I nodded, not trusting myself to speak. My nose, God damnit, appeared to be filling up with water.

'What was it, a treat or somethin'?'

In spite of myself I couldn't help thinking this was a quaint way to describe a sex romp.

I gulped and nodded. 'It might have made a nice change,' I squeaked – oh God, talking about it was fatal. Tears were threatening to break ranks any minute. I desperately fished up my sleeve for a non-existent hanky. *Don't cry Tess, don't cry!*

He sat up next to me and a comforting arm about the size of a tree trunk went round my shoulders. 'Hey, hey now, whatever it was can't have meant that much to you.'

'It did, it did!' I bawled, and that was it. The dam burst. 'It *did* mean a lot to me, and now it's all *spoilt*,' I sobbed into his soft Viyella shoulder. 'Nothing ever goes right for me any more and all I wanted was this one little thing and even *that's* been taken from me!' I knew I was behaving like a four-year-old but somehow I couldn't help it.

144

'Och now, there there,' he soothed, giving me a huge hug. 'Come on now, come on.' I'd heard him talk in the same way to his dogs who adored him, licked his boots, and now I knew why. I felt like licking them too.

'I *can't* come on,' I sobbed pathetically. 'I'm sick of coming on and bracing up and being strong and keeping a stiff upper lip, I'm sick of catering for everybody else's needs except my own!'

'Of course you are, of course,' he crooned, stroking my hair. 'It's only natural.'

'Just this one little thing,' I sobbed dramatically, 'of my own! For me! That was all I wanted!'

I was vaguely aware I was getting terribly out of control now, even perhaps wallowing in it a tiny bit, but then Willie didn't know what I was talking about so it didn't really matter. And it was so nice having my shoulder hugged like that and my hair smoothed like a child and being able to sob and bawl and lean my cheek against his soft shirt which smelled of grass and fresh air and – well, him, I suppose.

Gradually though, my sobs subsided and I began to feel a little foolish. I kept my head flat to his chest, sniffing quite a bit, not wanting him to see my tearstained face. I did feel an awful lot better for my outburst though, if a little weak. Crying always had such a debilitating effect on me, so much so that there wasn't a lot I could do about the fact that he was still stroking my hair, and actually, my neck too. Couldn't move a muscle. Or a finger. Oooh . . . that was lovely, bit lower – perfect. He tucked my hair back behind my ear and dropped a soft little kiss on the top of my head. Mmmm . . . a comforting, brotherly sort of kiss, you understand. I shut my eyes and nuzzled dreamily into his shoulder, wondering if it would happen again. Ah yes – there, lovely. As I leaned against him with half-closed eyes, I started to turn to goo inside. I felt so warm, so relaxed – rather like a hot water bottle, in fact.

Still he stroked and kissed and still I couldn't move, but little by little I began to realise that there was more on offer here than just tea and sympathy. But then again, I reasoned, eyeballing his Viyella checks rather nervously, I hadn't actually participated yet, had I? Hadn't done anything wrong? I stared at the small clear buttons on his shirt and watched his chest rise slowly up and down. Nerves turned to excitement. My tummy began to churn and presently, the moment came when he couldn't conceivably carry the show on his own any longer. Circumstances demanded he took my face in his hands and tilt it up towards him. I succumbed to the tilt and gazed, mesmerised. His moss-green eyes were soft, kind and enquiring, and his lips, when they came towards mine, so warm and comforting, and his tongue, so huge and hypnotic, that to be honest, there was damn-all I could do about it except fling my arms round his neck, lock them firmly together and pull him down roughly on top of me in the long, sweet grass.

Another soft kiss unfolded and another, and then he paused, possibly for breath, but also perhaps to search for that vital green light, the one that would give him the All Clear. What he got was more of a continental traffic cop, all beckoning white gloves and frantic whistles.

'Yes!' I gasped wantonly, then, lest there be misunderstanding, 'Yes, come on!'

After a few minutes I began to feel faint and realised I hadn't inhaled for a while. I came up for air and simultaneously felt a howling gale whistling around my midriff. I seemed to be losing some clothing.

'Not here,' I gasped. 'Too risky!' Not, notice, get off me right now, you mad fool, I must get home to my husband and children.

Willie nodded, and without so much as pausing in his exploration of my tonsils, scooped me up in his arms,

Tarzan style, and strode determinedly off down the river. It was at this moment, I'd like it recorded, that a very small piece of conscience did actually raise its tentative head to wonder what the hell I was up to. What on earth was I doing? Was this a good idea? For a moment I wasn't sure, then – wait; yes I was. I'd been planning on doing it with Patrick, hadn't I? What difference did it make if I did it with Willie the gillie instead? In the face of such brazenness that small, lone voice shrivelled and died, leaving the new, sex-crazed fallopian-tube-throbbing me to be carried into what I can only describe as a rude sod hut.

Willie kicked open the door and threw me down masterfully on a bed with a sheepskin rug on top. I caught a whiff and wasn't convinced the original owner had enjoyed rude health so I breathed through my mouth.

'Where are we?' I gasped, kneeling up on the bed and hastily unbuttoning my shirt.

'In the hut,' panted Willie.

His hands were quicker than mine and his shirt was off in a flash, then in an even quicker flash, his pants and trousers. He stood before me, huge, totally naked and unbelievably, gigantically, priapic.

My hands froze on my buttons, my eyes bulged, transfixed.

'Good God!'

He frowned. 'What?'

'Nothing! I'm just – religious!' I gasped, trying to tear my eyes away from what I imagined would make a very serviceable pogo stick. 'Good God bless us and keep us,' I went on, crossing myself and adding quickly – 'you too, Willie!' I really wished I hadn't said that. I was sure he was used to the sound of his own name but somehow under the circumstances . . .

He smiled and came towards me. 'Ay, I forgot you were a vicar's daughter.'

'Oh yes. Very much so!' I gulped, sounding more like a football manager now.

Still we didn't make contact. Perhaps it was a pogo stick after all? Perhaps he was just going to have a quick hop around the room then we'd sit down to a cosy cup of tea?

But such were the subtleties of dramatic effect; quite lost on me. A moment later he'd dropped to his knees on the bed in front of me, seized me in his arms, smothered me in frantic kisses, and from that moment on a cup of tea was clearly out of the question.

A dark and steamy tussle ensued with my own, recently much maligned body giving the performance of a lifetime – or a year or two at least. Zones which I'd imagined had long since ceased to be erogenous and hitherto had had to be jump – or even kick – started, roared into life with a momentum all of their own. I fizzed, crackled and spat with so much sexual energy it's a wonder I didn't spontaneously combust. Now and again, as we snaked and writhed, I'd catch a rather surprising glimpse of myself – a sleek thigh perhaps, or a snappy waist, a tight calf, a pleasantly rounded buttock turning swiftly in the moonlight and I'd gaze in wonder and think – good heavens, are those bits mine? Do they really belong to me, or am I having an out-of-body-and-into-someone-else's experience here?

It was then that it dawned on me. Of course. This was clearly the answer. Feeling a bit fat? A bit flabby? A bit unconfident? Simple, just hop into bed with the biggest man you can find, ideally the Incredible Hulk, because comparatively, you're bound to look petite, aren't you? At all costs though, I decided as I launched myself at Willie from the other end of the bed, I would avoid jockeys. That, I was sure, would be a serious morale basher. I wondered, as I rolled around wantonly in my particular Hulk's arms, if Robbie Coltrane might make himself available next year? After all, he was Scottish wasn't he? Or that huge man from *Whose Line Is It Anyway*, or any of the England scrum or – suddenly I froze. I went stiff in Willie's arms. What on earth was I talking about? What was I *thinking* about? I drew back. Was I seriously considering making a habit of rolling around in the sack with sixteen-stone giants by way of sexual therapy? By way of boosting my morale? I rocked back on my heels and stared down at Willie beneath me. He blinked up at me, flat on his back on the bed.

'What?' he panted. 'What's wrong?'

I shook my head. 'Willie, I – I can't!' I gasped.

Slowly he smiled. 'Och you're playing all provocative and hard to get now, aren't you? I know you London women with your sophisticated whip-lash ways, yull be tying me to the bed post and tickling me with yer feather duster next, come here, you little sex-machine, you little temptress you—' He made a grab for me but I shied away, jumping clean off the bed and taking the sheepskin with me for protection.

'No, Willie!' I gasped, clutching it to me.

He sat up and frowned at me in the moonlight. 'What is it? What's the matter?'

'Look, I'm terribly sorry, but I'm not sure I can go through with this.'

He stared at me. 'Not much more left, Tess, to tell you the truth. It's damn nearly over, bar the shouting.'

'I – I know, and I feel awful calling it off at the last minute, it's just that – well I don't think I can. Do it, I mean. I – think I've lost my bottle.'

I stared at him. Our eyes locked and suddenly he looked awfully huge sitting there stark naked in the moonlight. My heart began to hammer. I might have lost my bottle but I was damn sure he hadn't lost his, in fact I wondered if he might just have a handy one under the bed he could reach for and cosh me over the head with. Or perhaps he'd use his salmon-bashing implement? Or strangle me with his extremely able hands? He was after all a Scotsman and they weren't exactly renowned for their even tempers were they? I clutched the rug to me, trembling very slightly now, backing away.

'Talk about the eleventh hour, Tess.'

'I know, I know,' I whispered.

He gazed at me for a moment, then suddenly he smiled. He reached out for my hand. 'Och now don't be silly,' he said in a gentle voice. 'It's not important. Don't you go upsetting yourself over a little thing like sex.'

I blinked and stopped backing away. 'Really?' I whispered.

'Really.'

Slowly I took his hand and let him draw me down next to him. I sat on the bed beside him still wrapped in the sheepskin. 'You mean you're not – cross?'

'Of course not.' He shrugged. 'If you've changed your mind you've changed your mind, these things happen.'

I breathed in relief, squeezing his huge hand, 'Oh Willie, you're so sweet not to mind!'

'Och now don't push yer luck. I didn't say I didn't mind I just said I wasn't cross.' But he smiled. 'Come here.' He put his arm around my shoulders and kissed my cheek. We sat there companionably together for a moment. After a while he began to nibble my ear.

'Are ye quite sure now?' he mumbled.

I smiled but brushed him away. 'Quite sure.'

It was true too. My libido, which only moments before had been revving up like nobody's business, had sunk right down to join my heart, which all this time had been quietly watching from the sidelines, a spectator rather than a participant.

Willie sighed and abandoned my ear. 'Shame,' he reflected. 'Just what you needed really.'

I raised my eyebrows. 'A damn good seeing to you mean?'

He chuckled. 'Well, that was what you were after anyway, wasn't it? Only not with me?'

I opened my mouth to protest, but suddenly, couldn't be bothered. I smiled. 'Perhaps. I'm glad I didn't though.'

He shook his head wearily. 'You London women,' he mused. 'Yer like tight bloody springs when ye come up here, yer all so wound up with yer dinner parties and yer children and yer husband's office politics, you dinny know how to relax any more.'

'And you're the man to show us how are you, Willie? To uncoil our springs?'

He grinned at me sideways. 'Just yours, o' course.'

I smiled. 'Of course.'

I wondered, as we sat there together on the edge of the bed, just how many highly strung London women Willie had indeed worked his magic on. And whether he was right. Yes, maybe I would have felt better if I'd gone through with it, particularly if the warm up had been anything to go by, but in my heart I was glad I hadn't. I'd gone much too far already. I looked around for my clothes.

'I must get back.'

He held on to my shoulder, gently but firmly. 'Och now don't be running off just yet, Tess. Just because you got cold feet doesn't mean you have to scuttle away like a frightened rabbit. Lie down next to me for a few minutes and let's at least couch up and keep warm together for a bit, eh? Come on, we can still be friendly, don't leave me here on a sour note.'

I glanced across at him doubtfully. His eyes were warm and gentle. I wasn't convinced our definitions of friendly totally coincided since mine didn't usually extend to lying around stark naked with strange men in huts, but since his clearly did, it seemed rude not to somehow. I lay down hesitantly. Just for a moment or two. And anyway, I reasoned, he'd probably be asleep in a few minutes. I could slip away then.

I turned my head and glanced at him. Sure enough his eyes were closing rapidly, his chest expanding like a pair of giant bellows and his mouth dropping slowly open. A moment later he was fast asleep. I smiled. There was no way I was falling asleep, I had to get back. The trouble was I felt so damn sleepy all of a sudden. I sighed and started to raise myself up onto my elbows, but inexplicably, sank back again. My head seemed so thick and heavy, and totally opposed to movement. Perhaps I should stay and rest a moment longer? After all, it was so delightfully peaceful here in this little wooden hut by the river and I did feel so warm and relaxed and well – *safe* now that Willie was asleep. I turned my head – God, it was an effort just to do *that* – and gazed out of the grimy window to the huge pale moon that was coming up over the horizon, casting its path of milky light. Outside the birds were still singing determinedly and I could hear the river rushing by next to us. It was all so gloriously restful that I did just pull the rug up to my chin, curl my legs up and snuggle down. Slowly, gratefully, I shut my weary eyes. Just for a moment, of course.

Chapter Eleven

'No, she's definitely not here,' called a familiar voice.

'Let's walk along to the bridge and then come back on the other side,' came an equally familiar, but rather strained response. 'And then I think I'm going to ring the police, it's almost midnight.'

I opened my eyes blearily and blinked. David? Had that been David's voice? I frowned. What on earth was he doing wandering around shouting about the police – particularly if it was midnight? Why wasn't he here in bed with me? I flung my arm out for the light on the bedside table and as I did so, my hand froze. Suddenly I went cold. I sat bolt upright and the curtain came up on the nightmare. He wasn't here in bed with me because I was still in the rude sod hut with that rude sod Willie! A horrified eyes-right at the vast, inert, snoring mass beside me confirmed this terrifying truth. So David must be – I yelped silently – outside! Looking for me, searching for me, with my father. Shit! I damn nearly did. I sat for a moment, rigid with terror, then hurtled into action. I flew out of bed, and shot behind the door, waiting for the urgent rattle of the door handle for the commanding, 'Open up!' For basically, my comeuppance.

Seconds passed. Nothing happened. Nothing? No white-faced husband, no quivering, accusing finger, no fire and brimstone from the vicar? With a heart beating like a bongo drum I realised I was in some sort of reprieve here and I had to take advantage. I got a grip. First I gripped my shirt, then I gripped my pants, and then I ran for cover under the only window in the hut. I coaxed my trembling arms into my shirt-sleeves, willed my legs into my knickers, and slowly came up under the sill in silent prayer. I peered out. Oh please God, please don't let them be right outside peering in. Don't let our eyes meet! I hadn't quite grown accustomed to the dark and the window was thick with grime but after a moment, I could see that my prayer had been answered. Certainly there were a couple of shadowy figures out there wielding long sticks in the grass, certainly they did resemble my father and my husband – but thank the Lord, they were incontrovertibly *on the other side of the river.*

Oh thank you God, thank you, thank you! I fell to my knees in yet more prayer and as I did, spotted my skirt, hastily abandoned under the bed, and bent to put it on, just as David's voice rang out again across the water.

'You don't think she could be in the hut, do you, Ian? It's shallow here, I could just about wade across.'

My leg froze, poised as it was to plunge through the waistband of my skirt.

'Bound to be locked,' responded my father rationally. 'And anyway, we can try it on the way back. Come on, let's walk up to the bridge first.'

Oh bless you, Daddy, bless you and keep you in radiant health now and forever more for dissuading David from taking that retrograde step across the water and saving me from subsequent divorce proceedings!

I threw the rest of my clothes on any old how, fumbled with my buttons, managed a couple but gave up on the rest, and hastened to the door. I was off, I was out of here as they say in the movies, but as I reached for the latch, my hand stopped short. *Wait a minute, Tess.* What if they came back here and woke up Willie? I glanced over my shoulder at the huge, slumbering lump on the bed, face down, spreadeagled and snoring like a demon. What if he came round in a haze, rubbed his eyes sleepily and mumbled something like – 'Hmmm? Tess? Oh yes, she was here a moment ago. I should know, I was about to give her a damn good rogering!' Oh no, that would never do!

I grabbed his shoulder and shook it violently.

'Willie!' I hissed. 'Willie! You've got to wake up!'

I thumped him with all my might between the shoulder blades and then again in the kidneys, but I was as a flea to an elephant. He didn't so much as break the rhythm of his snores. Oh God! I looked around frantically for something to whack him with – an implement, something hard with spikes preferably. All I could see was a brace of pheasants hanging on a wall. A smutty rhyme about not being the pheasant plucker but the pheasant plucker's son sprang inconveniently to mind and only served to make me more desperate than ever to wake this pleasant fuc— this bastard up!

'Willie, for God's sake wake up!' I flung myself on top of him, straddling his back, bouncing hard, gripping with my knees in true Pony Club style.

'Willie, are you deaf? Are you dead? Wake up, will you!' I said, as loud as I dared in his ear. I bit the lobe savagely just for good measure.

'Eh, wha—?' he responded sleepily as I tugged hard at his hair.

'Willie, my husband's outside,' I gasped. 'He's got a gun!'

'Mmmm,' he mumbled. 'Not yet, Tess, later maybe.' He gave a faint sigh, smacked his huge chops and fell back to sleep, muttering something about 'insatiable bloody urban wenches'.

I clapped my hand to my mouth in horror. Oh God, this was exactly the sort of incoherent mumbling I was terrified of, I had to do something – fast! I thought wildly

155

for a second, then leaned over and cupped my hands to his ears.

'Poachers!' I hissed.

Willie's arm instinctively shot under the bed, he grabbed his gun and then rose up backwards like a monster from the depths, shaking me off his back like a drop of water. I fell with an almighty thump on the floor, landing smack on my coccyx.

'Ouch!' I yelped, as Willie strode stark naked to the door.

'Where?' he barked.

'No! No, not really!' I shrieked, flinging myself at his ankle and just managing to tackle it before he could push open the door and blow my husband's brains out. He tried to shake me off but I sank my teeth into his Achilles heel.

'Ow!'

'Then listen!' I pleaded. 'Not poachers, Willie, David! He's out there with my father – they're looking for me.'

Willie frowned down at me from his gigantic height. Slow thought processes began to engage. He scratched his huge, giant's head.

'David?'

For a moment I wondered if I wasn't in fact addressing Goliath here and I was about to get a front-row seat at a very modern stoning.

'Yes, David, my husband, you stupid great berk!' I croaked, very nearly croaking comprehensively right there and then on the floor-boards. My heart seemed very weak; I wasn't sure if it could take much more of this. Then I heard a truly terrifying sound. *Running footsteps.* And the voice accompanying the footsteps belonged to my husband.

'There's someone in the hut!' he shouted.

Willie and I stared at each other.

'Quick, under the bed,' Willie hissed, suddenly very much alive to the situation.

Sadly I was very much dead, paralysed from the brain down. Willie seized me and with his huge paws, folded me in half like a camp bed then shoved me under, just managing to kick a recalcitrant leg out of sight as the door flew open.

'Oi!' roared Willie as my husband and father flew in. 'What's going on?'

'Willie,' panted David, 'we're looking for Tess. Have you seen her?'

'Fock me, I thought you were poachers,' bellowed Willie convincingly enough, still stark naked and handily brandishing a gun. 'Nearly wasted the pair of ye!'

'Have you seen Tess?' demanded David again.

Under the bed I shut my eyes tight, pressed my nose hard into the floorboards and prayed to Almighty God that the rampant, nervous diarrhoea that was threatening to engulf me didn't, nor that my legs, which seemed to be twitching convulsively, would shoot out and kick my husband inadvertently on the ankle, thus giving the game away.

'Tess?' said Willie. 'No. Why, is she lost?'

David's voice when it came was harsh and unnatural. 'Been gone since teatime,' he said. 'Terrified she's fallen in the river. So dark.'

Oh my poor love, my poor love! I shed silent, guilty tears for my stricken, fearful husband. 'I'll make it up to you,' I sincerely promised an earwig which was trapped down a crack in the floorboards. Oh David, David, David, I'm so sorry. I'll make it up to you, I swear!

'Och noo, no danger of that,' soothed Willie. 'I've been up and doon this river all evening, had a feeling there was poachers about, ye see. Thought I'd kip in here to make sure and came in about half an hour ago. I'd know if there was somat amiss. If you ask me she's fallen asleep somewhere. Had she been drinking?'

'Well, yes,' David admitted, 'she had.'

'She'd had a whole damn bottle!' barked my father. 'Willie's right, she's asleep in some blasted field somewhere, and she won't come to till dawn with all that alcohol inside her. I'll tell you something, when she does, I'll give her a piece of my mind!'

I quaked silently under the bed.

'Well, I hope you're right.' David sounded slightly reassured.

'Tell you what,' suggested Willie. 'We'll try yellin' for her. You go off in that direction towards Frenche's Farm, I'll go back upriver, and you mark my words if we don't find her in some haystack or trip over her in a ditch or something.'

I hadn't actually taken a breath for a full, terrifying forty seconds now, but as things did seem to be reaching some sort of a climax, I allowed myself a brief inhalation lest I fall into a coma. This achieved, and still staying perfectly still, I swivelled my eyeballs up from the floorboards and right. Just eighteen inches away were my father's black boots, to the left of those, David's green ones, and completing the triangle, Willie's bare feet. I saw Willie's hand come down. He reached for his trousers, pulled them on, then seized his own boots and set them upright, dextrously flipping the white bra strap that was hanging decoratively out of the side of one inside and trampling it down with his foot. I whimpered silently to the earwig.

'Come on then, off we go, no point hanging about,' Willie ordered. 'We're not going to find her in here, are we?' And with that he ushered the search-party out of his hut.

This struck me as being a particularly sick joke, but I blessed him from the bottom of my overworked heart, knowing he was doing a damn good job of saving my bacon. I counted shakily to a hundred and when it was clear the posse of men would not be coming back with a search warrant, I crawled out from under the bed.

Still feeling very wobbly, I crossed over to the window and peered out just in time to see them disappear round the bend; Willie in one direction, David and my father in the other. With a last furtive look around in case I'd left something, I too slunk out. I tiptoed round the back of the hut, found my shoes where I'd kicked them off in a joyful moment in Willie's arms – thank God they'd missed those – and hastily slipped into them. Then I scurried off on very shaky legs in the direction of home and hopefully, safety.

I scampered along in the dark, my heart hammering high in my oesophagus. Dad and David were heading off to Frenche's Farm which meant I had to run like billyo to a destination somewhere in between there and the house so they could neatly trip over me on their way back, that much was clear. I hurtled along, leaping ditches, hurdling low stone walls and eventually came to the footpath I knew they'd take to get home. With a thumping heart I sank down in a ditch. This would have to do. This was just about the route they were bound to take back. I drew up my knees and hugged them hard, shivering wildly, my eyes huge with horror.

Let's get this straight then, Tess. You've just had a sexy romp with Willie the gillie, is that right? Interesting departure from the norm, but we'll discuss that later. For the moment though, here you are in a ditch. In a field. In the middle of the night. How on earth had this happened, I wondered in amazement. How on earth had this situation even *begun* to arise, let alone escalated into this? Right at this moment it just didn't bear thinking about. What did though, was how to successfully extricate myself from it. I had to keep my head, that much was clear. There'd be plenty of time for horror and remorse later.

Five minutes went by, then ten, until finally, I heard footsteps again. Numb with cold and terror, especially since my renown as an actress is not great, I began to make strange mumbling noises. As the footsteps got closer, I stretched my arms above my head and gave what I hoped was an accurate rendition of a sleepy yawn, but actually had more of a ring of a deranged harridan about it. The footsteps halted.

'What's that?' said David.

'What?'

I yawned and mumbled again.

'Over there, I heard something!'

I stretched widely this time. '*Ohhhh* . . . goodness gracious me. What a lovely sleep . . . mmmm, lovely.'

'Tess!'

In a moment the footsteps were a running stampede and in another, I was being scooped up into my husband's arms.

'Tess! Thank God!' He hugged me close.

'David? What?' I rubbed my eyes.

I hoped he wasn't hugging me close enough to notice that my heart was pumping unnaturally fast for someone who's just been raised from a deep, soporific slumber.

'What the hell happened to you? We've been looking everywhere for you!'

'You've got some explaining to do, my girl,' barked my father.

I cringed, but somehow this was infinitely preferable to David's relieved tones. Oh yes, give me a hair shirt right now, and knickers to match. I'd slip them on and wear them for ever.

Hating myself, I gazed at David and feigned a puzzled stare.

'Hello darling, what are you doing here?'

'I'm bloody looking for you, that's what I'm doing

here,' he burst out, relief quite rightly turning to outrage. 'I'm tramping up and down this sodding river all night wondering if my drunken wife has fallen in leaving two motherless children, that's what I'm bloody doing!'

I rubbed my eyes. 'Mmm, I must have fallen asleep. I came out for a walk and sat down here in the ditch and it was so lovely and peaceful and the stars were so beautiful, I must have drifted off . . .' I looked around in amazement. 'Goodness, it's pitch dark.'

David took me fiercely by the arm. 'Well, it would be, wouldn't it, it's one o'clock in the morning! Come on. We're going home.'

'I'll go and tell Willie,' muttered my father angrily. 'You *stupid* girl, Tessa.'

And with that he strode off in the other direction to tell Willie what he already knew.

David and I started for home in silence. He held on to my arm as I stumbled along in the dark, tripping over tufts of grass. I glanced up. His face was white and his lips very tight.

'Sorry, darling,' I said tentatively. 'I didn't mean to worry you.'

David's mouth remained tense. He looked straight ahead.

'David?'

'Unless you want to be on the receiving end of a torrent of abuse,' he snapped, 'I should bloody well keep quiet and let me seethe in private, OK?'

'OK,' I mumbled.

We walked quickly and quite soon were crossing the back lawn up to the house.

'The lights are all on,' I said in surprise.

'Well of course,' said David with scarce-disguised sarcasm. 'Piers is poised to ring the undertaker, Penny's planning her funeral outfit and your mother's choosing the hymns.'

'Oh David, I'm so sorry,' I gasped. 'I didn't realise I'd worried everyone so much.'

The back door swung open as we approached and Mummy peered out, white-faced in her dressing gown.

'Thank God!' she whispered, giving me a hug.

'Sorry, Mummy,' I murmured into her shoulder, feeling truly, deeply appalling now. 'I – I fell asleep.'

'Where?'

'In a field.'

'Darling!'

Penny and Piers were sitting at the kitchen table in their pyjamas. They gave me a pair of withering looks, then got up, yawned ostentatiously and made for the stairs.

'Sorry Penny, Piers,' I muttered after them. They didn't reply.

Mummy patted me on the shoulder, recovering slightly. 'Never mind. At least you're safe, that's all that matters.'

She smiled and rather shakily picked up her *Telegraph* from the table. She followed the others upstairs, using the banisters for support, I noted, rather more than she would normally. I gulped, mortified.

'Come on then,' said David gruffly. 'Let's go up too.'

We went upstairs together in silence. When we got to our room I went on through into the bathroom.

'I'm going to have a quick bath,' I muttered.

'What now?' he demanded. 'In the middle of the night?'

I nodded miserably as I peeled off my clothes and threw them at the foot of the bed.

'I must,' I whispered. 'Won't be long.'

I lay back in the hot, bubbly water and stared numbly at the bathroom ceiling. Great waves of shame and self-disgust swept over me. How awful. How completely despicable of me. How could I have done such a thing? Jeopardised my marriage, my family like that – and for what? A quick roll in the hay with a man I'd never even really noticed before, let alone fancied? Jesus, when you think about it, it could have been anyone, couldn't it – Edward, Piers – whoever had just happened to be strolling on by that night. *Oh, hello Tess, fancy a quick one? Sure, why not?* What was I, a tart or something? I groaned and sank down in the water, Badedas, shame and revulsion washing over me.

What on earth had got into me? Well, drink, obviously, a whole bottle in fact, and rejection too, of course. Patrick and Josie zooming off like that had really got my blood up, but – good grief, Tess, that's no excuse. I shouldn't even have been thinking about Patrick in the first place! I was a married woman. Suddenly I seized the soap. I had to be clean, really clean. I soaped and scrubbed every inch of myself, employing flannels, sponges, whatever cleaning equipment came to hand, a Brillo pad would have done nicely, but then just as suddenly, I stopped. I dropped the flannel in the water and sank down miserably into the bubbles. What was the use? I'd never be truly clean again, would I?

The full implications of what I'd done hit me. I'd cheated. I'd betrayed David. I'd had – not a fling, because that sounded so impulsive, so carefree – and not an affair because that sounded more serious, more intense, two people completely at the mercy of their romantic impulses . . . no, what I'd had was casual sex. Not all the way, granted. Happily I'd had the sense to resist that temptation, but quite a lot of the way nonetheless. I wondered, tentatively, if this made me, not a fallen woman but just a stumbling one? Since I hadn't actually gone the whole hog? Just a half hog?

I shivered even though the water was piping hot. No, that was undoubtedly a blessing but it was no mitigation.

I still had a hell of a lot of explaining to do. Oh dear God, I muttered silently, please forgive me. I eyed the ceiling nervously. It was a long time since I'd addressed Him properly, rather than just angrily in passing because I'd tripped over the carpet or lost my car keys. No, I hadn't prayed for a long time, chiefly because I always identified Him with my father. In fact, it seemed to me that even now, floating above me, was not an old man with a long white beard and a staff, but a middle-aged man with a bristling moustache and a dog collar. The Reverend Ian Fergusson. I winced.

Dear God, I struggled on, I'm well aware I've made a complete and utter pig's ear of things tonight, but I swear that I'll make amends. From now on I am determined to devote myself entirely to my husband and family. To be nothing more than a good wife and mother. I took a deep breath. I intend to darn socks rather than throw them away. I intend to make puddings rather than chuck yoghurts on the table and demand to know what's wrong with that? I intend to make plum jam – David's favourite – to fingerpaint, to throw away all the children's videos, particularly those Disney ones that immobilise them for a blissful eighty-six minutes, and instead I intend to read them storybooks for eighty-six minutes. I winced slightly at this but staunchly continued. I intend to indulge in frequent bouts of imaginative play with my children, to be Robin to Hugo's Batman, to be Barbie's pony, to neigh, whinny and trot on command and to indulge in frequent bouts of imaginative sex with my husband – not all at the same time, you understand, but I think you get the general idea. In short, I intend to subjugate my own wishes to those of my family and this, dear God, is something that I want You to know I do willingly. When I think how close I came to losing them, to ruining everything – oh dear God, it simply doesn't bear thinking about! With this I sank back in the water and covered my face with a flannel.

I lay there motionless for a while, when suddenly I heard a noise. I whipped the flannel off. There was a sort of rustling sound coming from the bedroom. I sat up. Good heavens, was David still awake? Was he waiting for me? Reading perhaps? Crikey, I'd been ages! I quickly hopped out of the bath and rubbed myself dry with a towel. I did hope he wasn't waiting to interrogate me or something, I'd rather hoped he'd be sound asleep by now. I stopped still for a moment and listened. No, it was all quiet again now, it must have been the sheets rustling as he turned over. He wouldn't interrogate me anyway, I thought gratefully, it wasn't in his nature. He always believed people, always thought the best of them. I wrapped a dry towel around me and crept back into the bedroom. Yes, my darling husband, he didn't have a suspicious bone in his body, he—

'David!'

I stopped dead in my tracks. My darling husband stood at the foot of the bed peering very suspiciously into my underwear.

'What's all this sheep's wool?' he enquired, picking up my shirt. 'Look, it's everywhere.'

I gazed down. All over the carpet and inside my clothes was indeed a huge amount of white fluffy stuff. I gulped. 'Ah, that'll be the sheep,' I croaked.

'What sheep?'

'The one I fell asleep on.'

'You fell asleep on a sheep?'

'Not a live one.'

'A dead one?'

'Er . . .' There didn't seem to be another option. 'Yes. A dead one. I didn't realise at the time, of course. Just thought it was a nice cosy pillow.'

'But . . . the field we found you in didn't have any sheep in it.'

'Ah, no, I moved. When I realised. Hopped over a wall into a different field.'

'Good God. And went back to sleep?'

I hung my head and shook it miserably. 'I was very, very drunk, you know.'

David briefly tore his hair. 'Clearly. God, it must have reeked.'

'Oh it did, and that's why I wanted a bath so much,' I went on quickly. 'To get rid of the pong.'

David dropped my clothes hurriedly. He shook his head in disbelief, sighed and got into bed.

'Why are you still awake?' I mumbled, climbing in next to him and quickly turning out the light so he couldn't see my flaming face.

'Because I wanted to tell you something.'

'What?' I sat up in alarm, my heart leaping into my mouth. He was leaving me. He'd seen through the whole charade.

'Peter rang when you were out.'

'Oh!' I relaxed. 'Your clerk?'

'Mmm. There's some case that's come up, he wants me to fly back and do it.'

I lay down again. 'Oh, what a bore. When?'

'Tomorrow.'

'Tomorrow! What did you say?'

'I said I would. I have to, Tess. It's a Court of Appeal thing that was supposed to have surfaced ages ago and didn't. Now it's suddenly reared its ugly head again.'

I lay there, realising I didn't have a leg to stand on. Normally I'd be incensed, argue long and hard about how his work was yet again ruining the only family holiday of the year and how on earth was I supposed to cope with the children on my own, et cetera . . .

'So you'll go tomorrow?' I said meekly.

'After breakfast. Just thought I'd mention it tonight in case you fancied a lie-in after your hectic night out with your dead sheep and woke to find your husband had packed his bags and gone. Just thought I'd let you know it's nothing personal,' he said grimly.

'Ah!' I laughed nervously. 'Righto, darling. Thanks for letting me know.'

'My pleasure,' he said darkly, before finally falling asleep.

Chapter Twelve

The following morning I awoke late to find that David had already gone. The covers on his side of the bed were thrown back and a couple of wet towels lay abandoned in a heap on the floor. Normally I'd smile, stretch lazily and think how nice it was to have the bed to myself, but on this particular morning I badly wanted to see him there next to me. The empty pillow looked at me reproachfully. I sighed, hating myself already, but although my conscience hurt like hell it was nothing to the physical state I was in. My head was throbbing like a New Wave disco, my mouth was desert-dry and my bladder so fit to burst I had to get out of bed that very second, and since our bathroom didn't possess a loo – that would be far too convenient – make my way as fast as possible down to the one at the end of the corridor.

I lumbered along the landing like some rough beast with my eyes half-shut and my hands already outstretched and groping for the door, when Penny suddenly stepped out in front of me, in true paparazzi style. She'd clearly been loitering around the airing cupboard for some time, waiting for a chance to doorstep me, to get an exclusive. Her eyes gleamed alarmingly as she barred the way with a mountain of ironing in her arms. I stumbled to a halt in front of her.

'Oh, good *morning*,' she chirruped, 'and how are we feeling today?'

'Er, fine, thanks Penny,' I lied. 'Has David gone?'

'Yes, Piers took him to the airport. We thought you might need a lie-in after last night.' She raised her eyebrows. 'Quite an adventure, eh? David said something about a dead sheep. Really setting your sights high this time, aren't you?'

'Ah, yes. Um, that was kind of Piers. To take David, I mean.' I tried to sidle past her but she sidled with me.

'Wasn't it?' she said beaming broadly, obviously on the brink of whipping out her microphone and asking one of her most probing questions.

'So tell me, Tess, what exactly – oi!'

With one quick flick I knocked the pile of ironing clean out of her hands and sidestepped around her.

'Oops, sorry, Penny! Hand slipped! Can't stop now, emergency!'

I sprinted on past her, but as luck would have it, arrived at the loo at precisely the same moment as Josie, whose bedroom was next door. Our hands simultaneously went for the handle.

'Sorry, go ahead,' I muttered.

'Oh hi, Tess. What happened last night?'

'Oh well, you know, this and that,' I said, grinning manically and hopping around from foot to foot. God, if I could just have a pee, was that too much to ask first thing in the morning? The place seemed to be swarming with budding interrogative journalists. Couldn't they organise a press conference later or something?

'Um, are you—?' I jerked my head towards the loo.

'No no,' she insisted. 'You first.'

'Thanks.' I dashed in. Oh, the relief . . .

When I came out she was still waiting. She smiled. 'My evening didn't amount to much either,' she said.

I stared at her blankly for a moment, then remembered. Of course, Patrick.

'Oh yes, how was it?' I asked politely. As if I cared! God, I never wanted to so much as *talk* to another man aside from my husband as long as I lived!

'It was OK,' she said, nodding without much conviction.

'Really?'

'Well,' she grimaced, 'maybe not. In the end we only went for a quick drink. I was back here by ten.'

'Oh!'

'Yeah,' she scratched her chin. 'He'd forgotten he had some phone calls to make to Italy, about his work. Galleries, that kind of thing.'

'Oh, right. Did you mind?'

She shrugged. 'Nah, not really. To be honest I think he's a bit old for me, or maybe I'm too young for him. Actually I don't even think he's that interested, I think he just thought I'd look good on the back of his bike.' She grinned good-humouredly.

That was what I liked about Josie, she had such refreshing Aussie candour.

'Well, you certainly did,' I said warmly. 'You looked great. I saw you go off.'

'He saw you too,' she said. 'Hey, I had no idea you two were an item?'

'Oh, er, yes. A long time ago.'

'Yeah, he said.' She folded her arms and leant on the wall as if we might be there for some time. 'In fact, he said—'

'Um, listen Josie,' I interrupted, unwilling to discuss any more of my menfolk, past or present, with anyone else on the landing that morning. 'I've got something I must do this morning. It's quite important. You wouldn't mind having the children on your own for a few hours, would you? I know you're due a morning off, but—'

'Nah, it's fine. We'll go down to the beach, go crabbing.'

'Oh thanks, you're a brick.'

She was. There was no malice in Josie's heart, and I

171

shuddered as I remembered how I'd maligned her last night. And then I shuddered some more as I remembered everything else about last night too . . . Still, that was all in the past now and would be firmly entrenched there for ever if I had anything to do with it.

I threw some clean clothes on and went down to breakfast. Thankfully, most people appeared to have eaten already. Piers had taken David to the airport, Penny, thwarted in her attempts to cross-examine me, was about to go shopping, and Mummy and Laura had gone fishing. Only my father and Edward remained, and I soon found out why. Daddy was in full swing, furiously brandishing the *Telegraph* and ranting away to poor Edward about some vicar who'd got more or less every girl in his parish pregnant. Happily he was far too incensed to remember anything about last night, let alone berate me. I slipped quietly into a chair, blessed the randy vicar from the bottom of my heart and began to butter some toast.

'Makes me spit!' he thundered, poking his finger at the newspaper. 'And it's not as if they'll even *do* anything about it, he probably won't even get his wrists slapped! Oh no, in all probability what he'll get is a nice spot of therapy, a caring shoulder to cry on so he can lay all his misdemeanours at society's door and explain exactly why he felt it was his bounden duty to knock up every single girl in the parish and all, mark my words, at the wretched tax payer's expense! Oh yes, the National Health Service will foot the counselling bill and then all the pregnant wenches will stagger into National Health hospitals to have his bastards and then they'll all be sent to bloody state schools, and who's paying for all that, eh?'

He glared at Edward who blinked nervously.

'I am, that's who and you, too, Edward! What's more you'll probably have to *teach* the bastards too! And all because a vicar, a man of the cloth, a *servant of God*, dips his wick in every passing fecund wench he fancies! MAKES MY BLOOD BOIL!' he bellowed.

Edward quaked into his porridge.

'He should be strung up, made an example of, eh?' He glared at the pair of us but I'd already propped up the *Guardian* Arts section on the Frosties packet and was well and truly unavailable for comment.

'Oh yes sir, definitely sir,' muttered Edward timidly.

'He should be setting an example – *noblesse oblige* and all that. Has he no concept of duty, of – where are you off to, Tess?'

I paused, halfway out of the door with a piece of toast in my hand. Damn. Thought I'd timed that rather nicely, actually.

'I have to go and see Willie.' Best not to lie.

My father raised his eyebrows enquiringly. 'Oh?'

'Yes. I left some of my best flies down by the river yesterday and I think he's probably picked them up.' Best to lie.

'Hrmph. Well, you won't find him at the river today, it's his day off. He'll be at home.' He frowned, suddenly remembering. 'Now then Tessa, what on earth was last night all about, eh? David and I spent the best part of two hours looking for you. Your mother was worried sick!'

I took a deep breath and was about to embark on an elaborate explanation when my eye suddenly lit on the same offending article in the *Guardian*. Marvellous. I screwed my eyes up quizzically.

'Oh look, there's a picture of that vicar in here too. Did you know him, Daddy?' I asked innocently.

My father glanced across at the unfortunate man's mugshot and came rapidly to the boil again.

'Makes me spit!' he roared, spitting indeed, a small piece of toast right across the table and hitting Edward squarely in the eye. He flinched in terror.

'No, I didn't know him, thank God! Dirty little scumbag, he was no friend of mine – but then that's hardly surprising, is it? A family man like me with no extra-marital affairs to speak of like most of the clergy – no prizes for guessing why I won't be the next Bishop of Durham, eh? No good at all to the modern church am I, eh? What?' He glared at the only person who hadn't dared to make an escape like everyone else.

I tiptoed out.

'Er, no sir, I mean yes sir, I'm sure you are sir,' I heard poor Edward mumble as I slipped down the hall.

My car keys were on the hall table. So Willie would be at home today, eh? Even better, even more private. I'd go and see him there. It was probably totally unnecessary but I wanted to make things crystal clear to that man. Warn him off. I was quite sure he knew how the land lay, that it had been a drunken mistake, I cringed – a never-to-be-repeated foolish escapade . . . but it wouldn't do any harm to make sure.

I ran down the stone steps into the drive and realised it looked remarkably empty. Damn, no cars. Piers had taken his to the airport so Penny had obviously taken mine shopping. That left Daddy's, which I wasn't convinced I was insured for. I was about to go back and ask him when I spotted the bicycles in the front porch. I paused. Yes, why not? I didn't particularly want to encounter Daddy again, and apart from anything else a cycle-ride would do me good. Blow the cobwebs away. When was the last time I'd had any decent exercise? Apart from last night, of course.

I wheeled a pretty ancient-looking contraption out into the drive and inspected it. No gears, naturally, but it appeared to have two wheels, a saddle and at least one brake, and it wasn't as if I was going to go very fast, was it? Anyway, Willie didn't live too far away. If I got sick of it I could abandon it in a hedge and pick it up later. I got on, wobbled precariously, then pedalled unsteadily down the drive. I went through the gate, round the corner and set off in the direction of Willie's house.

The first half-mile was easy enough – a doddle, in fact, I thought cheerfully as I gently pedalled along the lanes enjoying the fresh air. But then a hill appeared, followed by another and then another, and all of them went up, rather than down. I'd been past Willie's house once before in the car but I certainly hadn't remembered it enjoying quite such an elevated position, being quite so much in orbit as it were. God, I'd be on a different planet soon. On and on I pedalled and puffed, onwards and upwards, my legs going not so much like pistons as shivering lumps of cellulite. Finally I dismounted and pushed the wretched thing up the hill, once more bemoaning my lack of aerobics classes. Good grief, I'd need an oxygen cylinder soon. Surely no more hills? Just the one, a vertical one as it happened, around the next bend, and then just as I thought I might give up and collapse in a heap in the hedge, Willie's little bungalow came into view. It was clustered amongst ten or twelve other identical white bungalows – for moral support, almost – on this vast mountainside, looking as if just one little shove from behind would cause the whole lot to slide off down into the valley below.

I threw my bike down outside, boiling hot now and in a muck sweat, and fumbled gratefully with the garden gate. I was keen to be inside where there seemed less danger of plummeting into the abyss. I rapped smartly on the front door and as Willie opened it, realised I'd been so taken up with my epic journey I hadn't the faintest idea what I was going to say.

'Hi!' I gasped, discovering that actually I couldn't speak anyway. I bent double, clutched my knees for support and fought for oxygen.

Willie looked down at me in surprise, dressed as he

was in nothing but a green towelling dressing gown with a piece of toast in one hand, a mug of tea in the other.

'Tess! What on earth are you doin' here?'

I made some vague hand-movements to try to convey that I couldn't actually speak right now but would endeavour to do so just as soon as was humanly possible.

Willie looked over my bent back at my bike in the hedge. 'Good God, you didn't cycle here, did you?'

It was rather like being in the dentist's chair with half a ton of steel equipment in one's mouth and an invitation to speak at length on a chosen subject. He ushered me in and I followed, still speechless but boiling to death under my Guernsey after all that exertion.

'Just a second,' I panted, struggling to pull the wretched thing over my head. When I emerged from its woolly depths, a rather alarming light was gleaming in Willie's eye. 'Changed your mind, eh, Tess? Fine by me! Hang on, I'll just get rid of my breakfast and then I'll get my kit off too.'

He stuffed a whole piece of toast in his mouth and went for his dressing-gown cord. I recoiled. Oh no! He thought I'd come to finish the job! Thought I'd cycled feverishly up a mountainside to get to grips with his naked person only hours after I'd left it in the rude sod hut!

'No!' I shrieked. 'No, Willie. I—'

Too late. The cord was being loosened. I instantly clapped my hands over my eyes.

'Put it away,' I hissed. 'For God's sake, didn't you get enough of that last night? I know I did, now put it away!'

There was a pause.

'Has it gone?' I demanded.

'Well, I certainly can't see it,' said a female voice, 'unless it's very, very wee.'

I gasped in horror and swung around. A pretty dark-haired girl with freckles and a cheeky grin popped her

176

head out from the other side of the sofa where she'd clearly been reclining.

'Oh!'

'Tess, this is Kirsten,' Willie informed me, a wicked smile on his face. His dressing-gown was still firmly wound up, like me I realised. I blushed.

The girl swung her brown legs round, stood up and came towards us. Long dark hair, a waist, the shortest of denim skirts and a red gingham shirt tied in a knot above her midriff. I was old enough to be her mother, but probably far too ugly. She grinned at me.

'Don't mind me, I was just off.'

'Oh! No! Well, you don't have to,' I blustered, pushing my sweaty hair out of my eyes. 'I mean we weren't – I mean there's nothing—'

She winked. 'I should pick up where you left off last night if I were you. Bye Willie, have fun!'

She tapped him playfully on the cheek and sauntered out. I listened for a scream, hoping she might fall over the precipice but no such luck.

'Who was that?' I asked faintly.

'Kirsten,' said Willie with a grin. 'She . . . um,' he wrinkled his brow thoughtfully, 'she came to borrow some tea-bags.'

I stared at him. 'Oh yeah? Well, she forgot to take them with her, didn't she, unless she stuffed them in her handbag.'

'Yes, she did actually.' Willie calmly bent down to pick a couple of empty coffee mugs up off the carpet. He straightened up and looked at me. 'Kirsten's my cousin, Tess. She lives down the road.'

I flushed. 'Oh! Gosh, I'm sorry Willie. It's none of my business anyway.'

Willie went behind the breakfast bar to turn a whistling kettle off. 'Och, it's only natural,' he grinned. 'You don't want to feel one of many.'

'No, I don't! I mean, it doesn't matter if I am or not, if you see what I mean. That's what I came to tell you. What happened down by the river shouldn't have, should it? Well, I'm – sure you know that already, but I just thought I'd better come and make sure.'

He poured the boiling water into a teapot, watching me. Silent.

I licked my lips and laughed nervously. 'Come on, Willie, help me out here. I mean it was just a one off, wasn't it? Great fun and all that but it was a mistake, *my* mistake, and I don't want it to happen again,' I said decisively.

He put the kettle down and looked at me carefully. 'Aye, but it will though, won't it?'

'What?'

'Happen again.'

'No! Certainly not. That's what I—'

'Och, I don't mean with me, necessarily, but I'm pretty sure that's not the end of your extra-marital activity.' He smiled. 'Let's face it, Tess, up until you got cold feet you were absolutely panting for it.'

I flushed. 'How dare you! I was not!'

He laughed. 'Och now, don't get excited. Nothing wrong with being keen; nothing wrong with enjoying things, is there?' He winked.

'Certainly there's something wrong if it's outside the marriage bed,' I stormed piously. 'You can't just go around doing it with whoever takes your fancy, not when you've got responsibilities, a husband and family like I have. People could get hurt.'

'Of course,' he agreed, 'and that's why it's so much better to do it with me than with anyone else.' He twinkled knowingly at me. 'Especially the person you originally had marked out for the job.'

I flushed. 'What d'you mean?'

'Come on now.' He handed me a cup of tea. 'Don't

give me that. I knew damn well you'd been thwarted in some way yesterday. I also knew Patrick was back.'

'What's that got to do with it?'

He leaned on the breakfast bar and sighed. 'Tess, this is a small community. Everyone knows everything about everyone else. Everyone knows you had an affair with him years ago, everyone knows you never got over each other and everyone knows he's back. And so are you. Perhaps not everyone knows he chose to take your nanny out on a date late last night though.' He sipped his tea, regarding me thoughtfully over the top of his mug.

'That's got nothing to do with it,' I exploded. 'I was not looking for anything with Patrick, I was—'

He raised his eyebrows. 'Just looking forward to a bit of a treat, wasn't that what you said?'

I bit my lip and looked away. I could feel my face flaming.

Willie chuckled. 'Och Tess, I'm not laughing at you, really I'm not. Not unkindly anyway.' He came round from the other side of the bar and put his arm round my shoulder. 'And you're right, this is a serious business. That's why I'm tellin' you.' He turned me round to face him, his expression grim. 'Think carefully before you mess around with the likes o' Patrick Cameron.'

'What d'you mean?' I whispered. 'Not that I intend to,' I added quickly.

'What I mean is you might not be able to extricate yourself from his arms quite so easily as you did from mine.'

'I haven't the faintest idea what you're talking about,' I said sharply, shrugging his hands off my shoulders.

He sat down on a bar stool next to me and sipped his tea. 'Look at it this way, Tess. Sex with me is safe, isn't it?'

I laughed hollowly. 'I'm not so sure, judging by the

amount of women flitting in and out of your life.'

'What I mean is,' he went on, 'that you can almost regard me as a sort of service industry.' He flashed me an infuriatingly attractive grin. 'A bit of a meals-on-wheels if you like, or a mobile library. You have a need and I fill it, but with no strings attached. Certainly no heart-strings. It's just good old-fashioned lust, isn't it? But you fill that need with Patrick Cameron and mark my words, it'll be a whole new ball game. All those repressed emotions you two put the lid on years ago?' He shook his head. 'You open up that can of worms again and you won't know what's hit you.'

I smiled a superior smile. 'Willie, thank you for your concern but I assure you I have no intention of opening anything.' I took a gulp of tea. It was scalding hot and I burned my mouth.

He grinned. 'Oh good. I'm not sure I believe you, though. I still think you have a need.'

Suddenly I bridled. How *dare* he cross-examine me like this? I drew myself up haughtily.

'Yes, well, thank you so much for these pearls of wisdom about my life, Willie. I'm indebted to you, really I am, but rest assured I do *not* have a need and I certainly don't have one that requires filling with yours, or anyone else's "services" as you so quaintly put it. I require neither meals-on-wheels nor sex-on-tap which is, I take it, what you were offering. What happened last night was not only totally out of character but happened entirely under the influence of alcohol, something I do not generally indulge in. I want you to remember that.'

His mouth twitched. 'Och aye, I'll remember all right.'

'*That* is what I came here to tell you and that is all I have to say on the matter.' Was it my imagination or did I sound like Margaret Thatcher? 'Thank you for your concern but it's not necessary, do I make myself clear?'

He wrestled with a smile. 'Crystal.'

'Good.'

'Sorry if I spoke out of turn.'

'Not at all.'

'You're too kind.'

I turned away exasperated and drained my tea in silence. How did he manage to make me feel such a fool? It was infuriating! I was the educated, urbane, sophisticated one, wasn't I? He was just a blinking gillie, for heaven's sake . . . a keeper. What did he know about life in the real world? The one that went on beyond the trees and the fields and the river, the one that thinking, chattering people lived in? This wasn't real life, damn it, this was a ruddy Utopia, a holiday camp. What did anyone who lived like this know, aside from which pools to fish and what the weather would be like tomorrow? A silence fell. Eventually Willie cleared his throat.

'So what happens now?'

I looked up, miles away. 'What? Oh, yes.' I stood up. 'I must be going.'

'No, no, I didn't mean that, I meant in your life.'

I frowned. 'Sorry?'

'Well, you're married now, you've had your bairns, your second one's about to start school, you've got your nice house in Putney, presumably you've more or less finished tarting it up, painting the dado rails, quarry-tiling the floor, adding a conservatory and you don't need a country cottage 'cos your dad's got this place . . . so what happens next?'

'Why does anything have to happen next?'

He shrugged. 'It always has done, hasn't it? Up to now? You've always had something to occupy you, to look forward to. A wedding, a bairn, another bairn, a house – so what's next?'

I sighed and folded my arms, regarding him narrowly. 'Why is it, Willie, that I get the distinct impression we're back to sex again? You mean an affair, don't you?'

'It's either that or an art appreciation course, or Silk Screens Made Easy, or Opera for Beginners perhaps, and I know which I'd rather do!' He grinned.

I shook my head wearily and stood up. 'You really are incorrigible, and I don't know where you get your information about London women from, but you're woefully misinformed.'

Willie stood up. 'First-hand knowledge, Tess, not information. I see women like you all year round – and no, I don't sleep with them – but I observe them. Get a glimpse of their lives, their frustrations. I sympathise, really I do.' He put his arm round my shoulder as we walked to the door.

'Well gosh, Willie, I'm sure the entire female population of South East England will be truly comforted to know your thoughts are with us. That we can rely on your sympathy and understanding as we go about our boring, mundane lives.'

He chuckled, then as we reached the door, turned me around to face him. 'Seriously though, all I'm saying is that these are dangerous times.'

I raised my eyebrows at him. 'Oh really? For who?'

'For you, of course. At this stage in your life you're very vulnerable.' He bent down and kissed me on the cheek. 'Take care, Tess.' He stroked my cheek. 'I shall worry about you, you know.'

I smiled. He really was quite sweet. If a little simplistic. 'OK, I'll take care,' I assured him, humouring him.

He kissed me on the other cheek. 'See that you do.'

'I will, I will!'

He kissed me on the side of my mouth, softly. 'No, but really Tess,' he murmured, 'I mean it.'

'Yes, yes I mean it too,' I murmured back as he kissed me again. Heavens that was nice, all warm and soft and . . . No! I pushed him away, angrily, furious with myself. Willie was laughing, his eyes dancing.

'You see?' He wagged his finger. 'Very, very dangerous!'

'No, I do not bloody see!' I stormed, wrestling with the doorknob. 'I haven't the faintest idea what you're talking about and if you'll excuse me I've got a million things to do today. I've got shopping to do, meals to cook, washing to do – art appreciation – ha! I wish! Opera for Beginners – Jesus, if only I had time! What happens next? Good God, I haven't got time for what happens *now*! For your information, Willie, I am always on the bloody go, I never sit still, there is never a moment in my hectic life that is not catered for and— Oh for God's sake open this sodding door and let me out of here before—'

'Before?' he enquired mildly.

'Before I wring your neck,' I hissed.

He laughed, reached up and pulled back the bolt at the top. I fled down the path to my bike.

'Pedal carefully now, Tess,' he warned, watching as I lifted the bicycle out of the hedge and swung my leg over. 'Don't go charging up a tractor's backside in your hot and bothered state.'

I wobbled precariously. 'Who's hot and bothered!' I cried. 'I've never been so blinking calm in my life!'

'Oh, by the way – catch!' He threw something and a rather grey bra landed on my head. 'I found this bit of erotica in my boot!' I grabbed it furiously and stuffed it in my pocket. I didn't look back but out of the corner of my eye I caught sight of him, head thrown back, laughing like a drain as I took off down the vertical slope with a vengeance.

I sped off. How dare he! How dare he take the mickey out of me like that! How dare he presume to know me so well, to judge me – after one drunken night! Bloody nerve, bloody men – bloody typical! Give them an inch and they take half a bloody mile. And him, a hick from the sticks – what did he know? What did he know about running a household, about the incessant demands of a family, the constant juggling that went on – he was just a man on his own living in the middle of nowhere!

I pedalled furiously, round one bend, round the next one and on down the hill. Oh, I knew what he thought all right. He thought I was a frustrated housewife who spent her entire life rolling around with gillies and plumbers and washing-machine repair men. He probably thought last night had been just another in a long line of blue-collar interludes – Jesus!

My feet were going like pistons now, and it was only on the third bend that I realised the folly of this. I was on a more or less vertical slope here. One did not pedal furiously on such a slope, one did not give oneself a flying start down an incline of this nature. One got enough of a flying start from the angle itself. I desperately tried the brakes, I mean brake, but quickly realised it wasn't a brake at all but just a decorative feature on the handlebars bearing absolutely no relation to what was going on with the wheels.

The scenery was whipping past like a speeded-up video now and I felt quite sick with fear. How on earth was I supposed to stop the wretched thing? I hurtled down, quite out of control, each hairpin bend becoming more difficult to negotiate than the last and it seemed that no sooner had one been accomplished than another was upon me. Shit! Should I stick my feet out onto the road, I wondered, or would that send me catapulting high into the air? I gripped the handlebars tight, the wind whistling past my ears, my hair streaming out behind me. Suddenly I knew there was no way on earth I could possibly negotiate another corner. I'd have to go for a crash landing. Ahead of me was a field, to the left, another hairpin bend. Better to shoot straight across the road, crash into the field and collapse on the grass rather than veer round the bend and crash on the lethal Tarmac, I decided.

'*Ahh, ahh ahhhhh!*' I shrieked in terror, as I shot across the road Kamikaze-style, as just to my left, a car appeared up around the bend. I don't remember much, but I do remember the sickening crunch of metal on metal. I also remember flying through the air, somersaulting over the car and registering that it was red. Then the last thing I remember, before I fell with a thump in the field, was Patrick's shocked eyes over the steering wheel. After that, all I recall was the blackness.

Chapter Thirteen

As I opened my eyes Patrick was leaning over me. His hand snaked furtively up under the blanket, his face was close to mine, his breath on my cheek. I froze.

'Don't even think about it, Patrick Cameron,' I snarled. 'I wouldn't sleep with you if you were the last man on earth.'

He blinked. 'I was just checking to see if you were breathing, Tess.'

'And if I wasn't you'd have had me anyway, would you? Dead or alive?'

'Don't be silly, you must be delirious. You've had an accident.'

'Oh, don't give me that. Wh-what? An accident?' I clutched the blanket to me in panic, only I could see now that it wasn't a blanket, it was somebody's coat, and I couldn't be in a bedroom because there was far too much fresh air about, too much sky. A convalescence home, perhaps? By the sea?

'How long have I been like this?' I imagined months, years, a prolonged coma, paralysed from the neck down. Perhaps I was an old woman, with grown-up children? I imagined Clemmie and Hugo, middle-aged, coming to visit me in the twilight home, bearing grapes and bored, fidgeting grandchildren who were mesmerised by my teeth in a glass.

'About thirty seconds so far.'

'Is that all?' I sat up. 'Am I all right?'

'I don't know, you tell me.'

I clutched my head. 'Oooh, God no, that hurts like hell.'

'Well, at least you can sit up. Can you move everything?' he asked anxiously, crouched down beside me.

Despite the pain in my head and the general shock I couldn't help noticing that although I hadn't seen him for twelve years he really hadn't aged that much. Certainly not in a portly, hair-thinning sort of way anyway. There were a few extra lines fretted around his eyes but they were still as clear and blue as a summer sky, and although his hair had touches of silver at the edges, the majority was still jet black. He was as tanned as ever and in some ways, looked even more ruggedly handsome than ever. I noticed he was staring at me in much the same way. Digesting the changes. Rolling back the years. Finally he broke the silence.

'Tess?'

'Hmmm?'

'Can you move?'

I came back to life and concentrated hard on waggling bits of my body around. 'I think so,' I said doubtfully as I rotated my head. 'At least my neck's not broken and my arms are OK but – ouch!' I gasped. 'My ankle!'

'Broken?'

'No, I don't think so. I can move it but it's bloody agony!'

I've never been frightfully good at pain, shrieked the place down in childbirth in fact – very lower-class, apparently – and I had a nasty feeling I was about to be very lower-class again. I clenched my teeth and moaned low, trying to quell the scream.

'At least it's not broken,' said Patrick, rather heartlessly I thought. He jumped up. 'I think in that case we'll get you into the car. It'll take for ever to get an ambulance out here, I'll call the doctor from home.'

'No!' I cried, as he swiftly scooped me up off the grass and deposited me in the back seat of the car. 'Patrick, what are you doing? What about my bike and whose home are you talking about anyway?' I felt alarmed; events seemed to be galloping out of control here.

'Mine, of course,' he said as he threw the tangled bike in the boot and slammed it shut. He got into the driver's seat. 'The house is just over there, behind that hill. I was literally coming out of the back drive when you flew out like a bloody bazooka. We'll be there in a second and Mum can look after you until the doctor comes. She used to be a nurse, you know.'

He started the engine. I looked around quickly. Of course, this was probably all Gilduncan's land. I'd forgotten it stretched so far, but – I didn't want to go there!

'No!' I yelped as we pulled off. 'No, take me home. I don't need a doctor, or a nurse for that matter. Patrick, take me home!'

I scrabbled frantically for the door-handle but by the time I'd found it we'd already turned into some stone gates and were doing about twenty miles an hour up the back drive.

'Patrick, this is abduction!' I squealed, my voice slightly hysterical now.

'Don't be ridiculous. What makes you think I want to abduct you? I just don't particularly want to leave you lying on the side of the road for the rabbits to nibble, that's all. If the doctor says you're all right I'll take you home, OK?'

Suddenly I felt rather foolish. I cleared my throat. 'Uh, right. Thank you. Sorry. Um, must be the bump on the head,' I muttered.

He smiled at me in the rearview mirror. 'It's me who

should be apologising, but to be honest I just didn't see you. You seemed to come out of nowhere and the next thing I knew you were flying over the roof of the car. Lucky for you, you landed on the grass. If you'd hit the Tarmac it would have been a great deal messier. What on earth were you doing cycling around up there anyway? No one in their right mind attempts that hill on a bike.'

'I'd been to see Willie,' I muttered.

'Oh, really?' There was a pause. 'Any particular reason?'

I sighed. 'I thought he might have picked up some of my flies down by the river.'

'And had he?'

'No.'

We rode on in silence. God, this driveway seemed to go on for ever. He might just as well have driven me home. Panic began to rise in my breast again.

'Long way to go to get some flies,' he observed.

'They were particularly nice ones,' I replied tartly. Why on earth did I have to explain myself to him?

Finally we swept up the side of the house then around in a semi-circle to the front. We crunched to a halt on the gravel and I stared up at the façade of Gilduncan as it towered above us. I'd never actually been here before, just glimpsed it through the trees as we'd sped past the front gates in the car. As a girl the very mention of its name had been enough to make my heart perform backflips and triple somersaults and now here I was, about to enter it, and my heart was still energetic, but for different reasons.

It was a huge, greystone Baronial place, more of a castle than a house in fact, complete with turrets and most probably a drawbridge tucked away somewhere. I glanced warily at the slitty little windows at the top of the turrets. Any beady-eyed archers up there I wondered? I half expected a hairy man with bagpipes to appear on the battlements and blast out my arrival but instead, the oak front door swung back and two enormous lurchers flew down the steps, hurling themselves in a frenzy of delight at Patrick's shoulders. Following in the lurchers' enthusiastic wake was Madelaine, drop dead elegant in cream silk and pearls. She looked surprised.

'Patreek darling, what on earth are you doing back so soon?'

Patrick came round to open my door.

'I ran into Tess – quite literally actually. Knocked her off her bike at the bottom of the back drive.'

'*Ah, ma pauvre chérie!*' Madelaine was all consternation as Patrick revealed me in all my cringing glory.

'I'm perfectly all right, honestly,' I said, shakily attempting to get out. 'I don't know why Patrick didn't take me home.'

'She's sprained her ankle badly and she's got a nasty bump on her head. I'll call Dr McKlellen.'

'But I don't *need* a doctor,' I protested. God – had everyone gone deaf? Why wasn't anyone listening to me? 'And I certainly don't need to be carried,' I objected, as Patrick lifted me bodily from the car. 'Patrick, put me down this instant!'

Patrick ignored me as I thrashed vainly in his arms and marched up the front steps. He seemed to have an iron grip to match his iron will, but as we swept through a grey, flagstoned hall, he suddenly paused and looked down at me, lips twitching.

'Is it my imagination, or have you put on a bit of weight, Tess?'

'Put me down!' I spluttered.

'Now where shall we have you,' he mused, looking around thoughtfully. 'In my bedroom, perhaps?'

I stared at him in horror. 'No!' I gasped.

'Only joking,' he grinned. 'I'll put you on the sofa in the drawing room.'

He shouldered open the huge double doors in front of us to reveal an enormous light room that seemed to stretch the entire length of the house. He marched in, bent down and gently lowered me onto a cream sofa.

'I'll take you up to my bedroom later,' he whispered in my ear, 'and have my wicked way with you then, dead or alive!' He gave a melodramatic Vincent Price cackle and rolled his eyes manically. 'You will be mine, all mine!'

I glared at him. 'You're enjoying this, aren't you?' I spat. 'You haven't changed a bit, Patrick Cameron!'

He raised his eyebrows in mock injury. 'But it was your idea, Tess,' he said, 'back there on the road, don't you remember? Jabbering on about sleeping with me, dead or—'

'I know what I said,' I snapped, 'and I haven't the faintest idea what got into me.'

I blushed as he stood over me, grinning. 'Can't help you there, but a psychologist would probably say that before you got your bonk on the head you had another sort of bonking on your mind!'

'Don't be ridiculous!' I snorted. God, today had turned into a nonstop nightmare. Was this all part of my punishment?

'Now, Patrick, don't tease Tess,' said Madelaine, bustling in with a First-Aid box. 'She's had a nasty shock and the last thing she needs is you wittering on – oh my dear, you're shaking!'

She was right. For some reason I was in the grip of a rather embarrassing spasm. I couldn't stop it.

Patrick threw a tartan rug over me. 'It's just shock,' he said cheerfully. 'She'll be all right.'

You're damn right it's shock, I thought, teeth chattering. Shock of seeing you again, probably. My breath was coming in short sharp bursts now, my cheeks were wobbling violently and I couldn't control my shoulders which were shuddering like a pneumatic drill.

'I'll phone Dr McKlellen,' said Madelaine, regarding me anxiously. She put the First-Aid box down and hastened away again. Patrick perched on the arm of the sofa and watched me, which frankly was all I needed as I shook, rattled and rolled away like some kind of possessed washing machine in final spin. After a while however, the shaking subsided and came to a gentle tremble.

'How are you feeling now?' he asked kindly.

'Pretty groggy actually,' I whispered truthfully.

'The doctor will be here soon.' He patted my hand.

Stupidly I flinched away, which of course implied that it was far more than a friendly pat. He looked at me in surprise, then got up and walked over to the fire. He stood with his back to me, his hands clasped behind him.

A silence fell. I bit my lip. Oh, well done, Tess, I thought bitterly. That's really gone and opened up the chasm, hasn't it? The one that's absolutely brimming over with all those nice juicy memories. It was his fault, I reasoned, for being nice to me. It had been so much easier when he'd teased me and we'd snapped and sniped. I wondered how long it would be until we could get back to doing that again? It was infinitely preferable to this uneasy silence. I cleared my throat and tried to think of a suitably acerbic opening gambit, but what do you say to someone you haven't seen for twelve years when practically the last thing you declared was undying love? 'How's your life been?' 'What have you been up to all these years?' Mercifully, Madelaine returned and retrieved the situation, delivering us back to normality, to social graces, to the present.

'I got him on his mobile – he's at the McTavishes' in the village,' she announced. 'Isobel's just had her baby and he said he'll be up here as soon as he's finished.

What a stroke of luck. You can wait hours for a doctor around here!'

I smiled weakly. Madelaine had restored the equilibrium and the air was clearer, but physically I was feeling decidedly rough now. Patrick came back from the fire and sat down on the sofa with his mother as we waited for the doctor. They chatted away but I felt too queasy to join in. Everything in the room seemed to be moving around, conspiring to make me feel sick. Patrick and Madelaine's faces swam in and out of focus and quite often merged together in a rather surreal way before separating again. Occasionally I made a stab at coherent conversation but judging by the bemused expressions on my hosts' faces I was clearly talking utter gibberish.

'Try not to talk for a while,' said Madelaine kindly.

Well, if that wasn't a hint. Please God I hadn't been instructing Patrick in no uncertain terms to desist from ravaging me again. I shut my eyes and had just enough nous to tell myself to shut my mouth until the doctor arrived.

When the tweedy, grey-haired, Dr Finlay lookalike did indeed materialise, he poked, prodded and tutted quite a lot, before diagnosing a badly sprained ankle and mild concussion.

'Bed-rest for at least a week,' he announced, snapping his case shut and removing his stethoscope from his ears.

He eased himself up from the edge of the sofa where he'd been perching and looked down at me sternly.

'And then take it very easy indeed, young lady. If you get any blinding headaches or see flashing lights, let me know immediately. And keep that ankle up at all times.'

'Yes, Doctor,' I said meekly, thinking there was fat chance of that with two young children to look after.

'Well, you'll get no rest at all with two children to look after,' said Madelaine, uncannily echoing my thoughts. 'You'd better stay here.'

'Oh no,' I laughed. 'That's out of the question. No, I'm perfectly all right. I'll just totter off home now and—'

'You'll do nothing of the sort,' interrupted the doctor, 'and you certainly can't run around after children. Madelaine's right, you should stay here.' He smiled at her. 'She was an excellent nurse in her day, I'm sure she'll look after you splendidly. You really mustn't move at all for the present.'

'But I'm fine,' I protested, making a vain attempt to demonstrate how fine I was by trying to get up off the sofa and failing miserably. 'If I could just use the telephone—'

'I'll telephone,' said Patrick, striding off to the hall. 'I'll let them know where you are.'

'Tell them to pick me up,' I squeaked desperately. 'Ask Laura to come, or Penny.'

He disappeared and I flopped back into the pillows feeling totally helpless. Patrick returned a few minutes later.

'Laura agrees with me,' he announced. 'You should stay here for a few days to recover.'

'No!' I cried. Then, realising it must sound terribly ungracious to Madelaine: 'I – I mean under normal circumstances, I'd love to of course, but—'

'Tess, I insist,' said Madelaine firmly. 'Please, I'll hear no more on the matter.'

I stared up at the three determined faces thronged above me. 'What about the children?' I said faintly. 'David's gone to London – they'll be all alone.'

'Josie's there, isn't she?' said Patrick.

'Oh yes of course,' I said grimly, 'you've met Josie, haven't you?'

'Briefly,' he grinned. 'Nice girl. So that's all organised then. Oh goodbye Angus, are you off?'

He turned to shake hands with the doctor who was

keen to be away. Madelaine went to show him to the door.

'No, it's not OK,' I hissed at Patrick. 'I want to go home!'

'Look, Tess,' he said patiently, 'you go home and you'll be hobbling around on that ankle as soon as you get there, your head will be throbbing and you'll feel ghastly, you know you will. Stay here just for a day or two and then go home when you can at least walk, OK? Penny's coming over with some clothes for you.'

'Got everything organised haven't you?' I said bitterly, but actually, my resistance was fading fast. I didn't feel like going anywhere for a moment – in fact I felt quite sick again.

I gulped hard and shut my eyes. Oh please God, don't let me throw up all over Madelaine's immaculate creamy sofa. Please don't let me disgrace myself quite so comprehensively! I ignored Patrick, kept my eyes firmly shut, breathed deeply and counted to a hundred. When I opened my eyes again I felt a bit better. I looked around. Patrick had disappeared. On the telephone again, no doubt, arranging for all my worldly goods to be sent over forthwith, thereby ensuring I didn't leave for months.

I groaned. How on earth did I get myself into this mess? Talk about crashing into the lion's den, and what about the children? My poor babies, fatherless since this morning and now motherless too! Perhaps they could come and see me here tomorrow? I looked around and winced. Maybe not. The thought of Hugo and Clemmie jumping all over me and the cream sofa demanding chocolate biscuits and picking up everything in sight and me not having the wherewithal to spring up and whip priceless *objets d'art* from their grubby hands made me feel even iller. Perhaps they could come in a couple of days, when I felt a bit better. I cocked an enquiring eyebrow at myself. A couple of days eh, Tess? Got yourself ensconced here for that long already, have you? Didn't take much arm-twisting, did it?

I snuggled back into the sofa. Actually I had to admit that if one was going to be ill, this was certainly the place to do it. This room was supremely relaxing. I gazed around: Madelaine had done it beautifully. Whilst not exactly ignoring the uncompromising stone floors and walls, she nevertheless hadn't pandered to them either. There were no gruesome stags' heads sticking out of walls here, no crossed swords hanging above the fireplace and the place wasn't swathed in aggressive tartans either. Instead, she'd gone for cool creams and blues which complemented the cold granite beautifully. Faded duck-egg drapes hung at the tall French windows that ran the entire length of one wall, beyond which was a fabulous view of the mountains. No leaping salmon adorned the walls either; instead, beautiful and no doubt highly valuable Impressionist paintings hung from the picture rail, together with tapestries, perhaps Madelaine's own, which had also been made into cushions and were scattered over the sumptuous sofas. Yes, I thought dreamily, one could sink into one of these sofas and never surface again. I felt my eyes closing. How strange, I suddenly felt incredibly weary.

I must have fallen asleep because the next thing I knew, someone was knocking on my head. I opened my eyes. No, it wasn't my head, it was the door, but not the door to the drawing room. I was in a different room now, a rather pretty lemon-yellow bedroom, with sprigged curtains and a view of the mountains. I sat up. How on earth had I got here? More embarrassing weight-lifting from Patrick again? I groaned, imagining myself lying heavy in his arms, head lolling back, mouth open, perhaps a nice trickle of dribble coming out of one side. Terrific.

The knock came again, only this time, the handle turned. I quickly reached for the covers, pulling them up to my neck.

Penny popped her head around the door. 'It's only me,' she whispered, creeping in. 'Are you all right?'

I relaxed. 'Yes, I'm absolutely fine. I just can't *move*, that's all. It's maddening.'

'What on earth happened?'

'Patrick knocked me off my bike, that's what happened.'

'And now you're laid up here. What a lark!' She perched on the side of the bed grinning. 'Gosh, you jammy thing, I wouldn't mind lying in bed for a few days, especially in this place, it's like a blinking palace. And so quiet, no children running about. D'you get waited on hand and foot? I saw a couple of uniformed maids downstairs bustling around with silver dishes – bit different to Kilmarnoch, eh? What's the food like?'

I stared at her incredulously. 'Penny, this is Patrick's house, not a hotel and I haven't had any food. I'm sick, for heaven's sake!'

'Are you really?' She glanced furtively at the door. 'Or did you just kind of wait for his car then accidentally on purpose wobble out in front of it? I won't tell, honestly.'

'Penny!' I was aghast. 'How can you even suggest such a thing!'

'Well, when was the last time you went for a bike-ride, eh? Coincidentally passing the bottom of his drive?' She nudged me and winked. 'Kind of convenient, wasn't it, and now here you are, prostrate in his house, ordered not to move by the doctor, David in London and Josie on permanent duty with the children – marvellous! Tess, I really take my hat off to you, I think it's ingenious. It's sort of, literally flinging yourself at him, isn't it?' She laughed a merry, tinkling laugh.

I clenched everything I possessed under the blankets, speechless with rage. Eventually I found my vocal chords.

'If you don't shut that revolting mouth of yours I shall scream! I do not want to be here, they forced me, against my will, to stay and if you really think I threw myself under the wheels of his car – God, I might have been killed! Has your sewer-like mind considered that possibility?'

'All right, all right, don't get excited. It was just a thought.' She reached down and rustled around in a plastic M&S bag while I glared at her, breathing heavily.

'I brought you some clothes – jumpers, jeans, oh and a pair of pyjamas in case you want to wear something in bed.' She raised her eyebrows. 'But perhaps you don't?'

'I most certainly do!' I snarled, grabbing them from her.

She giggled. 'Oh, and I found this in my drawer.' She held up a tiny black, diaphanous nightie. 'Any good? For those warmer, balmy evenings perhaps?' Then seeing my face she went on hastily: 'Well, you decide. I'll just leave the bag here by your bed, OK? There are some shoes at the bottom and a couple of magazines Laura found. Oh, but I'll take this back. You won't be wanting this, will you?' She removed my make-up bag from the top.

'Why not?'

Penny frowned. 'Make-up, in bed? You, an invalid? Surely not.'

'Well I might just manage the occasional hobble downstairs, mightn't I, and I wouldn't want to frighten the servants. Just put it back, Penny, and stop being such a cow!'

She grinned. 'All right, all right, keep your hair on. I'm going now anyway, they've asked me to stay to lunch.'

She got up and smoothed her jumper down, sniffing the air speculatively. 'Mmm . . . salmon *en croûte* if I'm not very much mistaken, on the terrace apparently, and I saw some rather expensive-looking bottles of white wine going out too.'

'Really,' I said drily, gritting my teeth and wishing she'd go.

She sauntered round the room picking things up and putting them down again, then sat down on the stool at the kidney-shaped dressing table and peered at her reflection. She whipped her lipstick out of her bag, applied an extravagantly thick layer then set about combing her hair.

'I say, he's still awfully attractive, isn't he?' she murmured to me through her reflection. 'I went strangely gooey when he was talking to me downstairs. He's still quite wild and gypsyish, of course, but not so crazy-looking. Seems to have mellowed a bit with age, although he's still got that frightfully dominant manner, which is terribly sexy. I went all weak at the knees when he absolutely insisted I stayed for lunch. He was quite adamant, you know. Honestly, Tess, I really wouldn't say no myself and you know how loyal I am to Piers, so I wouldn't blame you, really I wouldn't. And it's not as if anyone would find—'

'Out!' I cried, pointing to the door with a quivering finger. 'Get out of here Penny, you're making my head ache!'

She raised her eyebrows at me in the mirror. 'Phew! What a nasty temper.' She fiddled around with her hair again, then put her comb back. 'All right, all right, I'm nearly ready.'

She stood up and preened again in the mirror, pressing her lips together to set her lipstick, then reached in her bag for her Chanel No. 5 spray and gave herself a quick blast behind the ears.

I moaned quietly. Would she ever be gone? Finally she bustled to the door, almost tripping over the black negligée which had fallen out of the bag.

'And take that with you,' I ordered.

'Sure?' She picked it up, grinning wickedly.

'Out! Now!'

She giggled and left, but then just as I was about to sink once more into the pillows, her hand came back around the door, hanging the nightie on the handle.

'Just in case,' she whispered, then beat a hasty retreat.

I groaned and thumped the bed with clenched fists. Oh *God*! Now I'd have to go and *get* it, before someone came in and wondered what on earth it was doing there! Slowly I began to manoeuvre myself out of bed, cursing Penny, when – bugger, too late. There was a quick rap on the door and Patrick appeared. I quickly flopped back, pulling up the covers. He glanced down at the nightie swinging gaily from the handle.

'What's this?' he asked, picking it up gingerly.

'It's Penny's. She left it behind. You might hand it back to her over the lunch-table.'

'But why bring it here?' he asked, bemused.

'Well, apparently she'd heard you had a rather attractive gardener, so she thought she might tempt him with it. You know Penny, dib dib dib, be prepared and all that.'

He grinned. 'God, she hasn't changed, has she? Well, she's been sadly misinformed. I'm afraid our gardener's nearly ninety.'

'Yes, that'll be the one,' I said grimly.

He laughed, then as the laugh faded, he leaned against the doorframe, just sort of looking at me. I raised my eyebrows enquiringly.

'Oh,' he straightened quickly. 'I, er, just came to tell you we're about to have lunch. D'you want anything brought up?'

I shook my head. 'No thanks. Still feel a bit queasy. Maybe later on.'

He nodded. 'I thought as much. Oh, and I brought you this.' He handed me a mobile phone. 'Thought you might want to ring your husband, tell him where you are.'

'Oh! Thanks.' I met his eye briefly as I took the phone and for some reason found myself blushing.

'He's called David, by the way,' I muttered.

'Ah.' He nodded. 'We've met then.'

I started. 'Where?'

'When I took Josie back. He came to the door.'

'Oh! Right.'

A silence fell. I gazed at the phone, twiddling the digits. Patrick cleared his throat.

'I'll be off then. If there's anything you need, just yell.'

'Will do.'

I smiled but couldn't help thinking you could scream yourself sick in this vast house and no one would hear. Patrick turned to go.

'Patrick—' I said suddenly. He turned back. 'I haven't been very . . . well, grateful. And you've been very kind. Thank you.'

He smiled. A proper smile. 'It's no trouble. In fact it's lovely to see you again, Tess.'

With that he closed the door and went down to lunch.

Chapter Fourteen

When he'd gone I stretched out in bed and stared at the mobile phone lying face down on the duvet. My hand twitched towards it, then unaccountably away, then back to it again. I grasped it firmly. Of course, once David knew where I was they'd have to let me go. He'd insist. It would be straight back to Kilmarnoch for me, and a good job too, I told myself sternly. Best place for me. Yes. Right. Go on then, Tess, punch out the number. Finally I did so and his clerk put me through.

'David Hamilton.'

'Darling, it's me.'

'Tess! I've just this minute walked in. How's things?'

'Not so good, actually. David, don't be alarmed, but I've had a bit of an accident. Not a bad one, but I've got a knock on the head and I've sprained my ankle pretty badly.'

'Good Lord. How on earth did you do that?'

'Well I was, um, knocked off my bike.'

'Your bike? What bike?'

I sighed. 'It's a long story, but basically the cars were all spoken for and I didn't have any choice so I cycled. I think I'm a bit rusty actually, I wobbled out in front of a car.'

'Good heavens! Are you badly hurt?'

'My ankle throbs like hell and I can't walk, but it's nothing serious.' I cleared my throat and braced myself.

'Actually, it was Patrick Cameron who knocked me off. I'm at his house now.'

'Patrick Cameron?'

'Yes, you remember. He and I—'

'Yes, I know,' he said quickly.

There was a silence.

I hastened on. 'You see, I was very near his house when the accident happened, that's why he brought me here, but it's so ridiculous, darling, there's absolutely no reason why I can't go home. I'm perfectly all right, but everyone's making such a stupid fuss. They say I have to stay here with my leg up till I'm better. It's maddening.'

'Has the doctor been?'

'Yes, and he said I should stay because I wouldn't get any rest at home, but what the devil does he know about my domestic arrangements? The whole point of bringing Josie was to give me a bit of a break and she's quite capable of looking after the children on her own, it's absurd!'

The line went quiet.

'David?'

'Yes, I'm still here, I was just thinking.' He sounded a long way away. There was another pause and I was about to say something when he spoke.

'You know, on balance I think the doctor's right. You'll get precious little rest at Kilmarnoch with the children running in and out of your room and I know you, you'll get up and start hobbling down to the kitchen to cook supper like a martyr, it'll drive Penny and Laura mad. I think you'd better stay put for a bit.'

I gawped. 'What d'you mean, for a bit? How long?'

'Until you're better. How long will your ankle take to recover? What did the doctor think?'

'He said I'd be flat on my back for a week,' I scoffed. 'I told him that was out of the question, but—'

'Then that's what you must do,' he interrupted firmly. 'It's no good getting up and making it worse. These things have a habit of recurring later if you're not careful.'

'But David, why can't I be in bed at Kilmarnoch?' I felt panicky. 'There's no earthly reason why I have to lie around in Patrick's house, is there?' I said 'Lie around' and 'Patrick' quite loudly in the hope that alarm bells might ring in what passed for his brain at the moment, but apparently he didn't hear them.

'There's every reason if it gives you a chance to rest,' he said briskly. 'The children will be fine with Josie. Just relax and take advantage of it, for heaven's sake. You're always banging on about how you never get a break from them, well now's your chance. Have you got something nice to read?'

'Yes, but—'

'Good. Darling I must go now, I'd love to chat but I'm due in court in a few minutes. Give me your number . . .'

I reeled it off in a daze.

'Right. I'll give you a ring tonight, OK? Now rest please, I don't want an invalided wife stumbling along behind me on a Zimmer frame!'

'But David—'

'Bye Tess, give my love to the children.' And he rang off.

I stared incredulously at the receiver. Good Lord. Did he have no idea? Did he not have a brain? He was supposed to be a barrister – an intelligent, probing man. Had he no grasp of the situation? Of the implications? I blinked. Or perhaps he did. Perhaps he wanted me to have an affair, perhaps it was some kind of kinky fantasy of his, to have me holed up with my ex-lover, trapped in his castle, bolts on all the doors, drawbridge raised, no possible means of escape. Perhaps he was hoping I'd be tied to a four-poster with a bit of bondage thrown in for good measure? I chucked the phone down in disgust.

That was the thing about men, I reflected, they were such simple creatures, so trusting. Any sensible, reasonably alert woman would have had sirens wailing and warning lights flashing within seconds of discovering my whereabouts, but not David, oh no. He just wondered if I had something nice to read. I gave a hollow laugh. It was quite clear he didn't think there was the slightest chance of me being tempted by Patrick or vice versa, which if you thought about it, was rather sweet. I smiled. Simple, but sweet. I turned around and plumped up my pillow. Not that there *was* a chance now, of course, I reflected – not after Willie. I snuggled down into the crisp linen. Yes, thank God for Willie. If it hadn't been for him, things might have been very different. I might have been lying here feeling deliriously happy about finding myself holed up in Patrick's spare room, unable to believe my luck. I might be preening myself even now, slapping on the fake tan, reaching for the mascara, working out the logistics of getting my one serviceable leg over – hell, what do I mean *might* be, WOULD be more like! I mean, let's face it – up until very recently I'd thought of nothing else. I shuddered. Well, I'd certainly had enough extra-marital activity to last me a lifetime. Oh yes, great fun and all that, but I couldn't be doing with all that guilt and shame that went with it, thanks very much.

In which case, I asked myself thoughtfully, was there any real harm in my being here? Whatever plans Patrick might harbour, I knew precisely where I stood, so was I therefore in any danger? I blinked as this radical thought dawned. No, none whatsoever. So why not just relax and enjoy it then? Why bother to resist? Why not, as everyone was so vehemently insisting, have a rest, put my feet up, and treat it as a holiday? After all, apart from one disastrously wet weekend with David in Dorset, this was the first break I'd had from the children since

Clemmie was born. Why not make the most of it?

With this rather reassuring thought in mind, I pulled the white bedcover up to my chin, yawned hugely and sank down into the gloriously sumptuous bed. For the first time I took a good look around the room, noting the beautiful paintings on the walls and the antiques that were scattered liberally around what might have been a spare room to the Camerons but was more like the size of your average bungalow. This wasn't so much faded grandeur as out-and-out unadulterated luxury, and for a couple of days at the most, would do very nicely, thank you.

I fingered the crisp white bedlinen. It was so sharp you could almost cut yourself on it and I couldn't help thinking it must be hell to launder, but then I didn't imagine that was Madelaine's problem, likewise the picking and arranging of that deep vase of flowers placed strategically in that pool of light over there. Their very presence struck me as extraordinary since surely no one could have had any idea that this room would be occupied? But then perhaps Madelaine insisted on flowers in every room, occupied or not? This was clearly a house where no expense was spared, a house that revolved around comfort. I had no doubt that in winter the heating would be on twenty-four hours a day, with windows open for fresh air if necessary, because this was not your average Scottish pile where you froze your goolies off, had cold baths and put on a third jumper if you were cold. Oh no, this was as close as Madelaine could come to transforming a Highland castle into a villa in the South of France, and whilst that might not appeal to the purists, in my present condition, who was I to complain?

Suddenly I frowned, listening. I craned my neck and tried to peer out of the window. I couldn't quite see, but I was almost sure I could hear splashing down there –

did they have a pool? And if so, how many days a year did they use it? My eyes boggled in astonishment. I mean yes, OK, we were having a warm spell now, but it must be the one week out of fifty-two, surely? What an extravagance! I could almost hear my father's reaction. 'A swimming pool,' he'd scoff, 'in Scotland? They must be mad!' I smiled. Mad or not, I found the whole sunshiny hedonistic environment very reassuring right now.

My ankle was beginning to hurt a bit so I leaned back and shut my eyes, propping up the heavy bedclothes with my healthy foot to stop them pressing against the bad one. I lay there, listening to the muffled sound of chatter below on the terrace. I didn't mean to fall asleep, but I obviously did, because when I opened my eyes again my ankle was throbbing like crazy and Penny was standing by my bed poking me hard in the shoulder with her fingernail.

'Tess, Tess! Oh good, you're awake.' She was swaying and her eyes looked very pink. 'I didn't wake you, did I? I just came to tell you I'm going now.'

'Eh?' I struggled to focus. The pain was excruciating. Someone seemed to be driving a stake through my ankle.

'I'm going,' she repeated breathlessly. 'I just came to tell you we had the most marvellous lunch, by the *pool*, would you believe! We sat there, drinking champagne under one of those glorious white Conran umbrellas and Tess, we were *waited* on by a couple of uniformed maids! God, I felt like a film star, and it wasn't salmon it was lobster which is my absolute favourite and oh, Tess, Madelaine is simply heaven!' Penny clasped her hands ecstatically then staggered and clutched the bedpost, clearly highly intoxicated. '*So* unbelievably chic – she's French you know, Parisian in fact, with an outrageous accent, and she's lent me these fabulous sun glasses . . .' Penny put them on and pouted, giving me the benefit of both profiles. 'She said I could hang on to them because they're old and she's got hundreds of them, but they're Yves St Laurent, for God's sake!' she squeaked. 'Look!' She waggled them around in my face so I could see the label, banging my nose with them.

'Penny,' I gasped, stretching past her for my painkillers which I couldn't quite reach on the bedside table. 'My ankle . . . You couldn't just—'

She flopped down on the side of the bed, knocking the pills out of my hand just as I'd managed to grasp them. I groaned as they fell to the floor.

'Honestly, Tess, these people are *simply* delightful,' she exclaimed breathlessly. 'I can't think why we haven't got together with them before. It's all our parents' fault, of course, fancy falling out with a family like this. Think of the fun we could have had here! Swimming parties, skinny-dipping, drinking – dancing even, Madelaine said they'd had some wild parties here with jazz bands and rose petals all over the pool. It sounded like something out of *Gatsby*! And as for Patrick – oooh!' She swooned and clutched her heart dramatically. 'Tess, he has *changed*!' she hissed, 'beyond *belief*! He is simply divine now and the perfect host, so considerate – shifting my chair into the shade and all that sort of thing because he thought I was going a bit pink – look.' She jumped up and unbuttoned her shirt to reveal a pair of enormous bright-red bosoms which had no doubt been out on permanent display. 'See my mark? And I was only in the sun for an hour or so.'

She left her blouse open and seized my hand playfully as I made another valiant attempt to reach my pills on the carpet.

'Oh – and Tess, he's so *funny*! You didn't tell me he was funny, did you, you sly old thing.' She waggled my wrist playfully and the pills slipped once again from my desperate grasp.

'He's *hysterical*! I nearly *wet* myself laughing at some of his stories, and you know how I *L-O-V-E* funny men.' She rolled her bloodshot eyes extravagantly. 'In fact, at one point he was being so hilarious and looking so mind-bogglingly handsome sitting there in his faded denim shirt with his tan and his bright blue eyes that I damn nearly threw down my lobster, leaped on his lap and told him to roger me senseless right there and then in front of his mother!'

'Well, you can tell him now,' I croaked. 'He's right beside you.'

Penny turned and giggled as Patrick came in, not remotely abashed. 'Oh hello, Patrick.' She linked arms with him and did a quick snuggling-up dive into his armpit. 'I was just telling Tess how you've changed. You used to be such a surly, aggressive chap and you've turned into a really lovely man, quite the hunk!'

He grinned. 'Why thank you, Penny, I'm glad I've turned out all right, and may I return the compliment by saying that you haven't changed one little bit?'

Mistakenly imagining this to be a huge compliment, Penny simpered girlishly and squeezed his arm, but Patrick was frowning. He leaned over and peered closely at me.

'Are you all right, Tess? You look awfully pale.'

I shook my head. 'Ankle,' I whispered. 'Agony.'

'Where are your pills?' he said quickly.

'Floor,' I managed, pointing down at Penny's feet.

He picked them up and went quickly to the bathroom for some water. My cousin, swaying violently without Patrick's support, bent down to peer at me. As she did so her bag slipped off her shoulder and bashed me hard on the side of the head. I yelped in pain.

'Yes, you do look a bit peaky, Tess,' she agreed, leering at me, hair all over her face, her breath reeking of booze. 'You should have been out by the pool getting some sun on your face instead of skulking away in here like a flipping killjoy. We had a marvellous time out there, didn't we Patrick? Honestly, we didn't stop laughing once. God, I was on form. Oh, and what was that *terribly* funny joke I told when your mother was banging on and on about getting older and being on her own and – oh yes! What's the similarity between a dog turd and an older woman? The older they get, the easier they are to pick up – HA HA! God, it was funny – although I'm not sure your mother appreciated it, Patrick. She looked a bit po-faced to me, and I was only trying to cheer her up. Maybe it's because she's no spring chicken herself, or perhaps it's the language barrier or—'

'Here.' Patrick brushed Penny rather roughly aside as he came back with the water. She overbalanced and clutched at the bedpost, just managing to stay upright, clearly not just a bit pissed but catastrophically drunk. He handed me the pills. 'Take these.'

Patrick supported my back and I guzzled them greedily. I hoped to goodness they'd work soon. My teeth were going through the Irish linen like a tatty old sponge and the pain was going to render me embarrassingly vocal soon.

'Come on.' Patrick turned to Penny and jerked his head. 'Tess needs some rest, I'll take you home.'

'Oh, we're not going, are we?' she asked, pouting. 'I was just limbering up for a nice little *digestif* – a touch of Calvados, perhaps. I bet your mother slips that down a treat eh, Paddy, being French and all that! Hey,' she whispered, grabbing his arm confidentially, 'has she got any lovers yet? Any toy-boys?'

I gasped at her, shocked despite the pain. 'Penny!'

'It's no good looking at me like that, Tess. You know what these Latin women are like, no sooner have they got their husbands safely stashed six feet under than they're swinging their Louis Vuitton bags over their shoulders and are off down the Champs Elysées sniffing around for a bit of *Jacques le garçon*! Ha ha! Know what I mean?' She elbowed Patrick in the ribs. 'How's about that Calvados then eh, Paddy? Don't be stingy!'

'Er, some other time perhaps,' said Patrick, hustling her quickly out of the room. 'Back in a bit,' he threw over his shoulder to me before they left.

I nodded weakly, in no position to argue.

A while later he was back, alone. He sat down gently on the side of the bed, taking care not to jar my ankle.

'How are you feeling now?'

'A bit better,' I gasped.

It was partly true, the pills had worked fast, but not quite fast enough. I hadn't realised quite how comprehensively I'd hurt myself.

He nodded. 'You must take these pills every six hours, that's what they're for. I broke my shoulder a few years ago so I know what it's like. It's not funny, is it?'

'Not remotely,' I whispered, 'and I'm afraid I'm a bit of a coward.'

'Don't worry – this is the worst bit. You'll feel better in the morning and then increasingly so every day.'

'Promise?'

'Scouts' honour.' He flashed me a gentle smile.

I gulped and turned away. Don't you flaunt those blue eyes at me, Patrick Cameron. Talk about taking advantage of a weak defenceless woman. You just wait till these pills start doing their stuff; there'll be no sitting on the side of my bed giving me those crinkly-eyed smiles then. Oh no, it'll be over to that chair in the far corner and nothing more than a tight little grimace, please. For the moment, however, I reflected, wincing again at the pain, he could stay.

'How's the head?'

'Not too bad.'

There was silence.

'Is talking difficult? D'you want me to go?'

I shook my head. A big mistake, it began to throb, but I didn't want to be on my own.

Patrick got up and strolled around the room, hands deep in his pockets. I watched as he peered at all the pictures and then at the view out of the window, almost as if he'd never been in this room before. But then perhaps he hadn't. The house was so flipping big, perhaps there were great wings he didn't even know existed. He paused at the round tripod table by the window, picked up a magazine and flicked through it.

'Did you ring David?' he asked casually.

'Yes.'

'What did he say?'

I laughed hollowly. 'Oh, he agrees with everyone else around here, says I should stay until I get better.'

Patrick looked up from the magazine in surprise. 'Ah well, there you are then. If your husband says you should stay . . .'

'Quite,' I said grimly.

He put the magazine down and gazed out at the mountains. Silence prevailed for a bit. After a while he turned.

'Does he . . . know about us?'

I looked at him squarely. 'He knows we went out together, if that's what you mean.'

'Ah.' He nodded.

I sat up a bit in the bed. The pills were working after all. My leg was easing up and I felt a lot stronger.

'Let's get this straight, Patrick,' I said calmly. 'There's nothing *to* know about us. Nothing more than the simple truth, which is that twelve years ago, we met on a beach and had a holiday romance – OK? There are no deep dark secrets waiting to be discovered, no nasty skeletons lurking in cupboards. Of course David knows about you, we don't have secrets from each other. He told me about his old flames and I told him about mine – husbands and wives do that, you know. In fact, an old girlfriend of his even came to our wedding. I would have asked you too,' I said lightly, 'but I wasn't sure how to get hold of you at the time.'

Patrick stared at me incredulously. Then he threw back his head and gave a shout of laughter.

I widened my eyes. 'What's so funny?' I enquired politely.

'Your wedding! Yes, well, that would have been um . . .' he searched for a word and nodded. 'Memorable.'

'Yes it was, very memorable. A fabulous day, happiest day of my life actually.'

'Really?' he grinned.

'Yes,' I snapped. 'Really. Never looked back.'

'If that's the case I couldn't be happier for you.'

'Yes of course it's the case, I just said so, didn't I?' I glared.

Patrick looked at me for a moment. He came over to the bed. 'Why are you being like this, Tess?'

'Like what?'

'All sort of – chippy. Defensive.'

'I'm not defensive, Patrick, but when I told you David was happy for me to be here you instantly asked me if he knew about us. As if there was something that perhaps he didn't know. Something that, had he been privy to it, might have made him think twice about encouraging me to stay.' I stared at him. 'Am I right?'

Patrick chuckled warmly. 'What an active mind you have, Tess. What an extraordinary supposition! I simply asked if he knew the situation.'

'And I'm simply telling you,' I said coolly, 'that there is no situation to know about. If there ever was a "situation" it ended twelve years ago, got it?'

'My God, Tess, you haven't lost any of your old fire,

have you? To be honest I was being entirely selfish. I didn't want to get into a cosy fireside chat with your husband and be on the receiving end of a "how do you know my wife?" enquiry, but since you've obviously made things crystal clear there'll be no danger of that, will there? Phew!' He mopped his brow and backed away towards the door, reaching for the handle and rattling it frantically, pretending he couldn't open it.

'Let me out of here,' he pleaded, 'she's gone mad! Penny, come back and rescue me, I'll do anything you want. Roger me senseless in front of my mother!'

I giggled in spite of myself. 'Shut up, you fool.'

'What?' he gasped, wrestling with the doorknob. 'You said you're sorry?'

'No, I didn't.'

'Did you say, "I'm sorry, Patrick, I overreacted" – is that what you said?'

'No, I bloody didn't, but—'

'But what?' He pounced, delighted.

I licked my lips. 'But – well, all right. Maybe I did overreact. Slightly. But I'm not sorry,' I added defiantly.

He grinned. 'Fair enough. I'd call that quite a capitulation for you.'

We eyed each other warily like a couple of prize fighters, sizing each other up, trying to get the measure of each other, both trying to weigh up the changes twelve years had made. In his case very little. Looks-wise he was much the same and – yes, I thought, shifting out of the glare of his steely blue eyes, mentally, he was just as I remembered too. Fiery, sparky, argumentative, irritating, amusing, challenging, exhausting but – invigorating too. No, he hadn't changed a bit.

'You haven't changed a bit, Tess,' he said quietly.

'Really?' I arched my eyebrows at him in surprise. 'How extraordinary – you have.'

He looked momentarily taken aback, then burst out

laughing. As he left the room he was still chortling and I could still hear great hoots of mirth as he went off down the stairs.

Chapter Fifteen

The following morning the telephone woke me. No one seemed to be answering it downstairs so after a few demanding rings I picked the one up by my bedside.

'Hello?' I enquired politely.

'What on earth are you doing *there*?' Laura's voice screeched into my ear. I instantly held the phone a couple of inches away. 'I mean – in Patrick Cameron's house, of all places!'

'I thought you might have heard by now – I fell off my bike,' I explained patiently.

'Oh yes yes, I know all about that, but it's a bit dodgy, isn't it? I mean what with you and him having been lovers, what with all that steamy rampant sex by the river and everything?'

'Yes all *right*, Laura,' I stopped her before she declined to mince her words further, 'thank you for pointing out the subtleties of the situation to me, they hadn't actually escaped me, and believe me – I would much rather have fallen off in Mary McTavish's front garden, or – outside the Campbells' house perhaps, but it just didn't happen like that, OK? Now I'm doing my level best to recover and get out of here, without, I might add, much co-operation from my family who seem to want me to be incarcerated here for as *long as possible!*' My voice at this point rose to an hysterical shriek.

'The sooner you're out of there the better,' she intoned darkly. 'I can remember a time when you two couldn't keep your hands off each other and you know what you're like when you're ill. You get all pathetic and vulnerable. Your defences are right down at the moment and who knows what else might follow . . .'

I fumed silently for a moment at her tacky insinuation, but eventually found what I hoped was a calm and level tone.

'Thank you for that supreme vote of confidence. However, you seem to have forgotten that not only is my leg in a bandage and my head throbbing like a pneumatic drill, but that I am also a married woman! I would have thought at least one of those tiny details might ensure my personal safety, wouldn't you?'

'Possibly,' she said doubtfully, 'but I'm not convinced. Personally I think you should be heavily chaperoned. I'm coming over.'

'Fine, fine,' I muttered weakly. 'Do what you like.'

'I'll be there in twenty minutes.'

'Terrific. Can't wait. Oh – and Laura?'

'What?'

'Bring the children with you, would you?'

'The children?'

'Yes, Hugo and Clemmie, my offspring, fruit of my loins and all that, remember? If it's all right with you I'd like to see my babies!' My voice quivered a bit at this because damn it, she was right – I *did* get rather pathetic when I was ill. It was my huge yellow streak, you see. I always feared the worst, sensed my mortality. Chicken pox, flu, it was always the same, even post-natal piles had had a seriously debilitating effect on my morale.

'All right, all right,' she said hastily. 'Don't worry, I'll bring them.'

'Thank you,' I bleated, and put the phone down.

I lay back on my pillow and sniffed a bit. My babies. My poor motherless little babies, missing me desperately, no doubt. I blew my nose and stuffed the hanky under the pillow. I sighed. That was the funny thing about children, I reflected. When you're with them all day long you dream of being without them; of having a cup of tea without having to share it with dolly; or taking a solitary trip to the loo without a captive audience demanding to know why you haven't got a willy; or having a house that looks like something out of *Homes and Gardens* rather than something out of Beirut, but then the moment they're not there – there you go, missing them like crazy. Their dear little faces, their winsome smiles, their . . . ooh dear! I reached under my pillow again for the hanky and gave in to a good old blub. When I'd finished I felt considerably better. I blew my nose sternly and stuffed the hanky back again.

It also wouldn't hurt, I decided, for Patrick to see them with me too. Yes, let him see what I'd done in twelve years, see what I'd produced. I couldn't help thinking that however badly the little darlings behaved they'd knock a few poxy watercolours into a cocked hat. Ha! Yes, put that on your palette and paint it, Mr Cameron. I bit my thumbnail thoughtfully. It was a shame I couldn't spirit up David, too, the devoted husband. Have the whole idyllic shooting match gathered round the bed in true *Hello!* style.

I was just wondering what the devil I was supposed to do about breakfast when my maid appeared – my *maid* for heaven's sake – to draw the curtains and deliver my bacon and egg. I made a big show of struggling to sit up and help with the tray, thanking her profusely, but knew full well that after a couple of weeks of this treatment I could quite easily be giving her a curt nod and demanding to know why the hell my egg wasn't sunny side up. She departed and was followed ten minutes later by Madelaine to check I'd taken my painkillers.

'And how are you feeling, my dear?' she asked

anxiously as she bustled over to check that the maid had delivered all that madame required.

'Oh much better, thank you,' I beamed, wiping my eggy mouth with my napkin. 'I really think I might be able to go home soon.'

She sat on my bed and patted my hand. 'We'll see. Rather selfishly I am not in so much of a hurry, you know. It's been a while since I had some company.'

I flushed, mortified. 'Oh! No, I didn't mean I was in a hurry, it's wonderful being here, it's just – well, my children, you know.'

'Ah, my dear, of course.' She clapped her hands in consternation. 'You must ask them over.'

'I have already, actually, if that's all right. With Laura. I hoped you wouldn't mind.'

'But of course not. They'll stay to lunch?'

Try and stop them, I thought grimly, but smiled. 'I'm sure they'd love to.'

'Splendid!' She got up hastily. 'I shall tell Cook immediately. So much to do.' She hastened to the door.

'Oh, Madelaine, I'm sure a sandwich, or a what d'you call it – a Croak Monsieur would be fine. Please don't go to any tr—'

But she'd gone, hurrying off no doubt to get the haunch of venison out of the cellar, slinging it over her shoulder and staggering up to the kitchen, or maybe she'd even go out onto the moors to kill it first with her own bare hands, because there was, it seemed, no end to the lavish hospitality of these Camerons. They were like frustrated hoteliers, thwarted for years by a lack of guests but with a sudden chance to fill up all those barren bedrooms and empty dining chairs. Well, if that was the case, they'd picked the right family. I was quite sure my lot would need absolutely no encouragement to lap it up.

After a while there was a crunch of gravel, a car door

220

slammed and great shrieks of delight drifted up from below, followed by the thump-thump-thump of tiny feet up the ancestral steps. I smiled. The little dears, they'd arrived. I sat up a bit, adjusted my pyjamas and clasped my hands together, smiling expectantly – maternally even – at the door.

Minutes passed and I was still smiling maternally at the door. I frowned. Oh well, perhaps they were having an orange juice in the kitchen. My children always seemed to need orange juice more or less intravenously the moment they set foot anywhere, and that, of course would prompt a biscuit, which would in turn prompt another, so we were probably talking – I glanced at my watch – ooh, a good five minutes now.

I glanced idly at the stack of books placed thoughtfully on my bedside table. *Persuasion*, *Vanity Fair* and *Middlemarch* – how extraordinary, three books I'd always meant to read at some stage but had never got round to. What a treat. I reached eagerly for *Persuasion* and scanned the blurb on the back.

Nineteen-year-old Anne Elliot falls in love with Captain Wentworth but is forced by her snobbish father to refuse his offer of marriage. Seven years later he makes a dramatic reappearance in her life, passions are rekindled and— Bloody hell!

I chucked the novel back on the table like a hot coal, wishing I had a crucifix handy, or perhaps a clove of garlic to rub on the cover. Had he put it there deliberately d'you suppose, hoping I'd pick it up, read it, consider the similarities of plot and – oh for heaven's sake, Tess, stop being so paranoid! What a thoroughly suspicious mind you have. He probably couldn't care less whether you were holed up in his spare room or not. He's probably longing for you to recover so he can get shot of you and your wretched family as soon as possible, have the house to himself and get a bit of peace and

221

quiet – speaking of which, where *were* those children?

What on earth could be keeping them? Why weren't they hurrying hot foot to see their poor injured mother? Had they been kidnapped too? Was this some hideous plot? I strained to listen. Ah, no, it was OK, I could hear them now. A gust of childish laughter drifted up from the terrace below my window. I heard Patrick's voice, then Laura's, laughing. They must be on their way. I settled back and rearranged my pillows and yet again, my smile, anticipating their worried little faces, their anxious enquiries, preparing to reassure them, to open my arms to their warm hugs.

Then I heard a splash. And another splash. Then shrieks of delight. I gasped. Good Lord, they weren't in the pool, were they? What, without even coming to see me first? But there was no disguising those whoops, those splashes, those cries of: 'Come on, Clemmie, there's a diving board up this end!'

Suddenly I knew exactly how poor old King Lear had felt, and how much sharper it was than a serpent's wotsit to have a thankless child. And my sister too, encouraging them! The Goneril, the – the Vegan, I seethed, getting my Shakespearean characters in a vegetarian twist. God, she couldn't even be bothered to shepherd them up here first! I mean yes, OK, there was no disputing the fact that Hugo and Clemmie were thoroughly sybaritic, always had been, took after their – no, I couldn't possibly blame David on this count. Who could I blame? Yes! Took after their aunt probably – but you'd think she'd at least encourage them to see how Mummy was, to – what was that? I sat up. I could have sworn I heard a loud 'pop!' Despite the pain I threw back the covers and hopped furiously on one leg to the window.

Down below, on a sun-drenched terrace, Patrick was pouring an overflowing champagne bottle into the greedily outstretched glasses of Laura and Edward, both of whom were already in their swimming costumes – Laura's, I noticed, being extremely minimal – and both of whom were already stretched out on bloody sun-lounger things. *Aaargh!*

I hopped furiously back to bed, teeth gnashing rhythmically. Oh, have fun won't you, I spat between the grinding molars. I mean, be my sodding guests! I flopped down on the pillows and stared at the ceiling. You bastards! You're only here because I'm here, remember? Would it be too much to ask you to pop up and see how the invalid is first? Jesus! I fumed silently, listening to the merriment from the holiday camp below, until finally it became too much and I reached for a box of tissues. I stuffed one manically in each ear. I just don't be*lieve* it, I seethed. Yes, Victor Meldrew was now playing King Lear.

Precisely forty-six minutes later, there was a thump-thump-thump up the stairs. A second later Hugo burst into my room in a wet bathing suit closely followed by Clemmie. Their smiles were radiant and their eyes shone, and as usual, I couldn't resist them, damn it. I sat up and they flew into my arms, soaking me comprehensively and then Clemmie sat squarely on my bad leg.

'Owww!' I screeched, as Laura sauntered in after them in her swimming costume and sarong, a glass in hand.

'Hey, Hugo, Clemmie, mind Mummy's leg,' she admonished vaguely, waving her hand a bit.

'Bit late now,' I gasped.

'Sorry,' she muttered with slightly more consternation as no doubt my face went green.

'I suppose it didn't occur to you to usher them quietly into their crippled mother's sickroom?' I hissed, wincing from the pain.

'Oh God, sorry Tess. Come on you two, get off Mummy's bed and sit here, look.' She patted a little chintz sofa at the foot of the bed.

'It's all right,' I said, recovering slightly. I curled my arms around each waist as they plonked themselves on my pillows. Clemmie kissed my cheek. I thawed and grinned.

'It's lovely to see you again, you little horrors.'

'Mummy, there's a pool!' said Hugo.

'So I gather.'

'And a lilo and a boat like a dolphin and a slide that goes zooming into the water and I went down it and Clemmie was too scared.'

'Was not!'

'Yes, you were!'

'No I wasn't, but, Mummy, he was going to push me, I know he was!'

'I was not!'

'You were, you—'

'All right, that will do!' I bawled.

Immediate silence. Nice to know I still had it in me.

'Now.' I went on calmly, 'Are you having a nice time at Kilmarnoch? Are you doing everything Josie says?'

Hugo stuck his finger up his nose and dug deep. 'No, not really, but she doesn't mind because you and Daddy aren't there to see. There aren't any rules really, it's great, like being an orphan. Everyone's nice to us, even Aunt Penny. I think I'd like to be an orphan.'

'Would you, Hugo? Yes, well I'm sorry I didn't oblige and go the whole hog, it's just the leg, I'm afraid.' I clasped my hands and smiled at them both. 'Now. Would you like a treat?'

'Oh yes!' Hugo and Clemmie leaped up in unison, eyes shining.

'If you look in that drawer –' they ran as one and yanked it open – 'you'll find some nice writing paper and some pencils. How about doing some drawing while you talk to me?'

'Oh.' They gazed in disappointment in the drawer.

'I thought you meant chocolate,' said Clemmie.

'Oh yuk, drawing. No thanks, we're going in the pool again, aren't we, Clem?'

'Y-E-SS!' she shrieked, and they tore out together, for once united in their pursuit of fun. It seemed that even my children were able to share an Olympic-sized swimming pool without civil war breaking out.

'Yes, well, lovely to see you too, darlings!' I called after them.

'You can't really blame them,' said Laura, sauntering over to the window and smiling down. 'This place is like a veritable pleasure dome for them. They really have got the most fabulous set-up here you know, Tess. You should see the pool – it's huge! What a bore you have to stay up here and miss it all.'

My lip was curling up like a brandy snap. 'Well don't let me keep you from your pleasure dome, Laura,' I bridled. 'Yes, perfectly well thank you, ankle throbbing like a traction engine, head about to explode, but other than that fine, absolutely fine. Off you trot!' I shooed her away with my hand.

She looked surprised. 'Oh, don't be like that, Tess. I'm not going yet and I was about to ask how you were. How are you?'

'In . . . great . . . pain,' I said in a measured voice.

'Ah.' She nodded and sat on the end of my bed. 'Does seem a shame though, doesn't it, that you're up here? I mean, I know it hurts and all that, but it's only a sprained ankle. Couldn't Patrick carry you down or something, then at least you could sit in the sun.'

'Only a sprained ankle,' I echoed. 'Laura, I was catapulted through the air at eighty miles an hour. *I nearly died.* And no, I do not want to be draped languidly in Patrick's arms, thanks very much. I don't think it's entirely fitting.' I declined to add that I'd already been languid and unfitting at least twice.

'OK, what about Edward then?'

'Edward! Good God, I should probably end up carrying *him*! What did you bring him for anyway, Laura? This isn't open house, you know.'

'Mummy made me. She said I'd been ignoring him too much lately, and anyway, Madelaine doesn't mind at all. She told me to bring anyone I wanted next time.'

'Next time? What is this, a permanent poolside arrangement?'

'Madelaine said to come every day, until you're better. To keep you company,' she added quickly. 'D'you think you'll be here for a while yet?' she asked hopefully, surreptitiously sneaking a bottle of sun tan lotion from the dressing table and applying it to her legs.

'Well now let's see, how long would suit everyone? A couple of weeks, perhaps?'

Laura looked up eagerly from the backs of her calves. 'Oh yes, that would be—' she began brightly, then saw my face. 'Er, no, no, of course not. We all hope you'll be back with us long before that.'

'Don't bank on it,' I said darkly. 'Hugo is keen to be an orphan and I might get so depressed I respect his wishes.'

'Don't be silly,' she said briskly, screwing the top back on the Ambre Solaire and popping it back. 'You'll be right as rain in a couple of days. Now, can I get you anything? Piece of toast? Glass of water, perhaps?'

'Laura, it's my leg that's the problem, not my digestive system. I'm sure I'll be having the same lunch as you.'

'Oh really?' She looked surprised. 'Potted shrimps and Dover Sole then, only Madelaine mentioned something about chicken soup for you.' She glanced at her watch. 'Actually I must go, she said it would be ready at one and I don't want to be late.'

'Yes, run along, you wouldn't want to miss the hors d'oeuvres,' I gnashed.

'Well, quite.' She hastened to the door, somehow missing the bucketload of sarcasm. 'I'll pop up and see you later then. Bye!'

And without a moment's hesitation she'd gone, just like that, her sarong whisking after her around the door.

I sat for a moment, fuming silently, listening to her bare feet padding down the corridor. Potted shrimps? I *adored* potted shrimps.

'Laura!' I bellowed.

She padded back and stuck her head round the door. 'What?'

'I'm coming with you.'

I threw back the covers and swung my good leg round, then holding my bandaged one carefully in my hands, swivelled it around and down to join the other.

Laura hovered nervously. 'Oh Tess, d'you think you should? Didn't the doctor say—'

'I don't give a damn what the doctor said. If you think I'm sitting up here while you lot quaff champagne and guzzle exotic sea food down there in paradise you've got another think coming. Now, hand me that shirt in that Sainsbury's bag – there, the red one, that's it – and that wraparound skirt thing . . . Now, tie it up for me . . .' she helped me into my clothes '. . . perfect! Now you'll have to kind of . . . that's it!'

She put one arm round my waist and I slung one of mine round her shoulders. Together we hobbled towards the door.

'Tess, how sensible is this?' she panted. 'We've got a flight of stairs to get down yet and you must be in terrible pain.'

'Just keep going,' I said through gritted teeth. 'The smell of the Dover Sole is doing wonders for keeping it at bay.'

Together we somehow hopped and struggled downstairs, with much yelping from me as the dagger in my ankle went too deep and much shrieking from her as she nearly dropped me. We staggered down the hall, out through the conservatory and finally emerged on the terrace where – oh look, a champagne bucket! My morale soared. I felt rather like John Mills and his cronies as they stumbled into the bar in *Ice Cold in Alex*.

'Made it!' I called out triumphantly.

All heads swivelled.

'Tess!' cried Patrick in astonishment as he sat chatting to Edward by the pool. 'What the hell are you doing?'

'Fancied a change of scene,' I gasped, feeling ready to faint. The pain was quite dreadful now and poor Laura was having a job to stay upright. Any minute now we'd be in the pool.

'Here!' He jumped up and seized me from her and in one deft movement I was languid in his arms again, damn it. He glanced towards a sunbed. 'Edward!' he yelled. 'Drag that bed over here please.'

Edward jumped, instantly recognising a command from a being higher up the evolutionary chain than himself. He made haste to assist with the bed. Patrick laid me gently upon it.

'You bloody idiot,' he muttered, 'what the hell are you playing at? Why didn't you call me? I'd have brought you down.'

'Sorry,' I muttered, trying to avoid his rather scrutinising gaze. His nose was inches from mine.

'So you should be. Here, hang on while I drag you out of the sun.'

'Sun's fine,' I said, quickly digging my good heel into the terrace.

'Really? And d'you think you should be drinking that?' Laura had surreptitiously slipped me a glass of champagne.

228

'Oh I do, I do.' I held on to it firmly and beamed up. 'Numbs the pain, Doctor.' I settled back on the bed. 'Ah, that's better!'

I took a sip of champagne and gazed around. Gosh, this really was terrific, wasn't it. Just look at the size of that pool! It stretched out before me, yards and yards of it, sparkling bright blue in the sunshine and contrasting wonderfully with a glorious wall of red bougainvillaeas that flanked it at the far end. How on earth did Madelaine do that in the Scottish Highlands? Did she have a private solar system or something? All around the pool, ancient urns spilled over with drifts of pale blue plumbagos, and up on the slightly raised terrace area where we were sitting, steamer beds were dotted conveniently about, covered in pristine white towelling like something out of an expensive Caribbean hotel. I half expected a little Negro punkah wallah to slide silently out of the shadows and fan me. Bliss.

'Your health!' I raised my glass merrily to one and all, ignoring Patrick's rather censorious gaze.

'And yours too,' he said sternly. 'Take it easy, Tess.'

It occurred to me to wonder who the hell he thought he was to tell me to take anything easy, but then this was his house so I let it pass. His house. I sipped my drink thoughtfully. Yes, I suppose it was now that his father had died. Quite an inheritance, eh?

Madelaine bustled around getting the children organised on a little table of their own. She seemed to be doing such a marvellous job I left her to it.

'Children,' she called, clapping her hands. 'Lunch!'

I watched in amazement, as without so much as a hint of prevarication, my offspring dutifully left the pool and sat quietly at their table whereupon they were immediately waited on by a maid, who, trying desperately to keep a straight face, served them fish fingers and chips from a silver salver. The pleases and thank yous flowed, albeit in hushed, overawed tones. Being treated like kings was having a curious effect on my children. They were displaying manners hitherto unheard of – in fact, I haven't the faintest idea where they found them.

'Tomato ketchup, Clemmie?'

'Yes please, Hugo. Thank you, Hugo.'

I half expected to hear, 'Not at all, Clemmie,' but that really would have been scary.

'This is clearly where you're going wrong,' Laura said *sotto voce*. 'You should be mincing round your kitchen dressed as a French maid doing silver service instead of screeching at them like a fishwife.'

'Quite,' I murmured back. 'I'm surprised Penelope Leach hasn't thought of it.'

Out of the corner of my eye I saw Patrick looking on with approval and was secretly and immoderately pleased. By God, if only he knew the blood that was spilled at home.

The second sitting then took their places and Madelaine fussed happily around finding me something to rest my foot on.

'This is so kind of you, Madelaine,' I murmured as I slipped my gammy leg under her white linen luncheon table, greedily counting the courses the array of silver suggested.

'Nonsense my dear, for me this is a rare treat! It's so wonderful to have some company. Usually you know I eat alone, which for someone who lives to eat is terrible.'

'Patrick doesn't join you?'

'Ah, Patreek. Usually he is painting. He goes out in the fields promising faithfully to be back for lunch and just about makes eet for supper. He gets lost you know, absorbed.'

'Really.'

I glanced across at him. He met my eyes and I chickened out, diverting my gaze to Edward instead.

Heavens, what a contrast! I almost jumped. His face was pink from too much sun, and his broken glasses slid around precariously on the beads of sweat on his nose. He'd put a polyester short-sleeved shirt on for lunch and it was clearly the one he'd deployed on every family holiday since he was about twelve. It gripped him firmly everywhere, particularly in the damp patches under the arms. I smiled, I hoped, kindly.

'All right, Edward? I say, you look frightfully hot. Crumbs, you've got socks on,' I said, suddenly noticing. 'You must be boiling.'

'I am a bit,' he admitted. 'Would anyone mind if I took them off?'

There was a silence. Why would we mind?

'Of course not,' I said quickly.

Laura was looking at him rather as one would a flasher who'd lost his nerve. Around the table the potted shrimps were ready for eating, but Madelaine was waiting for Edward. We watched as he bent down and carefully undid his Docksiders – something I've never before seen anyone do – peeled off a pair of damp grey socks, retied his Docksiders, rolled the socks into a neat little ball – and panicked. Perhaps he thought dropping them on the ground might be construed as litter? Who knows, but instead, he placed them carefully on the table, next to his side plate, nuzzling gently against the knife Madelaine was about to employ on her potted shrimps.

There was a nasty little pause. Just long enough, in fact, for the pong to make it from socks to nose. By golly, it was noxious. I held my breath and out of the corner of my eye saw Laura give him a look that was enough to freeze your underpants off. The tension mounted as everyone stared thoughtfully at the socks. How to get them off the table without thoroughly embarrassing Edward was the question. Suddenly, a hand appeared as if from nowhere and a maid slipped them onto her salver. She covered them gravely with a domed lid but before she slid away, she gave Edward a look of withering magnitude that clearly said she recognised a social incompetent when she saw one.

'OK now, Ed?' said Patrick jovially, giving him a pat on the back. 'All sorted out? Ginny will look after those for you. Now, how about some wine?'

Lunch finally began, and despite Edward's gaucheries was a huge success. Everyone seemed determined to enjoy themselves and Patrick was at his most amusing and cavalier. Laura and Madelaine roared with laughter as he gave an hilarious account of the volatile nature of everyday life in Italy where it seemed a simple hello could be misconstrued and result in a punch-up. I was determined not to laugh too uproariously but his stories were so hilarious that in holding back I found myself doing all sorts of unattractive nasal snorts and at one point even shot a mouthful of wine across the table.

As I surreptitiously mopped it up I watched the raconteuring continue. Laura, beside him, was shaking with laughter and Madelaine was wiping tears from her eyes. Of course, I reasoned, as I sipped my wine thoughtfully, he really couldn't fail with this audience, could he? A girl who hadn't spoken to a real man in years, his mother who clearly adored him, a mouse masquerading as a man, and me who – yes, well, me. He caught my eye and I was about to look away, when I grinned. OK Patrick, point taken. You're still as funny and irreverent as you ever were.

Later, when we'd all eaten and drunk too much we flopped down on the beds to snooze. At least, the women and Edward did. Patrick excused himself and withdrew to his studio to paint. As I lay on my bed watching him go, I found myself feeling faintly disappointed. Surrounded by other people I felt comfortable talking to Patrick, even joking and flirting with him. It was safe, and somehow it wasn't so safe when we were alone.

Ah well, I thought turning over on the bed, perhaps it was just as well we weren't all laid out here together. I was still lily white and in no condition to bare my body, but without his blue eyes boring into me, was daring enough to pull my skirt right up to my thighs and undo a couple of buttons on my shirt. I swivelled my head to look at Laura. Stretched out beside me she was altogether a different story. Her gold one-piece was cut high at the sides and had tiny shoe-string straps going up over her slim shoulders. With her shiny blonde hair and light tan she looked like a slim nugget of burnished gold lying next to me.

Beside her was Edward, still in the terrible shirt, lying on his back and peering at her longingly through half-closed eyes. He'd draped the *Telegraph* over his shorts but for all its careful positioning I couldn't help noticing that it peaked dramatically in the Sports section. I smiled and turned over. Poor chap, she must be driving him wild. The children sloshed noisily around in the shallow end with Madelaine supervising, enjoying her role as surrogate granny for the day. I shut my eyes. Marvellous. Perfect peace. I made a mental shopping note for Putney. One frustrated grandmother, one swimming pool, and one maid, and with that simple memo in mind, drifted off down the dark lanes of sleep.

Chapter Sixteen

When I opened my eyes I found there had been yet another dramatic scene change. This time, I was in the drawing room. I groaned inwardly. What was wrong with these Camerons? They weren't just frustrated hoteliers, they were frustrated flipping body-snatchers too. I only had to lower my eyelids and breathe regularly and they were sneaking up on me and hustling me off to a new location. How on earth had I been spirited in here? From the other side of the room a newspaper rustled. I looked across as a broadsheet lowered. Patrick smiled, folded it, and got up out of a pale-blue wing chair. As he crossed the room I glanced down – oh God, my skirt was still up around my knickers and my shirt was practically undone to my navel! I frantically sorted myself out, cursing Laura or anyone else who might have had the decency to make me look presentable. When I looked up, Patrick was standing over me.

'You're awake,' he said gently. 'How d'you feel?'

'Fine.' I hurriedly did up another button. 'A bit groggy, though. How did I get here?'

'Ginny and I wheeled the sunbed in. It started to get a bit chilly out there; we thought you'd be better off in here.'

I struggled to raise myself up onto my elbows.

'Chilly? The last thing I remember was blazing sunshine. How long have I been asleep?'

He consulted his watch. 'Ooh, about five hours. It's half-past seven now.'

'Five hours! Good grief.'

'Well, you obviously needed it. That bump on the head is not to be taken lightly, you know. You're still recovering.'

I peered around. 'So has everyone gone?'

'Yep, they all piled off about an hour ago, but we decided not to wake you. Mum gave the children tea in the kitchen and then sent them home loaded with Smarties and other teeth-corroding goodies, I'm afraid. You'd better watch out, she'll be knitting for them next.' He perched on the arm of a chair next to me and grinned. 'I must say they're lovely children, Tess. They're a credit to you.'

I beamed with pleasure. 'Thanks. Although I have to admit, we're talking best behaviour today.'

In fact we were talking totally unheard-of and unlikely ever to be seen again behaviour, but I didn't admit to that. Patrick was sitting quite close to my shoulder and he'd clearly had a bath and changed into some cotton trousers and a clean blue shirt. I suddenly felt foolish lying on a sunbed in the middle of the drawing room. I longed to wash my face and get out of these rather grubby clothes. I pretended to itch my cheek with my shoulder but surreptitiously sniffed my pits. Well, at least I didn't pong, that was something, but I still felt thoroughly disadvantaged. I sat up, hugging my good knee with my back towards him slightly. At least I could sit, I thought defiantly. I didn't have to lie around like a flipping invalid, did I?

'This is a beautiful room,' I said lightly, trying to deflect the attention away from me. It was the pale blue and cream drawing room I'd been brought into when I'd first had the accident.

Patrick glanced around surprised. 'Yes, I suppose it

is. I've lived here for so long I've never really noticed. Mum's got quite a good eye for colour though.'

'She has, and I just adore her pictures. They're so . . .'

'What?'

'Well, fresh. And original. Landscapes can be a bit dull and drab but there's a lot of light and colour in these. You just want to keep on looking at them.'

'Really?' He stared up at the one just above us.

'Yes, they draw the eye. So many pictures are just wall-coverings.'

'And these aren't?'

'No, they're vibrant, like that seascape over there with the sailing boats. It's—' I stopped suddenly. He was grinning.

'My God. They're not yours, are they?'

He scratched his chin. 'Well, actually . . .'

'Bloody hell, Patrick, did you do these? They're fantastic!'

He inclined his head in a mock bow, colouring slightly. 'Why, thank you.'

I sat up, delighted. 'You've gone all coy! I can't believe you're blushing, Patrick. Patrick Cameron, are you blushing?' I peered at him as he cleared his throat, recovering.

'Of course I'm not,' he said gruffly, 'but I suppose I was a bit nervous about you seeing them.'

'Why?'

He shrugged. 'Don't know. Value your opinion, I suppose.'

'Oh!' I was surprised. 'Thanks. Well, they're good. Very good. D'you exhibit a lot?'

'Quite a bit. Got a one-man show coming up in Cork Street in a couple of weeks actually.'

'Really?' I gazed around at the pictures. 'Hey, who's that?'

My eye snagged on a huge portrait at the far end of

237

the room. It was of a rather voluptuous nude, Rubenesque at the top with a huge bosom, but tapering down to a tiny waist, snake-like hips and long slim legs which curled gracefully on a sofa. She had masses of long dark hair tumbling over her shoulders and the face of an angel. She looked very young. Patrick glanced over.

'Oh, that's Luciana,' he said casually.

'You know her? Or she just sat for you?'

'Oh I know her, she was a girlfriend. For a while anyway, a year or so.'

'Heavens! She looks like a film star. Are they all like that?'

He laughed. 'You make it sound as if I've got a stable full!'

'But are they?' I persisted.

'Well, I suppose they've all been pretty, yes. I'm afraid I suffer from a curious condition which makes me allergic to unattractive women. I come out in a rash.'

'Patrick!'

He grinned. 'Terribly chauvinist, I know, but call it the artist in me. I have to be surrounded by the aesthetically pleasing.'

'That's no excuse.'

'I wasn't looking for one.'

A silence fell as I gazed up at the picture again.

'Like Josie, I suppose?' I said abruptly.

'What?'

'I was just thinking, most of your girlfriends would be like Josie. Sexy young au pair types.'

He frowned. 'You make them sound rather frivolous.' His mouth twitched. 'Young Josie has a degree, don't forget. Just because she's attractive doesn't mean she's an airhead. Think of all the Miss World contestants who've striven for world peace.'

'Yes, of course,' I said quickly, dimly aware he was winding me up, 'I know she's got a degree. What I meant was, I suppose most of them have been, well – young.' I wasn't at all sure where this line of questioning was getting me or why I was pursuing it, but I was finding it hard to resist.

He shrugged. 'I suppose they have.'

I smiled, satisfied. 'Ah. I thought so.'

'And what's that supposed to mean? Ah, I thought so?'

'Nothing.'

'Come on, Tess, what are you getting at?'

'All right, why is it that men like you don't go for women your own age? It's always the dolly birds, isn't it? What's wrong with a thirty-something like yourself? Too past it? Or are you trying to recapture some of your own youth with a nineteen-year-old?'

'Not at all,' he said calmly. 'It's just that there aren't many thirty-somethings left. Most women of my age are married with children, and the ones that are left tend to be hardened career women who frankly aren't my type.'

I pounced. 'Why's that? Feel threatened by them, do you? By their proper jobs? Their power suits?'

'No, I just find them rather tough and competitive. I prefer my women softer.'

'More pliable.'

'No,' he said evenly, 'just softer.'

I thought for a moment. He definitely meant pliable.

'That's rubbish anyway,' I said abruptly, 'what you said about career women. It's just a hackneyed old cliché. You can't possibly generalise like that. I mean – look at Laura. She's successful, got a terrific job, but she's not remotely tough.'

He stood up and walked over to one of his pictures on the wall. He thrust his hands in his pockets and stared up at it.

'Ah, but Laura's a totally different kettle of fish, isn't

239

she?' he murmured. 'She's one very mixed-up young lady.'

I stared at his back. 'What d'you mean?'

He turned and gazed down at his shoes. He shook his head. 'Nothing.'

'No, go on, what the hell d'you mean?'

He looked up sharply. 'Do you really want to know?'

'Of course I want to know!' I spluttered. 'And apart from anything else, there isn't anything I *don't* know. She's my sister, for God's sake!'

'Well then, you'll know that she's still a virgin, won't you?'

I stared at him in amazement. 'Oh don't be ridiculous,' I scoffed. 'Laura, a virgin. She's had heaps of men!'

'Hanging on to her arm, yes, but in bed,' he shook his head. 'I doubt it. What d'you think she's doing with that creepy Edward?'

'Well yes, OK, he is a bit wet, but there have been others—'

'Who were cast in much the same mould, I bet.' He raised his eyebrows. 'Am I right?'

I frowned. 'I suppose on the whole they have been a bit dim, but what's that got to do with her being a virgin?'

'Because a guy like Edward will expect precisely nothing from a girl like Laura. God, I bet he can hardly believe his luck just hanging around with her. He'll be happy just to be seen with her, be grateful for a hug, a chaste kiss on the cheek, then he'll go back to his room and do the rest himself.'

'Patrick!'

'I bet they're not even sleeping together.'

'Well, not now, but at the beginning of the holiday they were.'

'To keep up appearances, no doubt. Then after a couple of nights she told him to push off. You see if I'm not right, Tess. Edward is happy to stick with it in the vain hope that he might get somewhere one day, but he won't, just as no one before him has.' He went over to the sideboard and poured himself a couple of fingers of whisky from a decanter. 'Of course, she has to go for that type because no normal guy would stand for it, but with guys like Ed, she's safe.'

I stared at him. 'But why on earth wouldn't she want to, you know . . .'

He shrugged. 'Who knows? And if you don't, I shouldn't think anyone else does. You must be about the closest person to her, aren't you?'

'Yes, but—'

'Well then, why don't you ask her? I'm surprised none of this has occurred to you before.'

'Why should it have, for God's sake?' I was upset now.

'Well, you must have thought it odd that she went out with these no-hopers, a stunner like Laura?'

'Yes, I've asked – of course I have.'

'And?'

I desperately tried to remember. 'She just says . . . that she hasn't found the right man. That she's still looking, I think.'

He shrugged. 'Well, there you are then. Perhaps that's all there is to it. I don't know, Tess, I'm just hypothesising here. She's certainly changed though,' he commented, swilling his whisky around in his glass. 'Much more kind of deep, broody.'

'Oh Patrick, what would you know,' I muttered, unnerved by all this. 'You knew her as a child of fourteen, played games with her on the beach. Of course she wasn't deep and broody then.'

I frowned. It was true though. She'd become far more introverted. When did she get like that? Why hadn't I noticed?

'Oh no, I've seen her since then.'

I stared through the French windows, past the pool, to the mountains beyond. Suddenly his words registered. I swung round.

'What?'

'I said I've seen her since then.'

'Don't be ridiculous, when?'

'Oh, I don't know.' He paused to think. 'How old is Clemmie?'

'Four – why?'

'Then it was four years ago. You were just about to have her.'

My mouth fell open. 'You saw Laura then? Where?'

'I ran into her at a wedding in London. Recognised her immediately.'

'But I thought . . .' I was stunned. 'I thought you were in Italy!'

'Yes, sure, I live there,' he said impatiently, 'but it's not beyond the wit of man to get on a plane occasionally, is it? I do have friends in England, you know.'

'But . . . she never said.'

He shrugged. 'Why should she? You were practically in labour as I remember. She probably forgot all about it in the excitement.'

'Yes, but *never* to mention it . . .' It was extraordinary. 'Even later on.' I turned to him sharply. 'So you just saw her that once, at the wedding?'

'No, we went out for supper a few times. I was over for a couple of weeks.'

'No!'

'Yes. Why not?'

'Well, no reason, no reason at all,' I spluttered, 'but – well, my gosh, it just comes as something of a surprise, that's all. That she never said!'

'Why, do you talk to her about me then?'

I felt him looking at me carefully and blushed furiously. 'No, of *course* not!' I didn't, as it happened.

242

'So why should she mention it?'

Happily Madelaine hurried into the room at that moment and saved me from answering.

'Oh, there you are, Patreek. I've been looking everywhere for you. I hope you haven't been bothering Tess, she needs all the rest she can get. How are you, my dear?'

'Much better, thank you,' I said, feeling rather dazed.

'Oh good, I'm so pleased. Now, we're going to have supper soon, but I thought perhaps you might just like some soup in your room? Lunch did seem to knock you out rather. I wonder if Dover Sole and champagne wasn't just a leetle bit ambitious?'

I smiled. 'Far too ambitious, but delicious nonetheless and I wouldn't have missed it for the world. But you're right, I do feel a bit delicate now, and soup in my room would be perfect. But this time,' I said, wagging my finger sternly at Patrick, 'I'll get there under my own steam. I do not need to be lifted – Patrick, I said I do *not* – Patrick, put me *down*, will you? For God's sake, you're driving me mad!'

But it was no good, he'd swept me off the sofa and was even now marching upstairs. I kicked my bedroom door open viciously.

'I don't *need* this. I feel like the little woman, and I am *not* a little woman.'

He grinned as he dumped me on the bed. 'No Tess, that is not an accusation that could ever be levelled at you. It's simply that it's safer and more expedient to carry you up than to let you spend ten agonising minutes hobbling up on your own, OK?'

I gritted my teeth. 'I suppose so,' I muttered ungraciously.

He stood over me as I lay on the bed and our eyes seemed to lock, whether in combat or not I'm not sure, but it was too borderline for comfort and I looked sharply away. I could feel him watching me for a moment, then he walked over to the window. A silence fell. He fiddled with the catch on the casement.

'Your window doesn't close properly,' he remarked at length. 'I must do something about that.'

I watched his back. 'Yes, I suppose this is your house now. Your responsibility.'

'Effectively, yes. Mum doesn't want it, she only comes for a couple of months a year. Prefers hotter climes.'

'So . . .' I hesitated. 'Will you live here?'

'I don't know.' He turned around. 'It's too big for one person really. Needs a family. Children.'

'Perhaps you'll have some one day,' I said lightly.

'Perhaps.' He stared at me and I felt what lightness I'd managed to summon up drain away. We both looked away at the same moment. There was a long pause.

'Umm, Patrick,' I mumbled eventually, staring at the duvet, 'could you tell your mother to forget the soup, only I'm really not hungry. I think I'd much rather just read and then go to sleep.'

I'd had more than enough eye-contact with Patrick for one day, and there was always the chance he'd deliver the soup personally and perhaps embark on some more extremely personal and frighteningly acute observations about my family. Perhaps even about me, I thought nervously.

'Sure.'

He moved towards the door. Halfway out though, he stopped and glanced down at the books on my bedside table.

'What are you reading?'

'*Bleak House*,' I said firmly.

'Ah.' He smiled and left the room.

When he'd gone I picked up my book. I stared intently at the words on the page but nothing seemed to register.

I put it down and opened a magazine instead; perhaps something more frivolous would distract me. But even as I flicked through, gazing unseeingly at the debs and their delights my mind kept flying back to Patrick. I put *Harpers & Queen* down and gazed out of my open window. Not for the first time I tried to imagine what his life in Italy might be like. In my mind's eye I saw that apartment again, the one in Florence, high up, overlooking a piazza, with marvellous views across the city, the ancient duomo, the terracotta rooftops and down towards the river and the Ponte Vecchio. I saw a large roof garden, full of light and flowers with geraniums and jasmine tumbling over the railings. I imagined hot summer nights out there, with the city bustling and twinkling down below. Then I saw Patrick, on his terrace with friends, earnest young men, fellow artists perhaps and writers, with beautiful young girls on their arms, perched on their knees, slim arms flung around necks, chatting, flicking back reams of long silky hair, laughing and talking late into the night. I saw a girl chatting to Patrick, her back to the balcony, elbows resting on the rails, a slim, beautiful girl with dark, wavy hair and laughing brown eyes. The girl in the picture, Luciana.

By day, I imagined, he painted her and by night, slept with her, in a cool dark bedroom at the back of the apartment with the windows thrown open to the hot night, the sheets flung back. I tried not to think about how he'd be with her, how he'd lie with her in his arms, their dark heads together on the white pillows. Instead, I moved quickly on to the morning. I saw Patrick, on the terrace again, leaning over the balcony in a white towelling robe, listening to the bustle of the city below as it hummed into life, basking in that misty, soft-focus haze that heralds another baking hot Mediterranean day. Then I saw the girl, padding softly out onto the terrace in her own white robe, her hair long and loose, her feet

245

bare. She leaned over, kissed him lightly on the cheek before sitting down to breakfast on the terrace in the sunshine; the Italian papers, fresh bread, orange juice, strong black coffee. She'd laugh as he read bits out of the newspaper to her, they'd chatter softly in Italian.

Later I saw her get up from the table, disappear back into the apartment and return ten minutes later in a stunning cream linen ensemble, short skirt, baggy jacket, long brown legs. '*Ciao*.' She'd drop a kiss on the top of his head and waft back through the apartment. He'd lower his newspaper and watch her go, listening to her closing the front door, tapping lightly downstairs. Then he'd get up and lean over the balcony as she appeared beneath it. She'd look up, wave and smile, before disappearing into the crowd, turning back to wave once more, blowing him a kiss, looking like something out of Italian *Vogue*.

I sighed. Gosh, how wonderfully civilised. How blissfully romantic. Rather ruefully I then envisaged a comparable scenario in Pelham Road, Putney. An average morning might go something like this: I'd probably wake up in the grip of an affectionate stranglehold administered by my daughter, turn blue, wrench her off, glance at the clock, shriek with alarm, stagger downstairs and reach blindly for the coffee as the children banged spoons on the kitchen table demanding Hula Hoops for breakfast because you did once, Mummy, remember?

I'd lie that I remembered no such thing, fling Coco Pops in bowls, reach into the fridge for the milk bottle – empty – snatch the cereal bowls back and reach into the bread bin – empty – throw the Coco Pops back on the table and bellow, 'Don't be ridiculous they're delicious with water,' before blundering into the airing cupboard searching for school clothes, clean clothes, dirty clothes, *any* clothes. I'd quickly recycle a dress of Clemmie's by picking egg off the collar, get cornered by David in boxer shorts and socks enquiring if a clean shirt was out of the question for the *second* time that week, snap that this wasn't a flipping Chinese laundry, snatch one from the tumble drier, hastily iron the collar and cuffs and hand it back telling him it was a cold day and he was unlikely to take his jacket off, now was he?

I'd stalk back to the kitchen to let the-cat-who-refused-to-use-the-flap out of the back door for a poo, then realise there was little point because she'd already done it and it was even now squelching up between my bare toes. I'd shriek, curse, kick the cat, grab kitchen paper and bend down to mop up my feet and the floor, only to be booted in the backside by the back door opening and nosedive onto the terracotta tiles. Get up, turn around and see the Unigate milkman apologising for being late and bearing three pints, but also, a strange excited gleam in his eye. I'd realise I'd been up-ended wearing David's nightshirt with no knickers on underneath and resolve to switch to the Dairy Crest milkman immediately.

Then I'd dress the children, throw jeans and a jumper on over my nightshirt, tear around the house looking for car keys, hurtle out of the front door telling the children to *hurry up* or we'll be late *again*, dash down the path and be abruptly seized by my usual if-only-I-hadn't-had-that-last-cup-of-coffee desire for the loo. Hover at the gate, racked with indecision, buttocks clenched, the children waiting – will she or won't she chance it – then dash back into the house to be enthroned for the next five minutes with an audience of two urging me to, 'Push, Mummy, push, or we'll be late!'

After a degree of success I'd run out of the house with my trousers undone only to bump into the *other* milkman at the garden gate and see *his* eyes gleam too. As I pulled up my flies I'd realise, with a sinking heart, that my only option now was to buy the sodding milk myself.

I'd then drive dangerously fast to respective schools, dump the children in empty playgrounds, spy diligent children of organised mothers already crayoning away through lighted windows, dive under the dashboard in an effort to hide from Hugo's headmaster who already regards me as frivolous and beat a hasty retreat, only to be ambushed at the school gates by a new boy's mother who for some reason thinks I'm just the person to enlighten her on the opening times of the Natural History Museum (don't know) the whereabouts of the Philosophy for Children Centre (don't care), and the possibilities of cuboid maths tutoring (don't even know what it is). I'd then talk education for ten solid minutes until I felt I was going to pass out, excuse myself on the grounds of having left the cat in the oven, tear home, screech to an emergency stop outside the corner shop, run in, and make for the cake counter to secure a box of Mr Kipling's Fondant Fancies for the children's tea.

On arriving home I'd flick on Richard and Judy, rip the Mr Kipling box apart, devour the cakes, spy a huge pagoda of washing up and feel guilty but not guilty enough to spring up and do it but also relieved that Josie was doing the Sainsbury's shop and not around to see me playing Lady Muck. I'd then spray cake all over the carpet as she appeared in the sitting room having returned for her keys. I'd help her look, discover I'd picked them up by mistake in the mad, pre-school search for my own, apologise, mutter something about rampant PMT making me forgetful, guiltily offer her a Fondant Fancy, Richard and Judy, comfy sofa, grab my own car keys and dash off to do Sainsbury's myself, whence I would emerge an hour later looking bowed, bloodied, broken, and absolutely nothing like something out of Italian *Vogue*.

I sighed and sank back into my pillows, gazing out of the window to the mountains beyond. I chewed my lip reflectively and dredged up another deep sigh. It wasn't that I wanted a life like Patrick obviously had; I wasn't dissatisfied with my lot or anything, it was just that now and again I wouldn't mind savouring a *bit* of it. Just a week perhaps – not even that, a weekend . . . God, even half an hour would do. I wasn't jealous as such, no no, I wouldn't swap my lifestyle for a million years – I mean, who'd want Florence when they could have two children, a husband and Putney High Street, eh? Yes . . . well . . . I bit my thumbnail. One shouldn't make comparisons.

I opened *Bleak House* and tried again. '*London. Michaelmas term lately over, and the Lord Chancellor was sitting in . . .*' I looked up. And then there was Laura. What about all that, eh? Could Patrick possibly be right about that? Could he possibly have an insight into her that had completely passed me by? I put *Bleak House* down and this time, imagined Laura's life. Laura at home, in her flat in South Kensington, where I never really saw her because I was always too busy to go there . . .

I imagined her waking up in her pale blue Toile de Jouey bedroom. Was she alone? Somehow I couldn't see Edward's head on those White House pillows. I saw her slip her silk dressing gown on, make filter coffee in her galley kitchen, flick Classic FM on the radio, then sit, with a croissant, at the round table in the bay window overlooking the garden square. I tried to see Edward there with her, sitting opposite her perhaps, eating, what – cornflakes? Slurping them a bit? I shook my head. Somehow I couldn't see it; she still seemed alone.

I saw her take a quick shower, slip into something French and expensive, then run lightly down the stairs, out into the sunshine and into London's bustling streets. She'd walk across the park to work, arrive at her building, take the lift to her floor, then settle down at her huge desk; beautiful, composed, self-contained, efficient.

Would Edward ring? Maybe. Maybe I could see her talking to him on the telephone, and maybe later, he'd – what, meet her from work? No, I shook my head. No, I couldn't see him anywhere near her smart modern offices, nor having a drink with her colleagues either, and certainly not at any of the smart cocktail parties she went to, so – when then? When did she see him? Later on, perhaps.

Yes, maybe later she'd make an excuse, slip away from her drinks party, hop into a taxi and arrive at a rather unfashionable, out of the way Italian restaurant and there – yes, there, finally, I could see Edward. I imagined him waiting for her at a table in the window, in a mac, blinking behind his specs, reading *What Car?* I saw Laura slip into a seat opposite him, apologise for being late and I saw him flush with pleasure. She'd toy with a salad, drink Perrier, stare out of the window as he struggled to make conversation. She'd smile at him occasionally, distractedly; with him in body, but not really there at all.

Then I saw her look at her watch. He'd get the bill and up they'd get, he'd try to help her on with her coat but she'd already have it on and be halfway out of the door. Outside, Edward would look around vainly for a taxi but Laura would be the one to stop it, hail it, and then they'd trundle off in the direction of South Ken. But then this was the rub. Would he get out of the taxi? Would he come in? I hesitated. Certainly I hadn't been able to see him staying the night, waking up with her in the morning, sharing her breakfast table, but would he come in late at night for – you know, coffee?

The taxi door slammed. On the steps, Laura turned, waved and went into the white stucco block on her own. The taxi purred by the pavement for a moment, then drove away into the night. I frowned. Was that right? I wondered. Was that how it really was, or did he go up too? Could they hardly get up the stairs and into the flat for ripping each other's clothes off and making mad passionate love?

I sighed. Oh well, who knows. I certainly didn't, but one thing was for sure. I was going to – tactfully – find out. If Laura had some problem, some hang-up about sex, I wanted to know about it and I wanted to know the reason why.

The mobile telephone on my bed rang suddenly, making me jump. I stared at it for a moment. Was that for me? I was never quite sure in this place whether there was a switchboard somewhere, some lone operator in the basement putting calls through to my room. I picked it up nervously.

'Hello?'

'Darling?'

'David! Oh how lovely!'

'You sound surprised.'

'Well, I was rather.'

'Pleasantly, I hope?'

'Of course!' What a funny thing to say.

'How's the leg?'

'Much *much* better. I think I'll go home soon, maybe even tomorrow.'

'Well, don't . . .' The line began to break up, I strained to hear.

'What? Are you in the car?'

'Yes, sorry, on my way home. Terrible line. I said don't go until you're completely better.'

'No, OK, but—'

'No buts, Tess. You promised – OK? You're to stay put until you're completely well, until you're back on your feet again, all right? Promise me that now.'

'I promise,' I said slowly.

There was a pause.

'How's work?' I asked. 'When are you coming back?'

'Not just yet, I'm afraid. I'm up to my eyeballs here and the case is still going on. Tess, this line's appalling, I'll ring again in the morning.'

'Why not when you get home?'

'Well, you'll be going to sleep soon, won't you?'

I looked at my watch. Gosh, it was nine-thirty. He was coming back late from Chambers. 'Um, yes. I suppose so.'

'So I'll ring tomorrow. How are the children?'

'Fine, they came over today.'

'Good, good.' The line crackled. 'Bye then, Tess.'

'David—' But he'd gone.

I put the telephone down slowly, staring at it as I did so. Was he behaving oddly, or was it my imagination? How weird that he kept insisting I stay here. And no kiss. He always blew me a kiss if we were away from each other. He hadn't even minded that the children had been here. I'd wondered if he'd be angry that they'd been here, in Patrick's house. Oh, don't be silly Tess, I told myself. It's just David – he's such an innocent in many ways, thinks the best of everyone – and why shouldn't he, come to that? What was there to feel suspicious about? And of course he was rushed off his feet at the moment with all that work . . . Wistfully, for the third time that evening, I picked up *Bleak House*. I read precisely four lines, then fell asleep.

Chapter Seventeen

I was woken the following morning by a tremendous banging outside my door.

'What the – who's that?' I sat up and rubbed my eyes as Patrick stuck his head round the door. He grinned.

'Just testing them out, making sure they're sturdy.'

'What?'

'These.' He threw open the door and limped noisily in on a pair of ancient-looking crutches.

'Found them in the barn. They must be years old but there's nothing wrong with them apart from a bit of woodworm. Think you'll be able to handle them?'

He stood at the side of my bed grinning down at me. I pulled the covers up, irritated. It was extraordinary the way he just came barging into my room all the time without so much as a tap on the door.

'They look as though they're out of the Ark.'

'Doesn't matter, they're still functional. Come on, get up, you can't lie around in here all day. I'll be back in half an hour to take you for a walk.'

'Don't be ridiculous – a walk? I can't even—'

But he'd gone, limping noisily away down the corridor, whistling merrily to himself.

'Don't shut the door, will you,' I muttered, hopping out of bed and slamming it shut.

In the bathroom I grumbled to myself about the complete lack of privacy in this bloody place and the fact that I was supposed to need rest but didn't actually seem to be getting any. Yesterday I was told not to move at *all* – but today I was urged to get up and run a blinking marathon! Nevertheless, I managed a quick bath balancing on one leg and even attempted to wash my hair. I found a bag of fresh clothes Laura had brought me and was just towelling my hair dry when the door flew open again.

'Ready?'

'Suppose I hadn't been dressed!' I shrieked.

'Oh, I knew you would be. I gave you at least half an hour and you're not the titivating type. Coming?'

'Patrick, if you think for one moment I'm going anywhere on those crutches you're mistaken.'

What did he mean, I wasn't the titivating type? I could titivate for hours if I felt like it. Did he think I had nothing to titivate?

'Fine. How about we discuss it downstairs?'

'There's nothing to discuss.'

'Ah right, so you'll be staying up here all day, will you? Room service again, madam?'

He made to go. I hesitated.

'Come on, Tess, don't be wet. Just give it a go, eh?'

I narrowed my eyes and grabbed the crutches. 'Wet? Who's wet! I'll show you how to use these things, Patrick.'

I stuck them under my arms and clumped noisily out of the room. I had to admit, it was pretty easy once you got the hang of it and more to the point, it made me much more independent. I stomped down the passageway and turned at the top of the stairs.

'OK, I'll use them, but on one condition. You let me hop downstairs under my own steam, all right? We'll have no more heroic muscleman displays. If I can go for a walk I can get down the stairs on them.'

He grinned. 'Be my guest.'

I hesitated for a moment. The staircase was huge and sweeping and this time there wasn't the smell of Dover

Sole to entice me down it. I held on to the banister with one hand and then using only one crutch, made a gradual and slightly painful descent, conscious that Patrick was hovering behind me all the time. Finally I reached the bottom.

'There.' I felt rather elated. 'Nothing to it. Now,' I beckoned, 'my other crutch, please. Oh, and I'll need my purse if we're going out. It's over there on the hall table.'

His eyes widened. 'I say, Tess, you're getting rather used to the idea of servants, aren't you? Just call me Mellors,' he croaked, shuffling over and handing me the crutch and my purse. He doffed an imaginary cap. 'And consider me to be at your service, ma'am.'

I rested on the crutches and stared at him thoughtfully. 'You're full of the joys of spring this morning, aren't you?'

'And why not? It's a beautiful day!' He threw open the front door to demonstrate and the sun streamed in. 'Come on, Tess, stop bellyaching and get down those steps. We can go to the river for a bit.'

'Oh yes, what a splendid idea,' I said sarcastically, limping through the hall after him. 'Stony footpaths, lots of nice deep water for me to topple into, plenty of gorse bushes to manoeuvre. Terrific.'

In actual fact I was quite keen on the river idea. I tended to get withdrawal symptoms if I was away from it for too long in Scotland, but for some reason I didn't want to appear over-enthusiastic about anything Patrick suggested. If we were to go for a walk together I somehow felt it was terribly important I was a complete pain in the tubes. As vile as possible, in fact.

I manoeuvred the steps and then hobbled over to where Patrick was holding open the passenger door of a red Mercedes convertible.

'Oh Patrick, how delightfully obvious – a red sports

car! Precisely how long is it now? How much has this added to it?'

He laughed and helped me in. 'You can't live in Italy and not own a red sports car – and don't pretend you don't like them. All girls like the wind up their skirts, it makes them feel young and sexy.'

'Balls!' I spluttered as we roared off down the drive, my head catching up with my neck a few seconds later. 'That's the ad man's propaganda to lure the rich and brain-dead into the car showroom and you fell for it eh, Patrick? You were their number one mug. Well whaddya – hey, slow down, will you! Just stop showing off!'

But he paid no attention and we sped off down the winding country lanes that he knew so well at what seemed to be an extraordinarily dangerous speed. The rush of wind in my mouth did at least put paid to my stream of invective, which perhaps was the idea.

It was already a gloriously hot, sunny day and I had to admit it took years off me as we hurtled along under a clear blue sky with the yellow bracken beside us and the purple mountains making a stunning backdrop behind. Damn him. I felt young and – I hastily clutched my skirt which was billowing up – well, young. I snuck a sideways glance at my chauffeur. His arms were resting in denim shirt-sleeves on the car door and his blue eyes were narrowed against the wind. His face was lean and tanned. He caught my eye and grinned. I quickly looked away.

As we whipped around a corner and were about to make the descent down to the river, Patrick suddenly swung into the side of the road and stopped the car. He turned the engine off.

'Hey! I thought we were going to the river?'

'We are. But just look at that for a moment.'

I followed his eyes to the vista that stretched out before us. Down below in the deep well of the valley the river snaked and glistened, licking its way through the heather. On the valley floor, dotted with sheep, lay a bed of soft green fields, the sides of which rose gently up to rolling hills which rose in turn to majestic purple-topped mountains, soaring into the bright blue sky. I caught my breath.

'Oh God, it's heaven.'

He smiled. 'Isn't it just? Pure heaven.'

We were silent for a moment, just sitting, gazing out. Suddenly Patrick reached across. I jumped, absurdly, but his hand went on to the glove compartment and he pulled out a packet of cigarettes. He lit one and exhaled slowly, still looking straight ahead.

'Awful lot of questions you were asking me last night, Tess,' he said softly.

I blushed. 'Was I? Sorry, must have been the champagne.'

'Doesn't bother me, I just feel slightly disadvantaged. Haven't a clue what you've been up to for the last twelve years.' He took another drag and looked at me sideways.

'Oh, not a lot,' I muttered. 'Couple of babies, couple of houses, nothing very exciting.'

There was a pause.

'Do you work?' he asked at length.

'Oh yes,' I said with a hollow laugh, 'I work.'

'Really?' He turned, interested.

'Yeah, from home.'

'The writing? Great! What – articles, that sort of thing?'

'No, not the writing. I'm a mother.'

'Ah.' He smiled. 'I see.'

'Do you?' I raised my eyebrows. 'I think what you actually meant, Patrick, was do I earn, and the answer to that is of course no. My work is entirely voluntary and unpaid. In fact, I'm thinking of registering myself as a charity.'

He laughed. 'OK, OK, so why don't you earn, if that's the way you want it put? I mean, you could, couldn't you? You've got a nanny.'

'I've got a twenty-two-year-old au pair, not a surrogate, and neither would I want one, thanks very much,' I said tartly.

He exhaled. 'All right, all right, I was only asking.' He paused and stubbed his cigarette out. 'But there are other ways, aren't there? Of – you know, child-minding?'

'You mean a crèche? A sort of upmarket orphanage with pretty pictures on the walls, the only difference being that the children get to go home and sleep in their own beds at night? No thanks.'

'Wow, you're prickly about this, aren't you? To be honest I couldn't care whether you worked or not!'

'Ah, but you could, Patrick. It was your first question and believe me, it always is and I've sat at enough dinner parties to know that, "No, I'm a mother" is not a riveting-enough reply. It does not prevent the eyes of the man sitting next to you from glazing over as he summons up the energy to politely enquire which school little Johnny attends, although of course he's not remotely interested because he's got his own little Johnny at home and has quite enough child-rearing chat with his own wife, thanks very much. No, what he *really* wants to know is whether he should get into aggregates, or whether those Aerospace shares were a good buy, or what your latest marketing campaign is so he can immediately lean back and launch into his.'

'Oh come on, Tess, there are other things to talk about besides work.'

'Like what?'

'God – I don't know – politics, religion, art, sex . . .'

'Yes, but those don't tend to be opening gambits, do they? Those subjects tend to crop up a bit later on, when you know someone quite well. It's that first, ever-so-

258

mild, but ever-so-probing initial enquiry I'm talking about – *What do you do?* And it doesn't matter how scintillating you make child-rearing sound, you've instantly been pigeon-holed into a nice girl – because of course men like women who stay at home and look after kiddies, they tend to be softer, you see, Patrick, more pliable . . .' I gave him a beady look '. . . but on the interest scale you don't begin to score. In their eyes you're a cypher.'

'Rubbish!'

'I said in *their* eyes, Patrick, that's all.'

'Well, if that's how you feel you're perceived, why don't you do something about it?'

I shook my head and smiled ruefully. 'Can't. I'm trapped. It's the old cleft stick, I'm afraid. You see, I refuse to let someone else bring up my children – which, let's face it, is what it amounts to. Not that they wouldn't necessarily make a damn fine job of it – God, some of my friends work and have marvellous nannies and marvellous children come to that. Who knows, Hugo and Clemmie might even benefit from it, learn a few manners, but there's always a risk, isn't there?'

'What risk?'

'That they might turn round to me one day, aged about fifteen and say, "And where the hell were you when I needed you, Mummy?"' I shook my head. 'Frankly it's a risk I'm not prepared to take.'

Patrick scratched his head sheepishly. 'Look, Tess, if you want to bring your children up yourself that's fine by me, I'm certainly not asking for an explanation.'

'Yes, but I want to give you one, Patrick,' I said urgently, twisting round to face him in my seat. 'You're not just some stooge I'm sitting next to at a dinner party – and, to be perfectly honest, I don't care if most of them think I'm a flipping basket case – you're someone who knew me when I was young and enquiring and –

intelligent, damn it. I *want* to explain to you why it is that I can only talk about my pottery classes, or my plans for my garden. There is actually a reason, you know. I don't want to be brain dead, it's just force of circumstances, and yes I *do* feel bad about it, I feel I've betrayed my intellect. It's not just the working mothers who feel guilty about leaving their children behind, you know, it's the home-makers who feel guilty about leaving their brains behind. I left mine in that maternity hospital eight years ago and I haven't been able to lay my hands on them since. And that's another thing,' I ranted, well away now, finger wagging vigorously.

Patrick clutched his head with his hands. 'No, spare me, spare me,' he moaned.

'Not only has my mind deteriorated beyond belief, but my body has, too.'

He gasped in mock horror. 'No!'

'Oh yes.' I nodded vehemently, a trifle wild about the eyes now. 'Childbirth,' I raved, 'has left me with a body that even now has room for two. I'm stretched in places you can't imagine were designed to stretch, I'm overloaded at the bottom and underloaded at the top – God, even a Wonderbra has its work cut out doing wonders for me – so don't let anyone tell you breast-feeding doesn't affect your bust, Patrick, because it's a damn lie!'

'Thanks, I'll bear that in mind,' he muttered. 'Er, is this something else you've always wanted to say at dinner parties, Tess? Because I have to warn you, unless every-one's really tanked up on the old port it might not—'

'I do not keep fit,' I swept on, 'I keep fat, and aside from lugging shopping bags around and picking up bits of Lego from the floor I do no exercise whatsoever. My thighs move independently of my legs when I walk and I wouldn't be at all surprised if everything falls out at the bottom one day because let me tell you something

260

that very few people know, Patrick,' I hissed. 'When I was supposed to be doing my pelvic floors, I cheated!' I nodded triumphantly.

Patrick's eyes were wide. 'No! Your pelvic floors? I'm telling.'

'Don't you mock me, Patrick Cameron. These are intimate and serious shortcomings I'm admitting to here and yes,' I nodded solemnly, like some new recruit at Alcoholics Anonymous, 'yes, I know it's all my fault. I know I should take myself in hand and arrest the decline, go jogging, go to the gym, but I just can't bring myself to join that depressing queue. D'you know something, Patrick, twenty years from now our children will be shown videos of people in the 1990s, furiously stomping up and down imaginary steps, grimly riding imaginary bicycles, sweating like pigs in a mock-up of a hamster wheel, twenty to a room, each locked into their own cycling shorts and their own little egos, and they'll think we must have been completely bonkers. I went to one of those places once, just to see, and I thought it was the second most depressing room I'd ever been in.'

'The first being?' He nervously took the bait.

'The crèche.'

'Ah yes, of course.'

'So there you have it, Patrick, I am not the girl you knew. I have no job, no figure and have done absolutely nothing that you would regard as interesting with my life.'

Patrick cleared his throat. 'Personally, Tess, I've always thought that having children must be the most fulfilling thing a woman—'

'Oh, spare me the soft-soap crap!' I snapped.

I swung away from him and stared angrily out at the view. My teeth were clenched and I tried hard to control my breathing, to stop my nostrils from flaring. It was extraordinary, I mused, heart hammering hard, how I'd

261

managed to get so worked up about this. I actually didn't recognise myself. Was this me talking? To be honest I'd never really given a fig what people thought of me, couldn't care less if some pompous stockbroker wrote me off as a simple homemaker, so why did it suddenly matter so much now? Why, all of a sudden, did I mind that I hadn't done more with my life? Was it because Patrick reminded me of my youth? Of the plans I'd had for myself at nineteen, the travelling, the writing, the success, of all that potential that I'd willingly poured down the drain? Perhaps I was, rather late in the day, mourning the loss of my once more than adequate brain. I'd never questioned my decision to stay at home before because as far as I was concerned, it was all to do with instincts. My instincts kept me with my children, other people's took them out to work, so why then, suddenly, did I wish that just for the purposes of this conversation, I'd gone against my instincts? Why did I secretly wish I was sitting here as Head of Editorial at *Vogue* looking like I'd just Garboed out from between its covers? Why did I want to prove myself to this man?

'Why are you telling me all this?'

I jumped. 'What?'

'The warts and all stuff.'

'Don't want you to be under any illusions, I suppose.'

'Why should it matter what I think?'

I licked my lips and felt my colour rising. 'For the same reason, I imagine, that you valued my opinion about your pictures.'

There was a silence. We both looked straight ahead. A curlew was circling overhead, calling to its mate. I kept my eyes very firmly on that curlew.

'Tess,' he said at length, 'I have to admit I wasn't under any illusions about you. I didn't actually imagine that when you weren't stirring the baked beans you were moonlighting as a captain of industry or the first

262

housewife in space, and I do have eyes enough to see that you don't have the body of a supermodel.'

'Or even an Australian au pair.'

He frowned. 'Comparisons are always odious.'

'You can bet your life they would be in this case,' I muttered.

Patrick turned the key in the ignition. 'Come on,' he said, 'let's go down to the river.'

We drove the rest of the way in silence and as we roared along I tried to make sense of my mood. Why was I being so awkward? So defensive? I rested my head back and sighed. I wasn't exactly sure, and even if I had a vague idea, I felt nervous about pursuing the matter. Instead, I abandoned myself to the feeling of the wind rushing through my hair, only this time, I didn't feel quite so young, quite so lighthearted.

When we arrived at the river we were nowhere near the beat my family usually used because we'd had to go somewhere reasonably conducive to crutches. I looked around. I didn't recognise this place at all. Patrick came round to help me out, but I hopped out before he'd got there, declining his offer of an arm. No, if the idea was that I could manage this myself then manage I would. He strode off down the caked mud path that had been beaten smooth over the centuries along the riverbank and I limped slowly after him. Sensing my desire for independence, he didn't turn around and wait for me but when I arrived at a reasonably clear, grassy stretch, I saw him sitting at the water's edge. I flopped down next to him, chucking my crutches away.

'Phew! Made it,' I cried triumphantly.

He turned and smiled, chewing some grass. 'Knew you would.'

'These things aren't too bad once you get used to them actually,' I panted, patting my now trusty sticks. I lay down on my back in the long grass.

'Bliss! Listen to the river, and those birds. This is just what I needed, Patrick.'

'Thought it might be.'

I shut my eyes and let the sound of the water flow over me as it rushed over its bed of pebbles, licking at the bank. The lapwings called to each other, backwards and forwards across the river, and far away a woodpecker was tapping out its faint Morse Code. The sun was beating down on my face and I could smell the warm gorse and heather as it basked in the sunshine around me. Heaven. I could stay like this for ever, I thought. I did for a while, until I heard a different noise. Someone was laughing, a man. I sat up.

'What was that?'

Patrick quickly turned to me and put his finger to his lips. He was sitting up, his eyes narrowed, staring down to where the bank on the opposite side fell away and flattened out to fields, and then beyond to where the woods began.

'It's Willie.'

'Where?'

'In those woods over there,' he pointed.

I strained my eyes, following his finger. 'Oh yes. What's he doing in the woods, d'you think?' I lay down again. 'Besides talking to himself.'

'He's not talking to himself, he's got someone with him.'

I sat up again and shaded my eyes. 'Where?'

'There, look, just going into that copse. Keep quiet or they'll hear us,' he whispered.

I followed his gaze and sure enough, a girl's laugh rang out, shrill and clear. Whoever it was had her back to us. She was wearing jeans and a pink T-shirt and suddenly, the T-shirt rippled up and flew off over her head. The girl appeared from under it, shaking out a mane of blonde hair. She laughed again and turned around, bare-chested.

'Good God, it's Penny!' I gasped.

Patrick grinned. 'Well well well,' he murmured. 'The old devil.'

We watched as she ran skittishly through the bracken at the edge of the wood, swinging her T-shirt around on her finger, bouncing around spectacularly, clearly imagining she was some kind of heavily breasted wood nymph. Patrick's eyes were on stalks.

'Bloody hell!' he gawped.

Willie gamely played along, chasing after her like her swain, but looking somewhat bemused it has to be said. She turned and laughed girlishly, then disappeared into the wood, only to pop her head out from behind a tree a second later and beckon him on with a coy little smile. Then off she darted again, skipping and prancing around in the bracken. As they finally disappeared from sight Patrick gave a great guffaw of laughter.

'Oh, good for you, Willie,' he hooted, 'good for you! Blimey, she's unreal though, isn't she? She's like something out of a *Carry On* film! And did you see those socking great—'

'I can't believe it,' I breathed incredulously, eyes boggling, 'I mean Penny, of all people. I just can't believe it!'

Patrick wiped his eyes, still chuckling. 'Oh I don't know, she always was a bit of a goer, wasn't she? And of course Willie makes a point of bedding all the attractive London women who come up here every year.'

I swung around. 'No!' I gasped.

'Oh yes. And why not? Does them the world of good, a bit of *al fresco* rumpy pumpy with a great big hairy Scotsman. Must make a refreshing change from Peter Jones sheets and a balding merchant banker, don't you think? I'm surprised he hasn't tried you, Tess!'

'Don't be ridiculous,' I stuttered, flushing. 'The very idea!'

He grinned. 'Well no, perhaps not, he does tend to go for the more obvious types. She's not the first girl this week though, he had one in the hut a few days ago.'

I gazed at him, speechless with horror. My mouth felt dry, my throat tight.

'How d'you know that?' I whispered.

'I saw them, late one night. It was after I'd taken Josie out for a drink actually.' He lay back in the grass, clasping his hands behind his head. 'I didn't feel like going to bed so I wandered over for a dram with Willie. I do occasionally.' He grinned. 'Unfortunately, he was otherwise engaged. I was just about to open the door when I heard a girl's voice whooping away in there. Whooping and moaning actually, very vocal whoever it was, lots of Ooohs and Aaahs – *"Ahhh, Willie, oooh – ahhh . . . yes – YES!"*' he chuckled.

'How d'you know it wasn't Penny?' I croaked, feeling rather sick.

'Peeped through the window.'

'No!' My hand flew to my mouth. I sank my teeth into it.

He grinned. 'Couldn't resist it. Couldn't see much because it was so dark, but whoever it was had a whopping great bottom, much bigger than Penny's.'

My hand stayed firmly on my mouth. I froze and my eyes glazed over. 'Bigger than . . . Penny's?'

He chortled. 'Gives you some idea of the scale, doesn't it? We're talking *huge* here!' He illustrated the broadness of the beam with hands wide apart, like a fisherman demonstrating the size of his catch.

'Really?' I breathed as casually as possible, teeth gritted.

'Yes, and she was throwing it about like nobody's business. I must say, whoever it was had guts. If I had a bottom like that I wouldn't take it shopping let alone chuck it about like a beach ball – ha ha!'

My lip was curling uncontrollably now. 'Is that so?' I said. 'But perhaps it was the light? – perhaps you were deceived? After all, you did say it was very dark?'

He shrugged. 'Yes, OK, it was a bit dark, hard to tell I suppose. God, don't go all sisterhood-ish on me, Tess, I'm sure she was a very nice girl, heart of gold and all that. Just had a big bum, that's all.' He peered up at me. 'You look a bit sort of white and tense, are you all right? What's the matter, are you in shock? Doesn't this sort of thing happen in Putney?'

'Yes – yes of course it does!' I laughed nonchalantly. 'Happens all the time.' Bigger than Penny's! Wouldn't take it shopping! Bloody hell! I snarled inwardly but struggled on, forcing a bright smile. 'I'm just a bit surprised at Penny, that's all.'

'Well, I wouldn't go broadcasting it to the nation, no harm done. It's just a quick bonk, no point in rocking the marital bed. I expect she's having the time of her life right now – oh look, talk of the devil, she's back!' He sat up. 'Good heavens, that was quick – but no Willie. Has she left him for dead, d'you think? Ravished him rotten then spat him out?'

We watched as Penny tripped gaily out of the woods, T-shirt on this time but still frolicking girlishly, skipping along in the long grass, throwing back her blonde hair like Miss Piggy. Giddy with sexual gratification no doubt.

'Ah no, here he is,' grinned Patrick, 'the man himself, looking a bit worse for wear though.'

Willie staggered out of the woods after her. His hair was all over the place and his tongue and his shirt were both hanging out – the latter, I'd hazard, even from this distance, short of a few buttons. He looked distinctly dazed and I could have sworn he had scratches on his face.

'Looks like she's put him through his paces,' I murmured.

Patrick looked horrified. 'God, it's a terrifying thought, isn't it? I mean, if that's what she's done to a strong man like Willie in a matter of minutes, no wonder poor old Piers looks like he's not going to make it through the afternoon.' He scraped his hair back nervously. 'I tell you what, that man's gone up in my estimation. She's a flipping Rottweiler on heat.'

I giggled. 'Oh look – there's her car. Gosh, talk about obvious, she must be very sure no one's coming out this way.'

We watched as she skipped back to her car parked on the edge of the wood, turning and blowing kisses to Willie all along the way. So much for getting all that out of her system before she got married, I thought grimly. This was one leopard who hadn't remotely changed her spots. She got in, and we heard the engine turn over.

'There she goes,' murmured Patrick as the car pulled away, 'back to Pukey Piers – oh, and there goes Willie, back to Kirsten no doubt.'

Willie tucked his shirt in, adjusted his trousers and swung his leg over his bike. He grinned and waved to Penny then pedalled slowly, and it has to be said breathlessly, off up the hill that led to Invertarn.

I frowned. 'Kirsten? You mean the girl who lives down the road from him? She's not his girlfriend, she's his cousin.'

Patrick laughed. 'Cousin my eye! No, Kirsten's his regular bird when he's not going off piste with the holidaymakers. I think she's under the impression he might make an honest woman of her one day, but I have my doubts. Willie's got enough wild oats in his sack to sow a blinking prairie. He's into anything that moves.'

'Really?' I said with a tight little smile. 'Is that so?' My teeth, behind the smile, began imperceptibly to grind.

Patrick saw my face and grinned. 'My, what a sheltered life you've led, Tess. Still very much the vicar's daughter, eh?'

'Yes,' I laughed airily. 'Yes, I suppose I am.'

Up until last Thursday night that is, I thought grimly, when the vicar's daughter was throwing her whopping great bottom around with the man who's got enough wild oats to sow a blinking prairie. Thank God I'd stopped short of the seed sowing though, I thought with a surge of relief. That at least was a mercy. I wouldn't have been one of many, I'd have been one of flipping millions, and not only that but those flipping millions now included my cousin Penny. It was outrageous, the man was a sex fiend, unfit to be roaming the fields, he should be . . . oh well, what's the use? I caved in suddenly. Forget it, Tess. Stop ranting and forget it. What's done is done.

I lay back and breathed deeply, slowly, trying to calm myself down. I wondered if I could remember any of the breathing exercises I'd been taught at ante-natal classes designed to lower the blood pressure and – joke – relieve the pain. (And if that doesn't work we'll pop back and paralyse you from the waist down, OK?) Sort of – in through the nose and out through the mouth, wasn't it? Yes, something revolutionary like that. I practised for a while feeling the sun beating down on my face. I'd probably got a red nose by now but I couldn't be bothered to do anything about it. I breathed a bit more, and slowly, surely – amazingly – felt the irritants of the world slip away. Sod Willie. Sod Penny. Sod everyone, in fact. Gosh, yes, this was working, how marvellous. I breathed on.

So Willie had an insatiable sex drive – so what? So Penny was still a goer – what did it matter? So I had a big – no, steady Tess, don't think about that, keep breathing. Hard. Better. I began to calm down again.

Yes, what did anything matter when I could lie here and listen to that bullfinch calling to its mate? Or to that woodpecker, tapping out its persistent message and wasn't that a kingfisher? How marvellous, now that really took me back. I hadn't heard a kingfisher for years, not since . . . Slowly I opened my eyes. I raised myself up onto my elbows and gazed around. Yes, of course, I thought slowly, how stupid of me. Not since the last time I'd been here, twelve years ago. To this exact same stretch of river, except that we used to sit, or rather lie, on the opposite bank . . . and it was always dark . . .

Slowly I turned around. Patrick was watching me closely, had been watching me closely all this time, no doubt. My mouth dried.

'Patrick, why have you brought me here?'

'Why d'you think?'

'I – don't know.'

He smiled but there was an odd look in his eyes. 'Oh, I think you do, Tess. It's very simple. I brought you here to tell you I still love you. Always have done, actually. There's never been anyone else and at this rate,' he gave a strange half-laugh, 'I don't suppose there ever will be.' He shrugged. 'Sorry to be inconvenient, but there it is.'

Chapter Eighteen

My senses dazzled for a moment. I stared at him in horror. On one level I was totally stunned; but deeper down it didn't come as a complete surprise somehow. Of course. He'd waited for me. After all these years he'd waited for me to come back, and I hadn't even realised. The writing must have been graffitied on the walls in letters ten foot tall, yet somehow, I'd missed it. I turned and reached shakily for my crutches.

'Patrick, I – must go now. Take me back, please.'

He put a hand on my arm.

'Tess, just hear me out. There's no need to leap around like a frightened rabbit, I'm not going to jump on you or anything, I just want you to consider something. You don't have to give me an answer now, you can take your time. God, I've waited twelve years, any more won't make much difference, but please, let me speak, OK?'

He looked at me gently, kindly even.

I gulped and put down my crutches. 'Well, what is it then?' I whispered.

'I'd like you to think about coming to live with me. It doesn't have to be in Italy, I can see that might be inconvenient, but I'd like you to consider living with me here, in Scotland. With the children, of course.'

For a moment I couldn't believe he meant it, he was so cool, so – unemotional. Then I looked into his eyes, there was nothing cool about those, they were absolutely loaded with emotion. Oh yes, he meant it all right.

'Good God, you're mad,' I muttered.

'Why? Why am I mad? Because I know what's right? Because I can cut through the crap and say – look, this is how it should have been? Here are two people who loved one another and for reasons beyond their control – outrageous fortune, your father, whatever you want to call it – were kept apart. Why is that mad?'

'Because – because, Patrick, I have a family now,' I spluttered. 'Haven't you noticed? Have you no eyes in your head? You're twelve years too late. I have children, a husband, it's out of the question!'

Patrick stared into the middle distance and dragged on his cigarette.

'Well, I'd call that encouraging,' he said at length. 'It's not that you don't want to, it's because you can't. Because it's not possible.' He stubbed his cigarette out in the grass. 'And that in itself is not a problem, Tess, because anything's possible. It's just whether or not you want it enough, or are brave enough to make it happen. And there's certainly no such thing as too late.'

'Oh, don't talk nonsense, of course there is. Get real, Patrick, we're not a couple of lovestruck teenagers any more, we're adults! Middle-aged adults, and you may not have any responsibilities, but I certainly do!'

'Responsibilities,' he echoed, seeming to mull the word over in his head. 'Yes, that's about pleasing other people, isn't it? About putting other people's happiness before your own, like you did when you were eighteen. You pleased your father then, remember? Felt a responsibility – duty – towards him, and now when you have a chance of real happiness the second time around, you're prepared to please your husband and children instead of yourself, is that it?' He looked at me sharply. 'Because let's face it, you're not really happy are you, Tess?'

'Of course I'm happy!' I burst out. 'What a thing to say!'

'Really? Can you honestly look me in the eye and say you've never wondered what might have been? What life might have been like for the two of us together?'

'Well,' I blustered, 'well all right, I might have *wondered* occasionally, but – that's only natural, our relationship was so unresolved, but I've never for one moment wanted my life to be *other*wise, if that's what you mean!' I stared at him defiantly.

'Really?'

'Yes, really! Damn you.'

He dragged on his cigarette a bit. Then: 'Tell me, why did you marry David?'

'Because I loved him of course,' I said quickly.

'And because you were pregnant?'

I swung around. 'How did you know that?'

'I read *The Times*. I read about your engagement and then nine months later I read about the birth of your child. You don't have to be Einstein to figure that one out.'

'Yes, all right, I was pregnant. But I still loved him, OK?'

'So you'd have married him anyway.'

'Yes,' I cried. 'Yes, I'd have married him anyway! God, what do you want from me, Patrick?'

He shrugged. 'The truth, I suppose. Do you love me?'

I gazed at him, appalled. 'What, now?'

'Yes, now.'

'Patrick, what a question! I mean, years ago *yes*, of course, but now – no, no I don't! God, I haven't seen you for twelve years.'

'You can't separate people from their passions, Tess.'

I turned on him. 'And that's the problem with you, Patrick. As far as you're concerned, it's all about passion. Well, there are other types of love, you know, that are equally important. Love of children, parents, spouses—'

273

'*Spouses!* Is that how you think of your soul-mate? It's hardly romantic, is it?'

'Life isn't romantic,' I hissed. 'It isn't about travelling around hot countries, painting here, writing there, living off your trust fund in a sybaritic style under a sweltering sun, it's about domestic routine, schools, friends, mortgages . . .'

He shrugged. 'The children could go to school here. They'd have a marvellous life, they'd soon make friends, they'd—'

'They wouldn't have their father!' I shouted. 'You're talking about *taking them from their father*, Patrick!'

'Of course I'm not. All I'm saying is that they could have the same life up here as they do in London, only better. Think of them by the river every day, on the beach, think of the freedom. Children adapt, Tess, they—'

'Don't you dare plan a life for my family. Don't you dare mention my children again,' I said in a low, trembling voice.

'Why are you so angry?'

'Why am I so angry?' I stormed, tearing my hair briefly. 'God, you're asking me why I'm angry when here you are, questioning me, grilling me, asking me to justify my marriage, my whole existence, the very infrastructure of my life! You want to know if I'm deliriously happy, and if I can't tell you absolutely unequivocally that I'm quivering with joy every single second of the flipping day you want to know why it is I won't just up sticks and waltz off into the sunset with you. Well, I'll tell you why, *because you're twelve years too late, you stupid bastard!*' At that I broke off, and to my absolute horror, burst into tears.

For a while I just sat there sobbing, quite violently actually, and whilst I was horrified, it was such a relief. To do it, to get it all out. Thankfully he didn't try to comfort me or to stop the tears, he just sat next to me, and after a while as the sobs quietened into shuddering shoulder shakes, passed me a hanky. I took it gratefully, wiping my eyes. Then I blew my nose noisily.

'All right?' he asked gently.

'Yes, fine thanks,' I muttered. 'Sorry.'

I sniffed and wiped a bit more. We sat there, side by side, staring out at the water.

'It's funny,' he said eventually. 'I was so sure you'd come. It was such a shock, seeing that engagement announcement in the paper one morning. I couldn't believe it.'

'Yes, well you always were a cocky bastard,' I said, sniffing. 'I bet the only reason you're sitting here now is because I'm the only girl that's ever turned you down. And what exactly stopped you from coming to see me, eh? What stopped *you* getting on a plane?'

He shrugged. 'I didn't see the point. You knew where I was, you wrote to me—'

'And you never replied!'

'Of course I did. I wrote to you every bloody day, asking you to come, sent you enough frigging tickets—'

'What tickets?'

'Plane tickets. You didn't . . .' He stopped.

I shook my head, stunned. 'Daddy must have intercepted them.'

We were silent for a while. Remembering.

'Well,' I said at length, with another almighty sniff. 'That's that then.' I made to get up.

'That's a no then, is it?' he said quietly.

I turned. 'Yes, it's a no.'

He stared at me, slightly pale under his tan perhaps, but otherwise very composed.

'What did you expect?' I said, exasperated. 'I haven't seen you for twelve years and then you spring this on me as cool as a cucumber. I mean it's not even as if you're asking me for a quick roll in the hay here, you're asking me for total commitment, for a complete change in my life, it's unreal!'

'You mean you'd have considered a roll in the hay?'

I flushed. 'I didn't say that.'

He looked at me closely. 'You would, wouldn't you?'

'Don't be ridiculous!'

'How interesting. A brief interlude in your otherwise rather mundane life.' He gave a slight smile. 'Yes, perhaps I should have considered that. Perhaps I should have got you tipsy, snuggled up to you on the riverbank, whispered in your ear, reminded you of old times, slipped my hand round your waist, up your jumper – yes, we could have had an affair, couldn't we? And then when you were up to your neck in the quicksand, I could have just grasped you by the ankles and,' he gave a quick jerk down with his fist, 'pulled you under.' He smiled ruefully and shook his head. 'Sorry, Tess, I'm afraid that's not my style.'

'No, Patrick, I know. You're far too arrogant for foreplay.'

'No, it's not that at all, I just couldn't bring myself to do it. Smacks of dishonesty to me. Of lulling you into something messy until you're in too deep to get out. No, this is something that needs a good, long, calculating, clear view. You think twelve years is a long time, but you've got another fifty odd to go, you know. You want to get those right, don't you?' He paused. 'Think about it. You never know, you might change your mind. Take a couple of years if you like.'

I stared at him in amazement. 'And meanwhile you'll do what?'

He grinned. 'Oh, I won't save myself for you if that's what you mean. I'll carry on as normal, but in my heart I'll be monogamous. A bit like a swan really – they mate for life, you know. We found each other and it was right;

276

that's an undeniable truth, isn't it, Tess? Whatever else has happened in the meantime, we were a perfect match, weren't we?'

His eyes were clear and bright. I met them briefly, then looked away.

'Yes, we were,' I murmured. That was all I was prepared to admit. I cleared my throat. 'But I'm not a frigging swan, Patrick, and that was then and this is now. And fortunately for me, I fell in love again, a few years later. Unfortunately for you, you didn't.' I looked him straight in the eye. 'David and I are also a perfect match, you see. And now I'd like to go home, please.'

He gazed at me for a moment and I met the anguish in his eyes head on. Held it. Then it was his turn to be forced to turn away. There was a terrible silence.

After a while I slowly manoeuvred myself to my feet. He didn't offer his hand and I didn't look for it. He quickly got up and walked on ahead. I limped after him watching his stiff back. When I reached the car he was sitting in the driver's seat, staring straight ahead. The passenger door hung open for me. I limped round, threw my crutches in the back and slipped into the seat, slamming the door behind me. I knew that my last remark had been aggressive, brutal, even, but I also knew that it had to be said if I was to protect myself and my family. I couldn't afford to be soft, not for one moment. We drove back very fast to Gilduncan in silence. Five minutes later we crunched to a halt on the gravel.

'I think I'd better get your things from upstairs and take you back to Kilmarnoch, don't you?' he said in a gruff voice.

I nodded. 'Yes. I'd like to go home.' Why had I stayed so long? Why had I stayed at all? Deep down, I think I must have known all along. Known and half enjoyed it? I shook my head miserably.

'Patrick, I'm so sorry.'

'Don't, Tess,' he said, quietly. 'Let's leave it at that, shall we? I had to know if there was ever going to be a chance, and now that I know there isn't, I'd rather not prolong the discussion. No amount of damage limitation from you is going to make things any better.'

I nodded sadly. 'I'll get my things,' I offered.

But he was already out of the car. 'No, stay there. I'll ask Ginny to get your clothes.'

He disappeared into the house.

I stared down at the long treelined driveway. Sorry to be inconvenient . . . but I love you, I always will. I blinked. Patrick's cigarettes were in the open glove compartment. I pulled the packet out, fumbled for one and lit it with a shaky hand. They were strong, Italian, and I hadn't smoked for years, not since I was about eighteen but it didn't seem to have any effect on me. My senses seemed dazed, numb almost. I dragged in great lungfuls of the pungent smoke, then threw the butt out onto the gravel. It lay there, smouldering. A few minutes later Patrick reappeared. He chucked my Sainsbury's carrier bag in the back and jumped in without looking at me.

'I ought to say goodbye to your mother,' I faltered, 'thank her, at least.'

'She's not there,' he said briskly. 'You'll have to write to her.'

He started up the engine and off we flew. As we roared back down the lanes Patrick lit one cigarette after another, all of which lasted only a minute or so in the fierce wind. It was the only indication of any turbulence, any emotion beneath his set face. That, and the way his hand shook slightly as he lit them.

We roared up Kilmarnoch's driveway and screeched to a halt outside the house. Without wasting a moment Patrick jumped out and hoisted my bag out of the back seat. He carried it up to the top of the steps, dumped it there and then leaped down the steps again. I levered myself out of the car, my ankle throbbing painfully, and limped heavily up to the door.

'There'll be someone in, I take it?' he asked shortly, from the bottom.

'Oh yes, Penny's car's here . . .'

'Right, I'll be off then.' He jumped back in.

'Patrick—' As he started the engine, he glanced up and for the first time since we'd left the river our eyes met properly.

'I'm terribly sorry,' I whispered.

He shook his head briefly, indicating that I shouldn't say any more. His eyes were full of something dangerously close to water. He didn't speak. In a moment he'd turned the car around and I watched as in a cloud of dust and gravel it sped off down the drive, round the corner and away into the distance. I stood there on the step gazing out at the empty lane, stayed there for quite a few minutes. Then, with a sigh that seemed to come from the depths of my very soul, I picked up my bag and shouldered open the door.

The house seemed still, quiet, empty. I dumped the carrier bag down by the umbrella-stand and limped listlessly down the dark hall. Halfway down I paused. I could hear strange muffled cries coming from the drawing room. I limped on, stuck my head around the door and saw Penny, lying on the sofa with her head in a cushion. She didn't see me but her body was heaving, racked with sobs. It occurred to me that the last time I'd seen her, a few hours ago, she'd been tripping merrily through the bracken, bare-breasted, swinging her T-shirt round her finger. Had Piers found out? Had there been a dreadful scene? Had he left her? Oh God, I really didn't think I could cope with all that just now. I made to limp on but she heard my crutches, looked up, saw me. She threw down the cushion, jumped up and ran towards me, sobbing. Before she collapsed in my arms I saw that her eyes were full of pain.

'Daddy died!' she gasped into my neck.

Chapter Nineteen

Penny's sobs echoed in the silent house. I led her gently back through the drawing room and over to the window seat. She clung to me as we sat there together, sobbing into my neck. I rocked her gently and gazed over her head to the view of the mountains beyond. The view he loved. Tears filled my eyes. Uncle Robert. Dear, kind, lovely Uncle Robert, my father's beloved younger brother who was as mellow and calm as my father was sharp and irascible. Now, finally, after years of clinging to the wreckage, he'd gone, and with him such a large part of my childhood.

A great sigh engulfed me and the tears fled down my cheeks as I realised, with a jolt, that I'd never see him in this room again, at that table playing cribbage, in that chair with a book, or standing, laughing, with his back to the fire, warming his legs. A huge, clever, quiet man, not an opinionated bellower like my father, but a quiet, let's-get-on-with-it doer; a calming presence, and such an influence on me when I was younger.

When we were children it was always Uncle Robert who'd sit for hours with bicycle repair kits in the dark hall, fixing yet another inner tube, or a fishing net, or untangling a rod. I could see him there now, surrounded by children, with bits of twine and nails in his mouth and his Swiss Army penknife, patiently going through the rigmarole of showing us every single blade – including the hoofpick – before he could get on with the job in hand. It was Uncle Robert who'd sit doing all the sky in the jigsaw while we got on with the interesting bits and Uncle Robert who, when we were too tired to walk home from the river, would scoop all three of us up at once with a great roar, one riding on his shoulders, one under each arm, with my father crossly telling us to brace up and not be so feeble and us shrieking with laughter.

Later, after tea, when the other grown-ups were snoozing or reading books, Uncle Robert was the one we used to pounce on and drag protesting from his armchair, a child at each arm, another pulling his jumper, demanding he play round-the-table ping-pong, or come to the beach with us to collect mussels because the tide had gone out, or to the river on bikes because we weren't allowed to go without a grown-up . . . 'Now, *pl-ea-se*, Uncle Robert, *pl-ea-se!*'

Later, when we were older, he'd sit and help us with our CVs, get them typed for us, offer advice, work experience in his accountancy firm, anything, in short, that he could do in the way of practical hands-on help for his nieces – a course of action that was completely alien to my father. As far as he was concerned, we had teachers to help us with all that, and as for his niece, well, she had her own father, didn't she?

Daddy, I thought with a sudden lurch of pity. How on earth must he be feeling now? His adored younger brother and the perfect foil for him, if he did but know it. For Robert was the only person who could really temper Daddy's furious outbursts, who could admonish him to lower his high moral tone, who could reason with him to be more tolerant, more compassionate, as no one, not even my mother, could. What agonies must he be going through now?

And Penny. I looked down at Penny's fair head. Penny, who'd lost such an adored and adoring father. A man who'd unquestionably spoiled and pampered his only child, but who at the same time was the only one who could really keep her in check, curb her tantrums, her foot-stamping, her extravagances, her petulance, as surely her husband couldn't. Robert's was the only reproof that really shamed her.

But it was for my aunt that my heart really broke, for theirs was not a marriage to be taken lightly. When she was young, my mother had told me, Rachel had been so beautiful – a débutante, the society girl of her age, and bright, too – that she could have had almost anyone. But she chose Robert and later, once told me that if she couldn't have had him, she wouldn't have married at all. Theirs was the perfect match. Patrick's words came back to me. Yes, if anyone had found the real thing, they had, and now he'd gone, leaving his other half behind.

I bent my head on Penny's and the tears rolled down my face. Suddenly my heart ached for my own childhood. I longed to look for rock pools again, to hold on tightly to my uncle's hand as he led me cautiously over the barnacled rocks and slippery seaweed in my bare feet, when all that mattered was how many crabs I had in my bucket and whether my fish were bigger than Penny's and Laura's. I longed for simpler days.

Eventually Penny's sobs subsided. Her head lolled onto my shoulder and her eyes were half-closed. She looked almost weak from crying. I glanced up as my mother came quietly into the room. Her face was very pale. My eyes filled up again and we exchanged sad little smiles.

'Come on, Penny darling,' she said gently, 'come and have a lie down.'

'Not upstairs,' whispered Penny. 'Not on my own.'

'No no, dear, here, on the sofa. Tess and I will be close by.'

She led her to the vast red sofa in front of the fire,

laid her down like a child and put a blanket over her. I sat on the floor beside her, holding her hand, listening to her sobs gradually subside to the point where she was just catching her breath, watching her eyes close. Mummy sat behind me, perched on the arm of the sofa, her hands tightly clasped in her lap. When eventually Penny's breathing became regular, I turned and looked at her. She nodded and we tiptoed from the room.

In the kitchen we hugged each other hard.

'How's Dad?' I whispered.

She sat down, or rather lowered herself into a chair, and I suddenly thought, with an awful pang, how thin and frail she looked herself.

'Terrible,' she said sadly. 'I've never seen him like this, not since – well. Not for years. He won't speak to anyone, won't let go, just walks around the garden pretending he's pruning roses looking white and stricken.'

'Where is he now?'

'Still outside.'

'I'll go and—'

'No, Tess.' She put a hand on my arm. 'Give him a moment. He wouldn't want it, really.'

I sighed and nodded. 'OK. And the children?'

'Josie and Laura took them to the beach.'

'Do they know?'

'Oh yes, we told them. Hugo and Clemmie are all right, I mean they were upset, but they knew he'd been terribly ill and after all they only saw him once a year and death is so hard to grasp at that age, but Leonora . . .'

'Her beloved Grandpa,' I said softly.

'Quite. Who would have been such a good influence on her, don't you think?' she said quietly, looking up at me.

I nodded, knowing exactly what she meant. That she didn't always get the best of influences from her parents.

I put my hand on hers. 'Rachel will always be there for her.'

'Of course,' she rallied, 'and more so now. She'll put what's left of her heart and soul into that little girl.'

I blinked back the tears I wanted to cry for Rachel. For lost love. I sat down next to Mummy at the table and she grasped my hand. We sat still, remembering, in silence.

'Is Penny very upset that she wasn't there when he died?' I said eventually.

'Of course, but you know,' she glanced quickly at the door, 'I think Rachel would have wanted it this way. Penny would have been – well, upset, understandably.'

'Hysterical.'

'Exactly. This way, they could say their goodbyes quietly, alone.'

I nodded. A final, peaceful, loving goodbye. For a while we were quiet again. My mother rallied first. She straightened up and looked at me, as if seeing me for the first time.

'And how are you, darling? You're on crutches, I see – that's good. How's the ankle?'

'Better, much better.'

'And the head?'

'Fine.' I patted her hand, smiling. 'Don't you worry about me.'

'And the heart?'

I looked at her sharply. Her eyes held mine firmly.

'That's – all right,' I faltered in astonishment.

'Good.' This time she patted my hand.

She got to her feet. 'Now,' she said briskly, 'we must think what's the best thing to do. Have a plan of action. Penny will want to go back to London, of course, and your father too, I'm sure . . .'

She moved around the kitchen putting cutlery back in drawers, folding up tea towels, wiping surfaces, discussing the options. I watched her as if in a dream. Not so silly, my old mum. Not so silly at all. Why did I always underestimate her? Was it because Dad was always such a huge presence, such a main player? Because she was so often the background to his foreground?

'. . . so I think the best thing would be if you, Josie and the children stayed on with Laura and Edward for a bit, don't you? No sense in everyone dashing back immediately, the funeral won't be until next week and it seems a shame to cut short the only holiday the children have. Robert wouldn't have wanted that.'

'What?' I looked up at her, still dazed. 'Oh – no. No, you're right. And David will come back to drive us home, I hope.'

'Oh darling, of course, you can't drive. Well, Josie would do it surely, I mean if David doesn't want to come back?'

'Oh don't worry, I'm sure he won't mind, you know David. Anyway, I was thinking, I might let Josie go with Penny, sort of – loan her out for a week or two. I think Penny could probably do with the help and Leonora knows Josie so well now.'

My mother turned and smiled properly for the first time. 'Oh Tess, that would be so kind. Piers seems totally incapable of dealing with hysterical women, not to mention his sad little daughter. It's such a long drive home. Josie could play games with Leonora in the back and it would give Penny a chance to grieve quietly without upsetting Leonora.'

'Exactly.' I stood up, pleased to have done something positive. 'Does David know?'

'Yes, your father rang him earlier. We tried to get you at the Camerons' but you were out.'

'Yes, we – I was at the river.' I declined to meet her eye. 'I'll ring David now.'

'Oh, he's not in Chambers. His clerk said he'd taken

the day off to do some shopping.'

I turned to her, incredulous. 'Shopping? David? For what? I thought he was supposed to be so busy?'

She shrugged. 'Don't know, darling.'

I sighed. 'Oh well, I'll ring him later.'

I plucked an apple from the bowl and limped out into the garden. I sat down on the step that led down from the terrace to the lawn and ate it slowly in the sunshine. Down at the far end of the garden I could see my father, bobbing around in the bracken in his khaki hat. He had an old scythe in his hand and was swiping away at the brambles like a man possessed. The scythe was blunt and rusty and the brambles so thick and tangled it was a thankless, futile task. There was something pathetic about the spectacle. Once or twice I was sure he'd seen me but he didn't stop flailing away, didn't acknowledge me.

I drew up my knees to my chest, resting my chin on them. I gazed down at the old York stone that we'd played hopscotch on for hours as children. I knew every square of that stone, every line, every crack, just as my father probably did, and Robert too. Tears welled again. But it was funny, I mused, brushing them away, how on one level my heart ached for Robert, but on another, purely selfish level, I was grateful to him for his timing. By mourning his death, I didn't have time to think about my own life, about Patrick. Sorry, I could tell myself, but I haven't got time for all that heartsearching now; my uncle's died, you see. Yes, how weird. I looked up at the mountains. It was almost as if Robert was still around, still helping me out somewhere out there.

As I sat gazing into the distance, two very small, very familiar figures gradually came into sight. My face broke into a smile as I watched them race along the valley floor, Clemmie yelling for Hugo to wait, Hugo forging ahead, competitive to the last. They disappeared from view in the wood at the bottom of the garden for a second, then popped up again just below my father. He ignored them as they scrambled past him, racing up the lawn towards me.

I hugged them both as they flopped down beside me.

'Hello, pixies,' I murmured, kissing their heads hard.

'Uncle Robert's dead,' panted Clemmie. 'He's a dead man now, Mummy.'

'I know, darling.' I pulled her close.

'Is he with God? Up in heaven?'

'I'm sure he is.'

'No,' piped up Hugo. 'No, Mummy, he might be down—'

'Thank you, Hugo, that will do.'

'But he can't fly!' said Clemmie with anguished eyes. 'What will he do?'

'Oh Clem, he'll manage.' I squeezed her.

'Will God lend him some wings?'

'Well . . .'

'Like you said He would when Pericles and Roderick died?'

'Oh. Yes, probably.' Clearly I'd peddled that particular line of drivel when our pair of smelly homosexual guinea pigs had died so there was no going back now.

'And will Uncle Robert share a room with Pericles and Roderick?'

I laughed. 'Darling, I'm not sure there are rooms, as such, in heaven.'

'What then? Where will they sleep?' Her eyes were like saucers.

'Well . . .' Clouds sprang immediately to mind and I realised I hadn't actually updated my own view of heaven since I too was a four-year-old.

'Not at the airport!' she cried.

I frowned at her. 'No,' I said slowly, shaking my head, 'no, not at the airport. I'm sure they'll sleep – yes, in a

288

room.' I nodded firmly, unable to think of a suitable alternative.

'With on sweet bathroom and sea view?'

I stared at her in amazement.

'Cuntimental breakfast? Balcony and beeday?' she demanded.

I blinked. Good heavens, what a bourgeois child I'd raised! Balcony and bidet? How on earth did she even know what a bidet was?

'Yes, I expect so,' I said comfortingly.

'How lovely,' she breathed. 'Hugo, where's your sword?'

'Upstairs,' he muttered into the York stone, engrossed in the capturing of an ant. Clemmie raced off.

'Ow! It stung me!' he yelled, brushing it off with his hand.

'Hugo, where did she get all that heaven stuff from?' I asked. 'What have you been telling her?'

'Not me,' said Hugo, sucking his wounded finger. '*Wish You Were Here*, on the telly. That fat lady with the yellow hair shows you a hotel on a beach and then says it's heaven.'

'Oh!' I breathed. So we had Judith Chalmers to thank for this warped view of the after-life, did we? Terrific. No doubt Clemmie also thought wings would be available from reception for a quick flit around the bay followed by a barbecue on the beach with the heavenly host. Doubtless she expected Angel Gabriel to meet her at the airport in full nightie and halo regalia before standing at the front of the coach with a microphone saying: '*On your right we have the Copa Cabana disco . . .*' I groaned.

Clemmie was back in a twinkling, brandishing Hugo's sword. 'Hugo,' she ordered. 'Kill me.'

'Brilliant!' Hugo sprang up off the grass. 'No, hang on Clem, I'll strangle you if you don't mind. I'll just go and get my dressing-gown cord.'

'You'll do no such thing!' I roared.

He stopped in his tracks and turned. 'But she said—'

'I DON'T CARE! Now inside the pair of you, it's tea-time – and take off those wet sandals before you go in, Hugo.'

'But I want to die,' said Clemmie, her lip quivering. 'I want to do beach sports with Uncle Robert, just let me die!'

'Come on, Clemmie.' I tried to lead her in by her arm.

She went limp in my arms. '*I want to die!*' she bellowed at the top of her voice, dragging her legs behind her.

'Where's Josie?' I demanded, lugging my infant prima donna towards the house and looking around wildly. God, I'd only been back two seconds and already I was panting for the au pair.

'Upstairs, changing Clemmie's bed,' said Hugo. 'Clem tried to hatch some eggs last night. Thought if she lay on them all night she'd have some chickens in the morning.' He sniggered. 'But all she got was egg up her bum.'

'Oh Clem,' I sighed, 'you didn't, did you?'

She stood up. 'That's what hens do, isn't it?' she demanded.

I groaned. 'Oh God, I'd better go and give Josie a hand. Now listen, you two. Go inside and find Granny – take her in, Hugo – oh, and be very nice to Leonora, please. She's a bit sad today.'

'I gave her some of my old Easter egg,' sniffed Clemmie, wiping her eyes. 'It had gone all white but she didn't mind.'

'And I didn't put sand in her knickers like I usually do when she takes them off to put her swimsuit on,' said Hugo proudly.

'Excellent, excellent,' I muttered weakly. 'That's the

spirit, darlings, that's real progress.'

I trudged wearily upstairs thinking, not for the first time, how easy it would be to commit infanticide, particularly with one's own offspring.

I found Josie in Clemmie's room making a valiant attempt to get half a dozen eggs out of a mattress. The room smelled violently already. I perched on the bed opposite, held my nose, told her she was doing a marvellous job and then as casually as possible floated the Penny loan scheme with her. She paused and sat back on her heels, J-cloth in hand. I could see her hesitate and I didn't blame her. Leonora was a doddle of course, an absolute dream child to look after, but Penny, who got through about sixteen cleaners a year, was without doubt the employer from hell.

'All right,' she said finally, 'but for one week only, OK? That's my absolute limit. Otherwise I can see myself taking the bread-knife to her.'

'Absolutely,' I said quickly. 'One week only, you're a brick, Josie. And don't forget, you're still working for me, she's just borrowing you so don't take any, you know—'

'Shit.'

'Quite.'

We smiled at each other. She put the cloth down, folded her arms and looked at me squarely.

'So how was Patrick?'

I swallowed. Not ones to beat about the Outback, these Aussie girls, were they?

'Fine,' I said, smiling broadly. 'He was fine.'

She grinned. 'He's still crazy about you, isn't he?'

'Oh!' I shrugged. 'Well, yes, I suppose he is. A bit.' I nibbled the skin around my thumbnail. 'How did you know?'

'Oh, he more or less told me. More or less admitted that's why he'd asked me out. He wanted to make you jealous, let you see what you'd given up. Said he knew it was childish but he wanted to ram home the comparison – you know, there you were, middle-aged, jaded, careworn and all that, and there he was still young, free and single.'

I gulped. Clearly it was a comparison Josie could relate to too. 'Yes, well he did that all right,' I said, remembering my seething jealousy. 'He told you that, did he?'

'Yeah.' She dipped her cloth in the bucket and resumed her scrubbing. 'I could see he wasn't a bit interested in me so I asked him what he was up to. He came clean.' She laughed. 'I liked him all the more for it actually. We had a bit of a laugh after that, cleared the air. Had a game of darts in the pub then he took me home.' She looked up at me coyly. 'Not that I would have said no, though, Tess. I mean, Jeeze, that man is absolutely knockout.'

I blinked. 'Really?'

'Oh *what*?' She dropped her cloth incredulously. 'Tess, he's drop dead GORGEOUS, you must know that!'

'Er, yes.' I nodded. 'Yes, I suppose I do.'

She shook her head in amazement. 'He must really have been something else when he was younger. I'm surprised you didn't—' She broke off.

'What? Didn't what?'

'Nothing.' She bent her head and resumed her scrubbing. 'Don't think I'm gonna shift all this egg you know, Tess.'

'Oh, just soak it in Fairy Liquid and turn the mattress over. No one will ever know.'

She wrinkled her nose. 'It'll honk for ever, won't it?'

I shrugged. 'So what? Most people who stay here are so pissed by the time they fall into bed they'll just think it's all that salmon and port repeating on them.'

She giggled and I wandered out, leaving her to it. I walked slowly downstairs, chewing my nail. *I'm surprised you didn't pick him instead of David,* was what she'd been about to say. I paused on the landing halfway down and ran my finger round a picture frame, collecting a neat pile of dust. Well of course she would think that, wouldn't she? From a twenty-two-year-old's point of view Patrick was the obvious choice; attractive, wild, loaded, funny, whereas David – I smiled wryly. David was more of an acquired, sophisticated taste. Wouldn't appeal to a youthful palate at all. I grinned. More of a jaded, careworn old bag's palate perhaps.

As I hopped the last few steps into the hall I saw Piers through the open front door, packing up his car. I went out to him. He turned as he saw me and rather wearily put down the case he'd been struggling with. I gave him a big hug. He squeezed me gratefully. Piers had adored his father-in-law but it occurred to me that there would be no room at all for his grief. Penny's would be all-encompassing. I told him about Josie and he looked hugely relieved.

'Oh, thanks so much, Tess. I tell you, I wasn't looking forward to the drive back, or the next week or so, come to that. At least I won't have to worry about Leonora.'

'Exactly.'

'Just the week though?' he said hopefully. 'I couldn't persuade you to part with her for any longer?'

I hesitated, 'Well you could, but—'

'But she's not prepared to put up with my wife for any longer, and who can blame her?' He grinned. 'Just the lifetime of servitude for me, of course. Uh-oh, talk of the devil.' His expression softened as Penny, her face streaked with tears, came slowly down the front steps.

'All right, my darling?' he said gently, taking her arm.

'Yes, thank you,' she whispered. 'Are we off soon?'

'Just give me ten more minutes to organise the back of the car and then we'll be away,' he promised.

'OK,' she sniffed. She turned and disappeared back into the house.

'You're going now?' I asked in astonishment.

'Apparently,' he muttered. 'Don't ask me, Tess, I'm just following orders here.'

'Blimey. I'd better tell Josie.' I dashed back into the house and in the dark hall, collided with my father carrying a suitcase. His eyes were hollow with pain, his face white and contorted. It buckled as he looked down at me.

'Daddy!' I flew into his arms and felt his body stiffen as he tried to keep control. I hugged him hard.

'Cry,' I urged. 'Just cry!'

'Will do,' he said in a strange, strangled voice. He patted me on the shoulder. 'In my own good time, Tess, in my own good time.'

He disentangled himself and moved quickly on past me to the front door. I watched him go down the steps to the drive, his back as stiff as a door. I turned sadly and went off in search of Josie.

Finally, about an hour later, both parties left. Piers, Penny, Leonora and Josie – looking very doubtful – in one car, and my parents in the other. Laura and I stood on the steps and sadly waved them off. It wasn't the usual jolly Invertarn departure at all. There were no tooting horns, no children hanging out of windows waving, no jibes to 'beat you back to England!' just the gentle purr of the cars going down the gravel drive. Laura and I linked arms tightly and watched as they went round the corner, down the winding lane and disappeared off into the distance. Then we turned and walked slowly back into the house.

Laura sighed. 'So unfair, isn't it?'

'Well, life's a bitch, et cetera. You must know that by now.'

She nodded. 'I certainly do.'

That evening I rang David. We had a sober commiseration about Robert then I told him of Josie's departure.

'Are you mad?' he said irritably. 'How are you going to get home?'

'Well, you're coming back, aren't you?'

'Oh Tess,' he groaned, 'what's the point? You'll only be there for a few more days and then you'll be coming back for the funeral.'

'But you were coming back before, and we'd only have had a few more days then.'

There was a pause. I frowned.

'David?'

'Well . . .'

I stared at the receiver incredulously. 'You weren't intending to come back at all, were you?'

'Look, I'm so snowed under here you wouldn't believe it. Honestly, it would have been almost impossible to get away.'

'But not impossible to go shopping, eh? Mummy said you weren't even in court today!'

'Ah yes, well, today was – an exception. My case was taken out of the list. But as from tomorrow, God, I'm absolutely chock-a-block again.'

'David, I just don't believe this. You mean you're not coming back? How on earth are we supposed to get home?'

'Well, you were *supposed* to have an au pair but you seem to have given her away. Can't you ask Laura to drive you?'

'Laura!' I said hotly. 'Why the hell should she drive us? She'll want to go back with Edward!'

Laura popped her head round the drawing-room door on hearing her name. 'What's this? What will I be doing?'

'David wants you to drive us home so he doesn't have to come back. He's insane!'

'Oh yes, I'll do it,' she said eagerly. 'Anything rather than sit in a car with Enigmatic Ed for sixteen hours.' She grabbed the receiver. 'It's OK, David, you're off the hook. I'll drive them back with pleasure.'

'Laura!' I was appalled. 'Where is Edward? He'll hear!'

'No, he won't.' She handed me back the receiver. 'He's gone painting. Anyway, frankly my dear, I don't give a damn.' She sauntered back into the drawing room again.

'Well, there you are, darling, you have a driver,' drawled David's voice in my ear. 'Now don't rush back, I think it's as well the children stay up there as long as possible. It's baking hot in London at the moment. Now, any more problems? Anything else you'd like me to sort out long distance or d'you think you can cope now?'

I stared at the receiver in disbelief. Why was he being so weird? So . . . horrid?

'No,' I said coolly. 'No, that's fine, David. Everything is absolutely under control now. It's all just tickety-boo. You carry on window-shopping and filing your nails or whatever else it is you've been doing and don't you worry about us. This single-parent family is doing *just fine*!'

With that I slammed the receiver down and stalked back to the drawing room.

Laura raised her eyebrows. 'Problems?'

'The bastard!' I exploded. 'He's not coming back!'

'Well, you can hardly expect him to fly up here just to chauffeur you down again, can you?'

I stared at her. 'Whose side are you on?'

'No one's, but you can see his point, can't you?'

'No, I bloody can't,' I fumed, grabbing the newspaper and stomping upstairs. 'I can't see it at all!'

Chapter Twenty

Madelaine rang the following morning. The bush telegraph had reached Gilduncan and she wanted to offer her condolences. Laura took the call in the kitchen. She put her hand over the mouthpiece and turned to me as I fried bacon in my pyjamas at the stove.

'She wants to know if we'd like to go up for a swim,' she hissed.

'Jesus, no! Certainly not.'

'Shall I take the children?'

I swung around. 'No! Laura, for heaven's sake, I don't want the children up there.' Suddenly I felt panicky. I didn't want any of my family anywhere near that place.

'So what shall I say? It looks so rude, Tess—'

'Just say we're busy.'

She frowned and turned back to the telephone. 'Madelaine? Um, that would be lovely, but I'll come on my own if I may . . . Yes, look forward to it . . . OK, bye.'

She replaced the receiver and turned back to me, folding her arms. 'Just because you've fallen out with Patrick it doesn't mean we have to snub Madelaine again. It's not fair.'

'I think "fallen out" is putting it rather mildly when I've rejected his twelve-year love vigil, don't you?' I snapped. 'And I'm not snubbing Madelaine, I've written her a very fulsome thank-you letter, I just don't particularly want to see her son, that's all. But you go ahead, if you must.'

She grinned. 'I must. Think of me sipping my pre-lunch apéritif, won't you?' She pinched a piece of bacon from the pan and sauntered out of the room.

I threw the spatula in the sink. Oh terrific, I thought grimly. Just swan off up there when I've specifically asked you not to, and leave me here with your abandoned suitor and two quarrelsome children all day why don't you? Thanks very much. God, my sister was such a bloody teenager sometimes, so *thoughtless*.

I picked up the plate of bacon and marched down the passageway into the breakfast room. Yes, we had five more days to get through on our own up here now, with no grandparents to amuse the children, no au pair, no father, and I couldn't even drive. What on earth was I going to do with them? I slammed the bacon down in front of Hugo and Clemmie who were even now fighting over a free gonk from the Frosties packet with Edward making a futile attempt to referee.

'Um, Hugo, how about letting Clemmie have a little go first and then you could – oh dear, now look, you've pulled its leg off. Don't you think—'

'PUT THAT DOWN THE PAIR OF YOU!' I bellowed.

They dropped it like a hot coal and Edward recoiled in fright.

'Now, eat up your bacon –' Edward instantly picked up his knife and fork in terror – 'and then for heaven's sake go out to play or something. Isn't that what children are supposed to do?'

'We don't want to. There's no one to play with now,' whined Clemmie. 'Can we go to the beach?'

'Don't be ridiculous, how on earth am I supposed to get you there? No, you can play in the garden.'

Edward wiped his mouth with his napkin and cleared his throat. 'Er, might I be of some assistance?' he ventured timidly.

Three pairs of eyes regarded him doubtfully.

'In what sense, Edward?' I enquired as politely as possible.

'I wondered if they might like to go bird-watching. Apparently, there are some capercaillie over at Beacon's Top. I thought it might be worth trying to spot them.'

There was an awed silence. I held my breath. He might just as well have suggested four hours' devout prayer in Invertarn Church.

Hugo's eyes were wide. 'Bird-watching! I've never done that – what d'you do?'

'Watch birds,' I muttered darkly, 'and keep very still,' I added with a smirk. I could see my lot lasting precisely five minutes, but if Edward was game, by God so was I.

I dropped the smirk and beamed widely. 'What a marvellous idea. That would be lovely, wouldn't it, children? Come along, eat up all of you and off you go!'

And so it was that Edward, in a small, but intensely practical way, finally came into his own. To my amazement, he didn't just set off blindly up a mountainside with two bored children at his heels as I would have done, he did it properly. First he took them into Invertarn to buy little rucksacks, a bird book, pencils and paper to draw what they saw, and even special whistles to call the birds. Then he packed sandwiches in each dinky rucksack, found some old binoculars in a drawer, saw that the children had appropriate footwear and off they went. And not just once, but every day for four days. Yes, every morning after breakfast this ornithological trio would solemnly pack up their knapsacks, hold hands in a row, and more or less singing *The Happy Wanderer*, toddle off in search of lesser-spotted whatjamacalits, and every afternoon at about teatime they would return; happy, stimulated, and most important of all, exhausted, so that all I had to do was feed them, bath them, and pop them into bed. God, I could have kissed Edward, in fact I could have – no. Perhaps not.

'It's amazing,' I enthused to Laura as I came down from tucking the sleeping beauties into bed one night. 'I mean they really enjoy it, and what's more they enjoy *being* with him.'

'So he's a success with the under-fives,' she muttered from the depths of her newspaper. 'Terrific.'

'Oh, don't be such a bitch, Laura. He's really trying and the children are having a wonderful time, thanks to him.'

'Yes, well, he's a teacher, don't forget. It's the one thing he's supposed to be good at.' She folded her newspaper, threw it on the floor and stalked out of the room.

'Where are you going?' I called after her.

'Out!'

The front door slammed behind her and not for the first time I felt exasperated with my sister. I was well aware that a little irritation with a man could quickly flare into full-blown revulsion but it seemed to me she couldn't bear to be in Edward's company even for a moment. Not only did she make herself scarce during the day, 'when it isn't even as if he's *here*,' I reasoned, but she didn't come back until late in the evening either, by which time Edward had usually gone to bed.

'Where on earth do you go?' I demanded, as she finally put her head round the drawing-room door at half-past ten that night.

'Has he gone?' she whispered.

'Yes, he's gone. Where do you go?' I repeated. 'This is the third night in a row!'

'Oh,' she said airily, flopping down into the sofa, 'just around and about.'

I frowned down at her from the window seat where I'd been reading. Her cheeks were flushed and her eyes strangely bright, and if she'd been one of the children I probably would have taken her temperature.

'Yes, but where?'

She stared into space then turned dreamily. 'Hmmm? Oh, just down to the beach. I sit on the rocks or walk along the cliff tops. It's glorious in the evening, so quiet and peaceful, gives me a chance to think. And after all, we're not here for much longer, got to make the most of it.' She stretched her arms up above her head and yawned expansively. 'God, I'm tired though. Must be all that fresh air. I'm off to bed!' She jumped up with a sudden burst of alacrity.

I put down my book. 'Laura, I couldn't just talk to you for a sec, could I? It's just that I really need to—'

'Oh Tess, can't it wait till the morning? I'm absolutely bushed. Look, my eyes are closing as we speak.' She feigned sleep, staggering about a bit. 'I've really got to go up. G'night.'

''Night,' I muttered after her.

She went, and with a lump in my throat, I picked up my book and tried to read again, the same page I'd been trying to read for the last four days. I put it down. Why was I feeling like this? So depressed? I *never* felt depressed, damn it. Irritated, angry, stressed out, murderous even, but not depressed. Why then? I shook my head, banishing his face. His eyes. No. I would not think about him. I breathed deeply and got up, pacing around the dimly lit room. I paused at the window and looked out. In the night sky I saw him, serious, anguished, intense, down at the river.

'No, I will not *think* about him!' I repeated savagely, throwing my head back and scratching it energetically.

The stars winked back knowingly at me from the dark outside. I sighed. God, these last four days had been difficult to say the least. Thank heavens we were going home tomorrow. I leaned my hands on the windowsill

301

and peered out, pressing my nose to the glass. Actually, it wasn't the days that had been so bad; I'd kept very busy, hobbled around doing quite a bit of gardening one way and another. Dad was too stingy to employ a gardener so I'd taken on the role and had managed to get rid of much of my frustration by uprooting weeds and digging over what must once have been flower beds.

No, it wasn't the days, I thought, limping slowly round the room; it was the nights. These endless quiet evenings when he would keep popping into my mind. And having no one to talk to about it didn't help . . . I felt a tear roll down my cheek. I brushed it away furiously. Why did I keep doing that? Bursting into tears for no reason . . . why?

Of course, I reasoned, stooping down to turn off a lamp, there was bound to be a certain amount of shock. Patrick's admission had been a complete bolt from the blue; it had taken me flying back with a whoosh. It was like being in a time warp, suddenly, there I was, all those years ago. I was eighteen again. Yes, the whole thing had been very unsettling, but – I bit my lip and straightened up – somehow, in my heart, I knew I was reacting too violently.

Perhaps you're just missing David, I told myself sternly as I bent down to pick a newspaper up off the floor. That's what it is; you're up here on your own with the children, you've got a seriously sprained ankle, there was all that business with Willie, all that guilt, your uncle's just died and your husband's not around – God, it's no wonder you're bursting into tears every five minutes. But somehow, this didn't quite ring true either. I turned off the final light switch at the door, paused for a moment, gazing back into the dark room, then went slowly upstairs to bed.

It was, therefore, with a huge sense of relief that we finally swept floors, stripped beds, packed cases, loaded up the cars and set off back to London the next day. Edward had decided to do the whole journey in one go so he left at the crack of dawn, thereby missing out on any embarrassing goodbyes, much to Laura's relief. We'd decided to break the journey and stay overnight somewhere around Yorkshire, we thought vaguely. I was actually quite looking forward to driving back with Laura. It wasn't often we had the chance to be on our own and I was keen to pour my heart out to her, get it all off my chest.

I turned Vivaldi down slightly as we swept along the lanes towards Belgadoon.

'Strange, seeing Patrick again, wasn't it?' I mused.

'Hmmm,' she agreed, keeping her eyes firmly on the road.

'Did I tell you what happened down at the river?'

'Briefly.'

I sighed. 'Funny. I still can't seem to get him out of my head.'

She frowned at me, then jerked her head in the direction of the back seat, at the children. I glanced around.

'Oh, it's OK, they're plugged into their stereos.'

'Yes, but even so.' She turned Vivaldi up again.

I glanced sideways at her. She was staring straight ahead, humming away to the music. Oh well, I thought, leaning back with a quiet sigh, maybe later. And at least she was getting me out of this place, putting the miles between us. I turned and gazed out of the window at the mountains, the lochs, the valleys, letting *The Four Seasons* drift over me.

On and on we drove; the children behaved, the traffic was light, Laura really put her foot down and we ate up the miles, the result being that we drove far too far and in true Fergusson fashion left it much too late to find a bed and breakfast, let alone a hotel. Nine-thirty saw us

303

still frantically scouring the Yorkshire Dales when everything was either fully booked or shutting up for the night. Or so they said. I have to say, Laura's selection technique might well have put a few backs up. She would insist on cruising up to each prospective establishment in the BMW, purring down the electric window, and in a loud, expensive southern voice saying something like – 'Looks a bit shabby, the paint's coming off the walls. Still,' she'd sniff, 'there's not much else in this crummy old place, give it a go and don't forget to ask if the sheets are cotton or nylon.'

With a flushed face I'd dutifully hop out of the car – I'd dispensed with the crutches now but still did a certain amount of hopping – and convinced that every single curtain in the village was twitching with indignation, scurried dutifully up the garden path, while she sat in the car, drumming her fingers on the steering wheel, engine still running.

All the landladies looked exactly the same to me; floral housecoats, carpet slippers, corrugated iron curls, permanently folded arms and lips that had disappeared with years of pursing. Certainly the reaction I got on each doorstep was identical. They all stared at me as if I were barking mad.

'A room?' they'd repeat incredulously.

'No, two rooms actually.'

'Two rooms! What, for the night?'

'That would be helpful,' I murmured to this particular old bag who all but filled the doorway of her supposed guesthouse.

As if on cue the arms folded and the lips disappeared. She shook her corrugated curls firmly.

'Oh no, not two rooms, not for the night, any road.' For what then, I wondered? 'Try Tom Shilling's up the road, number thirty-two. It's not that clean mind, but beggars can't be choosers!'

And with that encouraging remark, she slammed the door in my face.

'Charmless old bitch,' I muttered as I hobbled down the path.

Laura stuck her head out. 'Well?' she demanded. 'What was she like?'

I nodded thoughtfully. 'Sweet. Very sweet. But unfortunately she's booked up. She said there was somewhere nice up the road though.'

I climbed back in, deliberately failing to inform her of the questionable hygiene standards at number 32, because at this stage, frankly, I was desperate. The children were over-tired, irritable and rapidly reaching fever pitch and I knew from experience that unless we found a room soon – any room, a cave would do – blood must surely spill.

Laura drove cautiously up to number 32 and pulled up outside. One of the bedroom windows was broken, there were at least four cats in the garden – OK yard – and an old lavatory was nestling lovingly up against the front door.

'Jesus,' she muttered, shifting into first gear again. 'Forget it.' But by this time I was already out of the car and halfway up the path.

'You must be joking,' she cried after me. 'I'm not staying there!'

'Let's just see, shall we?' I shouted back.

'Well, don't forget to ask about the sheets!'

I gave a confident backward wave as I galloped on, privately thinking – sheets? Blimey, dream on.

I rang the bell, literally a second before I spotted that the wire was hanging out of the wall, so I rapped instead on the distressed green door – and I don't mean that in a trendy paint effect sense. Hmmm, well this really was tourism at its most discerning, wasn't it? Off the beaten track and all that. Could be interesting.

Moments later the door swung back and I can't remember what struck me first, the fact that Tom Shilling was wearing a dress or the smell of dead cat that zoomed up my nostrils.

'Um – good evening!' I gasped, instinctively holding my breath. 'D'you have a couple of rooms for the night?' I tried hard not to stare at the thick hairy ankles that protruded from his pinny.

His moustache bristled. 'Plenty of rooms,' he barked, 'but I'd have to make up the beds, wouldn't I?'

'Do you have a problem with that?' I gasped obsequiously. Any sentence, however short, was a trial.

'No problem,' he growled menacingly, 'but I'd 'ave to ask me 'usband first!'

With this mind-boggling sentence still ringing in my ears I followed my host across the threshold and it was at this point – probably something to do with the sexless swing of the generous behind – that I realised my host was in fact my hostess, who just happened to have rather a lot of facial hair, a boozer's nose, rheumy eyes, thick ankles, bushy eyebrows and a baritone voice. I breathed a sigh of relief. I wasn't at all sure what Laura's views on cross-dressing landlords would be.

He – she, tapped on a closed door halfway down the corridor.

'Tom?' she growled. 'There's some folk here want to stay.'

There was a long, no doubt incredulous, pause.

'Stay?' came the gruff response eventually.

'Tha's right.'

Another pause.

'Wha' for?'

She shrugged. 'The night, most like.'

Another, much longer pause.

'Give 'em the rooms right at the top,' came the rather chilling response. I shivered.

She nodded curtly and turned to me. 'You can have the rooms right at the top. Want to see?'

'Please!' I said eagerly. I might be mad but I wasn't that mad and I didn't want to spend the rest of the summer de-fleaing my children or visiting them in hospital while they recovered from the first outbreak of typhoid England had seen for fifty years.

As I followed Mrs Shilling up the dark staircase she jerked her head backwards. ''E won't come out,' she hissed conspiratorially, 'on account of his halitosis!'

'Ah!' I responded sympathetically, although what difference it would make to this atmosphere I couldn't imagine.

It soon became clear that 'not that clean' had been the understatement of the century. Cat-litter trays decorated every landing together with tottering pagodas of old newspapers, saucers of rancid milk, bundles of blind kittens, piles of mangy old cat, in fact, every corner was a shrine to feline fecundity – what you could see of the corners, anyway. It was so impossibly dark I had to feel my way upstairs after her, a deliberate ploy, I suspected, to keep one from spotting the dirt.

Up and up we went, with me hugging the walls blindly as we passed landing after landing, until eventually we reached the top floor, where suddenly, something little short of a miracle began to happen. Perhaps it was something to do with the altitude or just call it wishful thinking but it seemed to me the air was thinning appreciably. The smell didn't seem nearly so pervasive, nor the cats so prolific – in fact they were positively extinct up here – and as I followed her down a corridor I distinctly saw a small shaft of light filtering bravely through a skylight.

I wanted to turn to her and shout joyfully – 'Oh, Mrs Shilling, I can breathe!' or, 'Oh, look – paintwork, and isn't that – yes it is, how charming – a window!'

I restrained myself however and limited myself to rather daringly lowering my hand from nose-clutching level to throat-clutching level, so that by the time she'd led me into two small adjoining rooms my hand was almost at my side and I was positively euphoric.

Although not spectacularly clean the rooms did appear to have at least seen a duster and a Hoover at some time in their lives, and what's more there was a window so that at least one could get a breath of fresh – oops! Perhaps not. As eagerly as I'd opened it I slammed it shut again as more cat pong zoomed up from the garden.

'Best to keep it shut, with kiddies,' remarked my landlady darkly.

'Oh! Yes, of course,' I agreed.

I nervously felt my way around the room. The beds had indeed not been made up yet and one swift glance at the pink nylon eiderdowns told me all I needed to know about the sheets. Laura's rigorous terms could not be complied with, but by this time I'd spotted a shade on the light bulb, something approaching a curtain at a window, a washbasin – albeit cracked – and it was too late.

'I'll take it,' I beamed confidently.

'Both of them?' She eyed me suspiciously.

'Both of them.'

'That'll be seventeen pounds fifty upfront then.' She promptly held out her hand.

I rummaged dutifully in my handbag.

'Like cats, do you?' she asked suspiciously.

'Oh yes, very much,' I gushed, 'in fact I've got one – or two,' I added quickly, lest one should sound amateurish. 'I miss them terribly when I'm away, they sleep on my bed you see.'

Her huge eyebrows shot up. 'Tha's not a problem, my two tabbies will sleep with you.' She jerked her head back downstairs. 'Tom too, most like.'

I stared at her aghast. 'T-Tom?' What, the halitosis-ridden husband?

'There's no extra charge,' she said sharply. 'I'll go and get him. Smells a bit, but he's a good ratter.'

'Oh!' I breathed as it dawned. 'You have a cat called Tom!'

'Large black one on the landing.' She folded her arms. 'Why, who did you think I meant?'

'Oh, I – wasn't sure!'

She eyed me sharply. 'Not after me husband are you?' she demanded.

'No! No of course not.'

She glared at me for a moment, then threw back her head and cackled loudly. 'Well you're welcome to that old bugger! I haven't been near him for fifteen years on account of his gums, but if he's your cup of tea, you have him. He'll be tickled pink when I tell him.'

'Please don't!' I squeaked, putting a restraining hand on her arm. 'Really Mrs Shilling, it was just a silly misunderstanding.'

She cackled some more then patted my hand. 'Aye well, perhaps it's best I don't, any road. Old Tom 'asn't had a whiff of a woman for so long, who knows what it might do to his ticker, not to mention his vitals.'

'Yes, well let's not upset his . . . vitals, shall we?' I muttered, feeling rather faint at the thought.

She tapped her nose conspiratorially. 'Your secret's safe with me, chuck,' she said, and with that she pocketed my seventeen quid and went chuckling downstairs.

I breathed a sigh of relief then followed her down. I hastened out to report to Laura and the children in the car. Now, how to phrase this . . .

'Not bad,' I said solemnly, head on one side. I nodded thoughtfully. 'Not bad at all. Heaps of character, very olde worlde.'

'Oh Tess, you can't be serious!' Laura protested. 'I can tell just by *looking* at it it's the pits!'

'Now that's unfair,' I scolded. 'Appearances can be very deceptive and once you get upstairs it's really rather pleasant. Come on, I'll lead the way.' I hopped back up the path.

'You mean you've taken it?' Incredulous, she followed at a safe distance with two very doubtful children hanging on to each hand. 'Have you seen the rooms? What about the beds?'

'She hasn't made them up yet – a good sign, don't you think?' I smiled brightly. 'Must mean they're clean.'

'Was there ever any doubt?' She cried as we crossed the threshold, 'Jesus, what's that SMELL!'

'There's no smell,' said a voice out of the darkness making us jump out of our skins. 'We keep a very clean establishment here, very clean indeed and if you don't like it you can go elsewhere.'

'Ah, Mrs Shilling!' I exclaimed as her moustache caught the light. 'This is my sister and my two children. May we go to our rooms, please?'

'You can do as you damn well please,' she retorted, disappearing into the depths of the cat-ridden bowels. A door slammed. I groaned. And just as we'd got to the cosy, husband-sharing stage.

'So refreshing,' I whispered as we groped our way upstairs, 'that sort of northern directness, don't you think?'

'Bloody rude, you mean,' snorted Laura. 'Tess, you must be out of your mind. And what the frigging hell was that, a transvestite or something?'

'Don't be silly,' I chortled merrily, 'she's just a bit *au naturel*, probably forgot to put her make-up on this morning. It happens, you know. Now, here we are,' we finally felt our way upstairs, 'right at the top. Isn't this nice? Hugo and Clemmie, you two are in here – look, a connecting door – isn't this exciting? See, here are your beds . . .' I groped around blindly in the dark and finally found a couple of flat things in each corner, 'one . . . two . . . and Laura and I will be just through here. OK, darlings?'

Through the gloom, two pairs of huge blue eyes blinked at me in disbelief.

'Are we really going to stay here, Mummy?' whispered Clemmie.

'Of course, my love.' I clapped my hands joyfully. 'It'll be an adventure! Now, come on, buck up, into your pye-jams' – I *never* call them that – 'clean your teeth till they're clean and sparkling and then hop into beddy-byes. *Won't* Daddy be sorry he missed this.'

Dumb with disbelief they slowly obliged and when I'd finally got them into bed having, on Clemmie's orders, looked in every single drawer, cupboard and under the beds for bears, ghosts, ghoulies and from my point of view, dead cats, I shut the connecting door, and with a huge sigh of relief leaned heavily against it.

Gazing up at me with equally shocked, disbelieving eyes was Laura, perched very gingerly on the edge of a chair, sucking hard on a cigarette. She'd put a hanky on the chair before sitting down so that her navy-blue Nicole Farhi trousers did not actually have to come into contact with it, and it was this last, small detail that finally did for me. Hysteria began to well up in my throat.

'Oh God!' I gasped, going weak at the knees. 'Isn't it awful, Laura? Isn't it just *awful*!' I clutched my mouth with one hand and held on to the door-handle for support with the other.

'It's disgusting,' she said firmly, but I distinctly saw her mouth twitch. 'Quite disgusting.'

'Quite!' Hysteria was rising fast now. 'Quite the most revolting place I've ever seen!'

Laura was not my sister for nothing and in seconds

311

we were clutching each other, crying with silent laughter, tears streaming down our cheeks, trying desperately not to wake the children.

'And what about that thing with the moustache!' she gasped. 'The one you said had probably forgotten her make-up!'

'More like her hormones!'

'Rather pleasant upstairs! Really rather pleasant, that's what you said, you lying cow!'

'Oh God, I feel sick,' I said weakly, clutching my throat and staggering to a chair. 'I don't know if it's the smell or because I've laughed too much!'

We finally fell into our pink nylon double bed at about ten-thirty, still giggling like schoolgirls.

'Where d'you think they sleep?' Laura whispered.

'With the cats, I expect. They're probably all tucked up in bundles of newspaper as we speak.'

She giggled. 'What d'you think Tom's like?'

'Ten to one he's ginger, but take it from me, he hasn't been neutered. His "vitals" are still intact, if a little rusty. Pussy Galore told me.'

'Oh yuk!'

'Still,' I mused quietly, 'awful though it is, I'd still rather be here than at Kilmarnoch. It went on for too long this year.'

'Oh no,' she said quietly. 'I could have stayed up there for ever.'

I turned my head towards her on my pillow. 'Don't be silly – you, in Scotland? You'd miss Sloane Street in seconds.'

'Oh, I don't know. I'm not so sure I haven't grown out of Sloane Street.'

'Well, you certainly haven't grown into a country bumpkin yet, so don't give me that.'

'I don't think you have to be a country bumpkin to live up there. Look at Madelaine.'

'Yes but she doesn't live there all the time.'

'Then perhaps that's the answer,' she murmured quietly. But I wasn't really listening.

'She seems to have mended her fences with Patrick, doesn't she,' I mused.

'Mmmmm . . .'

'Seemed pleased to have him back.'

She didn't answer.

I sighed. 'God, it was strange seeing him again after all this—'

'Oh, for heaven's sake Tess, stop banging on about it!' She sat bolt upright in bed.

I stared at her in the darkness. 'I'm not banging on, I'm just saying—'

'Yes, but you *keep* just saying. It's not fair to anyone, Tess – not fair to him, to David, to the children – anyone! You've made your decision so now for God's sake stick to it and let everyone else get on with their lives, OK?'

I sat up too. 'Hey, what's got into you? I mean, of course I'll stick to it, but it was after all a fairly momentous decision. I can surely discuss it, can't I?'

She turned on me, eyes blazing. 'Momentous, was it? Really? You mean there *really* was a chance you'd leave David for him? Sell the house, take the children away from their schools, make David an occasional father?'

'Oh Laura, of course I couldn't do that, but—'

'Well then, SHUT UP!' she exploded. 'Stop titillating yourself with the idea of him still being in love with you. Forget it. For ever!'

There was a silence. She lay down again in the bed and turned on her side, away from me.

I stared at her back.

'Why are you being like this?' I said after a while.

'Like what?'

'So . . . aggressive?'

She sighed. There was another long pause. 'Because

I'm sick of you just thinking about yourself. There are other people's lives at stake here, Tess, people who depend on your decision. You've got to stop playing with them. You've hankered after this man for twelve years now and—'

'That's not true Laura, I—'

'Yes you have! And now you've finally been offered the chance to have him. Well fine. Have him. Or *don't* have him, but for pity's sake make a decision one way or another and *stick* to it. Don't spend the rest of your life dithering and hankering and wondering what might or might not have been! Let him be, let him live again, let *everyone* live again and—'

'*AAAAAAHH!*'

A piercing scream cut her off in mid-diatribe. The connecting door flew open and there stood Clemmie, white-faced in her nightie.

I leaped out of bed and ran to her. 'Clemmie! What's the matter, darling?'

'There's a man.' She pointed, quivering. 'Outside the window! It's Burglar Bill, I'm sure it is!' She clung to me, sobbing.

'Don't be ridiculous, of course it isn't. Let me see.'

I dashed through the connecting door across to her window with Laura close on my heels.

'I wouldn't be at all surprised in this house,' she said in an undertone as we rubbed the filthy windowpane with Clemmie hugging my knees.

I peered out. There was definitely something going on out there. I couldn't see anything, but there was a sort of banging, scraping noise coming from directly beneath us in the garden. I strained my eyes and made out a shadowy figure, with a spade . . .

'Oh, it's all right darling,' I said with relief. 'It's just Mrs Shilling digging the garden.'

'At this time of night?' Laura said, peering out.

'Well she's probably getting the potatoes in or something. Perhaps she couldn't sleep and thought she'd get on with it, you know how it is. Come on, Clemmie, back to bed.'

She clung to me. 'I want to sleep with you, Mummy,' she whimpered.

I sighed and turned to Laura. 'Do you mind?'

She shrugged. 'Why not, the more the merrier.'

The three of us trooped back to the double bed and Clemmie snuggled in between us. I'd left the connecting door open and we could still hear Mrs Shilling scraping away outside.

'Surely you don't dig potatoes at this time of year, do you?' whispered Laura.

'Oh, I don't know.' I was still thinking about what she'd said earlier. About me. Hankering, wondering, dithering. I sighed. 'Perhaps she's burying cats.'

There was a pause. Then Laura sat up. 'Or worse!'

I stared at her back for a second then joined her in the bolt upright position.

'You mean . . .'

'Why not? It's always the back garden, isn't it? And they look mad enough.' She put a hand on my arm. 'Perhaps she's getting the holes ready! *Four* holes!'

I shook her off. 'Oh, don't be ridiculous, Laura. Honestly, you're worse than the children!'

I lay down again. A second later I shot back up again.

'HUGO!' I roared at the top of my voice.

'What?' came a sleepy response.

'Get in here this instant,' I bellowed.

'Why?'

'Because we're all sleeping together tonight. Now don't argue, just get in here!'

Chapter Twenty-one

Needless to say we were up and out of that place by seven o'clock the next morning, having politely declined to breakfast on dirt and dead cat, thank you very much. We said our goodbyes and instead, took our custom to a little café just down the road.

We piled into the small, already packed café, giggling about our close shave with the spade-wielding Shillings and got the last, Formica-topped table in the corner. The place was warm and steamy and the clientele a mixture of truckers and locals; all male and all resolutely working-class. They gave us a cursory glance as we walked in, but then got on with the serious business of hoovering up the traditional start to an English day – eggs-bacon-sausage-beans-tomato and half a gallon of steaming hot tea.

I smiled smugly as the children looked around in wonder. Oh yes, I prided myself on showing them all sides of life. We didn't just go to the Early Learning Centre and the Science Museum, oh no. There was an awful lot to be learned from this salt-of-the-earth stuff, and far be it from me to have cosseted children.

I did think rather longingly of my usual yoghurt and muesli as I sat down to an artery-furring plateful, but gamely played along and even mopped my fried egg up with my Mother's Pride. I had a nasty feeling it was going to play havoc with my bowels later though. We stuck out like sore thumbs naturally, but since everyone was minding their own business and getting on with the important things in life like eating as much as possible, burping loudly and reading the *Sun* from cover to cover before shuffling off to the Gents with it, no one took much notice of us. That is, until to my horror, my son abruptly took it upon himself to tweak up the atmosphere.

Short of the mandatory tomato ketchup for his sausage, Hugo held up his hand and summoned the waitress.

'Hey, servant!' he cried, in an imperious voice.

A horrible hush fell over the buzzing café. My mouth dried, as all around us knives and forks were lowered and teeth ground to a halt. All eyes were suddenly trained on the southern, middle-class table in the corner. Horrified, I swung around to Hugo.

'What the hell d'you think you're playing at?' I cried loudly, in what I hoped was a suitably outraged tone.

'Well, that's what we call them at school,' he retorted.

'What,' I glanced around nervously, 'servants?' I hissed, appalled.

He shrugged. 'Something like that.'

Something like that. I thought quickly. 'Oh, servers! You call them servers, darling!'

'That's what I said, isn't it?'

'He means servers!' I cried triumphantly, turning to what was now a decidedly hostile-looking crowd.

The waitress in question had been joined behind the counter by what appeared to be a huge steroid-tripping chef. His enormous muscles were rippling through his white overalls and he folded his arms grimly. God, he even seemed to have biceps in his eyes. I smiled brightly.

'It's what he calls the dinner ladies,' I trilled, 'at school,' I added quickly, in case he thought I meant at home, back at the Grade II Jacobean manor or something.

Steroid chef came no closer but his well-upholstered arms stayed folded and a sharp black knife twinkled in his hand. He kept up his penetrating stare. A low and dubious murmur began to circulate around the room. I kept on nodding and smiling in what I hoped was a conciliatory manner but no one looked mollified enough to resume their bacon and egg. Clearly the thought going through most people's minds was – what better excuse for a revolution?

'Shit,' muttered Laura, echoing my thoughts. 'They're probably sharpening the guillotine in the kitchen even now. Come on, let's get out of here.'

She rummaged in her expensive Mulburry purse for a wodge of money, then ostentatiously waved a twenty-pound note in the air with a flourish. She shoved it under a saucer. The murmur stopped and a disbelieving silence descended. The tension, if possible, mounted.

'For God's sake, Laura, I've already paid,' I hissed.

'I know,' she muttered. 'That's a tip,' she said loudly, beaming around magnanimously, like some wealthy benefactress.

'Are you mad? They'll think we're bragging, or trying to buy our way out of here or something.'

'Well, we are, aren't we?'

The low murmur resumed. It gained momentum around the room and to my mind it was far more ominous and sinister than the silence.

Laura and I slowly got up from the table. I grasped the children firmly by their shoulders and with a great deal of nodding, smiling and scraping back of chairs, reversed in the direction of the door, the street and hopefully, the free world.

'Delicious breakfast,' I chirped as we backed through the door. 'No offence meant!'

The door banged shut behind us. As we scuttled past the half-curtained window to the car, it seemed to me that most of the café surged across to the window to watch. My nervous fingers struggled with Clemmie's seat belt. I glanced back and between the faces at the window saw the waitress in question saunter over to our table and pick up the twenty-pound note. She looked at it for a moment, then stuffed it down the front of her dress. Then she looked around at the assembled diners and smirked. A shout of raucous laughter rang out and moments later the café was fairly heaving with hilarity. The joke, it appeared, was well and truly on us.

Scarlet with shame and rage I snapped the children quickly into their seats, marched round to the passenger seat and slammed the door shut. As Laura started the car I shook my head wearily. I was quite sure the good people of Yorkshire were full of the milk of human kindness, but it didn't seem to be flowing in our direction today and I wasn't at all sure I would be returning to this part of the world in a hurry.

We drove off, the children, for once, shocked into silence. Laura was clearly as pissed off as I was.

'Bloody peasants,' she muttered at length.

I sighed, thinking it was just as well she hadn't expressed that sentiment a few minutes earlier. I wondered if that was where Hugo was getting his arrogant ways.

I leaned my head back on its rest and shut my eyes. It was throbbing soundly now and I felt lousy. I'd been awake half the night listening on the one hand for sounds of knife-sharpening from the Shillings, and on the other hand going over and over in my mind what Laura had said. I snuck a sideways glance at her now as we drove along. What did she mean, let him live? Let everyone live? What difference did it make to her?

I brooded on it off and on for most of the journey, but lack of sleep had made my brain furry and it wasn't until we'd completed about 600 miles and were almost home, that a finger, rather like the one on the ceiling of the Sistine Chapel, suddenly appeared in my head and slowly slotted the piece of jigsaw into place. I turned and gazed at her as we drove over Putney Bridge. It was as if I were suddenly seeing her for the first time. My eyes widened with horror, my chest felt tight. She couldn't be . . . good heavens. In love with . . . Patrick? *Could she?*

I stared at her as she began to negotiate the network of roads that led up to the top of Putney Hill. Somewhere, deep down in my subconscious, I realised I'd known all along, suspected, but dismissed it out of hand, as something too painful to believe. But now it was as if I could no longer fail to see. I kept staring at her as she swung the wheel this way and that, thanking drivers for letting her through, smiling, her pink lips parting, white teeth gleaming, her bare arms slim and brown as they skilfully guided the wheel. So, had they . . . slept together? My tummy lurched. I gulped. In all probability, yes. And why not, I thought with a jolt. I hadn't wanted him, had I?

I turned away, unable to look at her any more. Of course, I thought feverishly, that's where she'd been going these past few days. Secretly, on her own, all day and then all evening. Ever since the day after Robert had died when she'd gone up to Gilduncan for a swim. That must have been when it all started, lying by the pool in her gold costume, Patrick stretched out beside her. I clenched my fists tightly on my lap. God, how stupid of me not to realise! Was this what she'd always wanted then? What she'd been looking for all this time, ever since she'd met him again at that wedding years ago, knowing she couldn't have him because in his heart he still belonged to me? But he didn't any more, did he? I'd rejected him categorically, and this time, he'd heard it from the horse's mouth. Not just from engagement notices and birth announcements in the newspaper, as he sat miles away in Italy wondering if I really wanted all that commitment or whether I'd been forced into it because I was pregnant; wondering if I was really happy, or if there was still a chance I might give it all up and come away with him. No, this time he knew for sure. It was well and truly over, and with that realisation ringing loudly in his ears, he'd gone home to Gilduncan. A sad, depressed, lonely man.

But not for long, eh? Oh no, not for long, because the very next day – guess what? Behold! A vision had appeared to him by the pool! A vision with the face of an angel, wearing a gold swimsuit, sipping a Martini and jangling a Rolex watch, and she said, 'Fear not, Patrick old boy, for I bring you tidings of great joy. A younger, prettier, cleverer, more toned-up version of the thing you crave has been delivered to you this day, and is sitting beside you even now on your very own terrace. Not the next best thing, but a far, far better thing – if you think about it.'

I swallowed hard and gripped my hands together tightly. My God, the scales must have fallen from his eyes with a plonk, straight into the pool as he beheld this fair – *virgin* – beside him. I snarled and dug my nails into the palm of my hand. He must have thought – of course! Stone the bleeding crows – Laura! Because deep down in his subconscious, he'd probably known all along that he'd been waiting to be let off the hook by me so that he was free to take my younger sister. After all, hadn't he been watching her secretly, all these years? Hadn't he told me himself of his speculations on her virginity? Hadn't he been quietly monitoring her progress? Well you don't do that unless you're pretty damn interested, do you?

So . . . I breathed hard and dug my nails deeper. Had he initiated it, the seduction? Or had she? I recalled her flushed cheeks as she'd come in at night, her bright eyes, her secret smile, her exhaustion. And of course, I thought, breathing fast now, if he *was* right, and she'd never done it before, it must have been rather marvellous, mustn't it? That first time, and then the second time, and then the third when she was just getting into her stride, going berserk, thrashing around – *Breathe, Tess, breathe!* I commanded. God, I was in danger of passing out here. I sucked in hard through my nose and out through my mouth; in through the nose, out through the mouth . . . Don't think about them, I told myself, don't think about them writhing and twisting in barns, in beds, in haystacks, by the river, *in* the river, covered in water, in weed, in frogspawn, in God knows what – but it was no good. By the time Laura pulled up outside our house, my teeth were gritted, steam was pouring from my nostrils, I was making strange, incoherent, animal noises and I was just about ready to kill her.

Laura turned off the engine and looked at me. 'You all right?'

'Fine,' I whimpered shrilly. 'Just fine!'

She frowned. 'You don't look it.'

The children, desperate to get out, were clambering over our heads as Laura opened her door.

'All right, all right,' she laughed as Hugo climbed into her lap and raced up the garden path. She turned to me and grinned. 'Looks like they're glad to be back.'

I nodded, unable to speak.

'I'm just going to drop you off if you don't mind, I'm dying to get home now and have a bath. I'll bring your car back later, OK?'

She smiled, but as I stared back at her, her eyes sort of slithered past me. Oh yes, now I knew. Laura never avoided my eye; she never looked past me like that. She was getting out of the car now, reaching into the back for various dolls and jigsaws the children had left behind. I watched as if she were in a film.

'God, it looks like a kindergarten back here,' she laughed.

'Laura, can I ask you something?' I muttered, not moving from my seat.

She poked her head in. 'What? Aren't you getting out?'

'Can I just—'

'David, hi!' She swung around and waved as he came smiling down the path to meet us.

'Hello, you two horrors!' He swept the children up joyfully in his arms and gave Laura a big smacking kiss on the cheek.

'Laura, please,' I said desperately.

David stuck his head into the car. 'Hello, darling. Aren't you getting out? Can't be that disappointed to see me, surely? How was the drive?'

I slowly got out of the car. My legs seemed to be full of lead, my mouth full of acid.

'Oh not bad,' Laura answered for me as they unpacked the boot together. 'With the exception of a couple of serial killers and a lynch mob in a café in Buckden, not bad at all!' She chuckled merrily. 'But please take your family away, David. Lovely though they are I've had enough of family life for a few weeks. I can't wait to get back to my flat for a spot of solitary confinement.'

And to ring *him*, I bet, I thought viciously as she snapped the boot shut with a grin.

I watched as she laughed and chatted to David on the pavement. I imagined her talking to Patrick like that. Flicking back her silky blonde hair with her tanned, jewelled fingers. An invisible hand took hold of my gut and twisted it hard. My upper lip curled unattractively. Oh no, I thought grimly, I'm afraid it's not that simple, Laura. You see, it doesn't matter that I don't want him any more, he's still my property – OK? You can't have him, *all right*! I tried the deep breathing again but it was no good, I was seething demonically now and although on one level I knew I was being selfish, irrational and a total dog in the manger, on another level I didn't give a stuff. I had to make it quite clear to her that he was mine. Just a word, a gesture, that would do the trick, she'd understand. Just like when we were young and she'd got a toy of mine. A quick swipe, a grab, that was all it took – hands off, tiddler, get one of your own.

She was hugging the children now, saying her goodbyes, promising to come and see us soon. Now she was hugging David, planting a kiss on each cheek, laughing, and now finally, it was my turn.

'Bye, Tess,' she cried, hugging me round the shoulders.

I stood there like a lump of granite. She kissed my cheek. The Judas kiss, I thought bitterly, the betrayal.

'Laura, don't do this,' I muttered in her ear. 'Please don't do this, I can't bear it.'

She drew back and dropped her hands from my shoulders. She stared. 'Do what?'

I flushed scarlet. David was standing close by, watching, listening.

'This . . . thing,' I whispered. 'You know.'

Our eyes locked in combat. She knew. Hers turned to stone.

'One of these days, Tess,' she said in a quiet, level voice, 'you'll realise that being my older sister does not give you the right to tell me how to live my life.'

She turned, got into the car and slammed the door. The window was open and I bent down. Her face was very pale.

'Laura—'

'I'll do as I damn well please!' she said icily. Then she

shunted into first gear and without looking back, sped off down the road.

David stared after her as the car shrieked around the corner at the end of the road.

'What the hell was that all about?'

'Nothing,' I said in a strangled voice. 'Nothing at all!'

I turned and barged past him, marching up the path to the front door. David scratched his head.

'Blimey, you sisters. You're either at each other's throats or you can't bear to be apart.'

He followed me to the door. 'So how was the journey?'

'Terrific,' I said, chucking my handbag down on the hall table. 'Just terrific, David, all five hundred and eighty-two miles of it.'

'Now look here, Tess,' he said irritably, 'there's no need to take your row with Laura out on me, is there?'

I rounded on him. 'Well, what do you *want* me to say? Actually it was a frigging long way, the children quarrelled non-stop, my foot was agony, my head ached and I would have been glad of your help? Is that what you want – the truth?'

He was dead right of course, I did need a vent for my anger. For my selfish, irrational, homicidal rage, and right this minute he would do very nicely thank you. Just stand right there, David, don't move an inch.

'Particularly,' I added venomously, 'since it appears you didn't have much work to do anyway.'

He stared at me. 'You really are a spoiled little girl, aren't you?' he said quietly. 'You really expected me just to drop everything and fly back to Scotland, with all the expense that that incurs, just to ferry you back again?'

'What I expect David,' I cried, 'is a little support. A little more loyalty, that's all. I expect that since I spend the best part of the year looking after the children we might, just once a year, have a holiday when we *share* the responsibility, when we can be a family. What I don't

326

expect is for you to bugger off back to London in order to do a spot of shopping, for God's sake! Had a nice quiet house all to yourself, did you? Saw a bit of the Test Match? Read a few good philosophy books? Snoozed in the garden with no children around to turn the hose on you or empty the sandpit on your head? Yes, well, actually *darling*, that's *my* idea of a holiday too, and I can't remember the last time I sodding well had one!'

I'd really lost it now. I was a loony woman, shaking, spitting, saying the very first thing that came into my head.

David regarded me coldly. 'You're a fine one to talk about loyalty, and as for the children, I thought you enjoyed looking after them. I didn't realise it was a chore. I thought that's why you didn't want to work.'

'Oh, don't be obtuse, David,' I yelled, 'we're not talking about me working here, we're talking about me having a flipping holiday! Yes, of course I like looking after them, I just don't want to do it to the exclusion of everything else, that's all. I wouldn't mind if there was just a little bit more to my life than these four walls and our two children. I wouldn't mind having a bit of life *outside* my bloody family, that's all. Is that too much to ask?'

He regarded me for a long moment. 'I don't know why you have to ask, Tess. *Alea jacta est.*'

He turned and walked towards the kitchen.

'And what's that supposed to mean?' I shrieked after him. 'Another one of your stupid smart-arse remarks that means *nothing*, David! Well, I'm sick of it, sick of your whole pompous attitude, OK!' I burst into tears and raced up the stairs.

'Nice to have you back, Tess,' he remarked before I slammed the bedroom door.

Sobbing with rage I looked around wildly for something to bash, to rip, or to maim. If I'd been a yob

I probably would have rushed out and beaten up a few phone boxes, but being a middle-class Putney housewife, I seized my hairbrush and beat the living daylights out of my Laura Ashley pillow. I can see that a phone box might have been more satisfying. Finally, I threw myself onto the bed and sobbed into the duvet.

Great shoulder-shaking, self-pitying sobs. As I lay there, crying like an idiot, I gradually got it out of my system. I felt it drain away. All that venom, all that rage, all that ghastly, pent-up, horrible self-pity went pouring down into the designer sheets. At length I sat up, grabbed a tissue and blew my nose loudly.

Suddenly I was mortified. It came over me like a wave. Oh God, how *awful*! What a bitch I'd been. Poor, poor David, what on earth had he done to deserve such a tirade? It wasn't as if it was anything to do with him, was it? It was Laura, Laura and Patrick. I flopped on my back and stared up at the ceiling. Was that how they were to be referred to then, in future? Laura and Patrick, a couple? To be said in one breath like that? I swallowed hard. Yes, what if this affair went from strength to strength, what if they really fell in love – married even . . . I gasped, jerked upright and stuffed a tissue in my mouth. What if they came here together for dinner, for Christmas, for the children's parties, what if – oh Christ – *they had children of their own*.

I bit hard on the tissue then spat it out. I got up and walked to the window. I felt ill. Really ill and sick. I breathed deeply to calm myself, pressing my hot face against the cool glass. I gazed out at the long row of identical terraced houses below, all pressed up against each other with their identical London families inside. Suddenly it wasn't so reassuring, it was depressing. I felt hemmed in. I stared at the cars crammed bumper-to-bumper in the street, at the gardens, every square inch utilised. Then I thought of Laura and Patrick in

328

Italy, in Scotland, with all that space, that love, that freedom. I turned my face and leaned my other cheek on the glass. And I'd always have them there before me, wouldn't I? As a shining example. Always be able to look at them, at their life and say – that could have been me.

Down below me the front door clicked. I looked out as David emerged from under the porch, a child swinging on each hand. They dragged him down the garden path and at the gate, turned right and trotted up the road. He was taking them to the park, no doubt. Off to the swings after their long sit in the car, then on to the corner shop for a lolly. I dredged a heavy sigh up from the soles of my feet. How like him to do that and what a cow I'd been to suggest he didn't. He did his share and more. I watched, wondering if he'd turn at the end of the road, look back at the house. I'd wave if he did, smile. I willed him to. He didn't.

I went back miserably to the bed and sat down again, tearing my tissue into shreds. More self-pitying tears were welling. God, this whole Patrick affair was conspiring to ruin everything. But I still couldn't bear it if it were true, I really couldn't. I bit my lip. Then I turned and stared at the telephone. Well, OK then, why not just ring Laura? Talk to her, reason with her, tell her it's simply too much for you to handle? Ask her to reassure you that it was just a holiday romance, nothing more than that? Yes, of course, I thought with a surge of relief, that was probably all it was. And here I was getting all het up about it! Ha! Silly me. Yes, and I could apologise too, I thought eagerly, for being so Draconian, so high-handed. We'd probably laugh, make up, everything would be fine again!

I quickly dialled her number. Engaged, damn. I drummed my fingers impatiently, then on a sudden impulse, rang Directory Enquiries and got Gilduncan's number. I rang that. Bloody engaged! I slammed the phone down in a fury.

'You bastards!' I shrieked into the empty house. 'You selfish, thoughtless, self-centred BASTARDS!'

Chapter Twenty-two

The following day was Robert's funeral. I limped, miserably, through the day, then at four o'clock went upstairs and dressed slowly, frowning critically in the mirror at my chosen outfit. Having never actually been to a funeral before, and not being a career girl with a limitless supply of little black suits to choose from, I'd had to improvise with an extremely limited wardrobe. If I'd been on speakers with Laura I could have borrowed something, but that was clearly out of the question. The only black skirts I possessed were a short cocktaily one, or a long maternity one. In the end I opted for the short one with a black shirt, black jacket and the tatty old shoes I'd been wearing all summer but which were supremely comfortable with my swollen foot. I was just looking doubtfully at my reflection when David came in.

'What d'you think?' I asked nervously, hoping he'd speak to me. 'Too tarty?'

He raised his eyebrows. 'Hoping to razz up the vicar?'

'Oh. Right,' I said sheepishly. 'OK, how about this then . . .' I swiftly changed into the maternity number.

'Now you could actually *be* the vicar,' he observed as he regarded my billowing black tent. 'The choice is vicar or tart, is it?'

'You could at least be constructive in your criticism,' I snapped, not one to stay sheepish for long.

'I'm not convinced you have to go for total blackout,

that's all,' he said, changing from his cords into a dark suit. 'How about your green suit or that flowery Liberty skirt with your navy blazer?'

'David, it's a funeral not a hula-hula party! Now hurry up and stop titivating, we're going to be late.'

I flounced down the stairs in my vicar's kit, knowing full well that he was being reasonable again and I was being *un*reasonable again. Damn it, I fumed, why was it always *me* who was in the wrong? Why was it always *me* who was left feeling like a heel?

As I marched down the stairs into the hall I almost tripped over Tricia, a friend's nanny, who in the absence of Josie had come in to look after the children for the day. She was crouched over Clemmie who was lying doubled up on her side, clutching her stomach, moaning and writhing around in agony.

'What is it?' I yelped, running fast. 'What happened? What's wrong!'

'I don't know.' Tricia looked up anxiously. 'I just found her like this.'

'Did she fall? Has she eaten something? Clemmie, what's wrong?'

I crouched over her, pushing her hair back so I could see her face. It was twisted with pain. She whimpered.

'Oh God!' I gasped. My heart hammered, my mind raced – appendicitis, meningitis – but what were the signs, the symptoms? Hugo came sauntering out of the kitchen.

'Hugo,' I yelled, 'get Penelope Leach for me quick – on the dresser!'

'Who's she?' he asked, strolling on.

'It's a book,' I screamed, 'for Clemmie! She's in agony, now *run*!'

Hugo regarded his sister on the floor. 'Oh, it's OK,' he remarked nonchalantly. 'She's in labour.'

'*What!*' I leaped up in horror.

'Yes, she saw it on *Home and Away*. Sandra's having a baby at the moment.'

I stared down at Clemmie, writhing in agony on the floor. Then I lunged down and hoicked her up under her arms.

'GET UP AT ONCE!' I bellowed, pulling her to her feet.

'Oh my baby, my baby!' she moaned, clutching her tummy. She wilted in my arms and rolled her eyes dramatically. 'Gas,' she gasped. 'Give me gas, quickly!'

'Stop that at once!' I shook her.

'Jesus,' muttered David, passing briefly through the hall to the kitchen. 'Why on earth are they allowed to watch these things?'

'It's not a question of being allowed,' I retorted, 'but short of becoming the television police I can't stop them.'

'Could have been worse,' offered Tricia reasonably. 'She could have been *making* a baby. I'm pretty sure they do that on *Home and Away* too.'

'Thank you, Tricia,' I said weakly as I delivered Clemmie into her arms. 'That really strengthens my case.' I turned to my husband.

'Ready?' I demanded.

'Ready,' he snapped.

I drove fast and furiously to Hanover Square where the funeral was taking place. Fast, because we were late as usual, and furiously because it was symptomatic of my mood. As a result, I succeeding in riling up quite a few of my fellow motorists, one of whom was so pissed off he deliberately followed me and carved me up in return at a roundabout.

'Right,' I snarled, in the grip of what I believe is now called road rage. 'We'll soon see about that, buster!'

I sped after the red car in question, eventually managing to carve him up and nearly causing an accident at the following roundabout.

'Tess,' began David, 'I really don't think—'

'Don't speak to me,' I hissed. 'Just don't speak, OK?'

He raised his eyebrows wearily. 'OK, OK.'

Moments later I was seething again. We were stuck, doing precisely two miles an hour down some Fulham back street, behind a lorry which was not only travelling at the speed of a snail but was slowly losing its load.

'Oh, for heaven's sake,' I muttered, beeping my horn loudly, 'he hasn't even noticed!'

The lorry didn't stop and cruised slowly on.

'Are you deaf as well as retarded?' I thumped my horn again. *Beep beep* BEEEEEEEEEEP!

Finally the lorry stopped. I leaped out and ran up to his cab. The driver stuck his head out.

'What's your problem, lady?' he shouted.

'You're losing your load, you moron!'

He stared at me. 'I'm gritting the road.'

I gasped. 'Oh!' I flushed, turned and ran back to the car, red-faced. 'He's gritting the road,' I muttered to David.

He raised his eyebrows. 'Clearly.'

'Why didn't you tell me?'

'You told me not to speak.'

I uttered some obscenities under my breath and drove on. After a while though I felt myself begin to simmer down slightly and knowing the usual row about parking was due to start shortly, resolved to wind my neck in and let David do the talking. Annoyingly he guided me expertly round the back streets of Regent Street and we parked, with comparative ease, on a meter just behind Hanover Square.

As David and I walked to the church and joined the solemn, family group assembled on the steps outside the main door, it occurred to me that at least our silence could be construed as a mark of respect rather than seething irritation with each other.

Daddy left the group and came to greet us, giving me a fleeting, economical peck on the cheek and David a quick handshake. He had his stony, far-be-it-from-me-to-show-any-emotion face on. I kissed him warmly then turned to Aunt Rachel.

'Rachel,' I whispered, taking her hand and kissing her. 'I'm so sorry . . .'

'Don't be,' she smiled, and pressed my hand with both of hers. 'It's what he wanted. It was time for him to go.'

I gazed up at her beautiful, composed face. Would I ever be like that, I wondered. Would I ever be anything like her?

I turned to Penny who was sobbing uncontrollably beside her, supported by Piers. Little Leonora was holding her hand tightly, looking baffled. I wondered at the suitability of bringing her but we all hugged each other, then I took Penny's other arm and we went into the church. As we all made our way down to the front pew I looked around for Laura. Late again as usual, I thought cattily, intent on making a dramatic entrance, no doubt. As we sat down, she hurried down the aisle. Sorry, no room, I thought childishly as I spread my handbag and service sheet along the pew, but David, who was on the end, smiled and beckoned her down. Laura slipped in beside him. She bent her head forward.

'Budge up!' she whispered.

I grudgingly moved an inch or two, then pretending I hadn't seen her lean across to kiss me, dropped to my knees and clasped my hands piously in prayer. Out of the corner of my eye I saw her look at David and raise her eyebrows. He sympathetically raised his in response.

Oh, so they think I'm behaving badly, do they? I thought savagely, well let them. Ask me if I care. They can go to hell, the lot of them! And with this truly Christian thought in mind, I bent my head in prayer.

The funeral was sad, but not tragic. Robert had been expected to die quite a lot sooner than he did and in fact there were some light and even humorous moments. Rachel's short address in particular was moving but also funny. As she recalled his rather unorthodox methods of teaching young children to fish by hanging sandwiches and even sausages on hooks, I laughed, remembering, and inadvertently caught Laura's eye. She smiled but I quickly turned away. Oh no, I thought, it's not going to be as easy as that.

I caught a glimpse of what she was wearing though, a sort of burgundy linen suit with a white body underneath. Well really. Did she honestly think that was appropriate? Had she *no* idea? I pursed my lips and looked around at my fellow mourners. It was then that I realised, with a jolt, that it was I who was inappropriately dressed. Everyone else seemed to be in smart, but not particularly sombre clothes, and certainly there was nothing quite like the ankle-length Widow Twanky kit I was in. God, I looked like something out of a Catherine Cookson period drama! I hastily hoicked my skirt up a bit and undid the top button of my shirt.

It was when my father got up to speak though, that everyone reached for their hankies. It wasn't so much what he said, which was predictably religious and prosaic, but the way he said it. As he struggled to be so formal and correct, every now and then his bottom lip would quiver or his face would buckle, giving him away. He'd pause as he struggled to regain his composure. No one dared breathe, wondering if he was going to break down. His voice shook with emotion every time he mentioned Robert's name. I gripped Mummy's hand tightly as together we mopped up the tears we were crying for Daddy, as much as for Robert.

By the time we all stumbled out of that dark church into the low, early evening sunshine, I for one was emotionally exhausted and in desperate need of a drink. All that sorrow had made me thirsty and I could quite see why the Irish were so keen on a wake. The plan was, apparently, to go on to Dukes Hotel for an early supper, but for the moment, everyone seemed content to mill around on the steps outside, chatting and commiserating with Rachel and no one looked inclined to move on. I hovered near the back, watching. What was the protocol here, I wondered. Was it rather like a wedding where one didn't want to get to the reception before the bride? Should we wait for Rachel? If I'd been on speaking terms with David I could have suggested a quick dart to the pub before going on to the hotel, and likewise with Laura, but obviously both options were out of the question.

I looked around for them. David was talking to an elderly aunt of mine, and Laura, to an old schoolfriend of Penny's. She looked distracted though, and once or twice I spotted her glancing at her watch. Another of Penny's friends interrupted their conversation and at that point, I saw Laura smile, murmur something apologetic, then with a brief glance around, turn and quickly slip away.

I watched, fascinated, as she sped down the steps at the side of the church. Where was she going, I wondered. Not for a solitary drink, surely? No, that was unlikely, but perhaps she'd decided to leave her car and walk to Dukes for some fresh air. Yes, this was far more like it and actually, just what I needed too. Suddenly I realised this was my one chance to talk to her. To catch her on her own, reason with her. It would be more or less impossible to talk later, surrounded by an army of relatives over supper. Yes, I'd do it now. I glanced across at David who was still deep in conversation. I waved, caught his eye and mouthed – *I'm going on, OK?* He frowned, but didn't mouth anything back, so I turned and slipped away with no further ado.

I hobbled determinedly after Laura, tracing her footsteps across the square. Yes, this was definitely the right thing to do. I'd nip this thing in the bud before it had a chance to blossom. The worst thing I could do would be to sit back and let the affair gain momentum, until it was too late to do anything about it. I quickened my pace as much as possible with my ankle, but as I did so, realised that I was losing my skirt. It was after all, a maternity skirt and the elastic had at one time catered for two and a half – all right, four stone of extra weight – and all this exertion was making it swivel down my hips, putting the hem somewhere around foot-level. As I hurried along I reached down to hoick it up but – too late – tripped over the hem and landed face down on the pavement with a resounding smack! Damn.

I picked myself up, shaken, distinctly embarrassed – this was after all practically Bond Street – but not badly hurt, so I hurried on. At least I did, until I felt something hot and runny trickle into my mouth. I put my hand up and looked at my fingers. Blood. Bother, a flipping nosebleed. I stopped in my tracks and quickly rummaged in my bag, still peering around for Laura who'd just disappeared round a corner. I found a tissue, ripped a piece off, rolled it into a ball and stuffed it up my nostril. There, that would have to do for the moment. I hurried on, looking around wildly – where the hell was she? I stopped still and gazed about. I was sure I'd seen her Manolo Blahnik heels trip this way, but now there was no sign of her. Blast. That little nasal interlude had cost me my prey. Where the devil had she got to?

I stood at the crossroads outside Fenwick's, looking around blindly. Had she gone up there, past Russell & Bromley, or over there towards Berkeley Square? I hesitated, then on a sudden impulse, plumped for a side street. There was a pub up this alleyway that we'd both been into once together. Perhaps she'd remembered it and slipped in for a quick one? I pushed open the frosted door. The gloom and the smoke hit me instantly. The bar was six deep with braying suits as surveyors, accountants and other West End businessmen thirstily sank their after-work pints. It looked like the relief of Mafeking. I let the door swing back. No, she wouldn't have gone in there, not on her own. Perhaps up here? I hastened up another side street, then another, then turned right, back onto Bond Street, at which point I realised, with a sinking heart, that I'd lost her.

I stopped running and clutched my side, panting hard. Damn and blast, where on earth was she? Oh well, I thought wearily, the only thing to do was to walk on to Dukes myself. You never know, I might be able to drag her into the ladies and threaten to beat the living daylights out of her if she so much as laid a finger on him again. I shrugged. Something like that anyway. I limped on.

My foot was excruciatingly painful now after all that activity and I was really having to limp. Added to this, my skirt, if left unattended, wanted to hover down by my thighs hipster-style, so I had to clutch the waistband in a ball with one hand and hold the tissue to my nose with the other. I stopped for a second to renew the tissue and a beautifully coiffured girl dressed from head to toe in Chanel stared as she walked past. What's the matter, I thought savagely, haven't you ever seen a nosebleed before? On the other hand, I thought with a jolt as I caught sight of myself in a shop window, I did look rather a strange sight. A tall, dark woman in outsized widow's weeds with half a ton of soggy red tissue up her nose dragging a gammy leg. I grinned. Not exactly *à la mode*, shall we say?

I moved slowly through the rush-hour crowd, looking around at the mixture of glamorous businesswomen in Armani suits, secretaries clip-clopping to the Tube in too-high heels, pinstriped businessmen, striding out, brandishing the *Evening Standard*, younger men in pale grey suits with white nylon shirts. It was rather nice not to be rushing with them, just to be passing through. A spectator rather than a participant.

As I hopped slowly along I gazed in the shop windows. I lingered for a second outside one particularly daft establishment with a silver body suit in the window complete with conical Madonna-like boobs. Hmmm . . . just right for getting to grips with the dusting. I could just see David's face when he came in of an evening to be greeted by that little ensemble frying up his liver and bacon. I grinned and moved on, feeling way out of touch. I passed another shop-front, brightly lit and thronging with people. I slowed down for a moment and blinked. Very glamorous people actually, and it was clearly a party of some sort, a new shop-opening perhaps. I moved slowly by, staring at the groovy, minimalist crowd. Most people seemed to be in either black or white – a touch uninspired to my way of thinking, but then who was I to be sartorially critical? There were one or two touches of colour, a man with an outrageous floral shirt, a girl in a fuchsia pink skirt that just about covered her bottom, and a blonde girl in a – *burgundy linen suit.*

I stopped and stared. What on earth was Laura doing in there? Did she know these people, or had she just barged in for a glass of champagne, uninvited? It wouldn't be difficult, she certainly looked the part but – no, she was chatting, laughing with someone as if she'd known him all her life. He had his hand in the small of her back. His own back was towards me, but I'd know it anywhere. He turned to lift a couple of glasses of champagne from a waitress's tray and I saw his face. It was Patrick.

I watched, rooted to the pavement as they laughed and chatted together. Patrick handed her a drink, they clinked glasses, toasting each other over the rims, gazing into each other's eyes. He leaned forward and whispered something in her ear, Laura threw her blonde head back, laughing, then she leaned forward and rested her hand on his shoulder, drawing him closer towards her so she could whisper something back. He laughed, nodded, agreeing with her, but as he bent his head to sip his champagne, his eyes strayed towards the window. They met mine. He froze over his drink. We stared at each other. Suddenly I was galvanised. With my heart pounding and the blood rushing up to my face I pushed through the plateglass door. I shoved my way roughly through the fashionable, tinkling throng and strode right over to them.

'So, Patrick,' I hissed, 'didn't waste much time getting over your broken heart, did you? Tell me, how do we compare in bed, as sisters I mean!'

Chapter Twenty-three

They stared at me in horror.

Patrick put his hand on my arm. 'Tess, slow down—'

'Don't you touch me!' I shook him off. 'How DARE you! How dare you even *look* at me after the lies you've told! Broken-hearted, eh? Waited for me for all these years, eh? Bullshit! You're an opportunist, Patrick, and you know it. You're a sad, despicable man, an aging, sex-crazed Lothario who's looking for some action, and when you couldn't get it with me you got it the very next day with my sister instead. That's about the size of it, isn't it!' My voice had risen; I was shaking with rage.

All around us conversation hushed and glasses stopped clinking. Elegantly coiffured heads turned and all eyes were on the madwoman in black. Laura took my elbow.

'Tess, you're making a fool of yourself,' she said in a low voice.

'Oh am I!' I spat, shaking her off. 'Then that's entirely appropriate, since I clearly *am* the fool here! Gosh, how you two must have laughed as you sneaked off to meet each other behind my back in Scotland! Oh yes, you must have thought it a huge joke. Well, it's not a joke, Laura, it's pitiful. Pathetic, deceitful and PITIFUL!' My voice, by now, had reached lunacy level and I was aware that I was very much the floorshow.

'Tess, for heaven's sake!' Laura coloured up and looked around nervously.

'For heaven's sake what!' I countered loudly, unstoppable now. 'For heaven's sake why shouldn't you sleep with him? Eh? Is that it?'

'Good God,' she muttered, mortified.

'No reason at all, Laura, none at all, expect perhaps for a tiny matter of sisterly loyalty. Ring any bells, hmmm? A little matter of sibling consideration or is that too difficult a concept for you to get your selfish head around? Well is it?' I cried.

'I've never been so embarrassed in all my life.' Laura's face was flaming now. 'Not only are you totally and utterly wrong, but—'

'Wrong, am I?' I raised my eyebrows in mock surprise. 'Oh yes of course, it's time for the big denial, isn't it – time to wriggle out. I wondered when we'd get to that. Well, come on then.' I stood back and folded my arms, waiting. 'Come on, Laura, show me how you do it. I'm keen to learn,' I nodded encouragingly. 'Come on, don't be shy!'

A few people behind us began to titter. Laura seized my arm in a vice-like grip.

'Out!' she muttered furiously. 'Come on, out. I've had enough of this. Help me, Patrick.' She began to drag me towards the door. I struggled but Patrick took my other arm. Between the two of them I began to slide doorwards, my skirt slipping down at the same time. The murmuring mass parted to make way for us.

I looked around wildly as I slid along the polished floor and out of the corner of my eye glimpsed a waiter, mouth open, balancing a tray of champagne. With a superhuman effort I wrenched a hand free, seized a glass, and threw it in Laura's face.

'Argh!' she squeaked, dropping my arm.

A gasp of shock rose up. She stood there, horrified and dripping, her face, hair and immaculate suit soaked.

'Tess!' Patrick thundered. 'What on earth—'

'And you can have one too, you bastard!' I grabbed another one from the bemused waiter and chucked it over him.

Another horrified gasp went up from the crowd. Patrick stared at me through his soaking-wet hair. It was plastered to his face and dripping rather satisfyingly all over his elegant Armani suit. Behind me I was dimly aware of camera bulbs flashing, then a little cry rang out.

'Patreek! Patreek, what ees going on! Who ees thees crazy woman?'

A little mustachioed Frenchman, all dusty pink suit and gleaming Gucci shoes came bustling over.

'*Allez-vous en!* Out!' he cried, poking me in the shoulder with a sharp, manicured finger. '*C'est trop, alors!* Get out, madwoman, get out!'

There was only one glass of champagne left on the tray and it seemed a shame not to use it.

'And I don't know who you are, you mincing little poofter, but you can have one too,' I panted, aiming it at the immaculate pink concoction.

His suit went a satisfying shade of dark red, his moustache drooped, his jaw dropped and his little wet brown eyes blinked at me in horror.

This time a rather delighted gasp went up from the crowd. I slammed the glass back down on the waiter's tray and with my head held high, limped, with as much dignity as I could muster, towards the door. The gaping throng parted nervously and everyone hung on like billyo to their glasses, just in case I should feel like lobbing some more around. Outside in the street I blundered into the traffic.

'That'll bloody teach them,' I muttered, dragging my leg across the road. All around me taxis honked furiously and fists waved. A car screeched to a halt inches from my feet.

'That'll wipe the smiles off their smug little faces, won't it?' I ranted on to one bemused taxi driver through his open window. 'They won't try that again in a hurry, will they?'

'I very much doubt it, luv,' he agreed, scratching his head.

Curious though, I thought limping on, because I'd never done anything like that in my life before, never made a huge scene in public, and it had proved not only satisfying, but quite easy. I must remember to do it more often. Behind me I became aware of running footsteps. I quickened my pace.

'Tess! Stop!' It was Patrick. He caught up with me, grabbed my arm and swung me around to face him.

'Get off me! Let me go!'

'Now just you LISTEN!' he thundered. 'For God's sake shut up AND LISTEN!'

'I don't want to listen,' I spat. 'I don't want to hear it!'

'You'll hear it whether you want to or not.' He dragged me forcibly to the side of the pavement where there were a few tables and chairs outside a café.

'Sit!' he ordered.

'No, I—'

'SIT!'

I sat. All around us cappuccino cups lowered, bacon sandwiches cooled and all chatter stopped, as once again, we became street theatre. The café clientele wasn't quite as elegant as it had been across the road, but it was just as interested and there's nothing élitist about my performances; I play to the cheap seats as well as to the boxes. The audience held their breath as the man in the wet Armani suit grasped the wrist of the lame woman in black. Holding on firmly to stop me escaping, Patrick sat down opposite me. He looked decidedly fierce. I mentally flexed my muscles. Not fierce enough to frighten *me* though.

'Laura and I are not having an affair, OK?'

His steely blue eyes bored into mine. Any coffee cups that hadn't already been lowered certainly were now. You could hear a napkin drop.

'There is nothing,' he said slowly, 'repeat, nothing, going on between us, have you got that? *Comprende?*' He thrust his finger to his temple and wiggled it around furiously.

'Oh yes, *comprende*, Patrick,' I sneered. 'That's why you were gazing so lovingly into each other's eyes just now, isn't it? That's why she kept sneaking off to meet you in Scotland, because you can't bear the sight of each other!'

'I was not gazing at her,' he said in a measured tone. 'I was merely looking at her, and she wasn't sneaking off to meet me in Scotland, she was sneaking off to meet someone else.'

'Oh sure,' I scoffed. 'Like who?'

'Like Willie.'

I stared at him. He rather tentatively relaxed his grip on my arm.

'Willie!' I gasped, staying still.

He nodded.

'Oh, don't be ridiculous!'

'What's ridiculous about it? Willie's a nice guy.'

'Yes, of course he is, but – but not for Laura,' I spluttered. 'He's not Laura's type at all!'

'And who is – Edward?'

'Well no, but—' I stared at him, flummoxed. My mind was spinning.

'So why not Willie? After all, countless other women have fallen for him. Look at Penny.'

'Yes, but that's sort of understandable,' I stammered, trying to digest this. 'You know what Penny's like, and he was just a bit of—'

'Rough?'

347

'Well—'

'A bit of rough on the side for married London women?'

I stared at him: he was serious. Good God, he was serious! It *had* been Willie . . . That's who Laura had been skulking off to meet, down at the river no doubt. Good heavens, I thought with a jolt, so we'd *all* got to grips with him – me, Penny and now Laura. What must he think of us? But *Laura*! I shook my head incredulously, trying to imagine the two of them together . . . and to my surprise, I found I could. Because when you think about it – why not? And who better, in a way? Particularly if it really was her first time and particularly if she really had been hung up about sex . . .

'Actually I reckon he was just the man for the job,' said Patrick with a grin. 'Just the man to break her in joyfully.'

'Oh Patrick, don't be so crude,' I snapped as he eerily echoed my thoughts.

'Who would you have preferred for her sexual debut, then? Some smooth bastard with a Porsche dragging her back from Draycotts to his pad behind Harrods, pinning her to his leather sleigh bed, peeling off his black Hom underpants?'

'No,' I said slowly, 'no, I wouldn't. It's just – so unexpected.'

I shook my head distractedly. Laura and Willie. So not Laura and Patrick. Suddenly I felt a rush of blood to my head. I almost gasped at its force and my hand inadvertently flew to my mouth. Oh – thank God! I stared at him across the table from me. He was still talking, laughing now, about Laura and Willie. I watched his lips move, studied his face as if in a dream.

'You see, rather amazingly, they conducted this little clandestine liaison at Willie's house,' he was saying. 'No fishing huts and gorse bushes for Laura, oh no, she must

348

have put her foot down about that, but I must say it's totally unlike Willie to be so indiscreet. He just walked her straight in through the front door apparently. The whole village is literally buzzing with the gossip and Kirsten's absolutely furious! I'm surprised you didn't hear about it sooner, Tess. I teased Laura about it the moment she walked into the gallery. That's what we were laughing about back there. I told her she was known locally as "the scarlet fisherwoman". She said she—'

'Hang on,' I interrupted. 'Did you say – in the gallery?'

'Yes, where we were just now, over the road.' He jerked his head back. 'Champagne-slinging alley.'

My jaw began to drop. 'I didn't know it was a gallery,' I breathed. 'I thought it was a party for the opening of a shop or something, one of Laura's dos.'

He grinned. 'No, it was one of my "dos" actually. My exhibition. I told you about it at Gilduncan.' He smiled ruefully and ran his fingers through his hair. 'Yes, my first night too, quite a stir you caused pitching up like that and dousing the artist.'

My hand flew to my mouth. I gazed appalled at his drenched suit. 'Oh Patrick! Oh God I'm so sorry! Your exhibition!' I stared at him, horrified. 'But – I didn't see – where were the pictures?'

'On the walls, that does tend to be the accepted thing. You were probably too busy chucking Bollinger about to do any art appreciation though.'

'But the window,' I blustered. 'I didn't even notice—' I swung around and stared back.

'Yes, only a small picture I grant you, but then Pierre likes to go for the minimalist look to get people to walk in. He's not keen on window shoppers.'

'P-Pierre?'

He grinned. 'Pink suit, moustache, French accent? Sorry, correction, *wet* pink suit.'

I cringed. 'Oh my God! That was Pierre Boulavère?'

'The very same.'

'Oh Patrick,' I gasped, 'what can I say? Have I ruined everything for you?'

He laughed, shrugging. 'Who knows? Possibly, but on the other hand possibly not. In fact, you may even have increased my chances of success. You may not have noticed, but quite a lot of the press were there, flashing away at the *moment critique*. It's not often they get a photo opportunity like that and you gave them three decent cracks at the whip too. If they weren't poised and ready when you went for the third glass they've no right to call themselves photographers. I bet you anything that'll be the shot that makes it to the Arts pages of the *Guardian*. Most people have wanted to do that to Pierre for years, particularly journalists. Anyway,' he lit a cigarette and blew the smoke out with a smile, 'you know what they say – all publicity is good publicity!'

Still aghast at what I'd done, I leaned my elbows on the table and groaned, clutching my head. I couldn't remember what had made me . . . Yes I could! I looked up and frowned suspiciously. 'So why was Laura there then?'

He shrugged. 'She just walked past. On her way to Dukes Hotel, she said, after your uncle's funeral. Unlike you she spotted the words *Patrick Cameron – One-Man Show*, at the top of the window. Popped in to wish me luck.'

'It was the way you were looking at her,' I murmured, feeling exhausted suddenly.

'Yes, one does tend to when one's talking to someone, don't you find? It's quite normal in polite society.'

Of course it was. But I'd been so eaten up with jealousy I'd imagined it was much more than old friends just having a laugh. I stared past him at the bustling crowds on the pavements. Patrick ordered us a couple of coffees. I was still staring into space when the waiter put the cappuccino down in front of me. My mind was taking a while to absorb all this. So . . . Laura and Patrick weren't together at all. I looked at him sitting opposite me, stirring his coffee. His still-damp hair was flopping into his eyes. He smiled up at the waiter as he left the bill. Suddenly a great black cloud seemed to lift up off my shoulders and a huge swell of relief flooded through me.

'Oh Patrick, I'm so relieved!' I blurted out, reaching across and grabbing his hand impulsively. 'I had visions, awful visions of you and Laura together, stupid, crazy thoughts – you know how your mind goes into overdrive. God, I had you practically engaged, married even! I imagined you coming to dinner together, kissing in the kitchen and then sort of breaking off when I came in, her jumping up off your lap, embarrassed in front of me, and then all of us sidling around each other, trying not to catch each other's eyes as we stacked the dishwasher, stupid childish things like that. God, I even had you coming for Christmas, sleeping together in the spare room, in the room next door to ours!'

He stared down at my hand on his. 'And that would have been so terrible?' he said quietly.

'Oh Patrick, horrendous,' I urged, squeezing his hand, still in the grip of my euphoric joy, 'don't you think?'

'I do, yes.'

'I mean, imagine,' I rushed on, 'you and her together, my *sister*! And me, always on the outside looking in – awful!'

'We'd certainly have seen a lot of each other, wouldn't we?' He was watching me very closely.

I laughed. 'Yes, but under what circumstances! It would have been ghastly! Always apart and never as we really want to—' I stopped abruptly, horrified.

'To what?' he said quickly, gripping my hand.

'To . . .' I stared down at our hands, together on the

351

tablecloth and felt the blood rush to my face. Slowly I pulled mine away. I shook my head.

'Tess?' he urged.

'Nothing,' I mumbled. I bit my lip and reached down on the pavement for my handbag. 'Patrick, I must go,' I faltered. 'It's my uncle's funeral . . .'

I stood up without looking at him, but as I made to go he came round the table and took one of my hands.

'You were going to say never as we really want to be – together – weren't you?'

I stared at the pavement in silence.

'Weren't you, Tess?' he insisted.

I slid my eyes up to the red-checked tablecloth. The pattern seemed to blur in front of my eyes. Tears flooded into them. I looked up.

'Patrick, I don't know what to do!' I blurted out.

There was a long silence. His eyes were full of love. And hope.

'Well, that's something, I suppose,' he said quietly, after a while. 'A few days ago you knew exactly what you wanted to do and it didn't include me. Now you don't know.' He smiled. 'It's not much, but it's a start.'

I licked my lips. 'Look, you won't . . . pressurise me, in any way?'

He shook his head. 'No, I won't, but—' Suddenly he seized both my hands and shook them urgently. 'Tess, you've got to do the right thing this time! This is for ever, it's important, you know that, don't you?'

I nodded dumbly. The right thing. What was the right thing? And for whom? There was another long pause.

'I have to go now,' I whispered eventually.

'Yes, I know.'

Neither of us moved. We stared at each other and it seemed to me he could see right into my soul. Everything went very quiet, very still. I could feel the blood pumping in my veins, my ankle gave a quick, sympathetic throb and my tissue twitched violently in my nose. Oh God, it was still there! Mortified, I longed to take it out but – would that look like an invitation?

As it was he didn't need one. He rested his hand gently on my face, tilted my head towards him, leaned forward, and his lips brushed mine.

We stood back. I blinked. There was a brief silence, then suddenly, raucous cheering broke out. We looked around, startled. All the people at the clutch of tables on the pavement were smiling and clapping, nodding their heads delightedly. I suddenly remembered our rather dramatic arrival at the café and blushed. Patrick grinned.

'Looks like I've got one or two supporters anyway.'

I glanced over his shoulder. 'Uh-oh, and there's one of mine,' I muttered, 'and he's coming this way.'

Behind Patrick, Pierre Boulavère, now dressed in a pale blue suit, was bustling over. He hadn't seen us yet, but he was getting closer, peering around, clearly looking for his artist.

'I'd better go,' said Patrick quickly. He squeezed my hand, gave me a last hot stare that was enough to singe my eyeballs off, then pointed quickly at my nose.

'That's pretty, incidentally.'

He gave a wicked grin, then turned on his heel and went swiftly back towards Pierre and his gallery.

I blushed and delicately removed the tissue from my nose. Then I bent down and picked up my bag and aware that some people were still looking, swung it as nonchalantly as possible over my shoulder. As I moved through the tables I surreptitiously put my fingers to my lips. Still there. They hadn't frazzled off with the heat then. My mind was racing and I didn't feel entirely with it. I shook my head as if trying to clear it. He was so adamant, so sure of himself, so convinced. But then of course, he always had been. And I wasn't, and never had been. I felt my lips again. I didn't want to consider the implications of that kiss, of what it meant, not just now. I could do that later. Plenty of time for all that. Right now I just wanted to savour it.

I limped slowly along the pavement, passing in a daze through the crowds, when suddenly I was pulled up short. My arms were both seized from behind.

I gasped. 'What the—'

'You little tart,' hissed a voice in my ear. 'You disgusting, filthy little tart!'

I froze in horror, and then with great force, was abruptly swung around. I stared.

'Daddy!' I gasped.

Chapter Twenty-four

'Shame on you,' he said fiercely, shaking me. His hands gripped my upper arms tightly. His face was contorted with rage; he looked almost possessed.

'A married woman,' he spat, 'kissing and flirting with another man. You little hussy!' He kept on shaking me, it was as if he couldn't stop.

'Daddy please,' I gasped, my head wobbling violently on my shoulders. 'Just let me explain.'

'Explain?' The force of his final shake flung me backwards and a couple of gaping tourists dodged nervously out of the way as I hit a shop window like a splattered fly, arms outstretched.

My father towered over me. 'Go on then,' he said threateningly. 'By all means have a go. Explain why you were canoodling with that ne'er-do-well when you should have been at your uncle's funeral!' He was trembling with fury. 'My own beloved brother,' he quavered, 'and neither of my children, it seems, can be bothered to turn up and pay their last respects. So finally, when in dumb disbelief I go looking for them, I find that one of them has been waylaid at some party or other and is covered in champagne, and the other is kissing and canoodling with that *degenerate*, in the middle of the street. You, Tessa! A wife, a mother, a supposedly respectable woman, have you no shame!'

By now a small and very interested crowd had gathered at a safe distance. I recognised a tourist from the café and saw her fish eagerly in her bag for her camera, keen, no doubt, to capture on celluloid this quaint English eccentric, the professional scene maker.

'Daddy, please—'

'And what about David?' he thundered on. 'What about Hugo and Clementine, have you thought about them? Have you considered the implications of anything beyond your own deceitful behaviour?'

'Hang on, Dad, just wait a minute, can't you? I'm trying to explain, just let me—'

'Oh, I've despaired of you before,' he went on with a tremor in his voice. 'I've prayed for you long and hard, my girl, but all along I've known you were a bad lot. In my heart I've known how rotten your soul is!'

'Bloody hell,' I muttered, my legs giving way a bit under all this fire and brimstone.

'I've prayed to God for forgiveness for you but I've always known the futility of it because you can't help yourself, can you?' he droned on relentlessly. 'It's in your nature, this dirty, lustful craving for sex. You just can't do without it.'

'Stop!' I cried, putting my hands over my ears, trying to block out his words. I'd never heard him talk like this before.

'But it's true, isn't it,' he urged, pulling my hands away from my ears. 'That's why you don't want to hear it! You've always longed for that man, haven't you?' His face was inches from mine and he had my wrists firmly. '*Haven't you!*' he insisted, giving me a little shake, as if somehow he could rattle it out of me.

I stared at him, his face was trembling with fury, but he looked – afraid, somehow, too. I drew myself up. All of a sudden I felt very calm.

I nodded. 'Yes, it's true,' I said, looking him in the eye. 'I've always wanted Patrick.'

He stared at me and for a moment I thought he was

going to hit me, but then abruptly, he let go of my wrists. His face crumpled, his shoulders sagged and for an awful moment I thought he might cry.

I stared at him. The fight had completely gone out of him. I straightened myself out and glanced around quickly. Our little audience was still with us and we were still in the middle of a busy West End street. This wasn't exactly the place for histrionics. I took him firmly by the arm.

'Come on,' I said decisively.

To my surprise he came like a lamb. He let himself be led very meekly through the murmuring, disappointed crowd and off down the road until I spotted what looked like a quietish side street with a pub in it; an empty bench stood outside. I hustled him down to it.

'Sit there,' I ordered.

He sat obediently and I went inside. The pub was practically empty and I was served immediately. I hurried back outside and handed him a glass of wine. When he drank it I noticed his hand was trembling but he sank half of it straight down in one go. I sat next to him and sipped mine, watching him. His face was very pale. He didn't look at me, just sat staring straight ahead. I dug deep for courage.

'This is all your fault, Daddy,' I said quietly. 'You realise that, don't you?'

He turned and looked at me, but it was as if he didn't quite recognise me. 'Hmm?'

'You should have let me go.'

He shook his head, puzzled. 'Go? Go where?' he muttered.

'To Italy, with Patrick. Years ago. You should have let me go.'

His face cleared. He shook his head and smiled, laughed almost. 'Oh no, Tess. No, no.'

'But don't you see?' I urged. 'If I'd gone I could have

found out for myself! I could have found out if Patrick and I were any good together, whether it would have worked. For all I know it might have fizzled out after a few months, or even a few years, but at least we'd have known for sure. Instead of which we're still dithering around in the dark, wondering if it was to be or not to be, and all because you insisted on putting the lid on it. Well, you can't just put the lid on something like that, not if it's still alive, still burning. All you get is an explosion when the lid flies off, and that's what's happening now!'

It was my turn to tremble a little now. 'And I've tried, Daddy,' I whispered, 'I really have. When Patrick told me in Scotland that he still felt the same way about me, I told him it was hopeless, but it's one thing to say it and another to feel something completely different.' I stopped and tore my hair briefly. 'And – and the crazy thing is I'm not even sure I *do* want him, necessarily. What I'm saying is that I don't know – and that's *your* fault. Because you never gave us a chance to find out, we're all reaping what you sowed twelve years ago – me, Patrick, David – all of us!'

He raised his eyebrows. 'Ah, I see. So you think I should have given you and Patrick a chance then, eh? Taken you to the airport, let your mother go with you as chaperone perhaps?'

'Yes! Yes I do!'

He smiled and shook his head. 'Oh no Tess, I couldn't do that.'

'But *why*? It wasn't as if we were under-age. God, I was eighteen, almost off to university – and let's face it, everyone shacks up with someone in their first term anyway, so what difference would it have made?'

He looked at me properly for the first time. 'A big difference, as it happens. You see, if you'd shacked up with someone at university I was pretty sure it wouldn't be your brother.'

For a moment I couldn't speak.

'My . . . brother?' I whispered eventually.

He didn't say anything. Just watched me. I shook my head incredulously.

'Oh no, no, that can't be . . .' I faltered. I searched his eyes. Oh God, it could be. *It was.*

'Madelaine?' I breathed incredulously.

He nodded. Suddenly his eyes wavered from mine and fled for the safety of the pavement. There was a terrible silence. Then: 'It was years ago,' he began softly, 'before your mother and I were married. Not before we were engaged, but before we were married. We were at Kilmarnoch with your grandparents. Madelaine was at Gilduncan. She was . . .' he sighed, shook his head slowly '. . . so beautiful you can't imagine, Tess – and so young. And he was – God, he was awful to her. Marcus, her husband.' He leaned back on the bench and gazed up at the sky, cradling his drink, remembering. 'He was away for most of that summer, on business or so he said – one never really knew with Marcus. So there she was, up there on her own, for weeks and weeks at a time in that big empty house. She'd just got married you see, a young bride, a young foreign bride and we felt so sorry for her; me, your mother, Rachel and Robert.' He paused, sipped his drink. 'We invited her for dinner once or twice and then it became a regular thing. She came a lot, most nights in fact. Your mother and she – they got on very well. They became great friends.' He paused. A muscle twitched in his face. 'Then one night, when everyone else had gone to bed, we stayed up, Madelaine and I, talking, by the fire. She told me about her marriage. About how cold it was, how empty. She said she knew she shouldn't have married him but now that she'd done it, she was afraid. Afraid to get out.' He narrowed his eyes, still staring at the sky. 'And then she cried,' he said softly. 'She cried and I held her, and she was so . . .' he shook his head, remembering '. . . so vulnerable. Lovable.' I watched in disbelief, as tears filled his eyes. Tears and something else, something so soft and so tender and so uncharacteristic, I almost didn't recognise it. 'And then later that night we went for a walk and – we made love.'

I stared. 'With Mummy back at Kilmarnoch?'

He nodded. 'My bride to be. In the room next to mine.' He looked down at his shoes. 'We met other nights too, Madelaine and I. All that summer, in fact.' He frowned. 'It was so strange, I just couldn't help myself you see, Tess. Just . . . couldn't . . . help myself. It was this dreadful craving I had – lust, I suppose.' He shot me a sudden look. 'And you have it too, I know you do. You see you're so *like* me,' he insisted. 'That's what frightens me.'

'And Mummy?' I whispered, ignoring this last observation. 'She never knew?'

He shook his head and sighed. 'No, she never knew. Still doesn't know. Marcus came back a few weeks later from abroad and Patrick was born in January.'

'Your son,' I breathed.

He nodded. 'My son. My only son.'

There was a silence. Tears welled in his eyes. He shook them away and with an effort, collected himself.

'But I had to hate him, you see. Had to hate Patrick. It was the only way for me to get over it. I couldn't stand by on the side-lines watching him grow up, knowing he was my boy, hankering after him. I washed my hands of him right there and then, called him "that little bastard" to myself. I refused to see him or have anything to do with him.'

'And Madelaine?'

'Madelaine too,' he said shortly. 'I knew it was madness. It was a madness that lasted a summer and that was it. After that I made sure we cut ourselves off from that family for good.'

'So . . . you didn't love her?'

'Good God no,' he said quickly. 'I didn't love her.' He gave a short, sharp laugh. 'How could I? Madelaine is everything I despise in a woman. She's flighty, insecure, flirtatious . . . No, she's not my sort of woman at all. She wouldn't have been remotely suitable.'

'Suitable? There's no agenda for falling in love, Dad.'

'Whereas your mother,' he went on as if I hadn't spoken, 'was everything I was looking for in a wife. Steady, practical, down to earth, and from good, sensible stock.' He nodded firmly. 'Oh, I married the right woman, there's no doubt about that. But I—' He stopped.

'You wrecked your life in the process.'

He gazed down at the pavement and frowned. 'Yes, I did.'

'And mine too,' I said.

There was a long silence. It had been hot all day but there was a sudden chill in the air that hadn't been there before. I shivered. I couldn't think straight, couldn't even begin to get my head around this.

'Why didn't you tell me? I said eventually. 'When I was eighteen, when I'd just met him, that time on the beach? Why didn't you take me aside, and tell me gently? I'd have understood.'

He shook his head. 'Couldn't,' he muttered gruffly. 'Couldn't have you think ill of me, Tess, know me for the sham I was.'

'I'd have thought *more* of you,' I said fiercely, 'much more! It would have helped a great deal to know you were human!'

He bowed his head.

'And I could have accepted it then, too, in the beginning. I could have accepted that there was no way Patrick and I could ever see each other, no way we could

361

ever fall in love. If you'd told me then I could have set my heart against him, maybe even loved him as a brother, been proud to have him as that, but now . . .'

'Tess, you must!' he cried, seizing my hand. 'You must!'

'But it's not so easy now!' I blurted, snatching my hand back. 'And so what if he is my brother,' I cried hopelessly, 'so what? I don't want more children, so it doesn't matter!'

'No!' he cried, appalled. He seized my shoulders. 'No! It's a mortal sin, brother and sister!'

I knew he was right but I wanted to hurt him. 'But we already have,' I said coldly. 'Sinned.'

He shrank back. 'You can't have done – I was so careful!'

'Not careful enough, Daddy. Needs must, as you well know. Like you, that summer with Madelaine. Who knows, perhaps we all picked the same spot – down by the riverbank, eh? In the middle of the night?'

He stared at me aghast. The blood drained from his face. 'Oh God,' he breathed, 'thank heavens nothing came of it.'

'No, nothing came of it,' I said flatly, 'but you see, the deed has already been done. We wouldn't be breaking new ground.'

'Tess, promise me you won't do this, promise me! Don't you see that in God's eyes it's damnable?'

I stared at him. 'In God's eyes, Daddy, you've got an awful lot to answer for. I don't know how you have the nerve to—' But I couldn't go on. His head was already bowed in shame.

'Preach,' he finished for me. 'I know, Tess, believe me, I know. I've lived with it for thirty-four years now and there hasn't been a day when I haven't thought about it.'

We fell silent. There was so much I wanted to say, to

reproach him for. I wanted to scream and yell, to pummel my fists on his chest, call him a hypocrite, a liar, a cheat, tell him I could see him for what he really was now. Not the strong, powerful figure occupying the high moral ground, that elevated position he'd always led me to believe I could never hope to reach even if I clawed my way up by my fingernails, but a weak, selfish, vain, flawed man. I wanted to tell him I knew all this, but more than anything I wanted to get away from him. I wanted to get away and think about where this left me.

Eventually I cleared my throat. 'Daddy, we must get back. Rachel will be wondering . . .'

He nodded. 'I know. You go on, Tess. Just give me five minutes to collect myself and I'll come on after.' He jerked his head. 'Go on.'

I gulped. After all this he was still telling me what to do! I wanted to shriek, 'No, damn it, you go on! What about *my* five minutes? What about *me* collecting myself?'

Out of habit, I put my glass down and got up. I started off down the street, doing as he'd asked.

'Tess!' he called after me suddenly. I turned. 'You won't say anything to your mother?' His eyes were pained, haunted.

Mummy. Oh God, Mummy. 'No,' I whispered.

'One more thing.' His face buckled. He fought with it. 'Will you forgive me?'

I looked back at him sitting there in his dark suit and dog collar, on a pub bench, looking so old suddenly, so lonely, so incongruous. He looked – pathetic. With difficulty, I nodded curtly. Still he held my gaze. It wasn't enough. He wanted a word. He wanted absolution. I took a deep breath.

'Yes,' I muttered.

Relief flooded his eyes. I turned and walked quickly on.

363

Chapter Twenty-five

Somehow, by putting one foot in front of the other and clicking onto automatic pilot, I made my way to Dukes. I limped slowly and methodically through the crowded streets; past Selfridges, through Berkeley Square, registering the shops, the parks, the statues, but not really seeing them, just dragging my foot and staring straight ahead. I felt numb with shock, but at the same time my mind was kaleidoscoping fragments of chaotic information around. I tried to assimilate them. Patrick was my brother. We shared a father. He was my father's son. Sister and brother. Brother and sister. Daddy and Madelaine.

I limped on and on and after a while, the numbness began to thaw; I started to get some feeling back in my mind. The shards of light stopped flitting around and settled down into some sort of cohesive order. Slowly, surely, I began to get the picture and as it came into focus I realised it wasn't very pretty. Rage began to well up from somewhere deep inside me. It started in the pit of my stomach and unfurled in waves, surging up through my throat until I felt I'd almost gag on it. *He'd done it again, hadn't he?* Once again my father had blocked me, stopped me in my tracks.

The first time, twelve years ago, he'd done it physically, by barring my way, refusing to let me leave the country – or even the house, for that matter – and now this time, when I was too old for such bullying tactics, he'd done it by presenting a stumbling block so awful and so insurmountable, that however much I'd insisted it would make no difference, I knew it would, despite my show of bravado. There was no earthly way Patrick and I could ever be together now, my father had seen to that. Once again he'd taken away my freedom of choice. Once again he'd steered the course of my life, taken the helm, put an end to everything, but in another way, he'd ensured that there was no end. He'd just made the waters even murkier, because he hadn't taken away our attraction for each other; he'd just highlighted it by its impossibility.

I'd want Patrick even more now I couldn't have him, wouldn't I, I thought bitterly. I'd probably dream about him all the time now, moon about the house in my nightie thinking about him, eat too much, take up smoking, die of chocolate, wonder what might have been, stare out of rain-streaked windows, pull myself together for just long enough to put a coat on over my pyjamas and take the children to school then sink back into wistful melancholia with a vengeance, surrounded by the washing up, yesterday's papers, crawling through the days, resenting my life with David . . . Oh yes, I thought sourly, there was no hope for me now. I'd end my days a twisted, bickering, frustrated old hag with a poor, henpecked husband who could do no right. That was the fate that awaited me and David, my father had seen to that. He'd condemned us to an unhappy marriage. My father, the preacher man, and all because his inflated pride and vanity had meant more to him than my happiness. All because he couldn't bear me to think he was anything less than The Right Reverend Perfect. Well thank you so much, Daddy.

I limped grimly into the hotel. The doorman gave me a quizzical glance but I swept past him, on and up the stairs to the suite where our party was gathered.

As I hobbled into what was now quite a noisy and

jolly throng – and certainly less than sober – I spotted David hovering near the doorway. He was waiting for me, looking around anxiously. My anger dissipated in a moment. I stopped for a second and looked at him without him seeing me. There he was, tall, elegant, poised, his chin raised as he peered around, with that kind intelligent face. My heart gave a sudden lurch. Poor, lovely David, my darling husband, who'd done nothing wrong apart from follow Patrick chronologically in my affections. Who'd loved me, given me children and was now caught up in this God-awful mess by dint of the fact that he'd met me second and not first.

'Tess!' His face cleared with relief as he saw me. He walked quickly over. 'Where on earth have you been? I've been worried sick.'

'Oh David, I'm sorry. I needed some air, went for a walk, but I ended up wandering around for a bit. Sorry.'

'But you've been ages, an hour at least, and you look terrible!'

'I know, I know. I – I think Robert's death affected me more than I imagined.' I cringed inwardly at my hypocrisy.

David took my arm and steered me towards the bar. 'Well come on, let's get you a drink, that's obviously what you need. You'll feel much better after a brandy. It doesn't do to dwell on these things for too long, you know. That's the whole point of a wake . . . you get pissed and it takes your mind off all that death. And you're probably starving too, which doesn't help either. You can't grieve on an empty stomach.' He produced a plate of salmon and salad from behind a potted palm. 'Everyone fell on the food like gannets when they arrived but I managed to save you some. Here, tuck into this.'

Tears welled up in my eyes. Right, so let's get this straight, Tess. While you've been out hand-holding with another man, your hunter-gatherer here has been storing up food, squirrelling it away behind plants, lest his homemaker – sorry, home*breaker* – should be the teeniest bit hungry when she arrives. Lest she should have even the remotest of hunger pangs. I mentally flogged myself and took the plate.

'Thanks,' I whispered.

What I really wanted to say was, 'For God's sake don't be so frigging nice to me, David. Why on earth didn't you spike the cucumber with arsenic, garnish the lettuce with a nice touch of cyanide, finish off your cheating, conniving witch of a wife once and for all, eh?'

He peered at me under my fringe. 'Sure you're all right? You look decidedly clammy if you don't mind me saying so.'

I felt my forehead. It was damp. God, how disgusting. I nodded and forced a smile. 'Fine, fine honestly.'

Silently I bent my head and toyed with the salad. At least with a plate of food I didn't have to look at him. At length, he broke the silence.

'Look, Tess, I'm sorry,' he said briskly.

I looked up. 'What for?'

'For everything. But mainly for not coming to help you back from Scotland. Leaving you in the lurch like that, with your leg and the children. It was just – well, it was a rather difficult time for me . . .'

I smiled. God, that seemed so long ago now. 'It's OK, David. I was just being a selfish cow as usual.'

'It won't make any sense now,' he went on hesitantly, 'but maybe later on you'll understand. I needed that time to – well. There were lots of things I wanted to sort out. For myself. Alone.'

I frowned up at him, watching his mouth twisting and turning awkwardly. How strange, he looked almost shifty. David never looked shifty. And what on earth was he going on about? What things? Sort what out? I sighed. No, I had enough chaos on my plate without trying to take on any more. Whatever it was would have to wait. I put down my salad.

'David, you've got nothing to apologise for. It's me who's behaved abominably.' Tears of shame and self-pity filled my eyes. I kept my head low and reached for my wine glass.

'That's not strictly true,' he said quietly, 'but there's a limit to the extent I can . . .' He hesitated.

'The extent you can what?'

He shook his head. 'Nothing. I should have come and got you, that's all. Shouldn't have left you there alone.'

'David, stop banging on about it, will you? You were right not to! It's about time you stopped jumping at my commands, for heaven's sake. I'm just a spoiled, arrogant girl who expects you to leap through hoops at a moment's notice and quite frankly I don't know why you put up with me. Most husbands would have shot me through the mouth long ago. Honestly, sometimes I haven't the faintest idea why you don't just bugger off and leave me.'

He smiled. 'Sometimes I haven't the faintest idea either.'

There was a pause.

'So – would you?' I said suddenly, recklessly.

He looked at me carefully. 'What exactly are you asking me here, Tess?'

I was playing with fire and I knew it. All at once the room seemed very still. It was as if we were the only two people in it.

'I'm asking you if you'd ever leave me,' I said breathlessly, feeling my colour rise.

'What sort of a question is that?' he said quietly.

I stared at him. Wasn't he going to answer it then? Why the hell not? My heart stopped for a second. Then I mentally shook myself. Why not? Because you're in a room full of relatives at your uncle's funeral, you fool, that's why not. And because there's a time and a place for everything. I could still feel his eyes burning into me. As abruptly as the madness had taken me, it left me. I felt my damp forehead as if maybe that was to blame.

'Oh, God, I'm so sorry, David,' I gasped. 'I don't know what came over me just then. Actually I'm feeling decidedly dodgy right now – it's all this emotion I suppose, makes me hormonal. You know what I'm like at weddings, I can get through a dozen hankies in one sitting. Must be the same with funerals, I suppose, only worse. Forget I said anything, I'm – I'm raving at the moment.' I looked up with the brightest smile I could muster.

He stared back at me. His face seemed white, colourless. I glanced away. *Don't talk to him now*, a little voice in my head said. *Don't say any more, not in this state. You'll spill the Patrick beans, blurt it out, confess it, you know you're dying to unburden yourself. You're just ripe for a confession but once it's out you can never un-say it and my God you'll live to regret it ...* And quite apart from anything else, I thought bitterly, there were precious few beans left to spill now, were there? My eyes, which had been preoccupied with my wine glass, took a quick flit to David's ashen face.

'Darling, I simply must go to the loo,' I muttered. 'I've got to do something about my face. I can feel how ugly I am without even consulting a mirror.'

He nodded and managed a thin smile beneath his pallor. 'You've looked better, I must say. Go on, I'll guard your food.'

'No, no, I don't want it really. You go and talk to everyone. I'll probably be a while.'

I turned and without looking back, elbowed my way through the throng in the direction of the Ladies.

Once inside I leaned heavily on the marble wash stand and stared at my battered, tear-stained face in the overlit mirror. I looked about a hundred years old and felt it too. I delved in my bag and found a blunt eyeliner and attempted a shaky line. I tried some mascara too, but made such a hash of it I wiped it off and ended up with black eyes. I slapped some lipstick on instead. Then I stared at my clown's face with its swollen eyelids and red mouth. It seemed entirely appropriate somehow.

'What a mess,' I whispered. 'What a God . . . awful . . . mess.'

I could see by my reflection that such wanton self-pity had triggered the tear ducts again so I hurriedly stuffed the make-up back in my bag and tempting though it was to stay in the safety of the Ladies for the next hour or so, turned and went back outside.

The hum of social chatter swirled around me. I took a glass of champagne from a waitress's tray, and then on an impulse, another. It was an old trick of mine at gruesome parties, to wander around with two glasses, and if accosted by the bore of the century, say I was actually just on my way to deliver a drink. I looked around nervously. And let's face it, there were plenty of people I simply couldn't speak to here, ones I really had to avoid, like David, Laura, Mummy. I was circling around the edge of the crowd when suddenly, my elbow was seized in a pincer-like grip. An ancient cut-glass voice barked in my ear.

'Trying the old two-glasses-at-a-party trick eh? That doesn't fool me. I've been looking for you.'

I swung around and my heart sank. 'Aunt Elspeth!'

I leaned forward and kissed the paper-thin cheek that was presented to me. Oh hell. Blind, boozy, belligerent Great-Aunt Elspeth, just what I needed. As usual she reeked of stale Chanel and pink gin, was smothered in jewels and had the usual eccentric hat complete with

371

ostrich feathers foaming out of the top like some kind of extravagant bantam cock. Still, I reasoned, at least she wasn't a member of my more immediate family and at least I wouldn't have to say anything to her. There was no such thing as a conversation with Elspeth; hers was the only voice that mattered so she simply held forth.

'How lovely to see you,' I lied.

Tall and thin she swooped down with her watery blue eyes and hawk-like nose.

'Don't lie, my dear, you know you avoid me like the plague, everyone does; but just think, it could have been worse. It could have been mad bad Uncle Arthur. At least I won't pinch your bottom. I might just pinch that extra drink, though. It's like the bloody Gobi desert in here.'

I grinned and passed it over to her. 'Be my guest.'

'But as it happens, my dear,' she took a huge slug of champagne and fixed me with her rheumy old eyes, 'I've got a bone to pick with you.'

I groaned silently and braced myself for a flurry of confusion. No one would ever be foolish enough to accuse Elspeth of being senile because in actual fact she was quite astonishingly on the ball. It was just that being half-blind, it was almost invariably the *wrong* ball. She tapped me with a heavily bejewelled hand.

'You must give up that dreadful job of yours. It'll be the ruin of you!'

I sighed. 'No, Elspeth, that's not me. That's—'

'Find yourself a nice young man. It's high time you were settling down and having babies, my dear. It's all very well swanning round in your designer suits fancying yourself as a captain of industry, but your biological clock is ticking away. You're running out of eggs, young lady!'

I groaned. 'Elspeth, it's Laura who's—'

'Yes I can see it's Laura. What d'you think I am, blind as well as old? Now look here, my girl, if you don't get yourself sorted out soon you're going to end up on the shelf like your poor Aunt Beatty and no amount of dusting off is ever going to get *her* down again!'

I cringed for poor Beatty, Elspeth's elder sister. I glanced around and – ah yes, as luck would have it she was standing right behind us. I tried to convey this to Elspeth with a series of extravagant head nods and winks, but to no avail.

'You know what happened to her, don't you?' she barked.

I saw Beatty's back stiffen. 'Elspeth, I really don't think—'

'She left it too late and then in desperation had a *disastrous* flirt with a married man. She threw herself at him, poor cow, absolutely *threw* herself; it was embarrassing to watch. Of course he swore blind he'd leave his wife for her but he never did. Pitiful it was – and in those days it wasn't even as if she had the satisfaction of a proper affair! Some decent hanky-panky! On no, it was all conducted in public, lots of feverish glances across a crowded room, sweaty palms, heaving bosoms – just one long, wretched, knee-trembling flirt, poor devil. Shall I tell you something,' she hissed loudly, putting her hand on my arm and glancing around furtively. I braced myself, knowing exactly what was coming. 'Poor old Beatty's never even had it up!'

Behind me I could almost hear Beatty's teeth grinding to dust. 'Elspeth, I know, you've told me before and—'

'Imagine,' said Elspeth loudly. 'Imagine going to your grave never knowing what it is to have a fuck!'

'Elspeth, please!' God, she was worse than ever. I took her arm and forcibly steered her to the side of the room where hopefully it was a little quieter and she could insult everyone to her heart's content. Unfortunately I inadvertently steered her into little Leonora who was kneeling up at a table drinking orange juice.

'Not that lack of sex will ever be your problem though, eh?' she observed loudly.

I cringed and tried to steer her away from Leonora's pricked-up ears, but the Perfect Child looked strangely delighted to see her great-great-aunt. She left her juice, climbed down from the table and followed us, attaching herself firmly to Elspeth's side. She gazed up at her intently.

'Eh? What? Quite the opposite I should imagine,' Elspeth roared on. 'You've probably been getting far too much and all from the wrong sorts of people! Who's this soppy teacher chappie I've been hearing about? Not a bloody Communist, is he?'

I sighed, recognising my father's intervention. 'No, Elspeth, he's not, but—'

'What? Don't whisper, girl! They're all Lefty bastards now, aren't they? Or so your father tells me. Can't abide bloody Communists, they should all be taken out and shot through the testicles.' She frowned down for a moment at Leonora who was staring up at her now with quite disconcerting intensity.

'What are you staring at me for, child?' she barked.

'I want to see you drink like a fish.'

Elspeth blanched. 'Eh? What's that?'

'Well, Daddy said—'

'Leonora, run along, darling,' I said hastily. 'I think Mummy's looking for you.'

'But Aunt Tess, Daddy said she could! He did, he said she could dri—'

'Leonora, please!' I snapped desperately. I turned her around, pointed her in the direction of her mother and gave her a little shove. 'Now run along.' God, this wake was going from bad to worse. All the same, I made a mental note to tell Hugo his pupil was coming along rather nicely.

'Hrmph!' snorted Elspeth. 'That child's going to turn out just like her mother if she's not careful.'

'Yes, well, anyway, Elspeth, look,' I muttered, desperately inching away, 'it's been lovely to talk to you but I really ought to go and ring the babysitter. I said I'd check in about now and—'

'You'll do no such thing, young lady. I haven't finished with you yet. Now just hold your horses a moment while I tell you what you need.' She seized my wrist in her bony old hand. There was no escape. 'What you need is a nice solid barrister like your sister. Doesn't matter what he looks like, as long as he works hard and he's got a bit of money, then you just knuckle down and get breeding, all right?' She leaned forward with a conspiratorial hiss. 'But for heaven's sake don't let yourself go to pot afterwards like she has. I shouldn't think she even shaves her legs any more, let alone her armpits. Talk about getting your man and breathing a monumental sigh of relief! No, no, that's not the way at all. You can still wear your fancy frocks and carry on chasing Lefties – if you must – but at least you'll have got the staples under your belt.' She tapped my hand. 'Know what I mean? It's no good helping yourself to the little luxuries in life without having the staples first!'

I grinned in spite of myself. Old Elspeth had notched up precisely three staples in her time; three rich, solid, boring, unquestioning husbands, who'd sat by and watched as she'd steadily peppered her life with a string of caddish luxuries, most of whom had had yachts in the Bahamas, castles in the Black Forest and villas in the South of France.

'I blame the pill,' she declared hotly, 'and the so-called sexual revolution.'

I looked around desperately, wondering if anyone else would like to hear this as many times as I had.

'Liberation,' she scoffed. 'Liberation for whom? For

men, that's who! Oh yes, they have a very cushy time of it now, don't they? They get a nice young gel to take to bed on a regular basis and all for the price of a bottle of Chablis and a Coq auVin. What could be more liberating than that? Wouldn't have happened in my day. Oh no, in *my* day if some fellow wanted to get you between the sheets he had to marry you first, he couldn't just scatter his seed around like some sex-crazed tomcat! I mean, that's all very fine for him but where does it leave you?'

'Exactly,' I murmured distractedly.

Out of the corner of my eye I spotted Laura and David, huddled in a corner over by the fireplace, talking earnestly. In fact it was Laura who was doing all the talking. David was just listening intently, his head tilted to one side. I went cold. What was she telling him? That I was so obsessed with Patrick I'd marched into a gallery like a scorned, jilted lover, doused her in champagne and accused her of having an affair with him? My heart stopped for a moment. She wouldn't do that, would she?

'Up the creek without a bloody paddle, that's where! With no ring on your finger and not even a bun in the oven to force his hand!'

But – if she wasn't telling him that – what was it then? What was so riveting that it was being related in such hushed tones and listened to so avidly? I watched their faces, trying desperately to read her lips.

'I tell you, if I was a young gel these days I'd throw that wretched pill packet away and have him marching up the aisle beside me with a bump under my dress. The next time you're bedding down with your drippy little teacher fellow you bear that in mind, my dear. After all, it's not as if *he'd* take the wretched thing, is it – so why should you? Don't swallow it!'

I turned back to Elspeth and blinked. 'What?'

'I said the next time you're in bed with your teacher chappie – don't swallow it!'

I gazed at her incredulously. Good heavens. Elspeth really had gone from bad to worse; she shouldn't be allowed out.

'Spit it out!' she barked.

My mouth hung open. Luckily I was saved from spluttering a reply by a cool hand on my arm.

'Darling – a word.'

'Mummy!'

'Elspeth, I'm so sorry to barge in but could I drag Tess away for just a moment?'

'You're going as barmy as I am, Daphne. It's Laura, not Tess, but yes, have her, by all means. See if you can talk any sense into the gel. I certainly can't!'

'I'll do my best,' purred my mother. 'Oh, and incidentally, I think Beatty's looking for you.'

She pushed Elspeth in the direction of Beatty's bristling back and steered me the other way.

'She's got worse, Mummy,' I muttered as we moved off. 'Honestly, some of the things she says . . . she's unreal!'

'Ah well, that's the arrogance of old age for you, makes you feel you've lived so long you can say what you like. To tell you the truth, I'm beginning to feel a little like that myself these days.'

She smiled as she linked arms with me and led me over to a window seat overlooking the street. She sat down and patted the cushion next to her. I perched gingerly beside her. She frowned.

'Why so grim, darling?'

'Me?' I forced a smile. 'Oh, no reason. I'm fine really. Fine.'

I couldn't look at her. What a bastard my father was. What a complete and utter first division shit. He didn't deserve someone like my mother.

'Really? You look a bit – distressed.'

I sighed. 'Oh I'm all right really, just a bit tired, I

suppose. This wretched ankle doesn't help and – oh I don't know. Everything seems to be getting on top of me at the moment, conspiring against me . . .' I trailed off, looking out of the window at the traffic in the street below.

'Is it Patrick?'

I swung round abruptly. 'Wh-what d'you mean?'

'Come on, Tess,' she said quietly. 'You don't think I don't know, do you?'

I looked away. 'Does . . . everyone know?' I muttered.

'If you mean David, I don't think so, no. But I've always known.'

We were silent for a moment.

'To be honest, Mummy, I hadn't really realised myself,' I said quietly. 'But now I can see that it's always been there, that sort of . . . dull ache. Sometimes it's hardly there at all. I can go for weeks, months, years even, without thinking about him, but then suddenly, like now, it just gets me in its grip and it's as if I can't breathe. Can't think rationally, it just – takes me over.' I caught my breath in a gasp.

God, it was a relief to talk about it, to tell someone. I looked down at my hands, twisted them together. But I mustn't talk too much, must I? I turned to her with a bright smile.

'But not any more. As from today that's all in the past. I intend to quit the habit; it's my New Year's resolution! No more pain, no more longing.'

She shook her head. 'I don't think so.'

'Oh yes, definitely. This holiday was the main culprit of course, seeing him again, bringing it all back, but I'm going to put it all behind me now. Get back to normal. You'll see.' I gave a brave little smile, but it shook a bit as she gazed into my eyes.

'I doubt it. It's not as simple as that, is it?'

'Oh, so what do you suggest then, Mummy,' I

said, exasperated. 'An affair? The break-up of my marriage – something jolly like that?'

'No,' she said calmly, 'but one way or another this will wreck your marriage anyway and you know it. The rot's already set in as far as I can see, and whether you go with Patrick now or just hanker after him silently for the rest of your life it doesn't make much difference. You're not giving your all to David.'

I hung my head in silence. It was true. But since there was no way I could be with Patrick anyway, what was the point of talking about it? But I couldn't tell her that.

Mummy put her hand on mine. 'Look, Tess,' she said gently, 'I just don't want you to be as trapped and frustrated as I've been, to think there's no way out. It's not true. You *do* have a duty to other people, of course you do, but your real duty is to yourself. Don't live the life of a martyr, it doesn't help anyone.'

'Like you have,' I said quietly.

'Like I have.'

There was a silence. I realised I'd always known that, just never acknowledged it. I looked at her.

'Do you wish you'd left Daddy then?'

She sighed and shook her head. 'Oh, it's too late now so what's the point in talking about it?' She lifted her chin and breathed deeply. Then she stared into the middle distance and nodded slowly. 'But yes, since you ask, there've been plenty of times when I thought if I didn't get out he'd drive me insane. Really insane.' She shrugged. 'But then, every time I was about to go I'd think of you and Laura. I thought you wouldn't survive the break-up, that you'd both be psychologically affected by it for the rest of your lives and that it would be all my fault. The usual thing.'

I nodded miserably. I couldn't even think about Hugo and Clemmie, just couldn't think.

'So, I just put up with him. Martyred myself to the

cause, marriage and family life.' She shook her head. 'Not a very healthy situation, but inside I consoled myself with the thought that I might actually do it one day, when you were older. Get up and go, have a life of my own. I kidded myself I had a secret hidden agenda. That kept me going.' She smiled sadly. 'Too late now, of course.'

I bit my lip. 'Mummy – David and I, we're not like that, like you and Daddy. Not at all, in fact. We love each other very much. It's just—'

She patted my hand. 'I know. You just can't get rid of Patrick, can you?'

'No, I can't, but Mummy, it's no good!' I blurted out suddenly. 'There's no point in even thinking about it.'

'Because?'

'Because – nothing.' I stood up. God, shut *up*, Tess, just shut *up*. I smoothed my skirt down. 'Come on,' I said gruffly, 'let's go and get another drink. I reckon I could drink this bar dry today. In fact, I look upon it as a positive challenge.'

She put a hand on my arm. 'Because of something your father's just told you?'

I whipped around and stared back at her. Slowly I sat down beside her again.

'How did you know?' I whispered.

'Well, I knew he went looking for you and I guessed you'd be with Patrick. I assumed he'd find you together and have to tell you.'

'So you know – about Patrick?'

She smiled. 'I've known for years. Since it happened, in fact.'

I stared at her. 'Does he know that you know?'

'No, of course not.'

I blinked. 'How did you find out?'

'Oh, it wasn't difficult. It was quite obvious at the time that he was having an affair with Madelaine. I knew

380

from the word go. I can remember the precise moment it started, in fact. She stayed late after supper one night at Kilmarnoch and they sat up talking together.' She smiled. 'After that it was just a joke. You know what your father's like, he's hopeless at subterfuge. He kept imagining he was sneaking noiselessly out of the house in the middle of the night, whereas in fact every floorboard was creaking violently and every door banging shut and he kept whispering "Bugger" under his breath as he stubbed his toes in the dark. It was enough to wake the dead. I had the room next to him and I used to get out of bed in my nightie and stand at the window, watching him disappearing down the drive to meet her.'

'And you didn't mind?' I said incredulously.

'Oh, I *minded* all right, I minded like anything, but what could I do? I was engaged to be married to him the following month and at the time assumed I was very much in love. You see, he was the only man I'd ever met really. I was very young, very confused and my parents were dead so I felt totally alone.' She shrugged. 'I thought – if I run out now, what will happen to me? Who will have me? I panicked, I suppose. I reckoned if I kept my head down and kept quiet, the affair would run its course and fizzle out, which of course it did.'

'Crumbs,' I breathed. 'I'm not sure I'd have been so stoical.'

'And neither should I have been, nor so forgiving, but when you're as young and naive as I was in those days . . .' She trailed off back into the past. Then with a start, collected herself and came back to the present. 'Anyway, Marcus returned from abroad and Madelaine went back to him. Your father and I got married and I thought I'd won. Thought I'd got what I wanted.'

'And you guessed that Patrick was their son?'

'Well, it wasn't hard. When we heard at a dinner party

381

that Madelaine was expecting, your father went as white as a sheet, was nearly sick in his soup and had to leave the table. He came back ten minutes later visibly shaken, couldn't eat a thing and looking as if he'd seen a ghost. Then for the next six or seven months he practically fought the paper boy for *The Times* in the morning, propped it up behind his boiled egg and scanned the births avidly, frowning with concentration and imagining he was being *so* discreet.'

I smiled in spite of myself. I could just imagine it.

'When it was finally announced the paper shook in his hand like a jelly. He dropped it straight into his coffee and ran upstairs. I reached across the breakfast table, picked up the sodden paper and read about Patrick's birth. I mean, what does he think I am, brain dead or something?'

'And Madelaine? Does she know you know?'

'Oh yes,' she smiled. 'I mean, it's never been mentioned, but it's very much understood.' She looked at me. 'You know, between women. Something unspoken. There was a little friction at first, but there's no animosity now. Quite the reverse in fact. In a way I think we both feel rather bonded.' She stared out of the window. 'And of course, we've both been too unhappy in our marriages to get in a state about that sort of thing now. We both know why it happened.'

'You'd say that then, would you?'

'What?'

'That you've had an unhappy marriage?'

She took a deep breath. 'I'd say that I've had a desperately frustrating, unfulfilled –' she hesitated – 'unhappy marriage, yes.' She looked at me intently. 'And I don't want that for you, Tess, however high the price. Take it from me, it's not worth it.'

'But then – don't you see?' I said desperately, 'for God's sake, there's just no way! Patrick and I – we're brother and sister. It's impossible, Mummy!'

She looked at me squarely. 'Ah, but you're not, you see.'

I stared. 'But you just said—'

'I said Patrick was his son, but—' Suddenly she faltered. She glanced away, then down at her hands. She twirled her wedding ring. I stared at her in mounting horror.

'But I'm not his daughter?' I breathed incredulously. 'Mummy!' I seized her hand, shook it. 'Mummy! Is that what you're saying? *That I'm not his daughter?*'

She looked up. Her face was composed, but very pale under her make-up. Her lips, bloodless. 'Yes that's right. That's exactly what I'm saying,' she said. 'You're not his daughter, Tess.'

Chapter Twenty-six

I gazed at her, my throat, mouth and lips as dry as sand. 'So,' I breathed, 'who is my father then?'

She glanced at me quickly, then away. 'This is very hard for me, Tess.'

'Mummy!' I squeezed her hand hard. 'For heaven's sake just tell me! Is it someone I know?'

She nodded. 'Yes, it's someone you know.'

I gasped. 'Good God! Who?'

'Hamish McPherson.'

For a moment the name meant absolutely nothing to me. My mind raced feverishly around, winding forwards, backwards, searching desperately for a face, but coming up with nothing. I blinked. 'Hamish McPherson?'

'The old gillie. Willie's father.'

I stared at her incredulously. 'Hamish – from the river? You mean – no! I don't believe it!'

'You don't believe it's Hamish, or you don't believe I'd do such a thing?' She was watching me carefully now.

'Good God – both,' I spluttered, briefly tearing at my hair. 'I mean,' I stood and paced up and down by the window seat, backwards and forwards, turning small circles, 'well, I just can't believe it, that's all. Any of it!'

'Having decided to tell you, it's hardly something I'd lie about, is it?' she said calmly. 'Hamish *is* your father, darling.'

I stopped pacing, turned and stared at her. For several seconds I was bereft of speech. Then I sat down next to her again. I thought of Willie's father, the old gillie, a huge bear of a man with grey woolly hair, a beard, a deep Scottish brogue. A nice man, quiet, kindly, twinkly-eyed, helpful always, but – my father? I dug deep and found some kind of a voice. It didn't sound like mine at all.

'But how on earth did you and he – how did you ever come to . . . I mean, with someone like that?'

She smiled. 'How did I ever come to sleep with someone as old and raddled as that? You forget, my love, that I too am old and raddled now but in those days we were both young and Hamish was extremely attractive. He was terrifically,' she hesitated, 'well, virile, I suppose. He had this huge powerful frame and a shock of blond hair – looked rather like his son does now, in fact.'

'Of course,' I breathed. 'Willie.'

'Not unattractive in his way, wouldn't you say?'

I blushed and glanced away. 'Er – no. No, I suppose not.' God, to think I'd nearly slept with my *brother*.

'And certainly your sister seems to find him so. Not really your type, of course – too rustic, not urbane enough, but still, he has a certain rakish charm, as did Hamish. And Hamish was such a gentle man, so unlike your father. He was tender and kind and – yes, passionate. And let's face it,' she brushed some imaginary crumbs off her immaculate navy skirt, 'passion was very lacking in my life at the time.'

I looked at her in amazement as she sat, gloves clasped on her lap, Dickins & Jones hat on, talking matter-of-factly to me about virility and tenderness and passion as if for all the world she was discussing the price of spring greens. I blinked. My mother, Mum, who cooked and sewed and gardened – what on earth did she want with things like that, was the question that sprung shamefully to mind.

'So,' I struggled to make sense of this, 'so all of

this happened the same summer that Daddy and Madelaine . . .'

'Oh dear me, no. No no, it was a few years after all that, three or four years, by which time I'd realised what a terrible mistake I'd made. That the man I'd married was not the man he'd purported to be. My fault too, of course,' she smiled. 'I hadn't read the small print properly, and I expected too much. Women always do though, don't they? It's only natural. We've all been spoonfed true romance from puberty and whether it's Mills and Boon or *Anna Karenina* one still comes to expect it as a matter of course. As a girl's divine right. So it comes as a bit of a shock to realise you're not necessarily going to get it. That this is as good as it gets. First you're angry, as I certainly was and there are rows, furious rows because you can't believe you've been so short-changed, but then a sort of post-purchase dissonance sets in. You're irritated, you'd like to take it back, get a refund, try something else, but at the end of the day it's just too much effort. So you live with it, let it grow on you, try to get used to it. And to some extent you do get used to it.' She looked over my shoulder, into the past, nodding slightly. Then her face hardened. 'But not that summer. No, no, that summer I hadn't got used to it at all. I was still at the good old angry stage. Gloomy resignation had not by any means set in and I was livid.' She looked at me sharply. 'And fed up with being constantly blamed for not having produced any babies!'

I jumped. 'Wh-what?'

'Your father was desperate for children. In all honesty I think that's probably why he married me. He took one look at my childbearing hips and thought, She'll do. Then when I still hadn't conceived after four years he made up his mind it was all my fault. Penny had just been born and we were all up at Kilmarnoch with the baby. Your father was at his most – well, cruel, actually. That's

387

the only word. He more or less pointed the finger in public, pondered aloud at dinner parties as to why it was that other women could have babies and I couldn't, wondered how the dickens he'd managed to marry a barren one, what on earth could be wrong with me.'

She swallowed hard and bit her lip. 'And of course, I naturally assumed it *was* my fault because I knew he'd fathered Patrick and he certainly thought it was my fault because he knew he'd fathered Patrick too.' She grinned. 'Sometimes I'd even deliberately irritate him, say something like – "But darling, how can you be so sure, it could be something to do with you, couldn't it? Couldn't you be firing blanks?" I'd watch him go absolutely puce in the face, clench his fists and almost implode as he struggled to resist the temptation to bellow – "No, you silly cow! It can't possibly be my fault because I already have a son!"' She laughed, but it tailed off into a sigh. 'Yes, that summer at Kilmarnoch. God, how I hated the place, year after year after bloody year!'

I blinked, shocked by her vehemence. 'But I thought you loved it there.'

She looked at me absently. 'Did you, darling? Yes, well, I suppose it wouldn't be quite true to say I loathe it now. I learned to tolerate it because you and Laura loved it so much but I'm afraid midges, driving rain and gutting fish on a riverbank is not actually my idea of a holiday. Give me India or Thailand any day.'

'Thailand!' I gasped. 'Have you ever been?'

'No.' She smiled. 'Probably never will now.'

I caught my breath, silenced. Not for the first time I realised there was much I didn't know about my mother. About how she'd subjugated herself for my father, for Laura and for me. But she hadn't had to do that for me, I thought fiercely, and I resented the fact that she had. God, if she'd so much as mentioned that she'd wanted to travel to any of those places I'd have been down at

388

the travel agents buying her the tickets – God, I'd have gone with her! Then a seeping doubt crept into my mind. Or would I? Might I not have dismissed it as one of Mum's funny ideas and not have bothered? After all, she never made a fuss, did she? My chest felt tight suddenly. It hurt me terribly that I'd never properly got to know her, never bothered to find out what made her tick. My own mum.

'And of course,' she went on, 'being up there by the river always reminded me of your father's affair with Madelaine. Not that it hurt any more, quite the opposite in fact. It just rammed home to me how stupid I'd been not to take my chance when I'd had it. It was as if fate had handed it to me right there on a plate, a month before I was due to be married and said: "Go on, Daphne, take it! Quick, run with it!" But I didn't. I fumbled it, dropped my chance . . . God, in my own quiet way I even *fought* for him.' She gave a hollow laugh. 'And for what?'

She looked beyond me, out of the window. Her eyes were far away. 'I used to go for walks that summer, solitary walks, down to the beach, along the cliffs, by the river, thinking, cursing myself for being such a fool. Telling myself I should get out now while I didn't have children. But I was still too scared. Scared of what everyone would think and say, scared of what would happen to me, but most of all – *scared of him*. I know it makes me sound like a complete wimp, Tess, but he was all I had, you see and he has – *had*,' she corrected herself, 'such a hold on me. Such power.' Her eyes swivelled back from the window and looked at me squarely. 'He's a bully, of course.'

I nodded. 'I know,' I whispered. Suddenly I had an awful thought. 'Not—'

'Oh no,' she said quickly. 'Not that. Just mentally.'

I nodded, relieved.

She grimaced. 'Just as bad in a way. The only thing is, you don't have the bruises to prove it.'

We were silent for a moment. I tried not to think about what she might have been through, how much I'd never known.

'Anyway,' she went on briskly, 'one day I was walking – and crying – by the river as usual and I bumped into Hamish.' She paused. 'No, that's not right, I didn't bump into him. I was sitting with my head on my knees, crying by the river when I suddenly realised he was there beside me. He didn't say anything, just stayed there while I sort of snivelled away next to him, trying to get control.'

I stared at her. 'Go on.'

She coloured slightly. 'Must I, darling? I mean it just sort of went from there. He comforted me, put his arm round me, I put my head on his shoulder, he stroked my hair as I remember and – well, that was that really.'

'You mean there? By the river?'

'Well, no, we went – somewhere.'

'To the hut?' I squeaked.

She looked at me quickly. 'Yes. How did you know?'

'Oh! I er – guessed, that's all.' My mind boggled. Talk about history repeating itself.

She looked at me sharply. 'You're shocked.'

'No! No, I'm not actually. Well, only in the sense that it's a surprise, so unexpected and you are after all my—'

'Mother.'

'Quite.'

We were silent for a moment, watching as the crowd milled around in front of us, ebbing and flowing, hats tilting this way and that, talking, drinking.

'If I told you that it was the happiest, most fulfilling time of my life would that make it any easier for you?' she said quietly.

I looked at her sharply. 'It's not a question of making

390

it easier for me. If you must know, I'm glad. I'm glad you had that time, had some happiness.' I paused and bit my lip. 'Does Hamish know?'

'That you're his daughter?' She shook her head. 'No, I never told him. But he's always been there for me, Tess, he's always been my friend.'

I nodded, thinking back to all the times I'd seen them fishing the river together, year after year, quite often on their own, upstream, on distant pools, shoulder to shoulder. I'd never given it a second thought.

'He's a good man you know, you mustn't be ashamed.'

I shook my head. 'I'm not.'

I was surprised, in fact, how totally unashamed, unshocked and unfazed I was by all this. If someone had told me at sixteen that my father wasn't my father I probably would have gone into a flat spin, got into a terrible mess, experimented with all manner of dubious substances, stuffed things up my nose, into my arms, down my throat, gone in for therapy and counselling, felt it was a marvellous excuse to get thoroughly mixed up, and consequently come out at the end a totally screwed-up individual. But now, at the ripe old age of thirty with two children of my own and set against my own heavy domestic backdrop, it really didn't seem too cataclysmic in the scheme of things. I mean, so what? My father wasn't my father, but I was still the same person, wasn't I? Yes, OK, maybe later on I might feel slightly taken aback, a bit rocked by it all, I might even get out the old holiday snaps, search feverishly for one of Hamish by the riverbank, look for resemblances. Doubtless I'd feel some delayed shock, feel bewildered, uprooted, cry a bit, maybe I'd even persuade Mummy to tell Hamish who I was. And then perhaps I'd want to get to know him better. Go on my own to Scotland, spend some time with him. Or, then again, maybe I wouldn't. Maybe I'd want to keep it all safely locked away in the past, where it had been for the last thirty years. Maybe I'd still want Hamish to be the retired gillie from the river and me to be the vicar's daughter from Claygate. Right at this moment, I didn't know. Because right now all that came shining through, clear as a megawatt light bulb, was not the fact that the man I'd been calling Daddy for the past thirty years was not actually biologically related to me, nor even that the old man by the river who helped me to wind in fish on a regular basis *was* my father . . . No, the one single, glorious light that lasered its way through this ghastly heap of old marriages, old affairs, old bitterness and old bones, was that Patrick was not in any way shape or form my brother. We were not, by any stretch of the imagination, related.

I felt excitement bubbling up inside me, but tried to calm it down, quell it. I turned to my mother.

'So, Patrick and I—'

'Are free to do exactly as you please.' She looked at me sharply. 'Not that I would necessarily encourage it, but it is your choice, Tess. You see, I wouldn't condemn it either.' She struggled to get a balance. 'All I mean is, whatever you do, don't get to my age and look back regretfully. It's not worth it.'

I looked at her sitting there in her smart navy suit, her small pillbox hat with veil perched on her grey curls, her discreet diamond brooch placed just so on her lapel, the perfect vicar's wife. Who would ever guess a life of heartache, misery and savage regrets?

'No, I won't,' I said quietly.

I reached across and gave her hand a sudden squeeze. She squeezed mine back. Our eyes watered simultaneously. We sat there, side by side in the window seat and I realised that, apart from when I was a small child, this was the closest I'd ever got to my mother. It was a glorious, joyous moment. She felt it too, I know

392

she did, and we sat there together, hands clasped, blinking back the tears, savouring it greedily.

Suddenly I knew that I wanted more of this. I wanted to feel this way with Patrick. I needed to see him now, to feel a similar sort of happiness, to get that rush of joy, to have just a few, wonderful, uncomplicated moments before things got oh so incredibly screwed up as they inevitably would. It was so long since I'd felt this happy and I wanted it to go on and on. I wanted to be selfish, to think about me. I could feel my heart beginning to pound. I stood up.

'Mummy, I think I'm going to slip away for a bit.'

She nodded, knowing exactly where I was going. She watched me.

I flicked my tongue nervously over my lips. 'Listen, you couldn't just tell David I felt a bit unwell, could you? Say I won't be long and – and that I'll make my own way home?'

She smiled. 'No, darling, I won't do that. You must make your own excuses.'

I flushed and looked at my feet, ashamed. 'OK, well I'll explain when I get home then,' I mumbled. It had begun already, hadn't it – the lying, the deceit; it was already getting underway. But I still wanted those moments, I thought desperately.

I bent down and kissed her cheek. 'Bye, Mummy.'

'Take care, Tess.'

'I will.'

I turned and disappeared into the crowd, giving her one last backward look as she sat watching me, framed by the window, hands clasped tightly in her lap. Then I slipped away.

Outside I flagged a taxi down.

'Where to, luv?'

I stared at the driver. Could I do this?

'Give us a clue, darlin'.'

'Cork Street, please,' I said decisively.

I jumped in. Yes, I could. I *could* do it, and I would. I sat in the back, my heart pounding with excitement. I wanted to run there, like I used to run on the beach when I was young, tearing along the London pavements, ducking and weaving through the crowds, but my ankle put paid to anything as impulsive and romantic as that so instead I leaned forward in my seat and urged my cab along.

'Come on, come on,' I muttered.

The driver's window shot back. 'Doing my best, luv, but these back streets are murder at this time of day. You'd be better off walking.'

We were stationary now. Would Patrick still be at the gallery? If not, where was he staying? Surely he wouldn't go straight back to Scotland? I looked around in desperation at the clogged streets. Damn it, I could hobble faster than this. I got out, pressed a fiver into the driver's hand and limped off like I'd never limped before. As I flashed past shop windows I caught sight of my reflection. It was still pretty strange sartorially speaking, but the odd thing was that my face had changed. It looked more alive, younger, more like – yes, more like Tessa Fergusson than Tessa Hamilton. Well there you are, I thought joyfully, sweeping my hair back off my forehead like I used to wear it when I was young. Perhaps I'd come back at last!

As I rounded the corner into Cork Street I literally bumped into a street-trader selling bright silk scarves.

'Ooops – sorry!'

I was about to move on, but a vivid length of fuchsia silk caught my eye and on an impulse, I bought it. It suited my mood. Grinning, I wound it around my neck and hurried off. I reached up and touched it as I neared the gallery. I'd remember this scarf, I thought. It would represent freedom, the first thing I bought after – after what, Tess? No decisions, remember, no plans, nothing remotely concrete.

I reached the gallery and stopped outside, peering through the window excitedly. It was dark, the lights had all been turned off except for a tiny lamp on the front desk and – oh God, it was empty. Everyone had gone. My heart stopped for a moment in panic, but then through the gloom at the back of the room, I spotted movement. Two men were talking, coming this way, and Patrick was definitely one of them. As they moved into the semi-light of the main front room I watched. Patrick's head was bowed; he was listening intently to the Frenchman. He stroked his chin thoughtfully, nodded, then threw his head back and flicked a piece of dark hair out of his eyes. I felt a sudden rush of – was it love? I didn't know, but whatever it was certainly had a proprietorial element to it. He could be mine again, I thought excitedly, if I wanted him. Here he was doing his own particular thing, painting his pictures, exhibiting them, seemingly on his own, except that with the wave of a wand I could be part of it, part of his life, if that's what I wanted. And the thing was that if I did, it would be *my* decision, *my* choice, no one else's and certainly not my father's.

So – how had he done, I wondered, at this, his first major exhibition? I glanced swiftly round the walls and for the first time saw the beautiful pictures which previously had been obscured by beautiful people. Landscapes and seascapes full of rich swirling colour abounded. As did the little red stickers. I puffed with pride. He'd done well.

Just then the Frenchman turned and gestured at a picture near the window and saw me standing there. His arm froze, high in the air in mid-gesticulation. His face darkened and he advanced towards me furiously.

'Pees off!' he shrieked, flicking me away with his hand

like a fly. 'Go on, pees off, you mad crazy woman!'

I grinned and gave him a dinky little wave back. He looked around furiously, desperate no doubt for a large heavy object to hurl through the window at me. It was probably just as well Patrick wasn't a sculptor. In the end he settled for the telephone.

'I call the poleece!' he squeaked, brandishing the receiver.

Patrick glanced over at me and put a restraining hand on his arm. He had a quiet word with his hot-blooded friend who, looking only slightly mollified, did at least remove his hand from the telephone, only to clench it into a fist and shake it furiously at me instead. He then seized Patrick by the shoulders, kissed him passionately on both cheeks and then with a final throat-slitting gesture at me – a nice touch, I thought – turned and stalked back into the dark of his back room again.

Patrick smiled and came out to meet me.

'He'd like me dead,' I breathed in awe.

'Oh no, much worse. He'd like you strung up on his walls as a live exhibit for people to throw darts at.' He shut the gallery door behind him. 'So you're back.'

'I am. I came to tell you something.'

'You've made a decision already?'

'Nope, that's what I came to tell you. Come on.' I breezed off in front of him, my hurt ankle forgotten. He fell in step beside me and I turned and grinned up at him as we went. 'I'm not going to make a decision, Patrick, because you see I can't. And since I can't make it, I won't. So instead, I've got a new set of rules.'

Patrick raised his eyebrows. 'Go on.'

'First of all we make no plans. We have no heavyweight discussions and no demands are made by either party.'

He frowned. 'Ever? Isn't that slightly unrealistic?'

'It may be but I'm fed up with realism. I'm sick to the back teeth of it, if you must know. I'm fed up with all the soul-searching and agonising it entails when all I really want to do is just *be* with you again, get to know you again, to talk, to laugh, to *enjoy* myself with you.'

His mouth twitched. 'I see. You're looking for undiluted frivolity, is that it?'

I laughed. 'Something like that. Something totally pleasurable, anyway. I'm fed up with being fed up. I want to laugh, for God's sake, not cry all the time!'

He shook his head, a wry grin on his face. 'No pleasure without pain, Tess.'

'That's as maybe but we can at least have the pleasure before we get to the pain, can't we? Not vice versa?' I glanced at my watch refusing to be deflated. 'And at the moment I've got precisely half an hour before I have to get back so let's make it snappy.'

He laughed. 'Right. So tell me, where exactly is this fun-packed half-hour to take place?'

'Oh, I don't know,' I said airily, enjoying myself already. 'Wherever you like, really. I had no fixed venue in mind but I suppose an attractive London park complete with bench and daisy-strewn grass would suit?'

'Fine. Limp on, Miss Macduff, I'm in your delightfully frivolous hands.'

Together we wandered towards Green Park. It was still warm and a mild evening breeze ruffled my hair. He didn't say anything as we walked but I was aware that he was looking at me.

'You look different,' he observed eventually.

'It's the scarf.' I put my hand up to my neck.

'No, more than that, something else. You look younger.'

I smiled. 'That's because I've changed my attitude. From now on, Patrick, I'm only allowing youthful thoughts to filter through my consciousness. I'm blocking out all the elderly, rational ones and going back to my instincts, which you've got to admit is much more fun.

You see, the way I see it, there's no point in letting this situation get to us. We just have to let it run, because at the end of the day,' I threw up my hands, 'what will be will be, and any other timeworn clichés you care to mention.'

'You mean go with the flow? Play it by ear? Lap of the gods and all that?'

I laughed. 'Perfect.'

'*Que sera sera*?'

I grinned. 'Maybe just a bit *too* timeworn, and anyway, we had it earlier in English. Perhaps you missed it, but I think you're getting the idea. There's simply no point in torturing ourselves. We'll just throw ourselves into it with gusto and see what happens.'

'Gusto, eh? I like the sound of that.'

My heart was beating wildly now. I felt scared but very excited. We'd reached the park. The deckchairs had all been stacked away but we found a handy bench that still had a smattering of sunlight on it. As I sat down I could almost feel my eyes shining, every nerve tingling. Yes, this was great, this was a glorious feeling. For the first time in ages I felt really alive and it felt terrific. He sat down next to me.

'Is this OK? I mean I'm new to this game, Tess, all right if I sit next to you like this?'

'Perfect.'

'And pass the time of day?'

'Exactly.'

'And as long as there are no searching questions . . .'

'I'll tell you no despicable lies.'

'So we just – meet and chat?'

'Almost.' I looked up at him quickly.

He held my eyes. 'Ah. I wondered.'

I felt myself flushing. 'Crazy not to, don't you think? Especially since we're talking about instincts here. And anyway, if we don't, how on earth will we ever know?'

My heart pounded as I looked at him. I'd almost dared myself to say it, to be a brazen hussy, to be selfish, to seize my bit of life at whatever the cost. And I had, I'd done it.

He stared at me. 'So you won't come away with me but you'd like an affair, is that it?'

'That's it.'

For an awful moment I thought he was going to turn me down. Claim his love was too high, too moral, too pure, that he could only exist on a more elevated, exclusive plane, that it was all or nothing with him. Then I saw his mind begin to whir in a different direction. Because after all, an affair is only despicable if one is not involved.

'I'll stay here in London,' he said quietly, thinking as he spoke. 'If I can paint in Italy I can paint here. I'll rent a studio, with a couple of rooms, maybe even a balcony. In Chelsea perhaps, with a view of the river. For the moment though, we can go to a hotel. I'm booked in at Claridges. We can go there.'

I gulped. A flat in Chelsea. Claridges. Why did such smart locations suddenly sound so . . . tacky? Horrified, I felt my bravado slipping, my frivolity ebbing away and taking – oh my God – my libido with it! No, no, come back, I thought desperately. I can do this, I know I can, I can have an affair! I can go to a hotel, piece of cake, honestly, and anyway I have to because otherwise – otherwise how on earth will I ever know? How on earth will I ever get him out of my system?

'Patrick, let's not talk about that now,' I said quickly. 'That can all be worked out later, can't it? Can't we just – well, enjoy being here together, for a few more minutes? I have to get back soon.'

He smiled and slid his hand along the back of the bench and nodded. 'Sure.'

I stared out at the evening haze over Green Park,

breathing heavily as his hand stroked my hair. So. An affair, eh, Tess? I shut my eyes trying to block out the word, trying not to let it spoil this moment. I felt his warm hand thread through my hair to the back of my neck, and after a while, it was all I could feel. The soft caressing, the exquisite lingerings. My body seemed to turn to liquid jelly. Bliss. I could hear myself breathing, in fact I was breathing so hard it was snorting out of my nostrils like a dragon. I seemed to have far too much air all of a sudden, but yes, this was definitely more like it. Let's have no more talk of hotels and flats, Patrick. Let's have no more planning, no more conniving, let's just encourage the passion to sneak up on us and sweep us off our feet, away and down into the abyss until we've fallen and it's much too late. Until it's not our fault. Let's take refuge in a grand passion, let's be overtaken by events, by the power of something much stronger than our intellects, so that in the end – oooh, yes, that's wonderful, keep on doing that, Patrick – so that in the end they can all just throw their hands up in despair and say, 'Well, the girl just simply . . . couldn't . . . help it . . .'

His hand slipped round from the back of my neck and turned my face towards his. One finger stroked my cheek. I gasped, whinnied almost – embarrassingly – all my senses sizzling with desire. He gazed down at me but still he didn't kiss me, he just looked, watched, drinking me in, and not just my face but all of me, my shoulders, my hands, my arms – up and down roved his eyes as if he wanted to roll back twelve years all in one glance. I tingled all over; it was as if his hands were caressing me. I began to tremble, my toes curled, my blood pumped. Come on, come ON, I urged, I can't take much more of this, when – suddenly, he froze. He frowned. Looked down at my feet. I blinked. What? Why had he suddenly got stuck down there? What was so compelling about my feet?

'Your shoes,' he muttered.

My shoes? God, what about them?

'What about them?' I breathed, still staring hard into his eyes, willing him to carry on. I was beginning to panic now. Come on, Patrick, get on with it! I've decided to do it now and it was no mean decision, I can tell you, so sodding well get on with it before I lose my nerve!

'I've seen them somewhere before.'

Realising that the moment was totally blown, I joined him in the contemplation of my footwear. Oh yes, charming. My filthy old red loafers complete with a cut down one side to get my foot into. Not at all the thing for smart London streets or even a funeral for that matter, but quite simply the only shoes I could get my swollen foot into.

'Russell and Bromley,' I muttered into his ear, nibbling it briefly. 'Last year's sale, thirty-nine ninety-nine.' Now come on, Patrick, let's go!

'Yes, that's it. Down by the river.'

I stopped in mid-nibble. What on earth did he mean?

His face had become terribly pale. He took his hand off my neck. Drew it back along the bench. His eyes were still on the shoes.

'Yes, outside the hut, that night when I—' Suddenly he turned to me aghast, his eyes incredulous. 'It was you, wasn't it?'

I stared at him. My mouth was dropping open now of its own accord.

'It was you I saw through the window, thrashing around in Willie's hut that night. It was you, Tess, *wasn't it?*'

Chapter Twenty-seven

I stared at him, aghast. After a moment of sheer immobilised terror, my mind went into frantic overdrive. It scuttled around like a pin-ball machine, looking for a way out. Had I perhaps lent the shoes to someone, to Laura perhaps, or Penny? Could either of them have kicked them off with gay abandon outside the hut and then frolicked around in the nude inside it? Both would fit the Willie bill, but . . . No. *He knew it was me.* His blue, piercing eyes were the trap and I was the rat. All of a sudden I had a violent desire to be watching *The Antiques Roadshow* at 42, Pelham Road with a gin and tonic in one hand and a packet of Phineas Fogg's in the other.

'It's not what you think,' I whispered.

He gave a thin smile. 'I see. Not what I think, eh? What is it then, exactly?' His face had gone very pale under his tan.

'Well,' I struggled, 'Willie and I – it wasn't planned, it just sort of happened.' God, this was awful. 'I bumped into him down by the river one evening and we just sort of – slipped into it.' I winced – that sounded terrible! Far too explicit. I hastened on. 'But the thing is I changed my mind and we never – well, we never actually did it.'

'Like hell!' he scoffed.

'It's true, I swear it! We just larked around a bit, then fell asleep together.'

'Oh, sweet,' he sneered. 'A little slumber party after

403

some energetic nude wrestling.'

'Look, I know it sounds unlikely, but it's the truth, I didn't—'

'Tess, I saw you! I was there, remember? I saw you with my own eyes! And whether you did the dirty deed or not, frankly, hardly matters, does it? You certainly weren't having a cosy cup of Ovaltine!'

'No,' I admitted, 'I wasn't, and I'm not proud of myself, it was a ghastly mistake, but – well, that's all it was, Patrick. A mistake, and to be honest, I don't even know why it happened. It just did!'

God, this was embarrassing.

Patrick's top lip curled in disgust. 'You fancied him.'

I shrugged uncertainly. 'Maybe it was just lust, but there was something else. Something . . .' I bit my lip. Suddenly it all flooded back – of course! I'd been crying – I'd been upset about Patrick.

'It was because of you, because you went off with Josie!'

'Ah, so it was my fault?' His mouth was set in a thin line now and a muscle was pumping away in his cheek.

'Well, indirectly, yes. I was jealous, and when Willie found me I was crying, and I suppose I just sort of – rebounded into his arms.'

He stared at me coldly. I licked my lips nervously.

'Look, Patrick, it was just sex, OK? And it's not as if we went the whole way. And any way, there was nothing meaningful about it so what difference does it make?' I said this desperately, aware that I was trying to brazen it out in a laddish sort of way. It lasted about half a second before one lad shrivelled under the other lad's penetrating blue gaze.

I stared down at the grass feeling my face flame, fiddling with the fringe of the pink scarf in my lap. There was a terrible silence.

'Is this really you speaking, Tess?' he said at length, a

slight tremor in his voice. 'Tessa Fergusson? Sweet, innocent Tess of one boyfriend and one husband? "Just sex"? Since when have you been so free with your sexual favours? So keen to resort to nothing meaningful?'

I stared at my shoes, those damn shoes.

'What are you, just another frustrated housewife who can't wait to get her leg over with the resident holiday stud because her husband's not paying her enough attention or something? That's why they all go to bed with Willie you know – *Willie*! Of all people, he's renowned for it – Jesus it's a local joke! How many London women will he get this summer . . . and now you,' he said bitterly. 'Another notch in his belt.'

'I've told you,' I muttered. 'I'm not another notch, and anyway I didn't go looking for sex, I was just upset and Willie just happened to be there. He comforted me, he—'

'Shagged you? Oh yes, I can see how that must have been very comforting, very comforting indeed,' he sneered.

I gazed down at my hands. How awful. We were rowing. He didn't believe me. I could feel him slipping away, distancing himself.

'Patrick, I'm sorry,' I pleaded. 'Can't you just forgive me? It happened, it was a mistake and I'm sorry, but what more can I say apart from apologise? I mean, these things happen. Look at you with your Italian harem, your Marias and your Lucianas!'

'These things happen to men and a certain type of woman,' he said coldly. 'Women who look for sexual release with any Tom, Dick or Harry. They do not happen to women like you, or so I thought. Clearly I was wrong. Tell me, how often have you felt this urge?' His face was very grim now.

I boggled. 'Never! Good heavens, never, I'm too flipping knackered most of the time. I've never slept with anyone other than you and David!'

'I said how often have you felt the urge, Tess, not how often have you done it,' he said harshly.

I looked at him over in the far corner of the bench. His black hair highlighted his white face and his eyes looked strangely pale. It was as if emotion was wiping away all the colour.

'I don't,' I whispered, 'feel the urge.' God, why was I whispering? And why on earth did this remind me of something?

'Don't lie,' he spat, his lip curling again. 'You feel it all the time, don't you? You lie in your marriage bed night after night dreaming about it, about doing it with other men – any man! You fantasise, don't you? Well, let me tell you something, Tess – that's tantamount to the real thing. You might just as well go out there and get your kit off and get on with it!'

I stared at him. He was right, of course – I'd done a terrible thing, a dreadful thing, but his reaction seemed over the top, somehow. Suddenly I realised who he reminded me of. Yes, it was my father. The hectoring tone of voice, the stream of vile invective. I glanced back at him. Well – why not? said a little voice in my head. He is after all your father's son, isn't he? A wave of revulsion threatened to wash over me. I looked away, told myself not to be ridiculous. This was Patrick, my Patrick, and he was justifiably furious. God, any man would be in his position. I'd just let him simmer down a bit. I'd sit here quietly, wouldn't say anything for a minute. I avoided his eye and stared straight ahead.

Just in front of us two little girls were playing on the gravel path, picking up the stones in handfuls and throwing them into the air. A woman, not their mother, a nanny possibly, was admonishing them, telling them to stop, brushing the dirt off their hands. I was aware that Patrick was staring at me but I concentrated like mad on those girls, looking to see if their hands were clean, if their dresses were dirty.

'Just the two of us, Laura said,' he muttered quietly, breaking the silence. 'Just David and me. Bullshit.'

I swung round, frowned. 'Laura? What are you talking about? When did she say that?'

'And now I find that there have been others. Lots of others, no doubt. And that you're no different from Penny and all the other sexed-up little tarts who can't wait for their husbands to go to work so they can slip their knickers off and hop into bed with the first travelling salesman or plumber or window-cleaner who takes their fancy.'

'Penny's not like that,' I said, horrified. 'And neither am I!'

'You're all the same,' he muttered. 'Scum.'

I gasped. 'What?' I gazed at his profile, hard and uncompromising. Rather shakily I found my voice.

'So one little indiscretion changes everything, does it? Suddenly I'm a sex-crazed tart. From being the only woman you've ever wanted I've rather unexpectedly plunged into the abyss. I'm a scarlet woman, fit only for Hellfire, is that it?'

He didn't answer, just sat staring into space, eyes narrowed.

'Look at me, Patrick,' I quavered. 'I'm still the same person.'

'Except Willie's had you,' he said bitterly.

I gazed at him, then nodded slowly. 'Ah yes, that's what it's all about, isn't it? Who's had what, little boys with their toys. Willie's had this one so it's not so good any more. And of course,' I went on, my voice trembling, 'you've always had all the best toys, haven't you? Always had every woman you ever wanted. God, you've turned them away in droves – Penny, Josie, half the Italian female population, no doubt – they all fell for the handsome, scowling, poor little rich boy and you could take your pick, couldn't you? Except for me. I was the one that got away. You wanted me, not because I was the best, but because you couldn't *have* me!'

'I loved you, Tess,' he said grimly.

I noted the past tense, whether deliberate or not, with a sharp intake of breath.

'If you loved me,' I went on quietly, 'this wouldn't matter as much as it clearly does. But this isn't about love, is it? It's about obsession. And about winning. But now that the prize has been tampered with, now that it's soiled, it's not so covetable, is it? You've had a space in your trophy cabinet for twelve years. Now you discover that the cup is a little bit tarnished and it's not the same thing, is it?'

He didn't reply.

'That's not love, Patrick, that's a spoiled child completing his collection.'

I stood up shakily and wound my scarf around my neck. He looked up quickly.

'Where are you going?'

'Home.'

He stared at me, wondering if I was calling his bluff or if I meant it. I meant it. He licked his lips. There was a silence.

'Look, all right,' he faltered eventually. 'I'm sorry. Sit down and we'll talk this through sensibly. I probably did overreact, but you did rather spring this on me.'

'I didn't spring anything on you,' I said coolly. 'You spotted my shoes.'

'Yes, well, whatever. I'm sorry, OK? I was surprised, that's all. Shocked.' He flicked his dark hair back from his face. 'But I think I can overlook it.'

I stared down at him. 'Well, I can't.'

'What?'

'Overlook your reaction.'

408

'My reaction!' He laughed. 'For God's sake, my reaction was perfectly understandable under the circumstances! I'm a red-blooded heterosexual male and I'm in love with you so I'm bound to be as jealous as hell, aren't I? What did you expect me to do, pat you on the back and say – terrific! So Willie's slipped you a length! Good on yer girl, have another crack at him next year?'

'No, but I didn't expect a stream of misogynist abuse either.'

'Misogynist? Me? Oh, don't be ridiculous.'

'Oh yes, you are,' I said warmly. 'Thank God, though.'

'Thank God for what?'

'Thank God you saw my shoes, that we had this conversation, that it's not too late.'

Patrick was on his feet now; he grabbed my hands. I pulled away, but he lunged at me and caught the ends of my scarf, drawing me towards him.

'I'm sorry,' he said desperately. 'Don't go, I really am sorry. I just couldn't bear to think you were like all the rest, but you're not really, I know that.'

'All the rest?'

'Oh everyone,' he said impatiently, 'Penny, Luciana, Kirsten – God, my mother even!' He gave a short hysterical laugh.

'Your mother?' I stared at him.

He backtracked quickly. 'No. Nothing. Forget I said that, I'm just – well, I'm upset.'

His *mother*? I gazed at him. He knew. He knew about Madelaine, that she'd had an affair, and he'd known all along. He'd known when he was just a boy, when I didn't know. When it would have mixed me up too, made me a bit crazy. When he was so hurt and rebellious, so dark and brooding, staring out to sea, loathing his parents, he'd known! Known he wasn't his father's son. But had he known about Daddy? No, he can't have done. And I certainly wasn't going to tell him. Suddenly I felt terribly sorry for him. For the pain and hurt he must have been through. His father hating him because he knew he wasn't his son and Patrick hating the pair of them for making it so. I felt compassion for him but I didn't feel love.

He was still holding on tightly to my scarf. 'Patrick, please let me go.'

He stared at me, knowing I meant it, that I was really going. I saw him tighten his grip. I stepped back, but as I did so, could feel the scarf, which was wound twice round my neck, tighten.

'Let me go,' I said quietly.

He blinked. I saw him glance down at the scarf in his hands. Then he looked up at me. All of a sudden the park seemed very quiet, very still. It was getting late now. Most people had gone home. My heart began to hammer. I licked my lips.

'Patrick, let go of my scarf and we'll sit down again,' I whispered. 'I promise I won't go home yet. We'll just sit and talk, OK?'

I looked into his eyes. Suddenly I felt very scared. There was something I didn't recognise there. And then I realised there was an awful lot I didn't know about this man. This man I'd known for just a month, twelve years ago. I gulped, but only just; the scarf was quite tight. I swivelled my eyes right then left, wondering if anyone would hear if I screamed, wondering if I should yank the scarf from his hands and make a run for it. Suddenly he let go.

His hands fell to his sides and his head dropped in defeat. I stepped back hurriedly, unwinding the scarf from my neck in relief. He hadn't hurt me but it had been quite tight.

He sat down on the bench again, his back hunched. My heart was pounding. I wanted to go, I badly wan to go, but I made myself stay.

'Do you want to talk?' I whispered.

For a moment he didn't answer, then he looked up with a strange, unnatural smile.

'No, there'll be no more talk today, Tess. If it's all the same to you I'll resist the offer of therapy, the few minutes of park-bench counselling. You've already heard more about me in the last few minutes than I care to reveal. It wouldn't do for you to hear any more – you might get me locked up or at the very least committed to long stretches on the psychiatrist's couch.' He gave a twisted smile. 'Go on, be off with you. Go back to David and your children.'

I looked down at him sitting there, shoulders hunched, hands tightly clasped. His hair was really quite heavily flecked with grey from this angle; funny how I'd never noticed it before. Suddenly he looked smaller too; thinner, older and his fashionable Armani suit looked exactly what it was. Expensive packaging designed to make the older man look younger. I had a lump in my throat, a lump of sadness, but at the same time never had I wanted to be somewhere else so badly.

I looked around. The park was nearly deserted now. Unfriendly, alien territory. I felt an awful wave of horror. What was I *doing* here, anyway? Why wasn't I at home, putting the children to bed, reading them stories, cooking David's supper? My hand went to my mouth, I felt sickened by myself. I looked down at his shoes – trendy, black Italian loafers and thought of David's dark brown English brogues. I fiddled with the strap on my handbag, scuffed the dirt with my toe.

'Well, I will go then actually, if that's all right.'

He gave me a wounded smile. 'Of course it's all right. You're free to do exactly as you please, you know that.'

I nodded. 'Right. Goodbye then.'

There was a pause.

'Goodbye, Mrs Hamilton.'

Perhaps it was a last-ditch attempt. Perhaps he said it to conjure up visions of bourgeois respectability, a straitjacket I'd never break out of now, but if that was the case, it backfired. All it conjured up for me was home, glorious home, my children, my husband, my garden, my security, my nest, and my dazzling, mind-boggling stupidity at putting it all at risk. I turned on my heel and walked quickly out of the park.

I went as fast as I could, breathing deeply, filling my lungs with clean fresh air. As I went through the park gate I paused to let the two little girls and their nanny pass through ahead of me. They smiled up cheekily as they pushed on ahead, and I found myself almost reeling as I watched them go. I had to hang on to the railings for support for a second. I touched my forehead briefly with my hand. Was I mad? Insane? How could I have been such a fool? Risked it all, the children, the whole fabric of my life for a man who'd just parachuted back into my life after twelve years of absence? A man who, because I'd loved him then, I assumed I still loved now? I walked on in a daze. But then, I'd always worked on that assumption, hadn't I? In some kind of warped, crazy way I'd assumed that because no conclusion had ever been reached, we must still be in love, back there in that same position or thereabouts, simmering away gently on the back burner, ready to bubble up into a boiling passion at a moment's notice.

I shook my head. What a fool I'd been. It wasn't as if I'd really known him properly then and I certainly didn't know him now – and how can you love someone you don't know? And what about the bits I *did* know now – what about those bits that reminded me of – horrors – my father?

I clattered down the steps to Green Park Tube. No, no, come on, Tess, that's not altogether fair. You're just trying to make your father's cap fit Patrick, force the jigsaw into place, make the picture more grisly than it really is but – all the same, I pondered, biting my lip, it was odd, wasn't it, the way Patrick had that same desire to control as Daddy did? The way he'd held my scarf back then, for instance? I was quite sure now that he wouldn't have hurt me . . . but it was enough to frighten me, and he must have known I was scared. And that strange way he had of suddenly spitting venom – just like Daddy, as if it was all simmering away inside waiting to spew out at a moment's notice, and that awful, warped way of looking at women, madonnas or tarts, and the way he— Suddenly I stopped, shocked at myself.

Good heavens, Tess, steady on. I mean, half an hour ago you were ready to jump into bed with the man and now he's a bully, a tyrant and a misogynist? I walked slowly onto the platform. Wasn't *I* the one who was overreacting a teeny bit here? How come I didn't feel more of a wrench? A spot of – oh gosh I'll always have a soft spot for Patrick – wouldn't that be more normal? Yes, perhaps it would, but I didn't. All I thought was – thank God for a lucky escape.

I blinked in astonishment at this revelation and stepped onto a Tube bound for Earl's Court as if for all the world it were bound for Damascus. Yes, how odd – he almost *repulsed* me. I sank down in a seat and leaned my head back on the window. How extraordinary. He'd rattled my cage for twelve long years, but finally, and in a matter of minutes, the rattling had stopped. All was quiet. He'd gone for ever. Relief flooded through me, euphoria even, and it was so overpowering that I laughed out loud.

'Ha ha ha!'

I sat up and looked around with a grin. Yes, I was certainly getting some odd looks from my fellow commuters. The Indian lady opposite, swaddled in silks with her incongruous M&S cardigan over the top was staring at me in terror, her husband beside her was looking boot-faced in the opposite direction and the young girl next to him was peering nervously at me over the top of her *Woman's Own*, twiddling her long bleached hair. All of them were clearly wondering how long it would be until the train pulled into the next station and they could nip into the adjacent carriage. I wanted to lean forward, smile and say: 'It's OK, I'm not a nutter. I'm just wildly, ecstatically, deliriously happy! You see, I'm shot of him now and I can get on with my life!'

Yes, the best thing about all this, I acknowledged joyfully, was that I could get on with everything now, without the ghost of Patrick Cameron constantly hanging over me. Because however much I'd always denied his presence, I knew he'd always been there in the background of my mind, putting me off my stride, holding me back from doing the things I'd always intended to do. Like writing articles and children's books, the ones I'd had in my head since I was nineteen, the ones I'd always meant to write but had somehow felt were too wrapped up with my dreams of Patrick. Yes, subconsciously I'd shied away from all that. I'd had some misguided notion that writing in the spare room in Putney wouldn't be quite the same as writing on a sun-drenched terrace in Florence with my lover painting masterpieces in the studio beyond, that it would be a pale shadow of my creative life as I'd imagined it. But I knew now that that was crap. I'd put my life on hold for no good reason and now I wanted to get cracking.

The train rattled along the tracks and my mind rattled with it. I'd write while Hugo and Clemmie were at school. I'd clear out the spare room, make it into an office, and when they came home I'd spend more time with them. I didn't need an au pair! With two children at school it was crazy, I could do it all myself. I'd enjoy it, throw myself into it, take them round London on buses, go to museums, teach them to cook – all the things I'd meant to do with my children but somehow had never got round to. And I wanted to spend more time with David too. I didn't want us to flop exhausted in front of the telly every night with our Marks & Spencer suppers on our laps, I wanted to eat in the kitchen, have candles even, make an effort, do a cookery course, test out the recipes on him and not sneer at all that but *enjoy* it. Enjoy all those things I'd secretly boycotted thinking they'd make me dull, suburban, a housewife, so very married.

I hastened up the steps at Putney Bridge. My ankle hurt like hell now. As I limped past a pub I spotted a bin outside and instinctively tore off the pink scarf and threw it in. I wouldn't be needing *that* any more, would I? As I rounded the corner into Pelham Road, I stopped for a moment gazing up at our house. There it was, slap bang in the middle on the left-hand side, pale yellow with a bright blue front door and a black wrought-iron balcony above. A huge, gnarled old wisteria snaked all over the front, and in the front garden a flurry of roses – my roses – pink, white and red, frothed over the small brick wall. God, it was pretty. And whenever people had told me so, I'd looked at them in surprise thinking – is it? Hmm, yes I suppose it is, but after all it's only a semi in a row of semis, it's no big deal. Suddenly, I could see that it was. It was a humungously big deal. It was *home*.

I walked on slowly, staring at it. There was still so much to do, of course. I'd always meant to paint the little railings on the wall outside, grow a clematis round the door, put pots of geraniums on the balcony. And inside, the drawing-room curtains were still minus a pelmet – they'd been like that for three years. Jane Churchill had a sale next week. I'd go, queue up if needs be and – oh, Clemmie's bedroom, I'd always meant to make her a quilt. I'd do that too now, collect scraps of fabric, enjoy doing it! Oh yes, I decided happily, I was going to crawl along in the slow, safe lane of domesticity from now on. I was going to throw off the horrors of that fast, dangerous, adulterous lane, the one I'd so nearly swerved into. I wanted to write, to bake, make marmalade, be on the school committee – I hesitated. No, not that. I couldn't *quite* bring myself to do that . . .

I hastened up the garden path and opened the front door. David was sitting on the hall chair, telephone in hand. He quickly put it down when he saw me. He stood up. Flushed.

'Tess! Where the devil have you been?'

'David, I'm so sorry,' I gasped, falling against him and wrapping my arms round his waist. 'Please – don't ask me where I've been. I don't want you to ask me anything, I just want you to know that everything's all right now, everything's fine!'

I held on tight, burying my head in his soft, lambswool shoulder, breathing in his smell. Oh God, I was married to such a nice man – how come I'd never seen that before? It was as if I'd always had a smear over the lens, and the smear had been Patrick, always obscuring my view. But now I'd wiped him away; in ten, glorious minutes I'd wiped away twelve years of grime – but how awful that it had obscured the most important years of my life!

'Delighted to hear it, but where have you been?'

'Oh, just walking,' I said breathlessly. 'Sorry I deserted you at the funeral, I just needed to get away.' I glanced at the telephone. 'Who was that?'

'Oh, no one. Wrong number. Good God, look at your ankle, Tess – it's swollen up like an elephant's! Have you been limping round London on that? You are a fool. Come on, come and sit down.'

I grinned and let him support me down the hall to the kitchen.

'I know – a mad, stupid fool but I promise you, David,

416

I intend to put all my foolish ways behind me now, once and for all.'

I lowered myself into a chair and looked around the kitchen. Blue and yellow, very pretty. Good choice, Tess. How odd, it was as if I was seeing it for the first time. God, that doorframe could do with a lick of paint though, and look at the state of those windows . . .

'Tea?' David reached for the kettle.

'Please.' I sank back happily into the wheelback chair. Yes, please. Tea, comfort, home, you. I watched his back as he filled the kettle, reached up for the teapot on the top shelf. How like him just to make a pot of tea. Not a scene, not to give me the third degree, not insist on knowing exactly where I'd been, just a pot of tea. I felt a rush of love.

'David?'

'Hmm?' He was staring blankly into the caddy. 'Extraordinary isn't it, how no one can replace the tea-bags when they run out? Everyone's capable of taking tea-bags *out* but not of putting fresh ones *in*. Why not get a new packet out of the cupboard, I ask myself, or is that too much of a radical concept?'

I grinned. 'Beats me, darling.'

He was on his hands and knees now, rifling around in the store cupboard. He stood up. 'It's no good, the war of attrition is still raging in that larder. Everyone's waiting for someone else to buy the sodding things. It'll just have to be coffee.'

'Fine, fine, darling. Just *listen* a minute.'

'What?' He reached for the Nescafé.

'Forget the bloody coffee.' I limped over and put my arms round him. He turned. I smiled, reached up and stroked the back of his neck. 'Why don't we just go to bed?'

I stretched up on tiptoe and kissed his surprised mouth. 'Hmm? Does that sound like a good idea? Why

417

don't we just go upstairs, take our clothes off and—'

'She's in my bed again!' bellowed an angry voice behind us.

We jumped. I turned around and saw Hugo standing in the passageway, indignant in his pyjamas.

'Get her out,' he ordered. 'Right now! She's brought all her stupid dolls in with her and that one with the hole in its bottom has peed on my pillow!'

We sighed and unclinched.

'I'll go,' said David. 'Come on, Hugo. Clemmie!' he yelled as he mounted the stairs. 'Get back to your own bed!'

Hugo followed grimly then stopped and turned back.

'Were you two kissing?'

'Trying to,' I agreed.

'Oh yuk.' He looked suitably disgusted and went on upstairs. Then he stopped again and popped his head through the banisters. 'Mummy?'

'What?'

'If you're going to do it, don't shut the door like last time, OK? It's not fair.'

'Jesus,' I muttered. 'Just go to bed please, Hugo. NOW!'

I walked wearily back into the kitchen as the telephone rang. I sank down into a chair and picked it up.

'Tess, we have to talk,' said a cold voice.

I sighed. Oh hell, Laura. What an awful lot of ruffled feathers there were around at the moment. Last time I'd seen her was when I'd doused her in the gallery. That would all have to be smoothed out, of course, but although I was very much in a sorting-out mood, now was actually not the time.

'Definitely,' I agreed, 'and Laura, I'm so sorry about all that. There really is quite a simple explanation, but I'm a bit busy at the moment. Could we—'

'*I'm* busy too!' she retorted, clearly trying to out-bus

418

me. 'I can't talk either. But I'll see you tomorrow, in my lunch-hour. Twelve-thirty in the Harvey Nichols restaurant, all right?'

'Fine,' I said meekly. I knew I had to be meek, oh God I'd have to crawl.

'See you there,' she said grimly, 'and don't be late.'

I put the phone down and scratched my arm. Oh well, I thought sheepishly, I deserved all I got from her, I supposed. I looked bleakly round the kitchen. Heavens this place was a mess. Look at all that crap on the dresser - unopened letters, school reports, free magazines, socks, mouldy apple cores, headless dolls, and the bin was positively overflowing with rubbish. Didn't anybody think to take it out? Did they think Mary Poppins would just sail in and do it? I rolled up my sleeves and got to work. By the time David came back down I had my head in the oven and was scrubbing away for England.

'Won't be long,' I called from inside my Mr Muscle cage. 'Someone's cooked God knows *what* in here and just let it drip everywhere!' As if that someone, of course, hadn't been me.

'I'll just catch the news then,' came the muffled response.

Half an hour later I emerged, covered in muck and stinking of detergent, but my God I was happy. I folded my arms triumphantly. Yes, I was cleaning up all right. This was definitely the life. I grinned, threw the cloth in the sink and went into the sitting room, just as Trevor McDonald was shuffling his papers and bidding me a very good night over his spectacles. David was sprawled in the armchair in front of him, fast asleep. I smiled. Oh well, that was the end of my romantic evening; there'd be no waking him now. He wouldn't stir till he'd had at least two hours of comatose slumber, and then he'd stagger up to bed at about midnight. I removed his glasses, turned the television off and went upstairs to bed.

419

Chapter Twenty-eight

The following morning I had every intention of embarking on some serious domesticity. That is, until I opened my cookery book. Practically every recipe seemed to begin with something like: *If you don't have a smoke-house* . . . or *Take two pints of fresh Venison stock* . . .

'Bugger off,' I muttered, slamming it shut with irritation. The doorbell rang.

'Yes, I'm coming!' I barked as the ringing persisted. 'Oh Josie, it's you.'

She fell through the front door and ultimately onto me. I staggered back as she hung on to my shoulders, gasping with relief and looking rather wild about the eyes.

'Tess! Oh God, it's wonderful to see you. I can't tell you what a terrible time I've had!'

She staggered past me into the kitchen and sank down on a chair, panting hard. Then she stood up again and instantly jettisoned rucksack, hold-all, carrier bags, and layer upon layer of sweat-shirts and jackets until she'd swiftly transformed the place into an Aussie youth hostel. I followed her through and found a chair amidst the sea of shell-suit paraphernalia. She sank down again and lit a shaky cigarette.

'Jesus Christ,' she gasped, 'your bloody cousin! She made me wash the kitchen floor twice a day, and not with a mop but on my hands and knees.' She sucked hard on a Malboro Light, eyes wide with horror. 'She wouldn't let me smoke and I had to bloody well cook supper every night and even scrub their front step! That's positively Dickensian, isn't it? Jeeze, I thought she'd have me up the chimney next!'

I tutted and murmured something sympathetic, at the same time reflecting that actually, this was what all of us lily-livered employers would *like* these Aussie girls to do, but only Penny had the guts to do it. Front step, eh? Kitchen floor? Good on yer, Pen.

'*And* I had to clean the fridge out and wash the bath and *dry* it too, for heaven's sake – and dust all her poxy china ornaments and cut tomatoes into flipping water lilies *and* I had to look after Leonora all day long, too. That woman didn't lift a frigging finger!'

'Terrible,' I muttered, patting her hand.

'Talk about the white slave trade. If I'd had to stay there a moment longer I would have reported her to the Australian High Commission.'

She stubbed her cigarette out on one of my best saucers and flung her Doc Martened foot up on a chair. She gazed around appreciatively.

'God, it's nice to be back, Tess. Penny's place is so bloody antiseptic and perfect and up-yer-bum. This place is – well, it's lived in, isn't it? It's a real home.'

I looked around despondently, realising that despite my efforts to the contrary there was already a tottering pile of washing up in the sink, a pile of children's pyjamas under the table, a runnerbean in the milk jug and a Power Ranger face down in the butter. I rescued him and tossed him wearily in the sink, secretly yearning for a little more up-yer-bumness myself.

'All right if I catch Richard and Judy before I pick Clemmie up? I haven't seen it for a week, she wouldn't *let* me!' Josie informed me incredulously.

'Sure, sure,' I said weakly, watching her pert little Levi'd backside undulate casually into the playroom. 'But perhaps before it starts you could tidy the children's bedrooms? If you've got time, that is.' I scratched my neck hopefully.

She plucked an apple from the fruit bowl and consulted her watch. 'Nah. It's just about to start, but tell you what, if I get time I'll have a go later, OK?'

So saying, she sank into the sofa, swung her long denim legs up over the arm and sighed happily. Then she zapped on the telly with the remote control and sank her perfect white teeth into the apple. She smiled up at me.

'It's *so* nice to be back, Tess,' she informed me again warmly, as if perhaps I should be pleased and proud. Then she turned back to the television.

Oh is it, I thought grimly, folding my arms and watching from the doorway. A certain amount of steel was creeping into my soul. Yes, well enjoy it while you can, Josie, because nice though you are your days here are numbered. This house is poised for some radical changes and jettisoning the eldest of my three children is going to be one of them!

I stalked back into the kitchen and set about tidying up the mess, *her* mess, until my eye caught the clock. Half-past eleven! Jesus! I dropped the dustpan and brush in horror. I was still in my dressing gown, I hadn't had a bath yet and if I didn't get a move on I was going to be late for Laura and our lunch-date. I flew upstairs in a panic, jumped into the shower, threw on the first thing that came to hand and blundered downstairs and out of the house.

Forty minutes later I burst through the swing doors into the terribly tasteful Fifth Floor Restaurant at Harvey Nichols, panting and cursing, looking like somebody's grandmother and at least ten minutes late.

'Sorry,' I gasped to my unamused sister who was perched neatly at a corner table.

Her white cotton shirt looked crisp and flawless, her hair was silky and unruffled and her distinctly tight lips were leaving only the faintest trace of lipstick on her low tar cigarette. A tiny blue suede bag was swinging delicately from a chain on the back of her chair. I blinked. Was that hers or her dolly's, I wondered?

As I sat down opposite her, I flung my own, huge leather sack onto the floor. Unfortunately I hadn't done the zip up and as it hit the metallic tiles, out popped quite a few things of an extremely intimate and feminine nature. They instantly rolled away in all directions, intent, it seemed, on having a good old roll around on this nice shiny surface. I dropped to my knees with a 'Bugger!' and grovelled around under occupied tables retrieving them, an appropriate menstrual blush enlivening my features.

'They do a discreet little travelling case for those,' Laura informed me patronisingly as I clumsily stuffed them back in my bag. 'I discovered it when I was about sixteen.'

'Yes I know, been meaning to get one,' I muttered, straightening up, still feeling distinctly self-conscious. I glanced across at her.

'Oh! Sorry, Laura, how are you?' I leaned forwards to peck the soft, flawless cheek that I suddenly realised she'd been resolutely proffering since I arrived. And I thought she'd just got a cricked neck or something. Oh well, at least we were still on kissing terms.

'Very well, thank you,' she replied icily.

I flopped back into my chair again feeling decidedly hot and sweaty now. I billowed my shirt about to get some air in.

'Phew!' I gasped, looking around. Then I stopped and sank into my Perrier. No, it wasn't really a 'phew' sort of place, was it?

I peered over the rim of my glass. The clientele here

was distinctly ladies wot lunched, not ladies wot sweated. There was also a fair smattering of smart young gels with their mummies, the former looking faintly bored but not *too* bored, since Mummy did after all control what went into those smart carrier bags plumped down beside the designer chairs, and one wouldn't want to get on the wrong side of her until a great deal more trendy gear had been safely stashed away. Instead, these expensive beauties were restricting themselves to gazing superciliously around, hoping perhaps to see a girl from the lower fourth whom they could studiously ignore and at the same time doing a lot of flicking back of long silky tresses. It occurred to me that Clemmie would be doing the 'flick' before she was much older; in fact I wondered nervously if I hadn't spotted an embryonic 'flick' just the other day.

'Warm Radicchio and Goat's Cheese salad and then the polenta, please,' murmured Laura.

I looked up to see another potential flicker standing right beside me. Crikey, they all looked the same, didn't they, these well-bred girls – except that this one had a white apron on, a pad in her hand and pale blue china eyes that looked even less friendly than Laura's. She also had a distinct – 'I may have failed my A's at St Mary's Wantage but I'm only working at Harvey Nicks until Daddy sorts out something at Sotheby's' – look about her. She obviously found it difficult to talk as well as pass exams because she simply raised her eyebrows enquiringly at me. I gazed back at her, wondering if there was anything behind those blank eyes besides a pile of old *Tatler* magazines, an Ascot race card and a Henley Regatta Members' Enclosure badge.

'Shall I order for you?' asked Laura, as if I'd never been to a restaurant before.

I jumped. 'Oh! No thanks. I'll um, well, I'll have some wine for starters,' I blurted oafishly.

Laura smiled. 'A glass of Sancerre,' she murmured to her friend the waitress as if I'd just come over on the boat from Bog-Land.

Her friend the waitress smiled back and nodded, full of understanding.

I rallied quickly. 'No, not Sancerre, I'll have a half-bottle of house red actually and –' I ran my eye down the hyperbolic menu '– I'm not sure I'm in the mood for fashion-victim fodder today so could I have a cheese omelette and chips, please?'

Pale blue eyes blinked. 'Aim not actually sure if we—'

'You've got eggs in the kitchen, haven't you?' I enquired brightly. 'And surely some cheese and potatoes?'

'Oh, yah but—'

'Perfect.' I snapped the menu shut and handed it back to her with a fixed smile that distinctly said, 'Don't get patronising with *me*, Blue Eyes, or I'll order off the beaten track, all right?' She flushed and stalked back to the kitchen.

'You're not in a Little Chef now, you know,' said Laura frostily.

'More's the pity,' I said briskly, feeling braver by the minute. No, I would *not* be intimidated by a seventeen-year-old waitress, nor by my little sister, come to that.

'So what's this all about then?' I demanded, folding my arms.

Laura stared at me incredulously. 'What's it all about! You've got a nerve. God, the last time I saw you, you threw wine in my face and accused me of having an affair with Patrick, you tell *me* what it's all about!'

She had a point. I caved in dramatically. 'Ah, yes, right. Sorry. I forgot about that.'

'Well, I haven't, so come on, what's going on? Are you having an affair with him or what?'

It was a relief to answer in the 'or what' category. 'No,' I said firmly. 'I'm not. It's fair to say I was considering it—'

'Panting for it.'

'But I've dismissed the whole idea out of hand. There is absolutely nothing going on between me and Patrick Cameron and there never will be now. The whole thing was preposterous in the first place and—' Suddenly I dropped the pompous tone and looked at her beseechingly. 'Look, Laura, I know I owe you an explanation but to be honest I haven't really got one. I'm off him, that's all, for various reasons but I don't want to talk about it right now. If I just said I was totally devoted to David and the children and I'll never look at another man as long as I live, would you let me off? Please?'

She stubbed her cigarette out and smiled snidely. 'I see. A born again married woman.'

I shrugged. 'If you like.'

'Ready to play Happy Families again.'

I looked at her sharply. 'There's no playing about it, we *are* a happy family – and anyway, what's it to you, Laura? Why does that get up your nose so much? Don't you like happy endings? Would you have preferred it if I'd disappeared over the horizon with Patrick?'

'No, but—'

'But what?'

'Well it all seems to revolve around you, doesn't it? Everything hangs on your decision, what *you* think, what *you* decide.'

I considered this. 'Yes, I suppose it does. Do you have a problem with that? As far as I can see, you call the shots in all your relationships. I don't suppose Edward wore the figurative trousers, did he?'

'Oh Edward,' she said dismissively.

'Or Phillip or Michael or any of the other poor

pathetic lost souls you gave the kiss of life to and then tossed back into the pool again?' Suddenly I felt angry. Annoyed with her supercilious attitude. 'I suppose you've got the same treatment lined up for Willie, have you? Or does he get a reprieve because he had the balls to give you one?' I tossed this out wildly, like a yob lobbing a firework into a bonfire.

Laura flushed from her white shirt upwards, her neck and face suddenly blotched and mottled. I hadn't seen her do that since she was a child, when Daddy was horrid to her. My tummy churned. Oh God, how awful – what was I doing? Bullying my little sister because I'd been afraid of her judging me?

I leaned across quickly and seized her hand. 'Laura, I'm so sorry. I shouldn't have said that – I didn't even mean it!'

She searched my eyes, then nodded quickly, forgiving me, knowing I was sorry, knowing it was just my repulsive tongue getting out of hand as usual. I let go of her hand and cursed myself. We were silent for a bit.

After a while Laura swallowed. 'Did Patrick tell you about Willie, then?'

I nodded. 'Yes, but Laura, why didn't *you* tell me? You didn't have to sneak off every night at Kilmarnock like that. You could have told me – I'd have understood.'

She shook her head. 'It was . . . special. I didn't want it spoiled.'

'And you thought I might do that?' My heart ached quietly.

'I thought you might have laughed. Or tried to put me off.'

I wondered, would I? Possibly, yes. It was all right for me, wasn't it, a quick fling with Willie, but for Laura?

I sighed. 'You may be right.' Then I grinned. 'I tell you what, if you're still keen on him next summer I promise not to say a word, OK?'

I stared down as an enormous cheese omelette suddenly appeared in front of me. Blue Eyes looked at me challengingly. I blinked at its proportions.

'Next summer? I'm going back on Thursday.'

I glanced up. 'What?'

'The day after tomorrow. I'm going back.' She took a sip of Perrier and calmly flicked back her hair.

'But can you do that? Will they give you the time off?'

She shrugged. 'Don't have to. I've resigned.'

'What!'

She popped a radicchio leaf into her mouth. 'Resigned this morning. Half an hour ago, in fact.' She chewed slowly, watching me.

I put my fork down. 'But Laura, what will you *do*? Your fabulous job – you loved it, it was your life!'

'Only because I didn't have any other life.'

'But – you were so good at it!'

She sighed. 'Because I had to be and because, to be honest, it was piss simple. You don't get it, do you, Tess? I'm in love with Willie.'

I gazed at her in amazement. 'Willie? Oh come on now, Laura. I know he's the first guy you've ever slept with and all that, and it *is* a bit emotional, but you're surely not suggesting . . .'

'I surely am. And I'm moving up to Scotland to be with him.'

I rocked back in my chair and stared at her aghast. A holiday romance yes, maybe even a bit on the side every other weekend, but to *live* with him?

'OK,' I said, as calmly as possible, 'OK, why not take a sabbatical? Take a month off, two even, try it out. Try living up there together –' try a cold winter, I thought privately – 'and if you don't like it, come back.'

She shook her head. 'Don't want to.'

'But—'

'Listen, Tess.' She leaned forward abruptly. 'I loathe

my job, OK? I loathe my designer flat, I loathe my life in London, I loathe a lot of the false, pretentious people I know and I loathe the poncy drinks-party lifestyle I lead, got it?'

'But then – why did you do it in the first place?' I said, flabbergasted.

There was a silence.

'Because you didn't.'

I stared at her. 'What?'

'Because it was something you hadn't done. You got the husband, the house, the children, I looked and couldn't find what you had so I did something completely different. I did the career bit instead, OK?'

I stared at her. I'd never known I'd had such an effect on her, that she should feel driven, by me, to such extremes. To compete. I'd never felt threatened by her lifestyle, so why had she felt threatened by mine? I struggled to understand.

'Was it – Daddy?'

She shrugged. 'Partly, I suppose. I suppose I wanted to shine in his eyes, succeed like he'd hoped you would after university. I think subconsciously, I decided to step into your shoes for him.' She looked up. 'But it was quite clear it was never quite the same. He was proud of me, but not enough. Not as much as if it had been you.'

'Laura, that's not true,' I whispered. But I knew it was.

'And the stupid thing is,' she laughed, 'I don't even really like him! Why should I care what he thinks? But I do.'

I nodded. 'I know.'

'It wasn't just Daddy, though. There was something else – something I had to get away from. I wanted to hide myself in my work.'

'What?'

She hesitated, looked for a moment as if she might

tell me, then shook her head.

'I'll tell you one day. Not now.'

I pushed the half-eaten omelette away miserably. Terrific. The second person in my family I'd failed. First Mummy and now Laura, and all the time, instead of trying to please my sister and my mother I'd been running round in circles trying to please the one person in the family who resolutely *refused* to be pleased, my father. And of course, that's what Mummy and Laura had been trying to do too, struggling to get some approval, some peace, some harmony, but there never would be peace and harmony in our family, would there, because none of us could ever match up to the one he'd lost. The one he'd always hankered for. The son. Patrick. I looked at her for a second.

'Laura, about Daddy.'

'Hmmm?' She was chasing a piece of goat's cheese round her plate, miles away.

I hesitated. 'There's – well, there's something fairly monumental I have to tell you about him.'

She looked up. 'What?'

'He's not, actually . . . my father.'

She stared at me blankly for a moment. 'What did you say?'

'I said he's not my father. You see, the thing is, Laura . . .'

'WHAT!' she shrieked, her fork clattering down onto her plate.

'Shhhh!' I put my hand on her arm and looked around nervously. Several well-bred ears were pricking up like frisky ponies; the next thing we knew we'd be in *Jennifer's* blinking *Diary*. 'Mummy told me yesterday,' I whispered. 'You're his daughter, but I'm not. Mummy had an affair.'

She stared at me in disbelief. 'I don't believe you.'

'It's true,' I said patiently. 'I didn't know whether to tell you or not but then I thought I couldn't go on for the rest of my life with me knowing and you not, so I decided I would.'

'Christ – you're very cool about this aren't you, Tess? I mean how d'you *feel*? It's a bit bloody cataclysmic isn't it, that Dad isn't your – Jesus!'

'I know, I know, and I suppose I am being calm, but I think the reason is . . .' I struggled to rationalise it. 'Well – in the first place I have a family, my own family, so perhaps it's not as momentous as it would be,' I was going to say 'if I were you' but I hurried on, 'if I wasn't married, but also Laura,' I hesitated, 'rather like you, I've decided I don't actually *like* him very much.' I shrugged. 'To tell you the truth, that helps enormously.'

She was still staring at me aghast, mouth open, cigarette suspending a good two inches of ash. She flicked the ash off.

'All right,' she said steadily, although her fingers trembled, 'if he's not your father, who is then?'

I looked at her squarely. 'Brace yourself.'

'What? WHO?'

'Hamish.'

'Who's he?'

'Willie's father.'

She stared at me. 'Hamish?' she shrieked. '*Hamish McPherson!* Oh, bugger off, Tess,' she scoffed. 'Mum and Hamish? It's outrageous!'

'Is it? Look at you and Willie.'

She started, flushed and looked down at her napkin. There was a silence.

'And you,' she said softly.

I looked at her sharply. 'He told you?'

She nodded.

I gulped. 'Laura, it was just a one-off, and we didn't go all the way. I bottled out—'

'I know,' she interrupted quickly. 'He told me. And anyway,' she went on, 'why should you have to explain?

It was before I came along, wasn't it?' She gave a wry smile. 'Just.'

Our pale-eyed waitress came back to gather up our plates. Having been such a troublemaker I, of course, had only eaten a few mouthfuls. She looked at me accusingly as she cleared away. We were silent when she'd gone. Laura, I knew, was thinking about Daddy not being my father. I was thinking about her and Willie. Was she running away? Was this another violent manifestation of wanting to compete with me again? And was this decision just as alien and unnatural to her as having a career had been? What would they be like together, the sophisticate and the country boy, and what about his harem – would he still be running that?

'Laura,' I said gently, 'about Willie. There have been others, I think.'

She grinned. 'Others? Don't be ridiculous, Tess, there've been hordes! I know, he's told me all about them. Kirsten, a wide variety of Wee-Marys, all the London women on holiday, Penny too.'

She grinned at my expression. 'I know – even Penny. Can you imagine? All that pink angora flying around, pearls swinging, reinforced black bra sailing into the gorse bushes . . .'

'Shrieking and whooping – I shouldn't imagine she's a quiet lover, would you?'

'Oh no, and terribly athletic I should think, in a jolly hockey sticks sort of way. Nude leap-frog, perhaps—'

'Or fireman's lifts through the woods, that big white bottom wobbling around on Willie's shoulder—'

'Yes, thank you, Tess, that will do. I'd rather *not* imagine any more, if it's all the same to you.'

We giggled and she reached across and helped herself to a large slug of my wine.

'Want some?' I asked.

'Mmm, why not.'

I poured her a glass. We sat quietly for a while, supping away together, closer by miles suddenly. I put my glass down abruptly.

'But where on earth are you going to *live*, Laura, have you thought about that? Not in that boxy little bungalow, surely?'

I knew I sounded like a complete snob, but I just couldn't imagine Laura sitting in one of those G Plan armchairs with the antimacassar on the headrest warming her designer shoes in front of the two-bar electric fire.

'Oh no, Willie's already looking at places. He's seen a row of old cottages that need renovating – he thinks we could make them into one house. It's over near Kilmaglen, on the coast. We might take that on, do it up together.'

'But what with? I mean, how would you buy it?'

'Oh I'd sell the flat of course.'

I looked at her. Of course. That's how they'd finance it. I took a sip of wine. The nasty, rather cynical side of my nature said what a super wheeze for Willie then; lots of lovely money, big pad, no worries, but then happily, the slightly bigger, more generous side of me suddenly got a glimpse of Laura. Laura, halfway up a ladder in an old pair of jeans and a large checked shirt of Willie's, hair tied up any old how, pot of paint in her hand, spot of magnolia on her nose, laughing down at Willie as he held the ladder and I thought – so what? How on earth could I begrudge her that? Having fun, being in love, turning a wreck into something decent in much the same way that David and I had done. How could I begrudge her the freedom from her stifling, lonely, single-girl life? What did it matter whose money it was? Why shouldn't she have a stab at happiness with a man she loved, and what could be better, really, than that man was Willie and not some anally-retentive merchant banker who

434

insisted she polished the silver every week and entertained his boss every month and who brought out all her uptight neuroses – of which she had her share – instead of her carefree girlishness, of which, if the truth be known, she had a lot more . . . The trouble was that all that free spirit had been hidden away for so long I'd almost forgotten it was there. Forgotten that that was the real Laura. And why should she work for ever, either? Why should she sacrifice real life on the altar of a career?

Suddenly I felt a rush of love and warmth for her and a real sense of relief too. She was out, she'd made it across to the other side, and now she was running like blazes, she was free.

I leant across and seized her hand. 'You're right, you're absolutely right. Go for it, Laura! This is the best decision you've ever made in your life. Get up to Scotland, to Willie, buy your house on the coast, have four children, make jam, bake bread and don't let anyone tell you that you've opted out! There's more peace and sense and dignity in all of that than there is in a lifetime of client meetings and expense-account lunches and warm radicchio sodding salad and – oh, anything else in the world!'

Laura flushed with happiness, and not that nervous, mottled flush of a moment ago, just a lovely pink glow. Her eyes watered and a smile shot across her face.

'Do you really think so?' she said happily. 'Oh Tess, I'm so glad you agree. I was so afraid you'd censure me and – and—'

'Put you down?' I said miserably. I'd had no idea that with no great thought on my part I'd manipulated her life so abominably up to now. That she'd set such store by what I thought.

'Willie's going to try and start a salmon farm,' she went on eagerly. 'Well, we both are actually. We're going to work together, except when the babies come along, of course, then I'll want to be at home. I expect . . . although the farm will hopefully *be* at home so maybe I can do both!'

I let her gush on happily, all her plans pouring out at once now, as if someone had opened the flood-gates. I listened, nodding, smiling, so pleased for her. For her happiness.

All the same, I reflected, swirling my wine around in my glass, I couldn't help thinking that after the initial shock, this was much easier to be pleased about than any of the God-awful Trevors and Vincents and Edwards she'd paraded before me in the past. I mean, snobbish reservations aside, Willie was undoubtedly a nice bloke, which was more than could be said for the rest of the motley crew.

'And whatever snobbish reservations people may have about Willie . . .' I looked up quickly; how on earth had she known I'd been thinking about that? '. . . he must be infinitely preferable to any of my past beaux, don't you think?' I knew she was wondering about Daddy, about what he'd say.

'Absolutely,' I said warmly. 'I must say, I never quite knew what you were up to with all those wallys before him. No one did. Patrick had a hunch you were looking for something you couldn't have.'

She smiled and sipped her wine.

'That's why I thought it was Patrick,' I went on, 'because he was my ex-boyfriend and you couldn't have him because he was still in love with me and all that jazz. I thought perhaps you two had had a bit of a fling when he met you in London, years ago at that wedding.'

She laughed. 'God no, you must be joking! What – Patrick, with all his hang-ups about his parents and that weird obsession he had with you? No thanks. No, he just took me out to supper a couple of times when I was at a loose end, but all he wanted to do was talk about

436

you. Honestly, Tess, I thought he was a bit unhinged. He even wanted to know how many men you'd been to bed with and was I absolutely sure it was only him and David and hadn't you perhaps bonked someone else at university and what did I think of your marriage, were you really happy . . . all that sort of thing.' She shook her head. 'Weird. No, I had no desire to get entangled with the ultimate mixed-up bad boy like you did.'

'And me neither, any longer,' I said with feeling. I shivered. God, it was as if he'd been keeping an eye on me, all this time.

'All the same,' she went on, 'Patrick was right. I *was* looking for something I couldn't have, but it wasn't him.' She stubbed her cigarette out in the ashtray and looked me right in the eye.

'It was David.'

Chapter Twenty-nine

I felt my mouth drop open. For a moment I had neither air nor words to call on. Was this some kind of a joke? Was she, in a rather warped sort of way, having me on? I stared at her. Her eyes told me she wasn't.

'David?' I whispered incredulously.

'Yes,' she said calmly. 'Didn't you know?'

I could still hardly speak. 'No – no, I didn't. *David!*'

'Oh it's OK, I'm over it now, but it's taken twelve years. Twelve years to meet what I should have realised from the start was the antidote, his antithesis – Willie, and all this time I've been out there searching for a replica.' She laughed. 'I was looking for a clone you see, a thoughtful, brainy, fount-of-all-knowledge sort of chap – a polymath no less, but with that crucial, fatal ability to make me double up laughing at a moment's notice. A sublime combination, of course, but one that I'd never have found in a million years.'

I was transfixed by her mouth, by the extraordinary words it was forming. 'David! But when did you—'

'Fall in love with him?'

I nodded, mute.

'Oh, more or less the moment I saw him, as soon as you brought him home, in fact. I remember it distinctly. You were coming back from university with "some chap" and Mummy was in a bit of a flutter getting tea organised in the garden. It was July, very hot and we were all sitting around in deckchairs on the lawn when you breezed in with him, this tall blond boy in cricket whites with grass stains on his knees and that shock of hair that he pushed back impatiently when it got in his eyes. He shook hands with us all and then sat down next to me. Mummy passed round scones with jam and cream and he chatted a bit about this and that – ghastly cricket teas and philosophy and RagWeek – being funny and disparaging about it all – and he smiled quite a lot and made us laugh even more and I just wanted to kill you. I wanted to plunge my butter-knife through your heart right there and then.'

'But – you were only a child, fifteen . . .'

'Sixteen – and I knew what I wanted. Always had done. Knew I'd recognise the man I wanted to marry the moment I saw him. Imagine how I felt when you led him into the garden that day – and then decided to marry him yourself?' She laughed. 'And always, from your point of view, as someone who, in the absence of Patrick, would probably do!'

'Is that what you thought?' I gasped.

'It's what everyone thought. It's what you thought too, if you're honest. You *deigned* to marry him, to have his children, to share a home with him.'

'Stop it, Laura!' I felt panic-stricken.

'I'm sure you did actually deign to love him, but it was always a bit of a condescension on your part, wasn't it?' She played ruminatively with some crumbs on the table, smiling down at them. 'I, on the other hand, was absolutely gagging to love him and to be loved by him. And I used to think – what if you hadn't got pregnant? What if you hadn't been stupid and naive enough to let that happen . . . might he not have loved me instead? Might you not have just been the catalyst, the middle man, bringing him home for *me* to love, delivering him to *me* in the garden that sunny afternoon before moving on to something else? Might not that have been the way it was destined to be? But no, you cocked up, didn't you. Forgot to take your Smarties and I had to content myself with being his sister-in-law.' She looked at me defiantly. 'But it didn't stop me living and dreaming that man every day for twelve years. In my mind I ate with him, drank with him and slept with him too. And I can tell you all this now, Tess, because I don't any more.' She lit a surprisingly steady cigarette and blew a stream of smoke reflectively over my shoulder.

'Oh I think I'll always love him,' she admitted, 'but not with that same terrible passion. That gnawing, compulsive, debilitating passion that takes over your whole life, swallows you whole, colours everything you do, everyone you meet . . .' She tapped the ash off the end of her cigarette, and gazed over my shoulder into the distance.

'Is that why you never went to bed with anyone?' I breathed.

'Yes,' she laughed. 'Crazy, isn't it? I was saving myself for my sister's husband. I never admitted that, even to myself, but I think it's probably true.'

'Did David know?' I whispered. I could barely speak.

'Oh, I'm sure he did. David's not stupid, is he? But he was always very, very kind about it. I only once made a terrible fool of myself,' she gave a twisted smile, 'just after Hugo was born. I think I knew then that that really was the end, had to be. I got extremely drunk one night, lurched round to your house – you were still in hospital – and literally threw myself at him, flung myself on his neck, covered him in frantic kisses, then broke down hysterically.'

'Wh-what did he do?'

She grinned. 'Patted me on the back, took me out into the garden and gave me a large brandy. Then he sat and talked to me under the apple tree and the stars for about two hours. Not about us, him and me, about what I'd said and done, but just about me. About my life, where it was going, what I wanted to do. He tried to find a path for me, steer me onto it, a nice solid safe one far away from him. He's always done that for me, in his own quiet way.'

I nodded. 'Yes, yes he would. He's a – lovely man.' My heart ached for him suddenly.

'The best,' she corrected. She grinned. 'Bar Willie, of course.'

I breathed deeply, struggling to comprehend. 'He – never said.'

'Well, he wouldn't, would he? Being David. Lesser men would have loved it of course, bragged about it – "Oh, your sister's got the hots for me" and all that sort of stuff – but not David.'

I gulped and looked down at my napkin. I'd've liked to have torn it into tiny shreds right there and then; only the fact that it was pure Irish linen stopped me. We were both silent for a moment.

Laura broke the silence. 'Quite a lot to take on board in one lunch-hour isn't it?' she said quietly.

I nodded dumbly. I badly wanted to see him. To get home. To claim him, to reclaim him. The idea of someone else wanting him was so terrifying it made my chest tighten, made breathing difficult.

'And you so nearly left him, didn't you?' she mused. 'I got so excited, thought that maybe there was a chance, that I could really have him after all these years. Given time, of course. We would have left a respectable gap, given you and Patrick a chance to go off to Italy, live together for a while, maybe even have a child. Then that would have been my moment, you see. I could have stepped quietly out from the shadows and picked up the pieces. It would have been the best thing for everyone under the circumstances. Aunty Laura.'

My hand shot to my mouth. I stared at her, horrified. 'No, Laura, don't!' I felt sick.

'Pipe dreams,' she said briskly, waving away my alarm. 'Don't worry, Tess, it would never have happened. I'm quite sure David would have found the idea as repellent as you do. I don't kid myself that he even remotely fancied me, but while we're here spilling the beans you may as well have the whole rotten canful. You may as well know what was going on in my crazy mixed-up head.'

'Is there any more?' I gasped. 'Only if there is, I shall have to order the other half of this bottle. Two glasses isn't going to be enough to sustain me!'

She hesitated for a moment, then shook her head. 'No. No, that's all.' She reached for her glass and took a quick sip of water. Too quick.

'What?' I pounced. '*What?* Come on, out with it, Laura. Is there a love child lurking about somewhere, or did you drug him, drag him back to your flat and bonk him senseless? Come on, I want the works.'

Her eyes flitted over me momentarily, then slithered over to the door. 'No, it's nothing like that.' She paused, shook her head. 'In fact, it's probably nothing at all.'

'WHAT!' I shrieked, seizing her wrist. 'I want the nothing at all, if you don't mind. I want the whole sodding lot!'

'OK, OK, stop shouting,' she muttered, looking around nervously, 'but listen, this is pure conjecture, OK?' She licked her lips. I waited, tortured beyond belief. 'I – just wonder if David . . . well, if you haven't taken your eye off the ball for too long. If you haven't left rejecting Patrick in favour of David too late.' She fidgeted miserably in her chair.

'What d'you mean?' I breathed.

'Well while you've been busy sorting out your own life, it wouldn't be unreasonable to assume he's been doing the same, would it?'

'You mean he's having an affair,' I whispered. I felt

faint. Could feel the life blood slipping away from me, draining out of my face.

'I don't know, for sure. It's just – well, when I got back to London, Janie – you know, the girl I work with – said: "Oh, I saw your gorgeous brother-in-law the other day, having lunch."'

'Where?'

'In Bibendum.'

'Bibendum! Oh don't be ridiculous,' I scoffed. 'David wouldn't be seen dead forking out for a trendy place like that.'

'With a blonde. Very young.'

My heart stopped. Then it raced on again. I shook my head. 'Rubbish! No, that's absurd, Laura. That's not David's style at all. If you'd told me he'd been spotted lurking round the fossils in the British Museum with a blue-stockinged, middle-aged brunette I might have believed it, but a blonde in Bibendum – no.' I shook my head firmly. 'She must have been mistaken.'

'She wasn't,' said Laura quietly. 'She knows David quite well and anyway I phoned and checked. He booked the table in his own name.'

'You – checked?'

'Yes, well I've known his movements for the past nine years now; it's a difficult habit to break.' She had the grace to blush.

I stared at her, two fierce emotions battling for supremacy in my breast. One, that unbeknown to me, my sister should have had such an obsession with my husband for so long and the other, that now someone else had one too. It was as if Laura had passed over the baton – here, take it Blondie, it's your turn now. Pick it up and run with it, he's all yours. I struggled to keep calm but I wanted to stand up and shriek: 'Hands *off*! Just bugger *off* will you, you greedy grasping bastards. He's *my* husband, all right? Get one of your own!' I touched my forehead with a shaky hand. It was damp with sweat; I felt awful.

Laura leaned across the table. 'Tess,' she said gently, 'I'm telling you all this in the hope that maybe you can do something about it. That it's not too late. I don't want you to go on blithely taking him for granted only to discover he's . . . well.'

'Leaving me for someone else,' I whispered. 'Yes, thank you Laura, I'm indebted to you. Grateful to be so – informed.'

I reached down for my sack on the floor and pulled it onto my lap. I found my purse and with a shaking hand managed to open the clasp. I pulled out a twenty-pound note and pushed it across the table to her. She pushed it back.

'Don't be silly,' she murmured, 'I'll get this. Listen, Tess, have another drink, a soft one perhaps. I'm not sure you should go back on your own yet.'

I shook my head. 'Got to. Got to get away. Have a think.' I could only speak in clipped little staccato sentences now. I had to control my mouth or God knows what would come out of it – sobs, curses, wails, invective and serpents too, no doubt. I could feel them writhing around inside me, twisting my gut, stealing my breath, looking for a way out. I stumbled to my feet.

'Tess, just let me pay this then I'll come with you, walk you to the Tube at least.' She looked at me anxiously, then around the restaurant, searching desperately for our waitress, waving the bill in the air.

'No, really, I'll be fine. Rather be alone. Bye.' I bent down to kiss her.

'I shouldn't have told you,' she whispered.

I managed a brave smile. 'Best thing you ever did. Brought me to my senses. Thank you.' I meant it.

I turned and made my way through the sea of sleek heads in their black velvet hairbands, noticing with a stab that most of them seemed to be blonde. I lurched through the swing doors. The first of a series of escalators snaked down in front of me and since the ability to put one foot in front of the other seemed to have temporarily deserted me, this was convenient. I stepped on and waited, wide-eyed and frozen like the mannequins I was slowly gliding past, stepping off one escalator and picking up another until ultimately I was safely delivered to the ground floor and Perfumery.

As I moved blindly through the counters I caught a faint whiff of Diorissimo, the pong of my choice when I'm in the mood and the one David always buys me for Christmas when he's stumped for ideas. I wondered what *her* choice was, whoever she was, this blonde, this lunch-time and probably night-time companion of my husband's. My husband's mistress. Suddenly I had to stop and clutch a make-up counter. Several exorbitantly priced lipsticks wobbled precariously in their display stand. I stood there, head bent, taking deep breaths, looking at the sparkling floor beneath me. For an awful moment I thought it was accelerating up to meet me, but in the nick of time I gritted my teeth, and thought hard about the ERM and John Major's Social Charter and the way he now wears nice stripy cotton shirts instead of grey Bri-nylon ones and the mixed blessing that must be for Norma, a pleasure to look at but a pain in the arse to iron – and gradually, such dull contemplation sobered me up and the wooziness left me. I slowly raised my head. No, I determined, I would not faint in the Perfume department of Harvey Nichols. I looked up and saw the heavily made-up girl behind the L'Oréal counter peering anxiously at me.

'Are you all right, madam?' she asked, blinking through her blonde fringe which hung rather seductively in her eyes. Blonde again. Everyone seemed to be blonde these days.

'Yes, yes I'm fine,' I said. 'Just a bit hot, that's all.'

I stared at her. Is it you? Are you the one, you bitch, you vixen, you cold-blooded husband-snatcher? Are you the one intent on breaking up my world?

'Only Madam looks a little pale . . .'

I managed a wobbly smile, thinking: yes, well, you'd look a little pale under the circumstances.

'No, I'm fine,' I nodded, baring my teeth and preparing to move on, but as I did, I caught a glimpse of someone in the huge mirror behind her. I stopped. How odd, she looked just like me but older, thinner and much more lined. I stared. It was me, of course, but how strange that I hadn't noticed how truly terrible I was looking. Why hadn't I noticed that? I reached up and stroked my face absently with my fingertips. Dry, middle-aged skin, whereas hers was no doubt young, soft and peachy.

'Perhaps Madam would like a make-over? There's no obligation and you could sit down for a moment – take the weight off your feet?'

She was talking to me as if I was an old dear, and yet I could only be – what – ten years older than her . . . I stared. What on earth did they say to one another, I wondered. What did David find to say that would interest someone like this? 'Read any good Kafka recently?' 'Nah, but I bought a brilliant new nail-varnish in Top Shop yesterday, whaddya think?' Or was there no need to speak; did they let their bodies do the talking? Was all communication on a far more primeval, carnal plain? Oh God, that floor was definitely coming this way again, and even Norma doing the ironing was going to have a job to stop it. I clung on to the counter with both hands, my knuckles white.

'Madam?'

I took the chair quickly. 'Go on then, a make-over,' I whispered.

My word was her command. In a second my little blonde friend had whipped a sheet around my neck and swung into action, organising herself with brushes and palettes, bottles and potions, for all the world like a surgeon marshalling his instruments.

'Now,' she murmured, swiftly wiping a piece of damp cotton wool over my face, deftly removing all traces of make-up, dirt and tears. 'Did Madam have any particular image in mind?'

'Yes, Madam had the image of a nineteen-year-old blonde in mind. Take twelve years off me and I'll do the rest at home with a bottle of peroxide,' I snarled.

The girl started, then gave a nervous laugh. 'Well, of course, I'll do what I can, but Madam must appreciate that although she has quite marvellous bone structure there's no guarantee I can—'

'Make a silk purse out of a sow's ear? Sorry,' I muttered quickly. 'Bad day. Just do whatever you can.'

'Party make-up perhaps,' she suggested.

'Oh yes,' I said ironically. 'Make it nice and jolly.'

I sat mesmerised as her slim white fingers swept over my face, oiling, massaging, colouring. Slim, white, ringless hands, girlish hands with soft, pink fingertips, expertly soothing and stroking and painting. I imagined similar hands on David, young and soft caressing his shoulders, massaging his back, running down his spine, gently turning him over, stroking his tummy, his—

'That's enough!' I cried suddenly.

I jumped up and tore the sheet from around my neck. The girl dropped her make-up brush in alarm and took a step back.

What was I *doing* here, for heaven's sake? My husband was having an affair and I was calmly getting a make-over in Harvey Nichols?

'So sorry,' I gasped, 'but I'm afraid I must be going. Supposed to be somewhere else you see, just remembered. I'll pay you, of course . . .'

'There's no charge, madam, but I've only done one eye. You can't go yet. At least let me—'

'Sorry, I have to go.'

I turned and hurried away, catching as I did a last glimpse of myself in the mirror. As she'd so rightly said, one eye was garishly made up, complete with glittering gold shadow, whilst the other one next to it looked naked, small and frightened.

I stumbled down Sloane Street and round the square, narrowly missing a bus, and then plunged into the dark abyss of the Tube station. As I reached the platform the train was just disappearing into the tunnel, leaving me alone for a moment, staring blankly down a dark hole. But this was lunch-time and within seconds the platform had filled up again as people poured down the escalators like rats down a drain. I stood and gazed unseeing as they surged around me; shoppers, tourists, office-workers in their lunch-hours, businessmen, executive women, two young men in pale grey suits surreptitiously munching sandwiches beside me, the unmistakable whiff of prawn mayonnaise on wholemeal wafting over, and next to them, an older man in expensive grey flannel, chatting to a young girl. His secretary? Perhaps. I stared. Or perhaps not.

He was tall, mid-forties with thinning grey hair but an attractive, slightly arrogant face and he was smiling down at his young companion who was small and fluffy, bright eyes in a sharp little face, thin painted lips and a too-short skirt. She was recounting something eagerly and he was listening with a superior smile, indulging her pea brain because of her splendid performance between the sheets no doubt. When she'd finished he gave what must have been a mocking response because she pouted indignantly and elbowed him in the ribs. He rocked back on his heels and roared with laughter, she pouted some more and he put his arm round her shoulders, giving her an affectionate little squeeze. I marched up to them.

'And does your wife know about this?' I hissed.

The train rattled noisily into the station. The pair looked at me blankly as I pushed furiously past them and waited for the doors to open. When they did it was a case of squeezing more minced human into the layers of lasagne, but I managed it somehow and as the doors closed behind me, I realised my lecherous friends had managed it too. We stood eyeball to eyeball.

'My wife died last year and my daughter periodically accompanies me to lunch,' he informed me icily.

As I opened my mouth to scoff I realised that not only were the two pairs of hazel eyes glaring at me identical, but that the slightly hooked Roman noses were too. There was no dodging the genes here.

'Ah,' I conceded weakly.

No more was said, but I had to stand chest to chest with them all the way to Earl's Court, at which point the daughter stepped off, leaving her father behind. She pecked him on the cheek and muttered something scathing about a 'stupid, barking, insulting old woman'.

The doors closed and I watched her go, frowning slightly. Old – me? Did she mean *me*? Suddenly it tore at me like barbed wire on skin. I felt tears of anguish well up into my eyes, filling my nose. I gulped them down. Old! Was that what I was, then? An older woman, being traded in for a younger model; was that tired old cliché to be my fate? Was I to be left on my own, an aging, single mother struggling to bring up her children, eking out the maintenance, hanging on to dear, middle-class life by her fingertips while her attractive, greying-round-the-temples, barrister husband strutted off into the sunset to set up home with his new model?

Don't be ridiculous, I thought. You're overreacting.

David has been seen having lunch, that's all, and already you've got him marching into the divorce courts. Now *buck up*! There could be some perfectly innocent explanation. I mean, perhaps she was just a friend? And maybe I could meet her? Yes, perhaps we could be civilised about this. Maybe she'd like to come to dinner and perhaps I could . . . my insides curdled, my fists clenched – '*kill her!*' I gasped.

It was loud enough to make the people standing around me flinch away in alarm and the man I'd already accused of rampant incest blinked nervously. I quickly improvised a song on a theme.

'Killer que-en, yes, she's a killer – que-e-en . . .'

I could tell that Grey Suit wasn't convinced. He looked from one garish, glittering eye to one naked, mad-as-hell eye and came to a reasonable conclusion. He tucked his newspaper firmly under his arm, put his head down and pushed determinedly through the scrum for the sanity of the other end of the carriage.

A half-suppressed guffaw snorted out from behind me. I glanced around to see three or four teenage boys in semi-school uniform, ties askew, blazers frayed, shoes scuffed, oozing with testosterone, giggling into their hands.

'Keep takin' the pills,' one of them blurted out, which sent the others into paroxysms of hilarity.

I ignored them, and then also studiously ignored the fact that they were clearly daring each other to prod me in the back. Gently at first – followed by a muffled guffaw, then a bit harder – followed by louder guffaws.

Mercifully I didn't have to bear this oafish behaviour for too long as moments later the train pulled into Putney Bridge station. I stepped thankfully onto the platform and as I did so, my full cotton skirt floated gently to the ground leaving me standing on the platform in my pop socks and knickers.

'What the—'

Horrified, I snatched the skirt back up and swung around just in time to see the Tube doors close. The boys were choking with laughter, clutching their stomachs, gasping for air, sick with glee.

'You bastards!' I roared as the train chugged out of the station.

Helpless with laughter they hung on to each other, waving and whistling as the train drew away.

'Those bastards undid my skirt!' I spat to no one in particular. Several passers-by gave me an amused look, but an equally wide berth. Tears were pricking my eyelids as I zipped my skirt up at the back again and trudged on up the station steps. I shook my head bitterly. God it was unreal, wasn't it? I mean, those yobbos were some poor mothers' adored sons, fruit of their wombs. Imagine how I'd feel if Hugo behaved like that in a few years' time! I blinked, realising with a shock of dismay that I could well imagine Hugo doing it *now* let alone in a few years' time.

And if he was like that now, I thought miserably, what would he be like without a father? And Clemmie too, my crazy, lovable wild child who could draw like a dream, sing like a lark but still ate with her fingers, slept with a toy gun under her pillow, stripped naked to go to the loo – something I could foresee becoming a problem at the job interview stage – and had waited three and a half years before she'd even bothered to talk? How would she fare without her beloved Daddy, without his pragmatic, calming influence?

Or maybe David would fight for custody, I thought with a sudden lurch of horror. Maybe he'd tell the court I was an unfit mother and that I once gave them Hula Hoops for breakfast, encouraged them to cheat at Patience, turned their muddy trousers inside out, failed to buy sugar-free Ribena, smacked in Sainsbury's, shrieked in Tesco's, bit in Waitrose, frisbied Jaffa Cakes straight from the packet at teatime by way of a cake – yes – maybe they'd *all* go off and leave me and I'd be left alone, a bitter, twisted old woman with only her gin bottles and memories for company.

And maybe the children would want to go? Maybe Clemmie would take one look at Blondie's collection of pink cuddly toys sitting on the love-nest windowsill and bond instantly. Maybe Hugo would be lured by the promise of Blondie's younger brother having a season ticket at QPR, or maybe . . . On and on scurried my poor overworked brain, dreaming up ever more lurid, mind-boggling nightmares as I made my way home, and all the time I knew I was egging myself on to be more outrageous, more melodramatic, because in my heart I knew things really couldn't be as bad as all that, and that if I let myself think the absolute worst, things could only be better, couldn't they?

Or could they? As I rounded the corner into our road I stopped dead in my tracks. I stared. There was my house, number 42, tasteful, wisteria-clad and just as I'd left it, except that right outside a black taxi was waiting. It was throbbing away ominously and pointing in the opposite direction. Standing on the pavement, leaning in through the open cab door and talking to a passenger in the back seat, was David. I quickly stepped back into a hedge to watch. He was wearing his suit, but minus his jacket, in shirt-sleeves and braces. I peered out from behind the privet, my heart hammering. I couldn't see who was in the back of the taxi, but I could just make out a vague outline. David was laughing, chatting, leaning on the taxi roof. Suddenly, he leaned in and . . . kissed whoever it was who was sitting in the back. My tummy gave a lurch. I watched as he straightened up, smiled broadly and seemed about to shut the door when suddenly he clearly remembered something because his finger shot up in a little start of alarm. He turned, dashed up the path to the house, disappeared inside and reappeared a moment later carrying a large suitcase. I blinked. It was our suitcase. He lugged it down the garden path then threw it into the back of the taxi, laughing. He leaned in again for another kiss – reckless now – then slammed the door shut. As the taxi drew away and purred down the road he stood watching, waving, smiling fondly as it disappeared around the corner. He stayed there for a moment or two, gazing reflectively after it, then turned and went back into the house. The front door closed behind him.

My knees buckled and I sat down on the small wall under the hedge. I knew, of course I knew. There was no real mental exertion needed here. The cab had contained the mistress, the suitcase had contained David's clothes, the destination of the cab had been the love-nest and the object of the exercise had been to pick up David's wardrobe. He'd known that I'd be out of the house having lunch with Laura and that the children were out having a picnic with Josie. The coast had been crystal clear and they'd no doubt even found time to have a quick one on the bed – our bed – before he'd popped her and the case in the taxi bound for Maida Vale, or Ladbroke Grove or wherever it was that clandestine relationships were conducted these days. Thus far was perfectly plain, except for one tiny point. That case had been far too big to contain simply a spare pair of underpants and a clean shirt to pop into the extra-marital wardrobe. No, that case had been stuffed to bursting with clothes. He was leaving me. There was no doubt about that. Leaving me for whoever had been in the back of that taxi.

Suddenly I felt very calm, very cold and very still. A profound sense of fatalism rose up from my soul. There was nothing I could do about it. Nothing at all. Suddenly

David's words came back to me. *Alea jacta est*. Of course. *The die is cast*. There was no going back. That must have been what he meant. I sat on the wall feeling not quite real somehow, as if this wasn't happening to me at all but to someone else and I was just an innocent bystander watching the scene being played to its conclusion. I gazed at the blue front door, waiting for it to open, waiting for David to reappear, as I knew he would.

And there he was, coming out with his suit jacket on now and a bundle of briefs under his arm, tied up with the distinctive pink ribbon. He shut the door behind him, locked it, pocketed the key, walked briskly down the path and turned right, in the direction of the station and ultimately, me.

At first he didn't see me, shielded as I was by the weeping ash and the overgrown hedge, but then, just as he was nearly past, he did.

'Tess!' He started, colouring up. 'How long have you been there?'

'Long enough.'

He frowned, but the guilt shone through. 'For what?'

'To see you with your mistress,' I hissed.

As I said it, all calm collected fatalism left me. In an instant I turned into the wronged, vengeful, tie-snipping wife and out poured the pure, smoking-white anger of rejection.

'Long enough to see you snogging and canoodling in the middle of the street, long enough to see the happily married, devoted father of two tickle some peroxide tart's tonsils!' I ranted. 'Long enough to catch sight of that bitch, that viper, that under-age blonde strumpet who you had the nerve to bring to *my* house . . .' My voice was rising hysterically now and behind me, I was aware of curtains twitching. 'And have sex with her in *my* bed, on *my* sheets, before packing her off in a taxi to your sordid little den of sin where no doubt at lunch-time tomorrow you'll be nipping round to SHAG HER SENSELESS!'

I bellowed this into his face, causing him to blink and step backwards into the road. He narrowly missed a car. Behind me an assortment of china dogs rattled violently on the windowsill as a curtain was hastily dropped in alarm.

'Tess, what are you talking about?'

'Oh, don't give me that wide-eyed incredulity crap!' I roared. 'I saw her with my own eyes! Who was it then, David, eh? If you're so screamingly, mind-bogglingly clever you tell me who that scheming little slut in the back of that taxi was! Who was that piece of filth!'

'That piece of filth was your mother.'

'What?'

'Your mother.'

Chapter Thirty

My mind battled, my head roared. I shook it, bewildered. Surely he wasn't having an affair with . . . my mother?

David watched the battle of the brain cells, saw the mystification in my eyes and sighed.

'No, you idiot, of course I'm not having an affair with your mother.' He took my arm, turned me around gently and led me back in the direction of the house.

'You know, Tess, I don't think you're very well. Did you know for instance that you've been out this morning with only half a face? You've got one gold eye and one . . .'

I shook his hand off my arm and pulled away angrily. 'Oh don't you try to distract me, David. Don't you try to fob me off with your smart-arse ways. My mother, indeed! You must think I was born yesterday! Who was in that bloody cab?'

'I've told you,' he said patiently. 'It was your mother. She stopped off at the house to say goodbye to you but you weren't there so I said goodbye instead.'

We were outside the front door now. I gazed up at him, stupefied. He opened it and pushed me gently inside. As he shut the door behind us I could have sworn I saw a hundred net curtains drop disappointedly back into place. I followed David numbly down the hall to the kitchen.

'Goodbye?' I repeated stupidly, lowering my bottom onto a chair at the kitchen table. I stared blankly as he opened the fridge and took out a bottle of wine. 'Why, where's she going?'

'She's leaving your father.'

'No!'

'Only for a couple of months to begin with. She says she'll reassess the situation after that.' He smiled as he wound in the corkscrew. 'What she actually said was she's taking a long sabbatical with a view to possibly renewing her contract at the end of it, but only on her terms.' He laughed. 'Not bad, eh? Not an all-out desertion but pretty monumental nonetheless - particularly for your mother. It'll certainly make your old man sit up a bit anyway.' He pulled the cork.

'But where's she going?'

'India.'

'India!'

'Yes, on a trekking and painting course with similar likeminded souls. Who knows, she might even find someone so likeminded she leaves your father altogether. Drink?' He sat down opposite me and pushed a glass over the table.

'Please.'

He poured us both a glass. 'She stayed with Rachel after the funeral, you see, never went back to Kent with your father. She said if she'd gone home she'd never have done it, wouldn't have had the guts to walk away.' He cradled his glass. 'I can see that actually, being in London probably felt as if she was halfway there. Anyway, she's noticed this painting holiday in the back of *The Times* few weeks ago, apparently. Got all the jabs done in secret and then chickened out. She rang yesterday on the off chance and amazingly they'd had a last-minute cancellation. So she borrowed some clothes from Rachel, bought a few more and now she's on her way to Delhi. Piece of luck, eh?'

'Delhi? Jesus! Daddy will freak!'

David shrugged. 'Of course he will, and it serves him right. She should have done it years ago, we all know that. No point in living a lie, is there? No point in living with someone you don't love or who doesn't love you, is there, Tess?'

He regarded me coolly over the rim of his glass and my heart just about stopped beating.

'David,' I began awkwardly, gripping the stem of my glass for courage. 'What were you doing here this lunch-time?'

'Collecting a brief,' he said calmly. 'I forgot to take it into Chambers this morning and I've got a conference with the client at four. I popped back here to get it and ran into your mother pushing a note through the letter box to let you know the score. She'd been shopping and had everything stuffed into plastic bags so I lent her our case.'

'Really?'

'Really.' He held my eyes. There was a silence.

'And David,' I plunged on again, taking a quick slurp of wine, 'Laura said that – well, Janie said actually, the girl she works with – that she saw you quite recently, having lunch, in Bibendum.'

He nodded. 'Yes, I saw Janie.'

'You were with a girl,' I breathed. 'A blonde.'

'Quite so.'

'Who – was that?'

'That was Lucy.'

In my mouth my wine suddenly turned to rat poison, to lighter fuel, to Domestos, to cat's piss. I spat it violently across the table.

'Lucy?' I roared. God, even the name was enough to make my insides knot, it was so deliciously juicy and luscious and suggestive and skittish and rampant and roly-poly in the hayish – Lucy!

'My new clerk.'

My heart stopped – then lurched on again dementedly. 'Your new clerk is . . . female?'

'Do you have a problem with that?'

I blinked. 'N-no. No, not at all! But you took her to . . . Bibendum?'

He smiled. 'Yes, I believe that's the name of the hugely expensive joint we were lunching in. It belongs to that Conran chappie who's always banging on about American Express on the telly. Bit of a flagship for him apparently, but it was news to me.' He grinned. 'I was stitched up, you see. Lucy arrived on her first day at work and as usual no one had bothered to organise anything by way of a "hello" so a few of us who weren't in court thought we ought to show willing and take her out to lunch. Simon suggested this place I'd never even heard of and got me to book a table. He then discovered he was in court and couldn't come, and then Ben and Dick discovered *they* conveniently couldn't come either so it was left to old muggins here to escort her. I did vaguely ask if they thought this place was quite the ticket but they assured me, with much guffawing and back-slapping, that it was just my cup of tea, terrifically cheap and cheerful, lots of nursery puddings, Spotted Dick, Jam Roly Poly and all that sort of thing, I'd *love* it.'

I smiled in spite of myself. I could just imagine the worldly Dick and Ben chortling with glee as they sent a bemused David off on his way to bankruptcy.

'I realised I'd been had the moment I glanced at the prices on the menu, but I squared my shoulders and thought, Right, you bastards, in for a penny in for a quarter of a million – and ordered whatever I felt like, urging Lucy to do the same. Between us we got through foie gras, duck, snails, grouse and got quietly plastered on a couple of bottles of very passable Burgundy. We stayed there for most of the afternoon and very pleasant it was too. Lucy's extremely good company and very easy on the eye and the whole thing was very convivial. When I finally mortgaged our way out of there at four o'clock and went back to Chambers, I told the grinning bastards that they were absolutely right; it had indeed been just my cup of tea and I was indebted to them to adding it to my list of eateries and wasn't it marvellous, incidentally, that Lucy had managed to swing it on Chambers' expenses. Mind you,' he added ruefully, taking a sip of wine, 'it might explain why the work appears to have dried up recently. Lucy obviously thinks she doesn't need to send any briefs winging my way as I've clearly got private means. Either that or she thinks I'm trying to get into her knickers and isn't amused.'

I swallowed and searched for my voice which I hadn't used for a while. 'So – you're not having an affair?'

'With Lucy?' He laughed. 'No.'

'With anyone?'

He regarded me thoughtfully. 'No, not with anyone, Tess.'

I stared at him for a moment, then threw my head back exultantly and gave a great gasp of joy.

'Oh!' I pulled my hairband out and shook my curls all over the place. 'Oh God, David, I'm so relieved! I can't tell you how worried I've been!' I slapped my hands down delightedly on the table, could almost feel my eyes dancing for joy.

'You see, Laura thought . . . well, we *both* thought actually, that – oh God, David, you've no *idea*!' I seized his hand. 'For the past couple of hours I've had you shacked up with some bimbo in a basement flat in Bayswater. I've had you squeezing into black 501s, spinning groovy discs and rolling joints on beanbags, I've had you rumpy-pumpying on a futon with your nubile little strumpet like some born again teenager – God, I think I even had you on the floor in Stringfellows, smoking pot, getting down, chilling out . . . I can't tell

461

you how berserk my imagination was going!'

David raised an eyebrow. 'Clearly,' he said drily.

'And as for me, oh God, there was no hope for me.' shook my head emphatically. 'No no, I was dead meat. was the deserted, passed-over droopy-boobed bab machine. I was last year's model, placenta brain, goo for nothing except slouching round the kitchen in m cheesy old dressing gown and socks, Rice Krispies i my pubic hairs, J-cloth in my hand mopping bottoms floors, puke and noses . . .' I got up and grabbed dishcloth from the sink and slouched around like Th Thing From The Swamp to demonstrate. 'Oh yes,' laughed joyfully, chucking the cloth back in the sink an flopping down into my chair. 'I was ancient history!'

'Really.'

'Yes, really! Honestly, David, you've no idea the he I've been through.'

'My heart bleeds.'

'You've no idea how arse-about-tit I'd got it all. Whe I saw you putting that suitcase in that taxi and lungin in for a kiss, I thought, Uh-oh, that's it, Tess.' I garrotte my neck with my finger. 'It's curtains for you, old girl It's happy single-parent families from now on, I'm afraid It's gritting your teeth as the paternal car rolls up outsid the house, forcing a smile as you wave the children of for some quality time with Daddy, biting your nails an hitting the sherry while they're dragged round the zo and stuffed with Big Macs and milkshakes and all th time wondering if *she's* there with them, watching then come back laden down with guilt presents, catching sigh of *her* in the car, holding on to the smile and th composure just long enough to shut the door then grillin them rigid – wanting to know and not wanting to kno – knocking seven bells out of them if they so much a admitted she was, "OK, I suppose", hitting the sherr again, crying myself to sleep . . . Oh God, David, I can' *tell* you how awful I thought it was going to be!'

'And it's not?'

'What?'

'It's not going to be like that?'

'Well, of course it's not,' I laughed. 'Why should it be if you're not—' I froze suddenly, glass poised at my lips. I lowered it. 'What d'you mean, David? Why should it be?'

He didn't say anything, just looked at me. I felt scared. 'Why should it be like that?' I whispered again.

'You tell me,' he said quietly. 'The way I see it, you've still got things pretty much arse-about-tit here. Shouldn't *I* be the one asking *you* the questions? Shouldn't I be asking you if *you're* having an affair?'

'Oh,' I breathed, as the dawn came up. 'Oh, I see . . . you mean Patrick. Oh no, don't be silly, I—'

'Silly?' His voice broke in harshly, making me jump. 'Silly? Is that what I'm being? Oh well, excuse me!'

He stood up and faced me furiously. His fists were clenched, his face pale, masklike. It didn't look like David at all.

'Nine years, Tess,' he said in a shaky voice. 'Nine years I've lived in that little turd's shadow, with him peering over my shoulder, lurking behind us all the way, watching our every move, lingering around like some bloody spy in a belted overcoat, quietly smoking in darkened doorways, waiting for you.'

I stared at him aghast. 'B-but he's never been here. He's always been in Italy. How can you—'

'He's always been *there* though, hasn't he?' He leaned over and jabbed me hard in the chest. His eyes were like two pieces of flint. 'He could have been in fucking Timbuktu and it wouldn't have made any difference. He's always been there in your heart, hasn't he, Tess? Oh, not your whole heart, I grant you; you very graciously shifted him over and made room for two when

463

I arrived and I like to kid myself that over the years I've managed to all but push him out, but not quite. You've always let him cling to the edge by the fingertips, haven't you, and let me tell you, that's been bloody hard to hack at times.'

I opened my mouth to deny it, then I saw his face daring me to do so. I hung my head in shame.

'I suppose I have rather carried a torch for him . . .'

'Torch,' he scoffed. 'A frigging *bon*fire, more like!'

'But not any more.' I looked up quickly. 'Really, not any more.'

David smiled and shook his head.

'It's true,' I said urgently, grabbing his hand. 'I swear to God, David. It's over, it's—'

'It's more alive than it's ever been,' he said drily, pulling his hand away roughly. He turned his back on me, staring out of the window. At length he spoke.

'Tess, I want you to go away for a while.'

I stared at his back. 'What?'

'I want you to go back to Italy with him.' He jerked his head in the direction of the door. 'Go on,' he said quietly, 'sod off.'

My mouth fell open. 'But David, why?'

'Because I'm tired of playing second fiddle, that's why. I'm tired of filling someone else's flashy Italian shoes with my rather mediocre grey woollen socks. I'm tired of trying to make you happy when all the time there's someone a mere plane flight away who could make you happier still.' He swung around to face me. 'You see, for some time, Tess, I've been wondering how I could throw the pair of you together. I even had a half-baked notion about taking a family holiday in Florence this summer, dragging the children round the Uffizi, taking in the duomo and then accidentally on purpose running into Him.' He smiled. 'Imagine my delight when I discovered I didn't have to go to all that

464

trouble. Imagine how thrilled I was when I heard his father had died and he'd be within spitting distance of us in Scotland. Imagine my glee as I watched you pant after him the moment we got there, tart yourself up for him, tear out at midnight to meet him in darkened fields and get lost in the process whilst I bust a gut looking for you, and then, throw into the equation the terrifically handy fact that you oh so conveniently fell off your bike and muscled into his spare room at Gilduncan . . . I'm sure you can imagine, Tess, that my rapture was complete. Oh, it was perfect. All I had to do was invent some spurious excuse to leave the stage, return to London and let you get on with it.'

'You mean you had no work to do here?' I whispered.

'Of course not. Most of the courts are shut in August and I'd finished all my paper work. No, I just mooched about a bit, watched the cricket, picked my nose, went to the pub and went quietly out of my mind.'

'So that's why you kept insisting I stayed there, at Gilduncan. You wanted me to have an affair with him. Go away with him.'

'I think you're finally getting the picture.'

'But – Jesus, David – supposing it had worked out? Supposing I had gone off with him, and taken the children. Talk about playing Russian Roulette with your family!'

He eyed me coldly. 'That was a risk I'd finally decided to take. This wasn't a sudden whim, Tess, this wasn't a spur-of-the-moment decision. This was something I'd considered for a very long time.'

I gulped. 'Was it that obvious then, my – you know . . .'

'Obsession with him? No, not all the time, but it had a way of rearing its ugly head every now and then. You'd go all quiet and moody and wilt a bit over the scrambled-egg pan, mutter on about the drudgery of being a common-or-garden Putney housewife, referring particularly, I'm sure, to the monotony of being married to a boring middle-class barrister, but being j-u-st about polite enough to refrain from mentioning that. But you didn't have to, Tess. I knew your heart wasn't in it. You may have looked like you were burning the bacon with one hand, ironing a vest with the other, kicking the door shut on the oven chips and shaking your head at the Jehovah Witness through the window, but I knew in reality you were on some balmy Italian balcony somewhere. I knew you were shooting Lover Boy ho looks over the gin and tonics, I knew you were furiously tearing your clothes off, thrashing around on wet canvases and making a terrible mess in the bougainvillaea.'

I looked at my hands and shook my head. 'Stupid,' muttered, 'naive.'

'Really?' He raised his eyebrows. 'How d'you know until you've tried it? Until you've tried living with spoiled, sullen brat of a man who's never had anything in life except his own way? A man who has a totally warped view of humanity and more particularly women How d'you know until you've tried living in a country where you can't speak the language and where, believe it or not, people *still* do the washing up and iron shirt and take children to school and go to the supermarket. Go on, Tess, off you trot. Get down to the travel agen and book a flight. I'll man the fort – try it for a bit.'

'I don't need to,' I whispered, 'I already know, an I'm over him, really I am. You must believe me, David

He looked at me squarely. 'Only yesterday I spoke t you at Robert's funeral. You certainly weren't over him then. I believe you even raised the subject of divorce does that ring any bells? Tell me, what's happened in th space of twenty-four hours that's so radically change your mind?' He leaned back on the sink and folded hi arms. 'Talk me through it, Tess, I'm all ears.'

'Well,' I faltered, 'after the funeral – I went to see him.'

'Ah yes. That must have been when you said you needed a walk. A little air.'

I nodded. 'Yes, that's right.' I swallowed hard, my brain spinning. I knew I had to tell him everything now, however implausible it sounded. A lot depended on this. I spread my hands on the table as if I were laying out my cards and tried to think clearly. 'At that time,' I said slowly, feeling my way, 'I really believe I was planning to have an affair with him.' I looked up.

'Yesterday,' he said with difficulty. 'Only yesterday.'

I nodded. 'Yes, that's right, but then something happened. Something . . .' I struggled to explain – think, Tess, think and *talk*, damn you, *tell* him. 'I saw something in him, in Patrick, that I'd never seen before. A totally unexpected, weird side of him.' I shook my head. 'It was as if I was looking back into his past, into his soul really. I could see how unloved he'd been, what an appalling upbringing he'd had and how badly that had affected him. *Twisted* him. I realised how he'd tried to hide all that before and why he was so obsessed by me. It wasn't love at all; it was more of a – crusade. I felt sorry for him but at the same time I found him creepy, odd. I tried to go, to leave him. We fought and he—'

'Your first quarrel,' he smiled. 'How very touching.'

'No, no, it was more than that. I – well, I felt completely repulsed by him, David. I couldn't bear the idea of him touching me.'

David raised his eyebrows sarcastically. 'How extraordinary! And yet only moments before you'd felt he was sexual temptation itself! But then – what, the scales literally fell from your eyes and you thought, Phew, that was a close shave. Quick, back to good old David. Back to good old doormat features. Back to Old Faithful.'

I looked at him squarely. 'If you like, except tha
when it looked like Old Faithful had got tired of hangin
around for Old Faithless and moved on to New Mode
I thought . . .'

'Yes?'

'I thought my world was coming to an end.' Tear
filled my eyes.

There was a silence. David turned and stared out o
the kitchen window. It had started to rain now and drop
were coming in through the open window into the sink
He didn't close it, just watched them drip onto th
windowsill, into the stainless steel sink, down the plug
hole.

'I don't know,' he said wearily. 'I just don't know.'

I looked at his straight back, at his square shoulders
his hands thrust deep in his pockets and suddenly I knev
I had to fight for this one. I had to fight for my marriage

I stood up behind him. 'Look, David,' I began in
low voice, 'just because I didn't do this thing properl
the way you'd planned it, just because I didn't clear m
wardrobe, take the children and come back six month
later saying, "Take me back, it was all a ghastly mistake,
you're disappointed, aren't you? Just because my eye
were opened in an instant it's not enough, is it? Yo
wanted me to go away, get it all out of my system, bu
don't you see,' I urged, 'I don't need to! In the sam
way that all I needed was a glimpse of you packing you
bags into a taxi to bring me to my senses all I neede
was that short sharp glimpse of Patrick! And I saw s
much in that short time. I saw it all. It doesn't take twelv
years to undo twelve years; nothing is relative in thi
game, there *are* no rules and it *can* all fall apart in
moment – you drop a stitch and the whole thing unrave
– I'm rid of him, David! I swear to God I'm shot of hir
for ever and I can't tell you how liberating that feels. It
as if I've finally exorcised him, he's really gone!'

In the silence I could hear the clock ticking, could almost hear my toes creaking in my shoes. Then I saw his head shake.

'I just want you to be sure,' he said softly. '*Really* sure.'

'I *am* sure.'

I flew to him and hung on tight, arms wound round his waist from behind. I rested my head on his back, shut my eyes and prayed to God, Buddha, Allah, anyone, and slowly, very slowly, he turned around. His arms closed about me. I looked up at him. Tears were taking their chance now and fleeing down my cheeks.

'I love you, David,' I gasped. 'I've been a bloody idiot, I know I have, but I do love you. I've always loved you, don't ever think I haven't, that I've been living a lie all these years because that's just not true!'

I saw him blink hard and swallow.

'But it will be so much better now,' I whispered, 'now that we've got rid of him, now that he's not around us any more.'

He stared down at me.

'Please believe me, darling. I know I'm full of shit and clichés and I can't think of any other ways of saying this but I love you so much and please don't make me go away, please! I'd be lost without you!'

He gazed down at me for a moment, then his head bent slowly towards me. Before his lips touched mine, however, he stopped. Frowned.

'You know, the funny thing is, Tess, I never had the faintest idea what you saw in him. He reminded me of your bloody father.'

I gasped, but it was lost as finally his lips met mine.

Later that evening, as soon as we'd read to the children and tucked them into bed, we crept quietly along to our room and made love. Afterwards, as I lay in his arms

contemplating his familiar, rock-like chest, David
squinted sideways at me.

'Did you sleep with the bastard?' he growled.

'No!' God it was a relief to be able to say that. 'No, of
course I didn't!'

David regarded me thoughtfully for a moment then
shut his eyes. 'Hmmm. Just checking.'

I snuggled down again relieved. It occurred to me to
wonder though, as I chewed my bottom lip reflectively,
if I shouldn't perhaps admit to Willie? I mean, since we
were coming clean and being all frank and fearless about
everything? On the other hand, men were a bit funny
about that sort of thing, weren't they? A touch sensitive
about who their wives cavorted naked with. I swallowed
hard and decided that on balance I might keep that one
to myself. There was no point in rocking the old marital
boat just when we'd got it nice and steady again. Instead
I curled up in his armpit, feeling warm and tired and
happy and heavy with sleep but not quite wanting to
give in to it just yet. I wanted to savour this feeling for a
bit longer. I gazed through the open window at the
gathering gloom in the street outside. Yes, I just wanted
to lie here and thank my lucky stars.

I sighed happily and after a while, heard regular deep
breathing from the hump beside me. I propped myself
up on one elbow and looked down at his sleeping form.
I smiled, watching the way his mouth quivered slightly
as he breathed out, the way his hair was just slightly
receding at the sides and becoming flecked with grey
and the way the laughter-lines round his eyes were
fanning out, almost to his temples now.

'Stop it.' David opened one eye sharply.

'Stop what?'

'Stop looking at me like that.'

'Like what?'

'In that soppy, doting sort of way people reserve for

their ancient golden retrievers.'

'I was not!'

'Yes, you were. I can tell. You were looking at me like a favourite old Leonard Cohen record or one of Clemmie's baby shoes and anyway, I was busy. You disturbed me.'

'Busy doing what?'

'Busy undoing Lucy's brastrap and letting her splendid, full young breasts fall into my outstretched hands.'

'David!'

'What?'

'That's outrageous!'

'Is it?' He paused. 'You're right, I should have kissed her first. The trouble with dreams though is that you don't always remember the formalities, you just bowl on in there and – ow! Oi, that was my ear you bashed then – Jesus, what is this – a fist-fight? I'll give you a fist-fight, I'll—'

'Oh great! Can we join in?'

David and I froze in mid-tussle as two small heads popped up from under the bed.

We stared at them.

'How long have you been there?' I breathed.

'Well, we missed the beginning but crawled in about halfway through, I think,' said Hugo. 'Clemmie got a bit bored but I thought it was great! Daddy, can you just tell me something though? You know when you bit Mummy's ear and she called you Stonky and you called her Tiger and then you sat on her and kind of—'

'OUT!' roared David, leaping up stark naked and chasing them from the room. 'OUT! GET BACK TO YOUR ROOMS BEFORE I LOSE MY TEMPER! I'M GOING TO COUNT TO THREE. ONE, TWO . . .'

Going Too Far

Catherine Alliott

From the bestselling author of The Old Girl Network;
'[An] addictive cocktail of wit, frivolity and madcap
romance' Time Out

'You've gone all fat and complacent because you've got
your man, haven't you?'

There are some things only your best friend can tell
you but this outrageous suggestion is met with indignation from Polly Penhalligan, who is recently
married, trying for a baby and blissfully happy in her
beautiful manor farmhouse in Cornwall. At least, she
was, until Pippa's unfortunate remark forces her to
realise that her idyllic life of gorging on chocolate
biscuits, counting her seemingly endless blessings
and not getting dressed until lunchtime could be
having a few unwelcome side-effects.

So Polly decides to razz things up a bit – and agrees
to allow her home to be used as a location for a commercial. Having a glamorous film crew around
should certainly put something of a bomb under rural
life, shouldn't it? But even before the cameras are set
up and the stars released from their kennels, Polly's
life and marriage have been turned upside down.
This time, it seems, she's gone too far . . .

0 7472 4607 6

HEADLINE

Rosie Meadows regrets . . .

Catherine Alliott

*Well, what could I say? If he was smitten then I could be
too, and I sank back into the whole cosy relationship with a
monumental sigh of relief. I didn't have to try too hard,
didn't have to be too witty, too amusing, too beautiful . . .
It was like landing on a feather mattress after all those years
of being Out There.*

Three years down the line, however, Rosie's beginning to think that 'cosy' isn't all it's cracked up to be.
Bridge parties have never really been her thing, and
it would be nice to feel beautiful just once in a while.
Enough is enough. It's time to get her life back.

'Alliott's *joie de vivre* is irresistible' *Daily Mail*

'Hilarious and full of surprises' *Daily Telegraph*

'A joy . . . you're in for a treat' *Express*

0 7472 5786 8

HEADLINE

Woman to Woman

Cathy Kelly

Best friends Aisling Moran and Jo Ryan think they have it all.

Aisling is deliriously happy with her brilliant editor husband, two beautiful ten-year-old sons and a home she's rag-rolled and stencilled to within an inch of its life. As a journalist with an Irish glossy magazine, Jo has a great career, independence and a drop-dead gorgeous boyfriend.

But that's all about to change.

One Friday morning, Aisling finds a receipt for expensive lingerie in her husband's suit pocket and Jo finds a blue line on her blue-for-positive pregnancy testing kit. By Friday night, it's all over – or has it only just begun?

'A page-turner' *Sunday Independent*

'A powerful story for the nineties woman; sharp, sexy and witty' *The Star*

0 7472 6052 4

HEADLINE

Suddenly Single

Sheila O'Flanagan

What do you do when you find yourself suddenly single?

Go suddenly suicidal?

Suddenly sex-crazed?

Or simply collapse in self-pity?

Alix Callaghan, who thought she was in control of her work-packed life, feels like doing all three when her long-term boyfriend insists on settling down to a sensible existence – complete with children, proper meals and early nights – but without her.

Though motherhood is the last thing on her mind, losing Paul hurts more than Alix will ever admit – especially to herself.

Now, with the men at the office eyeing up her job, not to mention the discovery of her first grey hair, she's beginning to wonder if being single again is all it's cracked up to be . . .

'Sparkling and inspiring . . . a must for the contemporary woman' *Ireland on Sunday*

'Fabulous . . . thoroughly enjoyable' *RTÉ*

'A rattling good read' *U Magazine*

0 7472 6236 5

HEADLINE